MARK 5

Evil Spirits Enter about 2,000 Swine and They Drown

11 Now there was there nigh [*near*] unto the mountains **a great** [*large*] **herd of swine** [*pigs*] feeding.

12 And **all the devils besought him, saying, Send us into the swine**, that we may enter into them.

13 And forthwith [*immediately*] **Jesus gave them leave** [*permission*]. **And the unclean spirits went out, and entered into the swine**: and the herd **ran** violently down a steep place **into the sea**, (they were about two thousand;) **and were choked** [*drowned*] in the sea.

> One might wonder why Jesus allowed the evil spirits He cast out of the man to enter into the pigs. We don't know. We do wonder what the people of that area were doing raising pigs, since pork was forbidden under the Law of Moses (see Leviticus 11:7–8). However, it also appears that most of the citizens of the area were not Israelites, so we will have to wait until another day for an authoritative answer on this issue.

14 And **they that fed the swine** [*those in charge of the herd of pigs*] **fled** [*ran away*], **and told it** [*what happened to the herd*] **in the city**, and in the country. And they [*the people who owned the swine*] went out to see what it was that was done.

15 **And they come to Jesus, and see him** [*the man*] **that** was possessed with the devil, and **had the legion** [*of evil spirits in him before Jesus cast them out*], **sitting, and clothed,** and in his right mind: and they [*the owners of the herd*] were afraid.

16 And they that saw it [*the people who had seen the whole thing as it happened*] told them [*the owners of the pigs*] how it befell [*what happened*] to him that was possessed with the devil, and also concerning the swine.

17 **And they began to pray** [*request*] **him** [*Jesus*] **to depart** out of their coasts [*area*].

> It would be nice if these people who owned the herd of swine had been spiritually sensitive enough to recognize the great miracle which had been performed by the Savior and had been converted. However, sadly, such was not the case. It seems that they were so set on material things that, rather than asking the Master to teach them, they simply requested that he leave their area so that they would not risk suffering another economic disaster.

> Next, beginning with verse 18, we see that the man who had been healed from the evil spirits wanted to go with Jesus. But the Master asked him to stay home as a witness of the healing that had taken place so that others in that region would have a better chance to hear and accept the gospel.

18 And **when he was come into the ship, he that had been possessed with the devil** [*evil spirits*] **prayed** [*requested*] him **that he might be with him.** [*The man healed of the evil spirits wanted to go with Jesus.*]

19 Howbeit [*however*] Jesus suffered [*allowed*] him not, but saith unto him, Go home to thy friends, and tell them how great things the Lord hath done for thee, and hath had compassion on thee. [*In other words, Jesus asked him to go home and be a witness of the healing so that others in that area could know of Christ.*]

20 And he [*the man who had been healed*] departed, and began to publish [*tell*] in Decapolis [*the country south and southeast of the Sea of Galilee*] how [*what*] great things Jesus had done for him: and all men did marvel.

21 And when Jesus was passed over again by ship unto the other side [*of the Sea of Galilee*], much people gathered unto him: and he was nigh [*near*] unto the sea.

The Healing of
Jairus' Daughter

22 And, behold, there cometh one of the rulers of the synagogue [*Jewish church building*], Jairus by name; and when he saw him, he fell at his feet,

23 And besought him [*pleaded*] greatly, saying, My little daughter lieth at the point of death: I pray thee, come and lay thy hands on her, that she may be healed; and she shall live.

24 And Jesus went with him; and much people followed him, and thronged [*crowded, pushed against*] him.

A Woman Who Had Been
Bleeding for Twelve Years
Is Healed by Touching the
Savior's Clothing

25 And a certain woman, which had an issue of blood [*had been bleeding for*] twelve years,

26 And had suffered many things of [*had suffered through treatments by*] many physicians, and had spent all that she had [*to pay the medical bills*], and was nothing bettered, but rather grew worse,

27 When she had heard of Jesus, came in the press behind [*pushed her way through the crowd and came up behind Jesus*], and touched his garment.

Next, we see the beautiful, simple faith of this woman.

28 For she said, If I may touch but his clothes, I shall be whole [*healed*].

29 And straightway [*immediately*] the fountain [*source*] of her blood was dried up; and she felt in her body that she was healed of that plague.

Next, the Savior, who is being crowded and pushed from every side by people in the huge crowd, startles His Apostles by asking who had just touched Him.

30 And Jesus, immediately knowing in himself that virtue [*strength*] had gone out of him, turned him about in the press [*crowd*], and said, Who touched my clothes?

31 And his disciples said unto him,

MARK 5

Thou seest the multitude thronging [*pressing against*] thee, and sayest thou, Who touched me?

32 **And he looked round about to see** her that had done this thing.

33 But **the woman** fearing and trembling, knowing what was done in her [*knowing that she had been healed*], came and **fell down before him, and told him all the truth** [*that she was the one who touched Him*].

Notice how tenderly and quickly the Savior puts this worried woman's mind and heart at ease. Perhaps you've noticed that He is anxious to do the same for you and me.

34 **And he said** unto her, **Daughter, thy faith hath made thee whole; go in peace** [*don't be afraid of me*], **and be whole** [*healed*] of thy plague.

Remember that Jesus was on His way to Jairus' home when He stopped to comfort the woman who had been hemorrhaging for twelve years and had touched His clothes. Now, as He comforts the woman, word comes that Jairus' daughter has died.

35 **While he yet spake, there came** from the ruler [*Jairus, verse 22*] of the synagogue's house **certain** [*people*] **which said, Thy daughter is dead**: why troublest thou the Master any further?

36 **As soon as Jesus heard** the word that was spoken, **he saith unto the ruler** of the synagogue [*Jairus*], **Be not afraid, only believe.**

Have you noticed that we are being taught lessons about the power of faith here?

37 And he suffered [*allowed*] no man to follow him, save [*except*] Peter, and James, and John the brother of James.

38 And **he cometh to the house** of the ruler of the synagogue, **and seeth the tumult** [*commotion*], and them that wept and wailed greatly [*the mourners, who, according to Jewish custom, were to make a big scene of noise and crying when someone had died*].

39 And **when he was come in, he saith** unto them [*the mourners*], Why make ye this ado [*fuss*], and weep? **the damsel** [*girl*] **is not dead, but sleepeth.**

Notice that the Savior now arranges for this to be a sacred, private miracle.

40 **And they laughed him** [*Jesus*] **to scorn** [*made fun of him*]. But when **he** had **put them all out**, he **taketh the father** and the **mother** of the damsel, **and them that were with him** [*Peter, James, and John—see verse 37*], and entereth in where the damsel was lying.

41 And he **took the damsel by the hand**, and said unto her, Talitha cumi; which is, being interpreted, **Damsel, I say unto thee, arise.**

42 And straightway [*immediately*] **the damsel arose, and walked**; for she was of the age of twelve years. And they were astonished

174   THE NEW TESTAMENT MADE EASIER THIRD EDITION, PART 1

with a great astonishment [*an understatement, no doubt*].

43 And he charged them straitly [*instructed them firmly*] **that no man should know it** [*that he had raised her from the dead, which he did—see heading to Mark, chapter 5 in our Bible*]; and commanded that something should be given her to eat.

We have not been told why Jesus instructed them not to tell anyone that he had actually raised her from the dead. Perhaps, as is often the case, it was a private, sacred matter for the parents and the three Apostles and was to be kept extra sacred by keeping it private.

MARK 6

Jesus will now return to His hometown of Nazareth, in Galilee, and be rejected there for the second time during His three-year ministry. At this point, we are still in the second year of Christ's mortal ministry.

The Second Rejection at Nazareth

1 AND **he** went out from thence [*from there*], and **came into his own country** [*his hometown, Nazareth*]; and his disciples follow him.

2 And when **the sabbath day** was come, **he began to teach in the synagogue** [*the local Jewish church building*]: and **many hearing him were astonished**, saying, From whence hath this man these things [*where does this man get all these teachings*]? and what wisdom is this which is given unto him, that even such mighty works are wrought [*done*] by his hands?

3 **Is not this the carpenter**, the son of Mary, the brother of James, and Joses, and of Juda, and Simon? and are not his sisters here with us? And **they were offended at him** [*felt that Jesus was an embarrassment to them and their community*].

Jesus had been trained as a carpenter by Joseph, Mary's husband. The citizens of Nazareth knew the family, including Jesus, and could not accept that Jesus was anything but a common man. They were disturbed that one of their own citizens was causing such an uproar in the country.

Verse three, above, gives us information about the size of Joseph and Mary's own family, which they had after Jesus was born. They had four sons, whose names are mentioned in this verse, and at least three daughters. The Greek plural form for the word "sisters" in verse three means three or more. It is also interesting to note that it is generally believed that James, one of Christ's half-brothers mentioned in this verse, was the writer of the book of James in the New Testament. See Bible Dictionary, under "James, Epistle of."

4 **But Jesus said unto them, A prophet is not without honour, but in his own country**, and among his own kin, and in his own house.

5 **And he could there** [*in Nazareth*]

MARK 6

do no mighty work, save [*except*] that he laid his hands upon a few sick folk, and healed them.

One of the important messages we can learn from verses 4–5, above, is that faith or lack thereof has a direct bearing on whether or not the work of the Lord goes forth.

6 And he marvelled [*NIV was amazed*] because of their unbelief. And he went round about the villages, teaching.

The Twelve Called and Instructed

7 And **he called unto him the twelve** [*the twelve Apostles*], and **began to send them forth by two and two**; and **gave them power over unclean** [*evil*] **spirits**;

This is a time of training for these twelve men. They will be sent out to serve, will run into some situations and problems they are not able to understand or solve, will return with an intense desire to learn more, and will be even more ready to be taught.

8 And commanded them that they should **take nothing** for their journey, **save** [*except*] **a staff** [*walking stick*] only; **no scrip** [*a bag, usually made of leather and used for carrying food—see Bible Dictionary, under "Scrip"*], **no bread, no money** in their purse:

9 But **be shod with sandals** [*wear sandals*]; and **not** put on **two coats**.

Sandals were worn by the common people in the days of the Savior and his Apostles. Shoes were very expensive and were worn only by the very wealthy.

It is apparent that He is teaching them to have faith in and be dependent on God. They will need this after He is gone.

10 And he said unto them, In what place soever ye enter into an house, there abide [*stay*] till ye depart from that place [*town or city*].

The Purpose of Shaking the Dust off their Feet, When Rejected

11 And whosoever shall not receive you, nor hear you, when ye depart thence, **shake off the dust under your feet for a testimony against them** [*as a witness that you tried to teach them the gospel but they rejected you*]. Verily I say unto you, It shall be more tolerable for Sodom and Gomorrha in the day of judgment, than for that city.

We understand from the scriptures that those who have a fair set of chances to hear, understand, and accept the gospel here in mortality, but reject it, will be in a worse position in spirit prison than those who did not have a chance here. Apostle Bruce R. McConkie explains this as follows: "It shall be more tolerable in the day of judgment, for heathen nations who had no opportunity to accept the gospel in this life, than for the more enlightened races who rejected the truths of salvation when such were offered to them" (*Doctrinal New Testament Commentary*, Vol. 1, page 327).

12 And **they went out, and preached** that men should repent.

13 And they **cast out many devils,** and **anointed with oil** [*part of the ordinance of administering to the sick—see James 5:14–15 for instructions on administering to the sick*] **many that were sick, and healed them.**

King Herod Fears that Jesus Is John the Baptist Returned from the Dead

14 And **king Herod heard of him;** (for his name was spread abroad:) [*Jesus had become famous*] and **he** [*Herod*] **said, That John the Baptist was risen from the dead,** and therefore mighty works do shew forth themselves in him [*King Herod had beheaded John the Baptist and was now worried that Jesus was actually John the Baptist come back alive*].

15 Others said, That it [*Jesus*] is Elias [*Elijah the prophet*]. And others said, That it is a prophet, or as one of the prophets.

16 But when **Herod** heard thereof, he **said, It is John, whom I beheaded: he is risen from the dead.**

Next, in verses 17–28, Mark tells us why Herod was so afraid that John the Baptist had returned from the dead.

17 For **Herod himself had**

sent forth and laid hold upon [*arrested*] **John, and bound him in prison for Herodias' sake** [*as requested by Herodias*], **his brother Philip's wife: for he had married her** [*Herod had married his own brother's wife, Herodias*].

18 **For John had said unto Herod, It is not lawful** [*legal*] **for thee to have thy brother's wife.**

19 Therefore **Herodias had a quarrel against him** [*was very angry at John the Baptist*], **and would have killed him; but she could not** [*could not talk her husband, King Herod, into having John killed*]:

20 For **Herod feared John, knowing that he was a just** [*righteous*] **man and an holy,** and observed [*protected; see Mark 6:20, footnote c*] him; and when he [*Herod*] heard him [*John*], he did many things, and heard him gladly [*Herod felt that John the Baptist was a prophet and gladly listened to his teaching*].

JST Mark 6:21
21 For Herod feared John, knowing that he was a just man, and **a holy man**, **and one who feared God and observed to worship him**; and when he heard him he **did many things for him**, and heard him gladly.

21 And when a convenient day was come, that **Herod on his birthday made a supper** to his lords, high captains, and chief estates of Galilee;

22 And **when the daughter of the said Herodias** [*her name was Salome; see Bible Dictionary,*

MARK 6

under *"Salome"*] **came in, and danced**, and pleased Herod and them that sat with him, **the king said** unto the damsel, **Ask of me whatsoever thou wilt, and I will give it thee.**

23 **And he sware** unto [*promised*] her, **Whatsoever thou shalt ask of me, I will give it thee, unto the half of my kingdom.**

24 **And she went forth, and said unto her mother** [*Herodias*]**, What shall I ask? And she** [*Herodias*] **said, The head of John the Baptist.**

25 **And she** [*Salome*] **came** in straightway [*immediately*] with haste **unto the king, and asked**, saying, I will that thou **give me** by and by [*immediately ("by and by" has changed in our day to mean "eventually")*] in a charger [*on a platter*] **the head of John the Baptist.**

26 And **the king was exceeding** [*very*] **sorry**; yet for his oath's sake [*because he had promised*], and for their sakes which sat with him [*because of peer pressure*], he would not reject her [*refuse granting her request*].

27 And **immediately the king sent an executioner, and commanded his** [*John the Baptist's*] **head to be brought**: and he [*the executioner*] went and beheaded him in the prison,

28 And **brought his head** in a charger, **and gave it to the damsel** [*Salome*]: and **the damsel gave it to her mother** [*Herodias*].

29 And when **his disciples** [*John's followers*] heard of it, they came

and **took up his corpse** [*body*], **and laid it in a tomb.**

Next, having given us an account of the death of John the Baptist, Mark returns to his account of the Apostles who have been out preaching and healing the sick (as instructed by the Savior— see verses 12 and 13), as they return and report what they have been doing to the Savior.

30 **And the apostles gathered themselves together unto Jesus, and told him all things**, both what **they had done, and** what they had **taught.**

Even though it may sound like an obvious and simple thing, the message in verse 31, next, that members in busy Church callings need time out to rest, is an important matter.

31 **And he said unto them, Come ye yourselves apart into a desert place** [*a quiet place where we can be alone*]**, and rest a while**: for there were many [*crowds of people*] coming and going, and they had no leisure [*time to themselves*] so much as to eat.

32 And they departed into a desert place by ship privately.

Watch the Savior's response now, in verses 33–34, as the people run in order to arrive in advance at the anticipated arrival point of Jesus and His weary Apostles when their ship comes to shore.

33 And the people saw them departing, and **many** knew him [*had heard*

of Jesus], and **ran afoot** [*on foot*] thither [*to where they figured Jesus and his Apostles were going in the ship*] out of all cities, **and outwent them** [*beat them to their destination*], **and came together unto him.**

34 **And Jesus, when he came out** [*of the ship*], saw much people [*the large crowd*], and **was moved with compassion toward them**, because they were as sheep not having a shepherd: and he began to teach them many things.

Feeding the 5,000

35 And **when the day was** now **far spent, his disciples came unto him, and said**, This is a desert place, and now the time is far passed [*the day is about over*]:

36 **Send them away, that they may go** into the country round about, and **into the villages, and buy themselves bread: for they have nothing to eat.**

Watch now as the Savior startles His Apostles-in-training by requesting that they feed the multitude (5,000 men plus women and children—see Matthew 14:21).

37 He answered and said unto them, **Give ye them to eat.** And **they say** unto him, **Shall we go and buy two hundred pennyworth of bread, and give them to eat?**

As you can see in verse 37, above, in reply, they told Him that enough bread to feed such a crowd would cost two hundred pennies. A penny, or

Greek denarius, was an average days wage for a workman—see Mark 6:37, footnote a. In our day, assuming an average day's wage to be about $150, the cost of feeding the crowd, which had gathered to hear the Savior, would be about $30,000 and would be somewhat overwhelming to the Apostles.

38 **He saith** unto them, **How many loaves** [*of bread*] **have ye?** go and see. And when they knew, they say, **Five, and two fishes.**

Perhaps there is a subtle message that might easily be missed in verses 39–40, next. It is that in order to receive nourishment (spiritual "bread") from the Savior, we must become part of His kingdom, which is well-organized here on earth. Notice how He has His Apostles organize these people by hundreds and by fifties. This can remind us of the fact that He organizes us in wards and branches, in order that the blessings of the gospel be made available to us.

39 **And he commanded them to make all** [*the people*] **sit down by companies** [*groups*] upon the green grass.

40 And they sat down **in ranks, by hundreds, and by fifties.**

41 And **when he had taken the five loaves and the two fishes, he looked up to heaven, and blessed, and brake** [*broke*] **the loaves, and gave** them to his disciples to set before them [*the people*]; and the two fishes divided he among them all.

MARK 6

179

42 And **they did all eat, and were filled**.

Among other possible messages, verse 42, above, can certainly be symbolic of the fact that when we come unto Christ and partake of His nourishment for us, our spiritual need can be completely filled (exaltation).

43 **And they took up** [*picked up the leftovers*] **twelve baskets full** of the fragments [*pieces of bread*], and of the fishes.

44 And they that did eat of the loaves were **about five thousand** men [*plus women and children; see Matthew 14:21*].

45 **And** straightway [*immediately*] **he** [*Jesus*] **constrained** [*asked*] **his disciples to get into the ship, and to go to the other side** [*of the Sea of Galilee*] before [*ahead of him*] unto Bethsaida, **while he sent away the people** [*while He dismissed the 5,000*].

It is helpful to remember that this is a time of training, learning faith, obedience, etc., for these Apostles. It was probably somewhat frustrating for them to get into the ship and leave for Bethsaida, on the northeastern side of the Sea of Galilee, leaving Jesus on the land with the multitudes who had just been fed. They may well have wondered how and when Jesus would catch up with them.

46 And **when he** [*Jesus*] **had sent them away** [*dismissed the crowd to go home*], **he departed** [*went*] **into a mountain to pray**.

Jesus Walks on the Water

47 And **when even** [*evening*] **was come, the ship** [*that his Apostles were on*] **was in the midst of the sea, and he alone on the land**.

48 And **he saw them toiling in rowing**; for the wind was contrary unto them [*they were struggling to row against the wind and waves, still trying to get to their destination*]: **and about the fourth watch of the night** [*between about 3 a.m. and 6 a.m.*] **he cometh unto them, walking upon the sea**, and would have passed by them.

The JST makes a rather helpful clarification to the last phrase of verse 48, above. From it we discover that Jesus intentionally acted as if He were going to walk on past them. He was the Master Teacher, and this certainly did get their attention and prepared them to be taught more about His power over the elements.

JST Mark 6:50
50 And about the fourth watch of the night he cometh unto them, walking upon the sea, **as if he** would have passed by them.

49 But **when they saw him walking upon the sea, they supposed it had been a spirit** [*ghost*], **and cried out** [*in fear*]:

The message given to these exhausted men in verse 50, next, is the same message the merciful Savior gives to all who are doing everything they can to come unto Him (these Apostles have been doing all in their power to row the boat against adversity in order to meet Him as instructed).

50 For [because] they all saw him, and were troubled [very worried]. And immediately he talked with them, and saith unto them, **Be of good cheer** [be happy, rejoice, cheer up]: **it is I; be not afraid.**

There is symbolism and comfort for us in these verses. We all go through "storms" of life and it is comforting to know that God is there to help and comfort us. He invites us to trust Him, cheer up, and stop being afraid.

Jesus Calms the Sea

51 And he went up unto them into the ship [got into the ship]; and **the wind ceased:** and they were sore [very] amazed in themselves beyond measure, and wondered. [The Apostles were very surprised at the power Christ had over the wind and sea.]

52 **For they considered not the miracle of the loaves: for their heart was hardened.**

The miracle of feeding the 5,000 hadn't yet sunk into their hearts as far as their understanding of the Savior's power was concerned. Again, we would do well not to criticize them for taking time to learn about the Master's power; rather, we ought to realize that these great men are in intense training now and are learning rapidly. The "learning curve" is steep!

53 And when they had passed over [completed the journey], **they came into the land of Gennesaret** [the fertile plain on the northwestern shore of the Sea of Galilee], and drew to the shore.

54 And when they [Jesus and his Apostles] were [had] come out of the ship, **straightway** [immediately] they [the people of that area] **knew him** [recognized Him],

55 **And ran through that whole region** round about, **and began to carry about** in beds **those that were sick**, where they heard he was [to where Jesus was].

56 And whithersoever [wherever] he entered, into villages, or cities, or country, **they laid the sick in the streets, and besought** [asked] **him that they might touch if it were but the border of his garment** [cloak, robe]: and **as many as touched him were made whole** [healed].

MARK 7

At this point, the Jewish religious leaders are so worried about the popularity of Jesus and what He is teaching that they have traveled all the way from Jerusalem to Galilee to try to trap Him and get Him arrested. It is easy to see that Satan has taken over their hearts and minds to the point that they are in an irrational frenzy to destroy Him and His work. Their actions are a sad reminder to us all that wickedness does not promote rational thought.

MARK 7

181

1 **THEN came together** [*working and plotting together*] **unto him the Pharisees, and certain of the scribes, which came from Jerusalem.**

The Pharisees and scribes were very influential religious leaders among the Jews. They are desperately trying to find ways to discredit Him and His disciples in front of the people. Watch what they choose to complain about, in verse 2, next.

2 And **when they saw some of his disciples** [*followers*] **eat bread** with defiled, that is to say, **with unwashen** [*unwashed*], **hands, they found fault** [*criticized Jesus for letting his followers eat without washing their hands first*].

Recognizing that some of his readers will not understand why the Pharisees and scribes criticized the Savior's disciples for not washing their hands before eating, he explains the situation to us in verses 3–4, next.

3 **For the Pharisees, and all the Jews, except** [*unless*] **they wash their hands oft, eat not, holding** [*following*] **the tradition of the elders.**

4 **And when they** [*the Jews*] **come from the market, except they wash, they eat not** [*if they don't perform the ritual washing of their hands, they don't eat*]. **And many other things** [*rules and laws*] **there be, which they have received to hold** [*to do, to obey*], as the washing of cups, and pots, brasen vessels, and of tables.

The "tradition of the elders" (end of verse 3, above) consisted of thousands of rules and regulations which had developed among the Jews over the centuries. Most of these rules were not in harmony with the Law of Moses, and were, in fact, opposite to God's will. They killed the spirit of the gospel. The scribes were generally the ones who interpreted these rules and prescribed penalties for those who violated them. As an example, they had so many specific rules for Sabbath day observance that it was virtually impossible for anyone to keep them all. A few of the things the Jews were forbidden to do on the Sabbath, according to the "tradition of the elders", are summarized in the following list:

The Tradition of the Elders
According to these laws and rules, which had been falsely added to the Law of Moses over the years, the Jews were forbidden on the Sabbath to:

- Sweep or break a single clod (it was planting)

- Pluck one blade of grass (it was harvesting)

- Cut a mushroom (a double sin-harvesting and planting because a new mushroom would grow in its place)

- Rub the ends of wheat stalks (guilty of threshing)

- Dip a radish in salt too long (guilty of pickling)

182   THE NEW TESTAMENT MADE EASIER THIRD EDITION, PART 1

- Rub mud off a dress (might bruise the cloth; however, if they let the mud dry and then carefully picked it off the dress so as to not bruise the fabric, it was ok).

- Spit on the ground, then rub it with the foot (guilty of farming, watering the ground; however, it was ok to spit on a stone, because nothing would grow as a result)

- Carry a legal burden more than 2000 cubits from home

- Replace wadding if it fell out of the ear

- Wear false teeth or wear a gold plug in a tooth

- Eat an egg that was laid on the Sabbath (unless the hen had been kept for eating rather than laying eggs, in which case the egg could be eaten because it was considered to be a part of the hen that had fallen off)

See *Mortal Messiah*, Vol. 1, pages 199–212 for many more examples of the laws and rules for the Sabbath that were a part of the "tradition of the elders."

5 Then **the Pharisees and scribes asked him, Why walk not thy disciples according to the tradition of the elders** [*why don't Your disciples keep the rules of the tradition of the elders*], **but eat bread with unwashen hands?**

Watch now as the Master (who gave the Law of Moses as Jeho-vah, the God of the Old Testament) responds to their charges, in verses 6–13.

6 **He answered** and said unto them, **Well hath Esaias** [*Isaiah*] **prophesied of you hypocrites** [*people who like to do evil, but want to look righteous*], as it is written [*you are fulfilling the prophecy which said (in Isaiah 29:13)*], **This people honoureth me with their lips, but their heart is far from me.**

7 Howbeit [*however*] **in vain** [*useless*] **do they worship me, teaching for doctrines the commandments of men.**

8 For **laying aside the commandment of God, ye hold the tradition of men,** as the washing of pots and cups: and many other such like things ye do. [*Your religious worship is useless. You don't keep God's commandments. You have replaced them with your own rules and laws.*]

9 And he said unto them, **Full well** [*absolutely*] **ye reject the commandment of God, that ye may keep your own tradition** [*tradition of the elders rules, and so forth*].

10 For **Moses said, Honour thy father and thy mother; and, Whoso curseth father or mother, let him die the death** [*death was the penalty given by Moses for being disrespectful or disobedient to parents; see Exodus 20:12*]:

The JST adds two verses (JST verses 10-11) here that are not found in the Bible, plus makes changes to Bible verse 10 (JST verse 12).

MARK 7

JST Mark 7:10-12

10 **Full well is it written of you, by the prophets whom ye have rejected**.

11 **They testified these things of a truth, and their blood shall be upon you** [*you are just as guilty as those who killed the ancient prophets who prophesied about you*].

12 **Ye have kept not the ordinances of God**; for Moses said, Honor thy father and thy mother; and whoso curseth father or mother, let him die the death **of the transgressor, as it is written in your law; but ye keep not the law**.

11 **But ye say, If a man shall say to his father or mother, It is Corban**, that is to say, a gift, by whatsoever thou mightest be profited by me; **he shall be free** [*of obligation to care for his parents; see note in this study guide after Matthew 15:6*].

12 **And ye suffer** [*allow*] **him no more to do ought** [*anything*] **for his father or his mother**;

13 **Making the word of God of none effect** [*destroying God's commandment to honor parents*] through your tradition, which ye have delivered [*require people to obey*]: and many such like things do ye [*you are guilty of doing all kinds of things like this*].

Now, Jesus turns from the Pharisees and scribes whom He has severely chastised, to the people who have gathered to watch and listen and addresses them.

14 And **when he had called all the people unto him, he said** unto them, Hearken [*listen and obey*] unto me every one of you, and understand:

15 **There is nothing from without** [*outside*] **a man, that entering into him can defile him** [*can make him unclean, unworthy*]: **but the things which come out of him** [*his thoughts, his words, etc.*], **those are they that defile the man**.

JST Mark 7:15

15 There is nothing from without, that entering into **a man**, can defile him, **which is food**; but the things which come out of him; those are they that defile the man, **that proceedeth forth out of the heart**.

16 **If any man have ears to hear, let him hear** [*the spiritually in tune will understand and obey*].

17 And when he was entered into the house from the people [*away from the crowds*], **his disciples asked him concerning the parable** [*asked Him to explain the parable in verse 15*].

18 And **he saith** unto them, **Are ye so without understanding also** [*don't you understand either*]? Do ye not perceive [*recognize*], that **whatsoever** [*whatever*] **thing from without** [*outside of us*] entereth into the man, it **cannot defile him** [*make him unworthy*];

19 **Because it entereth not into his**

184 THE NEW TESTAMENT MADE EASIER THIRD EDITION, PART 1

heart, but into the belly, and goeth out into the draught [*eventually passes out of the body*], purging all meats [*cleansing him from all food he has eaten*]?

In Bible language, "meat" means food. "Flesh" means "meat" as we now use the word.

20 And he said, **That which cometh out of the man, that defileth the man** [*your thoughts, words, actions, etc., are what can make you unclean, unworthy*].

21 For from within, **out of the heart of men, proceed evil thoughts, adulteries, fornications, murders,**

22 **Thefts, covetousness, wickedness, deceit** [*fraud, dishonesty*], **lasciviousness** [*pornography, lustful thinking, speaking, etc.*], **an evil eye** [*envy*], **blasphemy** [*speaking crudely, rudely, disrespectfully about God and sacred things*], **pride, foolishness:**

23 **All these evil things come from within, and defile the man** [*make him unclean and unworthy*].

24 And from thence [*there*] **he arose, and went into the borders of Tyre and Sidon** [*several miles north of the Sea of Galilee, on the coast of the Mediterranean Sea*], **and entered into an house, and would have no man know it** [*wanted to have some privacy*]: but he **could not be hid.**

JST Mark 7:22–23

22 And from thence he arose, and went into the borders of Tyre and

Sidon, and entered into a house, and **would that no man should come unto him**.

23 **But he could not deny them; for he had compassion upon all men**.

A Gentile Woman Asks Jesus to Heal Her Daughter

25 For **a certain woman, whose young daughter had an unclean** [*evil*] **spirit**, heard of him, and **came** and fell at his feet:

We would understand the "young" daughter to be over age eight, because D&C 29:46–47 tells us that Satan does not have power over children until they begin to become accountable, which we know to be age eight—see D&C 68:25–27.

Mark points out now that the woman is a Gentile, by way of background for what the Savior says to her.

26 **The woman was a Greek, a Syrophenician** by nation; and she besought him that he would [*asked Him to*] cast forth the devil out of her daughter.

27 But Jesus said unto her, **Let the children** [*the Jews, the covenant people, Israel—see JST quoted next*] **first be filled: for it is not meet** [*appropriate*] to **take the children's bread** [*the gospel, intended for the Jews only at this time in God's plan*], **and to cast it unto the dogs** [*give it to the Gentiles*].

MARK 7 185

JST Mark 7:26

26 But Jesus said unto her, Let **the children of the kingdom** first be filled; for it is not meet to take the children's bread, and to cast it unto the dogs.

As He states here, Jesus' mortal mission was limited to the house of Israel, specifically, the Jews. This limitation will be done away with later, as exemplified by Mark 16:15 and Peter's dream in Acts 10:9–48.

The word "dogs" in this context means "little dogs" or household pets (a term of endearment). A Bible scholar named Dummelow explains as follows:

"The rabbis often spoke of the Gentiles as dogs . . . [Jesus] says not 'dogs,' but 'little dogs,' i.e. house-hold, favourite dogs, and the woman cleverly catches at the expression, arguing that if the Gentiles are household dogs, then it is only right that they should be fed with the crumbs that fall from their master's table" (Dummelow, Commentary, pp. 678–79).

28 And **she answered** and said unto him, **Yes, Lord: yet the dogs under the table eat of the children's crumbs.**

29 **And he said** unto her, **For this saying** [*you have talked me into it (He probably said this with a twinkle in his eye)*] go thy way; **the devil** [*evil spirit*] **is gone out of thy daughter.**

30 And **when she was come to her house, she found the devil gone out**, and her daughter laid upon the bed.

31 And again, departing from the coasts of Tyre and Sidon, **he came unto the sea of Galilee**, through the midst of the coasts [*borders*] of Decapolis [*an area south and east of the Sea of Galilee*].

The Healing of the Deaf and Speech Impaired Man

32 And they bring [*brought*] unto him **one that was deaf**, and had an **impediment in his speech**; and they beseech him [*asked Jesus*] to put his hand upon him [*to heal the man*].

33 And **he took him aside** from the multitude, and **put his fingers into his ears** [*perhaps as a signal to the deaf man that He was going to heal his deafness*], and he **spit** [*the Jews believed that saliva had healing properties*], **and touched his tongue;**

34 And **looking up to heaven, he sighed, and saith unto him, Eph-phatha**, that is, Be opened.

35 And straightway [*immediately*] **his ears were opened** [*he could hear*], and the string of his tongue was loosed, **and he spake plain** [*he could speak plainly*].

36 And he charged them that they should **tell no man** [*Jesus gave them strict instructions not to tell anyone*]: but the more he charged them, so much the more a great deal they published it [*told others about it*];

37 And were **beyond measure**

astonished [*completely surprised*], saying, He hath done all things well: he maketh both the deaf to hear, and the dumb [*someone who can't talk*] to speak.

MARK 8

With the feeding of the 5,000, in Mark 6:41, the Savior was in the third year of His mortal ministry. In this chapter He is still ministering and teaching in Galilee as this third year of His earthly formal mission continues. Mark begins chapter 8 by reporting the feeding of the 4,000. Remember that the number 4,000 represents the number of men fed. Matthew informs us that there were also women and children fed in addition to the 4,000 (Matthew 15:38.)

Feeding the 4,000

1 IN those days **the multitude** being very great [*large*], and **having nothing to eat, Jesus called his disciples** unto him, and saith unto them,

2 **I have compassion on the multitude**, because **they** have now been with me three days, and **have nothing to eat**:

3 And **if I send them away** fasting to their own houses, **they will faint** by the way: for divers [*some*] of them came from far.

4 And **his disciples answered him, From whence can a man satisfy these men with bread here in the wilderness** [*where could we get bread since there are no markets*

here in the wilderness]?

5 And **he asked** them, **How many loaves** [*of bread*] **have ye?** And they said, Seven.

6 And he commanded the people to sit down on the ground: **and he took the seven loaves, and gave thanks, and brake** [*broke the loaves of bread into pieces*], **and gave to his disciples to set before them** [*to give to the people*]; and they did set them [*the pieces of bread*] before the people.

7 And **they had a few small fishes: and he blessed, and commanded to set them also before them**.

8 So **they did eat, and were filled**: and they took up of the broken meat [*food*] that was **left seven baskets** [*seven basketfuls of food were left over*].

One of the major messages for us in the above verses is that when we give the Savior what little we have, whether physical or spiritual efforts, He can make them into much more than we can alone. The left over food in verse 8, above, could symbolize the infinite blessings of exaltation for those who accept nourishment from the Master.

9 And they that had eaten were **about four thousand** [*in addition to women and children—see Matthew 15:38*]: and he sent them away [*dismissed them to go home*].

10 And straightway [*immediately*] **he entered into a ship with his disciples, and came into** the parts of **Dalmanutha.** [*Bible scholars'*

MARK 8

best guess is that Dalmanutha is in Galilee, on the west shore of the Sea of Galilee.]

Next, we see that the Pharisees have come to attempt to trap Jesus. By the way, they have come all the way up to Galilee from Jerusalem, a journey of several days, which shows how desperate they are becoming.

11 And **the Pharisees** [*Jewish religious leaders*] **came** forth, and **began to question with him** [*Jesus*], seeking of him a sign from heaven, tempting him [*to prove that he was from God*].

12 And **he sighed deeply** in his spirit, and saith, **Why doth this generation** [*the wicked people living in Israel at that time*] **seek after a sign?** verily I say unto you, **There shall no sign be given unto this generation**.

JST Mark 8:12
12 Verily I say unto you, There shall no sign be given unto this generation, **save the sign of the prophet Jonah; for as Jonah was three days and three nights in the whale's belly, so likewise shall the Son of man be buried in the bowels of the earth** [*a major sign for you will be that the Savior's body will be in the tomb for three days*].

13 And **he left them**, and entering into the ship again departed to the other side [*of the Sea of Galilee*].

14 Now **the disciples had forgotten to take bread, neither had** they in the ship with them more than one loaf.

Remember that the Apostles are undergoing a period of intense training in preparation for taking over the leadership of the Church after the Savior finishes His mortal ministry and is resurrected. Watch now as the Master Teacher creates the desire to learn more in the hearts and minds of the Twelve.

The Leaven of the Pharisees

15 And he charged [*instructed*] them, saying, Take heed, **beware of the leaven** [*the yeast that causes bread to rise*] **of the Pharisees, and** of the leaven of **Herod**.

The Savior's "students" are now at full attention, trying to figure out the meaning of what He just said to them. By the way, in the Jewish culture of the day, "leaven" often symbolized evil influence. For example, a little evil could spread and cause much evil.

16 And **they reasoned** [*talked*] **among themselves**, saying, **It is because we have no bread** [*He is saying this because we haven't enough bread with us*].

JST Mark 8:16
16 And they reasoned among themselves, saying, **He hath said this**, because we have no bread.

17 And **when Jesus knew it, he saith** unto them, **Why reason ye, because ye have no bread ?** [*You*]

are missing the point.] perceive ye not yet, neither understand? **have ye your heart yet hardened?** [*Are you still so spiritually insensitive that you can't understand the symbolism of what I say?*]

JST Mark 8:17
17 And **when they said this among themselves, Jesus knew it**, and he said unto them,

18 **Having eyes, see ye not** [*can't you see with spiritual eyes and understanding*]? and **having ears, hear ye not** [*can't you hear with spiritual ears and understanding*]? and **do ye not remember** [*can't you remember previous lessons I've taught you*]?

The Savior now reviews previous lessons with these Apostles.

19 **When I brake** [*broke*] **the five loaves among five thousand, how many baskets full of fragments took ye up** [*did you gather up*]? They say unto [*answered*] him, **Twelve.**

20 And when **the seven** [*loaves of bread*] **among four thousand, how many baskets full of fragments** took ye up? And they said, **Seven.**

21 And he said unto them, **How is it that ye do not understand** [*what I said regarding "leaven" in verse 15*]?

In Matthew 16:11–12, we see the rest of this account as follows:

11 How is it that ye do not understand that I spake it [*what I said about leaven, yeast*] not to you concerning bread, [*but, rather*] that ye should beware of [*watch out for*] the leaven [*influence*] of the Pharisees and of the Sadducees?

12 Then understood they [*the Apostles*] how that he bade them not [*was not warning them to*] beware of the leaven [*yeast*] of bread, but of the doctrine [*teachings*] of the Pharisees and of the Sadducees [*hypocritical Jewish religious leaders*].

In other words, just as a little bit of yeast can spread itself throughout the whole lump of bread dough, and thus influence it all, so also can the evil influence of corrupt religious leaders, such as the Pharisees and Sadducees, spread throughout the whole nation.

A Blind Man Is Healed

22 And he cometh to Bethsaida [*just north of the Sea of Galilee*]; and they bring **a blind man** unto him, and besought [*asked*] him to touch him.

You are about to see a rather rare physical healing by the Master, because it will be done in increments.

23 And **he took the blind man** by the hand, and **led him out of the town**; and when he had **spit** [*the Jews had a belief that saliva had healing properties*] **on his eyes, and put his hands upon him**, he asked **him if he saw ought** [*anything*].

24 And he looked up, and said, **I see men as trees, walking** [*I can see, but not clearly*].

MARK 8

189

25 **After that he put his hands again upon his eyes**, and made him look up: **and he was restored, and saw every man clearly**.

Perhaps this healing of the blind man in stages is symbolic of the fact that, usually, we are healed in stages. We grow "line upon line." We are gradually healed from our spiritual sicknesses such as lack of faith, meanness, inactivity, lack of charity, lustful thinking, and so on, until we see "clearly" as did the blind man.

26 And he sent him away to his house, saying, **Neither go into the town, nor tell it** [*that I healed you*] to any in the town.

Peter Bears Strong Testimony of Christ

27 And Jesus went out, and his disciples, into the towns of Cæsarea Philippi [*an area north and a bit to the east of the Sea of Galilee*]: and by the way [*as they were traveling*] he asked his disciples, saying unto them, **Whom do men say that I am?**

28 And they answered, John the Baptist: but some say, Elias [*Elijah*]; and others, One of the prophets.

29 And he saith unto them, **But whom say ye that I am?** And **Peter answereth and saith unto him, Thou art the Christ**.

30 And he charged [*instructed*] them that they should tell no man of him.

It would seem that this instruction to the Apostles was temporary

and for that particular time and circumstance. Perhaps they needed a bit of quiet time together for the Master to teach His disciples about His upcoming death (in about six months) and resurrection. Some manuscripts say "Don't go and tell anyone in the village."

Jesus Teaches His Coming Crucifixion and Resurrection

31 And **he began to teach them, that the Son of man** [*Christ; the "Son of Man." "Man" is "Man of Holiness" or Heavenly Father— see Moses 6:57*] **must suffer** many things, and **be rejected** of the elders, and of the chief priests, and scribes [*Jewish religious leaders*], and **be killed**, and after three days **rise again**.

32 And he spake that saying openly. And **Peter** took him, and **began to rebuke him** [*scold Him for saying such things*].

33 But when he had turned about and looked on his disciples [*implying that all the disciples shared Peter's expressed feelings*], **he rebuked Peter**, saying, Get thee behind me, Satan [*don't stand in My way like Satan does*]: for **thou savourest not** [*you are not considering*] **the things that be of God**, but the things that be of men.

Just a reminder that when you see a ¶ sign in your King James Version of the Bible, it means that there is now a change of topic.

Jesus Teaches What It Means to Truly Follow Him

34 And when he had called the people unto him with his disciples also, he said unto them, **Whosoever will come after me, let him deny himself** [*put aside his personal interests*], **and take up his cross** [*sacrifice whatever is necessary*], **and follow me.**

35 For **whosoever will save his life** [*pursue his own selfish interests*] **shall lose it** [*shall lose the real richness of eternal exaltation*]; **but whosoever shall lose his life** [*use his life*] **for my sake and the gospel's, the same shall save it.**

JST Mark 8:37–38 adds to verse 35 as follows:

JST Mark 8:37–38

37 For whosoever will save his life, shall lose it; **or whosoever will save his life, shall be willing to lay it down for my sake; and if he is not willing to lay it down for my sake, he shall lose it.**

38 But whosoever **shall be willing** to lose his life for my sake, **and the gospel**, the same shall save it.

36 For **what shall it profit a man, if he shall gain the whole world, and lose his own soul?**

37 Or **what shall a man give in exchange for his soul?**

JST adds a verse here:

JST Mark 8:40

40 Therefore deny yourselves of these, and be not ashamed of me.

38 **Whosoever** [*whoever*] **therefore shall be ashamed of me and of my words** [*will not accept Me and My teachings*] in this adulterous and sinful generation; **of him also shall the Son of man** [*Christ*] **be ashamed** [*Christ will not accept them into His kingdom*], **when he cometh in** the **glory** of his Father with the holy angels [*the Second Coming*].

The JST adds two verses here: (Remember that the verse numbers in the JST are sometimes different than in the King James Bible—the version that we use in English speaking areas of the Church.)

JST Mark 8:42–43

42 **And they shall not have part in that resurrection when he cometh.**

43 **For verily I say unto you, That he shall come; and he that layeth down his life for my sake and the gospel's, shall come with him, and shall be clothed with his glory in the cloud, on the right hand of the Son of man.**

MARK 9

This is a significant chapter. In it Mark tells us about the transfiguration of Christ starting with verse 2 and continuing through verse 8. As you read, you will

MARK 9

191

see that Peter, James, and John accompanied the Savior on this sacred occasion. It is clear that these three Apostles were in their "advanced training," so to speak, for the role they would take as the Presidency of the Church after the Savior returned to heaven following His crucifixion and resurrection. You will also see that Moses, Elijah, and John the Baptist appeared to the Savior and these men on the mount. Peter, James, and John watched as Jesus was transfigured before their eyes. They also heard the voice of Heavenly Father as He bore witness of the Son.

1 AND he said unto them, Verily I say unto you, That there be some of them that stand here, which shall not taste of death, till they have seen the kingdom of God come with power [*they will be alive until the Second Coming*].

The JST (Joseph Smith Translation of the Bible) places Mark 9:1 as the last verse of Mark, chapter 8. The Apostle John would be one of those to whom the Savior referred that would "not taste of death" until the Second Coming. We know that he was translated (see D&C 7:3) and is still alive.

Next, Mark records the transfiguration of Christ, which occurred about six months before His crucifixion. For more detail about what happened upon the mountain, see the note after Matthew 17:8 in this study guide.

The Transfiguration of Christ

2 And after six days **Jesus taketh** with him **Peter**, and **James**, and **John** [*the "First Presidency"*], and leadeth them **up into an high mountain** apart by themselves: and **he was transfigured** [*radiated tremendous light and glory*] **before them**.

3 And **his raiment** [*clothing*] **became shining, exceeding white as snow**; so as no fuller [*washer of clothes*] on earth can white [*bleach*] them.

4 And **there appeared** unto them **Elias** [*John the Baptist—see JST Mark 9:3, quoted below*] with **Moses**: and they were **talking with Jesus**.

JST Mark 9:3

3 And there appeared unto them Elias with Moses, **or in other words, John the Baptist and Moses**; and they were talking with Jesus.

As you can see, the JST Mark 9:3 informs us that John the Baptist, who had been killed (beheaded) by King Herod, also appeared on the Mount of Transfiguration. The "Elias" spoken of in Mark 9:3 was John the Baptist. The "Elias" spoken of in Matthew 17:3 was Elijah (see Matthew 17:3, footnote 3b). "Elias" is a title for one who is a forerunner, and can refer to any of several different prophets. See Bible Dictionary, under "Elias."

5 And **Peter** answered and **said** to Jesus, Master, **it is good for us to be here** [*we are grateful to be here*]: and let us make three tabernacles [*shelters*]; one for thee, and

one for Moses, and one for Elias.

6 For he wist [*knew*] not what to say; for they were sore afraid [*very frightened*].

The Father's Voice Is Heard, Bearing Witness of the Son

7 And there was a cloud that overshadowed them: and **a voice** [*Heavenly Father's voice*] came out of the cloud, **saying, This is my beloved Son: hear him.**

8 And suddenly, **when they had looked round about, they saw no man any more, save** [*except*] **Jesus only with themselves.**

JST Mark 9:6

6 And suddenly, when they had looked round about **with great astonishment**, they saw no man any more, save Jesus only, with themselves. **And immediately they departed**.

The enormous impact of this experience for these three Apostles may be difficult for us to entirely comprehend. In the Jewish culture, Moses was the main Prophet, the most important and significant prophet of all. You may have already noticed that the corrupt religious leaders of the Jews have been constantly quoting the teachings of Moses against the Savior's doings and teachings. It was a great and impactful teaching moment for Peter, James, and John to see Moses, as well as Elijah and John the Baptist, ministering to the Savior and acknowledging Him as the Messiah.

Both Moses and Elijah had been translated (taken up into heaven without dying) and still had their physical, mortal, translated bodies when they appeared on the Mount of Transfiguration and ministered to Jesus. John the Baptist would have appeared there as a spirit. All three, Moses, Elijah and John the Baptist were resurrected with Christ (see D&C 133:54–55).

Next, in verse 9, the Savior gives these three Apostles strict instructions not to tell anyone about the transfiguration until after His resurrection. This is perhaps a reminder to us that there are some sacred things that are best kept private.

9 And **as they came down from the mountain**, he charged them that they should **tell no man what things they had seen, till the Son of man** [*Christ; Son of Man*] **were risen** [*resurrected*] **from the dead.**

10 And **they kept that saying with themselves**, questioning one with another what the rising from the dead should mean. [*They didn't yet understand what resurrection meant or involved.*]

Next, these humble men ask the Master to teach them about a subject that has been confusing to them. The JST will help us understand the Savior's response to their question.

11 And they asked him, saying, **Why say the scribes that Elias must first come** [*what do the scribes mean when they say that Elias must come first*]?

MARK 9

12 And **he answered** and told them, **Elias** verily **cometh first** [*before Jesus*], and restoreth all things; and how it is written of the Son of man [*Christ; Son of Man*], that he must suffer many things, and be set at nought [*ignored, set aside, crucified*].

13 But I say unto you, That **Elias** [*John the Baptist*] **is indeed come, and they have done unto him whatsoever they listed** [*whatever they wanted to do*], as it is written [*prophesied*] of him.

JST Mark 9:10–11

10 And he answered and told them **saying**, Elias verily cometh first, and **prepareth** all things; **and teacheth you of the prophets** [*teaches about the prophecies of Old Testament prophets about the coming of the Messiah*]; how it is written of the Son of man, that he must suffer many things, and be set at naught.

11 **Again** I say unto you, That Elias is indeed come, **but** they have done unto him whatsoever they listed; **and even** as it is written of him; **and he bore record of me, and they received him not. Verily this was Elias**.

Matthew 17:13 tells us that the "Elias" referred to here was John the Baptist.

As the Savior, Peter, James, and John return from being up in the mountain, they come upon the scribes causing trouble for some of His disciples.

14 And when he came to his disciples, he saw a great multitude [*big crowd*] about them, and **the scribes** [*Jewish religious leaders*] **questioning** with **them**.

15 And straightway [*immediately*] all the people, when they beheld him [*Jesus*], were greatly amazed [*surprised*] and, running to him saluted [*greeted*] him.

16 And **he asked the scribes, What question ye with them** [*what are you debating with My disciples about*]?

An Evil Spirit Is Cast Out

17 And **one of the multitude answered** [*responded*] and said, **Master, I have brought unto thee my son, which hath a dumb spirit;**

18 And **wheresoever he** [*the evil spirit*] **taketh him, he teareth him** [*throws him on the ground, and he gets cut up*]: and **he foameth, and gnasheth with his teeth, and pineth away**: and **I spake to** [*asked*] **thy disciples that they should cast him out; and they could not.**

JST Mark 9:15

15 And one of the multitude answered, and said, Master, I have brought unto thee my son, who hath **a dumb spirit that is a devil**; and **when he seizeth him**, he teareth him; and he foameth and gnasheth with his teeth, and pineth away; and I spake to thy disciples **that they might cast him out**, and they could not.

19 **He answereth** him, and saith, **O faithless generation, how long**

shall I be with you? how long shall I suffer you? **bring him unto me.**

20 And **they brought him unto him**: and when he [*the son possessed by the evil spirit*] saw him [*Jesus*], straightway [*immediately*] **the spirit tare him** [*caused him to fall and get cut more*]; and he fell on the ground, and wallowed foaming [*at the mouth*].

21 And he [*Jesus*] asked his father, How long is it ago since this came unto him? And he said, Of a child [*when he was a child*].

22 And ofttimes it hath cast him into the fire, and into the waters, to destroy him: but **if thou canst do any thing, have compassion** [*mercy*] **on us, and help us.**

23 **Jesus said** unto him, If thou canst believe, all things are possible to him that believeth.

JST Mark 9:20
20 Jesus said unto him, If thou **wilt believe all things I shall say unto you, this is possible** to him that believeth.

24 And straightway [*immediately*] **the father** of the child **cried out,** and said with tears, Lord, **I believe; help thou mine unbelief.**

Verse 24, above, has a major message for us. Each of us, no doubt, at times have said or will say, "I believe; help thou mine unbelief." It is a beautiful, humble acknowledgment of our faith and yet our inadequacy to have as much faith as we would like to have.

25 When **Jesus** saw that the people came running together, he **rebuked the foul** [*evil*] **spirit,** saying unto him, Thou dumb and deaf spirit, I charge [*command*] thee, **come out of him**, and enter no more into him.

26 And **the spirit cried** [*shrieked*], **and rent him sore** [*caused the son to flop around and get cut up more*], **and came out of him**: and he [*the son*] was as one dead; insomuch [*to the extent*] that many said, He is dead.

27 But Jesus took him by the hand, and lifted him up; and he arose.

Next, when they have privacy, the disciples ask the Lord why they couldn't cast the evil spirit out.

28 And when he was come into the house, his disciples asked him privately, **Why could not we cast him** [*the evil spirit*] **out?**

29 And he said unto them, **This kind can come forth by nothing, but by prayer and fasting.**

The Prophet Joseph Smith mentioned something that might apply here. He said that there are times when people do not have sufficient faith for the desired miracle to be performed. Said he (**bold** added for emphasis):

"**If a man has not faith enough to do one thing, he may have faith to do another**: if he cannot remove a mountain, he may heal the sick. Where faith is there will be some of the fruits: all gifts and power which were sent from

MARK 9

heaven, were poured out on the heads of those who had faith" (*History of The Church*, Vol. 5, page 355).

Next, the Savior teaches His Apostles privately of His approaching crucifixion and resurrection

The Savior Prophecies His Crucifixion and Resurrection

30 And **they departed** thence [*left that place*], **and passed through** Galilee; and he would not that any man should know it [*wanted to have time alone with His Apostles*].

31 For he taught his disciples, and said unto them, **The Son of man** [*Jesus; Son of Man; "Man" means "the Father"—see Moses 6:57*] **is delivered into the hands of men, and they shall kill him**; and after that he is killed, **he shall rise** [*be resurrected*] **the third day.**

32 **But they** [*the disciples*] **understood not** that saying [*what Jesus had said about His death and resurrection*], **and were afraid to ask him.**

Next, Mark informs us about a debate among these disciples which caused them some embarrassment. Remember that Jesus is training them for when He leaves and they take over the leadership of His church on earth.

33 And **he came to Capernaum** [*on the north end of the Sea of Galilee*]: and being in the house [*very likely Peter's home, since he lived in Capernaum*] **he asked them, What was it that ye disputed**

among yourselves by the way [*what were you debating among yourselves as we were traveling*]?

34 But **they held their peace** [*didn't answer; obviously, they were embarrassed about it*]: **for** by the way [*while traveling*] **they had disputed** [*argued*] among themselves, **who should be the greatest.**

JST Mark 9:31
31 But they held their peace, being afraid, for by the way they had disputed among themselves, **who was the greatest among them**.

Watch as the Savior gently answers their question with a simple lesson.

35 And he sat down, and called the twelve, and saith unto them, **If any man desire to be first** [*the greatest in God's kingdom*], **the same** [*he*] **shall be last of all** [*should consider himself to be least important of all*], **and servant of all.**

36 And **he took a child, and set him in the midst of them**: and when he had taken him in his arms [*perhaps meaning hugging the child as it sat on His lap*], he said unto them,

37 Whosoever shall receive one of such children in my name, receiveth me: and whosoever shall receive me, receiveth not me, but him that sent me.

JST Mark 9:34–35
34 Whosoever shall **humble himself like one of these children**, and receiveth me, **ye shall**

receive in my name.

35 And **whosoever shall receive me, receiveth not me only**, but him that sent me, **even the Father**.

Next, John brings up an issue that perhaps you have also wondered about.

38 And John answered him, saying, Master, **we saw one casting out devils in thy name**, and **he followeth not us** [*perhaps meaning that he is not one of the Twelve*]: and **we forbad him** [*told him not to do it*], because he followeth not us [*perhaps meaning that he is not traveling with us*].

39 But **Jesus said, Forbid him not**: for there is no man which shall do a miracle in my name, that can lightly speak evil of me.

40 For **he that is not against us is on our part** [*is on our side*].

Apostle Bruce R. McConkie explained verses 38–40, above, as follows:

"On a previous occasion, Jesus taught that neither Satan nor his false ministers can cast out devils, for 'Every kingdom divided against itself is brought to desolation; . . . And if Satan cast out Satan, he is divided against himself' (Matthew 12:25–30). Now he adds in plainness what was necessarily implied in his previous discourse that only those who follow him and are legal administrators in his kingdom can perform the miracle of casting out devils in his name.

"He was not one of the Twelve to whom the express power had been given to cast out devils (Matthew 10:8); he was not one of the inner circle of disciples who traveled, ate, slept, and communed continually with the Master. Luke has it: "He followeth not with us"; that is, he is not one of our traveling companions. But from our Lord's reply it is evident that he was a member of the kingdom, a legal administrator who was acting in the authority of the priesthood and the power of faith. Either he was unknown to John who therefore erroneously supposed him to be without authority or else John falsely supposed that the power to cast out devils was limited to the Twelve and did not extend to all faithful priesthood holders. It is quite possible that the one casting out devils was a seventy. There is no New Testament record of the calling of the first quorum of seventy, but when Jesus (at a later day) called a second quorum of seventy into the ministry, he expressly gave them the power to cast out devils (Luke 10:1–20).

"Only righteous men who are members of the Church, who hold the priesthood, and who are keeping the commandments, have power to perform miracles. 'There was not any man who could do a miracle in the name of Jesus save he were cleansed every whit from his iniquity' (3 Nephi 8:1).

"Our Lord had many faithful followers who had power by faith to cast out devils" (*Doctrinal New*

MARK 9

Testament Commentary, Vol. 1, page 417).

41 For **whosoever shall give you a cup of water to drink in my name, because ye belong to Christ,** verily I say unto you, he **shall not lose his reward.**

Did you wonder how verse 41, above, fits in with what is being discussed here? It might be that the Master is dealing with the problem that often comes up among us and among many other groups. If we are not careful, we get to thinking that what others do can't be as valuable as what we do. It may be that the Savior is gently reminding these men that anyone, whether members of the Church or not, can do good, and that it is looked upon with favor by heaven, and such persons will be rewarded accordingly.

Next, Jesus refers to the little child on His lap and teaches another lesson.

42 And **whosoever shall offend** [*cause to stumble in their faithfulness—see Matthew 18:6, footnote 6a; many translations use "cause to commit sin" in place of "offend"*] **one of these little ones** that believe in me, **it is better for him that a millstone** [*a large grinding stone*] **were hanged about his neck, and he were cast into the sea.**

In the next verses, there is much symbolism where parts of the body represent people. The JST is very helpful in understanding verses 43–50. We will include the JST verses at the end of this chap-

ter. It tells us that people are represented by hand, foot, and eye. JST Matthew 18:9 gives additional interpretation which is represented in many of the brackets below.

43 And **if thy hand** [*your brother; friend*] **offend thee** [*causes you to sin*], **cut it off** [*stay away from him*]: it is better for thee to enter into life maimed [*crippled*], than having two hands to go into hell [*than following the sinful example of family members and going to hell with them*], into the fire that never shall be quenched:

44 Where their worm dieth not [*where they do not cease to exist*], and the fire [*their suffering*] is not quenched [*does not stop*].

45 And **if thy foot** [*friend; the person who is leading you*] **offend thee** [*leads you into sin*], **cut it off** [*stop associating with that person*]: it is better for thee to enter halt [*crippled*] into life, than having two feet [*sticking with the friend*] to be cast into hell, into the fire that never shall be quenched:

46 Where their worm dieth not [*where they do not cease to exist*], and the fire is not quenched [*the suffering never ends*].

47 And **if thine eye** [*parents, family members who lead you*] **offend thee** [*cause you to stumble in the faith, commit sin, etc.*], **pluck it out** [*leave them*]: it is better for thee to enter into the kingdom of God with one eye [*alone*], than having two eyes [*following parents' sinful example*] to be cast into hell fire:

48 Where their worm dieth not, and the fire is not quenched.

49 For **every one shall be salted** [*tested*] with fire, and **every sacrifice shall be salted** with salt [*every sacrifice we make for the gospel is part of our test*].

Apostle Bruce R. McConkie explains the phrase "salted with fire" as follows: "Every member of the Church shall be tested and tried in all things, to see whether he will abide in the covenant 'even unto death' (D&C 98:14), regardless of the course taken by the other members of his family or of the Church. To gain salvation men must stand on their own feet in the gospel cause and be independent of the spiritual support of others. If some of the Saints, who are themselves the salt of the earth, shall fall away, still all who inherit eternal life must remain true, having salt in themselves and enjoying peace one with another" (*Doctrinal New Testament Commentary*, Vol. 1, p. 421).

50 Salt is good: but **if the salt have lost his saltness**, wherewith will ye season it? Have salt in yourselves, and have peace one with another.

JST Mark 9:40–50

40 **Therefore**, if thy hand offend thee, cut it off; **or if thy brother offend thee and confess not and forsake not, he shall be cut off. It is better for thee t**o enter into life maimed, than having two hands, to go into hell.

41 For it is better for thee to enter into life without thy brother, than for thee and thy brother to be cast into hell; into the fire that never shall be quenched, where their worm dieth not, and the fire is not quenched.

42 And again, if thy foot offend thee, cut it off; for he that is thy standard, by whom thou walkest, if he become a transgressor, he shall be cut off.

43 It is better for thee, to enter halt into life, than having two feet to be cast into hell; into the fire that never shall be quenched.

44 Therefore, let every man stand or fall, by himself, and not for another; or not trusting another.

45 Seek unto my Father, and it shall be done in that very moment what ye shall ask, if ye ask in faith, believing that ye shall receive.

46 And if thine eye which seeth for thee, him that is appointed to watch over thee to show thee light, become a transgressor and offend thee, pluck him out.

47 It is better for thee to enter into the kingdom of God, with one eye, than having two eyes to be cast into hell fire.

48 For it is better that thyself should be saved, than to be cast into hell with thy brother, where their worm dieth not, and where the fire is not quenched.

49 For every one shall be salted with fire; and every sacrifice shall be salted with salt; but the salt must be good.

50 For if the salt have lost his

MARK 10

By now there are less than six months remaining in the third year of the Savior's formal mission. As you can see, in verse 1, next, He now leaves Galilee, where He has spent the majority of His mortal ministry, and journeys toward Judea, in the southern region of the Holy Land.

1 AND **he arose from thence** [*from where he was in Galilee*], **and cometh into** the coasts [*borders*] of **Judæa** [*the southern part of Israel*] by the farther [*eastern*] side of Jordan [*river*]: and **the people resort** [*came*] **unto him** again; and, as he was wont [*accustomed to doing*], **he taught them** again.

Concerning Divorce

2 And **the Pharisees** [*Jewish religious leaders*] came to him, and asked him, **Is it lawful** [*legal*] **for a man to put away** [*divorce*] **his wife?** tempting him [*trying to trap Him so they would have an excuse to have Him arrested*].

3 And **he answered** and said unto them, **What did Moses command you?**

4 And **they said, Moses suffered** [*allowed*] **to write a bill of divorcement** [*a legal divorce document*], **and to put her away** [*divorce her*].

5 And **Jesus answered** and said unto them, **For the** [*because of the*] **hardness of your heart he wrote you this precept** [*gave you this teaching*].

6 **But from the beginning of the creation God** [*Heavenly Father*] **made them male and female**.

7 **For this cause** [*for marriage*] **shall a man leave his father and mother, and cleave** [*be loyal*] **to** his wife;

8 And **they twain** [*the two of them*] **shall be one flesh** [*a family unit*]: so then they are no more twain [*two*], but one flesh.

9 **What therefore God hath joined together, let not man put asunder** [*destroy*].

10 And in the house his disciples asked him again of the same matter [*to explain more of what he had said about divorce*].

11 And he saith unto them, **Whosoever shall put away** [*divorce*] **his wife, and marry another, committeth adultery against her**.

12 And **if a woman shall put away her husband, and be married to another, she committeth adultery**.

For a discussion about the content of verses 11 and 12, above, regarding divorce, refer to the note after Matthew 5:31 in this study guide.

Little Children Welcomed

13 And **they** [*the people*] **brought young children to him, that he should touch them**: and his **disciples rebuked those** [*scolded them*] **that brought them.**

14 But when Jesus saw it, he was much displeased, and said unto them [*His disciples, who are still learning*], **Suffer** [*allow*] **the little children to come unto me, and forbid them not: for of such is the kingdom of God.**

15 Verily I say unto you, Whosoever [*whoever*] shall not receive the kingdom of God [*accept the teachings of the gospel*] as [*like*] a little child, he shall not enter therein.

16 And **he** took them [*the children*] up in his arms, put his hands upon them, and **blessed them.**

The Rich Young Man

17 And when he was gone forth into the way [*when he had gone on down the road*], there came one [*the rich young man in verse 22*] running, and kneeled to him, and asked him, Good Master, **what shall I do that I may inherit eternal life** [*exaltation*]?

18 And Jesus said unto him, Why callest thou me good? there is none good but one, that is, God. [*Jesus wants no glory for Himself, rather gives all glory and credit to the Father.*]

19 Thou knowest the commandments, **Do not commit adultery, Do not kill, Do not steal, Do not bear false witness** [*lie; accuse someone falsely*], **Defraud** [*cheat*] **not, Honour thy father and mother.**

20 And he answered and said unto him, Master, **all these have I observed** [*done*] **from my youth.**

21 Then Jesus beholding him loved him [*looked at him with kind, loving eyes*], and said unto him, **One thing thou lackest** [*there is one thing you haven't done yet*]: go thy way, **sell whatsoever** [*everything*] **thou hast, and give to the poor**, and thou shalt have treasure in heaven: and come, take up the cross [*take up My cause*], **and follow me.**

22 **And he** [*the rich young man*] **was sad at that saying** [*counsel*], **and went away grieved** [*troubled*]: for he had great possessions [*he was very rich*].

23 And **Jesus** looked round about, and **saith unto his disciples, How hardly shall they that have riches enter into the kingdom of God** [*how hard it is for rich people to enter the kingdom of God*]!

24 And **the disciples were astonished** [*surprised, startled*] at his words. But Jesus answereth again [*continued*], and saith unto them [*explained what He meant*], Children, **how hard is it** [*it is very difficult*] **for them that trust in riches to enter into the kingdom of God!**

This is a very important point. Some people believe that to be rich is somehow evil and against the Savior's teachings. That is not what the Master taught here.

MARK 10

To trust in wealth rather than God and to let wealth corrupt one's values and standards is the problem pointed out here by Jesus. See Jacob 2:16–20.

The Eye of a Needle

25 It is **easier for a camel to go through the eye of a needle, than for a rich man to enter into the kingdom of God**.

There is a common rumor that the "eye of a needle" was a small gate in the walls of Jerusalem, used for entry into the city by night, after the main gates were closed. The rumor states that it was very difficult for a camel to get down and scrunch through the gate. Scholars indicate that this rumor has no truth to it. They indicate that the word "needle," as used in verse 25, refers to an ordinary sewing needle in the original Bible languages.

The picture created in a person's mind of a large camel trying to get through the eye of a needle effectively demonstrates the impossibility of one entering heaven whose top priority is wealth. See JST Mark 10:26, quoted below.

26 And they were astonished out of measure [*could hardly believe what they had just heard*], saying among themselves, **Who then can be saved?**

27 And Jesus looking upon them saith, **With men it is impossible, but not with God**: for with God all things are possible

Watch what a difference the JST makes with verse 27, above!

JST Mark 10:26
26 And Jesus, looking upon them, **said, With men that trust in riches, it is impossible; but not impossible with men who trust in God and leave all for my sake, for with such all these things are possible**.

28 Then **Peter** began to say unto him, Lo, **we have left all, and have followed thee**.

Every Worthy Person Will Receive a Just Reward

29 And **Jesus answered** and said, Verily [*listen very carefully*] I say unto you, There is no man that hath left house, or brethren, or sisters, or father, or mother, or wife, or children, or lands, for my sake, and the gospel's,

30 But **he shall receive an hundredfold** [*a hundred times more*] now **in this time**, houses, and brethren, and sisters, and mothers, and children, and lands, with persecutions; **and in the world to come eternal life** [*eternal life*].

31 But many that are **first shall be last; and the last first**.

JST Mark 10:30–31
30 But there are **many who make themselves first, that shall be last**, and the last first.

The Savior Prophecies His Crucifixion and Resurrection Again

32 And **they were** in the way [*on the road*] **going up to Jerusalem**; and Jesus went before [*ahead of*] them: and they were amazed; and as they followed, they were afraid. And **he** took again the twelve, and **began to tell them what things should happen unto him,**

33 Saying, Behold, we go up to Jerusalem; and **the Son of man** [*Jesus, Son of Man*] **shall be delivered unto the chief priests** [*religious leaders of the Jews*], **and unto the scribes** [*Jewish religious leaders*]; and **they shall condemn him to death, and shall deliver him to the Gentiles** [*the Romans*]:

34 And they [*the Romans*] shall **mock** him, and shall **scourge** [*whip*] him, and shall **spit upon him**, and shall **kill him**: and **the third day he shall rise again** [*will be resurrected*].

James and John Ask a Favor

35 And **James and John**, the sons of Zebedee, come [*came*] unto him, saying, Master, **we would that thou shouldest do for us whatsoever we shall desire.**

36 And **he said** unto them, **What would ye that I should do for you?**

37 They said unto him, **Grant unto us that we may sit, one on thy right hand, and the other on thy left hand, in thy glory** [*in heaven*].

38 **But Jesus said** unto them, **Ye know not what ye ask**: can ye drink of the cup that I drink of [*can you really follow Me in everything*]? and be baptized with the baptism that I am baptized with [*go through what I have to go through*]?

39 And **they said** unto him, **We can.** And **Jesus said** unto them, Ye shall indeed drink of the cup that I drink of; and with the baptism that I am baptized withal shall ye be baptized:

40 **But to sit on my right hand and on my left hand is not mine to give; but it shall be given to them for whom it is prepared.** [*In other words, it is not to be given as a matter of favoritism or mere request; rather it will be given to those who earn it according to the laws established by the Father.*]

41 And when **the ten** [*other Apostles*] heard it, they began to be much **displeased with James and John.**

Watch now as the Savior, with kindness and skill calms the feelings of contention which have arisen among the twelve Apostles here and uses the occasion to teach the principle of "servant leadership," which is that those who want to be greatest among the people of God must be those who humbly and sincerely serve the others.

A Lesson About Serving

42 But **Jesus** called them to him, and **saith** unto them, Ye know that they which are accounted to rule over the Gentiles [*leaders among*

the gentiles] exercise lordship over them; and their great ones [most important leaders] exercise authority upon them.

43 But so shall it not be among you: but **whosoever will be great among you, shall be your minister:**

44 And **whosoever of you will be the chiefest, shall be servant of all.**

45 For **even the Son of man** [*Jesus*] **came not to be ministered unto, but to minister,** and to give his life a ransom [*payment*] for many.

Blind Bartimaeus Is Healed

46 And they came to Jericho [*east and down the mountain from Jerusalem, about 25 miles*]: and as he went out of Jericho with his disciples and a great number of people, **blind Bartimæus**, the son of Timæus, **sat by the highway side begging.**

47 And when he heard that it was Jesus of Nazareth, **he began to cry out** [*yell*], and say, Jesus, thou Son of David [*the promised Messiah, prophesied to come through David*], have mercy on me.

48 And **many charged him that he should hold his peace** [*told him to be quiet*]: **but he cried** [*shouted*] **the more** a great deal, Thou Son of David, have mercy on me.

49 And **Jesus stood still,** and **commanded him to be called.** And they call the blind man, saying unto him, Be of good comfort, rise; he calleth thee.

50 And **he,** casting away his garment [*throwing down his cloak, wasting no time*], **rose, and came to Jesus.**

51 And **Jesus** answered and **said** unto him, **What wilt thou** that I should do unto thee? **The blind man said** unto him, **Lord, that I might receive my sight.**

52 And Jesus said unto him, Go thy way; **thy faith hath made thee whole** [*healed*]. And **immediately he received his sight, and followed Jesus** in the way [*along the road*].

MARK 11

These next verses lead up to what is known as "the Triumphal Entry," the day when Jesus rode into Jerusalem accompanied by throngs of people shouting "Hosanna to the Son of David;" in other words, celebrating and cheering Jesus as the promised Messiah who would save them and free them from their enemies. Most Bible chronologies suggest that this day was Sunday, in our calendar system. The Passover was underway and throngs of Jewish pilgrims had arrived in Jerusalem from many lands to join in the Passover celebration and worship. This begins the last week of the Savior's mortal life.

The Triumphal Entry

1 AND when **they came nigh** [*near*] to **Jerusalem,** unto Bethphage and Bethany, at the mount of Olives [*a few minutes' walk east of*

Jerusalem], **he sendeth forth two of his disciples,**

2 And saith unto them, **Go** your way **into the village** over against you [*just ahead of you*]: and as soon as ye be entered into it, **ye shall find a colt** [*a young male donkey*] tied, whereon never man sat [*that has never been ridden*]; **loose** [*untie*] **him, and bring him.**

3 And **if any man say** unto you, **Why do ye this?** say ye that the Lord hath need of him; and straightway [*immediately*] he will send him hither [*here*].

Here is another miracle which is sometimes missed by people as they read. The young male donkey has never been ridden, yet when Jesus gets on him to ride into Jerusalem, the donkey does not object, rather, allows the Master to ride. This is another testimony of the Savior's power over all things.

4 **And they** [*the two disciples*] went their way, and **found the colt** tied by the door without [*outside*] in a place where two ways [*roads*] met; and they loose [*untied*] him.

5 And **certain of them that stood there** [*some people standing around*] **said** unto them, **What do ye, loosing the colt?**

6 And they said [*replied*] unto them even as Jesus had commanded: and they let them go.

7 And **they brought the colt to Jesus,** and cast their garments [*cloaks, robes*] on him [*the colt*]; **and he** [*Jesus*] **sat upon him.**

In Jewish culture and symbolism of that day, a donkey symbolized humility and submission. A horse, on the other hand, symbolized triumph and victory over enemies, in other words, military might and victory, in their culture.

Thus, the Savior's riding into Jerusalem on a donkey represents that He came in meekness and submission to carry out the Father's will in carrying out the Atonement, including being crucified. At His Second Coming, He is prophetically represented as riding on a white horse (Revelation 19:11), which symbolizes His triumph and victory over all enemies of righteousness, including Satan and his evil kingdom. White, by the way, symbolizes purity and righteousness, as well as celestial glory, in Biblical symbolism.

8 And **many spread their garments in the way** [*on the road*]: and **others cut down branches off the trees, and strawed** [*spread*] **them in the way** [*on the road in front of Jesus*].

9 And they that went before [*the people who went ahead*], and they that followed, cried [*shouted*], **saying, Hosanna** [*"Save us now." See Bible Dictionary, under "Hosanna"*]; **Blessed is he that cometh in the name of the Lord:**

10 Blessed be the kingdom of our father David, that cometh in the name of the Lord: **Hosanna in the highest.**

MARK 11

JST Mark 11:10–12

10 Hosanna! Blessed is he that cometh in the name of the Lord;

11 **That bringeth the kingdom of our father David** [*in other words, in effect, the prophesied Messiah is here, and will re-establish the kingdom of David and free us from Roman rule*];

12 **Blessed is he that cometh in the name of the Lord**; Hosanna in the highest.

11 And **Jesus entered into Jerusalem, and into the temple**: and when he had looked round about upon all things, and now the eventide was come, he **went out unto Bethany with the twelve.**

The Fig Tree Is Cursed

12 And **on the morrow** [*the next day*], when they were come from Bethany, **he was hungry:**

13 And **seeing a fig tree afar** off having leaves [*in other words, appearing as if it was a productive tree with figs on it*], **he came, if haply** [*to see if*] **he might find any thing thereon**: and when he came to it, he found nothing but leaves; for the time of figs was not yet.

14 And **Jesus** answered [*spoke*] and **said unto it** [*the fig tree*], **No man eat fruit of thee hereafter for ever.** And his disciples heard it. [*See more about this in verses 20–21.*]

JST Mark 11:14–16

14 And on the morrow, when they **came** from Bethany he was hungry; and seeing a fig tree afar off having leaves, **he came to it with his disciples; and as they supposed**, he came **to it to see if** he might find anything thereon.

15 And when he came to it, **there was** nothing but leaves; **for as yet the figs were not ripe**.

16 And Jesus **spake** and said unto it, No man eat fruit of thee hereafter, **forever**. And **the disciples heard him**.

Jesus Cleanses the Temple for the Second Time

15 And **they come to** [*arrived at*] **Jerusalem**: and **Jesus went into the temple**, and began to **cast out them that sold and bought** in the temple, and overthrew the tables of the moneychangers, and the seats of them that sold doves;

The temple had become a major marketplace for buying and selling birds and animals to be used for sacrifices. There was much of yelling and cheating, and so forth, which typically go along with such dealings; therefore, Jesus cleansed the temple from these moneychangers and their merchandise. John tells us (John 2:14–17) that Jesus cleansed the temple at the beginning of His ministry. Now, three years later, Jesus cleanses the temple again. This is the second time and the temple crowd obviously hadn't learned their lesson the first time.

16 And would not suffer [*allow*] that any man should carry any vessel [*container*] through the temple.

17 And **he taught**, saying unto them, Is it not written [*in the scriptures, in Jeremiah 7:11*], **My house shall be called of all nations the house of prayer? but ye have made it a den of thieves.**

18 And **the scribes and chief priests** [*Jewish religious leaders, who wanted desperately to arrest Jesus and have him executed*] **heard** it, and **sought how they might destroy him**: for they feared him, because all the people was astonished at his doctrine [*Jesus had become famous for His teachings*].

19 And when even [*evening*] was come, he went out of the city.

The Fig Tree Has Dried Up and Died, Overnight

20 And **in the morning**, as they passed by, **they saw the fig tree dried up from the roots.**

The fig tree is symbolic of the hypocritical Jewish religious leaders who pretend to look official but do not produce the fruit of the gospel. It is also symbolic of the Jewish nation, the covenant people, who are "barren" as far as the gospel is concerned. See *Jesus the Christ*, p. 443.

21 And **Peter** calling to remembrance **saith** unto him, Master, behold, **the fig tree which thou cursedst is withered away** [*has dried up and died*].

Jesus will now use the fig tree incident to teach His disciples about the power of faith.

A Lesson on the Power of Faith

22 And Jesus answering saith unto them, **Have faith in God.**

23 For verily I say unto you, That whosoever shall say unto this mountain, Be thou removed, and be thou cast into the sea; and shall not doubt in his heart, but shall believe that those things which he saith shall come to pass; he shall have whatsoever he saith.

24 Therefore I say unto you, **What things soever ye desire, when ye pray, believe that ye receive them, and ye shall have them.**

D&C 46:30 and 50:29–30 add to our understanding of this use of faith. In these Doctrine and Covenants verses we are instructed that, in order to have this kind of faith, the Holy Ghost must inspire us as to what is permissible for us to ask.

Next, beginning in verse 25, we are taught that in order to have the kind of faith spoken of in the above verses, we must forgive others. If we carry grudges in our heart, we cannot have this type of faith. One of the major messages here is that, since we need the constant forgiveness of God in our lives, if we ask for it and do not forgive others, we are hypocrites and cannot have the help of the Holy Ghost to sufficiently strengthen our own faith.

25 And **when ye stand praying** [*when you are asking God for blessings and help*], **forgive, if ye have ought** [*anything*] **against any: that your Father also which is in heaven**

MARK 12

may forgive you your trespasses. [*In other words, another message here is that if you want God to forgive your sins, you must forgive others.*]

26 But **if ye do not forgive, neither will your Father which is in heaven forgive your trespasses**.

Jewish Religious Leader Make Another Attempt to Trap the Savior

27 And they come [*came*] again to Jerusalem: and as he was walking in the temple, **there come to him the chief priests, and the scribes, and the elders,**

These Jewish religious leaders are now working closely together to do away with Jesus. Keep in mind that there are large crowds of people standing near who are listening carefully to what now goes on.

28 And say [*and the Jewish leaders said*] unto him, **By what authority doest thou these things? and who gave thee this authority to do these things?**

29 And **Jesus answered** and said unto them, **I will also ask of you one question,** and answer me, and I will tell you by what authority I do these things. [*If you will answer one question I ask you, then I will answer your question.*]

30 [*Here is my question to you:*] **The baptism of John, was it from heaven, or of men?** answer me. [*Was John the Baptist sent by heaven, or was he just a man who falsely claimed authority?*]

31 And **they reasoned with** [*talked it over among*] **themselves**, saying, If we shall say, From heaven; he will say, Why then did ye not believe him?

32 But if we shall say, Of men; they feared the people [*feared that the people would mob them*]: for all men counted John, that he was a prophet indeed.

33 And **they answered and said unto Jesus, We cannot tell** [*we cannot answer Your question*]. And Jesus answering saith unto them, **Neither do I tell you by what authority I do these things** [*then I will not answer your question either*].

MARK 12

In this next parable, known as the Parable of the Wicked Husbandmen, the Savior clearly compares the wicked Jewish religious leaders to the wicked husbandmen [*supervisors, foremen, stewards, those who run the business while the owner is away*] who kill the owner's son in an attempt to take the kingdom from him. The notes in brackets in the parable suggest possible interpretations of symbolism found in the parable.

The Parable of the Wicked Husbandmen

1 AND **he began to speak unto them** [*the Jewish leaders mentioned in Mark 11:27, who are trying to trap Jesus*] **by parables** [*stories which teach a lesson*]. **A certain man** [*Heavenly Father*]

planted a **vineyard** [*grape vines, symbolic of creating this earth and putting people on it*], and set an **hedge** [*protection from danger (Satan, temptation, etc.)*] about it, and **digged a place for the winefat** [*built a place to harvest the grape juice, in other words, planned for a good harvest of righteous people*], and built a **tower** [*so people could see enemies coming from far off and thus avoid being conquered; symbolic of prophets who see dangers and warn their people*], and **let it out to husbandmen** [*placed supervisors over it*], and went into a **far country** [*heaven*].

2 And **at the season** [*at harvest time*] **he sent to the husbandmen** [*supervisors, stewards*] **a servant** [*prophets*], that he might receive from the husbandmen of the **fruit of the vineyard** [*the harvest*].

3 And **they caught him**, [*the prophets*] and **beat him**, and **sent him away empty** [*wouldn't listen to the prophets*].

4 And again he sent unto them **another servant** [*more prophets*]; and **at him they cast stones**, and **wounded him** in the head, and **sent him away** shamefully handled [*reject them and badly abused them*].

5 And again **he sent another** [*more prophets*]; and **him they killed**, and **many others**; beating some, and killing some.

6 Having yet therefore one **son, his wellbeloved** [*Christ*], **he** [*the Father*] **sent him also** last unto them, saying, They will reverence my son.

7 But **those husbandmen said among themselves, This is the heir** [*the owner's son to whom all this will belong*]; **come, let us kill him**, and the inheritance shall be ours [*let's kill Jesus so we can keep our positions of power and leadership over the people*].

8 And **they took him** [*Jesus*], **and killed** [*crucified*] **him**, and cast him out of the vineyard [*got rid of Him from the earth*].

The Question and the Answer

9 **What shall therefore the lord of the vineyard** [*Christ*] **do? he will come and destroy the husbandmen** [*at the Second Coming*], and **will give the vineyard unto others** [*to the righteous, who will inherit the earth*].

10 And **have ye not read this scripture** [*in Psalm 118:22–23*]; **The stone** [*Christ*] **which the builders** [*the wicked husbandmen in verse two, and their people*] rejected **is become the head of the corner** [*the main part of the building*]:

11 **This was the Lord's doing, and it is marvellous in our eyes?**

12 And **they** [*the wicked Jewish religious leaders*] **sought to lay hold on him** [*tried to figure out a way to arrest Him*], but feared the people: **for they knew that he had spoken the parable against them:** and they left him, and went their way.

Having failed to stop Jesus themselves, these wicked chief priests, scribes, and elders now

MARK 12

recruit others to help them trap Jesus and get Him arrested. It is interesting to note that the Pharisees and Herodians (verse 13) normally are enemies. Now they have joined together to trap the Master. The Herodians were a political party among the Jews who supported the Herodian family as rulers (see Bible Dictionary, under "Herodians") which was very distasteful to the Pharisees.

13 And **they send** [*sent*] unto him **certain of the Pharisees and of the Herodians, to catch him in his words** [*to get Him to say something for which He could be arrested*].

Watch now as these leaders, oozing with hypocrisy, foolishly attempt to trap the Jehovah of the Old Testament, who is among them in the flesh, with cunning words.

14 And **when they were come** [*had arrived*], **they say** [*said*] **unto him,** Master, we know that thou art true [*honest*], and carest for no man [*You are not afraid to say what You think*]: for thou regardest not the person of men [*You don't care who You are talking to*], but teachest the way of God in truth: [*This is dripping with false flattery!*] **Is it lawful to give tribute** [*pay taxes*] **to Cæsar, or not?**

15 **Shall we give** [*pay*], **or shall we not give?** But he, knowing their hypocrisy [*trying to look righteous, but enjoying being evil*], said unto them, **Why tempt ye me? bring me a penny,** [*a Roman coin equal to a normal day's pay—see Bible*

Dictionary, under "Money"] that I may see it.

16 And **they brought it.** And he saith unto them, **Whose is this image and superscription** [*whose face and title are on the coin*]? And they said unto him, **Cæsar's.**

"Render to Cæsar the things that Are Cæsar's"

17 And Jesus answering said unto them, **Render** [*pay to*] **to Cæsar the things that are Cæsar's, and to God the things that are God's.** And they marvelled at him [*were surprised at how skillfully He got out of their trap*].

Next, the Sadducees come along to try their hand at trapping the Master. The Sadducees were another somewhat influential group of religious leaders among the Jews. They did not believe in the resurrection and were normally enemies of the Pharisees who did believe in resurrection. The Sadducees have now joined forces with the Pharisees in attempting to do away with Jesus. They will try to trap Him by posing a question about marriage in the next life.

18 **Then come** [*came*] **unto him the Sadducees,** which say there is no resurrection [*who didn't believe in resurrection*]; and **they asked him,** saying,

19 Master, **Moses wrote** unto us [*gave us a law, saying*], If a man's brother die, and leave his wife behind him, and leave no children, that his brother should take [*marry*]

his wife, and raise up seed [*children*] unto [*for*] his brother.

20 Now there were **seven brethren** [*brothers*]: and **the first took a wife, and dying left no seed** [*had no children before he died*].

21 And **the second took her** [*married her*], **and died, neither left he any seed**: and **the third likewise.**

22 And **the seven had her** [*all seven brothers eventually married her*], and **left no seed** [*children*]: last of all **the woman died also.**

The Question
23 **In the resurrection therefore, when they shall rise, whose wife shall she be of them? for the seven had her to wife.**

24 And **Jesus** answering **said** unto them, **Do ye not therefore err, because ye know not the scriptures, neither the power of God?**

JST Mark 12:28
28 And Jesus answering said unto them, **Ye do err therefore, because ye know not, and understand not the scriptures**, neither the power of God.

25 For **when they shall rise from the dead, they neither marry, nor are given in marriage; but are as the angels which are in heaven.** [*After everyone on this earth has been resurrected, there will be no more marrying for them.*]

Here is a major doctrinal point. Many religions use verse 25 to prove that there is no such thing

as eternal marriage and family in the next life. On the contrary, the simple fact that the Sadducees asked the Savior the question "Whose wife shall she be of them?" (when they are all resurrected), is proof that the Savior had indeed preached marriage in the resurrection, in other words, eternal marriage. Otherwise, their question would not make any sense at all! The next point of correct doctrine which needs to be understood here is that after everyone from this earth is resurrected, there will be no more eternal marriages performed for them, because such marriages have to be done by mortals for themselves, or by mortals who serve as proxies for those who have died—see D&C 128:15 and 18. Brigham Young said: "And when the Millennium is over, . . . all the sons and daughters of Adam and Eve, down to the last of their posterity (**bold** added for emphasis), who come within the reach of the clemency of the Gospel, [*will*] have been redeemed in hundreds of temples **through the administration of their children as proxies for them**" (Discourses of Brigham Young, p. 395). Since there will be no mortals left on earth after the resurrection is completed, there would be no one left to serve as proxies for eternal marriages.

The next point emphasized by the Savior here is particularly disturbing to the Sadducees, since, as previously mentioned, they do not believe in the resurrection of the dead.

MARK 12

26 And as touching **the dead**, that they **rise** [*get resurrected*]: **have ye not read** in the book of Moses, how in the bush [*the burning bush*] God spake unto him, saying, I am the God of Abraham, and the God of Isaac, and the God of Jacob [*Exodus 3:6*]?

27 **He is not the God of the dead, but the God of the living**: ye therefore do greatly err [*you Sadducees are making a big mistake in not believing in resurrection*].

JST Mark 12:32

32 He is not **therefore** the God of the dead, but the God of the living; **for he raiseth them up out of their graves**. Ye therefore do greatly err.

The Two Greatest Commandments

28 And **one of the scribes** [*prominent Jewish religious leaders*] **came**, and having heard them [*the Sadducees*] reasoning together, and perceiving that he [*Christ*] had answered them well [*had answered their question about the seven brothers skillfully*], **asked** him, **Which is the first commandment of all?**

29 And Jesus answered him, The first of all the commandments is, Hear, O Israel; The Lord our God is one Lord:

30 And **thou shalt love the Lord thy God with all thy heart, and with all thy soul, and with all thy mind, and with all thy strength**: this is the first commandment.

31 And **the second is like**, namely this, **Thou shalt love thy neighbour as thyself**. There is none other commandment greater than these.

32 And the scribe said unto him, Well, Master, thou hast said the truth: for there is one God; and there is none other but he:

33 And to love him with all the heart, and with all the understanding, and with all the soul, and with all the strength, and to love his neighbour as himself, is more than all whole burnt offerings and sacrifices [*is more important than all the laws of animal sacrifice*].

34 And when **Jesus** saw that he answered discreetly [*carefully and wisely*], he **said** unto him, **Thou art not far from the kingdom of God**. And no man after that durst [*dared*] ask him any question.

Jesus Teaches in the Temple

It must have been frustrating and even infuriating to the Jewish religious leaders at this point that Jesus boldly went back into the temple, which He had cleansed earlier in the week. It would have been an easy matter for them to have Him arrested there, but they did not dare.

Watch now as He poses a question to the people who have gathered in the courtyard of the temple, and then goes on to warn them about their religious leaders.

35 And **Jesus** answered [*spoke*] and said, while he **taught in the temple, How say the scribes** [*the Jewish religious leaders who interpreted the scriptures for the people*] **that Christ is the Son of David** [*what do the scribes mean when they say that Christ is the Son of David*]?

36 For David himself said [*Psalm 110:1*] by the Holy Ghost [*by inspiration*], The LORD [*Heavenly Father*] said to my Lord [*Christ*], Sit thou on my right hand, till I make thine enemies thy footstool [*until You conquer all Your enemies, including Satan*].

37 **David** therefore himself **calleth him Lord; and whence is he then his son** [*how can Christ be David's son if David himself calls him Lord*]? And **the common people heard him gladly** [*were pleased that Jesus was outsmarting their arrogant religious leaders*].

38 And **he said unto them** [*the people*] in his doctrine, **Beware of** [*watch out for*] **the scribes**, which love to go in long clothing, and love salutations [*to be greeted by the common people*] in the marketplaces,

39 And the chief [*the most important*] seats in the synagogues, and the uppermost rooms at feasts:

40 Which devour widows' houses [*take widow's houses away from them*], and for a pretence [*for show*] make long prayers: these [*wicked religious leaders*] shall receive greater damnation [*punishment*].

The Widow's Mite

41 And **Jesus sat over against the treasury** [*across from where people contributed money in the temple*], **and beheld** [*watched*] **how the people cast money into the treasury**: and many that were rich cast in much.

42 And there came **a certain poor widow**, and she **threw in two mites**, which make a farthing. [*Bible Dictionary, under "Money," tells us that one mite is equal to 1/64th of a day's pay.*]

43 And he called unto him his disciples, and saith unto them, Verily I say unto you, That **this poor widow hath cast more in, than all they which have cast into the treasury:**

44 For all **they did cast in of their abundance** [*they had plenty of money left over after they gave their contribution*]; **but she of her want** [*in her poverty*] **did cast in all that she had**, even all her living.

MARK 13

This chapter deals with many of the signs of the times (prophecies that will be fulfilled before the Savior's Second Coming). In the JST, the Prophet made many corrections and changes to this chapter. JST Mark 13, JST Matthew 24, and JS—Matthew in the Pearl of Great Price are the same. I created a parallel-column version of Matthew 24 in the Bible and Joseph

MARK 13

Smith—Matthew (the JST version) so you can "at-a-glance" study them side-by-side, and placed it at the end of Matthew 24 in this study guide for your convenience. If you do study this parallel-column comparison, you will see that Joseph Smith made many changes, including adding about 450 words to Matthew 24 in the Bible, combining some verses, rearranging the order of some of the verses, adding verses not found in the Bible, and so forth.

As we now study Mark 13, we will only include a few of the JST changes here (because all of them are found in Joseph Smith—Matthew, which is included at the end of Matthew 24 in this study guide).

1 AND as he went out of the temple, **one of his disciples saith** unto him, Master, see what manner of stones and what buildings are here!

Temple Destruction Prophecy

2 **And Jesus** answering [*responding*] **said** unto him, Seest thou these great buildings [*of the temple*]? there shall not be left one stone upon another, that shall not be thrown down.

JST Mark 13:1–5

1 And as **Jesus** went out of the temple, **his disciples came to him for to hear him, saying, Master, show us concerning the buildings of the temple.**

2 And **he** said unto **them**, **Behold ye these stones of** the temple, and all this great work, and buildings of the temple?

3 Verily I say unto you, they shall be thrown down and left unto the Jews desolate.

4 And Jesus said unto them, See ye not all these things, and do ye not understand them?

5 **Verily I say unto you,** There shall not be left **here upon this temple,** one stone upon another, that shall not be thrown down.

The Savior's prophecy that the buildings of the temple would be torn down was fulfilled by about A.D. 70 to 73 as the Romans finally conquered the Jews and destroyed many of their cities.

As you will see, four of the Master's Apostles came to Him privately and asked Him two specific questions.

3 And as he sat upon the mount of Olives over against [*across from*] the temple, **Peter** and **James** and **John** and **Andrew asked** him privately,

JST Mark 13:7

7 And as he sat upon the mount of Olives, **the disciples came unto him privately, saying,**

Two Questions

4 Tell us, [1] **when shall these things be** [*the things you have just prophesied*]? and [2] **what shall be the sign** when all these things shall

be fulfilled [*what are the signs to be fulfilled before the Second Coming*]?

JST Mark 13:8–9

8 Tell us, when shall these things be **which thou hast said, concerning the destruction of the temple, and the Jews?**

9 And what is the sign of thy coming, and of the end of the world, (or the destruction of the wicked, which is the end of the world?)

5 And **Jesus answering** them began to say, **Take heed** [*be careful*] **lest any man deceive you:**

Signs of the Times for Members of the Early Church at the Time of Christ

Verses 6–20 basically deal with prophecies of the near future for these Apostles and the early members of the Church back then. Beginning with verse 21, we see things that will happen in our day, prior to the Second Coming.

6 For **many shall come in my name**, saying, I am Christ; **and shall deceive** [*fool*] **many**.

7 And when ye shall hear of **wars and rumours of wars**, be ye not troubled [*don't be too concerned*]: for such things must needs be; but the end [*of the world*] shall not be yet.

8 For **nation shall rise against nation**, and **kingdom** against **kingdom** [*there will be widespread, numerous wars*]: and there shall be **earthquakes** in divers [*various*] places, and there shall be **famines** and **troubles**: these are the beginnings of **sorrows**.

9 But take heed to yourselves: for **they shall deliver you up to councils** [*you will be arrested*]; and in the synagogues [*Jewish church buildings*] ye shall be beaten: and ye shall be brought before rulers and kings for my sake, for a testimony against them.

10 And the **gospel must first be published among all nations**.

11 But when they [*your enemies*] shall lead you, and deliver you up [*arrest you*], take no thought beforehand what ye shall speak, neither do ye premeditate: but whatsoever shall be given you in that hour, that speak ye: for it is not ye that speak, but the Holy Ghost [*the Holy Ghost will help you know what to say*].

12 Now the **brother shall betray** the **brother** to death, and the **father** the **son**; and **children shall rise up against their parents**, and shall cause them to be put to death [*families will come apart and treat each other terribly*].

13 And ye [*Apostles and early members of the Church back then*] shall be hated of all men for my name's sake [*because of your loyalty to me*]: but he that shall endure unto the end, the same shall be saved.

MARK 13

14 But when ye shall see the **abomination of desolation**, spoken of by Daniel the prophet [*Daniel 11:31 and 12:11*], standing where it ought not, (let him that readeth understand,) then let them that be in Judæa flee to the mountains [*to escape*]:

> "Abomination of desolation" means terrible things which will cause much destruction and misery. The abomination of desolation spoken of by Daniel was to have two fulfillments. The first occurred in A.D. 70 when Titus, with his Roman legions, surrounded Jerusalem and laid siege to conquer the Jews. This siege resulted in much destruction and terrible human misery and loss of life. In the last days, the abomination of desolation will occur again (see Joseph Smith–Matthew 1:31–32), meaning that Jerusalem will again be under siege. See Bible Dictionary, under "Abomination of Desolation."

15 And let him that is on the housetop not go down into the house, neither enter therein, to take any thing out of his house [*just get away fast!*]:

16 And let him that is in the field not turn back again for to take up his garment [*robe, cloak*].

17 But woe to them that are with child [*pregnant*], and to them that give suck [*are nursing babies and small children*] in those days [*when these things happen to Jerusalem*]!

18 And pray ye that your flight be not in the winter [*when it is more difficult to flee*].

19 For in those days shall be affliction, such as was not from the beginning of the creation which God created unto this time, neither shall be.

20 And except that the Lord had shortened those days, no flesh should be saved [*the Lord will intervene so that some Jews will be left*]: but for the elect's sake, whom he hath chosen, he hath shortened the days.

Signs of the Times for Our Day

> Now the topic changes from the days when the Romans conquered and destroyed the Jewish nation, culminating in about A.D. 70 to 73, to the last days and signs preceding the Savior's Second Coming.

21 And then **if any man shall say to you, Lo, here is Christ; or, lo, he is there; believe him not** [*Christ will not come secretly or in just one place at the actual Second Coming; rather He will come and everyone will see Him at once*]:

22 For **false Christs and false prophets** shall rise, and shall shew signs and wonders, to seduce [*fool*], if it were possible, even the elect.

23 But take ye heed: behold, I have foretold you all things.

24 But in those days, after that tribulation, the **sun shall be darkened**, and the **moon shall not give her light**,

25 And the **stars** of heaven **shall fall**, and the powers that are in heaven shall be shaken. [*There will be many signs of the times, that is, prophecies fulfilled in the last days showing that the Second Coming is near.*]

Verse 26 jumps ahead to the Second Coming; then verse 27 goes back to the gathering of Israel in the last days.

26 And then shall they **see the Son of man** [*Jesus, the Son of Man— see Moses 6:57*] **coming** in the clouds with great power and glory.

27 And then shall he send his angels, and shall **gather** together **his elect** from the four winds, from the uttermost part of the earth to the uttermost part of heaven [*the righteous will be gathered*].

The Parable of the Fig Tree

28 Now learn a parable [*a story that teaches*] of the fig tree; **When her branch is yet tender** [*has new growth*], and **putteth forth leaves**, ye **know that summer is near**:

29 So ye in like manner, **when ye shall see these things** [*signs of the times*] come to pass, **know that it** [*the Second Coming*] **is nigh** [*near*], even at the doors.

30 Verily I say unto you, that **this generation** [*the dispensation of the fulness of times, the last dispensation*] **shall not pass, till all these things be done.**

31 Heaven and earth shall pass

away: but my words shall not pass away.

No One Knows Exactly When the Savior Will Come

32 But **of that day and that hour knoweth no man, no, not the angels which are in heaven, neither the Son, but the Father.**

Verse 32, above, is similar to Matthew 24:36, but adds that the Son, Jesus, won't know when the Second Coming will be, but only the Father.

33 Take ye heed [*pay attention*], watch and pray: for **ye know not when the time is** [*when the Savior will come*].

A Parable of the Coming

34 For **the Son of man** [*the Savior*] **is as a man taking a far journey**, who left his house [*went to heaven*], and gave authority to his servants [*the Apostles, leaders of the Church*], and to every man his work [*to all members their responsibilities*], and commanded the porter to watch.

35 **Watch ye therefore: for ye know not when the master of the house cometh** [*symbolic of the Savior at his Second Coming*], at even [*evening*], or at midnight, or at the cockcrowing, or in the morning:

36 **Lest coming suddenly he find you sleeping** [*not living righteously*].

MARK 14

37 And what I say unto you I say unto all, **Watch**.

MARK 14

The Feast of the Passover, mentioned in verse 1, was celebrated in the springtime at about the same time as we celebrate Easter. It commemorated the destroying angel's passing over the houses of the children of Israel in Egypt, when the firstborn of the Egyptians were killed. The Israelites in Egypt at the time were instructed by Moses to sacrifice a lamb without blemish and to put blood from the lamb which was sacrificed on the doorposts of their houses. See Bible Dictionary, under "Feasts." Thus, through the blood of a lamb, the Israelites were protected from the anguish and punishment brought to the Egyptians by the destroying angel. The symbolism is clear. It is by the "blood of the Lamb" (the sacrifice of the Savior) that we are saved, "after all we can do" (2 Nephi 25:23). Now, at the time of Passover in Jerusalem, the "Lamb of God," Christ, will present Himself to be sacrificed, that we might be saved. The Feast of the Passover brought large numbers of Jews from near and far to Jerusalem to join in the worship and celebration.

As you can see in verse 1, the religious leaders of the Jews are frantically plotting to get the Master executed. It is interesting to note that even though the Roman government had given the Jewish religious leaders many powers, they had not given them power to carry out capital punishment.

1 AFTER two days was the **feast of the passover**, and of unleavened bread: and **the chief priests and the scribes** [*religious leaders of the Jews*] **sought how they might take him** [*Jesus*] by craft [*quietly*], **and put him to death**.

2 **But** they said, **Not on the feast day** [*not on Thursday, the day of the Feast of the Passover*], **lest there be an uproar** of the people [*for fear that the people will riot*].

A Woman Anoints Jesus with Costly Spikenard

3 And being **in Bethany** [*a village a short distance from Jerusalem, just over the Mount of Olives*] **in the house of Simon the leper, as he sat at meat** [*as Jesus ate dinner*], **there came a woman** [*Mary—see John 12:3*] **having an alabaster box of ointment of spikenard** very precious [*expensive*]; and she brake [*broke*] the box, and **poured it on his head**.

The anointing of Jesus by Mary, in verse 3, contains much significant symbolism. Jesus is the Messiah. "Messiah" means "the Anointed One" (see Bible Dictionary, under "Messiah"). It would seem that this Mary understood what the disciples did not yet fully understand and symbolically "anointed" the Savior in preparation for His Atoning sacrifice. This sheds light on the divine nature and spiritual sensitivity of women.

As you can see, in verse 4, next, some in attendance were angry because of what they perceived to be a terrible waste of expensive ointment.

4 And there were **some** that **had indignation** within themselves [*who were angry*], and said, **Why was this waste of the ointment made?**

5 For **it might have been sold for more than three hundred pence** [*about a year's wages*], **and** have **been given to the poor.** And they murmured against her.

A Lesson in Perspective

6 And **Jesus said, Let her alone;** why trouble ye her? she hath wrought [*done*] a good work on me.

7 For **ye have the poor with you always**, and whensoever ye will ye may do them good: **but me ye have not always.**

8 She hath done what she could: she is come aforehand **to anoint my body to the burying.**

JST Mark 14:8

8 She **has** done what she could, **and this which she has done unto me, shall be had in remembrance in generations to come, wheresoever my gospel shall be preached; for verily** she has come beforehand to anoint my body to the burying.

9 Verily I say unto you, WhEresoever this gospel shall be preached

throughout the whole world, this also that she hath done shall be spoken of for a memorial of her.

Judas Iscariot Betrays Christ to the Chief Priests

10 And **Judas Iscariot,** one of the twelve, **went unto the chief priests** [*main religious leaders of the Jews*], **to betray him unto them.**

11 And when they heard it, **they** were glad, and **promised to give him money.** And **he sought how he might conveniently** [*watched for an opportunity to*] **betray him.**

Matthew 26:15 says they agreed to pay Judas thirty pieces of silver, which was the going price for a common slave. This devalued the Savior and was an insult to Judas.

The Savior Celebrates Passover with His Disciples

12 And the first day of unleavened bread [*Thursday*], when they killed the passover [*sacrificed the Passover lamb*], **his disciples said** unto him, **Where wilt thou** that we go and prepare that thou mayest **eat the passover** [*the Passover meal*]?

Watch as Jesus prophecies exactly what will happen as He sends two Apostles to make arrangements for them to celebrate the Passover meal together.

13 And **he sendeth forth two** of his disciples, and saith unto them, **Go ye into the city, and there shall**

MARK 14

meet you a man bearing [*carrying*] a pitcher of water: follow him.

14 And wheresoever he shall go in [*whichever house he enters*], say ye to the goodman [*owner*] of the house, The Master saith, Where is the guestchamber, where I shall eat the passover with my disciples?

15 And he will shew [*pronounced "show"*] you a large upper room furnished and prepared: there make ready for us.

16 And his disciples went forth, and came into the city, and found as he had said unto them: and they made ready the passover.

17 And in the evening he cometh [*came*] with the twelve.

Imagine the concern among the Twelve as Jesus made the statement in verse 18.

18 And as they sat and did eat, Jesus said, Verily I say unto you, One of you which eateth with me shall betray me.

19 And they began to be sorrowful, and to say unto him one by one, Is it I? and another said, Is it I?

20 And he answered and said unto them, It is one of the twelve, that dippeth [*that dips his bread*] with me in the dish.

21 The Son of man [*Jesus*] indeed goeth [*will be arrested, tried and crucified*], as it is written of him [*as it is prophesied in the scriptures*]:

but woe to that man by whom the Son of man is betrayed! good were it for that man if he had never been born.

The Last Supper and Sacrament

The Savior now introduces the sacrament to his Apostles. This meal for the Lord and His Apostles is known as the "Last Supper." Jesus introduces the sacrament as a "new testament" (verse 24) The word "testament" often means "covenant" (see Bible Dictionary, under "Covenant.") Thus, the sacrament becomes a "new covenant" and replaces the "old covenant" of animal sacrifice as a means of making covenants and pointing our minds and hearts toward Christ and our commitments to Him.

The Bread

22 And as they did eat, Jesus took bread, and blessed, and brake it, and gave to them, and said, Take, eat: this is my body [*this represents My body*].

The Wine

23 And he took the cup, and when he had given thanks, he gave it to them: and they all drank of it.

24 And he said unto them, This is my blood [*this represents My blood*] of the new testament [*the new covenant, associated with the full gospel which Christ had restored*], which is shed for many.

JST Mark 14:20–24

20 And as they did eat, Jesus took bread and blessed **it**, and brake, and gave to them, and said, Take **it, and** eat.

21 Behold, this is for you to do in remembrance of my body; for as oft as ye do this ye will remember this hour that I was with you.

22 And he took the cup, and when he had given thanks, he gave it to them; and they all drank of it.

23 And he said unto them, This is **in remembrance of my blood which is shed for many, and the new testament which I give unto you; for of me ye shall bear record unto all the world.**

24 And as oft as ye do this ordinance, ye will remember me in this hour that I was with you and drank with you of this cup, even the last time in my ministry.

JST verses 21 and 24, above, are not found in the Bible.

As you know, we now use water instead of wine for the sacrament. You may wish to read the heading for Doctrine and Covenants, Section 27, as well as D&C 27:2, for information regarding this change, as directed by the Lord.

Next, in verse 25, the Master informs His disciples that the next time He will partake of the sacrament with them will be in the kingdom of God. Apostle Bruce R. McConkie said that this will be during the council held at Adam-ondi-Ahman, shortly before the Savior comes for His Second Coming. (See *The Millennial Messiah: The Second Coming of the Son of Man*, Bruce R. McConkie, Deseret Book, 1982, 587.)

You may wish to read D&C 27, beginning with verse 5, in which the Savior speaks of a great sacrament meeting to be held in the future. Note that Mark 14:25 is footnoted in the Doctrine and Covenants as a cross-reference for D&C 27:5.

25 Verily I say unto you, **I will drink no more of the fruit of the vine, until that day that I drink it new in the kingdom of God** [*this is the last time the Savior will partake of the sacrament with them during His mortal life*].

A Hymn Is Sung

26 And **when they had sung an hymn,** they went out into the mount of Olives.

27 And **Jesus saith** unto them, **All ye shall be offended** [*stumble, leave, scatter, desert; see Strong's* Concordance, *#4624*] **because of me this night** [*all of you will scatter, desert Me tonight because of what happens*]: for it is written [*in Zachariah 13:7*], I will smite the shepherd, and the sheep shall be scattered.

28 But **after** that **I am risen** [*resurrected*], **I will go before you** [*ahead of you*] **into Galilee.**

MARK 14

29 **But Peter said** unto him, Although all shall be offended [*even if everyone else scatters and deserts you*], yet will not I.

30 And **Jesus saith unto him**, Verily I say unto thee, That this day, even in this night, before the cock crow [*a rooster crows*] twice, thou shalt deny me thrice [*you will deny knowing me three times before morning*].

Denying knowing Christ is forgivable and is not the same as denying the Holy Ghost. Peter was very disappointed by his behavior, as recorded in verses 66–72, but he went on to become a powerful Apostle and the president of the church after the Savior was resurrected and taken up into heaven. Perhaps Peter's example here can be a lesson to us. We think we are strong in the gospel and claim to be willing to live it at all costs. Yet, sometimes we falter and give in to temptation which disappoints us and makes us all the more determined to be stronger in the faith.

31 But he [*Peter*] spake the more vehemently [*strongly, emphatically*], If I should die with thee, **I will not deny thee in any wise** [*in any way*]. Likewise also said they all [*all the other apostles said the same thing Peter said*].

The Savior's Suffering in Gethsemane

32 And **they came to** a place which was named **Gethsemane** [*the Garden of Gethsemane*]: and he saith to his disciples, Sit ye here, while I shall pray.

"Gethsemane" means "oil press." There is significant symbolism here. The Jews put olives into bags made of mesh fabric and placed them in a press to squeeze olive oil out of them. The first pressings yielded pure olive oil which was prized for many uses, including healing and giving light in lanterns. In fact, we consecrate it and use it to administer to the sick. The last pressing of the olives, under the tremendous pressure of additional weights added to the press, yielded a bitter, red liquid which can remind us of the "bitter cup" which the Savior partook of. Symbolically, the Savior is going into the "oil press" (Gethsemane) to submit to the "pressure" of all our sins which will "squeeze" His blood out in order that we might have the healing "oil" of the Atonement to heal us from our sins.

33 And **he taketh with him Peter and James and John** [*the "First Presidency"*], and began to be sore amazed [*astonished*], and to be very heavy [*with depression and anguish—see Mark 14:33, footnote b*];

34 And saith unto them, **My soul is exceeding sorrowful unto death: tarry ye here, and watch.**

The JST gives verses 32–34 as follows:

JST Mark 14:36–38

36 And they came to a place which was named Gethsemane, **which was a garden; and the disciples began to be sore amazed**, and to be very heavy, **and to complain in their hearts, wondering if this be the Messiah**.

37 **And Jesus knowing their hearts, said** to his disciples, Sit ye here, while I shall pray.

38 And he taketh with him, Peter, and James, and John, **and rebuked them** [*perhaps because of their doubts expressed in JST verse 36, quoted above*], and **said** unto them, My soul is exceeding sorrowful, **even** unto death; tarry ye here and watch.

35 And he went forward a little, and fell on the ground, and **prayed that, if it were possible, the hour might pass from him.**

36 And he said, **Abba** [*an intimate, personal, tender term; "Daddy" in the Aramaic language of New Testament times—see Bible Dictionary, under "Abba"*], **Father, all things are possible unto thee; take away this cup from me: nevertheless not what I will, but what thou wilt.**

Apostle James E. Talmage describes the suffering of the Savior in Gethsemane as follows:

"Christ's agony in the garden is unfathomable by the finite mind, both as to intensity and cause. The thought that He suffered through fear of death is untenable. Death to Him was preliminary to resurrection and triumphal return to the Father from whom He had come, and to a state of glory even beyond what He had before possessed; and, moreover, it was within His power to lay down His life voluntarily. He struggled and groaned under a burden such as no other being who has lived on earth might even conceive as possible. It was not physical pain, nor mental anguish alone, that caused Him to suffer such torture as to produce an extrusion of blood from every pore; but a spiritual agony of soul such as only God was capable of experiencing. No other man, however great his powers of physical or mental endurance, could have suffered so; for his human organism would have succumbed, and syncope would have produced unconsciousness and welcome oblivion. In that hour of anguish Christ met and overcame all the horrors that Satan, 'the prince of this world' could inflict. The frightful struggle incident to the temptations immediately following the Lord's baptism was surpassed and overshadowed by this supreme contest with the powers of evil.

"In some manner, actual and terribly real though to man incomprehensible, the Savior took upon Himself the burden of the sins of mankind from Adam to the end of the world." (*Jesus the Christ*, page 613)

37 And **he** cometh, and **findeth them sleeping**, and saith unto

MARK 14

Peter, Simon, sleepest thou? couldest not thou watch one hour?

38 Watch ye and pray, lest ye enter into temptation. **The spirit truly is ready, but the flesh is weak.**

39 And **again he** went away, and **prayed**, and spake **the same words**.

40 And when he returned, he found them **asleep again**, (for their eyes were heavy,) neither wist [*knew*] they what to answer him.

No doubt these humble apostles were very tired by this time of the week [*Thursday night*]. It had been a difficult week for them, worrying about the Savior's safety and the plots to kill Him. No doubt they had had little sleep. Thus, in verse 40, "their eyes were heavy." In other words, they were very sleepy.

41 And he cometh **the third time**, and saith unto them, **Sleep on** now, and take your rest: it is enough, **the hour is come** [*the time for my arrest, trial, and crucifixion is here*]; behold, **the Son of man** [*Christ*] **is betrayed** into the hands of sinners.

42 Rise up, let us go; lo, he [*Judas Iscariot*] that betrayeth me is at hand [*is coming*].

43 And immediately, while he yet spake, cometh **Judas**, one of the twelve, and with him a great multitude with swords and staves [*sticks*], from [*sent by*] the chief priests and the scribes and the elders [*the Jewish religious leaders*].

44 And he [*Judas*] that betrayed him **had given them** [*the soldiers*] **a token** [*sign*], saying, **Whomsoever I shall kiss, that same is he** [*the person I kiss is Jesus*]; take him [*arrest him*], and lead him away safely [*don't let anyone take him away from you*].

45 And as soon as **he** [*Judas*] was come [*arrived*], he goeth straightway [*immediately*] to him [*Jesus*], and **saith, Master, master; and kissed him**.

46 And they laid their hands on him [*grabbed Him; arrested Him*], and took him.

Peter Cuts off the Ear of a Relative of the High Priest

47 And **one of them** [*Peter*] that stood by drew a sword, and **smote** [*struck*] **a servant of the high priest** [*one of the high priest's relatives—see John 18:10 and 26*]**, and cut off his ear.** [*Jesus healed this man's ear; see Luke 22:51.*]

<u>**JST Mark 14:53**</u>
53 But Jesus commanded him to **return his sword, saying, He who taketh the sword shall perish with the sword. And he put forth his finger and healed the servant of the high priest.**

JST verse 53, above, is left out of Mark in the Bible.

48 And **Jesus answered** [*responded*] and said unto them, **Are ye come out, as against a thief, with swords and with staves to take me?**

49 I was daily with you in the temple teaching, and ye took me not [*why didn't you arrest me during the daytime?*]: but **the scriptures must be fulfilled.**

50 And **they** [*the Apostles*] **all forsook him, and fled** [*as Jesus said they would in verse 27*].

51 And **there followed him** [*Jesus*] **a certain young man**, having a linen cloth cast about his naked body; and the young men [*soldiers or members of the mob*] laid hold on him [*grabbed the young man*]:

52 And he left the linen cloth, and fled from them [*the soldiers*] naked.

JST Mark 14:57

57 And there followed him a certain young man, **a disciple**, having a linen cloth cast about his naked body; and the young men laid hold on him, and he left the linen cloth and fled from them naked, **and saved himself out of their hands**.

The Trial before Caiaphas

53 And **they led Jesus away to the high priest**: and with him [*Caiaphas, the high priest*] were assembled all the chief priests and the elders and the scribes.

54 And **Peter followed** him [*Jesus*] afar off, even into the palace of the high priest: and he sat with the servants, and warmed himself at the fire.

55 And **the chief priests and all the council sought for witness against Jesus** to put him to death; and found none.

56 For many bare false witness against him, but their witness agreed not together [*the false witnesses they did get contradicted each other*].

57 And there arose certain, and bare false witness against him, saying,

58 We heard him say, I will destroy this temple that is made with hands, and within three days I will build another made without hands.

59 But neither so did their witness agree together [*they contradicted each other also*].

60 And **the high priest** stood up in the midst, and **asked Jesus**, saying, **Answerest thou nothing** [*aren't You going to say anything*]? what is it which these witness against thee?

61 **But he** [*Jesus*] **held his peace, and answered nothing.** Again the high priest asked him, and said unto him, **Art thou the Christ**, the Son of the Blessed [*the Son of God*]?

62 And Jesus said, **I am**: and ye shall see the Son of man [*Jesus; the Son of Man, meaning the Son of Man of Holiness (the Father; see Moses 6:57)*] sitting on the right hand of power, and coming in the clouds of heaven [*the Second Coming*].

63 **Then the high priest rent** [*tore*] **his clothes**, and saith, What need

we any further witnesses [*haven't we heard enough*]?

Tearing your clothing was a cultural way of expressing strongest emotion among the Jews.

64 **Ye have heard the blasphemy** [*this man claims to be the Son of God, the Messiah; he is mocking God!*]: what think ye? And **they all condemned him to be guilty of death**.

Blasphemy, showing blatant disrespect for God, mocking God, and so forth, was a crime punishable by death according to Jewish law.

65 And some began to **spit on him**, and to cover his face [*blindfolded him*], and to **buffet** [*hit*] **him**, and to say unto him, Prophesy [*tell us which one of us is hitting you; see Luke 22:64*]: and the servants did strike him with the palms of their hands.

Peter Denies Knowing Jesus Three Times

66 And as **Peter was beneath** [*in a lower room*] in the palace [*where the trial was taking place*], **there cometh one of the maids** [*servants*] of the high priest:

67 And when **she saw Peter** warming himself, she looked upon him, **and said, And thou also wast with Jesus of Nazareth** [*you are one of Jesus' followers*].

68 But **he denied**, saying, I know not, neither understand I what thou sayest. And he went out into the porch; and the cock [*rooster*] crew [*crowed*].

69 **And a maid saw him** [*Peter*] again, and began to say to them that stood by [*the bystanders*], **This is one of them** [*Christ's followers*].

70 And **he denied it again**. And a little after [*a while later*], they that stood by said again to Peter, **Surely thou art one of them** [*followers of Jesus*]: for thou art a Galilæan, and thy speech agreeth thereto [*we can tell by your Galilean accent*].

71 But he began to curse and to swear, saying, **I know not this man** of whom ye speak.

72 And the second time **the cock crew** [*a rooster crowed again*]. And Peter called to mind [*remembered*] the word that Jesus said unto him [*in verse 30*], Before the cock crow twice, thou shalt deny me thrice [*three times*]. And when he thought thereon, **he wept**. [*See note following verse 30.*]

MARK 15

This is Friday morning, the day on which they crucified the Savior. After conducting an illegal trial during the night at Caiaphas' palace (night time trials were illegal according to the Jews' own laws), the Jewish religious leaders now take the Master to Pilate, the Roman governor over that part of the Holy Land. Remember, as mentioned previously, the Romans at this time had not given the Jews the authority to inflict capital punishment (the death penalty). Therefore, the chief priests were very anxious to get Pilate to give the order that Christ be crucified.

1 AND **straightway** [*first thing*] **in the morning the chief priests held a consultation** [*a meeting*] with the elders and scribes and **the whole council**, and **bound Jesus** [*had Jesus tied up*], and carried him away, and **delivered him** [*turned him over*] **to Pilate** [*the Roman governor of that area*].

The Trial before Pilate

2 And Pilate asked him, **Art thou the King of the Jews?** And he answering said unto him, **Thou sayest it** [*in other words, "Yes I am";* *see JST, below, and John 18:37*].

JST Mark 15:4
4 And Jesus answering, said unto him, **I am, even as thou sayest**.

Jesus Refuses to Answer the Chief Priests

3 And **the chief priests accused** him of many things: **but he answered nothing**.

4 And **Pilate asked** him again, saying, **Answerest thou nothing** [*aren't You going to speak in Your own defense*]? behold [*look*] how many things they witness [*testify*] against thee.

5 But **Jesus yet answered nothing**; so that Pilate marvelled [*was surprised*].

The Release of Barabbas

6 Now **at that feast he released unto them one prisoner, whomsoever they desired**. [*It was customary for Pilate to release a prisoner of the people's choosing each year at this time.*]

7 And there was one [*criminal*] named **Barabbas**, which lay bound [*in prison*] with them that had made insurrection with him [*with those who had rebelled against the government with him*], who had committed murder in the insurrection.

The name "Barabbas" means "son of the father" [*see Bible Dictionary, under "Barabbas"*]. This may be symbolic in that the "imposter," Satan, stirred up the multitude to demand the release of an "imposter," Barabbas, while the true "Son of the Father" is punished for crimes which He did not commit.

8 And the multitude crying aloud began to desire him to do as he had ever done unto them [*release a prisoner*].

9 But **Pilate** answered them, saying, **Will ye that I release unto you the King of the Jews** [*mocking Jesus*]?

10 For he knew that the chief priests had delivered him for envy [*had had Jesus arrested because they were jealous of His power and popularity among the people*].

11 But **the chief priests moved** [*influenced*] **the people**, that he

MARK 15

should rather [*instead*] **release Barabbas** unto them.

12 And **Pilate** answered [*responded*] and said again unto them, **What will ye then that I shall do unto him** [*Jesus*] whom ye call the King of the Jews?

13 And they cried out again, **Crucify him**.

14 Then Pilate said unto them, **Why**, what evil hath he done? And they cried out the more exceedingly [*more loudly*], Crucify him.

15 And so **Pilate**, willing to content [*please*] the people, **released Barabbas** unto them, and **delivered Jesus**, when he had **scourged him** [*had him beaten, whipped, flogged*], **to be crucified**.

> "Scourging" was a very severe punishment, and many prisoners did not live through it. It consisted of being whipped with a whip which was composed of leather thongs with bits of metal, bone, etc., secured to the ends of the thongs.

The Soldiers Mock Jesus

16 And the **soldiers led him away** into the hall, called Prætorium [*a room in the governor's house*]; and they call together the whole band [*about six hundred Roman soldiers with a leader over them; see* McConkie, Doctrinal New Testament Commentary, *Vol. 1, p. 781*].

17 And they **clothed him with purple** [*in mockery of His claim to be "King of the Jews"*], and platted [*made, wove*] a **crown of thorns**, and put it about his head,

18 And **began to salute him** [*saying*], Hail, King of the Jews!

19 And they **smote** [*hit*] **him** on the head with a reed [*stick, mock scepter of kingly authority*], and did **spit upon him**, and bowing their knees **worshipped him** [*pretended to worship him*].

20 And when they had **mocked him**, they took off the purple from him, and put his own clothes on him, and **led him out to crucify him**.

21 And **they compel** [*forced*] one **Simon** a Cyrenian, who passed by, coming out of the country [*probably a foreigner* [*perhaps a Jew who had come for Passover*] who came from Cyrene, a city in northern Africa], the father of Alexander and Rufus, **to bear** [*carry*] **his cross**. [*After the suffering in the Garden of Gethsemane, the whipping, mocking, and so forth, Jesus was too weak to carry His own cross, which was a part of the legally required punishment and torture which went along with crucifixion.*]

The Crucifixion

22 And they bring [*brought*] him unto the place **Golgotha**, which is, being interpreted, The place of a skull.

23 And **they gave him** to drink **wine mingled with myrrh**: but **he received it not** [*refused it*].

This mixture of wine and myrrh was designed to drug the victim of crucifixion to lessen the pain somewhat. See *Jesus the Christ*, pp. 654–655.

24 And when they had crucified him [*hung him on the cross*], they parted his garments [*divided up his clothes*], casting lots upon them, what every man should take [*gambling to see who got what item of clothing*].

25 And it was **the third hour** [*about 9 A.M.*], and **they crucified him**.

26 And the **superscription** [*writing*] of his accusation [*what He was accused of*] was written over [*above Him on the cross*], **THE KING OF THE JEWS**.

The JST informs us that some of the Jewish chief priests were very frustrated about the sign above the Savior's head, as mentioned in verse 26, above. They wanted Pilate to modify it to read that Jesus "claimed" to be the king of the Jews.

JST Mark 15:29–31

29 And **Pilate wrote** his accusation and put it upon the cross, THE KING OF THE JEWS.

30 **There were certain of the chief priests who stood by, that said unto Pilate, Write, that he said, I am the King of the Jews.**

31 **But Pilate said unto them, What I have written, I have written.**

JST verses 30–31, above, are not found in the Bible.

The Two Thieves

27 And **with him they crucify two thieves**; the one on his right hand, and the other on his left.

28 And the **scripture** was **fulfilled** [*Isaiah 53:12*], which saith, And **he was numbered with the transgressors** [*killed with criminals*].

29 And **they that passed by railed on him** [*shouted, mocked him*], wagging [*shaking*] their heads, and saying, Ah, thou that destroyest the temple, and buildest it in three days,

These people obviously misunderstood what Jesus said regarding the temple. What He said is in John 2:19–21. He said that if they destroyed His body (the "temple of his body"), He would raise it up in three days (be resurrected in three days). By the time Jesus is on the cross, His statement has been misquoted and spread so that the mockers claim that He said He would destroy their massive temple in Jerusalem and rebuild it in three days.

30 **Save thyself**, and come down from the cross.

31 Likewise also **the chief priests mocking** said among themselves with the scribes, **He saved others; himself he cannot save.**

32 **Let Christ the King of Israel descend** [*come down*] **now from the cross, that we may see and**

MARK 15

believe. And they that were crucified with him reviled him [*mocked him*].

> One of the thieves seems to have softened his attitude a bit later. The Savior said to him, "Today shalt thou be with me in paradise." We will do more with this in Luke 23:43.

33 And when **the sixth hour** [*about noon*] was come, there was **darkness** over the whole land until the ninth hour [*about 3 P.M.*].

34 And at the **ninth hour** [*about three in the afternoon*] Jesus cried with a loud voice, saying, Eloi, Eloi, lama sabachthani? which is, being interpreted, **My God, my God, why hast thou forsaken me?**

> This had to have been a most difficult time for the Savior. Apparently, as part of the Atonement, Jesus had to experience what sinners do when they sin so much that the Spirit leaves them. At this point on the cross, we understand that all available help from the Father withdrew in order that the Savior might experience all things, including

> the withdrawal of the Spirit which sinners experience.

35 And some of them that stood by, when they heard it, said, Behold, he calleth Elias [*Elijah*].

36 And one ran and filled a spunge full of vinegar, and put it on a reed, and gave him to drink, saying, Let alone; let us see whether Elias will come to take him down.

37 And **Jesus cried with a loud voice, and gave up the ghost** [*left his body, died*].

38 And the **veil of the temple** was **rent** in twain [*torn in two*] from the top to the bottom.

39 And when the **centurion** [*Roman soldier*], which stood over against him [*across from Jesus*], saw that he so cried out [*had so much strength when he cried out*], and gave up the ghost, he said, **Truly this man was the Son of God**.

> It was common for victims of crucifixion to live two or three days before dying. The soldier was startled because he was experienced in crucifying people and it appeared to him that Jesus, who was still relatively strong, and after only six hours on the cross, had decided to leave His body and did so. That is exactly what happened and the Roman soldier apparently received a witness of Christ at that moment.

40 There were also women looking on afar off: among whom was **Mary Magdalene, and Mary** [*possibly the Savior's mother; see Mark 6:3*] the mother of James the less and of Joses, and Salome;

41 [*Who also, when he was in Galilee, followed him, and ministered unto him;*] **and many other women** which came up with him unto Jerusalem.

The Savior's Body Is Taken off the Cross

42 And now **when the even** [*evening*] **was come**, because it was the preparation, that is, the day before the sabbath,

43 **Joseph of Arimathaea**, an honourable counsellor, which also waited for the kingdom of God [*who also was a believer*], came, and **went in boldly unto Pilate, and craved** [*requested*] **the body of Jesus.**

44 And **Pilate marvelled if he were already dead** [*was surprised that Jesus was already dead*]: and calling unto him the centurion, he asked him whether he [*Jesus*] had been any while dead [*had been dead very long*].

45 And when he knew it of the centurion [*when the Roman soldier verified that Jesus was indeed dead*], **he gave the body to Joseph.**

46 And he [*Joseph of Arimathaea*] bought fine linen, and took him down [*from the cross*], and wrapped him in the linen, and laid him in a sepulchre [*tomb*] which was hewn [*carved*] out of a rock, and rolled a stone unto the door of the sepulchre.

47 And **Mary Magdalene and Mary the mother of Joses beheld** [*watched to see*] where he was laid.

MARK 16

This chapter contains Mark's account of the resurrection of the Savior. It is a glorious Sunday morning. The faithful women who had watched from a distance as Joseph of Arimathaea hurriedly took the Lord's body down from the cross and laid it in his own new tomb (Mark 15:42–47) have come very early Sunday morning to tenderly finish the customary final preparation of the Savior's body for burial.

The Savior's Resurrection

1 AND when the sabbath [*Saturday for the Jews*] was past, **Mary Magdalene**, and **Mary** the mother of James, **and Salome**, had **bought sweet spices**, that they might come and anoint him [*finish preparing Jesus' body for burial*].

2 And **very early in the morning** the first day of the week [*Sunday*], **they came unto the sepulchre** [*tomb*] at the rising of the sun.

The Stone Was Already Rolled Away

3 And they said among themselves, **Who shall roll** us **away the stone** from the door of the sepulchre [*so we can get into the tomb*]?

4 And when they looked, they saw that **the stone was rolled away**: for it was very great [*large*].

5 And **entering into the sepulchre** [*the tomb*], they saw a young man [*two angels—see JST quoted below*] sitting on the right side, clothed in a long white garment; and they were affrighted [*afraid*].

MARK 16

6 And he [*they*] saith unto them, Be not affrighted: Ye seek Jesus of Nazareth, which was crucified: **he is risen** [*resurrected*]; **he is not here**: behold [*look at*] the place where they laid him.

7 But **go** your way, **tell his disciples** and Peter **that he** [*Jesus*] **goeth** before you [*ahead of you*] **into Galilee**: there shall ye see him, as he said unto you [*in Mark 14:28*].

JST Mark 16:3–6

3 **But** when they looked, they saw that the stone was rolled away, (for it was very great,) and **two angels** sitting thereon, clothed in long white garments; and they were affrighted.

4 But **the angels said** unto them, Be not affrighted; ye seek Jesus of Nazareth, **who** was crucified; he is risen; he is not here; behold the place where they laid him;

5 **And** go your way, tell his disciples and Peter, that he goeth before you into Galilee; there shall ye see him as he said unto you.

6 **And they, entering into the sepulcher, saw the place where they laid Jesus** [*this verse is missing from Mark's account in the Bible*].

8 And **they went out quickly**, and fled from the sepulchre; for they trembled and were amazed: neither said they any thing to any man; for they were afraid.

Jesus Appears to Mary Magdalene

9 Now when Jesus was risen [*resurrected*] early the first day of the week, **he appeared first to Mary Magdalene**, out of whom he had cast seven devils [*Luke 8:2*].

10 **And she went and told them that had been with him** [*His disciples*], as they mourned and wept.

11 And **they**, when they had heard that he was alive, and had been seen of [*by*] her, **believed not**.

Jesus Appears to Two on the Road to Emmaus

12 **After that he appeared** in another form **unto two of them** [*two other disciples*], as they walked [*on the road to Emmaus; see Luke 24:13–35*], and went into the country.

13 **And they went and told it unto the residue** [*rest of the group*]: neither believed they them.

Jesus Appears to Eleven Apostles

14 Afterward **he appeared unto the eleven** [*Apostles*] as they sat at meat [*as they were eating*], **and upbraided** [*scolded*] **them** with their unbelief and hardness of heart, **because they believed not them which had seen him after he was risen.**

The Charge to Preach the Gospel to All the World

15 And he said unto them [*the Apostles*], **Go ye into all the world, and preach the gospel to every creature** [*person*].

Next, in verse 16, we are taught the vital importance of baptism (for those over age eight—see D&C 137:10).

Baptism Is Essential

16 **He that believeth and is baptized shall be saved; but he that believeth not shall be damned** [*will be stopped in their progress*].

17 And **these signs shall follow them that believe;** In my name shall they cast out devils [*evil spirits*]; they shall speak with new tongues [*foreign languages*];

18 They shall take up serpents [*the Apostle Paul had an experience with this in Acts 28:3–6*]; and if they drink any deadly thing, it shall not hurt them: they shall lay hands on the sick, and they shall recover. [*In other words, the Apostles will have divine protection as they carry out the work of the Lord.*]

The Ascension of Christ

19 So then **after the Lord had spoken unto them, he was received up into heaven, and sat on the right hand of God.**

20 **And they went forth, and preached** every where, the Lord working with them, and confirming the word with signs following. Amen.

THE GOSPEL ACCORDING TO
ST LUKE

Luke was a physician according to Colossians 4:14 and was a missionary companion to Paul. Most Bible scholars believe that he was of Gentile birth. He is also the author of Acts. His sensitivity as a physician to people and their needs shows in his writing. He gives emphasis to the role women played in the life and ministry of the Savior. Perhaps, because he is a physician, he alone of the gospel writers tells of Christ's bleeding during his agony in the Garden of Gethsemane. Luke was not an eyewitness to the Savior's ministry, rather learned from Paul and others about Jesus. It appears that he was writing to the Gentiles, especially the Greeks, to teach them of Jesus and His divine mission as our Savior and Redeemer.

LUKE 1

Here in chapter one, you will see an angel named Gabriel announce to Zacharias that he and his elderly wife, Elizabeth, will have a son (John the Baptist). About six months later, Gabriel (who was the prophet Noah—see Bible Dictionary, under "Gabriel") will also have the privilege of announcing to Mary that she will be the mother of the Son of God. Mary will visit Elizabeth (a relative) who is six months along and the child in her womb will respond to Mary as she enters Elizabeth's home.

You will see beautiful examples of revelation to these humble and righteous people in this first chapter of Luke. In a tender scene, Elizabeth will prophesy (verses 42–45) about Mary; then Mary will also prophesy (verses 46–55). After about three more months, John the Baptist will be born and his father, Zacharias, will prophesy (verses 67–79).

1 FORASMUCH as [*since*] many have taken in hand [*have undertaken*] to set forth in order a declaration of [*to write about*] those things which are most surely believed among us,

JST Luke 1:1
As I am a messenger of Jesus Christ, and knowing that many have taken in hand to set forth in order a declaration of those things which are most surely believed among us;

2 Even as they delivered them unto us, which from the beginning were **eyewitnesses** [*not all were eyewitnesses of Christ, but were eyewitnesses to the gospel and the growth of the Church*], and ministers of the word;

3 **It seemed good to me** [*Luke*] also, having had perfect understanding of all things from the very first [*I have been taught and understand all things from the birth of John the Baptist and from the birth of Jesus up to and including the crucifixion and resurrection of the Savior*], **to write unto thee** in order, most excellent **Theophilus** [*"friend of God," probably a Greek official of high rank*],

4 **That thou mightest know** the certainty [*that you might have a testimony*] of those things, wherein thou hast been instructed.

Having introduced the purpose of his letter to Theophilus, Luke now begins his account of the birth and life of Christ.

5 THERE was in the days of Herod, the king of Judæa, a certain priest [*in the Aaronic Priesthood*] named **Zacharias**, of the course of Abia [*a descendant of Aaron through Abijah*]: and his wife was of the daughters of Aaron [*was a descendant of Aaron*], and her name was **Elisabeth**.

The priests who served in the temple at the time of Christ were members of the Aaronic Priesthood. Zacharias was a righteous holder of this priesthood.

Those men who fulfilled priestly duties at the temple at Jerusalem were divided into 24 groups or "courses", each group assigned to serve for one week at a time. Zacharias was a member of the eighth "course" or group. Each group had upwards of 1400 men, so the privilege of officiating at the burning of incense in the temple might come once or never in the lifetime of a priest. (See *Jesus the Christ,* pp. 75-76.)

6 And **they were both righteous** before God, walking in all the commandments and ordinances of the Lord blameless.

7 And **they had no child, because that Elisabeth was barren** [*had not been able to have children*], and **they both were now well stricken in years** [*were quite old and had given up on having children*].

8 And it came to pass, that **while he** [*Zacharias*] **executed the priest's office** [*carried out his duties in the temple*] before God in the order of his course,

JST Luke 1:8
And while he executed the priest's office before God, in the order of his **priesthood,**

9 According to the custom of the priest's office, **his lot was** [*he had been selected*] **to burn incense when he went into the temple of the Lord.**

Since it was generally a once-in-a-lifetime opportunity for an Aaronic Priesthood priest to have the privilege of burning incense

in the temple, as mentioned in the note above, this would have been a very humbling and important day for Zacharias.

10 And the whole multitude of the people were praying without [*outside of the temple, watching for the cloud of smoke from the incense to rise from the temple, and waiting for Zacharias to come back out in a few minutes*] at the time of incense.

Gabriel Announces the Coming Birth of John the Baptist

11 And **there appeared unto him** [*Zacharias*] **an angel of the Lord** standing on the right side of the altar of incense.

This angel was Gabriel. He will also appear to Mary in a few months to tell her that she will be the mother of the Son of God. As mentioned previously, we are told that Gabriel is Noah. See Bible Dictionary, under "Gabriel."

12 And **when Zacharias saw him, he was troubled, and fear fell upon him.**

13 **But the angel said** unto him, Fear not, Zacharias: for thy prayer is heard; and **thy wife Elisabeth shall bear thee a son, and thou shalt call his name John.**

One of the important lessons we gain from verse 13, above, is that we should not give up praying for righteous desires of our hearts.

The instruction by the angel to call their son "John" was very

LUKE 1

definite. Otherwise, they would very likely have named him Zacharias, after his father.

14 And **thou shalt have joy and gladness; and many shall rejoice at his birth.**

Next, the angel prophecies to Zacharias about the wonderful son he and Elizabeth will have, after having waited all these years.

15 For **he shall be great in the sight of the Lord**, and **shall drink neither wine nor strong drink** [*a sign that he was dedicated to a special calling*]; and he shall be filled with the Holy Ghost [*see D&C 84:27*], even from his mother's womb [*before he is born*].

Elder Bruce R. McConkie teaches us more about John the Baptist, as quoted in the *Doctrine and Covenants Student Manual*, pp. 183:

"What concerns us above all else as to the coming of John, however, is that he came with power and authority. He first received his errand from the Lord. His was no ordinary message, and he was no unauthorized witness. He was called of God and sent by him, and he represented Deity in the words that he spoke and the baptisms he performed. He was a legal administrator whose words and acts were binding on earth and in heaven, and his hearers were bound, at the peril of their salvation, to believe his words and heed his counsels.

"Luke says: 'The word of God came unto John the son of Zacharias in the wilderness.' Later John is to say: 'He that sent me to baptize with water, the same said unto me,' such and such things (John 1:33). Who sent him we do not know. We do know that 'he was baptized while he was yet in his childhood [*meaning, when he was eight years of age*], and was ordained by the angel of God at the time he was eight days old unto this power [*note it well, not to the Aaronic Priesthood, but*] to over-throw the kingdom of the Jews, and to make straight the way of the Lord before the face of his people, to prepare them for the coming of the Lord, in whose hand is given all power' (D&C 84:24). We do not know when he received the Aaronic Priesthood, but obviously it came to him after his baptism, at whatever age was proper, and before he was sent by one whom he does not name to preach and baptize with water." (*Mortal Messiah*, pp. 384–85).

16 And **many of the children of Israel shall he turn to the Lord their God.**

17 And **he** [*John the Baptist*] **shall go before him** [*go ahead of Christ*] **in the spirit and power of Elias** [*one who prepares the way for even more important things; see Teach-ings of the Prophet Joseph Smith, pages 335-336; also see Bible Dic-tionary, under "Elias"*], to turn the hearts of the fathers to the children, and the disobedient to the wisdom

of the just [*righteous*]; **to make ready a people prepared for the Lord** [*Jesus*].

Zacharias is humbly puzzled by the announcement of the angel, since he and Elizabeth are old, and she is well-beyond the years when she could bear a child.

18 **And Zacharias said** unto the angel, **Whereby** [*how*] **shall I know this?** for **I am an old man, and my wife well stricken in years** [*we are beyond the years when we can have children*].

19 And **the angel** answering **said** unto him, **I am Gabriel** [*Noah; see note after verse 11 above*], that stand in the presence of God; and am sent to speak unto thee, and to shew thee these glad tidings.

While the limitation placed upon Zacharias, in verse 20, next, as a result of his hesitation to believe the words of the angel, might be viewed as a punishment, it might also be viewed as a kindness, as an assurance that he had indeed seen Gabriel and thus, that he and Elisabeth would surely have the promised son.

20 And, behold, **thou shalt be dumb** [*unable to talk*], and not able to speak, **until the day that these things shall be performed** [*until John is born*], because thou believest not my words, which shall be fulfilled in their season.

21 And **the people waited for Zacharias, and marvelled that he tarried so long in the temple** [*were wondering what was taking him so long*].

22 And **when he came out, he could not speak unto them**: and **they perceived** [*understood*] **that he had seen a vision in the temple**: for he beckoned unto them [*described with his hands that he had seen a vision*], and remained speechless.

23 And it came to pass, that, as soon as the days of his ministration were accomplished [*after his week of temple duties was over; see note after verse five above*], **he departed to his own house.**

Luke leaves it to our own imaginations to envision the scene that took place in the home of Zacharias and Elizabeth as he returned from his temple service and broke the good news to her.

24 And after those days his wife **Elisabeth conceived, and hid herself five months,** saying,

25 **Thus hath the Lord dealt with me** in the days wherein he looked on me, **to take away my reproach** among men [*to take away the social stigma of being childless*].

Six months after Elizabeth conceived, Gabriel appeared to Mary to tell her that she would be the mother of Jesus Christ. Imagine what a joy it was to Gabriel, or Noah, who preached the gospel and built the Ark in preparation for the Flood, to come back as the angel who had the privilege of announcing the coming birth of the Savior.

Gabriel Announces the Coming Birth of the Son of God

26 And in the sixth month **the angel Gabriel** [*Noah; see note after verse 11 above*] **was sent from God unto a city of Galilee, named Nazareth,**

27 **To a virgin espoused** [*engaged, promised*] **to** a man whose name was **Joseph**, of the house of David [*who was a descendant of David*]; and the virgin's name was Mary.

Being "espoused" [*verse 27*] was a much stronger commitment than engagement is in our day. An espoused couple was bound by covenants to each other even before their marriage and the espousal could not be broken off except through formal action similar to divorce.

28 And **the angel came in unto her, and said, Hail, thou that art highly favoured, the Lord is with thee: blessed art thou among women**.

29 And when she saw him, **she was troubled at his saying**, and cast in her mind what manner of salutation this should be [*wondered what kind of a greeting this was*].

30 And **the angel said** unto her, **Fear not, Mary: for thou hast found favour with God.**

His Name Is to be Jesus

31 And, behold, **thou shalt conceive** in thy womb, **and bring forth a son, and shalt call his name JESUS.**

Next, Gabriel gives Mary a brief description of her special Son. Mary would no doubt have recognized some of the ancient prophecies quoted by the angel, which would help her comprehend the significance of this announcement to her.

32 **He shall be great, and shall be called the Son of the Highest** [*the son of Heavenly Father*]: and the Lord God [*Heavenly Father*] shall give unto him the throne of his father [*ancestor*] David:

33 And **he shall reign over the house of Jacob** [*house of Israel; descendants of Jacob*] **for ever; and of his kingdom there shall be no end.**

34 **Then said Mary unto the angel, How shall this be, seeing I know not a man** [*I am a virgin*]?

35 And the angel answered and said unto her, **The Holy Ghost shall come upon thee, and the power of the Highest** [*the highest member of the Godhead, in other words, the Father*] **shall overshadow thee: therefore also that holy thing** [*holy child*] **which shall be born of thee shall be called the Son of God.**

JST Luke 1:35

35 And the angel answered and said unto her, **Of the Holy Ghost, and the power of the Highes**t. Therefore also, that holy **child that** shall be born of thee shall be called the Son of God.

Some people use verse 35, above,

to suggest that the Holy Ghost is the father of Jesus. That is a completely false doctrine. Apostle James E. Talmage teaches the following:

"That Child to be born of Mary was begotten of Elohim, the Eternal Father, not in violation of natural law but in accordance with a higher manifestation thereof; and, the offspring from that association of supreme sanctity, celestial Sireship, and pure though mortal maternity, was of right to be called the 'Son of the Highest.' In His nature would be combined the powers of Godhood with the capacity and possibilities of mortality; and this through the ordinary operation of the fundamental law of heredity declared of God, demonstrated by science, and admitted by philosophy, that living beings shall propagate—after their kind. The Child Jesus was to inherit the physical, mental and spiritual traits, tendencies, and powers that characterized His parents— one immortal and glorified— God, the other human—woman." (*Jesus the Christ*, p. 81)

Next, Gabriel tells Mary that her elderly cousin Elizabeth (actually a relative, not necessarily a cousin—see Luke 1:36, footnote a, in your Bible), is expecting a son.

36 **And, behold, thy cousin Elisabeth, she hath also conceived a son in her old age**: and this is the sixth month with her, who was called barren [*childless; Elizabeth is six months pregnant*].

37 For **with God nothing shall be impossible**.

Mary's Humble Response

There is probably not a greater example anywhere in scripture of humble faith and submission to the will of the Lord than the response given by Mary to the angel's announcement.

38 And **Mary said, Behold the handmaid of the Lord; be it unto me according to thy word.** And the angel departed from her.

Next, Mary will visit Elizabeth.

39 And **Mary arose in those days, and went into the hill country** with haste [*hurried*], into a city of Juda;

40 And **entered into the house of Zacharias, and saluted** [*greeted*] **Elisabeth.**

41 And it came to pass, that, when Elisabeth heard the salutation [*greeting*] of Mary, **the babe leaped in her womb** [*little John the Baptist jumped inside of Elizabeth*]; and **Elisabeth was filled with the Holy Ghost:**

Apostle Bruce R. McConkie teaches some comforting doctrine regarding stillborn children based on verse 41 above. It is as follows:

"(The babe leaped in her womb). In this miraculous event the pattern is seen which a spirit follows in passing from his pre-existent first estate into mortality. The

LUKE 1

spirit enters the body at the time of quickening, months prior to the actual normal birth. The value and comfort attending a knowledge of this eternal truth is seen in connection with stillborn children. Since the spirit entered the body before birth, stillborn children will be resurrected and righteous parents shall enjoy their association in immortal glory." (*Doctrinal New Testament Commentary*, Vol. 1, pp. 84–85)

Elizabeth Prophesies

42 And **she** [*Elizabeth*] spake out with a loud voice, and **said** [*note that Elizabeth will now exercise the gift of prophesy; see D&C 46:22*], **Blessed art thou** [*Mary*] **among women, and blessed is the fruit of thy womb** [*the child who will be born to you*].

43 And **whence is this to me, that the mother of my Lord should come to me** [*how do I rate the privilege of having the mother of the Son of God come visit me*]?

44 For, lo, **as soon as the voice of thy salutation** [*greeting*] **sounded in mine ears, the babe** [*John*] **leaped in my womb for joy.**

45 And blessed is she that believed: for **there shall be a performance of those things which were told her from the Lord** [*everything promised to you will be fulfilled*].

Just as Elizabeth was filled with the Spirit of prophecy, now Mary is given the gift of prophecy (one of the gifts of the Spirit—see

D&C 46:22) also. Her beautiful prophecies are recorded in verses 46-55.

Mary Prophesies

46 And **Mary said, My soul doth magnify** [*praise*] **the Lord,**

47 And **my spirit hath rejoiced in God my Saviour.**

JST Luke 1:46
46 And my spirit **rejoiceth** in God my Savior.

It is touching to realize that Mary's baby would be her Savior as well as her child. From the verses we are reading here, it seems clear that she was well versed in the scriptures and understood that these prophecies pertained to the son whom she would now bear.

48 For he hath regarded [*seen, considered*] the low estate [*humble condition*] of his handmaiden [*servant*]: for, behold, **from henceforth all generations shall call me blessed** [*from now on, all people will know me and know how blessed I am*].

49 **For he that is mighty** [*God*] **hath done to me great things; and holy is his name.**

JST Luke 1:48
48 For he **who** is mighty hath done to me great things; and **I will magnify his holy name,**

50 And **his mercy is on them that fear** [*respect and obey*] **him** from generation to generation.

240   THE NEW TESTAMENT MADE EASIER THIRD EDITION, PART 1

In verses 51–55, we continue gaining marvelous insights into the depth of Mary's understanding concerning the coming Messiah.

51 **He hath shewed** [*demonstrated*] **strength with his arm** [*has shown His power*]; **he hath scattered** [*punished*] **the proud** in the imagination of their hearts [*because of their pride*].

52 **He hath put down** [*humbled*] **the mighty** from their seats [*positions of power*], **and exalted them of low degree** [*blessed and lifted up the humble*].

53 **He hath filled the hungry** [*those who "hunger and thirst after righteousness"; see Matthew 5:6*] with good things; and the rich [*the rich who are prideful*] he hath sent empty away.

54 **He hath holpen** [*helped*] his servant **Israel** [*the covenant people*], in remembrance of his mercy;

55 As **he spake to** our fathers [*ancestors*], to **Abraham, and to his seed** [*posterity*] for ever.

56 And **Mary abode with her** [*stayed with Elizabeth*] **about three months, and returned to her own house.**

John the Baptist Is Born

57 Now **Elisabeth's full time came** that she should be delivered [*the time came for her to have her baby*]; **and she brought forth a son.**

58 And **her neighbours and her cousins** heard how the Lord had shewed [*showed*] great mercy upon her; and they **rejoiced with her.**

As you can see, in verse 59, next, the friends and neighbors of Zacharias and Elizabeth automatically assumed that their miraculous son would be named after his father. Remember, Zacharias has not been able to talk since the visit of Gabriel about nine months ago. Remember also that in verse 13, above, the angel instructed him to name his son "John." Based on what we see in verse 60, he had told Elizabeth about the name and she held firm to that instruction from the angel, even when well-meaning people tried to talk her out of it.

59 And it came to pass, that **on the eighth day they came to circumcise the child** [*John*]; and **they called him Zacharias**, after the name of his father.

60 And **his mother answered** [*responded*] and said, **Not so; but he shall be called John** [*his name is not Zacharias; it is John!*].

61 And **they said unto her, There is none of thy kindred that is called by this name.** [*Why name him John? You have no relatives named John.*]

62 And **they made signs to his father, how he would have him called** [*asked Zacharias what the baby's name should be*].

Next, Zacharias confirms what

LUKE 1

Elizabeth had told them, and he is immediately able to speak again.

63 And **he asked for a writing table** [*because he was still unable to speak*], and **wrote, saying, His name is John**. And they marvelled all [*were all surprised*].

64 And **his** [*Zacharias'*] **mouth was opened immediately, and his tongue loosed**, and he spake, and praised God.

65 And fear [*awe*] came on all that dwelt round about them: and **all these sayings were noised abroad** [*were spread*] throughout all the hill country of Judæa.

66 And all they that heard them laid them up in their hearts, saying, **What manner of child shall this be** [*what kind of special child is John*]! And **the hand of the Lord was with him**.

Zacharias Prophecies about John

67 And his father **Zacharias** was filled with the Holy Ghost, and **prophesied**, saying,

68 **Blessed be the Lord God of Israel** [*we are grateful to God*]; for he hath visited [*come; helped*] and redeemed his people,

Zacharias is prophesying about the future as if it had already taken place. This is a common form of prophecy in the Bible.

69 And **hath raised up an horn** [*"horn" was symbolic of safety,*

strength, and protection in Jewish culture] **of salvation for us** in the house of his servant David [*among us descendants of David*];

70 As which have been since the world began:

71 **That we should be saved from our enemies**, and from the hand of all that hate us;

72 **To perform the mercy promised** to our fathers [*ancestors*], and **to remember** [*fulfill*] **his holy covenant**;

73 **The oath** [*promise*] which he sware [*promised*] **to our father** [*ancestor*] **Abraham**,

74 That he would grant unto us, **that we** being delivered out of the hand of our enemies **might serve him without fear** [*without fear of being persecuted*],

75 **In holiness and righteousness before him, all the days of our life.**

76 And **thou, child** [*little John the Baptist*], **shalt be called the prophet of the Highest** [*God*]: for **thou shalt go before the face of** [*ahead of*] **the Lord** [*Jesus*] **to prepare his ways;**

77 **To give knowledge of salvation unto his people by the remission of their sins,**

78 **Through the tender mercy of our God**; whereby the dayspring [*rising sun, dawn*] from on high hath visited us [*this is the dawn of a new day for us*],

242   THE NEW TESTAMENT MADE EASIER THIRD EDITION, PART 1

79 To give light to them that sit in darkness [*spiritual darkness*] **and** in the shadow of death, **to guide our feet into the way of peace**.

Next, Luke gives a very brief summary of John the Baptist's life from birth to the beginning of his mission to formally prepare the way for the Savior. He does something similar with respect to the life of Jesus, in Luke 2:40 and 52.

80 And the child [*John*] **grew, and waxed strong** [*gained strength*] **in spirit, and was in** [*lived in*] **the deserts till the day of his shewing** [*beginning of his mission*] **unto Israel**.

LUKE 2

This chapter is probably one of the most well-known in the Bible. It has the "Christmas Story" about the birth of the Christ Child and the shepherds who came in from the fields to see baby Jesus. It also contains the account of twelve-year-old Jesus teaching in the temple.

1 AND it came to pass in those days, that **there went out a decree from Caesar Augustus** [*the ruler over the Roman Empire from 31* B.C. *to* A.D. *14*], **that all the world** [*everyone in the Roman Empire*] **should be taxed**.

2 [*And this taxing was first made when Cyrenius was governor of Syria*.]

3 And all went to be taxed, every one into his own city.

This was actually a process of registration or taking a census of all the people who were subject to the Roman government. Based on this census and registration, taxes were later assessed and then collected. The Roman government allowed people to register in the towns where they currently lived, but Jewish custom required that the Jews go to their hometowns to register and be counted. Thus, Joseph and Mary had to travel from Nazareth to Bethlehem, a distance of some one hundred plus miles. See *Jesus the Christ*, pp. 91–92.]

4 And Joseph also went up from Galilee, out of the city of Nazareth, into Judæa, unto the city of David, which is called Bethlehem [*thus fulfilling the prophecy in Micah 5:2 that Christ would be born in Bethlehem*]; (because he was of the house and lineage of David)

5 To be taxed with Mary his espoused [*married; see Matthew 1:24*] **wife, being great with child**.

Note: Mary was indeed "great with child", for the Savior was born while she and Joseph were in Bethlehem. It is highly likely that Mary was in labor during the long journey from Nazareth to Bethlehem.

6 And so it was, that, while they were there, the days were accomplished that she should be

LUKE 2

delivered [*the time came for her to have her baby*].

Jesus Is Born

7 And **she brought forth her first-born son, and wrapped him in swaddling clothes, and laid him in a manger; because there was no room for them in the inn** [*JST "inns"*].

> "Swaddling clothes" were bands of cloth in which a newborn baby was wrapped. The baby was placed diagonally upon a square piece of cloth. The bottom corner of the square cloth was folded up to cover the baby's feet, and the side corners were folded in to cover the baby's sides. Then bands of cloth were wound around the baby to make a warm, comfortable bundle.

The Birth of Christ Is Announced to the Shepherds

8 And there were in the same country [*in the Bethlehem area*] **shepherds** abiding [*staying*] in the field, keeping watch over their flock by night.

9 And, lo, **the angel of the Lord came upon them, and the glory of the Lord shone round about them: and they were sore** [*very*] **afraid.**

10 And **the angel said** unto them, **Fear not: for, behold, I bring you good tidings of great joy, which shall be to all people.**

11 For **unto you is born this day in the city of David** [*Bethlehem*] **a Saviour, which is Christ the Lord.**

12 And **this shall be a sign** unto you; **Ye shall find the babe wrapped in swaddling clothes, lying in a manger.**

Heavenly Choirs

13 And s**uddenly there was with the angel a multitude of the heavenly host praising God, and saying,**

14 **Glory to God in the highest, and on earth peace, good will toward men.**

15 And it came to pass, as the angels were gone away from them into heaven, **the shepherds said one to another, Let us now go even unto Bethlehem, and see** this thing which is come to pass [*which has happened*], which the Lord hath made known unto us.

The Shepherds Find Him

16 And **they** came with haste [*they hurried*], and **found Mary, and Joseph, and the babe lying in a manger.**

17 And when they had seen it, **they made known abroad the saying which was told them concerning this child** [*they told many others what the angel had told them about the birth of the Christ child*].

18 And **all they that heard it wondered** [*marveled and rejoiced*] at those things which were told them by the shepherds.

244   THE NEW TESTAMENT MADE EASIER THIRD EDITION, PART 1

19 But **Mary kept all these things, and pondered them in her heart.**

It is hard to imagine the flood of tender feelings which must have been in Mary's heart, as she looked at her newborn baby, realizing that this was the Son of God, the Promised Messiah, the Savior of the world. Yet, for the moment, it was her tiny, helpless baby boy, to hold and snuggle, to comfort and take care of, for her and Joseph to rear.

20 And **the shepherds returned, glorifying and praising God** for all the things that they had heard and seen, as it was told unto them.

21 And when **eight days** were accomplished [*were up*] for the circumcising [*see Bible Dictionary, under "Circumcision"*] of the child, **his name was called JESUS,** which [*who*] was so named of [*by*] the angel [*see Matthew 1:21 and Luke 1:31*] before he was conceived in the womb.

Both Joseph (Matthew 1:21) and Mary (Luke 1:31) were told by the angel to name the baby "Jesus." Jesus is the Greek form of Joshua or Jeshua, which means "God is help" or "savior." See Bible Dictionary, under "Jesus."

22 And when the days of her purification [*forty days; see Leviticus 12:1–4*] according to the law of Moses were accomplished [*finished*], **they brought him** [*Jesus*] **to Jerusalem, to present him to the Lord** [*at the temple*];

23 (As it is written in the law of the Lord [*Exodus 13:2*], Every male that openeth the womb [*firstborn male child*] shall be called holy [*shall be dedicated*] to the Lord;)

24 **And to offer a sacrifice** according to that which is said in the law of the Lord [*Leviticus 12:6–8, a pair of turtledoves, or two young pigeons.*

Next, a righteous, elderly man named Simeon, who had been promised that he would not die until he had seen the Christ, sees the Christ Child in the temple.

25 And, behold, there was a man in Jerusalem, whose name was **Simeon;** and the same man was **just** [*very exact in living the gospel*] **and devout** [*very faithful*], waiting for the consolation [*redemption; see verse 38*] of Israel: **and the Holy Ghost was upon him.**

26 And **it was revealed unto him by the Holy Ghost,** that he should not see death [*die*], before he had seen the Lord's Christ.

27 And **he came by the Spirit** [*was prompted by the Holy Ghost to come*] **into the temple:** and when the parents brought in the child Jesus, to do for him after the custom of the law [*to present Him in the temple as required*],

28 **Then took he him up in his arms** [*Simeon picked Jesus up*], and blessed [*praised*] God, **and said,**

29 **Lord, now lettest thou thy servant depart in peace,** according to

LUKE 2

thy word [*let me die in peace now, as You promised*]:

30 **For mine eyes have seen thy salvation** [*I have seen the Savior who will bring salvation to us*],

31 **Which thou hast prepared** before the face of all people [*for everyone*];

32 **A light** to lighten the Gentiles [*non-Israelites*], and the glory of thy people Israel.

33 And **Joseph and his mother marvelled** at those things which were spoken of him [*Jesus*].

34 And **Simeon blessed them**, and said unto Mary his mother, Behold, this child is set [*appointed*] for the fall and rising again of many in Israel; and for a sign which shall be spoken against [*He will run into much opposition*];

35 (Yea, a sword shall pierce through thy own soul also,) that the thoughts of many hearts may be revealed.

JST Luke 2:35

35 Yea, a **spear** shall pierce through **him to the wounding of thine own soul also**; that the thoughts of many hearts may be revealed.

Next, Luke reports that an elderly lady named Anna, who saw the child, Jesus, in the temple, likewise bore witness of Him as the Savior of the world.

36 And there was one **Anna**, a prophetess, the daughter of Phanuel,

of the tribe of Aser [*Asher, one of the twelve tribes*]: she was of a great age, and had lived with an husband seven years from her virginity [*for seven years, then he died*];

37 And she **was a widow** of about fourscore and four years [*was now about 84 years old*], which departed not from the temple, but served God with fastings and prayers night and day.

38 And **she** coming in that instant [*seeing Joseph and Mary with baby Jesus*] **gave thanks likewise** unto the Lord, **and spake of him** [*bore witness of Christ*] **to all them that looked for redemption in Jerusalem.**

Have you noticed so far in Luke that both men and women bear witness of the Savior, and that both have been given the gift of prophecy? Luke seems to have a special sensitivity to the role of righteous women as well as faithful men in teaching and bearing witness in the work of the Lord.

39 And when they had performed all things according to the law of the Lord [*when they had performed all the required rituals in the temple, in conjunction with the birth of Jesus*], **they returned into Galilee, to their own city Nazareth.**

Luke briefly summarizes the youth of Jesus, up until age twelve, in verse 40, next.

40 And **the child grew, and waxed strong in spirit, filled with**

THE NEW TESTAMENT MADE EASIER THIRD EDITION, PART 1

wisdom: and the grace of God was upon him.

In JST Matthew 3, we are given additional insights into the Savior's youth as follows:

JST Matthew 3:24–26
24 And it came to pass that Jesus grew up with his brethren, and waxed strong, and waited upon the Lord for the time of his ministry to come.

25 And he served under his father, and he spake not as other men, neither could he be taught; for he needed not that any man should teach him.

26 And after many years, the hour of his ministry drew nigh.

Jesus Teaches in the Temple, at Age Twelve

41 Now **his parents went to Jerusalem every year at the feast of the passover.** [*The Feast of the Passover is celebrated each year by the Jews in March or April, to commemorate the "passing over" of the angel of death over the Israelite homes in Egypt, when the firstborn of the Egyptians were killed. See Bible Dictionary, under "Feasts."*]

42 And **when he was twelve years old, they went up to Jerusalem** after the custom of the feast [*as was the custom, to celebrate the Passover feast*].

43 And when they had fulfilled the days [*when they were finished*], **as**

they returned [*to their home*], the child **Jesus tarried** [*stayed*] behind in Jerusalem; and Joseph and his mother knew not of it.

44 But **they**, supposing him to have been in the company [*they thought he was with friends or relatives in their traveling group*], **went a day's journey**; and they sought [*looked for*] him among their kinsfolk [*relatives*] and acquaintance.

45 And **when they found him not, they turned back again to Jerusalem, seeking him**.

46 And it came to pass, that **after three days they found him in the temple**, sitting in the midst of the doctors [*teachers, men of high education*], both hearing them, and asking them questions.

As you will see, as you read the JST for verse 46, above, it makes a significant change. Jesus was teaching them, rather than they teaching Him.

JST Luke 2:46
46 And it came to pass, that after three days they found him in the temple, sitting in the midst of the doctors, and **they were hearing him, and asking him questions**.

47 And **all that heard him were astonished** at his understanding and answers.

48 And when they [*Joseph and Mary*] saw him, they were amazed: and **his mother said unto him, Son, why hast thou thus dealt with us** [*why did you give us such*]

LUKE 3

a scare]? behold, thy father and I have sought thee sorrowing [*we have been looking for You, very worried!*].

49 And **he said** unto them, How is it that ye sought me [*why were you looking for me*]? **wist ye not** [*didn't you know*] **that I must be about** [*be doing*] **my Father's** [*Heavenly Father's*] **business?**

50 And **they understood not** the saying which he spake unto them. [*Joseph and Mary didn't understand His explanation.*]

51 And **he went down** [*home*] **with them, and came to Nazareth,** and was subject [*obedient*] unto them: but [*JST "and"*] his mother kept all these sayings in her heart.

52 **And Jesus increased in wisdom and stature, and in favour with God and man.**

When he was born, Jesus had the veil over his memory of the premortal life, just as all do. Elder James E. Talmage taught:

"He came among men to experience all the natural conditions of mortality; He was born as truly a dependent, helpless babe as is any other child; His infancy was in all common features as the infancy of others; His boyhood was actual boyhood, His development was as necessary and as real as that of all children. Over His mind had fallen the veil of forgetfulness common to all who are born to earth, by which the remembrance of primeval existence is shut off. The Child grew,

and with growth there came to Him expansion of mind, development of faculties, and progression in power and understanding." (*Jesus the Christ*, page 111)

President Joseph F. Smith said that Jesus did not know who He was as He lay in the cradle. See April 1901 General Conference. As stated in verse 52, above, He gained wisdom as He grew. No doubt the veil was gone before He reached age twelve, for He knew who He was and felt the urgency of being about His Heavenly Father's business, as expressed to Joseph and Mary in verse 49 above.

LUKE 3

In this chapter, Luke tells us that John the Baptist has come into the country, preaching and baptizing, and gives us an account of the baptism of the Savior. He informs us that Jesus began His formal mortal ministry at age 30 (verse 23) and then gives the Savior's mortal genealogy back to Adam.

1 NOW **in the fifteenth year of the reign of Tiberius Cæsar** [*about 29 AD*], Pontius Pilate being governor of Judæa, and Herod [*Herod Antipas, son of Herod the Great*] being tetrarch [*ruler*] of Galilee, and his brother Philip [*another son of Herod the Great*] tetrarch of Ituræa and of the region of Trachonitis, and Lysanias the tetrarch of Abilene,

John the Baptist Comes, Teaching and Baptizing

2 Annas and Caiaphas being the high priests [*the highest Jewish religious leaders*], **the word of God came unto John** [*the Baptist*] the son of Zacharias in the wilderness [*where he had been living since he was a small child*].

3 **And he came into all the country about** [*around*] **Jordan, preaching the baptism of repentance for the remission of sins;**

4 As it is written [*in Isaiah 40:3–5*] in the book of the words of Esaias [*Isaiah*] the prophet, saying, **The voice of one crying in the wilderness, Prepare ye the way of the Lord, make his paths straight.**

The JST adds a little over five verses here, which are left out of the Bible. They are as follows:

JST Luke 3:5–10
5 For behold, and lo, he shall come, as it is written in the book of the prophets, to take away the sins of the world, and to bring salvation unto the heathen nations, to gather together those who are lost, who are of the sheepfold of Israel;

6 Yea, even the dispersed and afflicted; and also to prepare the way, and make possible the preaching of the gospel unto the Gentiles;

7 And to be a light unto all who sit in darkness, unto the uttermost parts of the earth;

to bring to pass the resurrection from the dead, and to ascend up on high, to dwell on the right hand of the Father,

8 Until the fullness of time, and the law and the testimony shall be sealed, and the keys of the kingdom shall be delivered up again unto the Father;

9 To administer justice unto all; to come down in judgment upon all, and to convince all the ungodly of their ungodly deeds, which they have committed; and all this in the day that he shall come;

10 For it is a day of power;

5 Every valley shall be filled, and every mountain and hill shall be brought low; and the crooked shall be made straight, and the rough ways shall be made smooth; [*These things will literally happen at the Second Coming. See Isaiah 40:4, D&C 109:74. Symbolically, the pure gospel of Jesus Christ straightens out our spiritual lives and makes rough obstacles to salvation become smooth, through the Atonement.*]

6 And all flesh shall see the salvation of God.

Notice in the next several verses that people from all walks of life are coming to see John and ask him questions.

7 **Then said he** [*John the Baptist*] **to the multitude that came forth to be baptized of him, O generation of vipers** [*offspring of*

poisonous snakes, in other words, "you wicked people"], **who hath warned you to flee from the wrath to come** [*the punishments of God*]?

It can be puzzling why John scolds everyone in the crowd. But Matthew indicates that John's scolding was not directed at everyone, rather to some wicked Jewish religious leaders among the crowd. Matthew 3:7 tells us that John was speaking to the Pharisees and Sadducees among the people who had come out to listen to him. They were hypocritical religious leaders and insincere and deserved his scathing rebuke in verse 7 above. See note in this study guide, after Matthew 3:7.

An Invitation to Repent

8 Bring forth therefore fruits [*lives, deeds*] **worthy of repentance,** and begin not to say within yourselves, We have Abraham to our father [*we are related to Abraham, so we are automatically saved*]: for I say unto you, That God is able of these stones to raise up children unto Abraham. [*God could turn these rocks into descendants of Abraham. The message: You have to earn salvation yourselves. You will not get into heaven because Abraham was righteous and you descend from him.*]

JST Luke 3:13

13 Bring forth therefore fruits worthy of repentance, and begin not to say within yourselves, **Abraham is our father; we have**

kept the commandments of God, and none can inherit the promises but the children of Abraham; for I say unto you, That God is able of these stones to raise up children unto Abraham.

As mentioned above, it was strongly believed and taught among the Jews at this time that, because they were descendants of Abraham, they were automatically favored by God above all other people. In fact, they felt that they would be in the highest position in heaven, above any Gentile, even if the Gentile converted to God and lived a righteous life.

9 **And now also the axe** [*symbolic of the punishments from God*] **is laid unto the root of the trees** [*symbolic of wicked people*]: **every tree** [*person*] **therefore which bringeth not forth good fruit** [*does not live righteously*] **is hewn** [*cut*] **down, and cast into the fire** [*destroyed*].

10 And the people asked him, saying, **What shall we do then?**

As you can see, in the next verses, John teaches these people the very essence of living the gospel, in answer to their questions.

11 **He answereth** and saith unto them, He that hath two coats, let him impart [*give*] to him that hath none; and he that hath meat [*food*], let him do likewise.

12 **Then came also publicans** [*tax collectors*] to be baptized, and said

unto him, **Master, what shall we do?**

13 **And he said unto them,** Exact no more [*collect no more taxes*] than that which is appointed you [*than is legal; in other words, be honest with people*].

JST Luke 3:19–20

19 For it is well known unto you, Theophilus, that after the manner of the Jews, and according to the custom of their law in receiving money into the treasury, that out of the abundance which was received, was appointed unto the poor, every man his portion;

20 And after this manner did the publicans also, wherefore John said unto them, Exact no more than that which is appointed you.

14 And **the soldiers likewise demanded of** [*asked*] **him,** saying, And what shall we do? And he said unto them, Do violence to no man [*don't make anyone bribe you to keep you from hurting them*], neither accuse any falsely [*if they won't pay you "protection money"*]; and be content with your wages.

The explanations in parentheses in verse 14 above are taken from several other versions of the Bible which agree that John is telling the soldiers to be satisfied with their wages and not to go around intimidating people and making them pay money to keep the soldiers from hurting them.

Next, in verse 15, people are beginning to wonder if John the Baptist is actually the promised Christ.

15 And as the people were in expectation [*suspense*], and **all men mused in their hearts of John** [*were wondering about John*], **whether he were the Christ, or not;**

John the Baptist Teaches that He Is Not the Christ, but that Christ Is Coming

16 **John answered,** saying unto them all, **I indeed baptize you with water; but one mightier than I cometh** [*Christ*], the latchet of whose shoes I am not worthy to unloose: **he shall baptize you with the Holy Ghost and with fire:**

Just a note about the symbolism associated with the word "fire," at the end of verse 16, above. In the scriptures, the Holy Ghost is often compared to fire. The symbolism comes from the use of fire to purify gold. The gold ore is put in a container and fire is used to heat the container. The ore melts, the impurities float to the top, and the pure gold settles to the bottom. The impurities are then discarded and pure gold remains. Thus, the gold is purified by fire. Similarly, the Holy Ghost purifies us, if we allow it. Example: We commit sin. The Holy Ghost points it out and causes our conscience to burn within us. We respond by repenting. Thus we are purified, bit by bit.

17 **Whose fan is in his hand** [*who*

LUKE 3

is getting ready to harvest the earth], and **he will throughly purge** [*cleanse*] **his floor** [*the threshing floor, symbolic of the earth*], **and will gather the wheat** [*the righteous*] into his garner [*barn, symbolic of heaven*]; **but the chaff** [*the wicked*] **he will burn with fire** unquenchable [*and they won't be able to put the fire (punishment) out*].

18 And many other things in his exhortation [*warnings and teachings*] preached he unto the people.

John the Baptist Is Put in Prison

19 But **Herod the tetrarch** [*Roman ruler for that part of Palestine*], being reproved by him [*scolded by John*] for [*because of*] Herodias his brother Philip's wife, and for all the evils which Herod had done,

20 Added yet this above all [*added another huge sin to his collection*], that he **shut up** [*put*] **John in prison**.

Jesus Is Baptized

21 Now when all the people were baptized, it came to pass, that **Jesus** also being **baptized** [*Matthew 3:13–17*], and praying, the heaven was opened,

22 And **the Holy Ghost descended** in a bodily shape like a dove upon him [*Jesus; John the Baptist saw the Holy Ghost come upon Christ— see Matthew 3:16 in this study guide*], and **a voice** [*the Father's voice*] **came from heaven, which said, Thou art my beloved Son;**

in thee I am well pleased.

Next, in verses 23–38, Luke tells us that the Savior began His mortal mission at age thirty, and then gives His genealogy. Matthew also gives a genealogy of Jesus, in Matthew 1:1–17. Some people, who read these carefully, are confused because the two genealogies don't seem to agree completely. Matthew's account seems to be the royal lineage which would make Joseph, Mary's husband, the legal successor to the throne. He would have been king in Jerusalem if the Romans had not been in power. Thus, Jesus would be in line to be king of the Jews literally. According to Apostle James E. Talmage, Luke's genealogy of Christ seems to be the pedigree of Mary. For more on this, see *Jesus the Christ*, pp. 83–90.

Note that in verse 23, Luke tells us that those who did not realize that Jesus was the Son of God assumed that He was the son of Joseph.

23 And **Jesus** himself began to be about **thirty years of age**, being (as was supposed) the son of **Joseph**, which was the son of **Heli**,

24 Which was the son of **Matthat**, which was the son of **Levi**, which was the son of **Melchi**, which was the son of **Janna**, which was the son of **Joseph**,

25 Which was the son of **Mattathias**, which was the son of **Amos**, which was the son of **Naum**, which was the son of **Esli**, which was the son of **Nagge**,

26 Which was the son of **Maath**, which was the son of **Mattathias**, which was the son of **Semei**, which was the son of **Joseph**, which was the son of **Juda**,

27 Which was the son of **Joanna**, which was the son of **Rhesa**, which was the son of **Zorobabel**, which was the son of **Salathiel**, which was the son of **Neri**,

28 Which was the son of **Melchi**, which was the son of **Addi**, which was the son of **Cosam**, which was the son of **Elmodam**, which was the son of **Er**,

29 Which was the son of **Jose**, which was the son of **Eliezer**, which was the son of **Jorim**, which was the son of **Matthat**, which was the son of **Levi**,

30 Which was the son of **Simeon**, which was the son of **Juda**, which was the son of **Joseph**, which was the son of **Jonan**, which was the son of **Eliakim**,

31 Which was the son of **Melea**, which was the son of **Menan**, which was the son of **Mattatha**, which was the son of **Nathan**, which was the son of **David**,

32 Which was the son of **Jesse**, which was the son of **Obed**, which was the son of **Booz** [*Boaz, Ruth's husband*], which was the son of **Salmon**, which was the son of **Naasson**,

33 Which was the son of **Aminadab**, which was the son of **Aram**, which was the son of **Esrom**, which was the son of **Phares**, which was the son of **Juda**,

34 Which was the son of **Jacob**, which was the son of **Isaac**, which was the son of **Abraham**, which was the son of **Thara**, which was the son of **Nachor**,

35 Which was the son of **Saruch**, which was the son of **Ragau**, which was the son of **Phalec**, which was the son of **Heber**, which was the son of **Sala**,

36 Which was the son of **Cainan**, which was the son of **Arphaxad**, which was the son of **Sem**, which was the son of **Noe** [*Noah*], which was the son of **Lamech**,

37 Which was the son of **Mathusala**, which was the son of **Enoch**, which was the son of **Jared**, which was the son of **Maleleel**, which was the son of **Cainan**,

38 Which was the son of **Enos**, which was the son of **Seth**, which was the son of **Adam**, which was the son of **God**.

JST Luke 3:45
45 And of Enos, and of Seth, and of Adam, who was formed of God, and the first man upon the earth.

Some people have used the last part of verse 38, as it stands in the Bible, to teach that Adam was literally born to Heavenly Father and that is how he got his mortal body. The JST, quoted above, corrects this.

LUKE 4

In this chapter you will see that Jesus went into the wilderness to commune with His Father as He began His formal mortal ministry. Satan will tempt Him. He will visit His hometown of Nazareth and be rejected. Many will be healed and the fame of the Master will spread rapidly.

As we begin, you will see that a doctrinal question is answered in verse 1. Sometimes the question is asked as to whether or not the Holy Ghost was functioning during the time of the Savior's mortal mission. Based on Luke 4:1, next, the answer is definitely yes. For more on this subject, see Bible Dictionary, under "Holy Ghost." See also Acts 10:38.

1 AND **Jesus being full of the Holy Ghost** [*after His baptism; see Matthew 3:13-17*] returned from Jordan [*the Jordan River, east of Jerusalem*], and **was led by the Spirit into the wilderness,**

The Eighth Article of Faith states: "We believe the Bible to be the word of God as far as it is translated correctly . . ." Verse 2, next, is an example of a place where the Bible is not translated correctly. Jesus did not go into the wilderness to be tempted by Satan for forty days; rather He went into the wilderness, after His baptism, "to be with God" (JST–Matthew 4:1).

We will quote a number of JST (Joseph Smith Translation of the Bible) corrections and additions as we go along here. You will see that there are many significant doctrinal changes in the JST. Also, remember that not all of these JST corrections are given in footnotes in your Latter-day Saint Bible, because there is not enough room to include all the changes and additions the Prophet Joseph Smith made in the translation of the Bible. You may wish to obtain a copy of the complete JST from a Latter-day Saint bookstore or online.

2 Being forty days tempted of the devil. And **in those days he did eat nothing**: and when they [*the forty days of fasting*] were ended, **he afterward hungered** [*was hungry*].

JST Luke 4:2

2 **And after forty days, the devil came unto him, to tempt him**. And in those days, he did eat nothing; and when they were ended, he **afterwards** hungered.

Jesus Is Tempted by the Devil

As we continue, we will see that the devil tempted the Savior in three major categories in which he likewise tempts us.

1. Physical appetites (verse 3).

2. Materialism and power (verse 7).

3. Vanity and pride (verse 9).

But, as mentioned also in the note following Matthew 4:2, in this study guide, you will see another form of temptation associated with the above temptations. It is the word "if" in verses 3, 7 and 9. The devil challenged Jesus to prove that He was indeed the Son of God. This "if" challenge can be a very effective tool for Satan as he likewise challenges us to "prove it." People often find themselves committing sin or taking foolish chances in order to respond to someone who is challenging their courage or status, or whatever.

3 And **the devil said unto him, If thou be the Son of God, command this stone that it be made bread.** [*In other words, show me a miracle to prove you are Christ.*]

4 And **Jesus answered** [*responded to*] him, saying, It is written [*in Deuteronomy 8:3*], That **man shall not live by bread alone, but by every word of God.**

5 And the devil, taking him up into an high mountain, shewed [*showed*] unto him **all the kingdoms of the world in a moment of time.**

Verse 5, above, is another place where the Bible translation is incorrect. There is a big difference between the devil taking Jesus to a high mountain and the Spirit taking Him. If the devil were taking Him, it would indicate that the devil is in charge, which he is not! The JST reads:

JST Luke 4:5

5 And **the Spirit taketh him up into a high mountain, and he beheld** all the kingdoms of the world, in a moment of time.

6 And **the devil said** unto him, All this power will I give thee, and the glory of them [*the kingdoms of the world*]: for that is delivered unto me [*they are mine; see Revelation 13 heading*]; and to whomsoever I will I give it.

JST Luke 4:6

6 And the devil **came unto him, and** said unto him, All this power will I give unto thee, and the glory of them; for **they** are delivered unto me, and to whomsoever I will, I give **them**.

7 **If thou therefore wilt worship me, all shall be thine.**

8 And **Jesus answered** and said unto him, **Get thee behind me, Satan:** for it is written [*in Deuteronomy 6:13–14*], **Thou shalt worship the Lord thy God, and him only shalt thou serve.**

Have you noticed that the Savior is quoting scriptures to thwart the temptations the devil is attempting to use against Him? There is a major message for us in this. It is that there is great strength and safety against temptation for us in the scriptures.

9 **And he brought him to Jerusalem, and set him on a pinnacle of the temple,** and said unto him, If thou be the Son of God, cast thyself down from hence [*here*]:

JST Luke 4:9

9 And **the Spirit** brought him to Jerusalem, and set him on a pinnacle of the temple. **And the devil came unto him**, and said unto him, If thou be the Son of God, cast thyself down from hence;

10 **For it is written** [*in Psalm 91:11–12*], **He shall give his angels charge** [*responsibility*] **over thee, to keep thee:**

11 And **in their hands they shall bear thee up,** lest at any time thou dash [*strike*] thy foot against a stone.

12 And **Jesus** answering [*responding*] **said** unto him, It is said, **Thou shalt not tempt the Lord thy God.**

13 And when **the devil** had ended all the temptation, he **departed** from him for a season.

By way of review, we see three major forms of temptations plus a fourth in the verses above. First, temptation to gratify physical appetites as tempted by Satan. Second, the temptation for worldly power and glory. Third, the temptation to challenge God to make good on His promises, as if there were some doubt about how good His word is. Fourth, the phrase "If thou are the Son of God." This, for some of us, could be the most difficult temptation of all. Giving in to the challenge to inappropriately attempt to defend our own ego or position would be giving in to pride.

As Luke continues now, he will tell us that the Savior now returned to His home country of Galilee to preach and minister.

14 And **Jesus returned in the power of the Spirit into Galilee** [*an area in northern Israel*]: **and there went out a fame of him** [*He became famous*] through all the region round about.

15 And **he taught in their synagogues** [*Jewish church buildings*], being glorified of all [*everybody said He was great!*].

Jesus Tells the People of Nazareth that He Is the Promised Messiah

16 And **he came to Nazareth, where he had been brought up** [*His home town*]: and, as his custom was, **he went into the synagogue on the sabbath day, and stood up for to read.**

Watch now as the Master reads two verses of scripture from Isaiah in the synagogue of His hometown, and then tells the people gathered there that the verses apply to Him.

17 And **there was delivered unto him** [*brought to Him at His request*] **the book of the prophet Esaias** [*Isaiah*]. And when he had opened the book, **he found the place where it was written** [*Isaiah 61:1–2*],

18 **The Spirit of the Lord is upon me** [*Christ*], **because he hath anointed** [*called*] **me to preach the gospel to the poor; he hath sent**

256   THE NEW TESTAMENT MADE EASIER THIRD EDITION, PART 1

me to heal the brokenhearted, to preach deliverance [*remission of sins*] to the captives [*those under the bondage of sin*], and recovering of sight to the blind [*spiritually as well as physically*], to set at liberty [*redeem*] them that are bruised [*by sins*],

19 To preach the acceptable year of the Lord [*the time designated by the Father for Jesus to perform His mission on earth, as a mortal; see* Doctrinal New Testament Commentary, *Vol. 1, page 161*].

20 And he closed the book, and he gave it again to the minister, and sat down. And the eyes of all them that were in the synagogue were fastened on him.

21 And he began to say unto them, This day is this scripture fulfilled in your ears. [*In other words, I am the fulfillment of this prophecy of Isaiah.*]

22 And all bare him witness [*spoke well of him (for a few minutes)*], and wondered [*marveled*] at the gracious words which proceeded out of his mouth. And they said [*to each other*], Is not this Joseph's son?

The men of the synagogue, who heard Jesus claim to be the Messiah, after reading the passage from Isaiah, now begin to have doubts. They have heard of the many miracles and things a man named Jesus has been doing throughout the country. Now, when they see that He is the Jesus who grew up in their town,

they say, in effect, "Now wait a minute. Isn't this Jesus who is Joseph the carpenter's son? We know His family. He grew up here. He is just a common man, one of us. How can He possibly think He is the Messiah?"

23 And he said unto them, Ye will surely say unto me this proverb [*old saying*], Physician, heal thyself: whatsoever we have heard done in Capernaum, do also here in thy country. [*Prove that You are something special by doing the same miracles You have done elsewhere.*]

You have probably heard the last phrase of verse 24, next, many times. It is often quoted to mean that a person who is famous among people elsewhere is criticized and put down among people he or she grew up with.

24 And he said, Verily I say unto you, No prophet is accepted in his own country.

25 But I tell you of a truth, many widows were in Israel in the days of Elias [*Elijah*], when the heaven was shut up three years and six months, when great famine was throughout all the land;

26 But unto none of them was Elias [*Elijah*] sent, save [*except*] unto Sarepta, a city of Sidon, unto a woman that was a widow.

27 And many lepers [*people with leprosy*] were in Israel in the time of Eliseus [*Elisha*] the prophet; and none of them was cleansed, saving [*except*] Naaman the Syrian [*2 Kings 5:14*].

The point Jesus is making to these men of His hometown seems to be that it wasn't necessary for prophets such as Elijah and Elisha to heal every person in the land or perform the same miracles for everyone in order to be accepted as a prophet sent from God. So why should it be different with Jesus? Why should He be required to perform the same miracles for the people of Nazareth as for others, in order to be accepted by them. Couldn't they exercise faith in what had been done elsewhere?

28 **And all they in the synagogue,** when they heard these things, **were filled with wrath** [*were very angry*],

29 **And rose up, and thrust him out of the city, and led him unto the brow** [*cliff*] **of the hill whereon their city was built, that they might cast him down headlong** [*headfirst*].

30 **But he passing through the midst of them went his way,**

It will be interesting to get the rest of the details as to what happened here. This was a great miracle, if these wicked and hardhearted men would pay attention to it.

31 **And came down to Capernaum,** a city of Galilee, and taught them on the sabbath days.

32 And t**hey were astonished at his doctrine: for his word was with power** [*He taught with power and authority*].

A Man Possessed by Evil Spirits Is Healed

33 And **in the synagogue there was a man, which had a spirit of an unclean devil** [*was possessed by evil spirits*]**, and cried out with a loud voice,**

34 **Saying, Let us alone; what have we to do with thee, thou Jesus of Nazareth?** art thou come to destroy us? **I know thee who thou art; the Holy One of God.** [*One of the evil spirits bears witness of Christ.*]

35 And **Jesus rebuked him** [*sharply scolded*]**, saying, Hold thy peace** [*be quiet*]**, and come out of him.** And when the devil had thrown him [*tossed Him around*] in the midst, **he came out of him,** and hurt him not [*no more*].

36 And t**hey were all amazed,** and spake [*spoke*] among themselves, saying, What a word is this! **for with authority and power he commandeth the unclean spirits, and they come out.**

37 And **the fame of him went out into every place** of the country round about.

The Master Heals Peter's Mother-in-Law

38 **And he** arose out of [*left*] the synagogue, and **entered into Simon's** [*Peter's*] **house. And Simon's wife's mother** [*Peter's mother-in-law*] **was taken** [*sick*] **with a great fever; and they besought him for her** [*asked Jesus to heal her*].

39 **And he** stood over her, and **rebuked the fever** [*commanded the fever to leave*]; **and it left her: and immediately she arose and ministered unto them.**

The fact that Peter was married is significant. Some religions believe that celibacy (intentionally not getting married) is the highest form of dedication to God. This is not true. Living worthily of exaltation in a family unit forever is the highest form of dedication to God.

40 Now when the sun was setting, **all they that had any sick** with divers [*various*] diseases **brought them unto him; and he laid his hands on every one of them, and healed them**.

41 **And devils** [*evil spirits*] also came out of many, crying out, and saying, Thou art Christ the Son of God. And he rebuking them suffered them not to speak [*commanded them not to bear witness of Him*]: for they **knew that he was Christ**.

From verse 41, above, we learn that the veil, which erases our memory of our premortal life, is not upon Satan and the one third of premortal spirits who were cast out of heaven (Revelation 12:4) and down to the earth with him. They knew Christ in premortality and still recognize him here.

42 And when it was day [*the next day*], **he departed and went into a desert place: and the people** sought [*found*] him, and came

unto him, and **stayed him** [*stopped him*], that he should not depart from them.

43 And **he said unto them, I must preach the kingdom of God** [*the gospel*] **to other cities also**: for therefore [*that is the reason*] am I sent.

44 And **he preached in the synagogues** [*Jewish church buildings*] **of Galilee**.

LUKE 5

Here, Luke starts out by telling us about the calling of Peter, James, and John to be disciples. Later, they will be called and ordained as Apostles. Watch for the symbolism involved in fishing and the "gospel net."

1 AND it came to pass, that, as the people pressed upon him [*crowded and pushed against Him*] to hear the word of God, **he stood by the lake of Gennesaret** [*the Sea of Galilee*],

The Calling of Peter, James, and John

2 **And saw two ships** standing by the lake: but **the fishermen** were gone out of them, and **were washing their nets**.

3 And **he entered into one of the ships, which was Simon's** [*which belonged to Peter*], **and prayed** [*asked*] **him that he would thrust out a little from the land. And he**

LUKE 5

sat down, and taught the people out of the ship.

4 Now when he had left [*finished*] speaking, he said unto Simon [*Peter*], **Launch out into the deep, and let down your nets for a draught** [*a catch of fish*].

5 And Simon answering [*in response*] said unto him, **Master, we have toiled** [*worked hard fishing*] **all the night, and have taken nothing: nevertheless at thy word I will let down the net.**

By way of information, it was the practice at this time for those who fished for a living on the Sea of Galilee to fish during the night.

6 And when they had this done, **they inclosed a great multitude of fishes: and their net brake** [*started to break; see Luke 5:6, footnote 6a in your Bible*].

7 And they beckoned [*waved*] unto their partners, which were in the other ship, that they should come and help them. And **they came, and filled both the ships, so that they began to sink.**

There is beautiful symbolism here. As Peter and others follow the Savior's instructions in faith, they have great success in catching fish. Symbolically, as Peter and the others follow Christ, He will make them "fishers of men," and they will have a large "catch" of converts. See end of verse 10 below.

8 **When Simon Peter saw it, he** fell down at Jesus' knees [*very humble*], saying, Depart from me; for I am a sinful man, O Lord. [*I am not worthy to be in Thy presence.*]

9 **For he was astonished, and all that were with him**, at the draught [*catch*] of the fishes which they had taken:

10 **And so was** [*were*] **also James,** and **John**, the sons of Zebedee, **which were partners with Simon** [*Peter*]. **And Jesus said unto Simon, Fear not; from henceforth** [*from now on*] **thou shalt catch men.**

11 And when they had brought their ships to land, **they forsook all** [*left everything behind*], **and followed him.**

The Healing of a Leper

12 And it came to pass, when he was in a certain city, behold **a man full of leprosy**: who seeing Jesus fell on his face [*a cultural way of showing great humility*], and **besought** [*begged*] **him, saying, Lord, if thou wilt** [*if you are willing*], **thou canst make me clean.** [*This sick man has great faith in Christ.*]

Leprosy was one of the most dreaded diseases of the time. It was greatly feared by others, and a person who had the disease was required by law to warn others to stay clear so they would not accidentally touch the leper and risk catching the disease. Lepers were social outcasts. See "Leper" and "Leprosy" in Bible Dictionary.

13 And he [*Jesus*] put forth his hand, and touched him, saying, I will: **be thou clean. And immediately the leprosy departed from him.**

14 And he charged [*instructed*] him to **tell no man:** but go, and **shew thyself to the priest** [*as commanded in Leviticus 14:2*], and offer for thy cleansing, according as Moses commanded, for a testimony unto them.

15 But so much the more went there a fame abroad of him [*this healing caused Jesus to become even more famous*]: and **great multitudes came together to hear, and to be healed by him** of their infirmities [*sicknesses*].

16 And **he withdrew himself into the wilderness, and prayed.**

17 And it came to pass on a certain day, **as he was teaching,** that there were **Pharisees** [*religious leaders of the Jews*] **and doctors of the law** [*scribes—see verse 21; religious leaders who interpreted how to live the religious laws of the Jews*] **sitting by** [*watching*], which were come out of every town of Galilee, and Judæa, and Jerusalem [*who had come from all over, worried about Jesus and His growing popularity*]: and the power of the Lord was present to heal them [*the people from the area who had come to be healed or brought their sick to be healed*].

Jesus Heals a Man with Palsy

18 And, behold, **men brought in a bed a man** [*carried a man on a bed*] which was taken [*sick*] **with a palsy:** and they sought means to [*tried to figure out how to*] bring him in, and to lay him before [*in front of*] him [*Jesus*].

19 And when they could not find by what way they might bring him in [*when they couldn't figure out a way*] because of the multitude [*the crowd*], **they went upon the housetop, and let him** [*the sick man in the bed*] **down through the tiling** [*roof*] with his couch into the midst **before** [*in front of*] **Jesus.**

The Master Forgives Sins, Which Infuriates the Jewish Religious Leaders

20 And when he [*Jesus*] saw their faith, he said unto him, **Man, thy sins are forgiven thee.**

21 **And the scribes and the Pharisees** [*religious leaders who were trying to trap Jesus*] **began to reason** [*discuss among themselves*], saying, **Who is this which speaketh blasphemies? Who can forgive sins, but God alone?**

"Blasphemy," showing disrespect for God, mocking God, was a violation of law among the Jews which was punishable by death.

22 But when **Jesus perceived** [*read*] **their thoughts,** he answering said [*responded, saying*] unto them, What reason ye in your

LUKE 5

261

hearts [*why are such thoughts in your hearts*]?

23 Whether [*which*] **is easier, to say, Thy sins be forgiven thee; or to say, Rise up and walk?**

JST Luke 5:22–23

22 But Jesus perceived their thoughts, and he said unto them, What reason ye in your hearts?

23 Does it require more power to forgive sins than to make the sick rise up and walk?

The Savior is saying, in effect, "If I am a fraud, and imposter, as you say I am, which would be safer for Me to say, 'Your sins are forgiven.' or 'Rise up and walk.'? Which would be less likely to expose Me as a fake?" The obvious answer is "Your sins are forgiven," since there is no immediate way of telling whether or not that happens to the sick man. But as Jesus says "Rise up and walk," there will be immediate evidence as to whether or not He is an imposter. This creates a very tense situation. Notice also that in verse 24, next, Jesus clearly tells them that He is the Son of God.

24 But that ye may know that the Son of man [*I, the Son of Man, the Son of God; the Son of Man of Holiness (the Father—see* Moses 6:57*)*] **hath power upon earth to forgive sins,** [*He said unto the sick of the palsy,*] **I say unto thee, Arise, and take up thy couch** [*bed*], **and go into thine house**.

25 And immediately he rose up before them, and took up that whereon he lay [*his bed*], **and departed to his own house, glorifying** [*praising*] **God**.

26 And they were all amazed, and they glorified God, and were filled with fear, saying, We have seen strange things to day.

Matthew Is Called to Follow Christ

27 And after these things he [*Jesus*] went forth, and saw a publican [*tax collector*], named **Levi** [*Matthew*], sitting at the receipt of custom [*where they collected taxes*]: **and he** [*Jesus*] **said unto him, Follow me**.

28 And he left all, rose up, and followed him.

29 And **Levi** [*Matthew*] **made him** [*Jesus*] **a great feast in his own house**: and there was a great company of publicans [*tax collectors*] and of others that sat down with them.

30 But their **scribes and Pharisees** [*the Jewish religious leaders who are trying to trap Jesus*] **murmured** [*grumbled*] **against his disciples** [*didn't come directly to Jesus*], saying, **Why do ye eat and drink with publicans and sinners?**

These hypocritical Jewish religious leaders had strict rules for themselves to avoid associating with publicans and sinners. They considered it a matter of personal righteousness not to do so, and considered that Jesus and His disciples were exposing their sinful natures by eating and associating with such people.

31 And **Jesus** answering [*responding*] **said** unto them [*the Pharisees and scribes*], **They that are whole** [*well*] **need not a physician; but they that are sick.** [*If I am going to help people, I must associate with them.*]

32 **I** [*the Son of God*] **came not to call the righteous, but sinners to repentance.**

As you can see, in verse 32 above, Jesus states clearly again, very openly, that He is the Son of God, with power to call sinners to repentance and to forgive sins. This had to be very frustrating to these Pharisees and scribes!

33 And **they** [*the Pharisees and scribes*]**said unto him** [*Jesus*], **Why do the disciples of John** [*followers of John the Baptist*] **fast often, and make prayers, and likewise the disciples of the Pharisees; but thine eat and drink?** [*In other words, why don't you and your disciples follow the rules we do?*]

It is helpful to know that John the Baptist is in prison at this time and is soon to be beheaded at Herod's command.

34 And **he said** unto them, **Can ye make the children of the bride-**

chamber fast, while the bridegroom is with them?

35 But the days will come, **when the bridegroom shall be taken away from them,** and **then shall they fast in those days.**

Understanding a bit of Jewish culture will help with verses 34–35, above. Wedding imagery is involved. Jesus is the bridegroom, or groom, as we would say it. Faithful followers are the bride. "Bridechamber" would be the place where the wedding feast is held and, symbolically, would be the land of Israel where the Savior was performing His mortal mission. While the groom and the bride are together, much celebrating and feasting—hearing and understanding the Savior's teachings—would take place. It would not make sense to mourn and fast at this time. But, when the Savior is crucified and taken from them, the "children of the bridechamber," the faithful Saints, will mourn and fast.

Next, Jesus will teach that people who are set in their ways do not usually accept new ideas, in this case, the true gospel.

36 And he spake also a parable unto them; **No man putteth** [*attaches*] **a piece of a new garment** [*cloth*] **upon an old** [*symbolic of putting the true gospel into old lifestyles*]; if otherwise, then both the new maketh a rent [*tear*], and the piece that was taken out of the new agreeth not with the old [*is not compatible with the old piece*].

LUKE 6 263

New Wine in Old Bottles

37 And **no man putteth new wine** [*new gospel*] **into old bottles** [*scribes and Pharisees, who are set in their evil ways*]; else the new wine will burst the bottles, and be spilled, and the bottles shall perish.

38 But **new wine must be put into new bottles**; and both are preserved.

Leather bottles were used to store wine. Over time, the leather became hard and inflexible. If new wine were put in old leather bottles, the bottles would break because they could not stretch with the pressure generated by fermentation processes in the new wine.

39 **No man also having drunk old wine straightway** [*immediately*] **desireth new: for he saith, The old is better.** [*People who are set in their ways, don't like new ideas, in this case, the true gospel.*]

LUKE 6

In this chapter Luke focuses on the Savior's activities on several Sabbaths, pointing out how the leaders of the Jews attempted to discredit Him by using their Sabbath traditions against Him. This is ironic because He, as the premortal Christ, was the God of the Old Testament, Jehovah Himself, the One who gave the commandment in the Old Testament to keep the Sabbath day Holy. Additionally in this chapter, Jesus will choose the Twelve Apostles, and continue preaching, pointing out the blessings of living the gospel and the problems that come upon those who don't live it.

1 AND it came to pass **on the second sabbath** after the first, that he went through the corn [*grain*] fields; and **his disciples plucked the ears of corn** [*grain*], **and did eat, rubbing them in their hands**.

The Jews had developed thousands of laws over the years for observing the Sabbath, which were not in harmony with the laws for Sabbath observance given by the Lord to Moses. One of these laws was that it was forbidden to rub heads of wheat, barley or whatever grain together on the Sabbath because it was considered to be threshing grain (separating the grain kernels from the chaff) which violated the Sabbath.

Watch now as the Pharisees attempt to discredit Jesus regarding the Sabbath. And then watch in verse 5, below, as He tells them that He is the one who gave the commandments concerning the Sabbath.

2 And certain of the **Pharisees** [*religious leaders of the Jews*] **said** unto them, **Why do ye that which is not lawful** [*legal*] to do **on the sabbath** days?

3 And **JesuS** answering them **said, Have ye not read** so much as this, **what David did, when himself was an hungred** [*hungry*], **and they** [*his soldiers*] which were **with him**;

4 **How he went into the house of God, and did take and eat the shewbread** [*sacred bread used in the tabernacle and temple*], and gave also to them that were **with him; which it is not lawful to eat but for the priests alone?** [*Only the priests were allowed to eat the shewbread.*]

5 **And he** [*Jesus*] **said** unto them [*the Pharisees*], That **the Son of man** [*a short way of saying "Son of Man of Holiness" (the Father)— see Moses 6:57*] **is Lord also of the sabbath.** [*in other words, I am the God of the Sabbath.*]

Jesus Heals the Man with the Withered Hand

6 And it came to pass also **on another sabbath**, that he entered into the synagogue [*Jewish church building*] and taught: and there was **a man whose right hand was withered** [*crippled*].

7 And **the scribes and Pharisees** [*religious leaders*] **watched him, whether** [*to see if*] **he would heal on the sabbath** day; **that they might find an accusation against him** [*that they might get him arrested*].

8 But **he knew their thoughts, and said to the man which had the withered hand, Rise up, and stand forth in the midst** [*of the synagogue*]. **And he arose and stood forth.**

9 **Then said Jesus unto them** [*the scribes and Pharisees in verse 7*], I will ask you one thing; **Is it lawful** [*legal*] **on the sabbath days to do good, or to do evil? to save life, or to destroy it?**

10 **And** looking round about upon them all, **he said unto the man, Stretch forth thy hand. And he did so: and his hand was restored whole as the other.**

This must have been an intense scene. Just imagine how quiet it must have become, as Jesus slowly looked around at all of these wicked religious leaders and hypocrites who had gathered to trap Him, then said to the man with the crippled hand, "Stretch forth thy hand." And then the hand was healed.

11 **And they** [*the scribes and Pharisees*] **were filled with madness** [*anger*]; **and communed** [*discussed*] **one with another what they might do to Jesus.**

Jesus Calls the Twelve

12 And it came to pass in those days, that **he went out into a mountain to pray, and continued all night in prayer to God.**

13 And when it was day, he called unto him his disciples: and of them **he chose twelve**, whom also he named **apostles**;

14 **Simon**, (whom he also named Peter,) and **Andrew** his brother, **James** and **John**, **Philip** and **Bartholomew**,

15 **Matthew** and **Thomas**, **James** the son of Alphæus, and **Simon** called Zelotes,

LUKE 6

16 And **Judas** the brother of James, and **Judas Iscariot**, which also was the traitor [*who would betray Jesus*].

17 And **he came down** [*from the mountain*] **with them**, and stood in the plain, and the company of his disciples, **and a great multitude** of people out of all Judæa and Jerusalem, and from the sea coast of Tyre and Sidon, which **came to hear him, and to be healed of their diseases**;

18 And they that were vexed [*troubled, possessed*] with unclean spirits: **and they were healed**.

19 And **the whole multitude sought to** [*tried to*] **touch him**: for there went virtue [*power*] out of him, and healed them all.

The Sermon on the Plain

Luke next records what is often referred to as "the Sermon on the Plain." Scholars do not agree as to whether or not the Sermon on the Plain is the same as the Sermon on the Mount (Matthew 5, 6, and 7). Either way, we are given much help in understanding these teachings of the Savior by reading 3 Nephi, chapters 12–14. In 3 Nephi 12:1–2, it is clear that the Sermon on the Mount was given to members of the Church and was designed to help them obtain the kingdom of heaven; in other words, celestial glory. The notes in brackets in the next few verses demonstrate one possible way in which this sermon teaches members how to obtain celestial glory.

20 And he lifted up his eyes on his disciples, and said, **Blessed be ye poor** [*you poor in spirituality, who repent*]: **for yours is** [*you will obtain*] **the kingdom of God** [*celestial glory*].

21 **Blessed are ye that hunger** [*for personal righteousness*] **now: for ye shall be filled** [*with the Holy Ghost*]. **Blessed are ye that weep now** [*for your sins, then repent*]: **for ye shall laugh** [*rejoice*].

22 **Blessed are ye, when men shall hate you** [*because you are doing what is right*], **and when they shall separate you** [*reject you*] **from their company, and shall reproach** [*insult, criticize*] **you, and cast out your name as evil** [*ruin your reputation*], **for the Son of man's** [*the Savior's*] **sake.**

23 **Rejoice ye** [*be happy*] **in that day** [*when such things happen to you*], **and leap for joy: for, behold, your reward is great in heaven** [*it will all be worth it when you get to celestial glory*]: **for in the like manner** [*in the same way*] **did their fathers unto the prophets** [*their ancestors persecuted the prophets*].

24 But **woe unto you that are rich** [*the wicked who are rich*]! **for ye have received your consolation** [*your reward is your money here on earth, but it won't get you to celestial glory*].

25 **Woe unto you that are full** [*think you don't need the gospel*]! **for ye shall hunger** [*wish you*

266   THE NEW TESTAMENT MADE EASIER THIRD EDITION, PART 1

had repented]. **Woe unto you that laugh now** [*at righteous people, and at the gospel*]! **for ye shall mourn and weep** [*later in this life or in the next life*].

26 **Woe unto you** [*the wicked in verses 24–25*], **when all** [*wicked*] **men shall speak well of you** [*because you fit right in with them and their wicked lifestyle*]! **for so did their fathers** [*their ancestors*] **to the false prophets.**

27 **But I say unto you which hear** [*pay attention to My teachings*], **Love your enemies, do good to them which hate you,**

28 **Bless them that curse you, and pray for them which despitefully use** [*abuse*] **you.**

29 **And unto him that smiteth thee** [*hits you*] **on the one cheek offer also the other; and him that taketh away thy cloke forbid not to take thy coat also.**

30 **Give to every man that asketh of thee; and of him that taketh away thy goods ask them not again.**

The JST adds to and makes changes to verses 29–30, above.

JST Luke 6:29-31
29 And unto him **who** smiteth thee **on the cheek,** offer also the other; **or, in other words, it is better to offer the other, than to revile again.** And him **who** taketh away thy cloak, forbid not to take thy coat also.

30 **For it is better that thou suffer thine enemy to take these things, than to contend with him. Verily I say unto you, Your heavenly Father who seeth in secret, shall bring that wicked one into judgment.**

31 **Therefore** give to every man who asketh of thee; and of him who taketh away thy goods, ask them not again.

A major message taught in verses 27–30, above, and in the associated JST verses, is that we must develop self-control, character strength, and other such virtues to the point that our personalities and dispositions are not dependent upon our circumstances and how others are treating us.

The "Golden Rule"

31 **And as ye would that men should do to you, do ye also to them likewise.** [*In other words, treat others the way you would like them to treat you. This is known as "the Golden Rule."*]

32 **For if ye love them which love you, what thank have ye? for sinners also love those that love them.**

JST Luke 6:33
33 For if ye love them **only who** love you, **what reward have you? For sinners also do even the same.**

33 **And if ye do good to them which do good to you, what thank have ye? for sinners also do even the same.**

One important message we can get from verses 32–33 above is that if we love "only" (see JST verse 33) people who love us, and we are mean to everyone else, and if we only do good to people who are nice to us, that makes us like most everybody else and does not build Christ-like qualities in us.

34 And if ye lend to them of whom ye hope to receive, what thank have ye? for sinners also lend to sinners, to receive as much again. [*In other words, you are not truly generous if you only lend things to people in situations where you will profit by it.*]

JST Luke 6:34

34 And if ye lend to them of whom ye hope to receive, what **reward** have **you**? for sinners also lend to sinners, to receive as much again.

Love Your Enemies

35 **But love ye your enemies, and do good, and lend, hoping for nothing again; and your reward shall be great** [*because you are then truly loving and truly generous*], **and ye shall be the children of the Highest** [*you will obtain celestial glory and live in the presence of the Father*]: **for he is kind unto the unthankful and to the evil.**

The next verses contain more teachings about how to become Christlike and obtain celestial glory.

36 **Be** ye therefore **merciful**, as your Father also is merciful.

37 **Judge not** [*JST Matthew 7:2 "judge not unrighteously"*], and ye shall not be judged: **condemn not** [*judge someone worthy of being damned by God and hoping they don't get a second chance*], and ye shall not be condemned: **forgive,** and ye shall be forgiven:

38 **Give** [*be generous, kind, and forgiving*], **and it** [*your reward*] **shall be given unto you; good measure, pressed down, and shaken together, and running over** [*overflowing*], **shall men give into your bosom. For with the same measure that ye mete** [*give out*] **withal** [*how you treat others*] **it shall be measured to you again** [*given back to you by God*].

The phrase "pressed down, and shaken together, and running over" in verse 38, above, calls to mind someone cooking a delicious meal, who takes ingredients and packs them tightly in the measuring cup, shakes it to make sure there is no dead space, and then adds more ingredients until the cup runs over. Symbolically, the Lord will pack all kinds of rewards in the "cup" of the righteous so that their "cup runneth over" (Psalm 23:5) with blessings and eternal rewards.

39 And he spake **a parable** [*a story designed to teach a specific point*] unto them, **Can the blind lead the blind? shall they not both fall into the ditch?** [*Can the spiritually blind lead other spiritually blind people successfully?*]

40 The disciple [*follower; student*] is not above [*better than*] his master [*teacher*]: but every one that is perfect [*has been perfectly prepared*] shall be [*become*] as his master.

The Mote and the Beam

41 And **why beholdest thou** [*why do you look at*] **the mote** [*speck; symbolical of a little imperfection*] **that is in thy brother's eye, but perceivest not** [*don't notice*] **the beam** [*huge roof beam*] **that is in thine own eye?** [*Why are you so critical of little imperfections in others but can't see your own huge imperfections?*]

42 Either [*or else*] **how canst thou say to thy brother, Brother, let me pull out the mote that is in thine eye** [*let me fix your imperfections*], **when thou thyself beholdest not the beam that is in thine own eye** [*when you are so imperfect yourself*]? **Thou hypocrite, cast out first the beam out of thine own eye** [*straighten out your own life first*], **and then shalt thou see clearly to pull out the mote that is in thy brother's eye** [*then you will be able to help others effectively*].

The imagery of a small chip of wood and a huge beam of wood, in verse 42, above, is intentional exaggeration by the Master Teacher to help us see the importance of not criticizing others when we are so imperfect ourselves.

43 For **a good tree** [*symbolic of good people*] **bringeth not forth** corrupt fruit [*a wicked life*]; **neither doth a corrupt tree** [*a wicked person*] **bring forth good fruit** [*a good life*].

44 For **every tree** [*person*] **is known by his own fruit** [*the kind of life he or she leads*]. For of thorns [*from thorn bushes*] men do not gather [*harvest*] figs, nor of a bramble bush gather they [*harvest*] grapes. [*In other words, you can't expect a righteous reward on Judgment Day if you have lived a wicked life, including the hypocrisy of continuously judging others harshly.*]

45 A good man out of the good treasure of his heart bringeth forth that which is good; and an evil man out of the evil treasure of his heart bringeth forth that which is evil: for of the abundance of the heart his mouth speaketh. [*The true feelings and attitudes of our heart show up in the things we say about others.*]

46 And **why call ye me, Lord, Lord, and do not the things which I say?** [*Why do you pretend to follow Me when you don't do what I say?*]

47 Whosoever cometh to me, and heareth my sayings, and doeth them, I will shew [*show*] **you to whom he is like:**

House Built on a Rock

48 He is like a man which built an house, and digged deep, and laid the **foundation on a rock:** and when the flood arose, the stream beat vehemently [*fiercely*] upon that house, and **could not shake it: for it was founded upon a rock.** [*Symbolic of a life built upon Christ and His teachings, which cannot be destroyed by life's troubles.*]

House Not Built on a Rock

49 **But he that heareth** [*the Savior's teachings*], **and doeth not** [*does not obey them*], **is like a man that without a foundation built an house upon the earth**; against which the stream did beat vehemently [*violently*], and immediately **it fell**; and the ruin of that house was great. [*Much spiritual destruction came upon that person.*]

LUKE 7

In this chapter, you will see the Savior heal a Roman soldier's servant and raise the dead son of a widow living in the city of Nain. You will learn more about John the Baptist and see Jesus forgive sins.

1 NOW when he had ended all his sayings in the audience of the people, **he entered into Capernaum** [*on the northwest coast of the Sea of Galilee*].

Healing of the Centurion's Son

2 And a certain **centurion's servant**, who was dear unto him, **was sick, and ready to die.** [*A centurion was a Roman soldier in charge of one hundred soldiers.*]

3 And **when he heard of Jesus, he sent unto him the elders of the Jews, beseeching** [*asking*] **him that he would come and heal his servant.**

4 And when they came to Jesus, **they besought him** instantly [*asked Jesus right away to heal the centurion's servant*], **saying, That he** [*the Roman centurion*] **was worthy** for whom he [*Jesus*] should do this:

5 **For he** [*the centurion*] **loveth our nation, and he hath built us a synagogue** [*a church*].

As Luke continues, you will see that this Roman centurion was a very humble man with pure faith.

6 Then **Jesus went with them.** And **when he was now not far from the house, the centurion sent friends to him, saying** unto him, **Lord, trouble not thyself: for I am not worthy that thou shouldest enter under my roof** [*enter into my house*]:

7 Wherefore neither thought I myself worthy to come unto thee [*I didn't consider myself worthy to come to You so I sent friends*]: **but say in a word** [*give the word*], **and my servant shall be healed.**

8 For **I also** [*like you*] **am a man set under authority** [*who has authority*], having under me soldiers, and I say unto one, Go, and he goeth; and to another, Come, and he cometh; and to my servant, Do this, and he doeth it.

9 When Jesus heard these things, he marvelled at him, and turned him about [*turned around*], **and said unto the people that followed him, I say unto you, I have not found so great faith, no, not in Israel.**

10 **And they** [*the centurion's friends*] that were sent [*to Jesus*], returning to the house, **found the servant whole** [*healed*] that had been sick.

Widow's Son Is Raised From the Dead

11 And it came to pass **the day after,** that he [*Jesus*] **went into a city called Nain** [*a city in Galilee*]; and many of his disciples went with him, and much people [*large crowds of people*].

12 Now when he came nigh [*near*] to the gate of the city, behold, **there was a dead man carried out, the only son of his mother, and she was a widow**: and much people of the city was with her.

13 **And when the Lord saw her, he had compassion on her, and said unto her, Weep not.**

14 And **he** came and **touched the bier** [*the board being used to carry the dead man*]: and they [*the pall-bearers*] that bare [*carried*] him stood still. And **he said, Young man, I say unto thee, Arise.**

15 And **he that was dead sat up, and began to speak.** And he delivered him [*turned him over*] to his mother.

16 And **there came a fear on all: and they glorified** [*praised*] **God, saying, That a great prophet** [*Jesus*] **is risen up among us**; and, That God hath visited [*blessed*] his people.

17 And **this rumour** [*news*] of him [*Jesus*] **went forth throughout all Judæa** [*the southern region of the Holy Land*], **and throughout all the region round about.**

18 And **the disciples of John** [*John the Baptist*] **shewed** [*showed*] **him** [*told him*] **of all these things** [*about Jesus*].

Remember that John the Baptist is in prison at this time. From what we read here, it appears that his disciples had free access to him.

19 And **John** [*the Baptist*] **calling unto him two of his disciples sent them to Jesus, saying, Art thou he that should come** [*are you the Messiah*]**? or look we for another?**

20 **When the men** [*John the Baptist's disciples*] **were come unto him** [*Jesus*]**, they said, John Baptist hath sent us unto thee, saying, Art thou he that should come? or look we for another?**

Can you imagine what went through the hearts and minds of these disciples of John when, in answer to their question, they witnessed the Savior's healings in verse 21, next?

21 **And in that same hour he cured many of their** [*the people around Jesus at the time*] **infirmities and**

LUKE 7

plagues [*diseases*], and of evil spirits; and unto many that were blind he gave sight.

22 **Then Jesus answering** [*answering the question John the Baptist's disciples asked in verse 20 above*] **said unto them, Go your way, and tell John what things ye have seen and heard**; how that the blind see, the lame walk, the lepers are cleansed, the deaf hear, the dead are raised, to the poor the gospel is preached.

> Every time you read of the miraculous healings performed by the Savior, you may wish to consider them symbolic of His ability to heal all our spiritual "diseases," including spiritual blindness, failure to walk forward into the light of the gospel, grievous sins, spiritual deafness, spiritual insensitivity, and so forth.

23 And **blessed is he, whosoever shall not be offended in me** [*ashamed to accept Christ and His teachings*].

Jesus Praises John the Baptist

24 And **when the messengers of John were departed** [*to report back to John the Baptist*], **he** [*Christ*] **began to speak unto the people concerning John** [*the Baptist*], **What went ye out into the wilderness for to see?** A reed shaken with the wind [*a timid fellow, worried about what people think*]?

25 But **what went ye out for to see?** A man clothed in soft raiment [*high fashion clothing*]? Behold, they which are gorgeously apparelled [*are dressed in expensive clothes*], and live delicately [*an easy life*], are in kings' courts.

26 But **what went ye out for to see?** A prophet? Yea, I say unto you, and **much more than a prophet.**

27 **This is he, of whom it is written** [*prophesied, in Malachi 3:1*], **Behold, I send my messenger before thy face, which shall prepare thy way before thee** [*Christ*].

28 For I say unto you, **Among those that are born of women there is not a greater prophet than John the Baptist**: but he [*Christ*] that is least in the kingdom of God is greater than he [*John the Baptist*].

> Verse 28, above, can be a bit confusing, but the Prophet Joseph Smith explains it to us. He tells us that John the Baptist is the greatest prophet born of woman, but that He, Christ, who is considered by the Jews to be the least in the kingdom, is above John the Baptist. See *Teachings of the Prophet Joseph Smith*, pp. 275–276.

29 **And all the people that heard him**, and the publicans [*even the tax collectors*], **justified God** [*acknowledged that God's way is right*], being baptized with the baptism of John [*having been baptized by John*].

30 **But the Pharisees and lawyers** [*religious leaders among the Jews*] **rejected the counsel of God**

against [for] themselves, being not baptized of him [refused to be baptized by John].

31 And the Lord [Jesus] said, Whereunto then shall I liken the men of this generation? and to what are they like? [To what shall I compare the wicked of this day?]

32 They are like unto children sitting in the marketplace, and calling one to another, and saying, We have piped unto you [played the flute for you], and ye have not danced; we have mourned [sung a sad song] to you, and ye have not wept.

33 For John the Baptist came neither eating bread nor drinking wine [In other words, he came living the strict Nazarite code of abstaining from wine and certain foods, which was followed by those who had made specific vows to God. See Numbers, chapter 6.]; and ye say, He hath a devil.

34 The Son of man [Jesus] is come eating and drinking; and ye say, Behold a gluttonous man, and a winebibber [one who drinks too much wine], a friend of publicans and sinners!

The main point of verses 31–34 is this: Jesus is telling them (the Pharisees and lawyers in verse 30) that they are like children who are never satisfied. Just as the children who wouldn't dance to happy flute music, neither would they be affected by a sad song, so also are the Pharisees and lawyers. They criticize John

the Baptist and won't be affected by his teachings. They criticize Jesus and won't go along with His teachings. They are never satisfied. The righteous can never win, in the eyes of the wicked. No matter what the righteous do, the wicked still criticize them.

35 But wisdom is justified of all her children. [All things will work out the way they should, whether you like it or not.]

A Woman Anoints Christ's Feet With Expensive Ointment—Her Sins Are Forgiven

36 And one of the Pharisees desired him that he [Jesus] would eat with him. And he went into the Pharisee's house, and sat down to meat [to eat].

37 And, behold, a woman in the city, which was a sinner [was a known sinner], when she knew [found out] that Jesus sat at meat [was eating a meal] in the Pharisee's house, brought an alabaster box [an expensive flask—see Luke 7:37 footnote b, in your Bible] of ointment,

38 And stood at his feet behind him weeping, and began to wash his feet with tears, and did wipe them with the hairs of her head, and kissed his feet, and anointed them with the ointment [put the ointment on Christ's feet].

39 Now when the Pharisee which had bidden him [invited Jesus to

LUKE 7

273

eat with him] **saw it, he spake within himself, saying** [*he said to himself*], **This man, if he were a prophet, would have known who and what manner of woman this is that toucheth him: for she is a sinner.**

The Pharisees were very strict about not even touching a known sinner. They considered it a matter of personal righteousness to avoid contact with sinners.

40 **And Jesus** answering [*responding*] **said unto him, Simon** [*the Pharisee's name*], **I have somewhat to say unto thee. And he saith, Master, say on** [*go ahead*].

41 **There was a certain creditor** [*banker*] **which had two debtors** [*two people who owed him money*]: **the one owed five hundred pence, and the other fifty.**

A pence would be about a day's wages. See Luke 7:41, footnote a in your Bible.

42 **And when they had nothing to pay** [*couldn't pay*], **he frankly forgave them both. Tell me therefore, which of them will love him most?**

43 **Simon answered** and said, **I suppose** that **he, to whom he forgave most.** And **he said** unto him, **Thou hast rightly judged.**

44 And **he** turned to the woman, and **said unto Simon,** Seest thou this woman? **I entered into thine house, thou gavest me no water for my feet** [*you didn't wash My*

feet (a proper Jewish custom when entertaining guests)]: **but she hath washed my feet with tears, and wiped them with the hairs of her head.**

45 **Thou gavest me no kiss: but this woman since the time I came in hath not ceased to kiss my feet.**

46 **My head with oil thou didst not anoint:** but **this woman hath anointed my feet with ointment.**

47 **Wherefore** [*therefore*] I say unto thee, **Her sins, which are many, are forgiven;** for she loved much [*she showed much love and service to Me because she has much to be forgiven of and she knows it*]: **but to whom little is forgiven, the same loveth little.**

48 And **he said unto her, Thy sins are forgiven.**

49 And **they that sat at meat** [*dinner*] with him began to say within themselves, **Who is this that forgiveth sins also?**

50 And **he said to the woman, Thy faith hath saved thee; go in peace.**

It is logical to assume that this woman had heard Christ's teachings earlier and had already repented deeply. Her humble service to the Master, serving Him to demonstrate her love for Him because of His ability to cleanse and save her from her sins, can be symbolic of our serving the Savior in appreciation for the effects of His Atonement in our lives. Her willingness to appear in public, in spite of the embarrassment of having others gossip about her because of her reputation as a sinner, shows humility and resolve to serve the Savior at all costs.

LUKE 8

As the second year of the Savior's formal three-year mortal mission continues, Luke tells us in verse 1, next, that Jesus made another tour of Galilee, preaching and healing throughout the region. You will see that He is now making considerable use of parables in His teaching.

1 AND it came to pass afterward, that **he went throughout every city and village, preaching and shewing** [*showing*] **the glad tidings of the kingdom of God: and the twelve** [*Apostles*] **were with him,**

2 **And certain women, which had been healed** of evil spirits and infirmities, **Mary called Magdalene, out of whom went seven devils,**

The Savior had apparently cast seven evil spirits out of Mary Magdalene on an earlier occasion which is not recorded in the Bible.

3 And **Joanna** the wife of Chuza Herod's steward [*manager of his household*], and **Susanna, and many others**, which ministered unto him of their substance [*helped*

to support Jesus, using their own supplies].

4 And **when much people were gathered together,** and were come to him out of every city, **he spake by a parable** [*a story told to teach a specific lesson*]:

The Parable of the Sower

5 **A sower** [*farmer*] **went out to sow** [*plant*] his seed: and **as he sowed** [*planted*], **some fell by the way side** [*the pathway*]; and it was trodden down [*walked on*], and the fowls of the air [*birds*] devoured [*ate*] it.

6 And **some fell upon a rock**; and as soon as it was sprung up [*started growing*], it withered away [*dried up and died*], because it lacked moisture.

7 And **some fell among thorns;** and the thorns sprang [*grew*] up with it, and choked it.

8 And **other fell on good ground,** and sprang up [*grew*], and bare fruit [*produced a crop*] an hundredfold. And when he had said these things, he cried, **He that hath ears to hear, let him hear** [*he that is spiritually in tune will understand what I am saying*].

Jesus will explain this parable to his disciples, beginning in verse 11.

9 And **his disciples asked him, saying, What might this parable be** [*what does this story mean*]?

10 And **he said, Unto you it is**

LUKE 8   275

given to know the mysteries [*the basic teachings, principles, etc.*] of the kingdom of God: but to others [*I teach*] in parables; that seeing they might not see, and hearing they might not understand. [*The spiritually deaf and blind don't want to understand the basics of the gospel.*]

11 Now the parable is this [*I will now explain the parable*]: The seed is the word of God.

12 Those by the way side [*the seeds that fell on the pathway in the field*] are they [*people*] that hear; then cometh the devil, and taketh away the word out of their hearts, lest they should believe and be saved.

Missionaries see application of verse 12 often in their teaching. For instance, they are invited into a home. The people listen to the gospel message and are excited. They make an appointment with the missionaries to return. But when the missionaries return for the next appointment, the family is cold and asks them to leave and not return. Satan has quickly quenched the flame of desire to hear the gospel.

13 They on the rock are they [*people*], which, when they hear, receive the word with joy; and these have no root, which for a while believe [*stay active for a little while*], and in time of temptation fall away.

14 And that [*the seeds*] which fell among thorns are they [*people*], which, when they have heard [*the gospel*], go forth, and are choked with cares and riches and pleasures of this life, and bring no fruit [*fruit is symbolic of their lives*] to perfection.

15 But that [*seed*] on the good ground are they [*people*], which in an honest and good heart, having heard the word, keep it, and bring forth fruit with patience [*patiently remain faithful and produce righteous lives*].

The Prophet Joseph Smith gave additional insights into the Parable of the Sower, above. See the note following Matthew 13:23 in this study guide. Next, Jesus counsels us to let our light shine so that others might be attracted to the true gospel.

16 No man, when he hath lighted a candle, covereth it with a vessel [*container*], or putteth it under a bed; but setteth it on a candlestick, that they which enter in may see the light. [*In other words, let your good example of living the gospel be seen by others so that they can come unto Christ also.*]

17 For nothing is secret, that shall not be made manifest; neither any thing hid, that shall not be known and come abroad. [*God knows all things and all wickedness will eventually be exposed.*]

18 Take heed therefore how ye hear [*how you respond to the gospel when you hear it*]: for whosoever hath [*whoever lives the*]

gospel], **to him shall be given** [*more knowledge, testimony, etc.*]; **and whosoever hath not** [*does not remain faithful*], **from him shall be taken even that which he seemeth to have** [*see D&C 1:33*].

19 **Then came to him his mother and his brethren** [*his family; see Luke 8:19, footnote a*], **and could not come at him for the press** [*couldn't get through the crowd to talk to Jesus*].

20 **And it was told him** by certain [*people*] which said, **Thy mother and thy brethren stand without** [*outside*], **desiring to see thee.**

21 And **he answered** and said unto them, **My mother and my brethren** [*in other words, my "family"*] **are these which hear the word of God, and do it** [*see Mosiah 5:7*].

A verse similar to verse 21, above, is found in Matthew 12:50. We will include the JST equivalent here for Matthew 12:50 that adds important information for this situation.

JST Matthew 12:44
44 **And he gave them charge concerning her** [*asked them to take good care of His mother*], **saying, I go my way, for my Father hath sent me. And whosoever shall do the will of my Father which is in heaven, the same is my brother, and sister, and mother.**

Remember that there are only about 31 days of the Savior's life recorded in Matthew, Mark, Luke, and John. In verse 22, next, Luke

gives us an awareness that he is moving along, skipping several days in between events that he is recording for us. You can sense this when he says "on a certain day."

22 Now it came to pass **on a certain day**, that **he went into a ship with his disciples: and he said unto them, Let us go over unto the other side of the lake** [*Sea of Galilee*]. **And they launched forth.**

"Master, the Tempest Is Raging"

23 But **as they sailed he fell asleep: and there came down a storm of wind on the lake; and they were filled with water, and were in jeopardy** [*in danger of sinking*].

JST Luke 8:23
23 But as they sailed he fell asleep; and there came down a storm of wind on the lake; and they were filled with **fear, and were in danger**.

24 And **they** [*the disciples*] came to him [*Jesus*], and **awoke him, saying, Master, master, we perish.** Then **he** arose, and **rebuked** [*commanded*] **the wind** and the raging of the **water**: and they ceased, and there was a **calm**.

25 And **he said unto them, Where is your faith?** And **they** being afraid **wondered**, saying one to another, **What manner of** [*what kind of*] **man is this! for he commandeth even the winds and water, and they obey him.**

Jesus Heals a Man Possessed by Evil Spirits

26 And **they arrived at the country of the Gadarenes**, which is over against Galilee [*southeast of the Sea of Galilee*].

27 And when he went forth to land, **there met him out of the city a certain man, which had devils long time** [*had been possessed by evil spirits for a long time*], and ware [*wore*] no clothes, neither abode [*lived*] in any house, but in the tombs [*lived among the graves*].

28 **When he saw Jesus, he cried out, and fell down before** [*in front of*] **him**, and with a loud voice said, **What have I to do with thee, Jesus, thou Son of God most high? I beseech** [*beg*] **thee, torment me not**.

The evil spirit seems to be speaking through the man who is possessed here, and is speaking for several evil spirits who posses the man.

From the next verses, we understand that several evil spirits possessed this man. We see also from these verses that these evil spirits clearly recognize the Savior and do not have the veil over their memory of the premortal life. They know who Jesus is and obviously fear Him.

29 For **he** [*Christ*] **had commanded the unclean spirit to come out** of the man. For **oftentimes it** [*the evil spirit*] **had caught** [*seized*] **him: and he was kept bound with chains and in fetters** [*leg irons*]; and **he brake** [*broke*] **the bands, and was driven of** [*by*] **the devil** [*evil spirit*] **into the wilderness**.

30 And **Jesus asked** him [*the evil spirit*], saying, **What is thy name? And he said, Legion: because many devils were entered into him** [*many evil spirits were in the man*].

31 And **they** [*the evil spirits*] **besought** [*pleaded with*] **him that he would not command them to go out into the deep**.

Evil Spirits Enter into a Herd of Swine

32 And there was there an **herd of many swine** [*pigs*] feeding on the mountain: **and they besought** [*begged*] **him tHat he would suffer** [*allow*] **them to enter into them** [*the pigs*]. And he suffered them [*allowed them to do so*].

33 **Then went the devils out of the man, and entered into the swine:** and the herd **ran violently down a steep place into the lake, and were choked** [*drowned*].

Do you remember, at the end of verse 31, above, that for some reason, the evil spirits did not want Jesus to command them to go into the "deep"? "Deep" is another word for "abyss." (See Luke 8:31, footnote a. This footnote also sends us to Revelation 9:1 and "bottomless pit," found also in Revelation 20:3, which we understand to be the final destination of the devil and his evil followers.) With this in mind, we can see the panic in these evil spirits who do not want to be prematurely banished to their final destiny (see D&C 88:111–14). Thus, they are likely relieved to be allowed to enter the bodies of the pigs. Ironically, however, they don't know how to drive the physical bodies of the pigs and end up dashing pell-mell into the lake and drowning 2,000 of them.

34 **When they that fed them** [*the people whose job it was to take care of the pigs*] **saw what was done, they fled** [*ran*], **and went and told it** [*spread the news*] **in the city and in the country.**

35 **Then they** [*the city officials and owners of the pigs*] **went out to see what was done; and came to Jesus, and found the man**, out of whom the devils were departed [*had been cast out*], **sitting at the feet of Jesus, clothed, and in his right mind: and they were afraid.**

36 **They also** which saw it [*eyewitnesses*] **told them by what means he** that was possessed of the devils **was healed.**

37 **Then the whole multitude** of the country **of the Gadarenes** round about **besought** [*asked*] **him** [*Jesus*] **to depart** from them [*to leave their part of the country*]; for they were taken with great fear: **and he went up into the ship**, and returned back again.

It is sad that these men, rather than asking the Savior to stay

and teach them, after having performed such a beautiful healing for the man (symbolic of the fact that Christ can heal us from the effects of Satan's influence), instead asked Him to leave their city and go elsewhere. It was no doubt a major economic disaster to lose about 2000 pigs (Mark 5:13). But being materialistic, worrying more about wealth and possessions than spiritual, eternal things, can blind us to the value of the Savior and His Atonement.

38 Now **the man** out of whom the devils were departed **besought him** [*asked Jesus*] **that he might be with him** [*if he could stay with Jesus*]: **but Jesus sent him away, saying,**

39 **Return to thine own house, and shew how great things God hath done unto thee** [*stay here and be a witness of the fact that God healed you*]. And he went his way, and published throughout the whole city how great things Jesus had done unto him.

40 And it came to pass, that, **when Jesus** was **returned, the people gladly received him**: for they were all waiting for him.

Jairus' Daughter Is Raised from the Dead

41 And, behold, there came a man named **Jairus**, and he was a ruler of the synagogue: and he fell down at Jesus' feet, and **besought him** that he would [*humbly asked him to*] **come into his house:**

LUKE 8

42 For he had **one only daughter**, about twelve years of age, and she **lay a dying**. But as he went **the people thronged him** [*crowded and bumped against him*].

A Woman with an Issue of Blood Is Healed

43 And a **woman having an issue of blood** twelve years [*who had been bleeding for twelve years*], which had spent all her living upon physicians [*she had spent all her money to pay doctors*], neither could be healed of any [*no doctors had successfully treated her illness*],

44 **Came behind him, and touched the border of his garment** [*robe, cloak*]: and **immediately her issue of blood stanched** [*the bleeding stopped*].

45 And **Jesus said, Who touched me?** When all denied [*nobody admitted touching him*], Peter and they that were with him said, Master, the multitude throng thee and press thee [*people in this crowd are bumping You and pressing against You constantly*], and sayest thou, Who touched me [*what do You mean, "Who touched me"*]?

46 And **Jesus said, Somebody hath touched me: for I perceive that virtue** [*power; strength*] **is gone out of me.**

47 And when **the woman** saw that she was not hid [*that she had been discovered*], she **came trembling, and falling down before him**, she **declared** unto him before [*in front of*] all the people **for what cause** [*the reason why*] **she had touched him and how she was healed immediately.**

48 And **he said** unto her, Daughter, **be of good comfort: thy faith hath made thee whole** [*healed*]; go in peace.

49 While he yet spake, **there cometh one** from the ruler of the synagogue's house [*Jairus' house; see verse 41*], **saying to him, Thy daughter is dead; trouble not the Master** [*it is too late; don't bother Jesus*].

50 **But when Jesus heard it, he answered** [*responded to*] him, saying, **Fear not: believe** only [*just have faith*], **and she shall be made whole** [*will be healed*].

51 And when **he came into the house**, he suffered [*allowed*] no man to go in, save [*except*] Peter, and James, and John, and the father and the mother of the maiden [*the dead girl*].

52 And **all wept**, and bewailed her: but **he said, Weep not; she is not dead, but sleepeth.**

53 And **they** [*the mourners*] **laughed him to scorn** [*mocked and ridiculed Jesus*], knowing that she was dead.

54 And **he put them all out** [*sent the mourners out of the room*], and **took her by the hand, and called, saying, Maid, arise.**

55 And **her spirit came again,**

and **she arose** straightway [*immediately*]: and he commanded to give her meat [*food*].

In the language of our Bible, "meat" means any type of food. "Flesh" means meat, as in beef, lamb, chicken, etc.

56 And **her parents were astonished**: but **he charged** [*instructed*] them that they should **tell no man what was done.**

Some experiences with God are very private and personal and are to be kept to ourselves. Perhaps this is the reason the parents were so instructed by Jesus.

LUKE 9

As Luke, who was not an Apostle himself, continues, he reports some details to us concerning the training of the twelve Apostles by the Savior. As you can well imagine, this was an intense time of learning and training for these humble men, and the "learning curve" remained steep.

The Twelve Are Sent on Missions

1 THEN **he called his twelve disciples together, and gave them power and authority over all devils, and to cure diseases.**

2 And **he sent them to preach** the kingdom of God, **and to heal the sick.**

This is an important part of the Apostles' ongoing training, and will raise several questions in their minds for which they will seek answers as they return to the Master Teacher for more instruction. They will be ready to hear the answers.

3 And he said unto them, **Take nothing for your journey**, neither staves [*staffs*], nor scrip [*a bag in which to carry food; see Bible Dictionary, under "Scrip"*], neither bread, neither money; neither have two coats apiece.

4 And whatsoever house ye enter into, there abide, and thence [*from it*] depart.

5 And **whosoever will not receive you, when ye go out of that city, shake off the very dust from your feet for a testimony against them** [*as a witness that you tried to teach them the gospel; see D&C 60:15*].

6 And **they** departed, and **went** through the towns, **preaching** the gospel, **and healing** every where.

Just a reminder that the symbol, "¶" at the beginning of verse 7 and many other places in our Bible, means the beginning of a new topic.

7 ¶ Now **Herod** the tetrarch [*ruler in Galilee, under Roman authority*] **heard of all that was done by him** [*by Jesus*]: **and he was perplexed** [*worried*], **because that it was said of some, that John was risen from the dead;** [*Some people were saying that Jesus was John the Baptist, come back to life, whom Herod had had beheaded.*]

LUKE 9

8 And **of some, that Elias had appeared** [*some said that Jesus was Elijah the Prophet*]; **and of others, that one of the old prophets was risen again** [*had come back to life*].

9 And **Herod said**, John [*the Baptist*] have I beheaded: but **who is this,** of whom I hear such things? And **he desired to see him** [*wanted to see Jesus*].

The Twelve Report Back from Their Missions

10 And **the apostles, when they were returned** [*from their missions as mentioned in verses 2–6*], **told him all that they had done** [*reported back to Him*]. And **he took them, and went aside privately into a desert place** [*JST "a solitary place"*] belonging to the city called Bethsaida. [*Jesus wanted to have some private time with His Apostles.*]

11 **And the people**, when they knew it [*when they found out where Jesus was*], **followed him: and he received them**, and spake unto them of the kingdom of God, and healed them that had need of healing.

> Jesus demonstrated His compassion and kindness time and time again, putting aside His needs for rest and privacy, as in verse 11 above, to minister to the people.

The Feeding of the 5,000

12 And when the day began to wear away [*was about gone*], then came **the twelve**, and **said unto him, Send the multitude away**, that they may go into the towns and country round about, and lodge, and get victuals [*food*]: for we are here in a desert place. [*There is nowhere here to buy food.*]

13 **But he said unto them, Give ye them to eat.** [*This must have startled the Apostles!*] And they said, We have no more but **five loaves and two fishes**; except we should go and buy meat [*food*] for all this people.

14 For they were **about five thousand men**. [*Matthew 14:21 says there were about 5,000 men plus women and children.*] And **he said to his disciples, Make them sit down by fifties** in a company [*in groups of fifty*].

15 And they did so, and made them all sit down.

16 Then **he** [*Jesus*] **took the five loaves and the two fishes**, and looking up to heaven, he **blessed them, and brake, and gave to the disciples to set before the multitude.**

17 And they [*all the people*] did eat, and **were all filled**: and there was taken up of fragments that **remained** to them **twelve baskets** [*they gathered up twelve basketfuls of leftovers*].

Peter Bears Testimony that Jesus Is the Christ

18 And it came to pass, as he was alone praying, his disciples were with him: and **he asked** them, saying, **Whom say the people that I am?**

19 They answering said, **John the Baptist**; but some say, **Elias** [*Elijah*]; and others say, that **one of the old prophets** is risen again [*has come back to life*].

20 He said unto them, But **whom say ye that I am? Peter answering said, The Christ of God.**

21 And **he** straitly [*strictly*] **charged** [*told*] them, and commanded them to **tell no man** that thing;

JST Luke 9:21
21 And he straitly charged them, and commanded them to tell no man **of him,**

It would seem that this instruction (in verse 21, above) to the Apostles was temporary and for that particular time and circumstance. Perhaps they needed a bit of quiet time together for the Master to teach His disciples about His upcoming death (in about six months) and resurrection. Some manuscripts say, "Don't go and tell anyone in the village."

22 Saying, **The Son of man** [*Jesus*] **must suffer many things**, and be **rejected** of [*by*] the elders and chief priests and scribes [*religious leaders of the Jews*], and be **slain**, and be **raised** [*resurrected*] **the third day.**

23 And **he said** to them all, **If any man will come after me, let him deny himself** [*put aside his own needs*], **and take up his cross** [*sacrifice whatever is necessary*] daily, **and follow me.**

24 For **whosoever will save his life** [*preserve his own worldly lifestyle rather than following the Savior*] **shall lose it** [*will ultimately lose that way of life*]: but **whosoever will lose his life for my sake** [*will change his lifestyle and follow the Savior*], the same **shall save it** [*will keep the rich blessings of a righteous life forever*].

25 For **what is a man advantaged, if he gain the whole world, and lose himself** [*lose his soul*], or be cast away [*be cast away from heaven on Judgment Day*]?

JST Luke 9:24–25
24 For whosoever will save his life, **must be willing to lose it for my sake**; and whosoever **will be willing to** lose his life for my sake, the same shall save it.

25 For what **doth it profit a man** if he gain the whole world, and **yet he receive him not whom God hath ordained, and he lose his own soul, and he himself be a castaway?**

26 For **whosoever shall be ashamed of me** [*will reject me*] and of my words, **of him shall the Son of man be ashamed** [*he will be rejected by Jesus*], when he shall come in his own glory [*at the Second Coming*], and in his Father's, and of the holy angels.

JST Luke 9:26

26 For whosoever shall be ashamed of me, and of my words, of him shall the **Son of Man** [*Son of the Father, who is "Man of Holiness" in Moses 6:*57] be ashamed, when he shall come in his own **kingdom, clothed in the glory of his Father, with** the holy angels.

27 But I tell you of a truth, **there be some standing here, which shall not taste of death, till they see the kingdom of God.**

JST Luke 9:27

27 **Verily,** I tell you of a truth, there **are** some standing here **who** shall not taste of death, until they see the kingdom of God **coming in power**.

We know that John, the Apostle, was one in this group around the Savior who would "not taste of death" (has not yet died). He was translated and allowed to stay on earth to minister to people until the Second Coming. See D&C 7:3. We don't know who any of the others are, standing by the Savior at this moment in verse 27, who would be translated. We do know that the Three Nephites were translated as described in 3 Nephi 28.

The Mount of Transfiguration

28 And it came to pass about an eight days after these sayings, **he took Peter and John and James, and went up into a mountain to pray.**

It is now near October, and the Savior will be crucified the following April, thus ending His mortal ministry. Three of his Apostles, Peter, James, and John are already taking on the role of First Presidency. They will experience tremendous additional training now as the Master takes them with Him up on the mountain which is referred to as the Mount of Transfiguration. There, they will see Christ transfigured (shine with brilliant heavenly light) before their eyes, will hear the Father's voice, and will see the great prophets Moses and Elijah, who will minister to Jesus, and from whom they will receive additional priesthood keys. From JST Mark 9:3, we learn that John the Baptist was also there.

29 And as he prayed, the fashion of **his countenance was altered, and his raiment** [*clothing*] **was white and glistering** [*shining*].

30 And, behold, **there talked with him** two men, which were **Moses and Elias** [*Elijah*]:

31 Who **appeared in glory, and spake of his decease** [*death*] which he [*Jesus*] should accomplish at Jerusalem.

JST Luke 9:31

31 Who appeared in glory, and spake of his **death, and also his resurrection**, which he should accomplish at Jerusalem.

32 But **Peter and they that were with him** [*James and John*] were heavy with sleep: and when they

were awake, they **saw his glory, and the two men that stood with him**.

33 And it came to pass, as they [*Moses and Elijah*] departed from him [*Christ*], **Peter said unto Jesus, Master, it is good for us to be here**: and let us make three tabernacles [*small booths, typically used among the Jews for private worship during the annual Feast of Tabernacles*]; one for thee, and one for Moses, and one for Elias [*Elijah*]: not knowing what he said [*not understanding the situation*].

34 While he thus spake, there came **a cloud**, and **overshadowed them**: and they feared as they entered into the cloud.

The Father Bears Witness of the Son

35 And there came **a voice** [*the Father's voice*] **out of the cloud, saying, This is my beloved Son: hear him**.

36 And **when the voice was past, Jesus was found alone. And they kept it close, and told no man** in those days any of those things which they had seen.

For additional information about what took place on the Mount of Transfiguration, see the note after Matthew 17:8 in this study guide.

37 And it came to pass, that on **the next day**, when they were come down from the hill [*from the Mount of Transfiguration*], **much** [*many*] **people met him**.

An Evil Spirit Is Cast Out

38 And, behold, **a man** of the company [*in the crowd*] **cried out**, saying, Master, I beseech [*beg of*] thee, **look upon my son**: for he is mine only child.

39 And, lo, **a spirit** [*an evil spirit*] **taketh** [*possesses*] **him**, and he suddenly crieth out; and it teareth him that he foameth again [*it throws him around and makes him foam at the mouth*], and bruising him [*causes him to get bruised as he tosses around on the ground*] hardly departeth from him [*it hardly ever leaves him so he can have peace*].

40 And **I besought** [*begged*] **thy disciples to cast him out; and they could not**.

41 And **Jesus** answering **said**, O faithless and perverse [*wicked*] generation [*people*], how long shall I be with you, and suffer you [*put up with your lack of righteousness and faith*]? **Bring thy son hither** [*here*].

42 And as he [*the man's son*] was yet a coming, the devil [*evil spirit*] threw him down, and tare him [*threw him around some more*]. And **Jesus rebuked the unclean spirit** [*commanded the evil spirit to leave*], **and healed the child, and delivered him again to his father**.

43 And **they were all amazed at the mighty power of God**. But while they wondered every one at all things which **Jesus** did, he **said unto his disciples**,

Jesus Prophecies His Arrest

44 Let these sayings sink down into your ears: for **the Son** of man [*Jesus*] **shall be delivered into the hands of men** [*arrested and turned over to wicked men*].

45 **But they understood not** this saying [*didn't understand what He was saying*], and it was hid from them, that they perceived [*understood*] it not: and they feared to ask him of that saying [*were afraid to ask Him to explain what He meant*].

Who Is Greatest Among You?

46 Then **there arose a reasoning** [*a debate*] among them, **which of them should be greatest.**

47 And **Jesus,** perceiving the thought of their heart, **took a child, and set him by him,**

48 And said unto them, **Whosoever shall receive this child in my name receiveth** [*accepts*] **me: and whosoever shall receive me receiveth him** [*the Father*] **that sent me: for he that is least** [*humbly considers himself to be the least*] **among you all, the same shall be great.**

49 And **John** answered and **said, Master, we saw one** [*a person*] **casting out devils in thy name; and we forbad him** [*told him not to*], because he followeth not with us [*he is not one of us*].

50 And **Jesus said unto him, Forbid him not** [*don't tell him not to*]: for **he that is not against us is for us.**

51 And it came to pass, **when the time was come that he should be received up** [*perform the Atonement, be crucified, resurrected and taken up into heaven*], **he stedfastly** [*with determination*] **set his face to go to Jerusalem,**

Jesus and his Apostles have been serving in the Galilee area, in northern Israel. Now, Jesus has told them that they must go south to Jerusalem. Normally, the Jews avoided going straight south from Galilee, because that would require traveling through the province of Samaria. The Jews despised the Samaritans (people of Samaria) and the Samaritans despised the Jews. Thus, the Jews normally traveled around Samaria, to the east, and then south to Jerusalem. But this time, Jesus is heading straight south, right through Samaria, which would no doubt cause his Apostles some extra anxiety.

52 And sent messengers before his face [*ahead of Him*]: and **they** [*the messengers*] went, and **entered into a village of the Samaritans, to make ready for him** [*to prepare things for Him to rest, eat, etc.*].

53 **And they** [*the Samaritans in the village*] **did not receive him** [*were rude to Jesus and would not allow him and his followers to buy provisions*], because his face was as though he would go to Jerusalem [*because they knew He was a Jew and was heading toward Jerusalem*].

May We Destroy
Them With Fire?

54 And **when his disciples James and John saw this, they said, Lord, wilt thou that we command fire to come down from heaven, and consume them** [*these Samaritans*]**, even as Elias did** [*is it OK with You if we command fire to come down from heaven and destroy them like Elijah did to the fifty soldiers and their captain who were rude to him; see 2 Kings 1:10*]?

55 **But he** turned, and **rebuked** [*scolded*] **them,** and said, Ye know not what manner of spirit ye are of [*you don't realize how awful your attitude is*].

56 For **the Son** of man [*Jesus*] **is not come to destroy men's lives, but to save them.** And they went to another village.

Next, Luke will use examples for his account that emphasize that one must commit one hundred percent in order to successfully follow Christ.

57 And it came to pass, that, as they went in the way [*along the road*], **a certain man said unto him, Lord, I will follow thee whithersoever thou goest.**

58 And Jesus said unto him, Foxes have holes, and birds of the air have nests; but **the Son of man** [*Christ*] **hath not where** [*anywhere*] **to lay his head.**

59 And **he said unto another, Follow me. But he said, Lord, suffer** [*allow*] **me first to go and bury my father.**

60 Jesus said unto him, **Let the dead bury their dead: but go thou and preach the kingdom of God.**

There is probably more to the story than is recorded here. Perhaps "let the dead bury their dead" includes a message that following the Savior requires real commitment and sometimes requires one to leave the comforts of home and family and follow Jesus at all costs.

61 And another also said, Lord, I will follow thee; but **let me first go bid them farewell, which are at home at my house.**

62 And Jesus said unto him, **No man, having put his hand to the plough** [*plow*]**, and looking back, is fit for the kingdom of God.** [*Ultimately, we have to be committed to follow the Savior at all costs. If we achieve this level of commitment, all other things of eternal value, including family, will be ours forever.*]

LUKE 10

In this chapter, Jesus continues to organize the priesthood officers for the leadership of His church by calling the Seventy and sending them out two by two.

LUKE 10

The Seventy Are Called and Sent Out

1 AFTER these things **the Lord appointed** other **seventy** also, and sent them two and two before his face [*in advance of Him*] into every city and place, whither he himself would come.

2 Therefore said he unto them, **The harvest truly is great** [*the potential for converts is large*], **but the labourers are few** [*there are relatively few members, missionaries, etc., to spread the gospel*]: pray ye therefore the Lord of the harvest, that he would send forth labourers into his harvest.

3 Go your ways: behold, **I send you forth as lambs among wolves** [*you will be in danger at times*].

4 Carry **neither purse** [*money*], nor **scrip** [*food; see Bible Dictionary, under "Scrip"*], nor **shoes** [*wear sandals instead*]: and salute no man by the way [*don't stop to visit or delay the work you are assigned; see* Doctrinal New Testament Commentary, *Vol. 1, p. 433*].

5 And **into whatsoever house ye enter, first say, Peace be to this house.**

6 And if the son of peace [*a peaceful person*] be there, your peace shall rest upon it: if not, it shall turn to you again.

7 And in the same house remain, **eating and drinking such things as they give: for the labourer is worthy of his hire** [*it is worthwhile for people to support you*]. Go not from house to house. [*Don't go methodically from house to house. Go where the Spirit directs.*]

8 And **into whatsoever city ye enter, and they receive you**, eat such things as are set before you:

9 And **heal the sick that are therein**, and say unto them, **The kingdom of God is come nigh unto you** [*the true gospel is now available to you*].

You have perhaps heard of the missionaries wiping the dust off their feet as a testimony that people would not accept their gospel message. Verses 10–12, next, are an example of this.

10 **But** into whatsoever city ye enter, and **they receive you not, go your ways out into the streets** [*don't do it in front of them; it would just make things unnecessarily worse*] of the same, and **say,**

11 Even **the** very **dust of your city,** which cleaveth on [*sticks to*] us, **we do wipe off against you** [*as a witness that we tried to teach you; see D&C 60:15*]: notwithstanding [*even though you have rejected us*] **be ye sure of this, that the kingdom of God is come nigh unto you** [*the true gospel of Christ is here for you*].

12 But I say unto you, that it **shall be more tolerable in that day** [*Judgment Day*] **for Sodom, than for that city** [*it is a very serious thing to reject the gospel, knowingly*].

The JST adds a verse after verse 12, above, that is not found in the Bible.

JST Luke 10:13

13 **Then began he to upbraid the people in every city wherein his mighty works were done, who received him not, saying,**

13 **Woe unto** thee, **Chorazin!** woe unto thee, **Bethsaida** [*cities where Jesus had preached and done many miracles*]! for **if the mighty works had been done in Tyre and Sidon** [*non-Jewish cities*], **which have been done in you, they had** [*would have*] **a great while ago repented,** sitting in sackcloth and ashes [*would have humbled themselves*].

14 But **it shall be more tolerable for Tyre and Sidon at the judgment, than for you** [*because you have had great opportunities to know the gospel and they haven't*].

15 And **thou, Capernaum,** which art exalted to heaven [*whose inhabitants are prideful, cocky*], **shalt be thrust down to hell.**

16 **He that heareth you** [*pays attention to you, My disciples—see JST verse 17, next*] **heareth me; and he that despiseth you despiseth me; and he that despiseth me despiseth him that sent me** [*the Father*].

The JST adds an important change that helps us understand verse 16, above. Otherwise, it doesn't make sense. Remember that the verse numbering in the

JST is often different than in the Bible.

JST Luke 10:17

17 **And he said unto his disciples,** He that heareth you, heareth me; and he that despiseth you, despiseth me; and he that despiseth me, despiseth him who sent me.

The Seventy Return

The Seventy, who were sent out on missions by the Lord in verse 1, above, now return and report their missions to Him.

17 And **the seventy returned again with joy,** saying, Lord, **even the devils are subject unto us through thy name** [*when we do it in the name of Jesus Christ*].

Next, Jesus tells the Seventy that He was there when Lucifer was cast out as a result of his rebellion—see Isaiah 14–12, Revelation 12:7–9, D&C 76:25–27, etc. Among other things, the Savior is instructing these men in the fact that He has power and authority over Satan.

18 And **he said unto them, I beheld** [*saw*] **Satan** as lightning **fall from heaven.**

19 Behold, **I give unto you power to tread on serpents and scorpions, and over all the power of the enemy** [*Satan and all who work with him in opposing the work of the Lord*]: and **nothing shall by any means hurt you.**

20 Notwithstanding [*nevertheless*]

in this **rejoice not** [*don't get cocky or boastful*], **that the spirits are subject unto you**; but rather rejoice, because your names are written in heaven [*you will go to celestial glory*].

21 **In that hour Jesus rejoiced** in spirit, and said, I thank thee, O Father, Lord of heaven and earth, that thou hast hid these things from the wise and prudent, and hast revealed them unto babes [*humble people who have childlike faith*]: even so, Father; for so it seemed good in thy sight.

> Here again we see the powerful contribution of the Prophet Joseph Smith's translation of the Bible, changing just one phrase that makes a world of difference in our understanding (from "the wise and prudent" in verse 21, above, to "them who think they are wise and prudent" in the JST, as given next).

JST Luke 10:22

22 In that hour Jesus rejoiced in spirit, and said, I thank thee, O Father, Lord of heaven and earth, that thou hast hid these things from **them who think they are wise and prudent**, and hast revealed them unto babes; even so, Father; for so it seemed good in thy sight.

22 **All things are delivered to me of my Father**: and no man knoweth who the Son is, but the Father; and who the Father is, but the Son, and he to whom the Son will reveal him.

JST Luke 10:23

23 All things are delivered to me of my Father; and no man knoweth **that the Son is the Father** [*Jesus is the "father" of our salvation*], **and the Father is the Son** [*the "father of our salvation" is the Son of God*], **but him to whom the Son will reveal it**.

We will pause a moment and explain JST verse 23, above. As you know, some of our Christian brothers and sisters believe that the Godhead consists of three in one and one in three, the three being actually only one personage. Without understanding Bible language and imagery, it could be claimed that JST Luke 10:23, quoted above, supports that false concept.

The word "Father" is often used to mean the "creator of" or the "provider of." Even in modern English, we often use "father" in a similar way. For example, George Washington is the "father" of our country. Thomas Edison is the "father" of the electric light bulb. Eli Whitney is the "father" of, or inventor of, the cotton gin. Similarly, Jesus is the "father" of the Atonement, the one who provided the gift of forgiveness and resurrection to us. He is the "father" or creator of the earth, the "father" of our salvation, because He provided the way for us to return to our Heavenly Father.

Thus, in the Biblical language and imagery used in JST Luke 10:23, the "Son" (Jesus Christ) is the "Father" of our salvation, and the "Son" (the only Begotten Son of the Father) which gave Him the power to carry out the Atonement. You will see the same concept and doctrine taught in Mosiah 15:1–5.

Next, the Savior turns to His disciples and reminds them of the blessing they enjoy in knowing what they know about Him and in having seen what they have already seen.

23 And he turned him unto his disciples, and said privately, **Blessed are the eyes which see the things that ye see:**

24 For I tell you, that **many prophets and kings have desired to see those things which ye see, and have not seen them; and to hear those things which ye hear, and have not heard them.**

25 And, behold, a certain **lawyer stood up, and tempted him** [*tried to trick Jesus*], saying, Master, **what shall I do to inherit eternal life** [*to get to heaven and inherit exaltation*]?

26 He said unto him, **What is written in the law** [*to the Jews at the time, "the law" meant the books of Moses, namely, Genesis, Exodus, Leviticus, Numbers, and Deuteronomy*]? **how readest thou** [*what do you understand the scriptures to say on this matter*]?

27 And he answering said, **Thou shalt love the Lord thy God with all thy heart, and with all thy soul, and with all thy strength, and with all thy mind; and thy neighbour as thyself.**

28 And he [*Jesus*] said unto him [*the lawyer*], **Thou hast answered right: this do, and thou shalt live** [*get to heaven*].

The Parable of the Good Samaritan

29 But he, willing to justify himself [*wanting to make himself look good in front of the people who were standing around; see Luke 10:29, footnote a, which sends you to Luke 16:15 for a similar situation*], said unto Jesus, And **who is my neighbour?**

Jesus will now give the Parable of the Good Samaritan. It is helpful to know that the Jews despised the Samaritans and the Samaritans generally despised and made fun of the Jews. Samaria (the land of the Samaritans) was between Judea (in southern Israel) and Galilee (in northern Israel). When the ten tribes of Israel (who lived in Samaria) were taken into captivity (about 721 B.C.) by the Assyrians, some Israelites were left behind and intermarried with the Assyrian soldiers who occupied Samaria. This intermarrying over the years led the Jews to despise the Samaritans for breaking the Law of Moses in which marrying outside of covenant Israel was forbidden.

30 And Jesus answering said, **A certain man** went down from Jerusalem to Jericho, and **fell among thieves** [*was attacked by robbers*], which stripped him of his raiment [*clothing*], and wounded him, and

LUKE 10

291

departed, **leaving him half dead.**

31 And by chance there came down **a certain priest** [*Jewish priest*] that way: and when he saw him, he **passed by on the other side.**

32 And likewise **a Levite** [*another Jewish priest*], when he was at the place, came and looked on him, and **passed by on the other side.**

JST Luke 10:33

33 And likewise a Levite, when he was at the place, came and looked upon him, and passed by on the other side **of the way; for they desired in their hearts that it might not be known that they had seen him.**

Just a reminder. As mentioned a number of times already in this study guide, all of the JST corrections and additions are not contained in our Bible. There is not enough room for them, consequently there were some difficult decisions made by the Brethren as to what to include and what to leave out. The JST verse given above, which contains some more information about the priest and the Levite, is not in our Bible. In order to see all of the JST changes, you need to purchase a copy of the complete JST, possibly from a Latter-day Saint bookstore, or find it online.

33 **But a certain Samaritan** [*a man from Samaria; as mentioned above, Samaritans were despised by the Jews*], as he journeyed, came where he was: and **when he saw him, he had compassion on him,**

34 And went to him, and **bound up his wounds, pouring in oil and wine** [*gave him first aid*], and **set him on his own beast,** and **brought him to an inn, and took care of him.**

35 And on the morrow when he departed, he **took out two pence** [*money representing two days' wages*], **and gave them to the host** [*the innkeeper*], and said unto him, **Take care of him; and whatsoever thou spendest more** [*beyond what I have paid you*], when I come again, **I will repay thee.**

Did you notice that it costs to be a "good Samaritan"? Certainly, that is one of the important messages for us in this parable.

36 **Which now of these three, thinkest thou, was neighbour unto him that fell among the thieves?**

37 And he [*the lawyer*] said, **He that shewed** [*showed*] **mercy** on him. Then said Jesus unto him, **Go, and do thou likewise.**

Remember, as stated previously, that there are just 31 days of the Savior's mortal life and mission that are mentioned in Matthew, Mark, Luke, and John. Luke mentions another such event, next.

Mary and Martha

38 Now it came to pass, as they went, that **he entered into a certain village** [*Bethany, near the Mount of Olives, just outside Jerusalem*]: and a certain woman

named **Martha received him into her house.**

What happens next is a rather well-known situation, in which Martha complains to Jesus that her sister, Mary, is not helping with the chores associated with preparing a meal for Him. What follows is a lesson by the Savior on priorities and individual needs and personalities.

39 And **she had a sister called Mary,** which also **sat at Jesus' feet, and heard his word.**

40 But **Martha was cumbered about much serving** [*very busy with all the details that needed attention in order to feed the Savior*], and **came to him, and said** [*complained*], **Lord, dost thou not care that my sister hath left me to serve alone** [*doesn't it bother you that Mary is not helping me*]? **bid her** therefore **that she help me** [*tell her to help me*].

41 And Jesus answered and said unto her, **Martha, Martha, thou art careful and troubled about many things** [*you are meticulous and always fuss over the tiniest details*]:

42 But one thing is needful: and **Mary hath chosen that good part** [*has chosen to listen to Me and My teachings*], **which shall not be taken away from her** [*which is a wise thing for her to be doing with her agency*].

Elder James E. Talmage, a member of the Quorum of the Twelve Apostles from 1911-1933, spoke of Mary and Martha as follows:

"There was no reproof of Martha's desire to provide well; nor any sanction of possible neglect on Mary's part. We must suppose that Mary had been a willing helper before the Master's arrival; but now that He had come, she chose to remain with Him. Had she been culpably neglectful of her duty, Jesus would not have commended her course. He desired not well-served meals and material comforts only, but the company of the sisters, and above all their receptive attention to what He had to say. He had more to give them than they could possibly provide for Him. Jesus loved the two sisters and their brother as well. Both these women were devoted to Jesus, and each expressed herself in her own way. Martha was of a practical turn, concerned in material service; she was by nature hospitable and self-denying. Mary, contemplative and more spiritually inclined, showed her devotion through the service of companionship and appreciation." (*Jesus the Christ*, p. 433)

LUKE 11

We are now into the last months of the Savior's mortal life. As Luke continues, we will read "the Lord's Prayer" and feel the beauty of the gospel of love in contrast to the hypocritical attacks upon the

LUKE 11

Savior and His mission by the Jewish religious leaders.

1 AND it came to pass, that, as he was praying in a certain place, when he ceased, one of his disciples said unto him, Lord, **teach us to pray**, as John [*the Baptist*] also taught his disciples.

Jesus now gives what is commonly known as "The Lord's Prayer." It is an example of how to pray and of things which can be included in our prayers.

The Lord's Prayer

2 And he said unto them, When ye pray, say, **Our Father which art in heaven, Hallowed be [*holy is*] thy name. Thy kingdom come. Thy will be done, as in heaven, so in earth.**

3 **Give us day by day our daily bread.**

4 **And forgive us our sins; for we also forgive every one that is indebted to us. And lead us not into temptation; but deliver us from evil.**

JST Luke 11:4

4 And forgive us our sins; for we also forgive every one who is indebted to us. And **let us not be led unto** temptation; but deliver us from evil; **for thine is the kingdom and power. Amen**.

Next, Jesus will encourage his disciples to ask Heavenly Father for whatever they need.

He reminds them that Heavenly Father is a Father with tender feelings toward His children and who likes to bless and help them. He also encourages them to continue praying for things they need, even if at first they don't get them.

5 And he said unto them [*his disciples*], **Which of you shall have a friend, and shall go unto him at midnight, and say unto him, Friend, lend me three loaves [*of bread*]**;

JST Luke 11:5–6

5 And he said unto them, **Your heavenly Father will not fail to give unto you whatsoever ye ask of him. And he spake a parable, saying,**

6 Which of you shall have a friend, and shall go unto him at midnight, and say unto him, Friend, lend me three loaves;

6 **For a friend of mine in his journey is come to me, and I have nothing to set before him [*nothing to feed him*]?**

7 **And he [*the friend in verse 5*] from within [*inside his house*] shall answer and say, Trouble me not**: the door is now shut, and my children are with me in bed; **I cannot rise and give thee.**

8 I say unto you, Though he will not rise and give him, because he is his friend, **yet because of his importunity [*because he stays there and keeps knocking at the door and asking for help*] he [*the friend who**

has bread] **will rise and give him as many as he needeth.**

Ask, Seek, Knock

9 And I say unto you, **Ask**, and it shall be given you; **seek**, and ye shall find; **knock**, and it shall be opened unto you.

10 **For every one that asketh receiveth; and he that seeketh findeth; and to him that knock-eth it shall be opened.**

11 **If a son shall ask bread** of any of you that is a father, **will he give him a stone? or if he ask a fish, will he for a fish give him a ser-pent?**

12 **Or if he shall ask an egg, will he offer him a scorpion?**

13 **If ye then, being evil** [*being human, imperfect*], **know how to give good gifts unto your chil-dren: how much more shall your heavenly Father give the Holy Spirit to them that ask him?**

JST Luke 11:14

14 If ye then, being evil, know how to give good gifts unto your chil-dren, how much more shall your heavenly Father **give good gifts, through** the Holy Spirit, to them **who** ask him.

Did you notice that the JST verse above uses a period at the end rather than a question mark like in the Bible? Thus, it turns it into a statement rather than a question.

An Evil Spirit Is Cast Out

14 And **he was casting out a devil** [*an evil spirit*], and it [*the man*] was dumb [*couldn't talk*]. And it came to pass, **when the devil was gone out, the dumb spake** [*the man who had been possessed by the evil spirit was able to talk*]; and the people wondered [*the people were amazed*]

JST Luke 11:15

15 And he was casting a devil **out of a man, and he** was dumb. And it came to pass, when the devil was gone out, the dumb spake; and the people wondered.

Watch next, in verse 15, as some of these people, who have person-ally watched one of the most com-passionate of miracles, claim that Jesus was in partnership with the devil to deceive people by casting out devils through Satan's power in order to make it look like He was doing it with God's power. It's obvious that the devil caused such thoughts in their minds and hearts.

15 **But some of them said, He casteth out devils through Beel-zebub** the chief of the devils [*they claimed Jesus was using Satan's power to cast out evil spirits*].

16 And **others**, tempting [*testing Him*] him, **sought of him a sign from heaven.**

17 But **he, knowing their thoughts, said** unto them, Every kingdom divided against itse**lf is brought to desolation** [*is even-tually destroyed*]; and **a house divided against a house falleth.**

LUKE 11 295

18 **If Satan also be divided against himself** [*if Satan is casting out his own evil spirits*], **how shall his kingdom stand** [*survive*]? because ye say that I cast out devils through Beelzebub [*Satan*].

19 And **if I by Beelzebub** [*by the power of Satan*] **cast out devils, by whom do your sons cast them out?** therefore shall they be your judges.

From JST Matthew 12:22–23, we learn the correct interpretation of verse 19 above:

JST Matthew 12:22–23

22 And if I by Beelzebub cast out devils, by whom do your **children cast our devils?** Therefore they shall be your judges.

23 But if I cast out devils by the Spirit of God, then the kingdom of God is come unto you [*in effect saying that He is the promised Messiah*]. For they [*some righteous Jews*] also cast out devils by the Spirit of God, for unto them is given power over devils, that they may cast them out.

From the words in the JST, above, we find that there were righteous Jews, obviously baptized and faithful, who were enabled by the Spirit of God to cast out evil spirits. See *Doctrinal New Testament Commentary*, Vol. 1, p. 269.

20 But **if I with the finger** [*power*] **of God cast out devils, no doubt the kingdom of God is come upon you** [*you are seeing the true king-*

dom of God in action and you had better pay attention].

21 **When a strong man armed keepeth his palace** [*guards his palace*], his goods are in peace [*his possessions are safe*]:

22 **But when a stronger than he shall come** upon him, and overcome him, he taketh from him all his armour [*protection*] wherein he trusted, and divideth his spoils [*takes his possessions*].

23 **He that is not with me is against me**: and he that gathereth not with me scattereth.

24 **When the unclean spirit is gone out of a man**, he walketh through dry places, seeking rest; and finding none, he saith, I will return unto my house whence I came out.

JST Luke 11:25

25 When the unclean spirit is gone out of a man, **it** walketh through dry places, seeking rest; and finding none, **it** saith, I will return unto my house whence I came out.

25 And **when he cometh, he findeth it swept and garnished.**

26 **Then goeth he, and taketh to him seven other spirits more wicked than himself; and they enter in, and dwell there: and the last state of that man is worse than the first.**

JST Luke 11:26–27

26 And when **it** cometh, it findeth the house swept and garnished.

27 Then goeth the evil spirit, and taketh seven other spirits more wicked than himself, and they enter in, and dwell there; and the last **end** of that man is worse than the first.

Verses 24–26 above are especially difficult to understand without help. Matthew 12:43–45 is similar to Luke 11:24–26, and there is a note following Matthew 12:45 in this study guide which explains these verses as follows:

Matthew 12:43–45

43 **When the unclean spirit is gone out of a man**, he walketh through dry places, seeking rest, and findeth none.

44 Then he saith, I will return into my house from whence I came out; and when he is come, he findeth it empty, swept, and garnished.

45 Then goeth he, and taketh with himself seven other spirits more wicked than himself, and they enter in and dwell there: and the last state of that man is worse than the first. **Even so shall it be also unto this wicked generation**.

The JST will help us understand verses 43–45, above.

JST Matthew 12:37–39

37 [*Note: This verse is entirely missing from the Bible.*] **Then came some of the scribes**

[*Jewish religious leaders who specialized in interpreting the gospel doctrines and laws*] **and said unto him, Master, it is written that, Every sin shall be forgiven; but ye say, Whosoever speaketh against the Holy Ghost shall not be forgiven. And they asked him, saying, How can these things be?** [*In other words, what you, Jesus, are teaching contradicts our traditional written doctrines.*]

38 **And he said unto them**, When the unclean spirit is gone out of a man, he [*the evil spirit*] walketh through dry places, seeking rest and findeth none; but when a man speaketh against the Holy Ghost [*when a man reverts back to his evil ways to the extent of denying the Holy Ghost*], then he [*the evil spirit*] saith, I will return into my house [*the man in whom the evil spirit used to reside*] from whence I came out; and when he [*the evil spirit*] is come, he findeth **him** [*the man in whom the evil spirit formerly resided*] empty, swept and garnished [*was cleansed from sin, with a sure testimony given him by the Holy Ghost, but who is now speaking against that testimony*]; **for the good spirit** [*the Holy Ghost*] **leaveth him unto himself**.

39 Then goeth **the evil spirit**, and taketh with himself seven other spirits more wicked than himself; and they enter in and dwell there [*with the man who has denied the Holy Ghost*]; and the last **end** of that man is worse than the first [*the man is worse*

off now than he was before he gained a sure testimony from the Holy Ghost]. Even so shall it be also unto this wicked generation.

Elder Bruce R. McConkie helps us understand the above three verses as follows: "JST Matthew 12:37–39. Having already taught that every sin shall be forgiven except the sin against the Holy Ghost, Jesus now illustrates why. In effect he says: 'If you gain a perfect knowledge of me and my mission, it must come by revelation from the Holy Ghost; that Holy Spirit must speak to the spirit within you; and then you shall know, nothing doubting. But to receive this knowledge and revelation, you must cleanse and perfect your own soul; that is, your house must be clean, swept, and garnished. Then if you deny me by speaking against the Holy Ghost who gave you your revelation of the truth, that is if you come out in open rebellion against the perfect light you have received, the Holy Ghost will depart, leaving you to yourself. Your house will now be available for other tenancy, and so the evil spirits and influences you had once conquered will return to plague you. Having completely lost the preserving power of the Spirit, you will then be worse off than if you had never received the truth; and many in this generation shall be so condemned'" (*Doctrinal New Testament Commentary*, Volume 1, p. 276).

27 And it came to pass, as he spake these things, a certain woman of the company lifted up her voice, and said unto him, Blessed is the womb that bare thee, and the paps which thou hast sucked [*blessed is the woman to whom you were born and nursed you; praising Mary, the mother of Jesus; this is one of the fulfillments of Mary's prophecy in Luke 1:48*].

28 But he said, Yea rather [*that is true, but even more important*], blessed are they that hear the word of God, and keep [*obey*] it.

29 And when the people were gathered thick [*in a tight crowd*] together, he began to say, This is an evil generation: they seek a sign [*always are wanting proof that I am the Messiah*]; and there shall no sign be given it [*them*], but the sign of Jonas [*Jonah*] the prophet [*the signs they get will be miserable for them, like being swallowed by a whale was for Jonah, when he tried to reject God's call*].

30 For as Jonas was a sign unto the Ninevites [*the people to whom Jonah preached*], so shall also the Son of man [*Jesus*] be to this generation.

31 The queen of the south [*the queen of Sheba*] shall rise up in the judgment with the men of this generation, and condemn them: for she came from the utmost parts of the earth to hear the wisdom of Solomon; and, behold, a greater than Solomon [*in other words, the Son of God*] is here.

The point in verse 31 above seems to be that the Jews will be condemned (damned) by the good example of the Queen of Sheba, who came from far away to learn about God from Solomon, whereas the Jews have the Son of God in their midst, teaching them, and they ignore Him.

32 The men of Nineve [*Nineveh*] shall rise up in the judgment with this generation [*the Jews*], and shall condemn it [*by their good example*]: for they repented at the preaching of Jonas [*Jonah*]; and, behold, a greater than Jonas is here.

33 No man, when he hath lighted a candle, putteth it in a secret place, neither under a bushel, but on a candlestick, that they which come in may see the light.

34 The light of the body is the eye [*the eye takes in light so you can see where you are going*]: therefore when thine eye [*your spiritual eye*] is single [*focused on God's light*] thy whole body also is full of light; but when thine eye is evil [*you look for evil, to participate in*], thy body also is full of darkness.

35 Take heed therefore that the light which is in thee be not darkness.

36 If thy whole body therefore be full of light [*full of gospel light*], having no part dark [*avoiding evil*], the whole [*your whole life*] shall be full of light, as when the bright shining of a candle doth give thee light.

37 And as he spake, a certain Pharisee besought [*requested*] him to dine with him: and he went in, and sat down to meat [*to the meal*].

38 And when the Pharisee saw it, he marvelled [*was surprised*] that he had not first washed before dinner.

The Pharisees were very strict about washing before eating and had made it a very exact part of their religious rituals which made them look righteous in the eyes of others.

39 And the Lord said unto him, Now do ye Pharisees make clean [*wash*] the outside of the cup and the platter [*plate*]; but your inward part is full of ravening [*greed, seeking to rob and plunder the people*] and wickedness.

40 Ye fools, did not he [*God*] that made that which is without [*outside*] make that which is within [*inside*] also? [*God knows that you try to look clean on the outside but that you are filthy with wickedness on the inside.*]

41 But rather give alms of such things as ye have; and, behold, all things are clean unto you. [*In other words, if you would keep My commandments, you could be just as clean on the inside as you are on the outside.*]

JST Luke 11:42

42 But if ye would rather give alms of such things as ye have; and observe to do all things which I have commanded you, then would your inward parts be clean also.

Although tithing is not the main issue in verse 42, next, (hypocrisy is the issue) it is obvious that it was a common practice among the Jews in New Testament times. This can be helpful to us if non-Latter-day Saint acquaintances question why the Church requires tithing of its faithful members. We can show them this verse and tell them that tithe paying was commonly practiced in New Testament times.

Tithing

42 But woe unto you [*you are in much trouble*], Pharisees! for ye tithe [*pay exact tithing on*] mint and rue [*herbs*] and all manner of herbs, and pass over [*ignore*] judgment [*being fair to others*] and the love of God: these [*Christlike things*] ought ye to have done, and not to leave the other [*paying tithing exactly*] undone. [*In other words, you go through the motions of being religious but you are not!*]

43 Woe unto you, Pharisees! for ye love the uppermost seats [*the highest, most respected and prestigious seats*] in the synagogues [*Jewish meeting houses*], and greetings in the markets. [*You love to have people notice how important you are.*]

44 Woe unto you, scribes and Pharisees, hypocrites [*people who want to appear to others to be righteous, but in their hearts, they love to be wicked*]! for ye are as graves which appear not [*don't look like graves*], and the men that walk over them are not aware of them [*don't realize that there is rot and corruption just under the surface*].

45 Then answered one of the lawyers, and said unto him, Master, thus saying thou reproachest us also. [*By speaking so disrespectfully to the scribes and Pharisees, you are insulting us lawyers also!*]

46 And he said, Woe unto you also, ye lawyers! for ye lade men [*load people down*] with burdens grievous to be borne [*difficult to carry*], and ye yourselves touch not the burdens with one of your fingers [*you won't lift a finger to help*].

47 Woe unto you! for ye build the sepulchres of the prophets [*build big monuments to dead prophets*], and your fathers [*ancestors*] killed them. [*You pretend to be righteous and honor past prophets, but if you had lived back then, you would have joined your ancestors in killing them!*]

48 Truly ye bear witness [*through your wicked lives*] that ye allow [*agree with*] the deeds of your fathers: for they indeed killed them [*past prophets*], and ye build their sepulchres [*you build big monuments upon past prophets' grave sites to honor them*].

49 Therefore also said the wisdom of God [*God, in his wisdom, said*], I will send them [*the Jews*] prophets and apostles, and some of them they shall slay and persecute:

50 That the blood of all the prophets, which was shed from the foundation [*the earliest days*] of the world, may be required of this

THE NEW TESTAMENT MADE EASIER THIRD EDITION, PART 1

generation; [*Since you have murder in your hearts for the prophets and Apostles now, you are as good as guilty of participating in killing all the prophets whose blood has been spilt by the wicked since the beginning of time.*]

51 From the blood of Abel unto the blood of Zacharias [*John the Baptist's father*], which perished [*whom you had executed*] between the altar and the temple: verily I say unto you, It shall be required of this generation. [*You wicked people will answer for all this.*]

52 Woe unto you, lawyers! for ye have taken away the key of knowledge: ye entered not in yourselves, and them that were entering in ye hindered [*stopped*]. [*In other words, you won't get to heaven yourselves and you prevent others from going there too!*]

JST Luke 11:53

53 Woe unto you, lawyers! For ye have taken away the key of knowledge, the fullness of the scriptures; ye enter not in yourselves into the kingdom; and those who were entering in, ye hindered.

53 And as he said these things unto them, the scribes and the Pharisees [*Jewish religious leaders*] began to urge him vehemently [*strongly and angrily opposed Him*], and to provoke him to speak of many things [*and bombarded Him with many angry questions*]:

54 Laying wait for him [*trying to trap Him*], and seeking to catch something out of his mouth, that they might accuse him [*hoping Jesus would say something for which they could have Him arrested*].

LUKE 12

As this chapter begins, we see a warning to avoid hypocrisy. Some misinterpret "hypocrisy" to mean anyone who belongs to a church and still has faults and imperfections. Such is not the case. Hypocrisy means to actively attempt to appear righteous to others while secretly desiring to be involved in evil, and thus privately and intentionally participating in wickedness. Perhaps you have noticed that the Savior came down hard on hypocrites but was gentle and encouraging to those caught up in other types of sin. Thus, hypocrisy must be considered as one of the most damaging kinds of sin.

1 IN the mean time, when there were gathered together an innumerable multitude [*a huge group*] of people, insomuch that they trode [*were stepping*] one upon another, he began to say unto his disciples first of all, Beware ye of [*watch out for*] the leaven [*yeast*] of the Pharisees, which is hypocrisy.

Here the Master Teacher warns His disciples against the evil doctrines of the Pharisees (Jewish religious leaders). He compares these doctrines to leaven (yeast) which is put in bread dough to make it rise. As the leaven works its way through the entire lump of dough, it influences everything. So

LUKE 12

also with these hypocritical Jewish leaders, who are influencing everything in Jewish society. (See also Matthew 16:6.)

2 For there is nothing covered, that shall not be revealed; neither hid, that shall not be known. [*God knows all things and all unrepented-of evil deeds will eventually be exposed.*]

3 Therefore whatsoever ye have spoken in darkness shall be heard in the light; and that which ye have spoken in the ear in closets [*spoken secretly*] shall be proclaimed upon the housetops [*broadcast to everyone*].

4 And I say unto you my friends, Be not afraid of them that kill the body, and after that have no more that they can do [*that is all they can do to you*].

5 But I will forewarn you whom ye shall fear: Fear him, which after he hath killed hath power to cast into hell; yea, I say unto you, Fear him [*fear Satan and spiritual death*].

6 Are not five sparrows sold for two farthings, and not one of them is forgotten before God? [*God knows the little birds, so you can be assured that he knows and cares about you.*]

7 But even the very hairs of your head are all numbered. Fear not therefore: ye are of more value than many sparrows.

8 Also I say unto you, Whosoever [*whoever*] shall confess [*be faithful to*] me before men [*in the presence of others*], him shall the Son of man [*Christ*] also confess [*accept*] before the angels of God: [*In other words, he will be invited to live in heaven.*]

9 But he that denieth [*rejects*] me before men shall be denied [*rejected*] before the angels of God.

The JST adds two verses here. They are as follows:

JST Luke 12:10–11
10 Now his disciples knew that he said this, because they had spoken evil against him before the people; for they were afraid to confess him before men.

11 And they reasoned among themselves, saying, He knoweth our hearts, and he speaketh to our condemnation, and we shall not be forgiven. But he answered them, and said unto them,

10 And whosoever shall speak a word against the Son of man [*Jesus*], it shall be forgiven him: but unto him that blasphemeth against the Holy Ghost [*denies the Holy Ghost*] it shall not be forgiven.

JST Luke 12:12
12 Whosoever shall speak a word against the Son of man, and repenteth, it shall be forgiven him; but unto him who blasphemeth against the Holy Ghost, it shall not be forgiven him.

11 And when they [*arrest you, and*] bring you unto the synagogues, and unto magistrates [*public officials*], and powers [*the courts, etc.*], take

ye no thought how or what thing ye shall answer, or what ye shall say:

12 For the Holy Ghost shall teach you in the same hour what ye ought to say.

13 And one of the company [*a person in the crowd*] said unto him, Master, speak to my brother, that he divide the inheritance with me [*tell my brother to share his inheritance with me*].

14 And he [*Jesus*] said unto him, Man, who made me a judge or a divider [*arbitrator*] over you?

15 And he said unto them, Take heed, and beware of covetousness [*greed*]: for a man's life consisteth not in the abundance of the things which he possesseth [*worldly possessions are not what makes life worthwhile*].

Next, Jesus will give what is known as "The Parable of the Foolish Rich Man." It is given in Perea during the winter of A.D. 31. The main message is "You can't take it with you." The point is that we must avoid allowing our worldly possessions take the place of God in our lives.

The Parable of the Foolish Rich Man

16 And he spake a parable [*a story which teaches a certain lesson*] unto them, saying, The ground of a certain rich man brought forth plentifully [*grew very good crops*]:

17 And he thought within himself, saying, What shall I do, because I have no room where to bestow [*store*] my fruits [*crops*]?

18 And he said, This will I do: I will pull down [*tear down*] my barns, and build greater [*bigger ones*]; and there will I bestow [*store*] all my fruits and my goods.

19 And I will say to my soul [*to myself*], Soul [*self*], thou hast much goods laid up for many years [*you have enough to last for several years*]; take thine ease [*relax, take it easy*], **eat, drink, and be merry**.

20 **But God said** unto him, **Thou fool, this night thy soul shall be required of thee** [*tonight you will die*]: then whose shall those things be, which thou hast provided [*then who will all your stuff belong to*]?

21 **So is he that layeth up treasure for himself, and is not rich toward God.** [*So it is with people who allow their possessions to take the place of God in their lives.*]

22 And he said **unto his disciples**, Therefore I say unto you, **Take no thought for your life, what ye shall eat; neither for the body, what ye shall put on.**

This counsel applies to the Apostles and those involved in full-time service of God, such as missionaries. JST Matthew 6:25–27 makes this very clear as follows:

JST Matthew 6:25–27
25 And, again, I say unto you, Go ye into the world, and care not for the world; for the world

LUKE 12

303

will hate you, and will persecute you, and will turn you out of their synagogues.

26 Nevertheless, ye shall go forth from house to house, teaching the people; and I will go before you.

27 And **your heavenly Father will provide for you**, whatsoever things ye need for food, what ye shall eat; and for raiment, what ye shall wear or put on.

These verses do not apply to everyone. Occasionally, individuals or groups take this literally as applying to them and the results are tragic and disastrous. The Savior continues this counsel to His Apostles in verses 23–33, next.

23 The **life is more than meat** [*food*], and **the body is more than raiment** [*clothing*].

24 **Consider the ravens**: for they neither sow [*plant*] nor reap [*harvest*]; which neither have storehouse nor barn; and God feedeth them: **how much more are ye better than the fowls?** [*God takes good care of birds and you are much more important than they are.*]

25 And **which of you** with taking thought **can add to his stature** one cubit? [*Which of you could think and thus add inches to your height?*]

26 **If ye then be not able to do that thing which is least, why take ye thought for the rest?**

[*Since you can't do such an unimportant thing, why worry about the rest of your needs?*]

27 **Consider the lilies** [*flowers*] how they grow: they toil not [*they don't work*], they spin not [*they don't weave cloth for clothing*]; and yet I say unto you, that Solomon in all his glory was not arrayed [*dressed*] like one of these.

28 **If then God so clothe the grass** [*makes the grass beautiful*], which is to day in the field, and to morrow is cast into the oven [*is gone*]; **how much more will he clothe you**, O ye of little faith?

JST Luke 12:30

30 If then God so clothe the grass, which is **today** in the field, and tomorrow is cast in the oven; how much more **will he provide for you, if ye are not of little faith?**

29 And seek not ye what ye shall eat, or what ye shall drink, **neither be ye of doubtful mind** [*don't doubt that the Lord will do this for you*].

30 For all these things [*the things you need daily to take care of your physical needs*] do the nations of the world seek after: and **your Father knoweth that ye have need of these things**.

The JST adds an entire verse after verse 30, above.

JST Luke 12:33

33 **And ye are sent unto them to be their ministers, and the laborer is worthy of his hire; for**

the law saith, That a man shall not muzzle the ox that treadeth out the corn.

31 But rather **seek ye the kingdom of God; and all these things shall be added unto you.**

JST Luke 12:34
34 **Therefore seek ye to bring forth** the kingdom of God, and all these things shall be added unto you.

Notice how tender verse 32 is next as Jesus addresses His Apostles. It is a reminder that Heavenly Father is indeed our Father and truly loves us.

32 **Fear not, little flock; for it is your Father's good pleasure to give you the kingdom.**

33 **Sell that** [*what*] **ye have, and give alms** [*pay your offerings to God*]; provide yourselves bags which wax not old [*leather bags to carry food in*], a treasure in the heavens that faileth not [*doesn't ever run out*], where no thief approacheth, neither moth corrupteth [*ruins*].

The JST makes very significant changes to verse 33, above. Among other things, notice that it says "provide not for yourselves bags."

JST Luke 12:36
36 **This he spake unto his disciples, saying,** Sell that ye have and give alms; provide **not** for yourselves bags **which wax old, but rather provide** a treasure in the heavens, that faileth not;

where no thief approacheth, neither moth corrupteth.

34 For **where your treasure is, there will your heart be also.**

35 **Let your loins be girded about** [*be dressed and ready*], **and your lights burning** [*have your lamps burning, as in the parable of the ten virgins, in Matthew 25:1–13*];

36 **And ye yourselves like unto men that wait** [*are prepared*] **for their lord, when he will return** from the wedding; that when he cometh and knocketh, they may open unto him **immediately.**

The counsel and imagery here deal with our being prepared for the Second Coming. When the Savior actually does come, there will be no time for further preparation to meet Him. As indicated at the end of verse 36, above, we must be prepared to "immediately" open the door for Him, so to speak, when He comes. In other words, those who are prepared and worthy will "immediately" be taken up to meet him at his coming. See D&C 88:96.

37 **Blessed are those servants, whom the lord when he cometh shall find watching:** verily I say unto you, that he [*Christ*] shall gird [*prepare*] himself, and make them to sit down to meat [*eat, symbolic of partaking of the blessings of the gospel*], and will come forth and serve them.

The Joseph Smith Translation (the JST) adds much for verses 38–48 here. As we continue,

LUKE 12

305

we will put a few notes in these verses as they stand in Luke. Then, at the end of verse 48, we will include JST Luke 12:41–57 in its entirety, which covers Luke 12:38–48.

38 And if he shall come in the second watch [*in the middle of the night*], or come in the third watch [*the early morning hours before sunrise; see Bible Dictionary, under "Watches"*], and find them so [*watching and prepared*], **blessed are those servants**.

The scriptures are very clear that no one knows the exact timing of the Second Coming. See Matthew 24:36 and Mark 13:32.

39 And this know, that **if the goodman** [*owner*] **of the house had known what hour the thief would come, he would have watched** [*would not have been caught off guard*], **and not have suffered** [*allowed*] his house to be broken through [*into*].

40 **Be ye therefore ready** also: for **the Son of man** [*Christ*] **cometh at an hour when ye think not**.

Next, in verse 41, Peter asks Jesus if the advice on preparing for the Second Coming, given in the above verses, applies only to the Twelve, or to all people.

41 Then **Peter said** unto him, Lord, **speakest thou this parable unto us, or even to all?**

42 **And the Lord said,** [*I speak to those who are faithful—see JST,*

verse 49, quoted below] Who then is that faithful and wise steward, whom his lord shall make ruler over his household [*who will attain exaltation*], to give them their portion of meat [*their reward*] in due season [*when it is time*]?

43 **Blessed is that servant, whom his lord when he cometh shall find so doing** [*living righteously*].

44 Of a truth I say unto you, that **he will make him ruler over all that he hath** [*exaltation; see D&C 84:37–38*].

Do you realize how significant the doctrine taught in verse 44 above is? Many of us have friends who do not believe the teaching of our church that we can become gods like Heavenly Father. But here it is, right in the Bible! We refer to it as "exaltation," and it is receiving "all that he hath." In other words, we can become Gods, living in our own family units forever, having our own spirit children and raising them, teaching them, sending them to worlds like ours, and being gods over them just like Father is over us.

45 **But and if that servant say in his heart,** My lord delayeth his coming; and shall begin to beat the menservants and maidens, and to eat and drink, and to be drunken; [*In other words, if people live wickedly because they either don't believe the Lord will come, or think that they have plenty of time to repent after they have "enjoyed" wickedness.*]

46 **The lord** [*Christ*] **of that servant will come in a day when he looketh not for him** [*when he is not prepared*], and at an hour when he is not aware, **and will cut him in sunder** [*he will be destroyed at the Second Coming*], and will appoint him his portion [*punishment*] with the unbelievers.

47 And **that servant, which knew his lord's will** [*was accountable*], **and prepared not himself** [*those who knew the gospel but didn't live it*], neither did according to his will, shall be beaten with many stripes [*will be severely punished; in ancient times, each time a person was hit with a whip, it was called a "stripe"*].

This may sound harsh, but we are governed by eternal laws. The Savior has taught us over and over again in the scriptures, that mercy cannot rob justice, "Nay; not one whit" (Alma 42:25). He constantly extends His mercy to us (Jacob 6:4), and through His Atonement allows us to repent, be healed of the aftermath of sin, and become righteous, clean, new people. However, if we ignore the gospel and do not live as we know we should, then the Law of Justice must take over, and we have to suffer for our own sins, which suffering is beyond our ability to comprehend. (See D&C 19:15–19.)

48 But **he that knew not** [*did not know the gospel, therefore was not as accountable*], and did commit things worthy of stripes, **shall be beaten with few stripes.** [*All people are born with a conscience, and therefore have some degree of accountability, whether they know the gospel or not.*] For **unto whomsoever much is given, of him shall be much required** [*see D&C 82:3*]: and to whom men have committed much, of him they will ask the more. [*More is expected of them.*]

As stated in the note at the end of verse 37 above, JST 12:41–57, which covers verses 38–48, is included here and reads as follows:

JST 12:41–57

41 **For, behold, he cometh in the first watch of the night, and he shall also come in the second watch, and again he shall come in the third watch.**

42 **And verily I say unto you, He hath already come, as it is written of him; and again when he shall come in the second watch, or come in the third watch, blessed are those servants when he cometh, that he shall find so doing;**

43 **For the Lord of those servants shall gird himself, and make them to sit down to meat, and will come forth and serve them.**

44 **And now, verily I say these things unto you, that ye may know this, that the coming of the Lord is as a thief in the night.**

45 **And it is like unto a man who is an householder, who,**

LUKE 12

if he watcheth not his goods, the thief cometh in an hour of which he is not aware, and taketh his goods, and divideth them among his fellows.

46 And they said among themselves, If the good man of the house had known what hour the thief would come, he would have watched, and not have suffered his house to be broken through and the loss of his goods.

47 And he said unto them, Verily I say unto you, be ye therefore ready also; for the Son of man cometh at an hour when ye think not.

48 Then Peter said unto him, Lord, speakest thou this parable unto us, or unto all?

49 And the Lord said, I speak unto those whom the Lord shall make rulers over his household, to give his children their portion of meat in due season.

50 And they said, Who then is that faithful and wise servant?

51 And the Lord said unto them, It is that servant who watcheth, to impart his portion of meat in due season.

52 Blessed be that servant whom his Lord shall find, when he cometh, so doing.

53 Of a truth I say unto you, that he will make him ruler over all that he hath.

54 But the evil servant is he who is not found watching. And if that servant is not found watching, he will say in his heart, My Lord delayeth his coming; and shall begin to beat the menservants, and the maidens, and to eat, and drink, and to be drunken.

55 The Lord of that servant will come in a day he looketh not for, and at an hour when he is not aware, and will cut him down, and will appoint him his portion with the unbelievers.

56 And that servant who knew his Lord's will, and prepared not for his Lord's coming, neither did according to his will, shall be beaten with many stripes.

57 But he that knew not his Lord's will, and did commit things worthy of stripes, shall be beaten with few. For unto whomsoever much is given, of him shall much be required; and to whom the Lord has committed much, of him will men ask the more. [*End of JST quote.*]

We will now continue with Luke, chapter 12, verse 49, as it stands in the Bible.

49 I am come to send fire on the earth [*because people do not keep the commandments, they will be burned at His coming*]; and what will I, if it be already kindled?

JST Luke 12:58

58 For they are not well pleased with the Lord's doings; therefore I am come to send fire on the earth; and **what is it to you, if I will that** it be already kindled?

50 But **I have a baptism to be baptized with** [*I have a "baptism of fire," a most difficult task of My own, namely, to perform the Atonement.*]; **and how am I** straitened [*confined, can't go on to other things*] till it be accomplished [*I must not deviate at all from My assigned course, until I have accomplished it*]!

Next, we will be reminded that the gospel sometimes causes dissension and divisions rather than bringing peace (because of the agency of those involved).

51 **Suppose ye** [*do you suppose*] **that I am come** [*have come*] **to give peace on earth?** I tell you, **Nay; but rather division** [*to divide the righteous from the wicked or the uninterested from the interested, and so forth*]:

52 For from henceforth [*from now on*] **there shall be five in one house divided, three against two, and two against three.** [*In other words, some members of a family will accept the gospel and others will not. As a result, they will be divided against each other.*]

53 The **father** shall be **divided against the son,** and the **son against the father;** the **mother against the daughter,** and the **daughter against the mother;** the **mother in law against her daughter in law,** and the **daughter in law against her mother in law.**

54 And **he said also to the people,** When ye see a cloud rise out of the west, straightway [*right away*] ye say, There cometh a shower; and so it is. [*You predict the weather by looking at the signs in the sky.*]

55 And when ye see the south wind blow, ye say, There will be heat [*it will be hot*]; and it cometh to pass [*it happens*].

56 **Ye hypocrites,** ye can discern the face of the sky [*you can predict the weather by looking at the signs in the sky*] and of the earth; but **how is it that ye do not discern this time** [*why are you so blind to the signs about the coming of Christ, which are all around you*]?

57 Yea, and **why** even of yourselves **judge ye not what is right?** [*These signs are so obvious that you should be able to tell what's going on without help!*]

Next, the Savior gives counsel for us to be peacemakers. (Notice in your King James Bible that there is a paragraph mark at the beginning of verse 58. That indicates that there is a change to a new topic here.) He counsels us to work things out quickly with those with whom we have a disagreement, rather than letting it fester and drag on. If we have bad feelings, bitterness, hatred, or whatever toward others, and do not quickly work it out, it is like being thrown into prison. The longer it drags on, the more difficult it is to work through. We pay a much heavier price by allowing such things to go unresolved than if we would quickly and humbly work things out.

58 **When thou goest with thine adversary to the magistrate** [*when someone takes you to court; symbolic of when you have a disagreement with someone*], **as thou art in the way** [*as you are on your way to the courthouse*], **give diligence** [*try hard*] **that thou mayest be delivered from him** [*to make peace and work things out with him before you go to court*]; **lest he hale thee to the judge** [*for fear that he will take you in front of the judge*], **and the judge deliver thee** [*turns you over*] **to the officer, and the officer cast thee** [*puts you*] **into prison.**

59 I tell thee, **thou shalt not depart thence** [*you will not get out of the prison you allowed yourself to be put in*], **till thou hast paid the very last mite** [*until you have paid dearly every last bit of the punishment*].

LUKE 13

As we begin this chapter, we are taught an important lesson to the effect that people who suffer tragedy are not necessarily more wicked than others.

1 THERE were present at that season [*JST "at that time"*] **some**

that told him [*Jesus*] of the Galilæans, whose blood Pilate had mingled with their sacrifices [*who had been killed by Pontius Pilate, the Roman governor*].

2 And **Jesus** answering [*responding*] **said** unto them, **Suppose ye that these Galilæans were sinners above all the Galilæans, because they suffered such things?** [*Do you suppose that they were more wicked than other Galileans, and that's why they were killed?*]

3 **I tell you, Nay**: but, except ye repent, ye shall all likewise perish.

The reference to the fall of a tower in Siloam, in verse 4, next, is apparently referring to a tragedy that happened in the Jerusalem area.

4 **Or those eighteen, upon whom the tower in Siloam fell,** and slew them, **think ye that they were sinners above all men that dwelt in Jerusalem** [*worse sinners than anyone else in Jerusalem*]?

5 **I tell you, Nay**: **but, except ye repent, ye shall all likewise perish.**

This next parable is known as "The Parable of the Barren Fig Tree." The main point is that it is what you actually do that counts, not what you say you will do. If you claim to be spiritual and righteous, but your deeds are evil, you will end up being destroyed by your enemies (symbolic of Satan and his evil hosts). It was given in the winter of A.D. 32. The notes in brackets give one possible interpretation out of many possibilities.

The Parable of the Barren Fig Tree

6 **He spake also this parable** [*a story that teaches a particular point*]; **A certain man** [*symbolic of the Father*] **had a fig tree** [*the Jews*] planted in his vineyard [*on earth*]; and **he came and sought fruit** [*looked for righteous lives*] thereon [*among the Jews*], **and found none.**

7 **Then said he unto the dresser of his vineyard** [*symbolic of Christ; see Talmage, Jesus the Christ, p. 443*], Behold, **these three years** [*the three years of Christ's mission*] **I come seeking fruit** [*righteousness*] on this fig tree [*among the Jews*], **and find none: cut it down** [*John the Baptist said, "Now . . . the axe is laid unto the root of the trees"; Luke 3:9; in other words, destruction is almost here for the wicked Jews*]; **why cumbereth it the ground** [*why let it keep cluttering the earth*]?

8 **And he** [*Jesus*] answering **said** unto him [*the Father*], Lord, **let it alone this year also, till I shall dig about it** [*cultivate it*], **and dung it** [*nourish it; in other words, let's give the Jews one more chance to repent*]:

9 **And if it bear fruit, well** [*if they do, wonderful!*]: and **if not, then** after that [*this one more chance*] thou shalt **cut it down** [*destroy their nation*].

Did verses 6–9, above, seem familiar? We see similar symbolism in the allegory of the tame and wild olive trees found in Jacob, chapter 5.

The Jews did not take advantage of this last opportunity, at that time, to repent. They crucified Christ and persecuted His followers. The Romans completed the destruction of Jerusalem and the Jews about A.D. 70–73.

Christ Heals a Crippled Woman on the Sabbath

10 And **he was teaching** in one of the synagogues **on the sabbath.**

11 And, behold, **there was a woman which had a spirit of infirmity** [*had been weak and sickly*] **eighteen years**, and was **bowed together** [*was bent over*], **and could in no wise lift up herself** [*could not straighten herself out at all*].

12 And when **Jesus** saw her, he called her to him, and **said** unto her, **Woman, thou art loosed from thine infirmity** [*you are set free from being crippled*].

13 And **he laid his hands on her: and immediately she was made straight, and glorified** [*praised*] **God.**

14 And **the ruler of the synagogue answered** [*responded*] **with indignation** [*anger*], **because that Jesus had healed on the sabbath day, and said unto the people, There are six days in which men ought**

Luke 13

to work: in them therefore come and be healed, and not on the sabbath day. [*In other words, if you want to be healed in my synagogue, come on any of the six days of the week when work is permitted. But don't come to be healed on the Sabbath.*]

15 **The Lord** then answered him, and **said, Thou hypocrite, doth not each one of you on the sabbath loose** [*untie*] **his ox or his ass from the stall, and lead him away to watering?**

16 **And ought not this woman**, being a daughter of Abraham, whom Satan hath bound, lo, these eighteen years, **be loosed** [*freed*] **from this bond** [*the bondage of being crippled*] **on the sabbath day?** [*You treat your beasts of burden better that you treat this woman.*]

17 And **when he had said these things, all his adversaries** [*opponents*] **were ashamed: and all the people rejoiced for all the glorious things that were done by him.**

The Parable of the Grain of Mustard Seed

18 Then said he, **Unto what is the kingdom of God like?** and whereunto shall I resemble it [*unto what shall I compare it*]?

19 **It is like a grain of mustard seed** [*a very tiny seed; symbolic of very small beginnings for the Church*], **which a man** [*God*] took, and **cast into his garden** [*the*

earth]; **and it grew, and waxed a great tree** [*became a large tree*]; **and the fowls of the air lodged in the branches of it.**

Joseph Smith explained this parable:

"And again, another parable put He forth unto them, having an allusion to the Kingdom that should be set up, just previous to or at the time of the harvest, which reads as follows—'The Kingdom of Heaven is like a grain of mustard seed, which a man took and sowed in his field: which indeed is the least of all seeds: but, when it is grown, it is the greatest among herbs, and becometh a tree, so that the birds of the air come and lodge in the branches thereof.' Now we can discover plainly that this figure is given to represent the Church as it shall come forth in the last days." (For more of the Prophet's explanation, see *Teachings of the Prophet Joseph Smith*, pp. 98–99 and p. 159.)

The Parable of the Leaven

20 And **again he said, Whereunto shall I liken the kingdom of God?**

21 **It is like leaven** [*yeast*], **which a woman took and hid in three measures of meal, till the whole was leavened.** [*The Church will start out small but will expand into the whole world; see* Teachings of the Prophet Joseph Smith, *pp. 100 and 102.*]

22 And he went through the cities

and villages, teaching, and journeying toward Jerusalem.

23 **Then said one** unto him, **Lord, are there few that be saved** [*will just a few be saved*]? And **he said** unto them,

The Strait Gate

24 **Strive to enter in at the strait** [*narrow*] **gate: for many**, I say unto you, **will seek to enter in** [*into heaven*], **and shall not be able.**

JST Luke 13:24
24 Strive to enter in at the strait gate; **for I say unto you** Many **shall** seek to enter in, and shall not be able; **for the Lord shall not always strive with man**.

25 **When once the master of the house** [*the Lord*] is risen up, and **hath shut to the door** [*once your opportunities to repent and join Christ are over*], **and ye** begin to **stand without** [*outside*], **and to knock at the door, saying, Lord, Lord, open unto us**; and **he shall answer and say unto you, I know you not whence ye are** [*you don't belong to Me; you haven't made covenants with Me*]:

JST Luke 13:25
25 **Therefore**, when once the **Lord of the kingdom** is risen up, and hath shut the door **of the kingdom, then ye shall stand without**, and knock at the door, saying, Lord, Lord, open unto us, **But the Lord** shall answer and say unto you, **I will not receive you, for ye know not from whence ye are.**

26 **Then shall ye begin to say**, We have eaten and drunk in thy presence, and thou hast taught in our streets.

27 **But he shall say**, I tell you, **I know you not whence ye are;** depart from me, all ye workers of iniquity [*wickedness*].

JST Luke 13:27
27 But he shall say, I tell you, **ye know not from whence ye are;** depart from me, all workers of iniquity.

Did you catch the message in the JST change above? Bible verse 27, above, in context, says that God doesn't know the status of these wicked people, but, of course, He does. In the JST, it is these wicked people themselves who don't realize that they have procrastinated their repentance until it is too late.

28 **There shall be weeping and gnashing of teeth** [*grinding teeth together in great agony*], when ye shall see Abraham, and Isaac, and Jacob, and all the prophets, in the kingdom of God, and **you yourselves thrust out.**

29 And **they** [*righteous people who have made and kept covenants with the Lord*] **shall come** from the east, and from the west, and from the north, and from the south [*in other words, from all nations of the world*], and **shall sit down in the kingdom of God.**

The Last Shall Be First and the First Shall Be Last

30 And, behold, there are **last** [*the humble, righteous who are considered by the wicked to be the lowest*] which **shall be first** [*exalted*], and there are **first** [*the wicked who considered themselves to be superior to the righteous*] which **shall be last** [*will receive the lowest rewards on Judgment Day*].

31 The same day there came certain of the **Pharisees** [*Jewish religious leaders*], **saying unto him** [*Jesus*], **Get thee out**, and depart hence [*leave!*]: **for Herod will** [*the Roman governor desires to*] **kill thee.**

> Next, Jesus tells the hypocritical Pharisees to tell Herod, in effect, that He is the prophesied Son of God and will go about His mission regardless of what Herod plots against Him.

32 And **he said** unto them, Go ye, and **tell that fox** [*King Herod*], Behold, I cast out devils, and I do cures to day and to morrow, and the third day [*the day I am resurrected*] I shall be perfected.

33 **Nevertheless I must walk to day, and to morrow, and the day following** [*I will not leave; My work requires that I stay here to complete it*]: **for it cannot be that a prophet perish out of Jerusalem.** [*It is prophesied that I will be killed in Jerusalem, and so it must be.*]

> The JST adds a verse here:

JST Luke 13:34

34 This he spake, signifying of his death. And in this very hour he began to weep over Jerusalem.

34 [*JST "Saying"*] **O Jerusalem, Jerusalem**, which killest the prophets, and stonest them that are sent unto thee; **how often would I have gathered thy children** [*your people*] **together, as a hen doth gather her brood** [*chicks*] **under her wings, and ye would not** [*you would not come*]!

> There is beautiful symbolism here. The Savior compares Himself to a mother hen, with warm, soft feathers under her wings, where her chicks can be gathered to comfortable safety when danger comes. His invitation to the Jews has been to come to the warm, pleasant peace and safety of the gospel, but they have rejected His offer. As a result, He prophecies their fate, in verse 35, next.

35 Behold, **your house is left unto you desolate**: and verily I say unto you, Ye shall not see me, until the time come when ye shall say, Blessed is he that cometh in the name of the Lord.

JST Luke 13:36

36 Behold, your house is left unto you desolate. And verily I say unto you, Ye shall not **know** me, until **ye have received from the hand of the Lord a just recompense for all your sins**; until the time come when ye shall say, Blessed

is he that cometh in the name of the Lord.

LUKE 14

In this chapter we will see the Savior heal again on the Sabbath, which has infuriated the religious leaders of the Jews on many occasions before this. In this case, you will see Jesus directly confront the lawyers and Pharisees on the issue, asking them if it is permissible to heal on the Sabbath, before He heals the man. Their response to His question shows their extreme frustration and fear of public ridicule.

1 AND it came to pass, as **he** [*Jesus*] **went into the house of one of the chief Pharisees** [*a man very high up in religious leadership*] **to eat bread on the sabbath day**, that **they** [*the Jewish religious leaders who are trying desperately to find a way to get rid of Him*] **watched him.**

2 And, behold, there was a certain **man** before him [*in front of Him*] **which had the dropsy** [*probably edema accompanied by severe swelling*].

3 And **Jesus** answering [*responding*] **spake unto the lawyers and Pharisees**, saying, **Is it lawful** [*legal*] **to heal on the sabbath day?**

4 And **they held their peace** [*didn't reply*]. And **he** took him [*the man with dropsy*], and **healed him**, and let him go;

5 And answered them [*asked the lawyers and Pharisees*], saying, **Which of you shall have an ass or an ox fallen into a pit, and will not straightway** [*immediately*] **pull him out on the sabbath day?**

6 And **they could not answer him** again to these things [*they couldn't come up with a good answer*].

The Parable of the Chief Seats

7 And he put forth **a parable** to those which were bidden [*to the guests at the dinner*], when he marked [*noticed*] how they chose out the chief [*most prestigious*] rooms; saying unto them,

JST Luke 14:7

7 And he put forth a parable **unto them concerning those who were bidden to a wedding; for he knew how they chose out the chief rooms, and exalted themselves one above another; wherefore he spake unto them, saying,**

As you will see in the verses which follow, the Master is teaching a lesson in being humble.

8 When thou art bidden of [*invited by*] any man to a wedding, **sit not down in the highest room** [*the room reserved for the guests who were highest in authority in the community*]; **lest a more**

honourable man than thou [*one higher in authority than you*] be bidden of [*invited by*] him;

9 **And he that bade thee** [*the host*] and him [*the man higher in authority than you*] **come and say to thee, Give this man place** [*let this guest sit where you are sitting*]; and thou begin with shame [*with embarrassment*] to take the lowest room.

10 **But when thou art bidden** [*invited*], **go and sit down in the lowest room**; that when he that bade thee [*the host*] cometh, he may say unto thee, Friend, go up higher: then shalt thou have worship [*respect*] in the presence of them that sit at meat [*at dinner*] with thee.

The main point of the lesson is found in verse 11, next.

11 For **whosoever exalteth himself** [*pridefully presents himself to others as being important*] **shall be abased** [*put down, humbled*]; and he that humbleth himself shall **be exalted**.

The JST makes a subtle clarification to verse 12, next.

12 Then said he [*Jesus*] also **to him that bade him**, When thou makest a dinner or a supper, call not [*don't invite*] thy friends, nor thy brethren [*family members*], neither thy kinsmen [*relatives*], nor thy rich neighbours; lest they also bid thee again [*return the favor by inviting you to their place*], and a recompence be made thee [*you are thus repaid*].

JST Luke 14:12

12 Then said he also **concerning him who bade to the wedding,** When thou makest a dinner, or a supper, call not thy friends, nor thy brethren, neither thy kinsmen, nor rich neighbors; lest they also bid thee again, and a recompense be made thee.

Jesus is teaching here that true charity and generosity are demonstrated when you do kind things for others with no thought or chance for reward.

13 **But when thou makest a feast, call the poor, the maimed** [*crippled*], **the lame, the blind**:

14 **And thou shalt be blessed** [*by God*]; for **they cannot recompense thee** [*pay you back*]: for **thou shalt be recompensed at the resurrection of the just** [*your payment will be that you are resurrected with the righteous and enter celestial glory*].

15 And when one of them that sat at meat [*dinner*] with him heard these things, he [*Jesus*] said unto him, **Blessed is he that shall eat bread in the kingdom of God** [*lives worthy to be with God in heaven*].

This next parable given by the Master is known as the Parable of the Great Supper. The main point is that people who are indifferent to the invitation to participate in the Church and Kingdom of God will lose out and eventually suffer the consequences. The notes in brackets represent one possible interpretation. See Talmage, *Jesus the Christ*, pp. 450–452 for additional information. We understand that this parable was given in Perea (northeast of Jerusalem, and east of the Jordan River) in the winter of A.D. 33.

The Parable of the Great Supper

16 Then said he unto him, **A certain man** [*Heavenly Father*] **made a great supper** [*a great feast of gospel, covenants, etc., symbolic of the Father's plan*], **and bade** [*invited*] **many** [*the people of covenant Israel, including the Jews*]:

17 **And sent his servant** [*Jesus, the prophets, missionaries, etc.*] at supper time to say **to them that were bidden** [*invited*], **Come; for all things are now ready** [*the full gospel is here for you*].

Watch now as people in the parable make excuses for not coming to the feast of the gospel prepared for them.

18 And **they all** with one consent **began to make excuse.** The first said unto him, **I have bought a piece of ground**, and I must needs go and see it: I pray thee have me excused [*please excuse me*].

19 And another said, **I have bought five yoke of oxen**, and I go to prove them [*see how they perform*]: I pray thee have me excused.

20 And another said, **I have married a wife**, and therefore I cannot come.

21 **So that servant came, and shewed** [*showed*] **his lord these things** [*the excuses*]. **Then the master of the house** [*God*] being angry **said** to his servant, **Go out quickly into the streets and lanes of the city, and bring in hither the poor, and the maimed** [*crippled*], and **the halt** [*lame*], and **the blind** [*since the covenant people will not come, go into all the world and invite the Gentiles, who are looked upon by the covenant people as spiritually poor, maimed, halt and blind*].

22 And **the servant said, Lord, it is done** as thou hast commanded, and **yet there is room** [*we still have more room, symbolic of the fact that there is plenty of room in the celestial kingdom for everyone who wants to qualify to come*].

23 And **the lord** [*the Father*] **said unto the servant** [*Christ*], **Go out into the highways and hedges, and compel** [*urge, encourage*] **them to come in, that my house may be filled.**

The symbolism in the above verses is that the Savior, in His mercy, keeps trying to bring us to the feast of rich blessings prepared by the Father.

24 For I say unto you, That **none of those men which were bidden** [*invited*] **shall taste of my supper.** [*None of those of covenant Israel, who refuse to come unto Christ,*

LUKE 14

will partake of the "feast" of gospel blessings.]

By now, large crowds are following Jesus everywhere He goes. Next, He turns to them and explains that it can be difficult to truly follow Him by living His gospel, including when friends and family want nothing to do with it.

25 And there went **great multitudes** [*large crowds*] **with him: and he turned, and said unto them,**

26 **If any man come to me, and hate not his father, and mother, and wife, and children, and brethren, and sisters, yea, and his own life also, he cannot be my disciple** [*he cannot follow Me faithfully*].

JST Luke 14:26
26 If any man come to me, and hate not his father, and mother, and wife, and children, and brethren, and sisters, **or husband**, yea and his own life also; **or in other words, is afraid to lay down his life for my sake**, he cannot be my disciple.

27 And **whosoever doth not bear his cross, and come after me** [*whoever is not willing to sacrifice whatever is necessary to follow Me*], **cannot be my disciple.**

The JST adds a verse here, as follows:

JST Luke 14:28
28 **Wherefore, settle this in your hearts, that ye will do the**

things which I shall teach, and command you.

The whole point here is that if you are half-hearted about following the Savior, you will be unsuccessful.

Next, beginning with verse 28, the Master emphasizes again that one must plan and accept the cost in order to successfully follow Him.

28 For **which of you**, intending to build a tower, **sitteth not down first, and counteth the cost**, whether [*to see if*] he have sufficient [*enough money*] to finish it?

29 Lest haply, after he hath laid the foundation, and is not able to finish it, all that behold it begin to mock him,

JST Luke 14:30
30 Lest, **unhappily**, after he **has** laid the foundation and is not able to finish **his work**, all **who** behold, begin to mock him,

30 Saying, This man began to build, and was not able to finish.

JST Luke 14:31
31 Saying, This man began to build, and was not able to finish. **And this he said, signifying there should not any man follow him, unless he was able to continue; saying**,

31 **Or what king**, going to make war against another king, **sitteth not down first, and consulteth** [*looks the situation over*] whether

[*to see if*] he be able with ten thousand to meet him [*the enemy*] that cometh against him with twenty thousand?

32 Or else, while the other is yet a great way off, he sendeth an ambassage [*ambassador, negotiator*], and desireth conditions of peace.

33 **So likewise, whosoever he be of you that forsaketh not all that he hath** [*is not willing to sacrifice everything for the gospel*], **he cannot be my disciple.**

The JST adds the following after verse 33 and overlapping verse 34:

JST Luke 14:35–37
35 Then certain of them came to him, saying, Good Master, we have Moses and the prophets, and whosoever shall live by them, shall he not have life?

36 And Jesus answered, saying, Ye know not Moses, neither the prophets; for if ye had known them, ye would have believed on me; for to this intent they were written. For I am sent that ye might have life. Therefore I will liken it unto salt which is good;

37 But if the salt has lost its savor, wherewith shall it be seasoned?

34 Salt is good: but **if the salt have lost his savour, wherewith shall it be seasoned?**

35 **It is neither fit for the land, nor yet for the dunghill** [*the garbage dump*]; **but men cast it out. He that hath ears to hear, let him hear** [*if you are spiritually in tune, you will understand what I mean*].

JST Luke 14:38
38 It is neither fit for the land, nor yet for the dunghill; men cast it out. He **who** hath ears to hear, let him hear. **These things he said, signifying that which was written, verily must all be fulfilled**.

LUKE 15

In this chapter, you will see one of the best-known of the Savior's parables. It is the parable of the lost sheep, in which the shepherd leaves the ninety and nine to find the one that is lost.

1 **THEN drew near** unto him all the **publicans** [*tax collectors*] **and sinners** for to hear him.

2 And the **Pharisees and scribes murmured** [*grumbled*], saying, **This man receiveth** [*accepts*] **sinners, and eateth with them.**

The Pharisees and scribes were very strict about not associating with sinners, as a matter of religion. The following parable which the Savior gives is generally known as the Parable of the Lost Sheep. Joseph Smith tells us that it is directed to the Pharisees and scribes in verse 2 who are complaining that Jesus

LUKE 15

319

is associating with sinners. See *Teachings of the Prophet Joseph Smith*, p. 277.

The Parable of the Lost Sheep

3 And **he spake this parable unto them** [*the grumbling Pharisees and scribes in verse 2*], saying,

4 What man of you, having an **hundred sheep, if he lose one** of them, doth not **leave the ninety and nine** in the wilderness, and **go after that which is lost, until he find it?**

JST Luke 15:4

4 What man of you having **a** hundred sheep, if he lose one of them, doth not leave the ninety and nine, **and go into the wilderness after that which is lost**, until he find it?

5 And **when he hath found it**, he **layeth it on his shoulders, rejoicing.**

6 And when he cometh home, he **calleth together his friends and neighbours, saying unto them, Rejoice with me**; for I have found my sheep which was lost.

7 I say unto you, that **likewise joy shall be in heaven over one sinner that repenteth, more than over ninety and nine just persons, which need no repentance** [*who claim to need no repentance, like the Pharisees and scribes in verse 2, above*].

This parable can remind us of the quote from the Doctrine and Covenants dealing with the worth of souls. We will quote two verses:

D&C 18:10 and 15

10 Remember the worth of souls is great in the sight of God;

15 And if it so be that you should labor all your days in crying repentance unto this people, and bring, save it be one soul unto me, how great shall be your joy with him in the kingdom of my Father!

Reading verse 7 of Luke chapter 15, above, could make a person feel bad that a repentant sinner causes more joy in heaven than a righteous one. One could almost be tempted to commit an occasional sin so as to bring more joy to heaven when he or she repents. But wait! That is not at all what verse 7 is saying. Using the Prophet Joseph Smith's explanation that the ninety nine "just persons" represent the Sadducees and Pharisees "that are so righteous; they will be damned anyhow" (*Teachings of the Prophet Joseph Smith*, p. 277–78). We can then understand verse 7 as follows: "There is more joy in heaven over one humble sinner who repents, than over ninety nine self-righteous hypocrites like you Pharisees and Sadducees who claim to be just men who need no repentance!" This verse, then, is actually a scathing rebuke of these evil religious leaders of the Jews, whom the Savior called "whited sepulchres" (Matthew 23:27); in other words, whitewashed coffins which look clean on the outside, but inside are full of rot and filth.

This next parable is usually referred to as the Parable of the Lost Coin. Again, it is in response to the criticism of the Pharisees and scribes in verse 2, and reminds us that it is worth whatever effort is necessary to save one lost soul.

The Parable of the Lost Coin

8 Either [*here is another example:*] what woman having **ten pieces of silver** [*equal to ten days' wages for a workman—see Luke 15, footnote 8a in your Bible*] if she **lose one** piece, doth not light a candle, and sweep the house, and seek diligently till she **find it?**

9 And when she hath found it, she calleth her friends and her neighbours together, saying, **Rejoice** with me; for I have found the piece which I had lost.

10 Likewise, I say unto you, **there is joy in the presence of the angels of God over one sinner that repenteth.**

The Parable of the Prodigal Son

We will suggest some possible symbolism in this parable. No doubt you will be able to come up with other symbolism which would also fit in terms of gospel applications in our lives.

11 And he said, **A certain man** [*symbolic of God*] had **two sons** [*symbolic of different types of people*]:

12 And **the younger** of them said to his father, **Father, give me the portion of goods that falleth to me** [*give me my inheritance now, instead of waiting until you die; symbolism: I am not interested in future exaltation, but rather want to enjoy the ways of the world now*]. And **he** [*the father*] **divided unto them his living** [*divided up his property between his two sons; symbolism: our Father in Heaven respects our agency*].

13 And not many days after the **younger son gathered all together** [*put all his financial resources together*], **and took his journey into a far country** [*symbolism: he fell away from the Church and participated in the ways of the world*], and there **wasted his substance** [*financial resources; symbolism: his gospel heritage*] with **riotous** [*wild*] **living** [*symbolism: he wasted his potential for joy and happiness in the gospel for temporary worldly, sinful pleasures*].

14 And when **he** had **spent all** [*symbolism: when he was wasted away by his wicked lifestyle*], there arose a mighty **famine** in that land [*symbolism: Satan left him with no support, as taught in Alma 30:60*]; and he **began to be in want** [*in need, poverty, desperation*].

15 And he went and joined himself to [*got a job with*] a citizen of

LUKE 15

that country [*symbolism: he didn't yet turn to God for help*]; and he sent him into his fields to **feed swine.** [*Feeding pigs was about the lowest, most humiliating job a person from Jewish culture could have; symbolism: he was totally humbled.*]

16 And he **would fain have filled his belly with the husks that the swine did eat** [*he got so hungry that even the carob tree pods he was feeding the pigs started to look good to him*]: and **no man gave unto him** [*no one gave him anything to help him in his poverty; symbolism: there was no worldly source of effective help for him*].

17 And when **he came to himself** [*came to his senses; symbolism: he started repenting*], he said, How many hired servants of my father's have bread enough and to spare, and I perish with hunger [*I am starving*]!

18 **I will arise and go to my father,** and will say unto him, Father, I have sinned against heaven, and before thee [*I have been wicked; symbolic of sincere confession*],

19 And am **no more worthy to be called thy son** [*symbolism: I am not worthy of exaltation*]: **make me as** [*let me be*] **one of thy hired servants** [*symbolism: let me go into one of the other degrees of glory*].

20 And **he** arose, and **came to his father.** But when he was yet a great way off [*still a long distance off*], **his father saw him**

[*had been watching for him*], and **had compassion, and ran, and fell on his neck** [*hugged him*], **and kissed him** [*symbolism: the Father is merciful and kind and is anxious to "run" to us to help us return to Him*].

21 And **the son said unto him,** Father, I have sinned against heaven, and in thy sight, and am no more worthy to be called thy son [*symbolism: the son, thoroughly humbled by his wickedness, acknowledges his unworthiness to live with the Father in celestial exaltation*].

22 **But the father said** to his servants, Bring forth the **best robe,** and put it on him; and put a **ring** on his hand, and **shoes** on his feet:

23 And bring hither the **fatted calf,** and kill it; and **let us eat, and be merry** [*symbolic of joy and rejoicing on earth and in heaven when a sinner repents and returns*]:

24 For this **my son was dead** [*symbolic of being spiritually dead*], **and is alive again** [*symbolic of rebirth, through the Atonement*]; **he was lost, and is found.** And they began to be merry [*to celebrate*].

A question sometimes arises among members of the Church as to whether or not the returning prodigal son could ever repent sufficiently to gain exaltation, especially in view of his intentional wickedness. There is much symbolism in verse 22, above, which can help answer that question:

The "robe" is symbolic of royalty and status. It is also symbolic of acceptance by God, as in 2 Nephi 4:33 where Nephi says "O Lord, wilt thou encircle me around in the robe of thy righteousness! O Lord, wilt thou make a way for mine escape before mine enemies!" See also Isaiah 61:10. In Revelation 7:9, white robes are given to those who live in the presence of God (celestial glory). The "best robe" would be symbolic of potential for highest status, in other words, exaltation.

The "ring" is symbolic of authority to rule. Example: a signet ring which a king would use to stamp official documents and make them legal and binding.

"Shoes on his feet": Shoes were very expensive in the days of the Savior's ministry and were only worn by the wealthy and the rulers. Thus, shoes would be symbolic of wealth, power, and authority to rule.

Summary: The cultural symbolism in this verse would lead us to believe that the father was not only welcoming his wayward son back with open arms, but also that he was inviting him to repent and reestablish himself as a ruler in his household, symbolic of potential for exaltation. President David O McKay, in April Conference, 1956, speaking of the prodigal son, said, "The Spirit of forgiveness will be operative" when the prodigal son comes to himself and repents.

Elder Richard G. Scott, in October Conference 2002, speaking of Alma the Younger and the four sons of Mosiah, who he said "were tragically wicked," said that there are no "second-class" citizens after true repentance. Said he, "If you have repented from serious transgression and mistakenly believe that you will always be a second-class citizen in the kingdom of God, learn that is not true."

Thus, the prodigal son does not have to remain a "second-class citizen" in the Father's kingdom. However, the older brother may have to change his attitude if he plans to retain his status in the Father's kingdom.

25 Now **his elder son** [*symbolic of a member who has been active all his life*] was in the field: and as he came and drew nigh [*near*] to the house, he heard musick and dancing.

26 And he called one of the servants, and **asked what these things meant** [*what is going on?*].

27 And he said unto him, **Thy brother is come; and thy father hath killed the fatted calf,** because he hath received him safe and sound.

28 And **he was angry, and would not go in**: [*This is hardly appropriate behavior for one who is supposed to be a faithful son.*] therefore came his father out, and intreated [*pleaded with*] him.

29 And **he answering said to his father**, Lo [*now see here!*], **these many years do I serve thee, neither transgressed I at any time thy commandment: and yet thou never gavest me a kid, that I might make merry with my friends**: [*you never killed even so much as a young goat for me to have a party with my friends!*]

30 **But as soon as this thy son** [*implies "thy son," not my brother anymore*] **was come** [*came home*], **which hath devoured thy living with harlots** [*wasted his inheritance with prostitutes*], **thou hast killed for him the fatted calf.**

31 And **he said unto him, Son, thou art ever with me, and all that I have is thine.** [*This presupposes that the older son rethinks his attitude about his returning younger brother, repents, and helps him get reestablished in his father's household. Otherwise, anyone who has his attitude about someone who repents successfully would, of course, not make it to celestial glory.*]

32 **It was meet** [*needful, good*] **that we should make merry** [*celebrate*], **and be glad: for this thy brother** [*emphasizing that he is "your brother," not just "my son"*] **was dead** [*spiritually*], **and is alive again** [*has repented, is a new person*]; **and was lost, and is found.**

LUKE 16

The Savior continues teaching in parables. This next parable is known as the Parable of the Unjust Steward. This parable probably shouldn't be scrutinized for lots of details or various specific applications in our daily lives, but rather is probably best seen as a general message that people often are more resourceful in dealing with worldly situations than they are in working out their salvation. If we strain at finding detailed applications, we will probably come up with some that don't fit or that don't teach correct doctrine and lessons.

At this point in Luke, the Savior is in Perea (east of the Jordan River and north of Jerusalem), and it is now the winter of A.D. 33. The Savior will be crucified and resurrected in the spring (A.D. 34).

The Parable of the Unjust Steward

1 AND he said also unto his disciples, There was **a certain rich man**, which **had a steward** [*a man in charge of all his business dealings*]; and **the same was accused** unto him [*someone complained to the rich man*] **that he** [*the steward*] **had wasted his goods** [*was mismanaging the business*].

2 And **he called him, and said unto him, How is it that I hear this of thee** [*what's this I hear about you*]? **give an account of thy stewardship** [*give me a report on how the business is doing*]; for thou

mayest be no longer steward [*I am going to fire you*].

3 Then **the steward said within himself, What shall I do?** for my lord taketh away from me the stewardship: I cannot dig [*I can't do manual labor*]; to beg I am ashamed [*I would be embarrassed to be a beggar*].

4 **I am resolved what to do**, that, when I am put out of the stewardship, they may receive me into their houses [*I have a plan, so that, after I am fired, I will have friends who will take care of me*].

5 **So he called every one of his lord's debtors** [*people who owed the owner money*] unto him, and **said unto the first**, How much owest thou unto my lord?

6 And he said, An hundred measures of oil. And he said unto him, Take thy bill, and sit down quickly, and write fifty [*if you pay now, I will settle for half of what you owe*].

7 Then **said he to another**, And how much owest thou? And he said, An hundred measures of wheat. And he said unto him, Take thy bill, and write fourscore [*eighty*].

8 And **the lord commended** [*congratulated*] **the unjust steward, because he had done wisely: for the children of this world are in their generation wiser than the children of light** [*often, people in business worry more about their future security on earth than members of the Church worry about their future security in heaven; see* Jesus the Christ, *p. 463*].

9 And I say unto you, **Make to yourselves friends of the mammon of unrighteousness**; that, when ye fail [*when your life is over*], they may receive you into everlasting habitations.

Elder Talmage (see reference above in verse 8) suggests that verse 9 basically means that we should make "friends" in heaven by using money wisely and honestly, so that you can enter heaven. Money is often used dishonestly by others, and is thus referred to as "the mammon of unrighteousness."

10 **He that is faithful in that which is least** [*in small responsibilities*] **is faithful also in much: and he that is unjust** [*dishonest*] **in the least is unjust also in much.**

11 **If therefore ye have not been faithful in the unrighteous mammon** [*if you are not honest in your dealings with people*], **who will commit to your trust the true riches** [*how can you be trusted with the true riches of eternity, the gospel, covenants, etc.*]?

12 And **if ye have not been faithful in that which is another man's** [*in the daily world of business*], **who shall give you that which is your own** [*how do you expect to earn a place in heaven*]?

No One Can Serve Two Masters

13 **No servant can serve two masters**: for either he will hate the one, and love the other; or else he will hold to the one, and despise the other. **Ye cannot serve God and mammon** [*you cannot be righteous and worldly at the same time*].

Next, Luke records the Master's response as the Pharisees make fun of Him in public for the things He taught in the verses above.

14 And **the Pharisees** also, **who were covetous** [*greedy*], **heard all these things**: and they **derided** [*mocked*] **him**.

15 And **he said unto them, Ye are they which justify yourselves before men** [*make yourselves look righteous in public*]; **but God knoweth your hearts**: for **that which is highly esteemed among men is abomination in the sight of God** [*even though people respect you and think you are righteous, God knows that you are full of evil and wickedness*].

16 **The law and the prophets** [*the "law" means Genesis, Exodus, Leviticus, Numbers, and Deuteronomy (all written by Moses) and "the prophets" refers to the writings of prophets such as Isaiah, Jeremiah, Daniel, and so forth in the Old Testament at the time of Christ*] **were until John** [*were valid until John the Baptist came and started preaching*]: since that time the kingdom of God [*the full gospel of Jesus Christ, the gospel of salvation and exaltation*] is preached, and every man presseth [*strives to get*] into it.

17 And **it is easier for heaven and earth to pass, than one tittle of the law to fail.**

Verses 16 and 17, above, are very fragmentary. Much was left out of the Bible here. The JST adds the following:

JST Luke 16:16–23

16 And they said unto him, We have the law, and the prophets [*we have our scriptures*]; **but as for this man** [*Jesus*] **we will not receive him to be our ruler; for he maketh himself to be a judge over us**.

17 Then said Jesus unto them, The law and the prophets testify of me; yea, and all the prophets who have written, even until John [*up to and including John the Baptist*], **have foretold of these days**.

18 Since that time, the kingdom of God is preached, **and every man who seeketh truth** presseth [*seeks to get*] into it.

19 And it is easier for heaven and earth to pass, than **for** one tittle [*tiny bit*] of the law [*the words of God in the Old Testament*] to fail [*not be fulfilled*].

20 And why teach ye the law [*the Old Testament*], **and deny that which is written** [*that* *which is prophesied about Me; see verse 17]*; **and condemn him [*Jesus*] whom the Father hath sent to fulfill the law [*to fulfill the prophecies about Him given in the Old Testament*], that ye might all be redeemed?**

21 O fools! for you have said in your hearts, There is no God [*you secretly believe that there is no God*]. **And you pervert** [*pollute*] **the right way; and the kingdom of heaven suffereth violence of you** [*the kingdom of God is badly damaged by you*]; **and you persecute the meek; and in your violence you seek to destroy the kingdom; and ye take the children of the kingdom** [*righteous Saints*] **by force** [*you use force to stop righteous people from living their religion*]. **Woe unto you** [*you are in deep trouble!*], **ye adulterers!**

22 And they reviled [*angrily responded to*] **him again, being angry for the saying** [*what Jesus had just said*], **that they were adulterers.**

23 But he continued, saying, Whosoever putteth away his wife, and marrieth another, committeth adultery; and whosoever marrieth her **who** is put away from her husband, committeth adultery. **Verily I say unto you, I will liken you unto the rich man**.

We will now continue with the Bible version as it stands, paying close attention to verse 18 and noting some JST additions to it, given in JST, verse 18, above.

18 **Whosoever putteth away his wife, and marrieth another, committeth adultery: and whosoever marrieth her that is put away from her husband committeth adultery.**

The JST additions in JST verses 17–23, above, provide very important background for verse 18. When taken alone, as it stands in Luke 16:18, and applied to everyone, it becomes a real problem. It would then mean that anyone who is divorced and remarries is guilty of adultery. Divorce is a very serious problem today and in most cases is not justified. Yet, when things are in proper order in the lives of divorcees, and the individuals involved are worthy, the Lord through our prophets today allows people who have been divorced to remarry and be sealed in a temple. Certainly this would not be the case if the very ordinance, of marrying, immediately made them adulterers. The JST verses quoted above show us that Jesus was addressing the hypocritical Pharisees, who verbally attacked him in verse 14. Thus, we understand that, among other evil practices, the Pharisees were secretly involved in marrying and divorcing to make their sexual conquests seem legal. The Savior said they were adulterers and strongly condemned them for this evil at the end of JST Luke 12:21, which unfortunately was left out of the Bible.

Lazarus and the Rich Man

19 There was **a certain rich man** [*remember that the Savior is comparing the Pharisees with this rich man; see JST addition to verse 18, above*], which was clothed in purple and fine linen, and fared sumptuously [*lived in luxury*] every day:

20 And there was **a certain beggar** named **Lazarus**, which [*who*] was laid at his gate, full of [*covered with*] sores,

21 And **desiring to be fed with the crumbs which fell from the rich man's table**: moreover the dogs came and licked his sores. [*Symbolizing that dogs take better care of beggars and people in need than the Pharisees do.*]

22 And it came to pass, that **the beggar died**, and **was carried by the angels into Abraham's bosom** [*was taken to paradise*]: **the rich man also died**, and was buried;

23 And **in hell he lift up his eyes, being in torments**, and **seeth Abraham afar off, and Lazarus in his bosom** [*with Abraham in paradise*].

24 And **he cried** and said, Father Abraham, have mercy on me, and **send Lazarus**, that he may dip the tip of his finger in water, and cool my tongue; for I am tormented in this flame [*it is miserable here in hell*].

25 **But Abraham said,** Son, remember that thou in thy lifetime receivedst thy good things, and

likewise Lazarus evil things: but now he is comforted, and thou art tormented.

26 And **beside all this, between us and you there is a great gulf fixed**: so that they which would pass from hence to you cannot; neither can they pass to us, that would come from thence.

This "gulf" or barrier between spirit prison and paradise was bridged by the Savior during the time that His body lay in the tomb and His spirit visited the righteous in paradise. There, in paradise, He set up and organized missionary work and authorized the righteous spirits in paradise to go to spirit prison and teach the gospel there. See D&C, Section 138, 1 Peter 3:18 and 4:6.

27 **Then he said,** I pray thee therefore, father [*Abraham*], that thou wouldest **send him to my father's house** [*to warn them about what has happened to me*]:

28 For **I have five brethren** [*brothers*]; **that he** [*Lazarus*] **may testify unto them, lest they also come into this place of torment** [*hell, spirit prison*].

29 **Abraham saith** unto him, **They have Moses and the prophets; let them hear them.** [*They have already been given that message through the writings of the prophets in the scriptures.*]

30 And **he said, Nay, father Abraham** [*they don't pay much attention*

to the scriptures]: **but if one went unto them from the dead, they will repent.** [*That would scare them enough to repent.*]

31 And **he said** unto him, **If they hear not** [*pay no attention to*] **Moses and the prophets, neither will they be persuaded** [*converted*], **though one rose from the dead** [*even if one came back from the dead to them*].

LUKE 17

In this chapter you will see the Savior begin His final journey to Jerusalem from Perea (starting with verse 11), traveling into Galilee and Samaria as He goes. He will heal ten lepers (probably in Samaria) and will teach about His Second Coming.

In verses 1–10, as the chapter begins, Luke records the Master's teachings concerning things that cause people to commit sin, and then tells us of His teachings about forgiveness and faith.

1 **THEN said he unto the disciples, It is impossible but** [*unavoidable, inevitable*] **that offences will come** [*things will come along that cause people to sin*]: **but woe unto him, through whom they come!**

2 It were **better for him that a millstone were hanged about his neck, and he cast into the sea, than that he should offend** [*cause to commit sin; cause to stumble*

in the gospel; see Matthew 17:6, footnote a] **one of these little ones** [*children or righteous adult members who are childlike in their faith*].

3 Take heed to yourselves [*be careful*]: If thy brother trespass [*sins*] against thee, rebuke [*tell*] him; and if he repent, **forgive him.**

4 And if he trespass against thee seven times in a day, and seven times in a day turn again to thee, saying, I repent; thou shalt **forgive him.** [*Be forgiving.*]

5 And **the apostles said unto the Lord, Increase our faith.**

> Verses 6–10, next, seem to be instruction from the Lord on strengthening our faith. First He tells them the power of faith. Then He explains that they must avoid thinking that God owes them because they keep the commandments (see Mosiah 2:22–24). This counsel appears to be designed to keep them humble to enable them to better exercise faith.

6 And the Lord said, **If ye had faith as a grain of mustard seed,** ye might say unto this sycamine tree [*mulberry tree*], Be thou plucked up by the root, and be thou planted in the sea; and it should obey you.

7 But **which of you, having a servant** plowing or feeding cattle, will **say unto him** by and by [*immediately; see Luke 17:7, footnote b*], when he is come from the field,

LUKE 17

Go and sit down to meat [*sit down and eat your dinner*]?

8 And will not **rather** [*instead*] **say** unto him, **Make ready wherewith I may sup** [*prepare my dinner*], and gird thyself [*clean up*], and **serve me, till I have eaten and drunken; and afterward thou shalt eat and drink?**

9 **Doth he thank that servant** because he did the things that were commanded him? **I trow** [*think*] **not.**

10 So likewise ye, when ye shall have done all those things which are commanded you, say, **We are unprofitable servants**: we have done that which was our duty to do.

11 And it came to pass, **as he went to Jerusalem, that he passed through the midst of Samaria and Galilee.**

Healing of Ten Lepers

12 And as he entered into a certain village, there met him **ten** men that were **lepers** [*had leprosy*], which stood afar off [*by law they were not allowed to be near people who did not have leprosy*]:

13 And they lifted up their voices [*spoke loudly*], and **said, Jesus, Master, have mercy on us.**

14 And when he saw them, he said unto them, Go shew yourselves unto the priests [*as required by the Law of Moses; see Leviticus 14:2*]. And it came to pass, that, as they went, **they were cleansed** [*healed*].

15 And **one of them,** when he saw that he was healed, **turned back,** and with a loud voice glorified [*praised*] God,

16 And **fell down on his face** at his feet [*humbly laid down at Jesus' feet—a sign of deep humility in Jewish culture*], **giving him thanks: and he was a Samaritan.**

Samaritans were despised by Jews and Jews were despised by Samaritans (inhabitants of Samaria). Originally, about 700 years before Christ, the ancestors of the Samaritans were members of the tribes of Israel, especially Ephraim. When the Assyrians conquered the ten tribes and took them away into captivity, about 722 B.C., Israelites who were permitted to remain ended up intermarrying with the occupational armies. This led to their being shunned by the Jews and developed into the long-standing ethnic dislike and hatred prevalent at the time of Christ's mortal ministry.

17 And **Jesus** answering **said, Were there not ten cleansed** [*healed*]? but **where are the nine?**

18 **There are not found that returned to give glory to God, save this stranger** [*foreigner, non Israelite; this may imply that the other nine lepers were Jews*].

19 And he said unto him, Arise, go thy way: **thy faith hath made thee whole.**

Instruction Regarding the Second Coming

20 And when **he was demanded of** [*by*] **the Pharisees, when the kingdom of God should come** [*when the Second Coming will be*], **he answered them** and said, The kingdom of God cometh not with observation [*perhaps meaning you can't tell exactly when it will be through careful calculations and watching of the signs of the times*]:

21 **Neither shall they say, Lo here! or, lo there!** for, behold, the kingdom of God is within you.

JST Luke 17:21
21 Neither shall they say, Lo, here! or, **Lo**, there! For, behold, **the kingdom of God has already come unto you** [*has already been restored among you by the Savior's mortal mission*].

22 And **he said unto the disciples, The days will come, when ye shall desire to see one of the days of the Son of man** [*Jesus*]**, and ye shall not see it.** [*Perhaps meaning that there will be days when the disciples will long for a day with the Savior, or perhaps meaning that they will long for His Second Coming.*]

23 And **they** [*people*] **shall say** to you, **See here** [*Christ is here*]**; or, see there** [*Christ is there*]**: go not after them**, nor follow them [*don't believe them*].

24 For **as the lightning, that lighteneth out of the one part under heaven, shineth unto the other part under heaven; so shall also the Son of man be in his day** [*at the Second Coming*]. [*In other words, when the Savior comes again, it won't be a low-key event, with His appearing to a small group here or a little group there. Rather, when He comes, everyone will see Him at once, just like everyone, from horizon to horizon, sees a large lightning strike.*]

25 **But first** [*before His Second Coming*] **must he suffer many things, and be rejected of this generation** [*he must suffer, be rejected and crucified*].

26 And **as it was in the days of Noe** [*Noah*]**, so shall it be also in the days of the Son of man** [*at the time of the Second Coming*]. [*At the time of the Second Coming, people will be ignoring the gospel just like they did in the days of Noah.*]

27 **They did eat**, they **drank**, they **married** wives, they were given in marriage, **until the day that Noe** [*Noah*] **entered into the ark, and the flood came, and destroyed them all.**

28 **Likewise also as it was in the days of Lot** [*Abraham's nephew, who chose to live in Sodom; see Genesis 19:1*]; they did eat, they drank, they bought, they sold, they planted, they builded;

29 **But the same day that Lot went out of Sodom it rained fire and brimstone from heaven, and destroyed them all.** [*All the wicked in Sodom and Gomorrah*

LUKE 17

331

were destroyed (Genesis 19:24), just like the wicked will be at the Second Coming.]

30 Even **thus shall it be in the day when the Son of man is revealed** [*at the Second Coming*].

Next, in verse 31, we are taught that when the actual Second Coming arrives, it will be too late to make any additional preparations for it.

31 **In that day, he which shall be upon the housetop, and his stuff in the house, let him not come down to take it away**: and he that is in the field, let him likewise not return back.

32 **Remember Lot's wife** [*who looked back, in disobedience to very simple instructions from God; see Genesis 19:17 and 26*].

33 **Whosoever shall seek to save his life** [*by making his own rules*] **shall lose it** [*will lose salvation*]; and **whosoever shall lose his life** [*sacrifices whatever is necessary to follow God's laws*] **shall preserve it** [*will gain salvation*].

34 I tell you, in that night [*when the Savior actually comes*] there shall be **two men** in one bed; the **one shall be taken** [*taken up to meet Him; see D&C 88:96*], **and the other shall be left** [*to be burned*].

35 **Two women** shall be grinding together; the **one shall be taken**, and **the other left.**

36 **Two men** shall be in the field;

the **one shall be taken**, and **the other left.**

37 **And they answered** [*responded*] and said unto him, **Where, Lord?** And he said unto them, **Wheresoever the body is, thither will the eagles be gathered together.**

The JST clarifies the verses above. We will quote, beginning with JST verse 36, which offers clarification for verse 37, above. JST verses 38–40 are verses that were completely left out of the Bible.

JST Luke 17:36–40

36 And they answered and said unto him, **Where, Lord, shall they be taken?**

37 And he said unto them, Wheresoever the body **is gathered; or, in other words, whithersoever the Saints are gathered,** thither [*to that place*] will the eagles [*the Saints—see verse 38, next*] be gathered together; **or, thither will the remainder be gathered together.**

38 **This he spake, signifying the gathering of his saints; and of angels descending and gathering the remainder unto them; the one from the bed, the other from the grinding, and the other from the field, whithersoever he listeth** [*chooses*].

39 **For verily there shall be new heavens, and a new earth, wherein dwelleth righteousness** [*the Millennium*].

40 **And there shall be no unclean**

thing [*remaining on earth*]; **for the earth becoming old, even as a garment, having waxed in corruption** [*grown in wickedness*], **wherefore it** [*the wickedness*] **vanisheth away, and the footstool** [*earth*] **remaineth sanctified** [*made holy*], **cleansed from all sin** [*prepared for the Millennium*].

LUKE 18

This next parable is usually known as the Parable of the Unjust Judge. The main point as given in verse 1 seems to be that some situations in life require that we continue to pray for desired blessings over a long period of time, and we shouldn't give up.

The Parable of the Unjust Judge

1 AND he spake **a parable** unto them to this end [*with this purpose in mind*], that **men ought always to pray, and not to faint** [*give up*];

2 Saying, There was in a city **a judge**, which feared not God, neither regarded man:

3 And there was **a widow** in that city; and she came unto him, **saying, Avenge me of mine adversary** [*I have been wronged; please render judgment against my enemy*].

4 And **he would not for a while**: but afterward he said within himself, Though I fear not God, nor

regard man [*even though I'm not afraid of God or man*];

5 Yet **because this widow troubleth me** [*keeps asking me for help*], **I will avenge her** [*grant her request*], lest [*for fear that*] by her continual coming she weary me.

6 And **the Lord** [*Jesus*] **said** [*explained*], Hear [*pay attention to*] what the unjust judge saith.

7 And **shall not God avenge his own elect** [*will God not answer the prayers of His Saints for justice*], **which cry** [*pray*] **day and night unto him, though he bear long with them** [*even if it takes a long time before He grants their request*]?

8 I tell you that **he will avenge them speedily.** Nevertheless when the Son of man [*Jesus*] cometh, shall he find faith on the earth?

JST Luke 18:8

8 I tell you that **he will come, and when he does come,** he will avenge **his saints** speedily. Nevertheless, when the Son of man cometh, shall he find faith on the earth?

This next parable is known as the Parable of the Pharisee and the Publican. Remember that the Pharisees claim to be important religious leaders of the Jews, live in luxury, are secretly wicked and love to look righteous to others. On the other hand, the publicans are tax collectors and are despised by the Pharisees. This parable warns us against

The Parable of the Pharisee and the Publican

9 And he spake this **parable** unto **certain which trusted in themselves that they were righteous, and despised others**:

You will find the main point of this parable given in verse 14.

10 **Two men went up into the temple to pray**; the one **a Pharisee**, and the other **a publican**.

11 **The Pharisee** stood and **prayed thus** with himself [*like this, bragging about himself to God*], God, I thank thee, that I am not as other men are, extortioners [*thieves*], unjust [*unrighteous*], adulterers, or even as this publican [*this tax collector*].

12 I fast twice in the week, I give tithes of all that I possess [*I pay tithing on all I have*].

13 And **the publican**, standing afar off, would not lift up so much as his eyes unto heaven, but smote upon his breast [*a cultural sign of deep sorrow*], saying, **God be merciful to me a sinner**.

14 I tell you, **this man** [*the publican*] went down to his house **justified** [*in harmony with God*] **rather than the other** [*the Pharisee*]: for **every one that exalteth himself** [*is lifted up in pride*] **shall be abased** [*brought down, humbled*]; and **he that humbleth himself shall be exalted**.

"Suffer Little Children to Come Unto Me"

15 And **they** [*the people*] **brought unto him** also **infants**, that he would touch them: **but** when **his disciples** saw it, they **rebuked them** [*scolded those people*].

16 **But Jesus called them** [*his disciples*] **unto him, and said, Suffer** [*allow*] **little children to come unto me, and forbid them not: for of such is the kingdom of God**.

17 Verily I say unto you, **Whosoever shall not receive the kingdom of God as a little child shall in no wise** [*shall not*] **enter therein**.

18 And **a certain ruler asked him**, saying, Good Master, **what shall I do to inherit eternal life?**

19 And **Jesus said unto him, Why callest thou me good?** none is good, save [*except*] one, that is, God.

There is no agreement among scholars as to the reason Jesus scolded the ruler for calling Him "good." Perhaps there was a root word for "good" that, among the Jews, was reserved only for the Father. We will have to leave this alone until we are taught more.

20 **Thou knowest the commandments**, Do not commit adultery, Do not kill, Do not steal, Do not bear false witness, Honour thy father and thy mother.

21 And **he said, All these have I kept from my youth up.**

22 Now when **Jesus** heard these things, he **said** unto him, **Yet lackest thou one thing** [*there is one thing missing in your life*]: **sell all that thou hast, and distribute unto the poor, and thou shalt have treasure in heaven: and come, follow me.**

23 And **when he heard this, he was very sorrowful: for he was very rich.**

24 And when Jesus saw that he was very sorrowful, he said, **How hardly shall they that have riches enter into the kingdom of God** [*how hard it is for the rich to enter heaven*]!

Camel and an Eye of a Needle

25 For **it is easier for a camel to go through a needle's eye, than for a rich man to enter into the kingdom of God.**

There is a rumor circulating that the "eye of a needle" was a small gate in the walls of Jerusalem, used for entry into the city by night, after the main gates were closed. The rumor states that it was very difficult for a camel to get down and scrunch through the gate. Scholars indicate that this rumor has no truth to it. They indicate that the word "needle," as used in verse 25, refers to an ordinary sewing needle in the original Bible languages. Thus, the message is that it is

impossible for those who value wealth above all else to enter heaven—see JST version after verses 26–27, next.

26 And they that heard it said, **Who then can be saved?**

27 And he said, **The things which are impossible with men are possible with God.**

JST Luke 18:27
27 And he said **unto them, It is impossible for them who trust in riches, to enter into the kingdom of God; but he who forsaketh the things which are of this world, it is possible with God, that he should enter in.**

Next, you will see Peter catch the significance of what Jesus has just said and ask if he and his fellow Apostles will make it to heaven, since they left everything in order to follow Him.

28 Then **Peter said,** Lo, **we have left all, and followed thee.** [*This implies, "We have forsaken all to follow you, so, are we going to get into heaven?"*]

29 **And he said** unto them, Verily I say unto you, **There is no man that hath left house, or parents, or brethren, or wife, or children, for the kingdom of God's sake,**

30 **Who shall not receive manifold** [*much*] **more in this present time, and in the world to come life everlasting** [*exaltation*].

Jesus Prophecies His Death and Resurrection

31 Then he took unto him the twelve, and said unto them, Behold, **we go up to Jerusalem, and all things that are written by the prophets concerning the Son of man** [*Christ*] **shall be accomplished.**

32 For he shall be delivered unto [*turned over to*] **the Gentiles** [*the Romans*], **and shall be mocked, and spitefully entreated** [*insulted*], **and spitted on**:

33 And they shall scourge [*whip, flog*] **him, and put him to death: and the third day he shall rise again** [*shall be resurrected*].

34 And they understood none of these things: and this saying was hid from them, neither knew they the things which were spoken.

JST Luke 18:34

34 And they understood none of these things; and this saying was hid from them; neither **remembered** they the things which were spoken.

A Blind Man Is Healed

35 And it came to pass, that as he was come nigh [*near*] unto Jericho, a certain **blind man** sat by the way side [*side of the road*] begging:

36 And hearing the multitude pass by, he asked what it meant [*what was happening*].

37 And they told him, that **Jesus of Nazareth passeth by.**

38 And he cried, saying, **Jesus**, thou Son of David [*thou descendant of King David, in other words, "thou Promised Messiah"*], **have mercy on me.**

39 And **they** which went before [*ahead of Jesus*] **rebuked** [*scolded*] **him**, that **he should hold his peace** [*told him to keep quiet*]: **but he cried so much the more** [*even louder*], **Thou Son of David, have mercy on me.**

40 And **Jesus stood** [*stopped*], **and commanded him to be brought unto him**: and when he was come near, he asked him,

41 Saying, **What wilt thou that I shall do unto thee?** And he said, **Lord, that I may receive my sight.**

42 And Jesus said unto him, **Receive thy sight: thy faith hath saved thee.**

43 And **immediately he received his sight, and followed him**, glorifying [*praising, thanking*] God: and all the people, when they saw it, gave praise unto God.

LUKE 19

As we begin this chapter, Jesus is on His way to Jerusalem for the last time and will be crucified in about ten days. We meet a delightful little man (small in physical size) named Zacchaeus who is despised by all (in fact he would have been excommunicated from the Jewish church because he worked for the Romans as a tax collector) but who is deeply good. Watch how the Master honors him.

1 AND **Jesus** entered and **passed through Jericho.**

2 And, behold, there was a man named **Zacchæus,** which was the chief among the publicans [*the chief of the tax collectors*], **and he was rich.**

3 And he **sought to see Jesus** who he was [*tried to get where he could get a view of Jesus*]; and **could not** for the press [*because of the crowd*], **because he was little of stature** [*he was a little, short man*].

4 And **he** ran before [*so he ran ahead*], and **climbed** up into **a sycomore tree to see him:** for he [*Jesus*] was to pass that way.

5 And when **Jesus** came to the place, he **looked up, and saw him,** and **said unto him, Zacchæus,** make haste [*hurry*], and **come down; for to day I must abide** [*stay*] **at thy house.**

This is a rather tender scene. As mentioned in the note at the beginning of this chapter, the people hated tax collectors, considering them to be sinners, and Zacchaeus was the head tax collector. Jesus says, "I must stay at your house," implying that He himself, the Creator of heaven and earth, had a very strong desire to stay with this humble man and reassure him

of his worth to God. "I must stay at your house" can also convey the message that this action on the part of the Redeemer was essential for the well-being of Zacchaeus.

6 **And he made haste, and came down** [*out of the tree*], and **received him** [*Christ*] **joyfully.**

7 And when they saw it, **they all murmured** [*criticized*], saying, **That he was gone to be guest with a man that is a sinner.**

From the JST of verse 7, quoted next, we see that the disciples still had not finished learning the lesson that the Master judges by what is in the heart, rather than what others think.

JST Luke 19:7
7 And when **the disciples** saw it, they all murmured, saying, That he was gone to be a guest with a man **who** is a sinner.

8 And **Zacchæus** stood, and **said unto the Lord** [*Jesus*]; Behold, Lord, the **half of my goods I give to the poor; and if I have taken any thing from any man by false accusation** [*if I have mistakenly collected more taxes than I should from anyone*], **I restore him fourfold** [*I pay him back four times what I took*].

JST Luke 19:8
And Zaccheus stood, and said unto the Lord, Behold, Lord, the half of my goods I give to the poor; and if I have taken any

LUKE 19

337

thing from any man by **unjust means**, I **restore fourfold**.

9 And **Jesus said unto him, This day is salvation come to this house** [*I have come to this house*], forsomuch as [*because*] he also is a son of [*descendant of*] Abraham [*can also mean that Zacchaeus is righteous and honest like Abraham was, and thus will be saved*].

10 **For the Son of man** [*I, Christ*] is [*have*] **come to seek and to save that which was lost** [*those who are lost*].

You will no doubt notice some similarities between the parable of the pounds, which the Savior gives next, and the parable of the talents (Matthew 25:14–30) which Jesus will give a few days later on the Mount of Olives.

The Parable of the Pounds

11 And as they heard these things, he added and spake a **parable**, because he was nigh [*near*] to Jerusalem, and because they thought that the king**dom of God** [*the Second Coming; see footnote 11a in your Bible, referring you to 2 Thessalonians 2:2*] **should immediately appear.**

The JST clarifies who "they" refers to, as used in the last phrase of verse 11, above.

JST Luke 19:11

11 And as they heard these things, he added and spake a parable, because he was nigh to Jerusalem, and because **the Jews**

taught that the kingdom of God should immediately appear.

As indicated after verse 10, above, this next parable is known as the Parable of the Pounds. In addition to explaining to the disciples that the Second Coming is still a long way off, which is opposite of what some of the Jewish religious leaders have been teaching the people, this parable seems to have a major message to the effect that each of us is given an equal opportunity to labor diligently in the work of the Lord, and ultimately become gods. Even though we have this equal opportunity, the results of our efforts will vary because of differences in our talents and abilities. Nevertheless, each of us who tries and produces according to our abilities will be given a stewardship to rule over others; in other words, will become gods. On the other hand, those of us who do nothing to further the work of God with our talents and abilities will not become gods.

12 He said therefore, **A certain nobleman** [*symbolic of Christ*] **went into a far country** [*symbolic of heaven*] to receive for himself a kingdom, and to return.

13 And **he called his ten servants** [*symbolic of all people*], and **delivered them ten pounds** [*each got the same amount of money, one pound—see verses 16, 18, and 20—symbolic of the fact that each of us will ultimately have an equal opportunity to live the gospel*

and become gods], **and said unto them, Occupy till I come** [*put your pound to good use until I return*].

14 **But his citizens** [*symbolic of rebellious people on earth*] **hated him, and sent a message after him, saying, We will not have this man** [*Christ*] **to reign over us.**

15 And it came to pass, that **when he** was **returned** [*symbolic of the Second Coming*], having received the kingdom, then **he commanded these servants to be called unto him**, to whom he had given the money, **that he might know how much every man had gained by trading** [*symbolic of Judgment Day*].

16 Then came **the first** [*the first man*], saying, Lord, thy pound hath **gained ten pounds.**

17 And he said unto him, **Well, thou good servant: because thou hast been faithful in a very little, have thou authority over ten cities** [*you can be a god*].

18 And **the second** came, saying, Lord, thy pound hath gained **five pounds.**

19 And he said **likewise to him, Be thou also over five cities** [*you can be a god*].

20 And **another** came, saying, Lord, behold, **here is thy pound, which I have kept** laid up in a napkin:

21 For **I feared thee**, because thou

art an austere [*very strict*] man: thou takest up that thou layedst not down, and reapest that thou didst not sow. [*In other words, You don't miss a thing!*]

22 And **he saith** unto him, Out of thine own mouth will I judge thee, **thou wicked servant.** Thou knewest that I was an austere man, taking up that I laid not down, and reaping that I did not sow:

23 **Wherefore then gavest not thou my money into the bank** [*why didn't you invest My money; symbolically, why didn't you use the talents and abilities I gave you, to do good?*], **that at my coming I might have required mine own with usury** [*interest*]?

24 And he said unto them that stood by, **Take from him the pound** [*the opportunity to become a god*], and **give it to him that hath ten pounds.**

25 **(And they said unto him, Lord, he hath ten pounds.)** [*He has ten pounds already. He doesn't need more.*]

26 For I say unto you, That **unto every one which hath shall be given; and from him that hath not, even that he hath shall be taken away** from him. [*Those who become gods will continue to increase in the number of worlds they have, whereas, those who prove unworthy of exaltation will lose the blessings reserved for the faithful.*]

JST Luke 19:25

25 For I say unto you, That unto every one **who occupieth**, shall be given; and from him who **occupieth** not, even that he hath **received** shall be taken away from him.

The word "occupieth," as used in JST verse 25, above, seems to refer back to that same word as used in verse 13, and basically means "put to work to earn more."

27 **But those mine enemies, which would not that I should reign over them** [who didn't want Me to be their ruler; see verse 14], bring hither [here], and **slay them before me** [symbolic of the wicked who will be destroyed at the Second Coming].

28 And when he had thus spoken, **he went** before [ahead], ascending [climbing] **up to Jerusalem**.

Jerusalem was about twenty-five miles up the mountains from Jericho. Luke now gives us his account of the triumphal entry of the Savior into Jerusalem. First, he tells us of the instructions to the disciples for arranging for the donkey upon which the Master will ride. This is itself a rather under-discussed miracle.

29 And it came to pass, when he was come nigh [near] to Bethphage and Bethany, at the mount called the mount of Olives [just outside Jerusalem], **he sent two of his disciples,**

30 Saying, **Go ye into the vil-**lage over against you [across from you]; in the which at your entering **ye shall find a colt** [a young, male donkey] tied, **whereon yet never man sat** [which has not been broken to ride]: loose [untie] him, and **bring him hither**.

31 And **if any man ask you, Why do ye loose him?** thus shall ye **say** unto him, **Because the Lord hath need of him**.

32 And **they** [the two disciples] that were sent **went their way, and found even as he had said** unto them [just as Jesus had prophesied].

33 And **as they were loosing the colt** [untying the donkey], **the owners** thereof **said** unto them, **Why loose ye the colt?**

34 And **they said, The Lord hath need of him**.

35 And **they brought him** [the donkey] **to Jesus**: and they cast their garments upon the colt, and **they set Jesus thereon**.

This is what is referred to as the "Triumphal Entry," when Jesus rode into Jerusalem to the cheers and praises of multitudes who welcomed Him as the promised One who would free them from their enemies. It is early spring, Passover time, A.D. 34, when Jews from all over throng into Jerusalem to celebrate and worship. As Christ rides into Jerusalem, they spread their clothing and palm leaves (John 12:13) on the path in front of

Him, "thus carpeting the way as for the passing of a king" (Talmage, *Jesus the Christ*, p. 514). Many scholars believe that the Triumphal Entry took place on Sunday. This is the first day of the last week of the Savior's mortal life. He will be crucified on Friday.

The Triumphal Entry

36 And **as he went, they spread their clothes in the way** [*on the path in front of Him*].

37 And when he was come nigh [*near Jerusalem*], even now at the descent of the mount of Olives, **the whole multitude of the disciples began to rejoice and praise God** with a loud voice **for all the mighty works that they had seen**;

38 **Saying, Blessed be the King** that cometh in the name of the Lord: peace in heaven, and glory in the highest.

39 And **some of the Pharisees** from among the multitude [*in the crowd*] **said unto him, Master, rebuke thy disciples** [*tell your disciples not to say such things about You*].

40 And **he answered** and said unto them, I tell you that, **if these should hold their peace, the stones would immediately cry out.**

41 And when he was come near, **he beheld the city** [*Jerusalem*], **and wept over it,**

42 Saying, **If thou hadst known,** even thou, at least in this thy day, the things which belong unto thy peace [*if only your inhabitants had been righteous and had done things which would have brought you peace*]! but now they are hid from thine eyes [*peace is no longer available*].

43 For **the days shall come** upon thee, that thine enemies shall cast a trench about thee, and compass thee round, and keep thee in on every side [*you will be attacked by enemy armies who will lay siege against you, dig trenches around you, and surround you*],

44 And shall lay thee [*Jerusalem*] even with the ground [*will tear you down to the ground*], and thy children [*inhabitants*] within thee; and they [*enemy armies*] **shall not leave in thee one stone upon another**; because thou knewest not the time of thy visitation [*because you would not acknowledge that your day of punishment would come*].

Next, Jesus cleanses the temple again. Brother Talmage suggests that this takes place on Monday. See *Jesus the Christ*, pp. 524–529. John tells us (John 2:14–17) that Jesus cleansed the temple at the beginning of His ministry. Now, three years later, He cleanses it again. This is the second time, and the money changers obviously hadn't learned their lesson the first time. This cleansing of the temple would involve clearing the outer courtyard of the temple grounds of those involved in making these sacred grounds a "den of thieves." Money changers, who exchanged temple coins for foreign currency, and merchants who sold animals for sacrifices had reduced the temple grounds to anything but a sacred place.

Jesus Cleanses the Temple

45 And **he** [*Jesus*] **went into the temple, and began to cast out them that sold therein, and them that bought;**

46 Saying unto them, It is written [*in the scriptures; see Jeremiah 7:11*], **My house is the house of prayer: but ye have made it a den of thieves.**

47 And **he taught daily in the temple.** [*This must have been very frustrating to the religious leaders of the Jews, especially after Jesus had cleansed the temple.*] But **the chief priests and the scribes and the chief of the people sought to destroy him,**

48 And **could not find what they might do:** for **all the people were very attentive to hear him.** [*They couldn't figure out a way to destroy Jesus without causing a riot among the people.*]

LUKE 20

This is the last week of the Savior's life. The religious rulers of the Jews are getting desperate. Jesus'

popularity is increasing. The huge crowds, including Jewish pilgrims from many countries coming for Passover, are very excited about Jesus, and are no doubt talking enthusiastically about His cleansing of the temple yesterday. These hypocritical religious leaders have lost every public debate with Jesus in the past. They are still losing face with the people. Three groups of Jewish religious leaders, the chief priests, the scribes, and the elders now have joined together to confront the Master.

1 AND it came to pass, that **on one of those days** [*probably Tuesday; see Talmage,* Jesus the Christ, *p. 530*], **as he taught the people** in the temple, and preached the gospel, **the chief priests** and **the scribes** came upon him **with the elders,**

Watch as their first point of attack centers on where He claims to get His authority.

2 And **spake unto him,** saying, Tell us, **by what authority doest thou these things** [*including cleansing the temple yesterday*]? or **who is he that gave thee this authority?**

3 And **he answered** and said unto them, **I will also ask you one thing;** and answer me: [*I will ask you one question. If you answer Mine, I will answer yours; see Matthew 21:24.*]

It is helpful to remember that John the Baptist had been very popular among the common people. Thus, these Jewish leaders could cause a riot against themselves if they say anything against him.

4 **The baptism of John, was it from heaven, or of men** [*did John the Baptist have authority from heaven, or was he just an ordinary man*]?

5 **And they reasoned with themselves** [*talked it over among themselves*], saying, **If we shall say, From heaven; he will say, Why then believed ye him not?**

6 **But** and **if we say, Of men; all the people will stone us**: for they be persuaded [*the people believe*] that John was a prophet.

7 And **they answered, that they could not tell whence it was** [*they could not answer his question*].

8 And **Jesus said unto them, Neither tell I you by what authority I do these things.**

In this next parable, known as the Parable of the Wicked Husbandmen, the Savior clearly compares the wicked Jewish religious leaders to the wicked husbandmen who kill the owner's son in an attempt to take the kingdom from him. The notes in brackets in the parable represent one possible interpretation.

The Parable of the Wicked Husbandmen

9 Then began he to speak to the people this **parable; A certain man** [*symbolic of Heavenly Father*] **planted a vineyard** [*planted grape vines; symbolic of establishing Israel, especially the Jews (see Isaiah 5:7) in the Holy Land*], **and let it forth** [*turned Israel over*] **to husbandmen** [*farmers in charge of the vineyard; symbolic of the religious leaders of the Jews*], **and went into a far country** [*heaven*] **for a long time.**

10 And **at the season** [*at harvest time*] **he sent a servant** [*symbolic of prophets*] **to the husbandmen, that they should give him of the fruit of the vineyard** [*the harvest; symbolizing that the leaders were to have taught righteousness and brought people unto God*]: but **the husbandmen beat him, and sent him away empty** [*rejected the prophets*].

11 And again **he sent another servant** [*more prophets*]: and **they beat him also,** and entreated [*treated*] him shamefully, and **sent him away empty** [*rejected them too*].

12 And again **he sent a third: and they wounded him also, and cast him out.**

13 **Then said the lord of the vineyard** [*the owner; symbolic of the Father*], What shall I do? **I will send my beloved son** [*symbolic of Christ*]: it may be they will

reverence him [*respect and honor Him*] when they see him.

14 **But when the husbandmen** [*symbolic of the religious leaders of the Jews*] **saw him, they reasoned among themselves**, saying, **This is the heir** [*everything will belong to Him*]: come, **let us kill him**, that the inheritance may be ours [*let's kill Jesus so we can keep our power, authority and position over the people*].

15 **So they cast him** [*the son of the owner; symbolic of the Savior*] **out** of the vineyard, **and killed him. What therefore shall the lord of the vineyard** [*in this case, symbolic of Christ*] **do unto them?**

16 **He shall come** [*Second Coming*] **and destroy these husbandmen, and shall give the vineyard to others** [*righteous religious leaders; symbolic of the restoration of the gospel through Joseph Smith*]. **And when they heard it, they said, God forbid.**

17 **And he beheld them** [*looked at them*], **and said, What is this then that is written** [*in the scriptures; see Psalm 118:22*], **The stone** [*symbolic of Christ, the "Rock of our salvation"*] **which the builders** [*the Jews*] **rejected, the same is become the head of the corner** [*cornerstone; capstone*]?

"Capstone" could symbolize "the finisher of our salvation." Strong's *Concordance*, numbers 1137 and 1119, suggest a possible association of words to

imply "kneeling." This could tie in with the fact that "all shall bow the knee, and every tongue shall confess" that Jesus is the Christ. (See D&C 76:110 and Philippians 2:10–11.)

18 **Whosoever shall fall upon that stone** [*Christ*] **shall be broken; but on whomsoever it shall fall** [*the wicked*], **it will grind him to powder.**

One of the important messages in verse 18, above, is that Christ and His gospel will ultimately triumph over the devil and his kingdom (see Moses 4:21). A religious movie producer once said, in effect, that we cannot break the commandments of God. We can only break ourselves against them.

19 And the **chief priests** and the **scribes** the same hour **sought to lay hands on him; and they feared the people** [*they tried to figure out a safe way to arrest Him immediately, without causing a riot*]: **for they perceived** [*they understood*] **that he had spoken this parable against them.** [*In other words, they understood full well that they were the "wicked husbandmen" in the parable Jesus had just told them in verses 9–16 above.*]

20 And **they** [*the scribes, Pharisees, and elders*] **watched him, and sent forth spies**, which should feign [*pretend*] themselves just [*righteous, sincere*] men, **that they might take hold of his words** [*catch Jesus saying something for which He could be arrested*], **that**

so they might deliver him unto the power and authority of **the governor** [*the Roman governor, Pontius Pilate*].

21 And **they** [*the spies in verse 20*] **asked him**, saying, **Master, we know that thou sayest and teachest rightly,** neither acceptest thou the person of any [*You don't change Your teachings because of peer pressure*], but **teachest the way of God truly**: [*They were indeed pretending to be "just men," as instructed by their evil bosses in verse 20.*]

Watch now as these cunning men attempt to get the Master in trouble with the Roman government.

22 **Is it lawful** [*legal*] **for us to give tribute** [*pay taxes*] **unto Cæsar** [*the Roman emperor*], **or no?**

23 **But he perceived their craftiness** [*Jesus understood their sly intentions*], **and said unto them, Why tempt ye me** [*why are you trying to trick Me*]?

24 **Shew** [*pronounced "show"*] **me a penny** [*a Roman coin representing about a day's wage*]. **Whose image** [*picture*] **and superscription** [*writing on the coin*] **hath it? They answered and said, Cæsar's.**

25 And he said unto them, **Render** [*pay*] therefore **unto Cæsar the things which be Cæsar's, and unto God the things which be God's.**

26 And **they could not take hold of his words before the people** [*their plot didn't work*]: and **they marvelled** [*were stunned*] at his answer, and **held their peace** [*kept quiet*].

The three groups of Jewish religious leaders mentioned in verse one are now joined by yet another prominent group, the Sadducees, in their attempts to discredit Jesus and get Him arrested. Since the others have failed miserably, they will now try their hand.

27 **Then came** to him certain of the **Sadducees** [*another influential group of Jewish religious leaders*], **which deny that there is any resurrection** [*who did not believe in the doctrine of resurrection*]; **and they asked him,**

Seven Brothers, One Wife

28 Saying, Master, **Moses wrote** unto us [*taught us in the scriptures—Deuteronomy 25:5*], **If any man's brother die, having a wife, and he die without children, that his brother should take** [*marry*] **his wife, and raise up seed unto his brother** [*produce children for his dead brother*].

29 There were therefore **seven brethren** [*brothers*]: and **the first took a wife, and died without children.**

30 And **the second took her to wife** [*married her*], and **he died childless.**

LUKE 20

31 And **the third** took her; and in like manner **the seven also:** and **they left no children, and died.** [*Ultimately, all seven brothers married her in turn, had no children with her, and died.*]

32 **Last of all the woman died also.**

33 **Therefore in the resurrection whose wife of them is she? for seven had her to wife.**

Celestial Marriage

Here is a major doctrinal point. Many religions use these next three verses to prove that there is no such thing as eternal marriage and family in the next life. On the contrary, the simple fact that the Sadducees asked the Savior whose wife she would be when they are all resurrected (verse 33 above) is strong evidence that the Savior had indeed preached marriage in the next life, or, in other words, eternal marriage. Otherwise, their question would not make any sense at all!

34 And **Jesus** answering **said** unto them, **The children of this world marry, and are given in marriage:**

35 But they which shall be accounted worthy to obtain that world, and the resurrection from the dead, **neither marry, nor are given in marriage:**

JST Luke 20:35

35 But they **who** shall be accounted worthy to obtain that world, **through** resurrection from the dead, neither marry nor are given in marriage.

36 **Neither can they die any more: for they are equal unto the angels;** and are the children of God, being the children of the resurrection.

The above three verses can be confusing. Perhaps these verses are not translated correctly. Perhaps there are some things left out. Whatever the case, we have been given correct doctrine regarding eternal marriage (D&C 132:19–20). We have also been taught that, after everyone from this earth is resurrected, there will be no more eternal marriages performed for former residents of this earth, because such marriages have to be done by mortals for themselves, or by mortals who serve as proxies for those who have died—see D&C 128:15 & 18. Brigham Young said: "And when the Millennium is over, . . . all the sons and daughters of Adam and Eve, down to the last of their posterity, who come within the reach of the clemency of the Gospel, [will] have been redeemed in hundreds of temples through the administration of their children as proxies for them" (Discourses of Brigham Young, p. 395). Since there will be no mortals left on earth after the resurrection is completed, there would be no one left to serve as proxies for eternal marriages.

37 **Now that the dead are raised** [*the fact that the dead are resurrected; remember that Jesus is talking here to Sadducees, who do not believe in resurrection—see verse 27*], even Moses shewed [*showed; proved*] at the bush [*when he talked to God at the burning bush*], when he calleth the Lord the God of Abraham, and the God of Isaac, and the God of Jacob.

38 **For he is not a God of the dead, but of the living: for all live unto him** [*everyone will be resurrected*].

39 Then certain of the **scribes answering said, Master, thou hast well said.**

40 **And after that they** [*the spies, mentioned in verse 20 above, and perhaps others also in tHe crowd*] **durst not** [*didn't dare*] **ask him any question at all.**

41 And **he said unto them, How say they that Christ is David's son** [*what do people mean when they say Christ is King David's son*]?

42 **And David himself saith** in the book of Psalms [*Psalm 110:1*], **The LORD** [*the Father; see* Doctrinal New Testament Commentary, *Vol. 1, p. 612*] **said unto my Lord** [*Christ*], **Sit thou on my right hand,**

43 **Till I make thine enemies thy footstool** [*until all your enemies have been subdued under your feet*].

44 **David therefore calleth him**

Lord [*God*], **how is he then his son** [*how can He be David's son*]?

45 **Then in the audience** [*within hearing*] **of all the people he said unto his disciples,**

46 **Beware of** [*watch out for*] **the scribes** [*religious rulers among the Jews*], **which** [*who*] **desire to walk in long robes, and love greetings in the markets, and the highest seats in the synagogues, and the chief rooms at feasts** [*they love to appear very important in public*];

47 **Which devour widows' houses** [*take widow's houses from them*], **and for a shew** [*for show*] **make long prayers: the same** [*the scribes*] **shall receive greater damnation.**

LUKE 21

In this chapter, the Savior prophecies the destruction of the temple in Jerusalem and of the city of Jerusalem. He will give a number of the signs of the times, prophesies that will be fulfilled before His Second Coming. You may wish to review Matthew, chapter 24, which contains more of these signs of the times.

1 AND **he** [*Jesus*] **looked up, and saw the rich men casting their gifts into the treasury** [*depositing their donations in the public donation container at the temple in Jerusalem*].

The Widow's Mite

2 And **he saw** also a certain **poor widow casting in thither two mites** [*one mite was about one sixty-fourth of a day's pay; see Bible Dictionary, under "Money"*].

3 And **he said**, Of a truth [*certainly*] I say unto you, that **this poor widow hath cast in more than they all**:

4 For all **these** [*rich men*] **have of their abundance cast in unto the offerings of God** [*have taken just a bit, relatively speaking, from their wealth*]: **but she of her penury** [*poverty*] **hath cast in all the living that she had.** [*She has given everything she has to live on.*]

Next, in verses 5–6, Jesus will prophesy of the coming destruction of the temple in Jerusalem.

5 And as some **spake of the temple**, how it was adorned [*decorated*] with goodly [*beautiful*] stones and gifts, **he said**,

6 As for these things [*the huge stones used to build the temple*] which ye behold [*see*], **the days will come, in the which there shall not be left one stone upon another**, that shall not be thrown down [*the temple in Jerusalem will be destroyed*].

Signs of the Times

7 And they asked him, saying, Master, but **when shall these things be? and what sign will there be** when these things shall come to pass?

The Savior has just told His disciples about the coming destruction of Jerusalem by the Romans, which will be essentially complete by A.D. 73. Next, He will teach them many of the "signs of the times," meaning prophecies which will be fulfilled before the Second Coming. For more complete notes, see Matthew 24 in this study guide.

8 And he said, Take heed [*be careful*] that ye be not deceived: **for many shall come in my name, saying, I am Christ**; and the time draweth near: go ye not therefore after them. [*There will be many false Christs in the last days. Don't follow them.*]

9 But when ye shall hear of **wars and commotions**, be not terrified [*don't panic when you see the signs of the times being fulfilled*]: for these things must first come to pass [*must happen before the Second Coming*]; but the end is not by and by [*right away*].

10 Then said he unto them, **Nation shall rise against nation, and kingdom against kingdom** [*in the last days*]:

11 And great **earthquakes** shall be in divers [*various*] places, and **famines**, and **pestilences**; and **fearful sights** and **great signs** shall there be **from heaven**.

Next, in verses 12–24, Christ will prophesy things that will happen to His Apostles and disciples in their day after He is crucified and resurrected.

12 **But before all these** [*things which will happen in the last days*], they shall lay their hands on you [*the disciples*], and persecute you, delivering you up to the synagogues [*arresting you*], and into prisons, being brought before kings and rulers for my name's sake [*because of your service to Me*].

13 And **it shall turn to you for a testimony** [*it will work out so that you can bear testimony of Me*].

14 **Settle it therefore** [*determine*] **in your hearts**, not to meditate before [*think in advance*] what ye shall answer:

15 For **I will give you a mouth and wisdom**, which all your adversaries shall not be able to gainsay [*oppose, put down*] nor resist.

16 And **ye shall be betrayed** both by parents, and brethren, and kinsfolks [*relatives*], and friends; and some of you shall they cause to be put to death [*they will kill some of you*].

17 And **ye shall be hated** of all men for my name's sake [*because of your loyalty to Me*].

18 **But there shall not an hair of your head perish** [*without the Father noticing it—compare with Matthew 10:29-31; in other words, ultimately, you will be fine in the celestial kingdom*].

19 **In your patience** [*loyal service at all costs*] **possess ye your souls** [*you will earn exaltation; the high-est degree of glory in the celestial kingdom*].

20 And when **ye shall see Jerusalem compassed** [*surrounded*] **with armies**, then know that the desolation thereof is nigh [*the "desolation of abomination" spoken of by Daniel; see notes for Matthew 24:15 in this study guide*].

21 Then let them which are in Judæa **flee to the mountains**; and let them which are in the midst of it depart out; and let not them that are in the countries enter thereinto.

JST Luke 21:20

20 Then let them **who** are in Judea flee to the mountains; and let them **who** are in the midst of it, depart out; and let not them **who** are in the countries, **return to enter into the city**.

Many faithful Saints at the time of the Roman attacks followed the prophetic counsel in verse 21 above. They fled to Pella, east of Samaria, and thus escaped the Romans.

22 For these be the days of vengeance, that **all things** [*all the prophecies*] **which are written may be fulfilled**.

23 But **woe unto them that are with child** [*are pregnant, so they can't run fast*], **and to them that give suck** [*are nursing, thus have small children and can't run away fast with them in tow*], in those days! for **there shall be great distress in the land, and wrath upon this people** [*the Jews*].

LUKE 21

24 And **they** [*the Jews*] **shall fall** [*be killed*] **by the edge of the sword, and shall be led away captive into all nations:** and **Jerusalem shall be trodden down** of [*by*] the Gentiles, **until the times of the Gentiles be fulfilled.**

The JST adds a verse after verse 24, above. It helps us understand that many of the signs of the times given here by the Savior related to the times of the Apostles and early members of the Church immediately following the crucifixion and resurrection of Christ. And others of the signs relate to the last days, in other words, our day.

JST Luke 21:24
24 **Now these things he spake unto them, concerning the destruction of Jerusalem. And then his disciples asked him, saying, Master, tell us concerning thy coming?**

25 And **there shall be signs** [*in the last days*] in the **sun**, and in the **moon**, and in the **stars**; and upon the earth **distress of nations** [*much trouble between nations*], with **perplexity**; the **sea and the waves roaring** [*much trouble upon the oceans and waters*];

JST Luke 21:25
25 **And he answered them, and said, In the generation in which the times of the Gentiles shall be fulfilled** [*this refers to our day*], there shall be signs in the sun, and in the moon, and in the stars; and upon the earth distress

of nations with perplexity, **like** the sea and the waves roaring. **The earth also shall be troubled, and the waters of the great deep**;

26 **Men's hearts failing them for fear** [*people will be depressed, giving up hope*], and for looking after those things [*because of seeing the terrible things*] which are coming on the earth: for **the powers of heaven shall be shaken**.

27 And **then shall they see the Son of man** [*Jesus*] **coming in a cloud with power and great glory** [*the Second Coming*].

Every one will see the Savior, when He comes in glory at the time of His Second Coming, including those who caused His crucifixion. See Revelation 1:7.

28 And **when these things** [*prophecies*] **begin to come to pass** [*begin to happen*], then **look up, and lift up your heads; for your redemption draweth nigh.** [*The righteous can rejoice at the Second Coming, because their troubles, persecutions, etc., are over.*]

Next, Jesus gives the Parable of the Fig Tree. The main point is that, just as a farmer can tell when a fruit tree is about to start growing leaves, so also wise Saints will be familiar with the signs of the times so that they will recognize that the Second Coming is near.

The Parable of the Fig Tree

29 And he spake to them a **parable**; Behold **the fig tree**, and all the trees;

30 **When they now shoot forth** [*start putting on leaves and blossoms*], **ye see and know** of your own selves that **summer is now nigh at hand** [*close at hand*].

31 So **likewise ye, when ye see these things come to pass** [*the signs of the times*], **know ye that the kingdom of God** [*Second Coming*] **is nigh at hand** [*is getting close*].

32 Verily I say unto you, **This generation shall not pass away, till all be fulfilled** [*until all the signs of the times have been fulfilled*].

JST Luke 21:32
32 Verily I say unto you, this generation, **the generation when the times of the Gentiles be fulfilled**, shall not pass away till all be fulfilled.

The "times of the Gentiles" refers to the period of time in the last days when the gospel is being taken to everyone but the Jews. In the days of the Savior's mortal ministry, He and His Apostles took the gospel message only to the Jews. Then, after His resurrection, He instructed them to go into all the world (Mark 16:15.) Thus, the Jews were the "first" to get the gospel in the days of the Savior, and the Gentiles (everyone else) was "last." In the last days it will be just the opposite.

First, the gospel will be taken to the Gentiles, then it will go to the Jews. Thus, the "last" (Gentiles) will be first (in the last days) and the "first" (Jews) will be last to get it in the last days. The happy news is that all will ultimately get a chance to understand it and accept it.

33 **Heaven and earth shall pass away: but my words shall not pass away** [*what I say is absolutely reliable*].

34 And **take heed** to yourselves [*watch out*], **lest at any time your hearts be overcharged with surfeiting** [*wicked, lustful living*], **and drunkenness, and cares of this life**, and **so that day** [*the Second Coming*] **come upon you unawares** [*catches you off guard*].

JST Luke 21:34
34 **Let my disciples therefore** take heed to **themselves**, lest at any time their hearts be overcharged with surfeiting, and drunkenness, and cares of this life, **and** that day come upon **them** unawares.

35 For **as a snare** [*a trap which catches an unsuspecting animal totally by surprise*] **shall it come on all them** [*the wicked or foolish*] that dwell on the face of the whole earth.

D&C 106:4–5 differentiates between the "world" and the "children of light" as far as being caught off guard at the Savior's coming is concerned. The "world," meaning the wicked, will be caught off guard, similar to one who is caught unexpectedly by a "thief in the night" (D&C 106:4.) On the other hand, the "children of light" (D&C 106:5), meaning the Saints who are familiar with the signs of the times, are not caught off guard.

36 **Watch ye therefore, and pray always, that ye may be accounted worthy to** escape all these things that shall come to pass, and to **stand** [*worthily*] **before the Son of man** [*Christ*].

JST Luke 21:36

36 **And what I say unto one, I say unto all**, Watch ye therefore, and pray always, **and keep my commandments**, that ye may be **counted** worthy to escape all these things **which** shall come to pass, and to stand before the Son of man **when he shall come clothed in the glory of his Father**.

We understand that, at this point, it is most likely Tuesday evening of the last week of the Savior's life. See Talmage, Jesus the Christ, pp. 563 and 586.

37 And **in the day time he was teaching in the temple;** and **at night he** went out, and **abode** [*stayed*] **in the mount** that is called the mount **of Olives** [*just outside of Jerusalem*].

38 And **all the people came early in the morning to him in the temple, for to hear him.**

LUKE 22

In this chapter, Judas Iscariot will make arrangements to betray the Savior. Jesus will institute the sacrament, will suffer in the Garden of Gethsemane, will be betrayed, arrested, subjected to illegal trial, and will be brutally mocked. During the trial at night, Peter will deny knowing Jesus three times.

1 NOW **the feast of** unleavened bread drew nigh [*near*], which is called **the Passover.**

The Feast of the Passover was celebrated in the springtime at about the same time as we celebrate Easter. It commemorated the destroying angel's passing over the houses of the children of Israel in Egypt, when the firstborn of the Egyptians were killed. The Israelites in Egypt at the time were instructed by Moses to sacrifice a lamb without blemish and to put blood from the lamb which was sacrificed on the doorposts of their houses. See Bible Dictionary, under "Feasts." Thus, through the blood of a lamb, the Israelites were protected from the anguish and punishment brought to the Egyptians by the destroying angel.

The symbolism is clear. It is by the "blood of the Lamb" (the sacrifice of the Savior) that we are saved, after all we can do (2 Nephi 25:23). Now, at the time of Passover in Jerusalem, the "Lamb of God," Christ, will present Himself to be sacrificed, that we might be saved. The Feast of the Passover brought large numbers of Jews from near and far to Jerusalem to join in the worship and celebration.

2 And **the chief priests and scribes sought how they might kill him**; for they feared the people [*were afraid of causing a riot by arresting Jesus*].

3 **Then entered Satan into Judas** surnamed **Iscariot**, being of the number of the twelve [*who was one of the Twelve Apostles*].

4 **And he** [*Judas*] went his way, and **communed** [*plotted*] **with the chief priests and captains, how he might betray him** [*Jesus*] **unto them.**

5 And **they** were glad, and **covenanted to give him money** [*thirty pieces of silver*].

Thirty pieces of silver was the current price for an average slave. Thus, it was an insult to Judas and demeaning to the Master to offer him only the going price for a common slave in exchange for the Savior.

6 And **he** [*Judas*] promised [*agreed to the terms*], and **sought opportunity to betray him** [*Jesus*] **unto them in the absence of the multitude.** [*Judas looked for opportunities to betray Jesus quietly, out of sight of the public. We understand this to be taking place at the end of the third day of the last week of the Savior's life, probably Tuesday.*]

7 **Then came the day of unleavened bread, when the passover must be killed.** [*This is Thursday, the fifth day of the last week of the Savior's mortal life, when the actual feast of the Passover was eaten.*]

8 And **he** [*Jesus*] **sent Peter and John, saying, Go and prepare us the passover, that we may eat** [*find a place for us to eat the Passover meal*].

9 And they said unto him, **Where wilt thou that we prepare?**

Pay attention to the prophetic details which the Savior now provides as He directs Peter and John to prepare a place for them to eat the Passover meal.

10 And **he said** unto them, Behold, **when ye are entered into the city, there shall a man meet you, bearing a pitcher of water; follow him into the house where he entereth in.**

11 **And ye shall say unto the goodman** [*owner*] **of the house, The Master saith unto thee, Where is the guestchamber** [*room*], **where I shall eat the passover with my disciples?**

12 And **he shall shew** [*show*] **you a large upper room furnished: there make ready.**

13 And **they went, and found as he had said** unto them: and they made ready the passover.

The Last Supper

14 And **when the hour was come, he sat down, and the twelve apostles with him.**

15 And **he said unto them, With desire** [*deep emotion*] **I have desired to eat this passover with you before I suffer:**

16 For I say unto you, **I will not any more eat thereof, until it be fulfilled in the kingdom of God.**

JST Luke 22:16

16 For I say unto you, I will not any more eat thereof, until it be fulfilled **which is written in the prophets concerning me. Then I will partake with you,** in the kingdom of God.

Jesus now introduces the sacrament to His Apostles. This final Passover meal, partaken of with them, is known as the "Last Supper."

17 And **he took the cup, and gave thanks, and said, Take this, and divide it among yourselves:**

18 For I say unto you, **I will not drink of the fruit of the vine, until the kingdom of God shall come** [*this is the last time I will eat with you during my mortal life; see Matthew 26:29*].

The Sacrament

19 And **he took bread, and gave thanks, and brake it, and gave unto them, saying, This is my body** [*this represents My body*] which is given for you: this do in remembrance of me.

20 **Likewise also the cup after supper, saying, This cup is the new testament** [*the new covenant*] **in my blood** [*represents My blood*], **which is shed for you.**

21 **But, behold, the hand of him** [*Judas Iscariot*] **that betrayeth me is with me on the table.**

22 **And truly the Son of man** [*Christ*] **goeth** [*dies*], **as it was determined** [*planned*]: **but woe unto that man by whom he is betrayed!**

23 And **they began to enquire among themselves, which of them it was that should do this thing** [*betray the Savior*].

Who Is Greatest?

24 And **there was also a strife** [*an argument*] among them, **which of them should be accounted the greatest** [*which of them was the most important*].

25 And **he said** unto them, **The kings of the Gentiles exercise lordship** [*power, authority*] **over them; and they that exercise authority upon them are called benefactors.**

Those Who Serve Are Greatest

26 **But ye shall not be so: but he that is greatest among you, let him be as the younger; and he that is chief, as he that doth**

serve. [*If you want to be the greatest, you must consider yourself to be the lowest and serve others.*]

27 **For whether is greater** [*who is commonly considered to be the most important*], **he that sitteth at meat** [*is eating the meal*], **or he that serveth** [*who serves the meal*]? **is not he that sitteth at meat** [*answer: the person eating the meal*]? **but I am among you as he that serveth** [*I am among you as your servant*].

28 **Ye are they which have continued with me in my temptations** [*you are My loyal followers*].

29 And **I appoint unto you a kingdom** [*you will be exalted*], **as my Father hath appointed unto me;**

30 **That ye may eat and drink at my table in my kingdom, and sit on thrones judging the twelve tribes of Israel.**

We understand from JST Mark 14:30 that Judas Iscariot has already left the scene to betray the Master. Thus, Christ's statement to the Apostles that they are appointed a kingdom, verses 29–30 above, would apply to the eleven remaining Apostles, not to Judas.

31 And **the Lord said, Simon** [*Peter*], **Simon, behold, Satan hath desired to have you, that he may sift you as wheat:**

JST Luke 22:31
31 And the Lord said, Simon, Simon, behold Satan hath

desired **you, that he may sift the children of the kingdom as wheat**. [*Satan would like to destroy Peter's effectiveness, so that the members of the Church would be without his leadership.*]

32 **But I have prayed for thee, that thy faith fail not** [*so that Satan will not be successful*]: **and when thou art converted, strengthen thy brethren.**

It is significant that the Savior says to Peter, "When thou art converted, strengthen thy brethren." Peter feels that he is already completely converted and strong in the faith. Yet, this will be a most difficult night for him, as he denies knowing the Savior on three different occasions. Afterwards, he will be much stronger as we see in Acts, chapter 4 and elsewhere.

33 And **he said unto him, Lord, I am ready to go with thee, both into prison, and to death.**

34 And **he said,** I tell thee, **Peter, the cock** [*rooster*] **shall not crow this day, before that thou shalt thrice deny that thou knowest me.**

Denying knowing the Savior is not the same as denying the Holy Ghost. Denying the Holy Ghost, as described in D&C 76:31–35, is an unforgivable sin. Peter's denying that he knows the Savior and has been one of His followers for three years is not unforgivable, though so doing brought Peter deep anguish and tears.

LUKE 22

355

35 And **he said unto them, When I sent you** [*on your first missions; see Matthew 10:9-10*] **without purse** [*money*], **and scrip** [*a bag to carry food in; see Bible Dictionary, under "Scrip"*], **and shoes** [*a sign of wealth and power in the culture of the day*], **lacked ye any thing** [*were any of your needs not taken care of*]? **And they said, Nothing.**

36 **Then said he** unto them, **But now, he that hath a purse, let him take it, and likewise his scrip: and he that hath no sword, let him sell his garment, and buy one.** [*Things have changed, so from now on, equip yourselves as well as you can.*]

37 **For I say unto you, that this that is written** [*in Isaiah 53:12*] **must yet be accomplished in me** [*the prophecies about His atoning sacrifice must now take place*], **And he was reckoned among the transgressors** [*including the prophecy that he would be killed with transgressors (Isaiah 53:12), which was fulfilled by the two thieves on crosses*]: **for the things concerning me have an end.** [*The things that are going to happen to Me have a purpose, namely, they will lead up to My accomplishing the Atonement.*]

38 And **they said, Lord, behold, here are two swords. And he said unto them, It is enough.** [*The Apostles still don't seem to grasp the significance of what Jesus just told them, that He must go through with the Atonement. Otherwise,*

they would not have mentioned the swords for defending Him against the coming dangers.]

39 And **he** came out, and **went, as he was wont** [*as was His custom*], **to the mount of Olives; and his disciples also followed him.**

The Garden of Gethsemane

40 And **when he was at the place** [*the Garden of Gethsemane—see Matthew 26:36*], **he said unto them, Pray that ye enter not into temptation.**

"Gethsemane" means "oil press." There is significant symbolism here. The Jews put olives into bags made of mesh fabric and placed them in a press to squeeze olive oil out of them. The first pressings yielded pure olive oil which was prized for many uses, including healing and giving light in lanterns. In fact, we consecrate it and use it to administer to the sick. The last pressing of the olives, under the tremendous pressure of additional weights added to the press, yielded a bitter, red liquid which can remind us of the "bitter cup" which the Savior partook of. Symbolically, the Savior is going into the "oil press" (Gethsemane) to submit to the "pressure" of all our sins which will "squeeze" His blood out in order that we might have the healing "oil" of the Atonement to heal us from our sins.

41 **And he** was withdrawn from them about a stone's cast, and

kneeled down, and prayed,

42 Saying, **Father, if thou be willing, remove this cup from me: nevertheless not my will, but thine, be done.**

43 **And there appeared an angel unto him from heaven, strengthening him.** [*Apostle Bruce R. McConkie suggested that this angel might be Michael (Adam); see April 1985 General Conference*].

44 And **being in an agony he prayed more earnestly: and his sweat was as it were great drops of blood falling down to the ground.**

JST Luke 22:44

44 And being in an agony, he prayed more earnestly; and **he sweat** as it were great drops of blood falling down to the ground.

Some Christians wonder whether or not Jesus actually did sweat drops of blood, or if it was figurative, because of the wording in Luke. Mosiah 3:7 and D&C 19:18 clear up any doubt. He did bleed from every pore.

45 And **when he rose up from prayer, and was come to** [*returned to*] **his disciples, he found them sleeping for sorrow** [*exhausted by their worrying about Jesus and His safety*],

JST Luke 22:45

45 And when he rose up from prayer, and was come to his disciples, he found them sleeping;

for they were filled with sorrow;

46 **And said unto them, Why sleep ye? rise and pray, lest ye enter into temptation.**

The Betrayal

47 **And while he yet spake, behold a multitude** [*a group of soldiers and others, with swords and sticks, sent by and accompanied by the chief priests and elders; see Matthew 26:47, Luke 22:52*], **and he that was called Judas, one of the twelve, went before them** [*Judas led them*], **and drew near unto Jesus to kiss him.**

48 **But Jesus said unto him, Judas, betrayest thou the Son of man** [*Son of God*] **with a kiss?**

49 When **they which were about him** [*Jesus' Apostles*] saw what would follow [*what was about to happen*], they **said unto him, Lord, shall we smite with the sword?**

50 **And one of them** [*Peter*] **smote** [*struck*] **the servant of the high priest, and cut off his right ear.**

51 And **Jesus** answered and **said, Suffer ye thus far** [*let them arrest Me*]. **And he touched his ear** [*the servant's ear*], **and healed him.**

52 **Then Jesus said unto the chief priests, and captains of the temple, and the elders, which were come to him, Be ye come out, as against a thief** [*as if I were a thief, trying to hide from you*], **with swords and staves?**

53 When I was daily with you in the temple, ye stretched forth no hands against me [*Why didn't you arrest Me in broad daylight, when I was in the temple?*]: but this is your hour, and the power of darkness [*this is the evil hour you've planned, so go ahead with your plot*].

54 Then took they him [*they arrested Him*], and led him, and brought him into the high priest's house [*palace*]. And Peter followed afar off [*at a distance*].

Peter Denies Knowing Jesus

55 And when they [*the rowdy crowd who had come to help arrest Jesus*] had kindled a fire in the midst of the hall [*courtyard*], and were set down together, Peter sat down among them.

56 But a certain maid [*young lady*] beheld [*saw*] him as he sat by the fire, and earnestly looked upon him [*and stared at him*], and said, This man was also with him [*Jesus*].

57 And he denied him [*denied knowing Jesus*], saying, Woman, I know him not.

58 And after a little while another saw him, and said, Thou art also of them [*you are one of Jesus' followers*]. And Peter said, Man, I am not.

59 And about the space of one hour after another [*person in the crowd*] confidently affirmed [*spoke with confidence*], saying, Of a truth [*for*

sure] this fellow also was with him: for he is a Galilæan.

60 And Peter said, Man, I know not what thou sayest. And immediately, while he yet spake [*while he was speaking*], the cock crew [*the rooster crowed*].

61 And the Lord [*Jesus*] turned, and looked upon Peter. And Peter remembered the word of the Lord, how he had said unto him, Before the cock crow, thou shalt deny me thrice [*three times*].

62 And Peter went out, and wept bitterly.

The Mocking and Trial

63 And the men that held Jesus mocked him, and smote [*hit*] him.

64 And when they had blindfolded him, they struck him on the face, and asked him, saying, Prophesy, who is it that smote thee? [*Use Your power to tell us who hits You.*]

65 And many other things blasphemously [*mockingly*] spake they against him.

The Trial before Caiaphas

66 And as soon as it was day, the elders of the people and the chief priests and the scribes came together, and led him into their council [*this council was known as the Sanhedrin and was the highest court run by the Jewish religious leaders; see Bible Dictionary, under "Sanhedrin"*], saying,

67 **Art thou the Christ?** tell us. And **he said unto them, If I tell you** [*if I say "Yes."*], **ye will not believe:**

68 And if I also ask you, ye will not answer me, nor let me go.

69 Hereafter shall the Son of man sit on the right hand of the power of God [*after you are finished with Me, I will sit on the right side of the Father up in heaven*].

70 Then said they all, Art thou then the Son of God? And he said unto them, **Ye say that I am** [*"I am."—see Mark 14:62*].

71 And **they said, What need we any further witness** [*why do we need any more evidence*]? **for we ourselves have heard of his own mouth** [*we heard from His own mouth that He claims to be the Son of God*].

LUKE 23

In this chapter, Luke reports that Jesus was taken to Pilate, then to Herod, and back to Pilate again. Pilate releases a criminal named Barabbas in place of Jesus. He tells us of the crucifixion of the Savior and the burial in the garden tomb of Joseph of Arimathaea.

The Trial before Pilate

1 AND the whole multitude of them [*the Sanhedrin, Luke 22:66 above*] **arose, and led him unto Pilate** [*the Roman governor*].

Next, you will see that the Jewish leaders attempted to get Jesus convicted of high treason against the Romans. Under Roman rule they were not given the authority to execute prisoners, so they were attempting to get the Roman rulers to execute Jesus.

2 And they began to accuse him, **saying, We found this fellow perverting** [*undermining*] **the nation** [*the Roman Empire*], **and forbidding to give tribute to Cæsar, saying that he himself is Christ a King.**

In saying that Jesus told people not to pay taxes (tribute) to Caesar, these religious leaders show their true colors as liars. Christ had specifically taught "Render therefore unto Caesar the things which be Caesar's" (Luke 20:25).

3 And Pilate asked him, saying, **Art thou the King of the Jews?** And **he answered** him and said, **Thou sayest it.** [*John 18:37 records the Master's response as "To this end was I born, and for this cause came I into the world;" in other words, "Yes, I am."*]

4 Then said Pilate to the chief priests and to the people, I find no fault in this man.

5 And **they were the more fierce, saying, He stirreth up the people,** teaching throughout all Jewry, beginning from Galilee to this place [*from Galilee in the north to Jerusalem in the south*].

LUKE 23

6 When **Pilate** heard of Galilee, he **asked whether the man were a Galilæan** [*whether or not Jesus was a citizen of Galilee*].

What Pontius Pilate is trying to do here is avoid the responsibility of handling the case of Jesus by sending Him to the Roman governor of Galilee, who at that time was Herod, and who happened to be visiting Jerusalem.

The Trial before Herod

7 And as soon as he knew that he belonged unto Herod's jurisdiction, **he sent him to Herod**, who himself also was at Jerusalem at that time.

8 And when **Herod** saw Jesus, he was exceeding [*very*] glad: for he **was desirous to see him** of a long season [*he had wanted to meet Jesus for a long time*], because he had heard many things of him; and **he hoped to have seen some miracle done by him.**

9 Then **he questioned** with **him** in many words; **but he answered him nothing** [*Jesus refused to answer Herod at all*].

10 And **the chief priests and scribes stood and vehemently** [*extremely angrily*] **accused him** [*presented their case against Jesus to Herod*].

Second Hearing before Pilate

11 And **Herod with his men** of war **set him at nought** [*ridiculed him*], and **mocked him**, and **arrayed** [*dressed*] **him in a gorgeous robe, and sent him again to Pilate**.

12 And the same day **Pilate and Herod were made friends** together: for before they were at enmity between themselves [*they were enemies before this*].

13 And **Pilate**, when he had **called together the chief priests and the rulers and the people,**

14 **Said unto them**, Ye have brought this man unto me, as one that perverteth the people [*undermines the nation*]: and, behold, **I, having examined him** before you [*in front of you*], **have found no fault in this man** touching those things whereof ye accuse him [*I find no truth in the things you accuse Jesus of*]:

15 **No, nor yet Herod** [*neither did Herod find Him guilty*]: for I sent you to him; **and, lo, nothing worthy of death is done unto him** [*"by him"—see Luke 23, footnote 15a, in your Bible; in other words, Jesus has done nothing worthy of death*].

16 **I will** therefore **chastise** [*lightly punish*] **him, and release him.**

17 (**For of necessity** [*according to custom; see Matthew 27:15 in this study guide*] **he must release one** [*a prisoner*] **unto them at the feast.**)

18 And **they cried out all at once,** saying, **Away with this man, and release unto us Barabbas:**

19 (Who for a certain sedition [*undermining the government*] made in the city, and for murder, was cast into prison.)

The name "Barabbas" means "son of the father" (see Bible Dictionary, under "Barabbas"). This may be symbolic in that the "imposter," Satan, stirred up the multitude to demand the release of an "imposter," Barabbas, while the true "Son of the Father" is punished for crimes which He did not commit.

20 **Pilate** therefore, **willing to release Jesus, spake again to them.**

21 **But they cried**, saying, **Crucify him, crucify him.**

22 And **he said unto them the third time, Why, what evil hath he done? I have found no cause of death in him: I will therefore chastise him, and let him go.**

23 **And they were instant** [*insistent*] with loud voices, requiring [*demanding*] that he might be crucified. And **the voices of them and of the chief priests prevailed** [*won out, meaning that Pilate gave in*].

24 And **Pilate gave** [*passed*] **sentence that it should be as they required** [*demanded*].

Pilate was a weak leader, an embarrassment to the Roman Empire. About three years after this public show of weakness on his part, he was removed from office by the Roman Empire, and tradition has it that he was banished and later committed suicide. See Smith's Bible Dictionary, pp. 519–20.

25 **And he released** unto them **him** [*Barabbas*] that for sedition and murder was cast into prison, whom they had desired; **but he** [*Pilate*] **delivered Jesus to their will** [*turned him over to the people, as they had requested*].

26 And **as they led him away, they laid hold upon** [*seized*] one **Simon, a Cyrenian**, coming out of the country [*a foreigner; probably a Jew from the city of Cyrene, in northern Africa, likely in Jerusalem for the Passover*], **and on him they laid the cross** [*made him carry Jesus' cross*], that he might bear it after [*carry it behind*] Jesus.

The Savior would have been very weak, physically, by now, having suffered in Gethsemane, having been mocked and hit by the soldiers, Luke 22:64, and scourged (whipped), Matthew 27:26. Thus, He was too weak physically to carry His own cross, which was a normal part of the punishment of crucifixion, without resorting to His divine powers.

27 And **there followed him a great company of people, and of women, which also bewailed** [*cried*] **and lamented** [*mourned for*] **him.**

28 But **Jesus turning unto them said, Daughters of Jerusalem, weep not for me, but weep for yourselves, and for your children.**

LUKE 23

29 For, **behold, the days are coming, in the which they shall say**, Blessed are the barren, and the wombs that never bare, and the paps which never gave suck. [*In other words, women who never had children are the fortunate ones. This would be exactly opposite of Jewish culture of the day, in which women who had no children were considered to be the unfortunate ones and were looked down upon.*]

30 **Then shall they begin to say to the mountains, Fall on us; and to the hills, Cover us.** [*Conditions will get so bad in Jerusalem that people will desire death rather than face the persecutions and difficulties which will come.*]

31 **For if they do these things in a green tree, what shall be done in the dry?** [*If they do such wicked things in good times, what will they do when bad times come?*]

The JST adds another verse here that is not found in the Bible.

JST Luke 23:32
This he spake, signifying the scattering of Israel, and the desolation of the heathen, or in other words, the Gentiles.

The Two Thieves

32 And there were also **two** other, **malefactors** [*criminals*], led with him to be put to death.

The Crucifixion

33 And when they were come to the place, which is called **Calvary, there they crucified him, and the malefactors** [*thieves*], **one on the right hand, and the other on the left**.

34 **Then said Jesus, Father, forgive them; for they know not what they do.** And they parted his raiment, and cast lots.

The JST makes a very important doctrinal clarification to verse 34, above.

JST Luke 23:35
35 Then said Jesus, Father, forgive them; for they know not what they do. **(Meaning the soldiers who crucified him,)** and they parted his raiment and cast lots.

(Remember, as noted several times already in this study guide, that the JST verses often have different numbers than the equivalent verses in the King James Bible—the one we use in English-speaking areas of the Church—because Joseph Smith's additions and corrections often involved adding additional verses that are not found in the Bible.)

The statement, verse 34 (JST verse 35) above, which Jesus uttered from the cross, shows His compassion for those who were crucifying Him. As noted in the JST, Joseph Smith taught that it applied to the Roman soldiers rather than the Jewish religious leaders who arranged

His crucifixion and did, at least to some extent, know what they were doing.

The Savior's Statements from the Cross

Jesus uttered a total of seven recorded statements from the cross. These statements and the references for them are given next and are in chronological order:

1. **"Father, forgive them; for they know not what they do."** Luke 23:34.

2. **"Today shalt thou be with me in paradise."** Luke 23:43.

3. **"Woman, behold thy son!" Behold thy mother!"** John 19:26-27.

4. **"My God, my God, why hast thou forsaken me?"** Matthew 27:46.

5. **"I thirst."** John 19:28.

6. **"It is finished."** John 19:30.

7. **"Father, into thy hands I commend my spirit."** Luke 23:46.

35 And **the people stood beholding** [*staring*]. **And the rulers** [*religious leaders of the Jews*] **also with them derided** [*mocked*] **him, saying, He saved others; let him save himself, if he be Christ, the chosen of God** [*the Messiah*].

36 And **the soldiers also mocked him,** coming to him, and **offering him vinegar,**

37 And **saying, If thou be the king of the Jews, save thyself.**

38 And a **superscription** also was written over him [*a sign was put above Him on the cross*] in letters of Greek, and Latin, and Hebrew, **THIS IS THE KING OF THE JEWS.**

39 And **one of the malefactors** [*thieves*] which were hanged [*being crucified*] **railed on him** [*angrily yelled insults at Him*], saying, **If thou be Christ, save thyself and us.**

40 **But the other** [*thief*] answering [*responding*] **rebuked him** [*scolded the other thief*], **saying,** Dost not thou fear God, seeing thou art in the same condemnation?

41 And we indeed justly; for we receive the due reward of our deeds [*we are getting what we deserve*]: but **this man hath done nothing amiss** [*wrong*].

42 And **he said unto Jesus, Lord, remember me when thou comest into thy kingdom.**

43 And **Jesus said unto him,** Verily I say unto thee, **To day shalt thou be with me in paradise.**

It is a common belief that the thief on the cross went to paradise. This is not the case. Our Bible Dictionary explains this. It says: "The Bible rendering is incorrect. The statement would more accurately read, 'Today shalt

LUKE 23

363

thou be with me in the world of spirits' since the thief was not ready for paradise." See Bible Dictionary under "Paradise." No doubt, with his humble attitude, this thief accepted the gospel, which would soon be taught by missionaries in Spirit Prison.

44 And it was about the sixth hour [*about noon*]**, and there was a darkness over all the earth until the ninth hour** [*about 3 P.M.*]**.**

In the Jewish time system, the "sixth hour" would be about noon, the "ninth hour" would be about 3 P.M. in our time system. We understand that Jesus was nailed onto the cross at the "third hour" which would be about 9 A.M.

45 And the sun was darkened, and the veil of the temple was rent in the midst [*torn in two*]**.**

46 And when Jesus had cried with a loud voice, he said, Father, into thy hands I commend my spirit: and having said thus, he **gave up the ghost** [*died*]**.**

47 Now when the centurion [*Roman soldier in command of one hundred soldiers*] **saw what was done, he glorified God, saying, Certainly this was a righteous man.**

It apparently startled the Centurion that Jesus had so much strength that He could speak so loudly. Usually it took two to three days for victims of crucifixion to die, and near the end they were so exhausted they would

not be able to speak loudly at all. To this soldier, experienced at crucifying people, it was as if Jesus had voluntarily left His body when He so chose, which indeed he did—see John 10:18!

48 And all the people that came together to that sight, beholding the things which were done, **smote their breasts, and returned.**

Pounding on one's chest, "smote their breasts" in verse 48 above, was a cultural way of expressing deep fear and a feeling of impending doom, destruction, etc. It had gotten extremely dark and foreboding over the last three hours. And that, plus Christ's loud voice when He left His body must have terrified them. Thus they beat their chests, with a feeling of doom hanging over them as they left for home.

49 And all his acquaintance, and the women that followed him from Galilee, stood afar off, beholding these things [*watching these things*]**.**

Joseph of Aramathaea Donates the Tomb

50 And, behold, there was a man named **Joseph**, a counsellor [*a member of the council of the Jews*]; and he **was a good man, and a just:**

Luke 23, footnote 50a in your Bible, indicates that Joseph of Aramathaea was, in effect, a senator in the leading governing council of the Jews. He was a good man. This is a pleasant reminder that there were good men also among the leaders of the Jews at the time of Christ.

51 (The same **had not consented** to the counsel and deed of them;) [*Joseph had opposed the decision of the Jewish religious leaders to execute Jesus*] he was of Arimathæa, a city of the Jews: who also himself waited for the kingdom of God [*was a faithful, righteous man*].

52 This man **went unto Pilate, and begged** [*requested*] **the body of Jesus.**

53 And **he took it down** [*from the cross*], and wrapped it in linen, and **laid it in a sepulchre** [*a tomb*] that was hewn [*cut*] in stone, wherein never man before was laid.

54 And that day was the preparation, and **the sabbath drew on.** [*It was getting very late on Friday and the Sabbath was about to begin. The Jewish Sabbath was held on Saturday.*]

55 And **the women also, which came with him** [*Jesus*] **from Galilee, followed after** [*followed Joseph of Arimathaea*], and beheld [*saw*] the sepulchre, and how his body was laid.

56 And **they returned, and prepared spices and ointments; and rested the sabbath day** according to the commandment. [*It was too late for them to anoint Jesus' body with spices and ointments, as was*] *customary, because such work was forbidden on the Sabbath. So they went home and kept the Sabbath holy, and planned on coming back to the tomb early Sunday morning to finish final preparations for the Savior's proper burial.*]

LUKE 24

This chapter is the account of the Savior's resurrection. Luke, who was a physician, gives us several details that are not included in the accounts of Matthew and Mark. It is Sunday morning, and one of the most glorious days on earth ever recorded.

The Resurrection

1 NOW **upon the first day of the week** [*Sunday*], **very early in the morning, they** [*the women named in verse 10, below*] **came unto the sepulchre** [*tomb*], bringing the spices which they had prepared, and certain others with them.

2 And **they found the stone rolled away from the sepulchre.**

3 And **they entered in, and found not the body of the Lord Jesus.**

4 And it came to pass, as **they were much perplexed** thereabout [*they were very concerned about this*], behold, **two men** [*angels*] **stood by them in shining garments:**

5 And as **they** [*the women*] **were afraid**, and bowed down their faces to the earth, they [*the angels*]

said unto them, **Why seek ye the living among the dead?**

JST Luke 24:2–4

2 And they found the stone rolled away from the sepulcher, **and two angels standing by it in shining garments**.

3 And they entered into the sepulcher, **and not finding the body of the Lord Jesus, they were much perplexed thereabout**;

4 And **were affrighted,** and bowed down their faces to the earth. **But behold the angels said unto them,** Why seek ye the living among the dead?

Watch now as the two angels gently remind these faithful women about the Savior's prophecies of His crucifixion and resurrection to them. Imagine the look on these women's faces as they remembered and realization dawned that the Master was alive!

6 **He is not here, but is risen** [*has been resurrected*]: **remember how he spake unto you** when he was yet in Galilee,

7 **Saying, The Son of man** [*The Son of God*] **must** be delivered into the hands of sinful men, and **be crucified, and the third day rise again.**

8 **And they remembered** his words,

9 And returned from the sepulchre, **and told all these things unto the eleven** [*the eleven Apostles—Judas*

was no longer among them], **and to all the rest.**

10 **It was Mary Magdalene, and Joanna**, and **Mary the mother of James**, and **other women** that were with them, which **told these things unto the apostles.**

11 And their words seemed to them [*the Apostles*] as idle tales [*nonsense*], and **they believed them not.**

12 Then arose **Peter**, and **ran unto the sepulchre; and stooping down, he beheld the linen clothes** [*Jesus' burial clothing*] **laid by themselves** [*folded in a separate stack*], **and departed**, wondering in himself at that which was come to pass [*wondering what had taken place*].

By the way, John 20:3–8 tells us that John ran with Peter and beat him to the sepulchre but waited to go in so that Peter could be first to enter.

Two Traveling on the Road to Emmaus

13 And, behold, **two of them** [*two of Christ's disciples, not Apostles*] **went that same day to a village called Emmaus**, which was from Jerusalem about threescore furlongs [*about 7 miles from Jerusalem*].

14 And **they talked together of all these things** which had happened.

15 And it came to pass, that, **while they communed together** and

reasoned [*tried to figure out what had happened*], **Jesus himself drew near, and went** [*started walking*] **with them.**

16 But **their eyes were holden** that they should not know him. [*Jesus kept them from recognizing Him yet.*]

17 And **he said unto them, What manner of communications are these that ye have** one to another, as ye walk, **and are sad** [*what are you talking about that makes you so sad*]?

18 And the one of them, whose name was **Cleopas,** answering **said unto him, Art thou only a stranger in Jerusalem, and hast not known the things which are come to pass therein these days?** [*You must have just arrived or You would know the tragic things which have happened here in recent days.*]

19 And **he said** unto them, **What things?** And **they said** unto him, **Concerning Jesus of Nazareth, which** [*who*] **was a prophet mighty in deed and word** [*powerful in actions and teaching*] before God and all the people:

20 **And how the chief priests and our rulers delivered him** [*turned Him over*] **to be condemned to death,** and **have crucified him.**

As these two disciples of the Master continue chatting with this Stranger who has joined them, you can feel their disappointment as they express to Him their dashed hopes.

21 **But we trusted that it had been he which should have redeemed Israel** [*we were hoping that He would turn out to be the promised Messiah who would free us from our enemies*]: and beside all this, **to day is the third day since these things were done** [*and besides that, it has been three days now since He was crucified*].

We see from verses 22–24, next, that these two disciples were among "all the rest" in verse 9, above, when the breathless women excitedly told the eleven Apostles what the angels had told them.

22 Yea, and **certain women** also of our company [*of our group of followers of Jesus*] **made us astonished** [*told us an amazing story*], **which were early at the sepulchre** [*who went to the tomb early this morning*];

23 And when **they found not his body,** they came, saying, that they had also seen a vision of **angels,** which [*who*] **said that he was alive.**

24 And **certain of them** [*Peter and John—see John 20:2–8*] which were with us **went to the sepulchre, and found it even so as the women had said** [*found the tomb empty, just like the women said*]: **but him they saw not** [*but Peter and John didn't see Christ*].

The implication here is that since Peter and John didn't see Jesus, and the women's account couldn't be trusted, because of the emotional state they were in,

LUKE 24

the whole thing about Jesus has turned out to be a big disappointment for these two disciples on the road to Emmaus.

Watch now as the resurrected Christ teaches a firm lesson on faith, reminding these disappointed disciples of the numerous prophecies in the Old Testament which fit what has just happened.

25 **Then he said unto them, O fools, and slow of heart to believe all that the prophets** [*such as Isaiah and Jeremiah*] **have spoken:**

26 **Ought not Christ to have suffered these things, and to enter into his glory?** [*In other words, why is it so hard to believe that Jesus was the Christ, that He suffered, died, was resurrected, and has entered into His glory in heaven?*]

27 **And beginning at Moses and all the prophets** [*starting with the writings of Moses (Genesis, Exodus, Leviticus, Numbers, and Deuteronomy) and continuing with the other Old Testament prophets*], **he expounded unto them** [*taught them*] **in all the scriptures the things concerning himself** [*prophesying of Him*].

28 And **they drew nigh** [*near*] **unto the village** [*Emmaus*], whither they went [*which was their destination*]: **and he made as though he would have gone further** [*indicated that He was going to go farther*].

29 **But they constrained him** [*begged Him*], saying, **Abide** [*stay*] **with us: for it is toward evening,** and the day is far spent. **And he went in to tarry** [*stay*] **with them.**

30 And it came to pass, **as he sat at meat** [*supper*] **with them, he took bread, and blessed it, and brake, and gave to them.**

31 And **their eyes were opened, and they knew him; and he vanished out of their sight.**

32 And they said one to another, **Did not our heart burn within us**, while he talked with us by the way [*along the way*], and while he opened [*explained*] to us the scriptures?

33 And **they rose up the same hour, and returned to Jerusalem** [*about 7 miles from Emmaus*], and **found the eleven gathered together, and them** [*other members*] **that were with them,**

34 **Saying, The Lord is risen indeed**, and hath appeared to Simon [*Peter*].

35 **And they** [*the two disciples to whom Jesus had appeared on the way to Emmaus*] **told what things were done in the way** [*as they walked along the road to Emmaus*], **and how he was known of them** in breaking of bread [*how they finally recognized Jesus*].

The Resurrected Christ Appears to the Eleven and Others in the Room

36 And **as they thus spake, Jesus himself stood in the midst of them, and saith unto them, Peace be unto you.**

37 **But they were terrified and affrighted** [*frightened*], **and supposed that they had seen a spirit** [*thought they were seeing a ghost*].

38 And **he said** unto them, **Why are ye troubled? and why do thoughts arise in your hearts?**

39 **Behold** [*look at*] **my hands and my feet, that it is I myself: handle** [*feel*] **me, and see; for a spirit hath not flesh and bones, as ye see me have.**

40 And when he had thus spoken, **he shewed** [*showed*] **them his hands and his feet.**

A major doctrine is taught in verses 39–40, above, namely that the Savior now has a resurrected body of flesh and bone. The same is true of the Father. The Doctrine and Covenants confirms this.

D&C 130:22

22 The Father has a body of flesh and bones as tangible as man's; the Son also; but the Holy Ghost has not a body of flesh and bones, but is a personage of Spirit. Were it not so, the Holy Ghost could not dwell in us.

41 And **while they yet believed** not for joy [*they were so happy they could hardly believe what was happening*], **and wondered** [*marvelled*], **he said unto them, Have ye here any meat** [*do you have any food*]?

42 And **they gave him a piece of a broiled fish, and of an honeycomb.**

43 And **he took it, and did eat before them** [*before their eyes*].

44 **And he said unto them, These are** [*this is what I meant by*] **the words which I spake unto you, while I was yet with you, that all things must be fulfilled, which were written in the law of Moses, and in the prophets, and in the psalms** [*in other words, the Old Testament*], **concerning me.**

The Savior now teaches a vital summary of His mission and Atonement.

45 **Then opened he their understanding, that they might understand the scriptures,** [*then He taught them.*]

46 And said unto them, **Thus it is written, and thus it behoved Christ to suffer** [*Christ had to suffer*], **and to rise from the dead the third day:**

47 **And that repentance and remission of sins should be preached in his name among all nations, beginning at Jerusalem.** [*The Atonement had to be preached and accomplished in order for repentance and remission of sins*

JOHN 1   369

to be made available to all people, beginning at Jerusalem.]

48 And **ye are witnesses of these things**.

49 And, **behold, I send the promise of my Father upon you** [*the Martin Luther edition of the German Bible cross-references this verse with John 16:7, which refers to the Comforter, or, in other words, the Holy Ghost*]: **but tarry ye** [*wait*] **in the city of Jerusalem, until ye be endued with** [*clothed with, endowed with*] **power from on high**.

50 **And he led them out as far as to Bethany** [*about one to two miles*

from Jerusalem], **and he lifted up his hands, and blessed them**.

The Savior's Ascension into Heaven

51 And it came to pass, **while he blessed them, he was** parted [*separated*] from them, and **carried up into heaven**.

52 And **they worshipped him, and returned to Jerusalem with great joy**:

53 **And were continually in the temple, praising and blessing God** [*expressing gratitude to God*]. Amen.

THE GOSPEL ACCORDING TO
ST JOHN

John was one of the original twelve Apostles. Before that, he was a disciple of John the Baptist, along with Peter, James, and Andrew. He was a fisherman by trade, in partnership with Peter, Andrew [*Peter's brother*] and James [*John's brother*].

Whereas the gospels of Matthew, Mark, and Luke cover essentially the same material, presenting a narrative of the Savior's mortal life and teachings, the Gospel of John emphasizes the Savior's role in the overall plan of salvation and presents many more doctrines taught by Him. Matthew, Mark, and Luke

are sometimes referred to as the "Synoptic Gospels," meaning that they are "from the same view," in other words, they are similar.

According to D&C 7:3, John was translated [*has not died yet—is like the Three Nephites*] and will continue to preach the gospel on earth and help with the gathering of Israel until the Second Coming. In 1831, the Prophet Joseph Smith said that, at that time, John was working with the lost ten tribes, preparing them for their return. See *History of the Church*, Vol. 1, p. 176. John is the author of four other books in the Bible, 1 John,

370   THE NEW TESTAMENT MADE EASIER THIRD EDITION, PART 1

2 John, 3 John and the book of Revelation.

Note: As mentioned in the Introduction to Part 1 of this study guide, I have used **bold font** to suggest ways you might mark your own scriptures or to help you see at-a-glance the main concepts in each verse. As I mentioned then, I will not use **bold** for John and for Part 2 of this study guide, except occasionally to emphasize for teaching purposes and to show JST changes. The idea is that by now you will have learned much and will have your own ideas about what to mark and emphasize as you go along.

JOHN 1

This chapter contains John's introduction to the Savior's mortal life and mission. He introduces Him as the Creator of the world and gives many details about His work. He then tells us about the baptism of Jesus by John the Baptist and the calling of several men who would later become Apostles.

Joseph Smith made many additions and clarifications in verses 1–34. The JST (Joseph Smith Translation of the Bible) contains these changes. You can read JST John 1:1–34 in its entirety in the back of your Latter-day Saint English-speaking Bible in the section titled "Joseph Smith translation." We will include many of these JST changes as we study chapter 1. (Remember, I often use "we" when it is actually "I" who

am talking. Again, as mentioned previously, my parents taught me to avoid "I trouble," or, in other words, referring to myself too much.)

By the way, just by glancing at the large number of footnotes included in your Bible for John, chapter 1, you can tell that John's account contains a large number of doctrines.

1 IN the beginning was the Word, and the Word was with God, and the Word was God.

JST John 1:1

1 In the beginning was the **gospel preached through the Son. And the gospel was the word, and the word was with the Son, and the Son** was with God, and the **Son was of God**.

2 The same [*Christ*] was in the beginning with God [*the Father*].

3 All things were made by him; and without him was not any thing made that was made. [*Christ is the Creator.*]

4 In him was life; and the life was the light of men.

JST John 1:4

4 In him was **the gospel, and the gospel was the life**, and the life was the light of men;

5 And the light shineth in darkness [*in the spiritually dark world*]; and the darkness comprehended it not.

JOHN 1

JST John 1:5

5 And the light shineth in **the world**, and the **world perceiveth** it not.

6 There was a man sent from God, whose name was John [*John the Baptist*].

7 The same came for a witness, to bear witness of the Light, that all men through him might believe.

JST John 1:7

7 The same came **into the world** for a witness, to bear witness of the light, **to bear record of the gospel through the Son, unto all, that through him men** might believe.

8 He [*John the Baptist*] was not that Light, but was sent to bear witness of that Light.

9 That was the true Light [*Christ*], which lighteth every man that cometh into the world [*see D&C 93:2*].

The "Light of Christ" is often referred to as the "conscience" which is given to every person born into this world. This is true, and as a result, all people have a basic God-given ability to tell right from wrong, and thus are accountable to God to a certain degree for their behaviors. But the Light of Christ is much more than a conscience. A major purpose of it is to lead people to the true gospel, where they can be baptized and receive the Holy Ghost, which is a far more powerful "light."

10 He was in the world, and the world was made by him, and the world knew him not.

JST John 1:10

10 **Even the Son of God**. He **who** was in the world, and the world was made by him, and the world knew him not.

11 He came unto his own, and his own received him not [*His own people rejected Him*].

12 But as many as received him, to them gave he power to become the sons of God [*power to become exalted; see D&C 76:24*], even to them that believe on his name:

JST John 1:12

12 But as many as received him, to them gave he power to become the sons of God; **only** to them who believe on his name.

13 Which were born, not of blood, nor of the will of the flesh, nor of the will of man, but of God. [*In other words, Jesus was literally the Son of God, not just a highly successful man born to mortal parents.*]

JST John 1:13

13 **He was born**, not of blood, nor of the will of **the flesh**, nor of the will of man, but of God.

14 And the Word [*Christ*] was made flesh [*received a mortal body*], and dwelt among us, (and we beheld his glory, the glory as of the only begotten of the Father,) full of grace [*ability to help us*] and truth.

Sometimes confusion arises between Christ's being the "Only Begotten of the Father" and our being spirit sons and daughters of God. In other words, we are also begotten of the Father. So, how can we be begotten of the Father if Christ is the "Only Begotten" of the Father? The answer is simple. In premortality, all of us, including Jesus, were begotten and born as spirit children of our heavenly parents (see Proclamation on the Family, September 23, 1995, second paragraph). But Jesus was the only mortal whose father was Heavenly Father. Thus, Jesus is the "Only Begotten of the Father (as a mortal), and that is what the phrase "Only Begotten" means, wherever we find it in the scriptures and in the teachings of the leaders of the Church.

15 John [*the Baptist*] bare [*bore*] witness of him [*Christ*], and cried [*preached*], saying, This was he of whom I spake, He that cometh after me is preferred before me [*is higher in authority than I am*]: for he was before me.

JST John 1:15
15 John bear witness of him, and cried, saying, This **is** he of whom I spake; He who cometh after me, is preferred before me; for he was before me.

16 And of his fulness have all we received, and grace for grace. [*We have been taught the fulness or the complete gospel by Christ, thus*

are in a position to proceed step by step until we gain exaltation.]

JST verse 16, next, is not found in the Bible.

JST John 1:16
16 **For in the beginning was the Word, even the Son, who is made flesh, and sent unto us by the will of the Father. And as many as believe on his name shall receive of his fullness. And of his fullness have all we received, even immortality and eternal life, through his grace.**

17 For the law [*of Moses, Genesis, Exodus, Leviticus, Numbers, and Deuteronomy*] was given by Moses, but grace and truth [*the full gospel*] came by Jesus Christ.

JST John 1:17-18
17 For the law was given **through** Moses, but **life** [*eternal life, which means exaltation*] and truth came through Jesus Christ.

18 For the law was **after a carnal commandment, to the administration of death; but the gospel was after the power of an endless life** [*eternal life, exaltation*], **through** Jesus Christ, **the Only Begotten Son, who is in the bosom of the Father**.

Verse 17 and JST verse 18, above, are basically saying that the Law of Moses was a schoolmaster law to help prepare the Israelites for the higher law which the Savior restored to earth. No one could be saved

JOHN 1

in celestial exaltation through the Law of Moses. It is only through the full gospel, with all covenants and ordinances, that we can be exalted. By the way, this would not be a particularly popular thing for John the Baptist to say, because people of his day would look upon it as a "put down" for Moses, whom they considered to be their most important prophet.

18 No man hath seen God at any time; the only begotten Son, which is in the bosom of the Father, he hath declared him.

JST John 1:19

19 And no man hath seen God at any time, **except he hath borne record of the Son; for except it is through him no man can be saved**.

Many Christians use verse 18 above, as it stands in the Bible, to argue that Joseph Smith could not have seen Heavenly Father. Most of them won't accept the JST change, which clears up the matter. Therefore, it is sometimes helpful to invite them to turn to Acts 7:55-56, and show them that Stephen saw both the Father and the Son.

19 And this is the record of John [*the Baptist*], when the Jews sent priests and Levites [*religious leaders of the Jews*] from Jerusalem to ask him, Who art thou?

20 And he [*John the Baptist*] confessed, and denied not; but confessed, I am not the Christ.

JST John 1:21

21 And he confessed, and denied not **that he was Elias**; but confessed, **saying**; I am not the Christ.

The word "Elias," among other definitions, means "one who prepares the way." See Bible Dictionary, under "Elias." Obviously, the Jewish religious leaders were familiar with prophecies that said that an Elias would prepare the way before the Messiah (example: Isaiah 40:3), and thus, when they heard all the talk about John the Baptist, they sent some of their men to ask him some questions.

21 And they asked him, What then? Art thou Elias? And he saith, I am not. Art thou that prophet? And he answered, No.

JST John 1:22

22 And they asked him, **saying; How then art thou Elias?** And he **said, I am not that Elias** [*Christ*] **who was to restore all things. And they asked him, saying,** Art thou that prophet? And he answered, No.

Verse 21 above may need a bit of clarification. First of all, as you can see in the JST, Joseph Smith added "I am not that Elias who was to restore all things." This is very helpful, because it lets us know that we are dealing with two different definitions of "Elias" in these verses. One Elias is a "preparer." The other "Elias" is a "restorer." John the Baptist is the "preparer" while Jesus is the "restorer." See Bible Dictionary, under "Elias." So, what John the Baptist is emphatically saying to the questioners in verse 21 is "No, I am not the Messiah! Rather, I am the Elias who is preparing the way for Him."

22 Then said they [*the messengers sent from the Jewish religious leaders in verse 19 above*] unto him, Who art thou? that we may give an answer to them that sent us. What sayest thou of thyself [*tell us about you*]?

23 He said, I am the voice of one crying in the wilderness, Make straight the way of the Lord, as said the prophet Esaias [*Isaiah; see Isaiah 40:3*].

24 And they which were sent were of the Pharisees. [*Pharisees were another group of religious leaders among the Jews.*]

25 And they asked him, and said unto him, Why baptizest thou then, if thou be not that Christ, nor Elias neither that prophet? [*In other words, why are you baptizing if you are not the prophesied Messiah?*]

JST John 1:26
26 And they asked him, and said unto him, Why baptizest thou then, if thou be not **the** Christ, nor Elias **who was to restore all things, neither that prophet?**

26 John answered them, saying, I baptize with water: but there standeth one among you, whom ye know not; [*referring to Jesus, who is*

just preparing to begin His mortal ministry.]

27 He it is, who coming after me is preferred before me [*is higher in authority than I*], whose shoe's latchet [*sandal buckle*] I am not worthy to unloose.

JST John 1:28
28 He it is **of whom I bear record. He is that prophet** [*Jesus Christ*]**, even Elias, who, coming after me,** is preferred before me, whose shoe's latchet I am not worthy to unloose, **or whose place I am not able to fill; for he shall baptize, not only with water, but with fire, and with the Holy Ghost**.

28 These things were done in Bethabara beyond Jordan, where John was baptizing.

Jesus Is Baptized

29 The next day John seeth Jesus coming unto him, and saith, Behold the Lamb of God, which taketh away the sin of the world. [*John the Baptist bears witness of Jesus to the crowd around him.*]

30 This is he of whom I said, After me cometh a man which is preferred before me: for he was before me.

31 And I knew him not: but that he should be made manifest to Israel, therefore [*this is the reason, in answer to the question in verse 25*] am I come baptizing with water.

JST John 1:30

30 **And John bare record of him unto the people, saying**, This is he of whom I said; After me cometh a man who is preferred before me; for he was before me, and **I knew him, and** that he should be made manifest to Israel; therefore am I come baptizing with water.

Remember that the verse numbers of the JST are not always the same as the Bible verse numbers.

Look carefully at JST John 1:30, quoted above and compare it with John 1:31, above. Did you see the difference? It is a very important change. The Bible says, "I knew him not," which would indicate that John the Baptist did not recognize Jesus. However, the JST gives the true account and says, "I knew him," indicating that John the Baptist did know and recognize Jesus. See also verse 33 and compare with JST, verse 32. (Remember, as explained previously many times in this study guide, the JST verse numbers are sometimes different than the equivalent verses in the Bible because of the Prophet Joseph Smith making corrections to, combining, and adding several verses not found in the Bible to the JST text.)

32 And John bare record, saying, I saw the Spirit descending from heaven like a dove, and it abode upon him.

JST John 1:31

31 And John bare record, saying; **When he was baptized of me,**

I saw the Spirit descending from heaven like a dove, and it abode upon him.

Sometimes people ask whether or not the Holy Ghost, on occasions, changes into a dove. The answer is "No." The Prophet Joseph Smith taught:

"The Holy Ghost is a personage, and is in the form of a personage. It does not confine itself to the *form* of the dove, but in *sign* of the dove. The Holy Ghost cannot be transformed into a dove; but the sign of a dove was given to John to signify the truth of the deed, as the dove is an emblem or token of truth and innocence." (*Teachings of the Prophet Joseph Smith*, 1976, pp. 275–276.)

33 And I knew him not: but he that sent me to baptize with water, the same said unto me, Upon whom thou shalt see the Spirit descending, and remaining on him, the same is he which baptizeth with the Holy Ghost.

JST John 1:32

32 And **I knew him**; **for** he **who** sent me to baptize with water, the same said unto me; Upon whom thou shalt see the Spirit descending, and remaining on him, the same is he **who** baptizeth with the Holy Ghost.

34 And I saw, and bare record that this is the Son of God.

Although John already was acquainted with Jesus (see JST

in verses 31 and 32 above), the Holy Ghost bore strong witness of the Savior to John at the time he baptized Christ.

35 Again the next day after John stood, and two of his disciples [*the day after he baptized Jesus, John the Baptist was standing with two of his own followers*];

36 And looking upon Jesus as he walked [*and seeing Jesus as He walked by*], he [*John*] saith, Behold [*look!*] the Lamb of God!

37 And the two disciples [*John's followers*] heard him [*John the Baptist*] speak, and they followed Jesus.

38 Then Jesus turned, and saw them following, and saith unto them, What seek ye [*what can I do for you*]? They said unto him, Rabbi, (which is to say, being interpreted, Master,) where dwellest thou [*where do you live*]?

It may be that the two disciples of John the Baptist who left John and began following Jesus were caught a bit off guard when the Master turned and asked what He could do for them (verse 38, above). Perhaps, at a loss for something to say, they quickly stammered, "Uh, where do You live?" Of course we don't know if this was the case, but it brings a bit of a smile to our faces when we consider this as a possibility.

Whatever the case, He was very kind to them and invited them to "Come and see" (verse 39, next).

39 He saith unto them, Come and see. They came and saw where he dwelt [*lived*], and abode [*stayed*] with him that day: for it was about the tenth hour [*about 4 P.M.*].

40 One of the two which heard John speak, and followed him, was Andrew, Simon Peter's brother. [*Andrew will become one of the Savior's original twelve Apostles, as will Peter.*]

JST John 1:40
40 One of the two **who** heard John, and followed **Jesus**, was Andrew, Simon Peter's brother.

41 He first findeth his own brother Simon [*Peter*], and saith unto him, We have found the Messias [*the promised Messiah*], which is, being interpreted, the Christ [*"the Anointed One"*].

Anointing is a very significant thing in the Bible. It means "being prepared for" a future event or blessing. David was "anointed" to become king some years before he became king. When we administer to the sick, we "anoint" him or her first, in preparation for the actual blessing. Christ was the "Anointed One," meaning he was prepared in advance to actually perform the Atonement when the time was right for his mortal mission.

42 And he [*Andrew*] brought him [*Peter*] to Jesus. And when Jesus beheld [*saw*] him, he said, Thou art Simon the son of Jona: thou

shalt be called Cephas, which is by interpretation, A stone.

JST John 1:42

42 And he brought him to Jesus. And when Jesus beheld him, he said, Thou art Simon, the son of Jona, thou shalt be called Cephas, which is, by interpretation, a **seer, or** a stone. **And they were fishermen. And they straightway left all, and followed Jesus**.

It is interesting to watch the Master at work, building Peter's self-image and confidence. Imagine Peter saying to himself afterward, "Wow! He called me a rock. That means He thinks I am a 'rock solid' person. Well, I'll just make sure I am!"

43 The day following Jesus would [*decided to*] go forth into Galilee, and findeth Philip, and saith unto him, Follow me.

44 Now Philip was of Bethsaida, the city of Andrew and Peter [*the same city where Andrew and Peter lived*].

JST John 1:44

44 Now Philip was **at** Bethsaida, the city of Andrew and Peter.

45 Philip findeth Nathanael, and saith unto him, We have found him [*the Messiah*], of whom Moses in the law [*the first five books of the Old Testament*], and the prophets [*Old Testament prophets such as Isaiah and Jeremiah*], did write, Jesus of Nazareth, the son of Joseph [*the carpenter of Nazareth*].

When Nathanael asks his question, in verse 46, he gets a very important answer which can apply to all of us.

46 And Nathanael said unto him, Can there any good thing come out of Nazareth? Philip saith unto him, Come and see.

47 Jesus saw Nathanael coming to him, and saith of him, Behold an Israelite indeed, in whom is no guile!

48 Nathanael saith unto him, Whence knowest thou me [*how do You know me*]? Jesus answered and said unto him, Before that Philip called thee, when thou wast under the fig tree, I saw thee [*I saw you sitting under a fig tree before Philip talked to you*].

49 Nathanael answered and saith unto him, Rabbi, thou art the Son of God; thou art the King of Israel.

50 Jesus answered and said unto him, Because I said unto thee, I saw thee under the fig tree, believest thou? thou shalt see greater things than these.

51 And he saith unto him, Verily, verily, I say unto you, Hereafter ye shall see heaven open, and the angels of God ascending and descending upon the Son of man [*Christ; the JST corrects this to read "Son of Man"*].

Note: Jesus is often referred to as "the Son of man" in the New Testament. Moses 6:57 in the Pearl of Great Price teaches us what it means and how it should be written. It says, "For, in the language of Adam, Man of Holiness is his name [*Heavenly Father's name*], and the name of his Only Begotten is the Son of Man, even Jesus Christ." Therefore, the full name of the Savior, in the language of Adam, would be "Son of Man of Holiness." For whatever reason, the printers of the King James Bible neglected to capitalize "Man" and thus printed it "Son of man."

JOHN 2

Next comes one of the most famous miracles performed by the Master. It is the turning of water into wine. After telling us of this miracle, John will speak of the cleansing of the temple in Jerusalem, as Jesus begins His three-year ministry. He will cleanse the temple again during the last week of His mortal life (see Matthew 21:12–16 and Luke 19:45–46) after His triumphal entry into Jerusalem. In this chapter the Savior will prophesy His death and resurrection.

The JST will add very important items to the account of this first recorded miracle of the Savior (see verse 11), as He turns water to wine. Pay special attention to the difference in meaning between verse 4 and JST verse 4.

The First Recorded Miracle

1 AND the third day there was a marriage in Cana of Galilee; and the mother of Jesus was there:

JST John 2:1
1 And on the third day **of the week**, there was a marriage in Cana of Galilee; and the mother of Jesus was there.

2 And both Jesus was called [*invited*], and his disciples, to the marriage.

Some have wondered if this could be Jesus' marriage. Several factors combine to suggest that this would not be the case. For one thing, in the culture of the day, the marriage would be held at the groom's home town. If it were Jesus' wedding, it would have been held in Nazareth. Another thing against this notion is that Jesus and His disciples were invited to attend (verse 2). This would be a bit strange if He were the groom. Yet another factor is that the master of ceremonies of the festivities called the groom over to talk to him (verse 9), and there is no indication that this was Jesus. And finally, if it were Christ's wedding, one would expect the Gospel writers to mention it.

It does appear from the next verses that Mary, Jesus' mother, had a role in helping to host the guests at this wedding celebration. Perhaps she was a good friend of the family. Whatever the case, she knew who her Son was, and when they ran out of wine, she requested His help.

3 And when they wanted wine [*when they ran out of wine*], the mother of Jesus saith unto him, They have no wine.

JOHN 2

4 Jesus saith unto her, Woman, what have I to do with thee? mine hour is not yet come [*I have time to help*].

JST John 2:4
4 Jesus said unto her, Woman, what **wilt thou have me to do for thee? that will I do**; **for** mine hour is not yet come.

We understand that the phrase, "mine hour is not yet come," in verse 4, above, is a way of saying, in effect, that Jesus had not yet begun His formal mission. Verse 13 marks the beginning of His formal three-year mortal mission. It is also helpful to note that the word "woman" was a term of high respect in the days of Jesus.

5 His mother saith unto the servants, Whatsoever he saith unto you, do it [*do whatever He says*].

6 And there were set there six waterpots of stone, after the manner of the purifying of the Jews, containing two or three firkins apiece.

When we do the math, we see that this was apparently a rather large wedding celebration. Wedding feasts customarily lasted the better part of a week and there were apparently more guests than expected at this one. A "firkin" was a little more than 8 gallons. See Bible Dictionary, under "Weights and Measures," then under "bath" and "firkin." So, there were six containers, with a capacity of 16 to 24 gallons each. This would make a total of about 96 to 144 gallons of water which Jesus turned into wine. Thus, we sense that this was a rather unexpectedly large group, which apparently caught the host off guard when it came to having sufficient wine for the festivities.

Imagine the looks on the servants' faces as they carried out the Master's instructions, next.

7 Jesus saith unto them [*the servants*], Fill the waterpots with water. And they filled them up to the brim.

8 And he saith unto them, Draw out now, and bear unto the governor of the feast [*take wine out of the containers and take some to the master of ceremonies*]. And they bare it.

JST John 2:8
8 And he **said**, Draw out now, and bear unto the governor of the feast. And they bare **unto him**.

9 When the ruler [*host, master of ceremonies*] of the feast had tasted the water that was made wine, and knew not whence it was [*didn't know where it came from*]: (but the servants which drew the water knew;) the governor of the feast called the bridegroom [*the groom*],

10 And saith unto him, Every man at the beginning [*of the celebration*] doth set forth good wine; and when men have well drunk, then that which is worse: but thou hast kept the good wine until now.

Since wine was expensive, the common practice was to set good wine out at the beginning of the feast, then when the guests had drunk enough to become less discriminating, less expensive wine was served to save on expenses. The master of ceremonies was surprised that the groom was serving the best wine at this point of the feast.

11 This beginning of miracles [*the first miracle*] did Jesus in Cana of Galilee, and manifested forth his glory; and his disciples believed on him. [*This was a faith-promoting miracle for His disciples.*]

JST John 2:11
11 This beginning of miracles did Jesus in Cana of Galilee, and manifested forth his glory; **and the faith of his disciples was strengthened in him**.

12 After this he went down to Capernaum, he, and his mother, and his brethren [*probably His half-brothers, children of Joseph and Mary; see John 2:12, footnote a in your Latter-day Saint Bible*], and his disciples: and they continued [*stayed*] there not many days.

The Beginning of the Savior's Formal Three-Year Public Mortal Mission

13 And the Jews' passover was at hand, and Jesus went up to Jerusalem,

This marks the beginning of the Savior's formal three-year

public ministry. The Feast of the Passover was celebrated in the springtime at about the same time as we celebrate Easter. It brought large numbers of Jews from near and far to Jerusalem to join in the worship and celebration. It commemorated the destroying angel's passing over the houses of the children of Israel in Egypt, when the firstborn of the Egyptians were killed. The Israelites in Egypt at the time were instructed by Moses to sacrifice a lamb without blemish and to put blood from the lamb which was sacrificed on the doorposts of their houses. See Bible Dictionary, under "Feasts." Thus, through the blood of a lamb, the Israelites were protected from the anguish and punishment brought to the Egyptians by the destroying angel. The symbolism is clear. It is by the "blood of the Lamb" (the sacrifice of the Savior) that we are saved, after all we can do (2 Nephi 25:23). This is the first Passover attended by Jesus after he began His three-year ministry. Three years from now, at the time of Passover in Jerusalem, the "Lamb of God," Christ, will present Himself to be sacrificed that we might be saved.

The First Cleansing of the Temple

14 And found in the temple [*the outer courtyard or "temple grounds"*] those that sold oxen and sheep and doves, and the changers of money sitting:

JOHN 2

Because Jews came from all over, including many other countries to worship at the temple in Jerusalem, it had become big business for merchants to sell sacrificial animals and to exchange foreign money for temple coin. It was a wild, boisterous scene of animal sounds, merchants yelling at patrons to buy from them, etc., anything but reverent and worshipful, which met the Savior's eyes as He approached the temple. He will cleanse the temple again in three years during the last week of His life.

15 And when he had made a scourge [*whip*] of small cords, he drove them all out of the temple, and the sheep, and the oxen; and poured out the changers' money, and overthrew the tables;

16 And said unto them that sold doves, Take these things hence [*get these things out of here*]; make not my Father's house an house of merchandise [*a common market place*].

17 And his disciples remembered that it was written [*in the scriptures*], The zeal of thine house hath eaten me up [*Psalm 69:9*].

18 Then answered the Jews [*the Jewish religious leaders responded*] and said unto him, What sign shewest thou unto us, seeing that thou doest these things [*where did You get authority to cleanse the temple*]?

19 Jesus answered and said unto them, Destroy this temple, and in three days I will raise it up. [*In other words, Jesus is telling them that He is the Messiah. That is where He gets His authority. When they kill Him, as prophesied, He will resurrect in three days.*]

20 Then said the Jews [*who missed the point completely*], Forty and six years was this temple in building [*it took forty six years to build this temple*], and wilt thou rear it up [*rebuild it*] in three days?

21 But he spake of the temple of his body.

John indicates in verse 22, next, that when the disciples first heard this prophecy from Him that He would be resurrected three days after His death, it did not sink in. But when He was actually resurrected, they remembered back upon this prophecy and that He had told them it would take place.

22 When therefore he was risen from the dead [*resurrected*], his disciples remembered [*recalled*] that he had said this unto them; and they believed the scripture, and the word which Jesus had said.

23 Now when he was in Jerusalem at the passover, in the feast day [*on Thursday, the day of the actual Passover feast*], many believed in his name, when they saw the miracles which he did.

24 But Jesus did not commit himself unto them [*did not let down His guard*], because he knew all men,

JST John 2:24

24 But Jesus did not commit himself unto them, because he knew all **things**,

25 And needed not that any should testify of man: for he knew what was in man [*He knew their thoughts*].

JOHN 3

Many members of the Church are extra familiar with this chapter because of verse 3, which is much quoted in teaching the necessity of baptism.

1 THERE was a man of the Pharisees [*who was a Pharisee*], named Nicodemus, a ruler [*leader*] of the Jews:

The Pharisees were prominent religious leaders among the Jews. Jesus' popularity has begun to threaten their position of power and control over the Jews. They will play a prominent role in getting Him crucified. However, Nicodemus is a good man and will oppose the majority of the Pharisees. He now sincerely seeks Jesus out to ask Him questions. He is probably many years older than Jesus. In about three years, he will help Joseph of Arimathea take Christ's crucified body, prepare it for burial and gently place it in the tomb. See John 19:38–42.

2 The same [*Nicodemus*] came to Jesus by night, and said unto him,

Rabbi [*"my master," a humble, respectful term for "my teacher"*], we know that thou art a teacher come from God: for no man can do these miracles that thou doest, except God be with him.

3 Jesus answered and said unto him, Verily, verily, I say unto thee, Except a man be born again, he cannot see the kingdom of God.

Simply put, being "born again" means to be baptized and then to be directed by the Holy Ghost to become a new person, cleansed from sin and worthy to comfortably enter into the celestial kingdom.

In effect, Jesus is saying to Nicodemus, "I want you to be My child, spiritually, to be born again spiritually, and then let the Holy Ghost teach you in the ways of righteousness so that you can live with Me in celestial glory." (Compare with Mosiah 5:7.)

Obviously, Nicodemus does not understand the symbolism at first, and so asks a good question, seeking clarification.

4 Nicodemus saith unto him, How can a man be born when he is old? can he enter the second time into his mother's womb, and be born?

Baptism and the Gift of the Holy Ghost are Essential

5 Jesus answered, Verily, verily [*this is the main point; listen carefully*], I say unto thee, Except a man be born of water [*baptized*] and of

JOHN 3

383

the Spirit [*receive the gift of the Holy Ghost*], he cannot enter into the kingdom of God [*he cannot be taught the things he must do to become celestial*].

6 That which is born of the flesh is flesh; and that which is born of the Spirit is spirit [*there is a difference between being a common person and being a spiritual person*].

7 Marvel not that I said unto thee, Ye must be born again.

8 The wind bloweth where it listeth [*where it will*], and thou hearest the sound thereof, but canst not tell whence it cometh [*where it comes from*], and whither it goeth [*where it is going*]: so is every one that is born of the Spirit. [*Perhaps meaning that that is how it is with one who has the gift of the Holy Ghost. Promptings come and inspiration is given. We don't demand it or control it any more than we can control the wind, but it does come and it comes according to the will of the Lord.*]

9 Nicodemus answered and said unto him, How can these things be?

10 Jesus answered and said unto him, Art thou a master [*religious ruler*] of Israel, and knowest not these things? [*Nicodemus was a member of the Sanhedrin, the chief ruling body of religious leaders over the Jews; see Bible Dictionary, under "Sanhedrin."*]

11 Verily, verily, I say unto thee, We speak that [*what*] we do know,

and testify that we have seen; and ye [*the people of the world*] receive not our witness [*do not accept our testimony*].

> Verses 11–21 seem to be a direct quote which would be familiar to Nicodemus. See John 3:11, footnote b. We don't know where it comes from, but the Savior used it to teach this good man.

12 If I have told you earthly things [*simple basics such as faith, repentance, and baptism*], and ye believe not, how shall ye believe, if I tell you of heavenly things?

13 And no man hath ascended up to heaven, but he that came down from heaven, even the Son of man which is in heaven. [*Christ bears witness that He is the Son of God.*]

14 And as Moses lifted up the serpent in the wilderness [*Numbers 21:8–9*], even so must the Son of man [*Christ*] be lifted up: [*Christ will be crucified as part of His Atonement.*]

15 That whosoever believeth in him should not perish [*spiritually*], but have eternal life [*exaltation*].

> By the way, "eternal life," as used in the scriptures, always means exaltation in the highest degree of glory in the celestial kingdom. "Immortality" is the term that is used for "living forever" after being resurrected. All people who have ever been born into mortality will eventually be resurrected and will thus have immortality, regardless of whether they go to a degree of

glory or even to outer darkness. (See D&C 88:28–32.)

Keep in mind that the Savior is continuing to answer Nicodemus' question in verse 9, above. As mentioned after verse 11, verses 11–21 appear to be a direct quote from scriptures that Nicodemus would recognize. Verse 16, next, is beautiful and is often quoted in our day. If you are marking verses in your own Bible, you may wish to mark this one now.

16 For God so loved the world, that he gave his only begotten Son, that whosoever believeth in him should not perish, but have everlasting life [*exaltation*].

17 For God sent not his Son into the world to condemn the world; but that the world through him might be saved.

18 He that believeth on him is not condemned [*stopped in progress*]: but he that believeth not is condemned already, because he hath not believed in the name of the only begotten Son of God.

JST John 3:18
18 He **who** believeth on him is not condemned; but he **who** believeth not is condemned already, because he hath not believed **on** the name of the Only Begotten Son of God, **which before was preached by the mouth of the holy prophets; for they testified of me.**

The JST addition, "testified of

me" is a most significant addition, because it tells us that Jesus was telling Nicodemus clearly that He, Jesus, is the Son of God.

19 And this is the condemnation [*this is the reason people get condemned, in other words, stopped in their spiritual progress*], that light is come into the world [*because the gospel is presented to them*], and men loved darkness rather than light [*and people choose wickedness rather than the gospel*], because their deeds were evil.

20 For every one that doeth evil hateth the light [*wickedness, by its very nature, makes you hate light and truth*], neither cometh to the light, lest his deeds should be reproved. [*People involved in wickedness won't come to the light because they don't want to face the consequences of their sins.*]

21 But he that doeth truth [*lives righteously*] cometh to the light, that his deeds may be made manifest [*made known*], that they are wrought in God [*accomplished through God's help*].

JST John 3:21–22
21 But he **who loveth** truth, cometh to the light, that his deeds may be made manifest.

22 **And he who obeyeth the truth, the works which he doeth they are of God**.

The Savior's personal teaching session with Nicodemus ends with verse 21 (JST 21–22), above. We are left not knowing the outcome, but we do know that he defended Jesus to the Pharisees (John 7:50) and that he assisted with the Savior's burial (John 19:39).

22 After these things came Jesus and his disciples into the land of Judæa [*the southern province of the Holy Land in which Jerusalem was located*]; and there he tarried [*remained*] with them, and baptized.

For a short period of time here, the missions of John the Baptist and Jesus overlapped.

John the Baptist

23 And John [*the Baptist*] also was baptizing in Aenon near to Salim [*in the Jordan River, about half way between the Sea of Galilee and the Dead Sea*], because there was much water there: and they came, and were baptized.

The fact that John the Baptist was baptizing in a place where there was "much water" is another reminder that he was baptizing by immersion. In fact, the word "baptize" means to immerse. See Bible Dictionary, under "Baptism."

24 For John was not yet cast into prison [*the Baptist hadn't yet been put in prison*].

25 Then there arose a question between some of John's disciples [*John the Baptist's followers*] and the Jews about purifying. [*In other words, a debate as to whether or*

not direct descendants of Abraham, such as the Jews, even needed baptism in order to be "purified."]

The "purifying," mentioned in verse 25 above, refers to the purifying power of baptism. A long-standing apostate Jewish tradition taught that only Gentile converts needed to be baptized, and that direct descendants of Abraham, such as the Jews, were exempted from baptism. In fact, they had substituted other washing and cleansing rites for themselves. See Mark 7:1–8. See *Doctrinal New Testament Commentary*, Vol. 1, p. 146.

26 And they [*John's disciples*] came unto John, and said unto him, Rabbi [*"my master;" see Bible Dictionary, under "Rabbi"*], he [*Jesus*] that was with thee beyond Jordan, to whom thou barest witness [*of whom you bore testimony*], behold, the same baptizeth, and all men come to him.

<u>JST John 3:27</u>

27 And they came unto John, and said unto him, Rabbi, he **who** was with thee beyond Jordan, to whom thou bearest witness, behold, the same baptizeth, **and he receiveth of all people who come unto him**.

Perhaps John's followers are a bit jealous or concerned that "all men come to him." In other words, they are saying, "Everybody is coming to Jesus." Perhaps they are worried that Jesus is taking away from John's popularity.

27 John answered and said, A man can receive nothing, except it be given him from heaven [*each of us only does the work assigned to us by God*].

28 Ye yourselves bear me witness [*you are my witnesses*], that I said, I am not the Christ, but that I am sent before him. [*In effect, saying that Jesus' mission is to be the Messiah. My mission is to prepare the way for Him.*]

29 He that hath the bride [*He to whom the Church belongs*] is the bridegroom [*Jesus*]: but the friend [*John the Baptist*] of the bridegroom, which standeth and heareth him, rejoiceth greatly because of the bridegroom's voice: this my joy therefore is fulfilled. [*In effect, John is saying that he is very happy just to be a friend of Jesus and to hear Him preaching.*]

Verse 30, next, is one of the sweetest, most humble statements ever uttered. Among other things, John the Baptist is saying that his own mission and popularity are drawing to a close, and he humbly accepts that fact.

30 He must increase, but I must decrease.

31 He [*Jesus*] that cometh from above [*from heaven*] is above all [*is in charge of all things here*]: he that is of the earth is earthly [*I am just an ordinary man*], and speaketh of the earth: he that cometh from heaven is above all.

32 And what he hath seen and heard, that he testifieth; and no man receiveth his testimony [*people will reject Christ*].

JST John 3:32
32 He **who** cometh from above is above all; he who is of the earth is earthly, and speaketh of the earth; he **who** cometh from heaven is above all. And what he hath seen and heard, that he testifieth; and **but few men receive** his testimony.

Did you notice that JST verse 32, above, changes "no man receiveth his testimony" to "but few men receive his testimony"? This is a significant doctrinal change.

33 He that hath received his testimony hath set to his seal that God is true. [*Those who accept Christ's testimony certify that this is God's work.*]

34 For he [*Christ*] whom God [*the Father*] hath sent speaketh the words of God: for God giveth not the Spirit by measure unto him. [*Jesus is not limited like we are in how much of the Spirit of God He has.*]

JST John 3:34
34 For he whom God hath sent, speaketh the words of God; for God giveth **him not the Spirit by measure, for he dwelleth in him, even the fullness**.

35 The Father loveth the Son, and hath given all things into his hand [*has given Jesus full authority to accomplish his mission*].

JOHN 4 387

36 He that believeth on the Son hath everlasting life [*will receive exaltation*]: and he that believeth not the Son shall not see life [*will not be exalted*]; but the wrath [*punishment*] of God abideth on him [*will come upon him*].

JST John 3:36

36 And he **who** believeth on the Son hath everlasting life; **and shall receive of his fullness**. But he who believeth not the Son, shall not **receive of his fullness; for the wrath of God is upon him**.

JOHN 4

In this chapter, among other things, John gives us the account of the woman at the well. It is a well-known, delightful, and deeply moving story. We will watch as the Master teaches her about "living water." Perhaps you are already noticing that John gives much about the Savior's ministry that is not contained elsewhere in the New Testament.

As the chapter opens, we see that opposition to Jesus is mounting in Judea, and, as a result, He determines to go north to the province of Galilee. In so doing, He chooses to go through Samaria, rather than skirting it as is normally the practice among the Jews at the time. Once again, the JST will be very significant to our correct understanding of what John writes.

1 WHEN therefore the Lord knew how the Pharisees had heard that Jesus made and baptized more disciples than John,

2 (Though Jesus himself baptized not, but his disciples,)

Verse 2 above is a mistranslation in the Bible. The JST corrects this as follows (note that JST verses 2 and 4 have been left out of the Bible):

JST John 4:1–4

1 When therefore the Pharisees had heard that Jesus made and baptized more disciples than John,

2 They sought more diligently some means that they might put him to death; for many received John as a prophet, but they believed not on Jesus.

3 Now the Lord knew this, though he himself baptized not so many as his disciples;

4 For he suffered them for an example [*Jesus set the example for them*], preferring one another.

3 He left Judæa, and departed again into Galilee.

4 And he must needs go through Samaria.

JST John 4:6

6 And said unto his disciples, I must needs go through Samaria.

Normally, the Jews avoided going through Samaria. The Jews despised the Samaritans (people of Samaria) and the Samaritans despised the Jews. Thus, the Jews normally traveled around Samaria in order to get to Galilee. But this time, Jesus is heading straight north, right through Samaria, which would no doubt cause His Apostles some extra anxiety.

5 Then cometh he to a city of Samaria, which is called Sychar, near to the parcel of ground that Jacob gave to his son Joseph [*who was sold into Egypt*].

The fact that the Master is weary as they arrive at Jacob's well is a reminder that He suffered "hunger, thirst, and fatigue" (Mosiah 3:7) during His mortal sojourn, and thus understands our physical trials through His own personal experience. As He sits down on the side of the well, the stage is set for each of us to drink deeply from the well of "living water" offered us by the Savior.

The Woman at the Well

6 Now Jacob's well was there. Jesus therefore, being wearied with his journey, sat thus on the well: and it was about the sixth hour [*about noon*].

7 There cometh a woman of Samaria to draw water [*to get water from the well*]: Jesus saith unto her, Give me to drink [*please give Me a drink*].

8 (For his disciples were [*had*] gone away unto the city to buy meat [*food, provisions*].)

The following account of the Savior and the Samaritan woman is both delightful and profoundly moving. For our purposes, we will imagine her to be somewhat feisty and a bit sharp-tongued. We might imagine also a bit of a twinkle in the eyes of the Savior as He begins this conversation.

9 Then saith the woman of Samaria unto him, How is it that thou, being a Jew, askest drink of me, which am a woman of Samaria? for the Jews have no dealings with the Samaritans. [*In other words, why would a Jew like You ask a Samaritan woman like me for a drink? Don't You know that Jews don't have anything to do with us?*]

JST John 4:11
11 Wherefore he being alone, the woman of Samaria said unto him, How is it that thou being a Jew, askest drink of me, who am a woman of Samaria? The Jews have no dealings with the Samaritans.

Watch, now, as the Savior gets her curiosity up.

10 Jesus answered and said unto her, If thou knewest the gift of God, and who it is that saith to thee, Give me to drink; thou wouldest have asked of him, and he would have given thee living water. [*In effect, if you knew about the gift Father in Heaven has for you, and who I am, you would have asked Me for a drink, and I would have given you "living water."*]

The phrase "living water" was a familiar Old Testament phrase, having been used by Old Testament prophets to describe the blessings which flow from Jehovah to His faithful people. We will quote Jeremiah as an example:

Jeremiah 2:13

13 For my people have committed two evils; they have forsaken me the fountain of living waters, *and* hewed them out cisterns, broken cisterns, that can hold no water.

We will quote from the Institute of Religion's New Testament student manual regarding the term "living water."

"Israel's prophets had repeatedly declared that the Lord was as a fountain of living water that Israel had rejected. (See Jeremiah 2:13; Isaiah 8:6.)

"Jesus himself, as Jehovah, had pled with ancient Israel to repent and return to him so that he could nourish and sustain them. And in his pleading, Jehovah had used the word water as a figure of speech. (See Isaiah 58:11.)" (*Life and Teachings of Jesus and His Apostles*, p. 38)

Bruce R. McConkie taught about "living water." He said:

"His solemn invitation, 'If any man thirst, let him come unto me, and drink,' was a plain and open claim of Messiahship. In making it he identified himself as the very Jehovah who had promised drink to the thirsty through an out pouring of the Spirit. After such a pronouncement his hearers were faced with two choices: Either he was a blasphemer worthy of death, or he was in fact the God of Israel" (*DNTC*, 1:445–46).

You can find other references in the Topical Guide under "Living Water." As you know, we use the phrase often today in referring to the gospel of Jesus Christ which brings blessings that flow from heaven into our lives, providing refreshment, cleansing, and eternal life to the faithful.

11 The woman saith unto him, Sir, thou hast nothing to draw with, and the well is deep: from whence then hast thou that living water? [*Sir, You don't even have anything to get water out of the well. It is way too deep. So, from where do You think you are going to get me some of Your so-called "living water"?*]

12 Art thou greater than our father Jacob, which gave us the well, and drank thereof himself, and his children, and his cattle? [*In effect, do You think Your "living water" is better than the water Jacob provided us here in this well? It was good enough for Jacob and his family and his animals. In other words, what makes You think Your water is better than the Prophet Jacob's?*]

Watch as the Master Teacher takes her from being curious to a state of deep desire to partake of what He has to offer. She is still thinking of literal water, but the transition from the literal to the symbolic is about to take place in her mind.

13 Jesus answered and said unto her, Whosoever [*whoever*] drinketh of this water shall thirst again [*will just get thirsty again*]:

14 But whosoever drinketh of the water that I shall give him shall never thirst [*will never be thirsty again*]; but the water that I shall give him shall be in him a well of water springing up into everlasting life [*eternal life*].

15 The woman saith unto him, Sir, give me this water, that I thirst not, neither come hither to draw.

As you can see, the woman still doesn't get it. She thinks Jesus is talking about some kind of magical water that, when someone drinks it, he or she will never get thirsty again. She wants some so that she doesn't ever have to come to the well again and do the hard work of getting water. Watch how the Savior really gets her attention by the next things He says to her. A wonderful teaching moment has been quickly generated by the Master Teacher! She is about to learn that He truly is "a prophet."

16 Jesus saith unto her, Go, call thy husband, and come hither [*go get your husband and bring him back here*].

17 The woman answered and said, I have no husband. Jesus said unto her, Thou hast well said, I have no husband [*you were certainly right when you said that you have no husband*]:

18 For thou hast had five husbands; and he whom thou now hast is not thy husband [*you are not married to the man you are living with now*]: in that saidst thou truly [*you were certainly telling the truth when you said you have no husband*].

19 The woman saith unto him, Sir, I perceive that thou art a prophet. [*Sir, it just dawned on me that you are a prophet.*]

20 Our fathers [*ancestors*] worshipped in this mountain [*worshipped here in Samaria, rather than in Jerusalem*]; and ye [*you Jews*] say, that in Jerusalem is the place where men ought to worship.

A little review of history is helpful here. After King Solomon died, the twelve tribes split into two nations, Israel (ten of the tribes) in the north, with headquarters in Samaria, and Judah (the tribeof Judah and part of Benjamin) in the south, with headquarters in Jerusalem. There was much animosity between the two nations. Consequently, the people of the northern kingdom, Israel, even refused to come to Jerusalem to worship. Instead, they set up an apostate temple and apostate priests in their own country of Samaria and worshipped there.

21 Jesus saith unto her, Woman, believe me, the hour cometh, when ye shall neither in this mountain [*here in Samaria*], nor yet at Jerusalem, worship the Father. [*In other words, there will be a complete*

JOHN 4

apostasy such that no one will have correct knowledge of God, thus, no one can worship correctly.]

22 Ye worship ye know not what: [*because of apostasy and ignorance, you Samaritans don't really know who or what you worship*] we [*Jews*] know what we worship: for salvation is of the Jews [*salvation comes from the Jews, through Christ*].

23 But the hour cometh, and now is, when the true worshippers shall worship the Father in spirit and in truth [*the time has arrived when Jesus will restore the true gospel, so that sincere people can worship the Father by the power of the Holy Ghost with true doctrines*]: for the Father seeketh such to worship him.

The next verse has often been used to discredit Joseph Smith's testimony that "the Father has a body of flesh and bones" (D&C 130:22). This is another place where the Bible was not translated correctly (8th Article of Faith). JST verse 26 straightens this out.

24 God is a Spirit: and they that worship him must worship him in spirit and in truth.

JST John 4:26
26 **For unto such hath God promised his Spirit. And they who worship him, must worship** in spirit and in truth.

25 The woman saith unto him, I know that Messias [*Messiah*] cometh, which is called Christ: when he is come, he will tell us all things. [*This woman is familiar with the prophecies about the coming of the Messiah, who will be known as Christ.*]

26 Jesus saith unto her, I that speak unto thee am he [*the Messiah, Christ; the Jehovah of the Old Testament; see John 4:26, footnote a, in your Bible*].

JST John 4:28
28 Jesus **said** unto her, I **who** speak unto thee am **the Messias**.

27 And upon this [*just as Jesus finished saying this to the woman*] came his disciples, and marvelled [*were surprised*] that he talked with the woman [*that He would talk with a Samaritan woman*]: yet no man said, What seekest thou? or, Why talkest thou with her? [*But none of the disciples dared scold Him for so doing.*]

Watch now as this rather surprised and amazed Samaritan woman hurries back into the city and tells the men that she has met a prophet at Jacob's Well who is no doubt the Messiah spoken of in the scriptures.

28 The woman then left her waterpot [*left it at the well*], and went her way into the city, and saith to the men,

29 Come, see a man, which told me all things that ever I did [*who knows everything about me*]: is not this the Christ?

30 Then they went out of the city, and came unto him [*Jesus*].

31 In the mean while his disciples prayed him, saying, Master, eat [*urged Him to eat the food they had bought*].

32 But he said unto them, I have meat [*food*] to eat that ye know not of.

Here, the Master Teacher creates a teaching moment to help His disciples understand more about Him and His mission, as well as their mission. At first, they miss the point completely, thus are "off balance" and in a state of readiness to learn.

33 Therefore said the disciples one to another, Hath any man brought him ought [*anything*] to eat? [*The Savior said He has food (verse 32), so the disciples assume someone else must have brought Him something to eat while they were gone buying food.*]

34 Jesus saith unto them, My meat [*that which the Savior must partake of*] is to do the will of him that sent me, and to finish his work.

The implication here is that the "meat," which the Savior has been given, is to partake of all the work and suffering necessary, as assigned Him by the Father, to accomplish the Atonement.

35 Say not ye, There are yet four months, and then cometh harvest? behold, I say unto you, Lift up your eyes, and look on the fields; for they are white already to harvest. [*In effect, you say that harvest is four months away. I say that harvest time*

is now. In other words, it is time to start "harvesting souls," gathering converts into My Church now.]

36 And he that reapeth [*he who helps the Savior gather converts*] receiveth wages [*receives a reward*], and gathereth fruit unto life eternal [*stores up blessings for himself in heaven, namely exaltation*]: that both he that soweth [*the prophets of old, who laid the foundation by planting the gospel seeds—see JST verse 40, at the end of verse 38 below*] and he that reapeth [*he who harvests*] may rejoice together.

The main message in verse 36, above, seems to be that those who plant the gospel seed, but don't get to be around long enough to see it grow to maturity in the people, will rejoice together with the missionaries and others who actually bring the people into the Church.

37 And herein is that saying true, One soweth, and another reapeth [*one person plants and another person harvests*].

38 I sent you to reap that whereon ye bestowed no labour [*I sent you to harvest where you did not do any of the work to plant and nourish the crop*]: other men laboured [*prophets of old laid the foundation*], and ye are entered into their labours [*you finish what they started*].

JST John 4:40
40 I **have** sent you to reap that whereon ye bestowed no labor; **the prophets have labored**, and ye **have** entered into their labors.

JOHN 4 393

Having listened in as Jesus taught His disciples some important lessons, in the verses above, we now watch as Samaritans from the city arrive and meet the Savior themselves.

39 And many of the Samaritans of that city believed on him for [*because of*] the saying of the woman, which testified, He told me all that ever I did.

40 So when the Samaritans were come unto him, they besought him that he would tarry with them [*they asked Him to stay with them*]: and he abode [*remained*] there two days.

41 And many more believed because of his own word;

42 And said unto the woman, Now we believe, not because of thy saying: for we have heard him ourselves, and know that this is indeed the Christ, the Saviour of the world.

Certainly one of the major messages we learn from the example of the Samaritan woman is the great power of personal testimony shared with others, which invites them to come and learn for themselves from the Master.

43 Now after two days he departed thence [*He left there*], and went into Galilee.

44 For Jesus himself testified, that a prophet hath no honour [*is rejected*] in his own country.

Jesus' "own country" was His home town of Nazareth. Indeed, the people there rejected Him. (See Luke 4:16-30.)

45 Then when he was come into Galilee, the Galilæans received him, having seen all the things that he did at Jerusalem at the feast [*at the Passover feast*]: for they also went unto the feast.

The Healing of the Nobleman's Son

46 So Jesus came again into Cana of Galilee, where he made the water wine [*see John 2:1–11*]. And there was a certain nobleman, whose son was sick at Capernaum.

47 When he heard that Jesus was come out of Judæa into Galilee, he went unto him, and besought [*begged*] him that he would come down, and heal his son: for he was at the point of death.

48 Then said Jesus unto him, Except ye see signs and wonders, ye will not believe.

49 The nobleman saith unto him, Sir, come down ere my child die [*please come before my child dies*].

50 Jesus saith unto him, Go thy way; thy son liveth [*has been healed*]. And the man believed the word that Jesus had spoken unto him, and he went his way [*headed home*].

51 And as he was now going down, his servants met him, and told him, saying, Thy son liveth.

52 Then enquired he of them the hour when he began to amend [*the nobleman asked his servants when his son began to get better*]. And they said unto him, Yesterday at

the seventh hour [*about 1 p.m.*] the fever left him.

53 So the father knew that it was at the same hour, in the which Jesus said unto him, Thy son liveth: and himself believed, and his whole house [*he and his household were converted to Christ*].

54 This is again the second miracle [*the first one, according to John, was turning water into wine; see John 2:11*] that Jesus did, when he was come out of Judæa into Galilee.

JOHN 5

This is the beginning of the second year of the Savior's mortal mission. He begins this year by traveling to Jerusalem for the feast of the Passover. As you have probably learned already from Matthew, Mark, and Luke, the leaders of the Jews were extremely opposed to the healings which Jesus performed on the Sabbath. They felt that such activity violated the Lord's holy day. Little did they know that Jesus was the God of the Old Testament, Jehovah Himself, who gave the commandment to keep the Sabbath Day holy. They were caught up in what they considered to be the letter of the law and completely missed the spirit of the law. We will see this now as the Savior heals a man on the Sabbath.

1 AFTER this there was a feast [*Passover*] of the Jews; and Jesus went up to Jerusalem.

Healing a Crippled Man on the Sabbath

2 Now there is at Jerusalem by the sheep market a pool, which is called in the Hebrew tongue Bethesda, having five porches.

3 In these [*porches*] lay a great multitude of impotent [*crippled*] folk, of blind, halt [*lame*], withered, waiting for the moving of the water.

4 For an angel went down at a certain season into the pool, and troubled the water: whosoever then first after the troubling of the water stepped in was made whole [*healed*] of whatsoever disease he had.

Apparently there was a false belief which gave sick and crippled people hope that they would be healed if they were the first to get into the water after the water started being moved by an unseen angel. This is superstition and is not the way God works.

5 And a certain man was there, which had an infirmity thirty and eight years [*had been an invalid for thirty-eight years*].

6 When Jesus saw him lie [*lying there*], and knew that he had been now a long time in that case [*in that situation*], he saith unto him, Wilt thou be made whole [*would you like to be healed*]?

7 The impotent [*crippled*] man answered him, Sir, I have no man, when the water is troubled, to put me into the pool: but while I am coming,

JOHN 5

another steppeth down before me [*when I try to get into the water first, someone else always beats me to it*].

8 Jesus saith unto him, Rise, take up thy bed, and walk.

9 And immediately the man was made whole [*was healed*], and took up his bed, and walked: and on the same day was the sabbath [*this all happened on the Sabbath*].

10 The Jews [*religious leaders of the Jews, Pharisees—see Matthew 12:2 and 10*] therefore said unto him that was cured [*the man who had been healed*], It is the sabbath day: it is not lawful [*legal*] for thee to carry thy bed.

11 He answered them, He that made me whole [*the man who healed me*], the same said unto me, Take up thy bed, and walk.

12 Then asked they him, What man is that which said unto thee, Take up thy bed, and walk?

13 And he that was healed wist not who it was [*didn't know the name of the man who had healed him*]: for Jesus had conveyed himself away, a multitude being in that place [*Jesus had left right after healing him and was quickly lost in the crowd by the pool*].

14 Afterward Jesus findeth him [*the man He had healed*] in the temple [*in the temple courtyard*], and said unto him, Behold, thou art made whole [*you have been healed*]: sin no more, lest a worse thing come unto thee.

This had to be a specific case in which future sinning on the part of the man who had been healed would cause physical punishment. We must avoid generalizing this situation to apply to all people. Otherwise, we would come to believe, as did the Jews at the time, that all illness is caused by sin. Imagine the gossip which would go around about anyone who was sick if we believed this false notion!

15 The man departed, and told the Jews that it was Jesus, which had made him whole. [*Now that the healed man had met Jesus on the grounds of the Temple, and thus knew His name, he apparently found the Pharisees and told them the name of the man who had healed him.*]

16 And therefore did the Jews persecute Jesus, and sought to slay him, because he had done these things on the sabbath day.

The Tradition of the Elders and the Sabbath Day

Over the centuries, the Jewish religious leaders had imposed upon the Jews literally thousands of rules and laws concerning Sabbath behavior. These became known as the "tradition of the elders." See Matthew 15:2, Mark 7:5. They were caught up in the "letter of the law" as opposed to the "spirit of the law" regarding the Sabbath. As evidenced in verse 16 above, it was against the law to heal on the Sabbath. A few additional examples of these "traditions of the elders" follow:

Things a faithful Jew was not allowed to do on the Sabbath (according to the Tradition of the Elders):

1. Scatter two seeds (it was considered to be planting).

2. Sweep or break a single clod of dirt (it was considered to be plowing).

3. Pluck one blade of grass.

4. Water fruit or remove a dead leaf.

5. Pick fruit or even lift it from the ground.

6. Cut a mushroom (it was a double sin, one of both harvesting and of planting, because a new one would grow in place of the old one).

7. Roll wheat together to take away the husks (guilty of sifting with a sieve).

8. Rub the ends of wheat stalks (guilty of threshing).

9. Throw wheat stalks up in the air (guilty of winnowing).

10. Dip a radish in salt for too long a time (could be dipped into salt as long as it was not left too long which would make one guilty of pickling).

11. Rub mud off a dress (mud on a dress might be crushed in the hand and shaken off, but the dress must not be rubbed for fear of bruising the fabric).

12. Spit on the ground then rub it into the soil with the foot (it was considered irrigating because something might grow where you spit; however, it was legal to spit into a handkerchief, or spit upon rocks because nothing would grow).

13. Put a plaster on a sore.

14. Write a big letter, leaving room for two small ones (but it was okay to write one big letter occupying the space of two small letters).

15. Carry a burden that was heavier than a fig.

16. Carry a piece of food larger than the size of an olive.

17. Carry objects that could be put to practical use, for instance, two horse hairs (because they could be made into a bird trap), a scrap of clean paper (because it could be written on), a small piece of paper already written upon (because it could be made into a wrapper).

18. Carry enough ink to write two letters.

19. Carry enough wax to fill up a small hole.

20. Carry a pebble (because you might aim it at a little bird).

JOHN 5

21. Carry a small piece of broken pottery (because you could stir coals of a fire with it).

22. Write two letters, either with the right or left hand (but you could write letters in sand, because they would not remain). It was also permitted to write letters with the hand turned upside down, or with the foot, or with the mouth or the elbow.

23. Save a house or its contents from fire (however, you could rescue the scriptures and phylacteries (tiny leather boxes with scripture scrolls in them which the Jews tied to their foreheads or left arms) and the cases that contained them, plus food and drink needed for the Sabbath. Also, if food were in a basket, the whole basket could legally be carried out with everything in it. Only absolutely necessary clothing could be saved, however, a person might put on a dress, bring it out, take it off, go back in and put on another, save it and so on.

24. Carry a legal burden more than a Sabbath day's journey, which was 2,000 cubits (about 3,000 feet). (However, on Friday, a person could deposit food for two meals 2,000 cubits from his house. Then, on the Sabbath, he could go the 2,000 cubits, sit down and eat, and then that would be considered to be his residence and so he could go another 2,000 cubits from that point).

25. Provide first aid, unless the person's life was in danger.

26. Set broken bones.

27. Perform a surgical operation.

28. Wear a plaster on a wound or sore (unless the purpose was to prevent the wound from getting worse rather than an attempt to heal it).

29. Wear false teeth or wear a gold plug in a tooth.

30. Replace wadding if it fell out of the ear.

31. Light a fire.

32. Keep an oven warm.

33. Eat an egg that had been laid on the Sabbath (unless the hen had been kept for eating rather than laying eggs, in which case the egg could be eaten because it was considered to be a part of the hen that had fallen off).

(Adapted from *The Mortal Messiah*, pp. 199–212)

17 But Jesus answered them [*in answer to the Jewish religious leaders' criticism of His healing on the Sabbath, verse 16*], My Father worketh hitherto, and I work [*in effect, My Father has done much of His work on the Sabbath, and I will continue to do so too*].

18 Therefore [*because of Jesus' reply*] the Jews sought the more [*even more*] to kill him, because he not only had broken the sabbath, but said also that God was his Father [*claims to be the Son of God*], making himself equal with God.

In the next verses, Jesus humbly gives credit and honor to His Father and explains Their relationship as They work together in complete harmony for the salvation of our souls.

19 Then answered Jesus and said unto them, Verily, verily, I say unto you, The Son can do nothing of himself, but what he seeth the Father do: for what things soever he [*the Father*] doeth, these also doeth the Son likewise. [*In other words, the Son does nothing that is not in complete harmony with the Father's will. See* Doctrinal New Testament Commentary, *Vol. 1, p. 192.*]

Occasionally, members of the Church use verse 19 above to suggest that Heavenly Father was the Savior of the world upon which He grew up. Their reasoning is: Since Jesus said that He does nothing but what He sees the Father do, and since Jesus is our Savior, the Father had to have been the Savior on the world upon which He grew up as a mortal. Of course it is possible that the Father was the Savior on His world, but to use this verse to "prove" it is not sound thinking. Brigham Young said, "The Savior told his disciples as he saw the Father do, so does he, and

as Joseph Smith saw Jesus do, so did Joseph do, and as I saw Joseph do, so do I also." (Taken from remarks which appear to have been given at the dedication of the Seventies Hall in Nauvoo, late December, 1844. See *BYU Studies*, Winter 1978, Volume 18, No. 2, pp. 177–78.) Joseph Smith was not crucified. Brigham Young was not martyred in Carthage Jail. From that same volume of *BYU Studies*, p. 176, Joseph Smith says, "For the Savior says, the work that my Father did, do I also, . . . He took himself . . . a body and then laid down his life that he might take it up again, . . . We then also took bodies to lay them down, to take them up again."

The point of verse 19, above, is that Jesus was, in all things, in perfect harmony with the Father's will.

20 For the Father loveth the Son, and sheweth [*shows*] him all things that himself doeth [*that He Himself does*]: and he will shew him greater [*more*] works than these, that ye may marvel.

21 For as the Father raiseth up the dead [*resurrects people*], and quickeneth them [*causes them to become alive spiritually*]; even so the Son [*Christ*] quickeneth [*gives eternal life to*] whom he will.

Since every person who has ever been born on earth will be resurrected (1 Corinthians 15:22), in other words, will be "quickened," the last phrase in verse 21 above cannot mean that Jesus will be selective as to whom He resurrects. Another scriptural use of the word "quicken" is "to be made alive spiritually," which, in turn, leads to eternal life (exaltation). Jesus will be our final judge, and as such will give exaltation to "whom he will," according to the laws of justice and mercy.

22 For the Father judgeth no man, but hath committed all judgment unto the Son: [*The Father has given all the responsibility for final judgment to Jesus.*]

23 That all men should honour the Son, even as they honour the Father. He that honoureth not the Son honoureth not the Father which hath sent him.

24 Verily, verily, I say unto you, He that heareth my word, and believeth on him that sent me [*Heavenly Father*], hath everlasting life [*exaltation in the highest degree of glory in the celestial kingdom*], and shall not come into condemnation [*will not be stopped from eternal progress*]; but is passed from death unto life.

Gospel to be Preached in Spirit Prison

25 Verily, verily, I say unto you, The hour is coming, and now is, when the dead [*in spirit prison; 1 Peter 3:18–21, D&C 138*] shall hear the voice of the Son of God: and they that hear [*obey*] shall live.

26 For as the Father hath life in himself [*is "an immortal,*

resurrected, exalted being" (Doctrinal New Testament Commentary, *Vol. 1, p. 194*)]; so hath he given to the Son to have life in himself [*Jesus has power over death*];

27 And hath given him authority to execute judgment also, because he is the Son of man [*the Son of God*]. [*See Moses 6:57 for an explanation of why Jesus is called the Son of Man.*]

Resurrection for All

28 Marvel not at this: for the hour is coming, in the which all that are in the graves shall hear his voice,

29 And shall come forth [*everyone will be resurrected*]; they that have done good, unto the resurrection of life [*eternal life, exaltation*]; and they that have done evil, unto the resurrection of damnation [*those who will have limits placed on their progression; see D&C 76:112*].

30 I can of mine own self do nothing [*Jesus follows the Father's commands exactly*]: as I hear, I judge: and my judgment is just [*completely fair*]; because I seek not mine own will, but the will of the Father which hath sent me.

31 If I bear witness of myself, my witness is not true [*valid*]. [*The law of witnesses requires that there be at least two witnesses.*]

32 There is another [*the Father*] that beareth witness of me; and I know that the witness which he witnesseth of me is true.

33 Ye sent unto John [*the Baptist*], and he bare witness unto the truth.

34 But I receive not testimony from man: but these things I say, that ye might be saved.

JST John 5:35

35 **And he** [*John the Baptist*] **received not his testimony of** [*from*] **man, but of God, and ye yourselves say that he is a prophet, therefore ye ought to receive his testimony**. These things I say that ye might be saved.

35 He [*John the Baptist*] was a burning and a shining light: and ye were willing for a season to rejoice in his light.

36 But I have greater witness than that of John [*than that which John the Baptist gave of Me*]: for the works [*restoring the gospel, performing the Atonement, and such.*] which the Father hath given me to finish, the same works that I do, bear witness of me, that the Father hath sent me.

JST John 5:37

37 But I have **a** greater witness than **the testimony** of John; for the works which the Father hath given me to finish, the same works that I do, bear witness of me, that the Father hath sent me.

37 And the Father himself, which hath sent me, hath borne witness of me. Ye [*the Jews*] have neither heard his voice at any time, nor seen his shape [*meaning that the Father has "shape," a resurrected, physical body; see D&C 130:22*].

JST John 5:38

38 And the Father himself **who** sent me, hath borne witness of me. **And verily I testify unto you, that** ye have **never** heard his voice at any time, nor seen his shape;

38 And ye [*the Jews*] have not his word abiding in you [*do not have the Father's gospel in your hearts*]: for whom he [*the Father*] hath sent, him ye believe not [*you refuse to believe what I am teaching you*].

Verse 39, next, needs to be read carefully, in order to understand what is actually being said. Remember that the Master is addressing the hypocritical religious leaders of the Jews who are proud of their knowledge of the scriptures but who violate the gospel constantly in daily living.

39 Search the scriptures; for in them ye think ye have eternal life [*since you won't listen to Me, go ahead and keep studying your scriptures, the Law of Moses, and so forth, without help, thus perpetuating your spiritual blindness; you think you can be saved that way; it won't work*]: and they are they which testify of me. [*If you understood the scriptures correctly, you would see that they testify of Me.*]

40 And ye will not [*refuse to*] come to me, that ye might have life [*eternal life*].

41 I receive not honour from men. [*I am not honored by men like you.*]

JOHN 6

42 But I know you [*the Jews who are angry because Jesus healed the invalid on the Sabbath, and now want to kill Him; see verse 16 above*], that ye have not the love of God in you [*I know the evil which is in your hearts.*]

43 I am come [*have come*] in my Father's name, and ye receive me not [*you reject Me*]: if another shall come in his own name, him ye will receive. [*You accept false leaders and false prophets who build themselves up in the eyes of the people for personal gain, who practice priestcraft; see Alma 1:12 and 16.*]

44 How can ye believe, which receive honour one of another, and seek not the honour that cometh from God only? [*How can you believe and trust those who join together to build themselves up, rather than seeking God?*]

45 Do not think that I will accuse you [*I will not even need to bear witness against you*] to the Father: there is one that accuseth you, even Moses, in whom ye trust [*because the teachings of Moses about Me, which you blatantly misinterpret and refuse to believe, will bear witness against you*].

46 For had ye believed Moses [*if you believed Moses, who clearly taught about Me*], ye would have believed me: for he wrote of me.

47 But if ye believe not his writings, how shall ye believe my words? [*If you won't believe Moses, how can you possibly believe Me?*]

Moses was the most important prophet in Jewish culture. In fact, the Jews were constantly angered by the fact that Jesus did not do things the way Moses taught, forgetting that many of the things Moses gave them were "schoolmaster" laws (Galatians 3:24), specifically designed to prepare them for the higher laws the Messiah would give them.

JOHN 6

This is the beginning of the third year of the Savior's mortal ministry. As you can see, John's account deals mostly with the final year of the Master's mortal ministry (John 5 dealt with the second year of His formal mortal mission). In this chapter, you will see the feeding of the 5,000 and the Savior's walking on the water. The Bread of Life sermon will be given and Peter will testify that Jesus is the Christ. The JST will continue to be a great blessing to us as we study the life of Christ. By this stage of His mortal mission, large crowds of people are constantly following Him.

1 AFTER these things Jesus went over the sea of Galilee, which is the sea of Tiberias.

2 And a great multitude followed him, because they saw his miracles which he did on them that were diseased [*sick*].

3 And Jesus went up into a mountain,

and there he sat with his disciples.

4 And the passover, a feast of the Jews, was nigh [*near*].

Feeding of the 5,000

5 When Jesus then lifted up his eyes, and saw a great company [*huge crowd*] come unto him, he saith unto Philip, Whence [*where*] shall we buy bread, that these may eat [*to feed all these people*]?

In verse 6, next, John points out to us the Master Teacher's technique as He provides learning opportunities for His Apostles. They are, in effect, involved in a three year "MTC" training.

6 And this he said to prove [*test*] him: for he himself knew what he would do.

7 Philip answered him, Two hundred pennyworth of bread is not sufficient for them, that every one of them may take a little. [*Two hundred days' wages would not buy enough for everyone to have more than a little—see Mark 6:37, footnote a.*]

8 One of his disciples, Andrew, Simon Peter's brother, saith unto him,

9 There is a lad here, which hath five barley loaves, and two small fishes: but what are they among so many?

10 And Jesus said, Make the men sit down. Now there was much grass in the place. So the men sat down, in number about five thousand [*plus women and children; see Matthew 14:21*].

11 And Jesus took the loaves; and when he had given thanks, he distributed to the disciples, and the disciples to them that were set down; and likewise of the fishes as much as they would [*everyone ate as much as they wanted*].

12 When they were filled [*when the people in the crowd were full*], he said unto his disciples, Gather up the fragments that remain, that nothing be lost [*wasted*].

13 Therefore they gathered them together, and filled twelve baskets with the fragments [*leftovers*] of the five barley loaves, which remained over and above unto them that had eaten.

14 Then those men, when they had seen the miracle that Jesus did, said, This is of a truth that prophet that should come into the world [*this is definitely the Messiah*].

Unfortunately, as you will see in verse 15, next, most of the multitude failed to see the spiritual symbolism involved in the Savior's feeding all of them until they were full. Their minds and hearts were so focused on immediate physical needs and desires that they missed the spiritual implications.

15 When Jesus therefore perceived that they [*the members of the multitude who had just been fed*] would come and take him by force, to make him a king, he departed again into a mountain himself alone.

Apparently, the multitude felt that

JOHN 6

if they could have Jesus for their king, He would feed them every day and take care of all their needs so they wouldn't have to work. Therefore, they tried to force Him to be their king. They missed the symbolism that Christ can indeed take care of all our spiritual needs by giving us the "bread of life" on a daily basis.

16 And when even [*evening*] was now come, his disciples went down unto the sea,

17 And entered into a ship, and went over the sea toward Capernaum [*on the northwest side of the Sea of Galilee*]. And it was now dark, and Jesus was not come to them [*had not joined them*].

The Tempest Rages

18 And the sea arose by reason of a great wind that blew [*a terrible storm came up*].

Jesus Walks on the Water

19 So when they had rowed about five and twenty or thirty furlongs [*about three to four miles from shore*], they see Jesus walking on the sea, and drawing nigh [*getting close*] unto the ship: and they were afraid.

20 But he saith unto them, It is I; be not afraid.

21 Then they willingly received him into the ship: and immediately the ship was at the land whither they went [*the ship was suddenly at its destination, a miracle recorded only by John*].

22 The day following [*the day following the feeding of the 5,000*], when the people which stood on the other side of the sea [*near where they had been fed by the Master the day before*] saw that [*realized that*] there was none other boat there, save [*except*] that one whereinto his disciples were entered, and that Jesus went not with his disciples into the boat, but that his disciples were gone away alone; [*In other words, the next day the crowd came to see if Jesus was still there, so they could get Him to feed them again. They knew that the disciples had taken the only boat available the night before and had headed toward Capernaum without Jesus. At any rate, they saw that neither Jesus nor His disciples were there, so they determined to try to find them.*]

23 (Howbeit [*however*] there came other boats from Tiberias nigh unto the place where they did eat bread [*some boats from Tiberias came that morning and came to shore near the site of the feeding of the 5,000*], after that the Lord had given thanks:)

24 When the people therefore saw that Jesus was not there, neither his disciples, they also took shipping [*got aboard the boats from Tiberias*], and came to Capernaum, seeking for Jesus.

25 And when they had found him on the other side of the sea, they said unto him, Rabbi, when camest thou hither [*when did You come here*]?

26 Jesus answered them and said, Verily, verily [*this is very important; listen carefully!*], I say unto you, Ye seek me, not because ye saw the miracles, but because ye did eat of the loaves, and were filled. [*You are not looking for Me because you want to obey My gospel, but rather just to be fed again. In other words, you are looking for Me for the wrong reasons.*]

JST John 6:26

26 Jesus answered them and said, Verily, verily, I say unto you, Ye seek me, not because ye **desire to keep my sayings, neither** because ye saw the miracles, but because ye did eat of the loaves and were filled.

27 Labour not for the meat which perisheth [*don't spend all your effort working for worldly things which do not last*], but for that meat [*food, symbolic of spiritual priorities*] which endureth unto everlasting life [*which brings exaltation*], which the Son of man [*Christ*] shall give unto you: for him hath God the Father sealed [*sent*].

Now begins a brief series of interesting questions and answers between the spiritually blind and insensitive crowd and the Master Teacher.

Question
28 Then said they unto him, What shall we do, that we might work the works of God? [*What would it take to teach us how to multiply loaves and fishes?*]

Answer
29 Jesus answered and said unto them, This is the work of God, that ye believe on him whom he hath sent. [*You must develop faith in Jesus Christ.*]

Question
30 They said therefore unto him, What sign shewest thou then, that we may see, and believe thee? what dost thou work? [*They are getting a bit irritated that He is stalling and not teaching them how to multiply loaves and fishes. They challenge Him to show them a sign to prove to them that He has not lost the power which He had yesterday when He fed them.*]

31 Our fathers did eat manna in the desert; as it is written, He gave them bread from heaven to eat. [*In other words they seem to be taunting Jesus, saying in effect, "Hint, hint. Moses gave our ancestors bread (manna) every day when he was their leader. What's the matter? Aren't You as capable as Moses?"*]

What follows in verses 32–58 is known as the "Bread of Life" sermon. It is famous and contains tremendous symbolism. Have you noticed that the Savior masterfully uses familiar objects and everyday settings as background for teaching gospel doctrines and principles? We see this method throughout His teaching.

JOHN 6

Answer

The Bread of Life Sermon

32 Then Jesus said unto them, [*Answer:*] Verily, verily, I say unto you, Moses gave you not that bread from heaven [*Moses didn't give you that manna*]; but [*furthermore*] my Father giveth you the true bread [*symbolic of Christ*] from heaven.

33 For the bread of [*from*] God is he [*Christ*] which cometh down from heaven, and giveth life [*resurrection and the possibility of eternal life*] unto the world.

Question

34 Then said they unto him, Lord, evermore give us this bread [*give us bread so we will never get hungry again*].

As you can see from verse 34, above, they still don't get the point (see also verse 52). They don't understand the symbolism that Christ and His gospel will nourish them spiritually forever in celestial glory.

Next, Jesus explains His role as the Redeemer, and that He has been sent to earth by the Father to enable us to return to Him. In effect, He is giving them a short course in the Plan of Salvation.

35 And Jesus said unto them, I am the bread of life: he that cometh to me shall never hunger [*spiritually*]; and he that believeth on me shall never thirst [*spiritually*]. [*In other words, those who hunger and thirst after righteousness and eternal life and come unto Christ will be nourished eternally.*]

36 But I said unto you, That ye also have seen me, and believe not.

37 All [*all the righteous people*] that the Father giveth me shall come to me; and him that cometh to me I will in no wise [*never*] cast out [*of my kingdom*].

38 For I came down from heaven, not to do mine own will, but the will of him [*the Father*] that sent me.

39 And this is the Father's will which hath sent me, that of all which he hath given me [*all the righteous Saints*] I should lose nothing [*none of them*], but should raise it up again at the last day [*resurrect them in the resurrection of the righteous*].

40 And this is the will of him that sent me, that every one which seeth the Son, and believeth on him, may have everlasting life [*eternal life, or, in other words, exaltation*]: and I will raise him up at the last day.

JST John 6:40

40 And this is the will of him that sent me, that every one which seeth the Son, and believeth on him, may have everlasting life; and I will raise him up **in the resurrection of the just** [*exaltation*] at the last day.

The "resurrection of the just" as used in JST verse 40, above, is a term which means those who will attain exaltation, which is the highest degree of glory in the celestial kingdom.

Sadly, as you can see from verses 41–42, next, these people still don't get it. They are typical of people who are so focused on material things that they can't see the spiritual.

41 The Jews then murmured [*grumbled*] at him, because he said, I am the bread which came down from heaven.

42 And they said, Is not this Jesus, the son of Joseph, whose father and mother we know? how is it then that he saith, I came down from heaven? [*How can Jesus have come down from heaven? We know His parents. We've known Him all His life.*]

43 Jesus therefore answered and said unto them, Murmur not among yourselves [*don't criticize Me among yourselves for saying what I've said*].

44 No man can come to me, except the Father which hath sent me draw him: and I will raise him up at the last day.

The JST makes major changes to verse 44, above:

JST John 6:44

44 No man can come unto me, except **he doeth the will of my Father who hath sent me. And this is the will of him who hath sent me, that ye receive the Son; for the Father beareth record of him; and he who receiveth the testimony, and doeth the will of him who sent me, I will raise up in the resurrection of the just** [*those who are going to receive exaltation*].

45 It is written in the prophets [*in the Old Testament; Isaiah 54:13*], And they shall be all taught of God. Every man therefore that hath heard, and hath learned of the Father, cometh unto me. [*Everyone who has properly understood Old Testament prophets will be motivated to come unto Me.*]

46 Not that any man hath seen the Father, save he which is of God [*except he who is worthy, such as Stephen in Acts 7:55–56*], he hath seen the Father.

47 Verily, verily, I say unto you, He that believeth on me [*Christ*] hath everlasting life [*will be exalted, will be placed into the highest degree of glory in the celestial kingdom and will become a god— see D&C 132:20*].

48 I am that bread of life. [*Symbolism: Jesus is the spiritual "bread" sent to us by the Father, that, when we eat it, that is, when we internalize it and make it part of our lives, we are exalted.*]

49 Your fathers [*ancestors, mentioned in verse 31*] did eat manna in the wilderness, and are dead [*and still died spiritually*].

50 This is the bread [*symbolic of Christ's gospel and His Atonement*] which cometh down from heaven, that a man may eat thereof [*internalize it*], and not die [*not die spiritually*].

51 I am the living bread which came down from heaven: if any man eat of this bread, he shall live

JOHN 6

for ever [*shall have eternal life*]: and the bread that I will give is my flesh, which I will give for the life of the world. [*Jesus will sacrifice His body through suffering in the Garden of Gethsemane and crucifixion in order to accomplish the Atonement and provide eternal life for those who qualify.*]

52 The Jews therefore strove [*argued*] among themselves, saying, How can this man give us his flesh to eat? [*They still don't get the point!*]

Just as the Savior repeated the message time and time again in the previous verses, so He will repeat it several times in the next verses. He is giving these spiritually insensitive people every chance to understand that they must accept His Atonement and His gospel in order to be saved. They must symbolically eat Him ("he that eateth me," verse 57), that is, eat or internalize everything He is and offers them and make it a part of their lives, in order to receive eternal life. Sadly, many of them will still not get the point, even after so much repetition, and will leave him (verse 66).

53 Then Jesus said unto them, Verily, verily, I say unto you, Except [*unless*] ye eat the flesh of the Son of man [*Christ*], and drink his blood, ye have no life in you. [*Unless you take advantage of the Atonement and make it part of your lives, you will not have the life and light of the gospel here in mortality or in the world to come.*]

54 Whoso eateth my flesh, and drinketh my blood, hath eternal life; and I will raise him up at the last day.

JST John 6:54
54 Whoso eateth my flesh, and drinketh my blood, hath eternal life; and I will raise him up **in the resurrection of the just** at the last day.

55 For my flesh is meat [*symbolic of spiritual food*] indeed, and my blood is drink [*symbolic of spiritual drink*] indeed. [*This is sacrament symbolism.*]

56 He that eateth my flesh, and drinketh my blood, dwelleth in me, and I in him. [*He becomes one with Me, united with Me in the gospel.*]

57 As the living Father hath sent me, and I live by the Father: so he that eateth me [*internalizes My gospel*], even he shall live by me [*will be saved through living in accordance with My gospel*].

58 This is that bread which came down from heaven [*this is the Savior who was sent to earth from heaven*]: not as your fathers did eat manna [*physical nourishment*], and are dead: he that eateth of this bread [*spiritual nourishment*] shall live for ever [*will have eternal life, exaltation*].

59 These things said he in the synagogue [*Jewish church building*], as he taught in Capernaum.

60 Many therefore of his disciples [*followers*], when they had heard this [*the Bread of Life Sermon*], said, This is an hard saying; who

can hear it? [*This is too deep for us. Nobody can understand what He is saying.*]

61 When Jesus knew in himself that his disciples murmured at it, he said unto them, Doth this offend you [*are you bothered, offended by what I have taught about the Bread of Life*]?

62 What and if ye shall see the Son of man ascend up where he was before? [*Would it offend you if you saw Me go back up into heaven where I came from? Jesus will do exactly that after His resurrection.*]

Next, we are taught the necessity of having the help of the Holy Ghost in order to understand the message of salvation that the Savior is giving these people. This is an important reminder of the vital role the gift of the Holy Ghost plays in our lives. Those who do not have it cannot understand the depth and beauty of these things.

63 It is the spirit that quickeneth [*it is the Holy Ghost that gives you understanding*]; the flesh profiteth nothing [*you can't possibly understand what Jesus just said from an intellectual, academic basis*]: the words that I speak unto you, they are spirit [*spiritual*], and they are life [*they bring eternal life*].

64 But there are some of you that believe not. For Jesus knew from the beginning who they were that believed not, and who should betray him.

65 And he said, Therefore said I [*this is the reason I said*] unto you, that no man can come unto me, except it were given unto him of my Father.

JST John 6:65

65 And he said, Therefore said I unto you, that no man can come unto me, except **he doeth the will of my Father who hath sent me**.

As you can see from verse 66, next, many people deserted Jesus after He gave the Bread of Life sermon, above.

66 From that time many of his disciples went back [*left him*], and walked no more with him.

67 Then said Jesus unto the twelve, Will ye also go away? [*Is this doctrine of the Bread of Life so hard to accept that you, too, will leave Me?*]

Peter's Testimony

68 Then Simon Peter answered him, Lord, to whom shall we go? thou hast the words of eternal life. [*This is the right answer!*]

69 And we believe and are sure that thou art that Christ, the Son of the living God.

Next, Jesus prophesied that one of the Twelve would betray Him. In verse 71, John explains who it was to whom the Master was referring.

70 Jesus answered them, Have not I chosen you twelve, and one of you is a devil?

JOHN 7

71 He spake of Judas Iscariot the son of Simon [*not Peter, the Apostle, rather, a different Simon*]: for he it was that should [*would*] betray him, being one of the twelve.

JOHN 7

It is fall now and Jesus will be crucified and resurrected in the spring. He is traveling and teaching in Galilee, but will go to Jerusalem for the Feast of Tabernacles. As John begins this chapter, he informs us that many of the Savior's own close relatives do not believe that He is the Messiah.

1 AFTER these things Jesus walked in Galilee: for he would not walk in Jewry [*in Judea, in the Jerusalem area*], because the Jews sought to kill him.

2 Now the Jews' feast of tabernacles was at hand.

The Feast of Tabernacles was held in the fall at harvest time in Jerusalem. See Bible Dictionary, under "Feasts." It drew large crowds and was a week-long celebration of thanksgiving which included daily animal sacrifices, and a ceremony where people waved palm, myrtle, willow, and citrus branches toward the cardinal points of the compass (north, south, east and west), symbolizing the presence of God throughout the universe.

Next, in verses 3–5, there may be a hint of criticism on the part of Jesus' close relatives, likely including His own half-brothers, who do not believe in Him (verse 5), as they tell Him, in effect, that He really ought to go to Jerusalem for the Feast of Tabernacles so He can parade Himself in front of His disciples as well as huge numbers of people. There is a hint that these family members and close relatives were embarrassed that Jesus was part of their family.

3 His brethren [*close relatives, probably including his own brothers; see McConkie*, Doctrinal New Testament Commentary, *Vol. 1, p. 437*] therefore said unto him, Depart hence [*leave*], and go into Judæa, that thy disciples also may see the works that thou doest.

JST John 7:3
3 His brethren therefore said unto him, Depart hence, and go into **Judea**, that thy disciples **there** also may see the works that thou doest.

4 For there is no man that doeth any thing in secret, and he himself seeketh to be known openly [*no man keeps to himself who wants everybody to know who he is*]. If thou do these things, shew thyself to the world [*get out in public and let them see you*].

5 For neither did his brethren [*His half-brothers, the sons of Joseph and Mary*] believe in him.

6 Then Jesus said unto them, My time is not yet come [*perhaps meaning that the time for His atoning sacrifice in Jerusalem has not*]

yet arrived—compare with Matthew 26:18]: but your time is alway ready [*you can go to Jerusalem any time, so you go ahead and go for the Feast of Tabernacles*].

7 The world cannot hate you [*the people of the world don't hate you because you are just normal people and most of them don't even know you*]; but me it hateth, because I testify of it, that the works thereof are evil [*but they hate Me because I tell them they are wicked*].

8 Go ye up unto this feast [*the Feast of Tabernacles in Jerusalem*]: I go not up yet unto this feast; for my time is not yet full come [*it is not time for Me to go*].

9 When he had said these words unto them, he abode still [*still remained*] in Galilee.

10 But when his brethren were gone up [*after His brothers had departed for Jerusalem*], then went he also up unto the feast, not openly, but as it were in secret. [*The religious leaders of the Jews had already indicated that they wanted to kill Him; see verse 1.*]

11 Then the Jews sought him [*looked for him*] at the feast, and said, Where is he?

12 And there was much murmuring [*much talk*] among the people concerning him: for some said, He is a good man: others said, Nay; but he deceiveth the people [*He is a fraud*].

13 Howbeit [*however*] no man spake openly of him for fear of the Jews.

14 Now about the midst of the feast [*the middle of the week-long festivities*] Jesus went up into the temple, and taught.

15 And the Jews marvelled, saying, How knoweth this man letters, having never learned [*how does Jesus know so much; He hasn't had the formal training that our religious leaders have*]?

16 Jesus answered them, and said, My doctrine is not mine, but his that sent me. [*My Father is My teacher.*]

Verse 17, next, is a simple formula for gaining a testimony of the gospel.

17 If any man will do his will, he shall know of the doctrine, whether it be of God, or whether I speak of myself. [*If any one will live the gospel, he will find out that it is true.*]

18 He that speaketh of himself [*teaches his own, man-made doctrines*] seeketh his own glory: but he [*Christ*] that seeketh his glory that sent him [*the glory of the Father*], the same is true [*He is a true messenger, one you can trust*], and no unrighteousness is in him.

19 Did not Moses give you the law [*the first five books of the Old Testament*], and yet none of you keepeth the law [*none of you obey it*]? Why go ye about to kill me?

20 The people answered and said, Thou hast a devil [*you are crazy*]: who goeth about to kill thee [*what makes You think anybody is out to kill You*]?

JOHN 7

411

Next, the Master points out the hypocrisy of the Jews who are accusing Him of breaking the Sabbath.

21 Jesus answered and said unto them, I have done one work [*I healed the crippled man on the Sabbath*], and ye all marvel.

22 Moses therefore gave unto you circumcision; (not because it is of Moses, but of the fathers;) [*in other words, not because it originated with Moses, rather with Abraham*] and ye on the sabbath day circumcise a man.

23 If a man on the sabbath day receive circumcision, that the law of Moses should not be broken; are ye angry at me, because I have made a man every whit whole on the sabbath day? [*You have your priorities mixed up. You allow a man to be circumcised on the Sabbath, but you get angry at Me for healing a man on the Sabbath.*]

24 Judge not according to the appearance, but judge righteous judgment.

JST John 7:24
24 Judge not according to **your traditions**, but judge righteous judgment.

25 Then said some of them of Jerusalem [*who were from Jerusalem*], Is not this he, whom they seek to kill?

26 But, lo, he speaketh boldly [*look, He is speaking out boldly in public*], and they [*the Pharisees, etc.*] say nothing unto him. Do the rulers know indeed that this is the very Christ? [*Maybe they think He actually is Christ and are afraid of Him.*]

27 Howbeit [*regardless of what they think*] we know this man whence he is [*we know where Jesus comes from, namely Nazareth*]: but when Christ [*the promised Messiah*] cometh, no man knoweth whence he is [*no one will know where he comes from*].

It was a false tradition among the Jews that no one would know where the true Christ came from.

28 Then cried Jesus in the temple [*Jesus spoke loudly so everyone could hear*] as he taught, saying, Ye both know me, and ye know whence I am: and I am not come of myself [*I have not come on My own*], but he that sent me is true, whom ye know not [*rather, I have been sent by the Father, whom you do not know because of your wickedness*].

29 But I know him: for I am from him, and he hath sent me.

30 Then they sought to take him [*wanted to arrest him*]: but no man laid hands on him, because his hour was not yet come. [*No one was able to seize him because it was not time yet for His trial and crucifixion.*]

31 And many of the people believed on him, and said, When Christ cometh, will he do more miracles than these which this man hath done? [*In other words, this has to be the Christ.*]

32 The Pharisees heard that the people murmured [*were saying*] such things concerning him; and the Pharisees and the chief priests sent officers to take him [*to arrest Him*].

33 Then said Jesus unto them, Yet a little while am I with you, and then I go unto him that sent me [*then I will return to My Father in Heaven*].

34 Ye shall seek me, and shall not find me: and where I am, thither [*there*] ye cannot come.

Here again, as in so many other places, John is pointing out to us that we are watching a group of people who are very learned in the letter of the law and the scriptures but haven't a clue what it is really about because they don't understand anything about the simple Plan of Salvation. Watch now, as they again stumble over details because they do not understand or accept the "big picture."

35 Then said the Jews among themselves, Whither [*where*] will he go, that we shall not find him? will he go unto the dispersed among the Gentiles, and teach the Gentiles [*will He go to the Greeks and teach them; see John 7:35, footnote a*]?

36 What manner of saying is this that he said [*what does He mean by saying*], Ye shall seek me, and shall not find me: and where I am, thither ye cannot come?

37 In the last day [*the eighth and final day of the Feast of Tabernacles, the climactic finale to the*

celebrating—see Bible Dictionary under "Feasts"], that great day [*the culmination*] of the feast, Jesus stood and cried, saying, If any man thirst, let him come unto me, and drink.

38 He that believeth on me, as the scripture [*Isaiah 44:3, 55:1*] hath said, out of his belly shall flow rivers of living water.

Picture if you will, throngs of Jews crowding the grounds around the temple, watching in rapt attention as water from the stream of Siloam (symbolic of water drawn from the wells of salvation—see Isaiah 12:3) was carried to the altar and then poured upon it, flowing down off it onto the ground, in a great ritual show symbolic of the living waters, including the Holy Ghost, which flow from the altar of God onto the earth to quench the spiritual thirst of the faithful—see Isaiah 44:3, 55:1. Perhaps, at that very moment, Jesus stood, and, with a loud voice, spoke to the onlookers saying, "If any man thirst, let him come unto me, and drink (verse 37, above)." There could not have been a more dramatic setting. Jesus was openly claiming to be the Messiah and to be the Jehovah of the Old Testament who had promised to give "living waters" to the faithful.

39 (But this spake he of the Spirit, which they that believe on him should receive: for the Holy Ghost was not yet given; because that Jesus was not yet glorified.)

JST John 7:39

39 (But this spake he of the Spirit, which they that believe on him should receive; for the Holy Ghost was **promised unto them who believe, after that Jesus was glorified.**)

The phrase "the Holy Ghost was not yet given," in verse 39 above, causes some to believe that the Holy Ghost was not here at all during the time Jesus was here. This is not the case. The Holy Ghost was obviously functioning and active on earth during the Savior's mortal ministry. The Holy Ghost attended the Savior's baptism (Matthew 3:13–17). The Savior was "full of the Holy Ghost" in Luke 4:1. Thus, our understanding is that, while the Holy Ghost did function during Christ's mortal ministry, the full power of the Gift of the Holy Ghost was not here. See Bible Dictionary, under "Holy Ghost."

In the next verses, we watch a debate among the people as to who this Jesus really is.

40 Many of the people therefore, when they heard this saying [*what Jesus said in verses 37 and 38 above*], said, Of a truth this is the Prophet [*some prophet who was to come before Christ; see* Doctrinal New Testament Commentary, *Vol. 1, p. 448*].

41 Others said, This is the Christ. But some said, Shall Christ come out of Galilee?

42 Hath not the scripture said, That Christ cometh of the seed of David [*would be a descendant of David*], and out of the town of Bethlehem, where David was? [*Referring no doubt to the prophecy in Micah 5:2 that Christ was to be born in Bethlehem, and thus, they thought, should come from Bethlehem, not Nazareth in Galilee.*]

43 So there was a division among the people because of him.

44 And some of them [*the officers in verse 45*] would have taken him [*arrested him*]; but no man laid hands on him.

45 Then came the officers [*soldiers*] to the chief priests and Pharisees [*Jewish religious leaders*]; and they said unto them, Why have ye not brought him [*why didn't you arrest Jesus*]?

46 The officers answered, Never man spake like this man [*nobody ever taught like He does*].

47 Then answered them the Pharisees [*then the Pharisees and chief priests said to the soldiers*], Are ye also deceived [*has Jesus got you fooled also*]?

48 Have any of the rulers or of the Pharisees believed on him [*have any of us rulers been deceived by him*]?

49 But this people who knoweth not the law are cursed. [*The people don't understand the teachings of Moses. That's why they are subject to being deceived by Jesus.*]

Nicodemus Defends Jesus

Next, Nicodemus will defend Jesus, which is a very risky thing to do under the circumstances. Perhaps you remember that Nicodemus was the Pharisee who came to Jesus by night and was taught the necessity of baptism and the gift of the Holy Ghost (see John 3:1–21). He will also help Joseph from Aramathea prepare the body of the crucified Lord for burial (see John 19:39).

50 Nicodemus saith unto them, (he that came to Jesus by night, being one of them [*Nicodemus was a member of the Pharisees*],)

51 Doth our law judge any man, before it hear him, and know what he doeth? [*Why are we violating our own laws? We haven't even given Jesus a fair trial and already we are judging Him.*]

52 They answered and said unto him, Art thou also of Galilee [*has He converted you too*]? Search, and look: for out of Galilee ariseth no prophet. [*Check the scriptures. There is no mention of a Prophet who comes from Galilee.*]

53 And every man went unto his own house.

JOHN 8

It is the day after the Feast of Tabernacles and large crowds of people gather to listen to Jesus as He teaches in the courtyard of the temple in Jerusalem. The scribes and Pharisees are very frustrated because, despite repeated attempts to discredit Jesus and get Him arrested, they continue to fail to reach their goal. John now reports yet another attempt to trap Him in His words, as these Jewish leaders drag a woman taken in adultery to Jesus, in front of the crowd, and ask what He recommends be done to her. Their hope is that they can get Him to say something in opposition to the Law of Moses concerning punishment for adultery, in order that they can have Him arrested. Watch and see what happens.

1 JESUS went unto the mount of Olives [*just a few minutes' walk east of Jerusalem*].

2 And early in the morning he came again into the temple [*the courtyard of the temple*], and all the people came unto him; and he sat down, and taught them.

The Woman Taken in Adultery

3 And the scribes and Pharisees [*hypocritical religious leaders of the Jews*] brought unto him a woman taken in adultery; and when they had set her in the midst,

JST John 8:3

3 And the scribes and Pharisees brought unto him a woman taken in adultery; and when they had set her in the midst **of the people**,

4 They say unto him, Master, this

JOHN 8

415

woman was taken in adultery, in the very act [*we caught her right while she was doing it*].

One has to wonder why these Jewish leaders didn't also bring the man who was involved with this woman to the Savior. Perhaps he was one of their own. In JST Luke 16:21, Jesus called these leaders "adulterers." We don't know if the man was a fellow Pharisee, but it is pure hypocrisy to single out the woman for embarrassment and humiliation, and let the man escape.

Next, they remind Him of what the Law of Moses said regarding the matter, and then ask a question.

5 Now Moses in the law commanded us, that such should be stoned: but what sayest thou?

These evil men are still trying to trap Jesus by getting Him to say something against Moses and his laws. Imagine how quiet it was as the crowd hushed in an attempt to watch and hear the Master's response. Imagine also how frightened the woman was.

6 This they said, tempting him [*trying to lure Him into a trap*], that they might have to accuse him [*in order for them to build a legal case against Him*]. But Jesus stooped down, and with his finger wrote on the ground, as though he heard them not.

"He That Is Without Sin... First Cast a Stone"

7 So when they continued [*kept*] asking him, he lifted up himself [*stood up*], and said unto them, He that is without sin among you [*perhaps implying whoever has not committed the same sin; see* Doctrinal New Testament Commentary, *Vol. 1, p. 451*], let him first cast a stone at her.

8 And again he stooped down, and wrote on the ground.

9 And they which heard it, being convicted by their own conscience, went out [*left*] one by one, beginning at the eldest, even unto the last: and Jesus was left alone, and the woman standing in the midst.

JST John 8:9
And they which heard it, being convicted by their own conscience, went out one by one, beginning at the eldest, even unto the last; and Jesus was left alone, and the woman standing in the midst **of the temple**.

10 When Jesus had lifted up himself [*had stood up*], and saw none but the woman, he said unto her, Woman, where are those thine accusers? hath no man condemned thee? [*Where did the men go who wanted to stone you? Didn't any of them condemn you to death?*]

11 She said, No man, Lord. And Jesus said unto her, Neither do I condemn thee: go, and sin no more.

JST John 8:11

11 She said, No man, Lord. And Jesus said unto her, Neither do I condemn thee; go, and sin no more. **And the woman glorified God from that hour, and believed on his name**.

Jesus did not forgive the woman at this point. Obviously, she has some serious repenting to do. But He did not condemn her, meaning that she still had time and opportunity to repent. The Joseph Smith Translation, cited above at the end of verse 11, confirms that she began believing, which includes repenting.

Next, Jesus teaches that He is the light of the world.

The Light of the World

12 Then spake Jesus again unto them, saying, I am the light of the world: he that followeth me shall not walk in darkness [*spiritual darkness*], but shall have the light of life [*eternal life*].

13 The Pharisees therefore said unto him, Thou bearest record of thyself; thy record is not true. [*You are not following the law of witnesses.*]

14 Jesus answered and said unto them, Though I bear record of myself, yet my record is true: for I know whence I came [*where I am from*], and whither I go [*and where I am going*]; but ye cannot tell whence I come, and whither I go.

15 Ye judge after the flesh [*you are judging Me by worldly standards*];

I judge no man [*perhaps meaning that the day of final judgment has not yet arrived and the opportunity to repent and change their ways is still available*].

16 And yet if I judge, my judgment is true [*valid*]: for I am not alone, but I and the Father that sent me. [*Jesus has another witness of Himself and His mission, namely, the Father.*]

17 It is also written in your law, that the testimony of two men is true. [*This is the law of witnesses the Jews were referring to in verse 13.*]

18 I am one that bear witness of myself, and the Father that sent me beareth witness of me.

19 Then said they unto him, Where is thy Father? Jesus answered, Ye neither know me, nor my Father: if ye had known me, ye should have [*would have*] known my Father also.

20 These words spake Jesus in the treasury [*one of the temple buildings*], as he taught in the temple: and no man laid hands on him; for his hour was not yet come [*John is reminding us that the time for the Savior's arrest, trial, crucifixion, and resurrection was not yet here at this time*].

21 Then said Jesus again unto them, I go my way, and ye shall seek me [*to kill Me*], and shall die in your sins: whither I go, ye cannot come. [*You can't come to heaven because you refuse to repent.*]

22 Then said the Jews, Will he kill himself? because he saith, Whither

JOHN 8

I go, ye cannot come. [*Does He mean that He is going to commit suicide, and that is how He will get away from us so that we can't follow Him around?*]

23 And he said unto them, Ye are from beneath; I am from above: ye are of this world; I am not of this world. [*In effect, we are worlds apart.*]

24 I said therefore unto you, that ye shall die in your sins: for if ye believe not that I am he [*the Messiah*], ye shall die in your sins.

25 Then said they unto him, Who art thou? And Jesus saith unto them, Even the same that I said unto you from the beginning. [*I already told you.*]

26 I have many things to say and to judge of you: but he [*the Father*] that sent me is true; and I speak to the world those things which I have heard of him.

27 They understood not that he spake to them of the Father.

Have you noticed that John places great emphasis on the Savior honoring His Father and bearing witness of Him? 3 Nephi, chapter 15, likewise teaches of this.

28 Then said Jesus unto them, When ye have lifted up [*crucified*] the Son of man [*me*], then shall ye know that I am he [*the Messiah*], and that I do nothing of myself; but as my Father hath taught me, I speak these things. [*In effect, you will know that I am God's Son and*

that I bring you His word.]

29 And he that sent me is with me: the Father hath not left me alone; for I do always those things that please him.

30 As he spake these words, many believed on him.

31 Then said Jesus to those Jews which believed on him, If ye continue in my word, then are ye my disciples indeed;

The Truth Sets Us Free

32 And ye shall know the truth, and the truth shall make you free.

Verse 32 is one of the most profound verses in all the scriptures. It is a simple and powerful fact. The truth sets us free. For example, if people believe that a baby who dies without baptism is forever damned from returning to heaven, D&C 137:10 sets them free from the anguish and lingering guilt of having neglected this rite for the child.

If one has lived a life of serious sin, and upon repenting and changing lifestyle, still believes that he or she will forever be a "second-class" citizen in the Church, Isaiah 1:18 will set him or her free from feelings of being permanently limited by past lifestyle. So will Elder Richard G. Scott's talk in October Conference, 2000, set such persons "free," in which he taught: "If you have repented from serious transgression and mistakenly believe that you will always be a second-class citizen in the kingdom of God, learn that is not true."

As we move on to verse 33, next, a little background is helpful. The Jews at the time of Christ had a very strong tradition that they were privileged above others because they were direct descendants of Abraham. Watch now as they put this false notion into action, and watch the Savior's response to them.

33 They answered him, We be Abraham's seed [*we are descendants of Abraham*], and were never in bondage [*slavery*] to any man [*we don't need to be set free*]: how sayest thou [*what do You mean when You say*], Ye shall be made free?

34 Jesus answered them, Verily, verily, I say unto you, Whosoever committeth sin is the servant of sin [*is a slave to sin*].

35 And the servant abideth not in the house for ever [*slaves don't live in the master's house*]: but the Son abideth ever [*but the Son lives in the Father's house*].

36 If the Son therefore shall make you free, ye shall be free indeed. [*If I make you free from sin, you are free indeed!*]

37 I know that ye are Abraham's seed [*descendants*]; but ye seek to kill me, because my word hath no place in you [*because you have rejected Me*].

38 I speak that which I have seen with my Father: and ye do that which ye have seen with your father [*the devil; see verse 44*].

39 They answered and said unto him, Abraham is our father [*we are direct descendants of Abraham, implying that that fact gives them special privilege*]. Jesus saith unto them, If ye were Abraham's children [*true followers*], ye would do the works of Abraham.

40 But now ye seek to kill me, a man that hath told you the truth, which I have heard of God [*from the Father*]: this did not Abraham [*Abraham would not try to kill Me*].

41 Ye do the deeds of your father [*the devil; see verse 44*]. Then said they to him, We be not born of fornication [*we have not "stepped out" on God; in other words, we are not apostates*]; we have one Father, even God. [*We are completely loyal to God.*]

Just a brief note about the word "fornication," as used in verse 41, above. It is obvious that these Jews knew the symbolic use of the term as often found in the scriptures. The words "fornication" and "adultery" are often used in the Bible to refer, symbolically, to complete disloyalty to God. Example: Revelation 14:8, Jeremiah 3:8-9. See Bible Dictionary, under "Adultery."

42 Jesus said unto them, If God were your Father [*if you were true followers of God*], ye would love

JOHN 8

me: for I proceeded forth and came from God; neither came I of myself, but he sent me.

Next, Jesus poses a question to these people, and then answers His own question. The JST makes an important one-word change to verse 43. It teaches us that there are some people who, because of their beliefs or lifestyle, simply can't stand the truth.

43 Why do ye not understand my speech? even because ye cannot hear my word.

JST John 8:43
43 Why do ye not understand my speech? even because ye cannot **bear** my word.

Next, in verse 44, the Savior gives us a rather brief but concentrated description of the devil.

44 Ye are of your father the devil, and the lusts of your father ye will do [*you live the wicked lifestyle sponsored by your "father," the devil*]. He was a murderer from the beginning, and abode not in the truth, because there is no truth in him. When he speaketh a lie, he speaketh of his own: for he is a liar, and the father of it. [*The devil is the father of lies.*]

45 And because I tell you the truth, ye believe me not.

46 Which of you convinceth [*convicts—see John 8:46, footnote a, in your Bible*] me of sin? And if I say the truth, why do ye not believe me?

47 He that is of God [*the righteous*]

heareth God's words: ye therefore hear them not, because ye are not of God.

JST John 8:47
47 He that is of God **receiveth** God's words; ye therefore **receive** them not, because ye are not of God.

The change from "hear" to "receive" by the Prophet Joseph Smith in verse 47, above, is a major message for us. As learners, we have the obligation to actively receive the gospel when we hear it, rather than simply hearing it.

48 Then answered the Jews, and said unto him, Say we not well that thou art a Samaritan [*You are an apostate Yourself—see verse 41*], and hast a devil?

The phrase "thou art a Samaritan" in verse 48 above is saying, in effect, that Jesus is "illegitimate," and God is not his father. The Samaritans came from remnants of the ten northern tribes of Israel, who intermarried with non-covenant people, mainly Assyrian occupational armies, beginning in about 722 B.C., and apostatized. Thus, Samaritans were considered by the Jews to be former members of the House of Israel who had "stepped out on God" by marrying nonmembers and thereby had polluted the race. They were "illegitimate" children, therefore, were despised by the Jews.

49 Jesus answered, I have not a

devil; but I honour my Father, and ye do dishonour me.

50 And I seek not mine own glory: there is one that seeketh and judgeth.

51 Verily, verily, I say unto you, If a man keep my saying, he shall never see death [*spiritual death*].

52 Then said the Jews unto him, Now we know that thou hast a devil [*now we know that You are possessed by a demon*]. Abraham is dead, and the prophets; and thou sayest, If a man keep my saying, he shall never taste of death [*will never die*].

> Next, these people who are completely missing the point about spiritual death retort back to Jesus that Abraham was righteous and he died, so what He is saying about death can't be true.

53 Art thou greater than our father Abraham, which is dead? and the prophets are dead: whom makest thou thyself [*who do You think You are*]?

54 Jesus answered, If I honour myself, my honour is nothing: it is my Father that honoureth me; of whom ye say, that he is your God:

55 Yet ye have not known him [*you don't follow Him, you don't know Him*]; but I know him: and if I should say, I know him not, I shall be a liar like unto you: but I know him, and keep his saying [*follow His instructions*].

56 Your father [*ancestor*] Abraham rejoiced to see my day [*saw My day in vision*]: and he saw it, and was glad.

57 Then said the Jews unto him, Thou art not yet fifty years old, and hast thou seen Abraham?

58 Jesus said unto them, Verily, verily, I say unto you, Before Abraham was, I am [*in effect, I am the God who appeared to Abraham*].

> "I am" in verse 58 above is usually written "I AM," and is another name for Jehovah, the God of the Old Testament. See John 8:58, footnote b, in your Bible. See also Exodus 3:14. Jesus has just told the Jews, in terms they understand, that He is Jehovah, the God of the Old Testament, and that the reason He has seen Abraham (verse 57 above) is that he is the God of Abraham and appeared to him. Because the Jews finally understand clearly who Jesus is claiming to be, they are furious with Him, as shown in verse 59, next.

59 Then took they up stones to cast at him: but Jesus hid himself, and went out of the temple, going through the midst of them, and so passed by.

JOHN 9

Yet again Jesus will heal on the Sabbath, and the Jews will accuse Him of violating the Sabbath as a result. You will find the dialogue between the Jewish leaders and the blind man who was healed fascinating. They will interrogate him

JOHN 9

and attempt to get him to discredit Jesus, but he will refuse. Finally, since he refuses to go along with them, they will excommunicate him from their church (verse 34).

It may be that verse 1, next, is a connection back to chapter 8, verse 59. If so, then it is saying that as Jesus was escaping from the angry Jews who were trying to stone Him at the end of chapter 8, He saw a blind man and stopped.

1 AND as Jesus passed by, he saw a man which was blind from his birth.

Some people have come to believe the false notion that physical illness in general is caused by sin. This was a common belief among the Jews in New Testament times. We see this reflected in verse 2, next.

2 And his disciples asked him, saying, Master, who did sin, this man, or his parents, that he was born blind?

The Savior straightens out this mistaken idea in the case of the blind man, and then bears witness that the Father sent Him to be the light of the world.

3 Jesus answered, Neither hath this man sinned, nor his parents: but that the works of God should be made manifest [be shown] in him.

4 I must work the works of him that sent me, while it is day: the night cometh, when no man can work.

JST John 9:4

4 I must work the works of him that sent me, while **I am with you; the time cometh when I shall have finished my work, then I go unto the Father**.

5 As long as I am in the world, I am the light of the world.

A Blind Man is Healed

6 When he had thus spoken, he spat on the ground, and made clay of the spittle, and he anointed the eyes of the blind man with the clay,

There is perhaps symbolism in the use of "clay", in verse 6 above. "Clay" is symbolic of this earth as well as of our mortal bodies. Touching the blind man's eyes with the clay so he could see can symbolize the fact that those who are faithful in this mortal experience will eventually be enabled to "see" as God sees as they enter into exaltation.

7 And said unto him, Go, wash in the pool of Siloam, (which is by interpretation, Sent.) He went his way therefore, and washed, and came seeing [could see].

Did you notice that the word "sent," in verse 7, above, is capitalized? It is capitalized because it refers to Christ. Thus, we see symbolism here. Among the possible symbolism is: If we "wash" our spiritual eyes in the "living water" from Christ, we will be able to see the things of eternity clearly.

Watch now as people take the focus from a simple and beautiful miracle and ruin it by interrogating the once-blind man to the point of excommunicating him because of his simple, honest answers.

8 The neighbours therefore, and they which before had seen him that he was blind, said, Is not this he that sat and begged [*isn't this the blind man who used to be a beggar*]?

9 Some said, This is he: others said, He is like him [*he just looks like that blind man*]: but he [*the blind man*] said, I am he [*I am the one who was healed*].

10 Therefore said they unto him, How were thine eyes opened?

11 He answered and said, A man that is called Jesus made clay, and anointed mine eyes, and said unto me, Go to the pool of Siloam, and wash: and I went and washed, and I received sight.

12 Then said they unto him, Where is he? He said, I know not.

13 They brought to the Pharisees him that aforetime was blind. [*Some Jews brought the formerly blind man to the Pharisees.*]

14 And it was the sabbath day when Jesus made the clay, and opened his eyes. [*Jesus had healed the blind man on the Sabbath.*]

15 Then again the Pharisees also asked him how he had received his sight. He said unto them, He [*Jesus*] put clay upon mine eyes, and I washed, and do see [*and I can see*].

16 Therefore said some of the Pharisees, This man is not of God, because he keepeth not the sabbath day [*Jesus can't be sent by God, because He breaks the Sabbath by healing people on it*]. Others said, How can a man that is a sinner do such miracles? And there was a division among them.

17 They say unto the blind man again, What sayest thou of him, that he hath opened thine eyes [*what's your opinion of Jesus*]? He said, He is a prophet.

The Jewish religious leaders are trying desperately to discredit Jesus in the eyes of the people and it is not working. They now try to discredit the blind man's parents by suggesting that they don't really know for sure that their son was born blind.

19 And they asked them, saying, Is this your son, who ye say [*claim*] was born blind? how then doth he now see [*if he was really blind, how could he see now*]?

20 His parents answered them and said, We know that this is our son, and that he was born blind:

21 But by what means he now seeth, we know not [*we don't understand what happened so that he can now see*]; or who hath opened his eyes, we know not: he is of age; ask him: he shall speak for himself. [*Ask him. He is old enough to speak for himself.*]

JOHN 9

22 These words spake his parents, because they feared the Jews [*the religious rulers of the Jews*]: for the Jews had agreed [*plotted*] already, that if any man did confess that he was Christ, he should be put out of the synagogue. [*Anyone who says Jesus is the prophesied Messiah will be excommunicated.*]

23 Therefore said his parents, He is of age; ask him. [*The parents were afraid of getting excommunicated, so they told the Pharisees to ask their son what happened.*]

By now it must have become very bothersome to the blind man who was healed to have such a negative fuss made over a beautiful and straightforward miracle through which his sight was restored. You can sense his frustration in the next verses and perhaps some disgust with these distracters. Surely we can admire the boldness in his replies as he steadfastly maintains his position that Jesus healed him, thus risking his membership in the Jewish church.

24 Then again called they [*the Pharisees*] the man that was blind, and said unto him, Give God the praise: we know that this man [*Jesus*] is a sinner. [*Give God the praise for your being healed, but don't give this imposter, Jesus, any credit.*]

25 He answered and said, Whether he be a sinner or no, I know not [*whether or not Jesus is a sinner, I don't know*]: one thing I know, that, whereas I was blind, now I see [*but one thing I do know: I was blind*

and now I can see]. [*This formerly blind man is not intimidated by the Jewish rulers, which must have been frustrating for them.*]

26 Then said they to him again, What did he [*Jesus*] to thee? how opened he thine eyes?

27 He answered them, I have told you already, and ye did not hear [*what's the matter, are you dense?*]: wherefore would ye hear it again [*why do you want me to tell you again*]? will ye also be his disciples [*are you being converted to Him too*]?

28 Then they reviled him [*insulted him*], and said, Thou art his disciple [*you have become a follower of Jesus*]; but we are Moses' disciples.

29 We know that God spake unto Moses: as for this fellow, we know not from whence he is [*we don't know where He comes from*].

We sense that this blind man might well have been one of the "noble and great ones" (Abraham 3:22) from our premortal existence as we watch him now boldly take on these Jewish religious leaders who have been battering him constantly to try to get him to renounce Jesus.

30 The man answered and said unto them, Why herein is a marvellous thing [*well, this is getting more interesting all the time*], that ye [*the big religious leaders who are supposed to know these things*] know not from whence he is, and yet he hath opened mine eyes.

31 Now we know that God heareth not sinners: but if any man be a worshipper of God, and doeth his will, him he heareth. [*If Jesus were a sinner, God would not support Him in such miracles.*]

32 Since the world began was it not heard that any man opened the eyes of one that was born blind.

JST John 9:32
32 Since the world began was it not heard that any man opened the eyes of one that was born blind, **except he be of God**.

33 If this man [*Jesus*] were not of God, he could do nothing.

34 They answered and said unto him, Thou wast altogether born in sins, and dost thou teach us [*you, a complete sinner, have the gall to pretend to teach us*]? And they cast him out. [*They excommunicated him.*]

Watch now as the Savior seeks out the formerly blind man who humbly receives the Master's message of salvation.

35 Jesus heard that they had cast him out; and when he had found him, he said unto him, Dost thou believe on the Son of God?

36 He answered and said, Who is he, Lord, that I might believe on him?

37 And Jesus said unto him, Thou hast both seen him [*NIV "thou hast now seen him"*], and it is he that talketh with thee. [*You are talking with Him now.*]

38 And he said, Lord, I believe. And he worshipped him.

39 And Jesus said, For judgment I am come into this world [*I have come to the world so that all people can receive a fair judgment*], that [*so that*] they which see not might see [*so that the spiritually blind, who repent, can see spiritual things*]; and that they which see [*who claim to see, but are in spiritual darkness*] might be made blind [*can use their agency to remain spiritually blind*].

Watch now as some of these Pharisees, having caught on to what the Savior said in verse 39, above, openly ask if they fit into the category of those who are spiritually blind.

40 And some of the Pharisees which were with him heard these words, and said unto him, Are we blind also?

41 Jesus said unto them, If ye were blind, ye should have no sin: but now ye say, We see; therefore your sin remaineth. [*If you were ignorant of the truth, you would not be accountable, but it is as you say; you are sinning against light, therefore you remain accountable.*]

JOHN 10

Next, the Master uses the imagery of a shepherd leading his sheep to illustrate that He is the Good Shepherd, and other, unauthorized shepherds [*Pharisees, etc.*] try to sneak in and lead the sheep

JOHN 10

astray. In the days of Jesus, it was a common practice for several shepherds to keep their sheep overnight in the same enclosure, so that only one guard would have to be on duty through the night. The next morning, each shepherd would come to the enclosure, identify himself to the guard, and then literally call his own sheep to come out of the herd to him, often calling each of his sheep by its own name. His sheep recognized his voice and came out of the herd and followed him throughout the day as he led them to pasture and water. It is a fascinating sight in the Holy Land, even today, to see sheep following a shepherd who is leading his sheep, rather than herding them from behind.

In this chapter you will find the reference to the Nephites in the Americas (verse 16).

The Parable of the Good Shepherd

1 VERILY, verily, I say unto you, He that entereth not by the door into the sheepfold, but climbeth up some other way, the same is a thief and a robber [*is not authorized by God to lead the sheep; symbolic of Satan, apostates, and others, who try to lead us astray*].

2 But he [*Christ*] that entereth in by the door [*is authorized by God*] is the shepherd of the sheep.

3 To him the porter [*guard*] openeth; and the sheep hear his voice: and he calleth his own sheep by name, and leadeth them out.

4 And when he putteth forth his own sheep, he goeth before them [*leads them, rather than herding them*], and the sheep follow him: for they know his voice.

5 And a stranger will they not follow, but will flee from him: for they know not the voice of strangers.

6 This parable spake Jesus unto them: but they understood not what things they were which he spake unto them.

Next, Jesus explains the parable of the good shepherd.

7 Then said Jesus unto them again, Verily, verily, I say unto you, I am the door of the sheep [*symbolic of the door to heaven*].

8 All that ever came before me are thieves and robbers [*any others who have come before Me and claim to be the doorway to heaven are false shepherds*]: but the sheep did not hear them [*My true followers don't come to them when they call*].

9 I am the door: by me if any man enter in, he shall be saved, and shall go in and out, and find pasture [*will be nourished by God*].

10 The thief [*symbolic of Satan, the wicked, and so forth*] cometh not, but for to steal, and to kill, and to destroy: I am come that they might have life [*to bring the faithful eternal life*], and that they might have it more abundantly.

11 I am the good shepherd: the good shepherd giveth his life for the sheep

426 THE NEW TESTAMENT MADE EASIER THIRD EDITION, PART 1

[*Jesus will give His life for us*].

12 But he that is an hireling [*a hired servant*], and not the shepherd, whose own the sheep are not [*who does not own the sheep*], seeth the wolf coming, and leaveth the sheep, and fleeth: and the wolf catcheth them, and scattereth the sheep.

13 The hireling fleeth [*runs away when danger comes*], because he is an hireling, and careth not for the sheep [*he doesn't love the sheep like the owner does*].

14 I am the good shepherd, and know my sheep, and am known of mine [*the Savior's true followers know His voice and come when He calls*].

15 As the Father knoweth me, even so know I the Father: and I lay down my life for the sheep [*Jesus will give His life for His people as He performs the Atonement*].

Other Sheep

16 And other sheep I have, which are not of this fold [*are not on this continent*]: them also I must bring, and they shall hear my voice; and there shall be one fold, and one shepherd [*all of my righteous followers will ultimately come together with me in celestial glory*].

We know from 3 Nephi 15:21 that Jesus was referring to the Nephites on the American continent when He said, "Other sheep I have, which are not of this fold; them also I must bring, and they shall hear my voice;" (verse 16 above). We know also that there

were yet other sheep besides the Nephites. To the Nephites, Jesus said, "I say unto you that I have other sheep, which are not of this land, neither of the land of Jerusalem" (3 Nephi 16:1). As we read 3 Nephi 17:4, we are told that Jesus was referring to the lost ten tribes.

17 Therefore [*for this reason*] doth my Father love me, because I lay down my life, that I might take it again.

Verse 18, next, is significant doctrinally. In the strictest sense, no one killed Jesus or took His life. No one could. He gave it as a free-will offering for our sins.

18 No man taketh it from me, but I lay it down of myself. I have power to lay it down [*to leave my body*], and I have power to take it again [*I have power to resurrect*]. This commandment have I received of my Father. [*This is what My Father asked Me to do.*]

19 There was a division therefore again among the Jews for [*because of*] these sayings [*because Jesus said that no one could kill Him, rather, He would give His life willingly, then resurrect Himself*].

20 And many of them said, He hath a devil [*He is possessed by an evil spirit*], and is mad [*has lost His mind*]; why hear ye him [*why do you even listen to Him*]?

21 Others said, These are not the words of him that hath a devil. Can a devil open the eyes of the blind?

JOHN 10

427

Verse 22, next, begins a new topic. In your Latter-day Saint King James Version of the Bible (English), you will see a paragraph mark at the beginning of the verse signaling a new subject to you, the reader.

It is the winter before the crucifixion and the Savior is in Jerusalem at the time of the Feast of Dedication. It was eight days of festivities celebrating the dedication of a new altar of burnt offering in 165 B.C. after the old one had been desecrated by Antiochus Epiphanes, the king of Syria in 168 B.C. No fasting or mourning for any calamity of the past was allowed, which would mar the great gladness and rejoicing accompanying the celebration. Huge torches illuminated the streets and public gathering places in the city, and thus it became known as the Feast of Lights. (See Bible Dictionary, under "Feasts.")

Watch now as Jesus attends the Feast of Dedication.

22 And it was at Jerusalem the feast of the dedication, and it was winter.

23 And Jesus walked in the temple in Solomon's porch.

24 Then came the Jews round about him, and said unto him, How long dost thou make us to doubt [*how long are You going to keep us wondering about who You really are*]? If thou be the Christ, tell us plainly.

25 Jesus answered them, I told you, and ye believed not [*in effect,*

I have told you many times and in many ways that I am Christ, but you won't believe Me]: the works [*miracles and teaching*] that I do in my Father's name, they bear witness of me [*they tell you who I am*].

26 But ye believe not, because ye are not of my sheep, as I said unto you. [*You have been in apostasy so long that you no longer even recognize the voice of the Good Shepherd when He calls.*]

27 My sheep hear my voice, and I know them, and they follow me:

28 And I give unto them eternal life; and they shall never perish [*they will never suffer spiritual death*], neither shall any man pluck them out of my hand [*no one can take them away from Me*].

29 My Father, which gave them me, is greater than all; and no man is able to pluck them out of my Father's hand.

30 I and my Father are one. [*The Father and Son are completely united in all things.*]

Next, the Jews accuse the Savior of blasphemy (mocking God) which, under their law, was a crime punishable by death.

31 Then the Jews took up stones again to stone him [*to throw rocks at Him and kill Him*].

32 Jesus answered them, Many good works have I shewed [*shown*] you from my Father; for which of those works do ye stone me? [*In effect, I have done many wonderful*

miracles and much good; for which of these things are you going to stone Me?]

33 The Jews answered him, saying, For a good work we stone thee not; but for blasphemy; and because that thou, being a man, makest thyself God. [*We are not stoning You for those things, rather because You have mocked God and claim that You are God.*]

34 Jesus answered them, Is it not written in your law [*Psalm 82:6*], I said, Ye are gods [*you can become gods*]?

This is a very important doctrinal point. Many Christians are very offended by our teaching that we can become gods (D&C 132:20). Here in the Bible itself is a statement, confirmed by the Savior Himself, that we can become gods. He reaffirms what had already been given in Psalm 82:6.

35 If he called them gods, unto whom the word of God came, and the scripture cannot be broken; [*If your scriptures teach that you can become gods, why is it blasphemy (mocking God) for me to say I am a God?*]

As mentioned previously, blasphemy, according to Jewish law, was a sin which could get a person executed.

36 Say ye of him [*Me*], whom the Father hath sanctified [*prepared*], and sent into the world, Thou blasphemest; because I said, I am the Son of God [*are you saying that I mock God by claiming to be His Son*]?

37 If I do not the works of my Father [*if what I do doesn't remind you of the Father*], believe me not [*then don't believe Me*].

38 But if I do [*remind you of the Father*], though ye believe not me, believe the works: that ye may know, and believe, that the Father is in me, and I in him.

39 Therefore [*because of what He said*] they sought [*attempted*] again to take [*arrest*] him: but he escaped out of their hand,

40 And went away again beyond Jordan into the place where John at first baptized; and there he abode [*stayed*].

41 And many resorted [*went*] unto him, and said, John did no miracle [*John the Baptist didn't do miracles*]: but all things that John spake of this man [*Jesus*] were true [*everything he said about Jesus turned out to be true*].

42 And many believed on him there.

JOHN 11

As this chapter begins, Jesus and His disciples are staying in Perea (across the Jordan River, east of Jericho—see John 10:40, roughly 30 miles from Jerusalem), where there is relative safety from the Jews in Jerusalem who had recently attempted to stone Him. It is the Master's last winter during His mortal ministry.

JOHN 11

John, chapter 11, is a chapter that especially touches the heart. You will see the Savior's love for Mary, Martha, and Lazarus as He weeps with tender emotion (verse 35) and then watch His power over death as He raises Lazarus from the dead. Lazarus had become very ill, and his sisters, Mary and Martha, had sent for the Master to come heal him. Jesus did not come immediately, as they hoped He would, and Lazarus died. Watch now as a great lesson unfolds concerning the Savior's tender mercy and His power to bring resurrection to all.

Lazarus Is Sick

1 NOW a certain man was sick, named Lazarus, of Bethany [*about two miles outside of Jerusalem on the far side of the Mount of Olives, on the road to Jericho*], the town of Mary and her sister Martha [*the town where Mary and Martha lived*].

2 (It was that Mary which anointed the Lord with ointment, and wiped his feet with her hair [*Matthew 26:7, John 12:2-3*], whose brother Lazarus was sick.)

JST John 11:2

2 **And Mary, his sister, who** anointed the Lord with ointment and wiped his feet with her hair, **lived with her sister Martha, in whose house her** brother Lazarus was sick.

3 Therefore his sisters sent unto him [*Jesus*], saying, Lord, behold, he [*Lazarus*] whom thou lovest is sick.

4 When Jesus heard that, he said, This sickness is not unto death, but for the glory of God, that the Son of God might be glorified thereby. [*In effect, He won't be dead very long. He will die, verses 13–14, and this situation will help many to believe in God and to have a chance to be much more aware of who I am.*]

5 Now Jesus loved Martha, and her sister, and Lazarus.

6 When he had heard therefore that he was sick, he abode [*stayed*] two days still in the same place [*Perea*] where he was.

7 Then after that saith he to his disciples, Let us go into Judæa [*to the Jerusalem area*] again.

8 His disciples say unto him, Master, the Jews of late [*just recently*] sought to [*attempted to*] stone thee; and goest thou thither [*there*] again?

His disciples are very worried about His safety and don't want Him going to Mary and Martha's house in Bethany, because it is only two miles from Jerusalem where the Jews are who have already tried to kill Him.

9 Jesus answered, Are there not twelve hours in the day? If any man walk in the day, he stumbleth not, because he seeth the light of this world. [*In effect, I must keep right on going with My work.*]

10 But if a man walk in the night, he stumbleth, because there is no light in him.

11 These things said he: and after that he saith unto them, Our friend Lazarus sleepeth; but I go, that I may awake him out of sleep.

12 Then said his disciples, Lord, if he sleep, he shall do well [*if he is just sleeping, he will be ok, implying again that they don't want Him going near Jerusalem*].

13 Howbeit [*however*] Jesus spake of his death: but they thought that he had spoken of taking of rest in sleep.

Lazarus Is Dead

14 Then said Jesus unto them plainly, Lazarus is dead.

15 And I am glad for your sakes that I was not there, to the intent ye may believe [*in effect, I am glad he is dead, because what is going to happen will strengthen your testimonies*]; nevertheless let us go unto him.

16 Then said Thomas, which is called Didymus [*the twin*], unto his fellow disciples, Let us also go, that we may die with him.

JST John 11:16

16 Then said Thomas, which is called Didymus, unto his fellow disciples, Let us also go, that we may die with him; **for they feared lest the Jews should take Jesus and put him to death, for as yet they did not understand the power of God**.

This Apostle of Christ, Thomas, is usually known mainly as "doubting Thomas," because he refused to believe that Jesus had been resurrected unless he could see Him personally and feel the wounds in His hands and side. (See John 20:25–28.) Here we see Thomas in a much different light. He is a man of courage and conviction, and encourages the other disciples to join him in going to Jerusalem with Jesus so that they could all die with Him.

17 Then when Jesus came [*arrived in Bethany at Martha's house*], he found that he [*Lazarus*] had lain in the grave four days already.

JST John 11:17

17 **And** when Jesus came **to Bethany, to Martha's house, Lazarus had already been in the grave four days**.

Four days is very significant because of Jewish beliefs about death. They had a false belief that the spirit must remain by a dead person's body for three days. After that, the person is for sure dead. The fact that Lazarus had been dead for four days, and in fact, had already begun to stink (verse 39) left no doubt in the minds of the mourners that he was dead.

18 Now Bethany was nigh [*near*] unto Jerusalem, about fifteen furlongs off [*two miles away*]:

A "furlong," as used in verse 18, above, is about 607 English feet (see John 11, footnote 18a, in your Bible). Thus, 15 times 607 is 9,105 feet, or about 1.7 miles.

JOHN 11

19 And many of the Jews came to Martha and Mary, to comfort them concerning their brother.

20 Then Martha, as soon as she heard that Jesus was coming, went and met him: but Mary sat still in the house.

21 Then said Martha unto Jesus, Lord, if thou hadst been here, my brother had not died [*if You had come quickly, when I first sent word to You of Lazarus' illness, he would not have died*].

Next, Martha expresses her great faith in Jesus. We see that she has been taught the doctrine of resurrection as she responds to the Master's assurance that Lazarus will be resurrected.

22 But I know, that even now, whatsoever thou wilt ask of God, God will give it thee. [*Martha has great faith, and hints that she believes that even now, Lazarus could be brought back to life.*]

23 Jesus saith unto her, Thy brother shall rise again.

24 Martha saith unto him, I know that he shall rise again in the resurrection at the last day.

Verse 25, next, is a very well-known verse in the Bible. You may wish to mark it in your own scriptures. In a significant way, it is a very brief summary of the Savior's purpose and mission. Through His Atonement, all will be resurrected and eternal life (exaltation) is made available to all, contingent on repenting and living the gospel.

"I Am the Resurrection and the Life"

25 Jesus said unto her, I am the resurrection, and the life [*in effect, I have power over death and can give eternal life*]: he that believeth in me, though he were dead, yet shall he live:

26 And whosoever liveth [*is spiritually alive*] and believeth in me shall never die [*spiritually*]. Believest thou this?

Martha's Testimony of Christ

27 She saith unto him, Yea, Lord: I believe that thou art the Christ, the Son of God, which should come into the world. [*I believe that You are the promised Messiah.*]

28 And when she had so said, she went her way, and called Mary her sister secretly, saying, The Master is come, and calleth for thee.

29 As soon as she heard that, she arose quickly, and came unto him [*Jesus*].

JST John 11:29
29 As soon as **Mary** heard that **Jesus was come**, she arose quickly, and came unto him.

30 Now Jesus was not yet [*had not yet*] come into the town, but was in that place where Martha met him.

31 The Jews then which were with her in the house, and comforted her, when they saw Mary, that she rose up hastily and went out, followed her, saying, She goeth unto the grave [*to Lazarus' tomb*] to weep there.

32 Then when Mary was come where Jesus was, and saw him, she fell down at his feet, saying unto him, Lord, if thou hadst been here, my brother had not [*would not have*] died.

33 When Jesus therefore saw her weeping, and the Jews also weeping which came with her, he groaned in the spirit, and was troubled [*This was a very emotional time for Jesus.*],

34 And said, Where have ye laid him [*where have you buried him*]? They said unto him, Lord, come and see.

35 Jesus wept.

Verse 35 is the shortest verse in the Bible. It is a reminder of the great kindness and compassion the Savior has for us.

36 Then said the Jews, Behold how he loved him!

37 And some of them said, Could not this man, which opened the eyes of the blind, have caused that even this man should not have died [*couldn't Jesus have prevented Lazarus from dying if He had been here*]?

Lazarus Is Raised from the Dead

38 Jesus therefore again groaning in himself cometh to the grave. It was a cave [*tomb*], and a stone lay upon it.

39 Jesus said, Take ye away the stone [*open the tomb*]. Martha, the sister of him that was dead, saith unto him, Lord, by this time he stinketh: for he hath been dead four days.

40 Jesus saith unto her, Said I not unto thee, that, if thou wouldest believe, thou shouldest see the glory of God [*you would see the power of God in action*]?

Imagine the hush and the looks on people's faces as they watch with rapt attention as the stone is rolled away!

41 Then they took away the stone from the place where the dead was laid. And Jesus lifted up his eyes, and said, Father, I thank thee that thou hast heard me.

As you have no doubt noticed, the Son humbly gives credit to the Father in all things, pointing our minds past Him and to the Father. Here we are seeing it again.

42 And I knew that thou hearest me always: but because of the people which stand by I said it [*I said it out loud for the benefit of the people who have gathered around*], that they may believe that thou hast sent me.

43 And when he thus had spoken, he cried with a loud voice, Lazarus, come forth.

44 And he that was dead came forth, bound hand and foot with graveclothes: and his face was bound about with a napkin. Jesus saith unto them, Loose him [*unwrap him*], and let him go.

45 Then many of the Jews which came to Mary, and had seen the things which Jesus did, believed on him.

JOHN 11

46 But some of them went their ways to the Pharisees, and told them what things Jesus had done.

The Pharisees are beside themselves with frustration and anger. All their attempts to stop Jesus have failed. And now He has raised a man from the dead, and many people saw it happen.

47 Then gathered the chief priests and the Pharisees a council [*the chief religious leaders of the Jews called an emergency meeting*], and said, What do we [*what can we do about Jesus*]? for this man doeth many miracles.

48 If we let him thus alone [*if we don't do something*], all men will believe on him: and the Romans shall come and take away both our place [*our positions of authority*] and nation. [*They are concerned about their own power and prestige. They are an example of the fact that wickedness does not promote rational thought.*]

49 And one of them, named Caiaphas [*the highest religious leader among the Jews at that time*], being the high priest that same year, said unto them, Ye know nothing at all [*You are a pack of idiots!*],

50 Nor consider that it is expedient for us, that one man should die for the people, and that the whole nation perish not. [*The solution is clear. It is better that Jesus die, than our whole nation be disrupted and destroyed by the Romans.*]

51 And this spake he not of himself: but being high priest that year, he prophesied that Jesus should die for that nation;

52 And not for that nation only, but that also he should gather together in one the children of God that were scattered abroad.

Verses 51–52, above, present a problem. The way it is written, it sounds like the wicked high priest, Caiaphas, is actually prophesying that it is necessary for Jesus to die in order to gather the righteous from all the world and save them, which is true. In verse 51, John says that Caiaphas spoke "not of himself," implying perhaps that, by virtue of his office, the Spirit came upon him and caused him to prophesy truth. Apostle James E. Talmage helps us understand this matter. He taught:

"The chief priests, who were mostly Sadducees, and the Pharisees with them assembled in council to consider the situation created by this latest of our Lord's great works. The question they discussed was: "What do we? for this man doeth many miracles. If we let him thus alone, all men will believe on him: and the Romans shall come and take away both our place and nation." As stated by themselves, there was no denying the fact of the many miracles wrought by Jesus; but instead of earnestly and prayerfully investigating as to whether these mighty works were not among the predicted characteristics of the Messiah, they thought only of the possible effect of Christ's influence in alienating the people from the established theocracy, and of the fear that the Romans, taking advantage of the situation, would deprive the hierarchs of their "place" and take from the nation what little semblance of distinct autonomy it still possessed. Caiaphas, the high priest, cut short the discussion by saying: "Ye know nothing at all." This sweeping assertion of ignorance was most likely addressed to the Pharisees of the Sanhedrin; Caiaphas was a Sadducee. His next utterance was of greater significance than he realized: "Nor consider that it is expedient for us, that one man should die for the people, and that the whole nation perish not." John solemnly avers that Caiaphas spake not of himself, but by the spirit of prophecy, which, in spite of his implied unworthiness, came upon him by virtue of his office, and that thus: "He prophesied that Jesus should die for that nation; and not for that nation only, but that also he should gather together in one the children of God that were scattered abroad." But a few years after Christ had been put to death, for the salvation of the Jews and of all other nations, the very calamities which Caiaphas and the Sanhedrin had hoped to avert befell in full measure; the hierarchy was overthrown, the temple destroyed, Jerusalem demolished and the nation disrupted. From the day of that memorable session of the Sanhedrin, the rulers increased their efforts to bring about the death of Jesus, by whatever means they might find available. They issued a mandate that whosoever knew of His whereabouts should give the information to the officials, that they might promptly take Him into custody (*Jesus the Christ*, 1982 edition, p. 498).

53 Then from that day forth they [*the council of the Pharisees, known as the Sanhedrin; see Bible Dictionary, under "Sanhedrin"*] took counsel together for to put him to death.

54 Jesus therefore walked no more openly among the Jews; but went thence [*from there*] unto a country near to the wilderness, into a city called Ephraim [*about 15 miles north of Jerusalem*], and there continued [*stayed*] with his disciples.

55 And the Jews' passover was nigh [*close*] at hand: and many went out of the country up to Jerusalem before the passover, to purify themselves [*to prepare themselves to properly observe Passover week*].

This is the final Passover for the Savior during His mortal life. He will spend the final week of His life teaching the people during the Passover week festivities and worship in Jerusalem. He will be crucified on Friday of that week. The religious rulers of the Jews will be watching for Jesus to see if He will come to Passover this year.

JOHN 12

56 Then sought they [*they watched*] for Jesus, and spake [*spoke*] among themselves, as they stood in the temple, What think ye, that he will not come to the feast? [*They were wondering whether or not Jesus would show up in Jerusalem, because of the danger to Him.*]

JST John 11:56

56 Then sought they for Jesus, and spake among themselves, as they stood in the temple, What think ye **of Jesus**? **Will he not** come to the feast?

57 Now both the chief priests and the Pharisees had given a commandment, that, if any man knew where he were [*if any one spotted Jesus*], he should shew it [*report it*], that they might take [*arrest*] him.

JOHN 12

This chapter begins the last week of the Savior's mortal life. It is Passover time in Jerusalem and Jews from many countries have joined the huge crowds in Jerusalem in preparation for the festivities and worship. The Passover meal itself will be held on Thursday. It is eaten in celebration of the passing of the destroying angel over the homes of the children of Israel in Egypt when the firstborn sons of all the families of the Egyptians were slain in order to persuade Pharaoh to let the Israelite slaves go free.

There is much symbolism associated with the Passover. The children of Israel were held in bondage (slavery) by the Egyptians, symbolizing the bondage of Satan and the accompanying abuse of agency. After repeated attempts by Moses to get Pharaoh to let the Israelite slaves go free, the children of Israel were instructed by Moses (Exodus 12:5) to select and sacrifice a male lamb (symbolizing Christ), without blemish (symbolizing that Christ was perfect), of the first year (symbolizing that Christ was in the prime of life when He accomplished the Atonement). They were to take hyssop (Exodus 12:22), a sponge-like plant (associated with Christ on the cross, see John 19:29), dip it in the blood of the lamb, and then put the blood on the lintel (top of the door frame) and on the door posts of the front door of their dwelling (Exodus 12:7 and 22). This blood of the lamb provided protection for their household.

The ensuing death of the firstborn of Pharaoh and all other Egyptian families caused the Israelite slaves to be set free. The death of the "firstborn" is symbolic of the death of the Savior, the "Firstborn" of the Father in the spirit world (Colossians 1:15). The Savior is referred to as "the Lamb of God." It is through the blood of the Lamb of God that we are set free from the bondage of sin. During the Passover, at the very time the Jews are celebrating being set free from Egyptian bondage by the blood of lambs, the Lamb (Christ) will present Himself to be sacrificed in order that all of us might be set free from physical death and from the bondage of sin.

John begins this chapter by informing us that Mary, Martha's sister, anointed the Savior's feet with very expensive ointment, and Judas Iscariot was irritated because he considered such use of expensive ointment to be a waste of money.

1 THEN Jesus six days before the passover [*this would probably be on Saturday, since Passover was on Thursday*] came to Bethany, where Lazarus was [*lived*] which had been dead, whom he raised from the dead.

2 There they made him a supper; and Martha served: but Lazarus was one of them that sat at the table with him.

3 Then took Mary [*the sister of Martha and Lazarus*] a pound of ointment of spikenard, very costly [*very expensive; see note in verse 5*], and anointed [*poured it on*] the feet of Jesus, and wiped his feet with her hair: and the house was filled with the odour of the ointment.

4 Then saith one of his disciples, Judas Iscariot, Simon's son, which should betray him [*the one who would betray Christ*],

5 Why was not this ointment sold for three hundred pence [*about 300 days' wages*], and given to the poor?

6 This he said, not that he cared for the poor; but because he was a thief, and had the bag [*the money purse*], and bare what was put therein. [*Judas Iscariot was apparently the treasurer of the Twelve.*]

7 Then said Jesus, Let her alone: against the day of my burying hath she kept this. [*She has anointed My body in preparation for My death and burial.*]

JST John 12:7

7 Then said Jesus, Let her alone; **for she hath preserved this ointment until now, that she might anoint me in token of my buria**l.

It would appear here that Mary is more sensitive and aware of what is going to happen to Jesus than most of the others are at this time.

8 For the poor always ye have with you; but me ye have not always.

9 Much [*many*] people of the Jews therefore knew that he was there: and they came not for Jesus' sake only, but that they might see Lazarus also, whom he had raised from the dead. [*People didn't come just to see Jesus, but they were also curious to see Lazarus who had been brought back to life after having been dead for four days.*]

Having Lazarus around, healthy and very much alive, after he had been dead for four days, did not help the cause of the Jewish religious leaders at all. Therefore, as you will see in verse 10, next, they make plans for him.

10 But the chief priests consulted [*plotted*] that they might put Lazarus also to death;

JOHN 12

11 Because that by reason of him many of the Jews went away, and believed on Jesus. [*They wanted to get rid of Lazarus due to the fact that many Jews were being converted to Jesus because of His raising Lazarus from the dead.*]

Next comes what is known as the "Triumphal Entry" of Jesus into Jerusalem. Excitement about Jesus was making its way through the large crowds in Jerusalem, and when word came that Jesus was even now approaching the city, large numbers of people lined the streets and threw pieces of clothing along the way in front of the Master. They took palm branches and laid them in the path also. Symbolically, in Jewish culture, palm branches represent triumph and victory over enemies. In effect, the people were excitedly welcoming Jesus as a king.

The Triumphal Entry

12 On the next day [*probably Sunday*] much people that were come to the feast [*of Passover*], when they heard that Jesus was coming to Jerusalem,

13 Took branches of palm trees, and went forth to meet him, and cried, Hosanna: Blessed is the King of Israel that cometh in the name of the Lord.

The Hosanna Shout

In conjunction with the dedication of our temples, we participate in what is known as the Hosanna

Shout. See *Mormon Doctrine*, p. 368. "Hosanna" means "Lord, save us now." See Bible Dictionary, under "Hosanna." Another translation of Hosanna is "O, please, Jehovah, save (us) now, please!"

During the dedication of the Kirtland Temple on March 27, 1836, Joseph Smith gave a dedicatory prayer. In the prayer (D&C 109), the Prophet pled with the Lord "that we may be clothed upon with robes of righteousness, with palms in our hands, and crowns of glory upon our heads, and reap eternal joy for all our sufferings" (D&C 109:76). The prayer was followed by the Saints standing and participating in the Hosanna Shout. Afterward, they sang "The Spirit of God," which includes the phrase, "Hosanna, Hosanna to God and the Lamb!" (See *Mormon Doctrine*, p. 368, for more about the Hosanna Shout.)

Today, worthy members are invited to bring clean, white handkerchiefs with them to temple dedications. These handkerchiefs are symbolic of palm branches, and represent victory and triumph over our enemies of sin and weakness through the Atonement of Christ.

14 And Jesus, when he had found a young ass [*a young, male donkey, which had never been ridden; see Luke 19:30*], sat thereon; as it is written [*prophesied—see Zechariah 9:9*],

JST John 12:14

14 And Jesus, when he had **sent two of his disciples and got a young ass**, sat thereon; as it is written,

15 Fear not, daughter of Sion: behold, thy King cometh, sitting on an ass's colt.

Next, in verse 16, John indicates that when this was actually happening, he and the other disciples did not realize that they were watching prophecy being fulfilled.

16 These things understood not his disciples at the first: but when Jesus was glorified [*had been resurrected*], then remembered they that these things were written of him, and that they had done these things unto him.

17 The people therefore that was with him when he called Lazarus out of his grave, and raised him from the dead, bare record. [*The people who were with Jesus when he raised Lazarus from the dead, spread the word among the Passover crowds that Jesus was coming into Jerusalem.*]

18 For this cause the people also met him [*this is why the crowds came to meet Him as He arrived*], for that they heard that he had done this miracle [*because they heard that He had raised a man from the dead*].

19 The Pharisees therefore said among themselves, Perceive ye how ye prevail nothing [*we can't seem to do anything about Jesus*]? behold, the world is gone after him [*everybody is starting to follow Him*].

20 And there were certain Greeks among them that came up to worship at the feast:

21 The same came therefore to Philip [*an Apostle; see John 1:44*], which was of Bethsaida of Galilee, and desired him, saying, Sir, we would see Jesus [*we would like to see Jesus*].

22 Philip cometh and telleth Andrew [*an Apostle*]: and again Andrew and Philip tell [*told*] Jesus.

23 And Jesus answered them, saying, The hour is come, that the Son of man [*Christ*] should be glorified [*the time has come for Jesus to finish His mortal mission*].

Next, the Master Teacher explains why He must die and be buried.

24 Verily, verily, I say unto you, Except a corn [*kernel*] of wheat fall into the ground and die, it abideth [*remains*] alone: but if it die, it bringeth forth much fruit [*if it dies and is buried, it grows and produces much wheat*].

25 He that loveth his life [*selfishly lives according only to worldly desires*] shall lose it; and he that hateth his life in this world [*prioritizes on spiritual, eternal values*] shall keep it unto life eternal.

26 If any man serve me, let him follow me; and where I am, there shall also my servant be [*if we follow Jesus, we will be with Him in heaven*]: if any man serve me, him will my Father honour [*with celestial glory and exaltation*].

Next, Jesus gets quite personal as He shares His thoughts with His close followers.

27 Now is my soul troubled [*this is getting very difficult; see D&C 19:18*]; and what shall I say? Father, save me from this hour [*in effect, should I ask My Father to save Me from what I am now going to have to go suffer*]: but for this cause [*the Atonement*] came I unto this hour [*to this point in My mortal life*].

The Father's Voice is Heard

28 Father, glorify thy name. Then came there a voice [*the Father's voice*] from heaven, saying, I have both glorified it, and will glorify it again.

29 The people therefore, that stood by, and heard it, said that it thundered: others said, An angel spake [*spoke*] to him.

30 Jesus answered and said, This voice came not because of me, but for your sakes. [*In other words, you were allowed to hear My Father's voice to strengthen you.*]

31 Now is the judgment of this world [*the Savior's accomplishing of the Atonement now will finish qualifying Him to judge the world*]: now shall the prince of this world [*Satan; see John 12:31, footnote a*] be cast out. [*In other words, the Savior's Atonement will pave the way for righteous people to overcome Satan and cast him out of their lives through repentance.*]

32 And I, if I be lifted up from the earth [*crucified; see verse 33*], will draw all men unto me. [*Through His Atonement, He will have power to bring all people to Himself, then on to the Father, if they will repent.*]

33 This he said, signifying what death he should die [*indicating that He would die by crucifixion*].

Next, some of the people challenge Him, quoting an Old Testament verse that says that Christ will remain forever. That they don't understand the context of that verse is clear. What they are saying, in effect, is that if He were the Christ, He would remain with them forever, and would not be killed and thus leave them. Therefore, He cannot be the prophesied Messiah.

34 The people answered him [*responded to what He had just said and then asked*], We have heard out of the law [*the Old Testament, 2 Samuel 7:16*] that Christ abideth [*will remain*] for ever: and how sayest thou [*so, why are You saying that*], The Son of man must be lifted up? who is this Son of man?

35 Then Jesus said unto them, Yet a little while is the light with you [*He will be with you for just a little bit longer*]. Walk while ye have the light [*take advantage of this time*], lest [*for fear that*] darkness come upon you: for he that walketh in darkness knoweth not whither he goeth.

36 While ye have light, believe in the light [*believe in Him*], that ye may be the children of light [*in order that you might become His righteous followers; compare with Mosiah 5:7*]. These things spake Jesus, and departed, and did hide himself from them.

37 But though he had done so many miracles before them, yet they [*the majority*] believed not on him:

38 That the saying of Esaias [*Isaiah*] the prophet might be fulfilled, which he spake [*Isaiah 53:1*], Lord, who hath believed our report [*who believes us prophets*]? and to whom hath the arm of the Lord been revealed [*who recognizes the hand of the Lord in things*]?

39 Therefore they could not [*did not*] believe, because that Esaias [*Isaiah*] said again [*in Isaiah 6:10*],

40 He hath blinded their eyes, and hardened their heart; that they should not see with their eyes, nor understand with their heart, and be converted, and I should heal them [*it is just as Isaiah was told by the Lord when he received his call to preach to hard-hearted Israel*].

Referring to verse 40 above, it is important to understand that God does not make people spiritually blind nor harden their hearts. They are given agency and can become that way by ignoring the gospel.

41 These things said Esaias [*Isaiah*], when he saw his [*Christ's*] glory [*Isaiah 6:1–5*], and spake of him [*spoke of Christ*].

42 Nevertheless among the chief rulers also many believed on him; but because of the Pharisees they did not confess him, lest they should be put out of the synagogue: [*By now, many of the chief religious rulers of the Jews had come to believe that Jesus was the Messiah, but they would not admit it for fear of being excommunicated.*]

43 For they loved the praise of men more than the praise of God.

44 Jesus cried [*spoke loudly*] and said, He that believeth on me, believeth not on me, but on him that sent me. [*If you believe in Jesus, you believe in the Father.*]

45 And he that seeth me seeth him that sent me [*if you see Jesus, it is as if you were seeing the Father*].

While the message above is clear, namely, that if you believe in the Savior and follow Him, you are, in effect, believing in the Father and following Him, there is a literal aspect also to verse 45. We are told by the Apostle Paul, in Hebrews 1:3, that Jesus is "the express image" of the Father. In other words, the Savior and His Father are exact look-a-likes. See *Doctrinal New Testament Commentary*, Vol. 3, p. 138.

46 I am come a light into the world, that whosoever believeth on me should not abide in darkness [*will not live in spiritual darkness*].

47 And if any man hear my words, and believe not, I judge him not [*it is not yet time for final judgment; such*

people may still rethink and repent]: for I came not to judge the world [*at this time*], but to save the world.

Jesus will be our final Judge. See John 5:22.

48 He that rejecteth me, and receiveth not [*does not accept*] my words, hath one that judgeth him: the word that I have spoken, the same shall judge him in the last day. [*People are made accountable when they hear and understand the gospel. Therefore, the words of the Savior will be a witness against them on final Judgment Day, if they have not responded and come unto Christ.*]

49 For I have not spoken of myself [*on My own*]; but the Father which sent me, he gave me a commandment, what I should say, and what I should speak.

50 And I know that his commandment is life everlasting [*leads to eternal life*]: whatsoever I speak therefore, even as the Father said unto me, so I speak.

JOHN 13

John now tells us what happened after the Passover meal had been eaten by the Savior and His Apostles. It is later Thursday evening, and, as soon as Judas Iscariot leaves (verse 30), Jesus will expound many of the doctrines of the gospel to the remaining eleven Apostles, comprising the rest of chapter 13 through chapter 17. This will be a culminating time of learning for them and for us, as the Lord's mortal ministry draws to a close.

First, before Judas leaves, the Redeemer, the great Jehovah, the Creator and Savior of worlds without number (D&C 76:24), will humbly wash the Apostles' feet. Notice Peter's response at first, and then see how quickly he changes his mind as he is taught a true principle. He is a wonderful example to all of us of immediate change upon learning a gospel truth.

1 NOW before the feast of the passover, when Jesus knew that his hour was come that he should depart out of this world unto the Father, having loved his own which were in the world, he loved them unto the end.

2 And supper being ended [*they had finished eating the Passover meal*], the devil having now put into the heart of Judas Iscariot, Simon's son, to betray him;

3 Jesus knowing that the Father had given all things into his hands, and that he was come from God, and went to God [*and would return to God*];

Jesus Washes the Apostles' Feet

4 He riseth [*arose*] from supper, and laid aside his garments; and took a towel, and girded himself.

5 After that he poureth water into a bason [*basin*], and began to wash the disciples' feet, and to wipe them with the towel wherewith he was girded.

This must have been an especially tender time, when the

Master of all demonstrated that He was the servant of all. The washing of the dusty, tired feet of guests was a gesture of hospitality and service in the culture of the Jews. Among other things, the Savior was demonstrating by His actions that He was a humble servant to His Apostles.

6 Then cometh he to Simon Peter: and Peter saith unto him, Lord, dost thou wash my feet [*are You going to wash my feet too*]?

7 Jesus answered and said unto him, What I do thou knowest not now [*you don't understand now*]; but thou shalt know hereafter [*but later you will understand*].

8 Peter saith unto him, Thou shalt never wash my feet. [*Peter apparently felt that it was not necessary for Jesus to wash his feet—see JST below.*] Jesus answered him, If I wash thee not, thou hast no part with me. [*Symbolically, if he is not cleansed by the Savior, he will not be with Him in eternity.*]

JST John 13:8

8 Peter saith unto him, **Thou needest not to wash my feet**. Jesus answered him, If I wash thee not, thou hast no part with me.

9 Simon Peter saith unto him, Lord, not my feet only, but also my hands and my head. [*In that case, please wash me completely.*]

10 Jesus saith to him [*Peter*], He that is washed [*is clean spiritually*] needeth not [*needs no more*] save [*except*] to wash his feet, but

is clean every whit [*every bit. In other words, Peter, you are spiritually clean, and all I need to do is wash your tired dusty feet here this evening as a token of My being your servant; more is not necessary*]: and ye are clean, but not all [*you Apostles are "clean," except for Judas Iscariot—see verse 11*].

JST John 13:10

10 Jesus saith to him, He that **has washed his hands and his head**, needeth not save to wash his feet, but is clean every whit; and ye are clean, but not all. **Now this was the custom of the Jews under their law; wherefore, Jesus did this that the law might be fulfilled**.

11 For he knew who should [*would*] betray him; therefore said he, Ye are not all clean.

12 So after he had washed their feet, and had taken his garments, and was set down again, he said unto them, Know ye what I have done to you?

13 Ye call me Master and Lord: and ye say well; for so I am. [*They are correct in calling Him Master and Lord, because He is.*]

Serve One Another

14 If I then, your Lord and Master, have washed your feet; ye also ought to wash one another's feet. [*You ought to serve one another.*]

15 For I have given you an example, that ye should do as I have done to you.

JOHN 13

16 Verily, verily, I say unto you, The servant is not greater than his lord [*no servant is greater than his master*]; neither he that is sent greater than he that sent him [*the messenger is not greater than the one who sent him*].

17 If ye know these things, happy are ye if ye do them.

18 I speak not of you all: I know whom I have chosen: but that the scripture [*Psalm 41:9*] may be fulfilled, He [*Judas Iscariot*] that eateth bread with me hath lifted up his heel against me [*has become my enemy*].

19 Now I tell you before it come [*Jesus is prophesying this before it happens*], that [*so that*], when it is come to pass [*has happened*], ye may believe that I am he.

JST John 13:19
19 Now I tell you before it come, that, when it is come to pass, ye may believe that I am **the Christ**.

20 Verily, verily, I say unto you, He that receiveth whomsoever I send [*His servants, missionaries, Apostles, etc.*] receiveth me; and he that receiveth me receiveth him that sent me [*the Father*].

One of Them Will Betray Him

21 When Jesus had thus said, he was troubled in spirit [*was sad*], and testified, and said, Verily, verily, I say unto you, that one of you shall betray me.

22 Then the disciples looked one on another [*at one another*], doubting of whom he spake [*trying to figure out which one of them He meant*].

23 Now there was leaning on Jesus' bosom [*laying his head on Jesus' chest*] one of his disciples, whom Jesus loved [*John*].

From verse 23, above, you can see an interesting aspect of John's writings. He is so humble that he never directly gives his name, rather always refers to himself indirectly.

24 Simon Peter therefore beckoned to him [*motioned to John*], that he should ask who it should be of whom he spake. [*Peter signaled to John, who was leaning his head on the Savior at the moment, to quietly ask Him who it was that would betray Him.*]

25 He then lying on Jesus' breast [*had his head on Jesus' chest or on the front of his shoulder*] saith unto him, Lord, who is it [*which one of us is it*]?

26 Jesus answered, He it is, to whom I shall give a sop [*a small chunk of bread, used to dip into gravy, juice, or whatever*], when I have dipped it. And when he had dipped the sop, he gave it to Judas Iscariot, the son of Simon.

Jesus must have whispered the answer to John, because none of the others at the table seemed to have heard his answer—see verse 28, below.

27 And after the sop [*after Judas had taken the sop*] Satan entered

into him [*Satan's influence came upon him strongly*]. Then said Jesus unto him, That thou doest, do quickly [*what you have in mind to do, do quickly*].

28 Now no man at the table [*none of the others*] knew for what intent he spake this unto him.

29 For some of them thought, because Judas had the bag [*the money purse; apparently Judas handled the finances for the Twelve*], that Jesus had said unto him, Buy those things that we have need of against [*for*] the feast; or, that he should give something to the poor.

Judas Leaves to Betray Jesus

30 He [*Judas*] then having received the sop [*accepted the sop from Jesus*] went immediately out: and it was night.

As stated in the introductory notes to this chapter in this study guide, the Lord will now proceed to teach these brethren many important doctrines. It is, in effect, their final major classroom instruction in their three-year "MTC" training before they go on their missions after the Savior departs.

31 Therefore, when he was gone out [*when Judas had left*], Jesus said, Now is the Son of man [*the Son of God; Son of Man of Holiness; see Moses 6:57*] glorified, and God is glorified in him. [*The time has arrived for His Atonement, in which He will be glorified, and in which He will bring glory to His Father.*]

32 If God be glorified in him, God shall also glorify him in himself, and shall straightway [*right away*] glorify him.

33 Little children [*in effect, My dear Apostles, who still have much to learn*], yet a little while I am with you. Ye shall seek me: and as I said unto the Jews, Whither [*where*] I go, ye cannot come [*they cannot come to heaven with Him now*]; so now I say to you.

Love One Another

34 A new commandment I give unto you [*He renews a very old commandment*], That ye love one another; as I have loved you, that ye also love one another.

35 By this shall all men know that ye are my disciples, if ye have love one to another.

Did you catch how important it is to show love one to another, as taught in verse 35, above? The simple fact is that if we don't, we are not followers of Christ.

36 Simon Peter said unto him, Lord, whither goest thou? Jesus answered him, Whither I go [*where I am going*], thou canst not follow me now [*in other words, Peter can't follow Jesus to heaven now*]; but thou shalt follow me afterwards [*after he has finished his mission, he can come to heaven*].

We see Peter's basic boldness and courage in verse 37, next.

37 Peter said unto him, Lord, why cannot I follow thee now? I will lay down my life for thy sake. [*Peter apparently thinks Jesus is telling him that He, Jesus, must go it alone in Jerusalem, and Peter wants to stay close to Him and defend Him with his life if necessary.*]

Before the Cock Crows

38 Jesus answered him, Wilt thou lay down thy life for my sake? Verily, verily, I say unto thee, The cock [*rooster*] shall not crow, till thou hast denied me thrice [*three times*].

Denying knowing the Savior is not the same as denying the Holy Ghost. Denying the Holy Ghost, as described in D&C 76:31–35, is an unforgivable sin. Peter's denying that he knows the Savior and has been one of His followers for three years is not unforgivable, though so doing brought Peter deep anguish and tears.

JOHN 14

You may find many of the Savior's teachings in this chapter quite familiar. Many of these verses are quoted often in talks and lessons in the Church. As mentioned earlier, the Master is teaching His remaining eleven Apostles many things now, before He goes to Gethsemane and then is betrayed and arrested.

1 LET not your heart be troubled [*don't worry*]: ye believe in God

[*the Father*], believe [*have faith*] also in me.

2 In my Father's house are many mansions: if it were not so, I would have told you. I go to prepare a place for you.

Joseph Smith explained the meaning of verse 2 above, wherein it says "In my Father's house are many mansions." He said it should be, "In my Father's kingdom are many kingdoms." Also, "There are mansions for those who obey a celestial law, and there are other mansions for those who come short" (Teachings of the Prophet Joseph Smith, p. 366). We know from D&C 76 that there are three degrees of glory, each of which has some degree of reward and glory. Even the telestial kingdom is so glorious that it "surpasses all understanding" (D&C 76:89). We know from D&C 131:1 that even the celestial kingdom has three "mansions" or degrees. Thus, the Father's "house," or kingdom, does indeed have "many mansions" or categories. Obviously, Jesus will prepare a place for His faithful Apostles, whom He will leave shortly, in the highest mansion (exaltation) of His Father (see verse 3 below).

3 And if I go and prepare a place for you, I will come again, and receive you unto myself; that where I am, there ye may be also.

<u>JST John 14:3</u>
3 And **when** I go, **I will** prepare a place for you, **and** come again and receive you unto myself; that where I am, ye may be also.

4 And whither I go ye know, and the way ye know. [*They have been taught where He is going, and how to get there themselves.*]

These wonderful Apostles are still undergoing intensive training by the Savior. To those of us who are familiar with the concepts in these verses because we have been taught them most of our lives or since we joined the church, there may be a temptation to wonder why it is taking so much time and repetition for these brethren to catch on. We must remember that they grew up in an environment of apostate Judaism very foreign to these simple truths.

5 Thomas [*one of the Apostles*] saith unto him, Lord, we know not whither thou goest; and how can we know the way? [*We don't know where You are going, so how can we know the way to get there?*]

6 Jesus saith unto him, I am the way, the truth, and the life [*Christ has everything we need*]: no man cometh unto the Father, but by me [*except through Him*].

7 If ye had known me [*in effect, if you had truly known Me and understood Me and what I have been teaching you*], ye should have [*would have*] known my Father also: and from henceforth [*from now on*] ye know him, and have seen him [*because you have seen Me*].

8 Philip [*one of the Apostles*] saith unto him, Lord, shew us the Father, and it sufficeth us [*and that will be sufficient for us*].

9 Jesus saith unto him, Have I been so long time with you, and yet hast thou not known me [*and you still don't understand*], Philip? he that hath seen me hath seen the Father; and how sayest thou then [*so why do you say*], Shew [*show*] us the Father?

10 Believest thou not that I am in the Father, and the Father in me? the words that I speak unto you I speak not of myself: but the Father that dwelleth in me, he doeth the works. [*In effect, Don't you understand that the Father and I are a team and we work together in perfect unity? Everything I do is, in effect, what the Father is doing for you.*]

11 Believe me that I am in the Father, and the Father in me: or else believe me for the very works' sake. [*In effect, if you can't believe that I and my Father are perfectly unified in the work we do, at least believe Me because of the works you have seen and heard Me do, which could come from no one but the Father.*]

12 Verily, verily, I say unto you, He that believeth on me, the works that I do shall he do also; and greater [*additional*] works than these shall he do; because I go unto my Father.

The word "greater" in verse 12 above can have at least two meanings. In addition to meaning more significant or more spectacular or more powerful, higher, etc., it can also mean additional or on-going, continued, etc. It is used this way in D&C 7:5 where the Savior tells Peter that John the Beloved

JOHN 14

447

will stay on the earth until the Second Coming, and thus "do more, or a greater work" than he has done up to now.

For more on this, see Strong's *Exhaustive Concordance of the Bible*, word #3187, where "greater" is also defined as "more."

There is also another aspect of the word "greater" as used by the Master in this promise to His Apostles. When they are exalted, and have become gods, they will indeed do greater works, in the common sense of the word. They will have spirit offspring, will create worlds, and as gods, will do even greater, more magnificent and higher things than they ever saw Christ do while He was among them. See Joseph Smith's teachings on this in Lectures on Faith, pp. 64–66.

13 And whatsoever ye shall ask in my name, that will I do, that the Father may be glorified in the Son.

14 If ye shall ask any thing in my name, I will do it.

Verses 15–26, below, will speak of two different "Comforters." One of these Comforters is the Holy Ghost. The other is the Savior Himself and includes the Father on occasions.

Verses 16, 17, and 26 speak of the Holy Ghost.

Verses 18, 21, 23, and 28 speak of the Savior.

For more on this, see *Teachings of the Prophet Joseph Smith*, pp. 149 to 151.

15 If ye love me, keep my commandments.

16 And I will pray the Father, and he shall give you another Comforter [*the Holy Ghost—see* Doctrinal New Testament Commentary, *Vol. 1, p. 737*], that he may abide [*be*] with you for ever;

17 Even the Spirit of truth; whom the world cannot receive [*the world, meaning those who are not members of the Church, cannot receive the Gift of the Holy Ghost*], because it seeth him not, neither knoweth him: but ye know him; for he dwelleth with you, and shall be in you.

18 I will not leave you comfortless: I [*Jesus*] will come to you. [*This is spoken of as the "Second Comforter." See* Doctrinal New Testament Commentary, *Vol. 1, p. 738.*]

19 Yet a little while, and the world seeth me no more [*in effect, I will be crucified and gone, as far as most people are concerned*]; but ye see me [*you will see Me after I am resurrected*]: because I live [*resurrect*], ye shall live also. [*Because of the Atonement, they will resurrect also and have eternal life.*]

20 At that day ye shall know that I am in my Father, and ye in me, and I in you. [*Jesus is still responding to Thomas's question in verse 5 and to Philip's request in verse 8.*]

21 He that hath my commandments, and keepeth them, he it is that loveth me: and he that loveth me shall be loved of my Father, and I will love him, and will manifest myself to him [as the "Second Comforter"].

22 Judas [one of the faithful Apostles] saith unto him, not Iscariot [not Judas Iscariot who has already left to betray Jesus], Lord, how is it that thou wilt manifest thyself unto us, and not unto the world?

JST John 14:22
22 Judas saith unto him, (not Iscariot,) Lord, how is it thou wilt manifest thyself unto us, and not unto the world?

23 Jesus answered and said unto him, If a man love me, he will keep my words: and my Father will love him, and we will come unto him [the "Second Comforter," and make our abode with him].

24 He that loveth me not keepeth not my sayings [does not keep My commandments]: and the word [gospel] which ye hear is not mine [did not originate with Me], but the Father's which sent me [originated with the Father who sent me].

25 These things have I spoken unto you, being yet present with you [while He is still with them].

What the Holy Ghost Does for Us

26 But the Comforter, which is the Holy Ghost, whom the Father will send in my name, he shall teach you all things, and bring all things to your remembrance, whatsoever I have said unto you. [This is a description of some of the things the Gift of the Holy Ghost can do for us.]

27 Peace I leave with you, my peace I give unto you: not as the world giveth, give I unto you. Let not your heart be troubled, neither let it be afraid.

28 Ye have heard how I said unto you, I go away, and come again unto you. [The Apostles had the "Second Comforter" for forty days, after Christ's resurrection, see Acts 1:3, as the Savior ministered personally to them and taught them.] If ye loved me, ye would rejoice, because I said, I go unto the Father: for my Father is greater than I.

29 And now I have told you before it come to pass [I have told you ahead of time that I will be arrested, tried, crucified, and resurrected], that [so that], when it is come to pass [after it has all happened], ye might believe.

30 Hereafter I will not talk much with you [we can't keep talking much longer]: for [because] the prince of this world [Satan] cometh, and hath nothing in me. [In effect, the Savior is saying, "We can't talk much longer because Satan is bringing Judas Iscariot and the high priests with their soldiers to arrest Me. Satan has no power over Me, but you are still vulnerable to his temptations."]

JST John 14:30

30 Hereafter I will not talk much with you; for the prince of **darkness, who is of this world**, cometh, **but hath no power over me, but he hath power over you**.

31 But that the world may know that I love the Father; and as the Father gave me commandment, even so I do [*Jesus is completely obedient to the Father*]. Arise, let us go hence [*let us go to the Garden of Gethsemane*].

JST John 14:31

31 **And I tell you these things, that ye may know** that I love the Father; and as the Father gave me commandment, even so I do. Arise, let us go hence.

Mark 14:26 tells us that they sang a hymn at this point. Luke 22:39 tells us that Jesus then led his eleven remaining Apostles to the Mount of Olives. Matthew 26:36 informs us that they went to Gethsemane, a garden with olive trees, near the foot of the Mount of Olives. The time is getting short, because, as Jesus knows, Judas Iscariot and the high priests and their soldiers will be coming shortly.

JOHN 15

The Savior continues teaching His Apostles in this, His last major discourse of His mortal mission. The time of His betrayal through Judas is now even closer. As chapter 15 begins, we see an allegory in which the Lord illustrates the absolutely essential relationship between His Apostles and Himself and between Himself and His Father. In this, we are also taught that without the Savior, we would be like green branches cut off from the tree which provides nourishment to us. Without it, we would dry up and shrivel away. Apostle James E. Talmage discussed this allegory. He taught:

"In superb allegory the Lord thus proceeded to illustrate the vital relationship between the apostles and Himself, and between Himself and the Father, by the figure of a vinegrower, a vine, and its branches: 'I am the true vine, and my Father is the husbandman. Every branch in me that beareth not fruit he taketh away: and every branch that beareth fruit, he purgeth it, that it may bring forth more fruit.' A grander analogy is not to be found in the world's literature. Those ordained servants of the Lord were as helpless and useless without Him as is a bough severed from the tree. As the branch is made fruitful only by virtue of the nourishing sap it receives from the rooted trunk, and if cut away or broken off withers, dries, and becomes utterly worthless except as fuel for the burning, so those men, though ordained to the Holy Apostleship, would find themselves strong and fruitful in good works, only as they remained in steadfast communion with the Lord. Without Christ what were they, but unschooled Galileans, some of them fishermen, one a publican, the rest of undistinguished attainments, and all of them weak mortals? As branches of the Vine they were at that hour clean and healthful, through the instructions and authoritative ordinances with which they had been blessed, and by the reverent obedience they had manifested.

" 'Abide in me,' was the Lord's forceful admonition, else they would become but withered boughs. 'I am the vine,' He added in explication of the allegory; 'ye are the branches: He that abideth in me, and I in him, the same bringeth forth much fruit: for without me ye can do nothing. If a man abide not in me, he is cast forth as a branch, and is withered; and men gather them, and cast them into the fire, and they are burned. If ye abide in me, and my words abide in you, ye shall ask what ye will, and it shall be done unto you. Herein is my Father glorified, that ye bear much fruit: so shall ye be my disciples.' Their love for one another was again specified as an essential to their continued love for Christ. In that love would they find joy. Christ had been to them an exemplar of righteous love from the day of their first meeting; and He was about to give the supreme proof of His affection, as foreshadowed in His words, 'Greater love hath no man than this, that a man lay down his life for his friends.' And that those men were the Lord's friends was thus graciously affirmed; 'Ye are

my friends, if ye do whatsoever I command you. Henceforth I call you not servants; for the servant knoweth not what his lord doeth: but I have called you friends; for all things that I have heard of my Father I have made known unto you.' This intimate relationship in no sense modified the position of Christ as their Lord and Master, for by Him they had been chosen and ordained; and it was His will that they should so live that whatever they asked in the name of the holy friendship which He acknowledged should be granted them of the Father." (*Jesus the Christ*, 1982, pp. 604–605)

We will now proceed with our study of this chapter, adding notes giving some possible symbolism for the elements of the allegory. There are no JST changes for chapter 15.

Jesus Is the True Vine

1 I AM the true vine [*grape vine; symbolic of the fact that the true gospel comes from Christ*], and my Father is the husbandman [*farmer, owner; symbolic of the fact that the Father owns the earth*].

2 Every branch [*branch growing from the vine; symbolic of people*] in me that beareth not fruit [*people who live wickedly*] he taketh away [*the wicked will be destroyed*]: and every branch [*every person*] that beareth fruit [*who lives righteously*], he purgeth it [*prunes it, cuts out inappropriate behaviors and sin, nourishes it, shapes it, and so forth*], that it may bring forth

JOHN 15

more fruit [*symbolic of continuing progress in the lives of the Saints*].

3 Now ye are clean [*you have become clean*] through the word [*through the gospel with the Atonement*] which I have spoken [*taught*] unto you.

4 Abide in me, and I in you [*stay connected with the True Vine and He will continue to nourish you*]. As the branch cannot bear fruit of itself, except it abide in [*stay attached to*] the vine; no more can ye, except ye abide in me. [*Just as a branch of a vine cannot live without remaining attached to the vine, so we cannot live righteous lives unless we stay connected to Him.*]

The beautiful symbolism in verse 4 above is vitally important for us. How do we attach ourselves to the "vine" so that we can remain securely fastened to Christ? Answer: "Ye shall bind yourselves to act in all holiness before me—" (D&C 43:9). How do we "bind" ourselves to the true vine (Christ, verse 1, above)? Answer: We make and keep covenants. Thus, by making covenants, we bind ourselves securely to the True Vine, receive constant nourishment from His roots, and are privileged to be pruned, shaped, and strengthened by the Husbandman so that we can return to live with Him forever.

Jesus continues this explanation in the next verses.

5 I am the vine, ye are the branches: He that abideth in me, and I in him,

the same bringeth forth much fruit [*produces much good*]: for without me ye can do nothing.

6 If a man abide not in me, he is cast forth as a branch [*is cut off and thrown away*], and is withered [*and dries up*]; and men gather them, and cast them into the fire, and they are burned [*symbolic of the destruction of the wicked*].

7 If ye abide in me [*if we stay faithful to Him*], and my words abide in you [*and we are faithful to His gospel*], ye shall ask what ye will [*want*], and it shall be done unto you.

8 Herein is my Father glorified [*this is how His Father is glorified*], that ye bear much fruit; so shall ye be my disciples. [*This reminds us of Moses 1:39 which says: "For behold, this is my work and my glory—to bring to pass the immortality and eternal life of man."*]

9 As the Father hath loved me, so have I loved you: continue ye in my love [*remain faithful to Him*].

10 If ye keep my commandments, ye shall abide in my love; even as I have kept my Father's commandments, and abide in his love.

11 These things have I spoken unto you, that my joy might remain in you, and that your joy might be full.

Love One Another

12 This is my commandment, That ye love one another, as I have loved you.

13 Greater love hath no man than this, that a man lay down his life for his friends. [*This is exactly what Jesus will do in a few hours.*]

14 Ye are my friends, if ye do whatsoever I command you.

As you read verse 15, next, notice what is happening in terms of the relationship between Christ and His eleven Apostles. In a very real way, this is a "graduation."

15 Henceforth [*from now on*] I call you not servants; for the servant knoweth not what his lord doeth: but I have called you friends; for all things that I have heard of my Father I have made known unto you [*in effect, I have taught you everything*].

This is a significant change in status, from servants to friends. The Savior said the same thing to early members of the Church in our day in D&C 84:77.

16 Ye have not chosen me, but I have chosen you, and ordained you, that ye should go and bring forth fruit [*bring converts into the Church, help members to come unto Christ*], and that your fruit should remain: that whatsoever ye shall ask of the Father in my name, he may give it you.

"Ye have not chosen me, but I have chosen you, and ordained you" in verse 16 above is a most important matter for people to understand. We do not set up our own church and then choose the Savior to be our leader. It is

the other way around. He is the leader, and invites us to join Him for our salvation. Unfortunately, all other churches have been built up by people. The authority of the priesthood flows from Christ to us, not from us to Christ.

Love One Another

17 These things I command you, that ye love one another.

Next, the Master explains why so many people hate righteous people.

18 If the world hate you, ye know that it hated me before it hated you. [*If they were not doing what is right, the world would not hate them.*]

19 If ye were of the world [*if you were worldly and wicked*], the world would love his own [*the world would love you because you would be just like they are*]: but because ye are not of the world, but I have chosen you out of the world, therefore [*that is why*] the world hateth you.

20 Remember the word that I said unto you [*remember when I taught you*], The servant is not greater than his lord [*Matthew 10:24*]. If they have persecuted me, they will also persecute you; if they have kept my saying [*obeyed My teachings*], they will keep yours also.

21 But all these things will they do unto you for my name's sake, because they know not him [*the Father*] that sent me.

JOHN 16

453

22 If I had not come and spoken unto them, they had not had sin [*they would not have been account-able*]: but now they have no cloke [*cover or excuse*] for their sin.

23 He that hateth me hateth my Father also.

24 If I had not done among them the works which none other man did, they had not had sin [*they would not have become account-able*]: but now have they both seen and hated both me and my Father.

25 But this cometh to pass, that the word might be fulfilled that is written in their law [*this is a fulfillment of the prophecy in Psalm 35:19*], They hated me without a cause.

More About the Function of the Holy Ghost

26 But when the Comforter [*the Holy Ghost*] is come, whom I will send unto you from the Father, even the Spirit of truth, which proceedeth from the Father, he shall testify of me:

As you saw in verse 26, above, another function of the Holy Ghost is to testify to us of Christ. John 14:26 and 16:13 explain additional functions. You may wish to cross-reference them to verse 26, here.

Because of the wording in verse 26, some students of the gospel wonder if the Holy Ghost was functioning on earth while the Savior was here in mortality. The Holy Ghost was function-

ing on earth during the Savior's ministry as exemplified by the Holy Ghost descending like a dove at the Savior's baptism. See Matthew 3:16. See also Luke 4:1 which informs us that the Holy Ghost was upon the Savior. Apparently, though, the full power of the Gift of the Holy Ghost was not present until after Jesus was taken up. (See Bible Dictionary, under "Holy Ghost.")

27 And ye also shall bear witness, because ye have been with me from the beginning.

JOHN 16

As Jesus continues His discourse before they arrive at the Garden of Gethsemane, He cautions the Eleven to avoid falling away because of the coming persecution upon them, and teaches more about the mission of the Holy Ghost, which will be a major source of strength for them.

1 THESE things have I spoken unto you, that ye should not be offended [*fall away; stumble, crumble under the coming pressure and persecution*].

The word "offended", as used in verse 1 above, means to stumble, to crumble under pressure, to fall away, to apostatize. It is used the same way as in Matthew 11:6, where the Savior says "And blessed is he, whosoever shall not be offended in me." Footnote a, for Matthew 11:6, sends the reader to Isaiah 8:14

and Matthew 24:10 where the above definitions are verified.

2 They shall put you out of the synagogues [*Jewish church buildings and centers of learning*]: yea, the time cometh, that whosoever killeth you will think that he doeth God service.

3 And these things will they do unto you, because they have not known the Father, nor me.

4 But these things [*these warnings of coming persecutions*] have I told you, that when the time shall come, ye may remember that I told you of them. And these things I said not unto you at the beginning [*of His mission*], because I was with you.

5 But now I go my way to him that sent me [*to the Father*]; and none of you asketh me, Whither goest thou?

6 But because I have said these things unto you, sorrow hath filled your heart.

7 Nevertheless I tell you the truth; It is expedient [*necessary*] for you that I go away: for if I go not away, the Comforter [*the Holy Ghost*] will not come unto you; but if I depart, I will send him unto you. [*See note following John 7:39 about whether or not the Holy Ghost functioned on earth during Christ's mortal ministry.*]

8 And when he is come, he will reprove [*convict*] the world of [*with respect to*] sin, and of [*with respect to*] righteousness, and of [*with respect to*] judgment: [*in effect, after the full Gift and power of the Holy Ghost has come upon you, it will inspire and direct you and bear witness through you such that your teachings and deeds will stand as a witness against the wicked of the world for rejecting righteousness and refusing to believe that the day of judgment will come.*]

9 Of sin, because they believe not on me; [*They will be accountable, convicted, of their sins because the Holy Ghost will bear witness to them as you preach.*]

10 Of [*with respect to*] righteousness [*your teaching of Me and My gospel*], because I go to my Father, and ye see me no more; [*They will be held accountable for your testimonies and teachings, because I am no longer here to teach them.*]

JST John 16:10
10 Of righteousness, because I go to my Father, and **they** see me no more;

11 Of [*with respect to*] judgment, because the prince of this world [*Satan, see John 12:31, footnote a*] is judged. [*They will reject the witness of the Holy Ghost which will accompany your testimonies and will thus be judged for their sins, like Satan, whom they choose to follow, is judged for his sins.*]

Apostle Bruce R. McConkie suggested some possibilities for interpreting verses 9–11, above. He said:

JOHN 16

"These are difficult verses which have come to us in such a condensed and abridged form as to make interpretation difficult. The seeming meaning is: 'When you receive the companionship of the Spirit, so that you speak forth what he reveals to you, then your teachings will convict the world of sin, and of righteousness, and of judgment. The world will be convicted of sin for rejecting me, for not believing your Spirit-inspired testimony that I am the Son of God through whom salvation comes. They will be convicted for rejecting your testimony of my righteousness—for supposing I am a blasphemer, a deceiver, and an imposter—when in fact I have gone to my Father, a thing I could not do unless my works were true and righteous altogether. They will be convicted of false judgment for rejecting your testimony against the religions of the day, and for choosing instead to follow Satan, the prince of this world, who himself, with all his religious philosophies, will be judged and found wanting'" (*Doctrinal New Testament Commentary*, Vol. 1, p. 754).

12 I have yet many things to say unto you, but ye cannot bear them now [*you are not ready for them now*].

More About the Function of the Holy Ghost

13 Howbeit [*however*] when he [*the Holy Ghost*], the Spirit of truth, is come [*when the gift of the Holy Ghost has come upon you in full power*], he will guide you into all truth: for he shall not speak of himself; but whatsoever he shall hear [*from Heavenly Father and Jesus*], that shall he speak: and he will shew [*show*] you things to come.

14 He shall glorify me [*bear witness of Christ*]: for he shall receive of mine [*He gets His instructions from Me and My Father, see verse 15*], and shall shew it unto you.

15 All things that the Father hath are mine: therefore said I [*that is why I said*], that he shall take of mine, and shall shew it unto you.

16 A little while, and ye shall not see me: and again, a little while, and ye shall see me, because I go to the Father.

Verse 16, above, is a short verse but is saying a lot. Among other things, it says that in just a short while He will be crucified and will thus be separated from them while He goes as a spirit to the spirit world and visits the spirits in paradise (1 Peter 3:18-21; D&C 138:18-30). Then, when He is resurrected, He will come and they will see Him again. Verse 17, next, informs us however, that the Eleven did not understand what He meant.

17 Then said some of his disciples among themselves, What is this that he saith unto us, A little while, and ye shall not see me: and again, a little while, and ye shall see me: and, Because I go to the Father?

18 They said therefore [*they continued to wonder, among themselves*], What is this that he saith, A little while? we cannot tell [*understand*] what he saith.

Next, John lets us feel the kindness of the Master, as He, knowing that His Apostles were reluctant to ask, explains what He meant to them.

19 Now Jesus knew that they were desirous to ask him, and said unto them, Do ye enquire among yourselves of that I said [*about what I just said*], A little while, and ye shall not see me: and again, a little while, and ye shall see me?

20 Verily, verily, I say unto you, That ye shall weep and lament [*when the Savior is crucified*], but the world shall rejoice: and ye shall be sorrowful, but your sorrow shall be turned into joy [*when He is resurrected and they see Him again*].

21 A woman when she is in travail [*is in labor*] hath sorrow, because her hour is come [*because the time for her baby to be born has arrived*]: but as soon as she is delivered of the child [*as soon as her baby is born*], she remembereth no more the anguish, for [*because of*] joy that a man is born into the world.

22 And ye now therefore have sorrow [*you will indeed have sorrow because of what will happen in the next few hours*]: but I will see you again, and your heart shall rejoice, and your joy no man taketh from you.

23 And in that day ye shall ask me nothing. Verily, verily, I say unto you, Whatsoever ye shall ask the Father in my name, he will give it you.

JST John 16:23
23 And in that day ye shall ask me nothing **but it shall be done unto you**. Verily, verily, I say unto you, Whatsoever ye shall ask the Father in my name, he will give it you.

24 Hitherto have ye asked nothing in my name [*up to now, you have not had to ask Father for things in My name, because I have been here with you*]: ask, and ye shall receive, that your joy may be full.

25 These things have I spoken unto you in proverbs [*with examples and illustrations*]: but the time cometh, when I shall no more speak unto you in proverbs, but I shall shew you plainly of the Father.

26 At that day ye shall ask in my name: and I say not unto you, that I will pray the Father for you: [*Then, you will pray directly to the Father, in the name of Jesus Christ, rather than having Him pray to the Father for you.*]

27 For the Father himself loveth you, because ye have loved me, and have believed that I came out from God.

28 I came forth from the Father [*I am the Father's Son*], and am come [*have come*] into the world: again, I leave the world, and go to [*return to*] the Father.

JOHN 17

29 His disciples said unto him, Lo, now speakest thou plainly, and speakest no proverb. [*Yes! Now you are speaking clearly without relating it to other things we understand.*]

30 Now are we sure that thou knowest all things, and needest not that any man should ask thee: by this we believe that thou camest forth from God.

31 Jesus answered them, Do ye now believe?

32 Behold, the hour cometh [*the time is coming*], yea, is now come [*in fact, has now arrived*], that ye shall be scattered, every man to his own, and shall leave me alone: and yet I am not alone, because the Father is with me.

33 These things I have spoken unto you, that in me ye might have peace. In the world ye shall have tribulation [*many troubles*]: but be of good cheer [*be happy, optimistic*]; I have overcome the world.

JOHN 17

It is still Thursday evening (see Talmage, *Jesus the Christ,* 1982, p. 593). By way of review, the Passover meal, known as the Last Supper, was eaten by Jesus and the twelve Apostles. During the evening, Jesus introduced the sacrament and tenderly washed the Apostles' feet. Sometime during the evening, Judas Iscariot left to betray Jesus to the Jewish high priests and their soldiers. After Judas had left (John 13:30-31),

Jesus began teaching the remaining eleven Apostles great doctrines which stretched their minds and strengthened their understandings. These teachings are recorded, beginning with John 13:31 and continuing to the end of John, chapter 16. Sometime, during or after this discourse, the Savior led the Eleven to the Mount of Olives, just outside of Jerusalem, where He "lifted up his eyes to heaven" and gave what is known as "The Great Intercessory Prayer." It is recorded in John 17:1-26. In the first three verses, Jesus formally offers Himself as the great sacrifice for our sins, in order that we might have eternal life. He is the one who intercedes for us, allowing the law of mercy to act on our behalf. Thus, it is called the "intercessory" prayer.

After finishing this prayer, the Master will lead His little band of faithful Apostles back down the Mount of Olives to a garden which was named Gethsemane, where He will suffer and bleed at every pore. Shortly thereafter, the Master will be arrested and taken to the ruling high Priest's palace for trial.

The JST has no changes for this chapter.

The Great Intercessory Prayer

1 THESE words spake Jesus, and lifted up his eyes to heaven, and said, Father, the hour is come [*the time to begin the Atonement has arrived*]; glorify thy Son, that thy Son also may glorify thee:

2 As thou hast given him [*Christ*] power over all flesh [*over all people*], that he should give eternal life [*exaltation*] to as many as thou hast given him.

Just a reminder. The term "eternal life," as used in verse 2, above, always means exaltation when it is used in the scriptures. Exaltation is the highest degree of glory in the celestial kingdom (see D&C 132:19-20). Those who attain it will be gods and will live in the family unit forever.

Verse 3, next, is a famous verse. You may wish to mark it in your own scriptures if you have not already done so.

3 And this is life eternal, that they might know thee the only true God, and Jesus Christ, whom thou hast sent.

In D&C 132:24, the phrase "this is life eternal" is rendered with a bit different wording. It is "this is eternal lives," which emphasizes the fact that the faithful Saints who earn "eternal life" will have "eternal lives," meaning there will be no end to the spirit children they will have in eternity. See last two lines of D&C 132:19.

4 I have glorified thee on the earth: I have finished the work which thou gavest me to do.

5 And now, O Father, glorify thou me with thine own self with the glory which I had with thee before the world was.

6 I have manifested thy name unto the men [*the Apostles*] which thou gavest me out of the world: thine they were, and thou gavest them me; and they have kept thy word [*the Eleven have remained faithful*].

Next, the Savior emphasizes that the Eleven now have firm testimonies.

7 Now they have known that all things whatsoever thou hast given me are of thee.

8 For I have given unto them the words which thou gavest me; and they have received [*accepted*] them, and have known surely that I came out from thee, and they have believed that thou didst send me.

9 I pray for them: I pray not for the world [*He is not referring to the world at this point of His prayer*], but for them which thou hast given me; for they are thine.

10 And all mine are thine, and thine are mine; and I am glorified in them.

11 And now I am no more in the world [*I am leaving*], but these are in the world [*My Apostles have to stay here*], and I come to thee. Holy Father, keep through thine own name those whom thou hast given me, that they may be one, as we are.

It is obvious that the Savior is speaking so that the Apostles can hear Him. You may wish to imagine, in your mind's eye, the faces of these humble Eleven as they listen to this powerful prayer, given in their behalf.

12 While I was with them in the

JOHN 17

459

world, I kept them in thy name: those that thou gavest me I have kept, and none of them is lost, but [*except*] the son of perdition [*Judas Iscariot*]; that the scripture might be fulfilled.

13 And now come I to thee; and these things I speak in the world [*within hearing of My Apostles, while I am still here on earth*], that they might have my joy fulfilled in themselves.

14 I have given them thy word; and the world hath hated them, because they are not of the world [*they are not worldly*], even as I am not of the world.

15 I pray not that thou shouldest take them out of the world, but that thou shouldest keep [*protect*] them from the evil.

16 They are not of the world, even as I am not of the world.

17 Sanctify them [*make them holy, pure, and fit to be in Thy presence*] through thy truth: thy word is truth.

18 As thou hast sent me into the world, even so have I also sent them into the world.

In verse 18, above, we see the Savior saying, in effect, that just as the Father sent Him into the world on a mission, so also has He sent His Apostles into the world on a mission.

19 And for their sakes I sanctify myself, that they also might be sanctified through the truth.

20 Neither pray I for these alone, but for them also [*everyone*] which shall believe on me through their word [*through their teachings*];

21 That they all [*all the righteous*] may be one [*united in purpose*]; as thou, Father, art in me, and I in thee, that they also may be one in us [*so that all of them can be united in purpose with us*]: that the world may believe that thou hast sent me.

22 And the glory which thou gavest me I have given them; that they may be one [*united*], even as we are one:

The Prophet Joseph Smith taught that the word "one," as used in these verses, means "agreed as one." (See *Teachings of the Prophet Joseph Smith*, p. 372.)

23 I in them, and thou in me, that they may be made perfect in one [*agreed, in unity, harmony*]; and that the world may know that thou hast sent me, and hast loved them, as thou hast loved me.

24 Father, I will [*desire*] that they also, whom thou hast given me, be with me where I am [*live with Me in celestial glory*]; that they may behold my glory, which thou hast given me: for thou lovedst me before the foundation of the world [*in the premortal life*].

25 O righteous Father, the world hath not known thee: but I have known thee, and these [*Apostles*] have known that thou hast sent me.

26 And I have declared unto them thy name, and will declare it: that the love wherewith thou hast loved me may be in them, and I in them.

We will quote from the New Testament student manual used by the Institutes of Religion of the Church for a brief summary of the Savior's prayer in verses 1–26, above.

"With a perfect understanding of his mission and that the time of his atonement was 'at hand,' Jesus concluded the teaching portion of his ministry with a prayer that has sometimes been referred to as the high-priestly or great intercessory prayer. (See John 17.) These designations are not inappropriate, for, as we shall see, Jesus, our Great High Priest, first offered himself as an offering; then, as Mediator, he interceded on behalf of worthy members of his kingdom. The pattern for this had been established in ancient Israel.

"Once each year, the presiding high priest in ancient Israel entered into the holy of holies, the most sacred place within the tabernacle. There he would perform certain rites in connection with the Day of Atonement, a day set aside for national humiliation and contrition. Having bathed himself and dressed in white linen, he would present before the Lord a young bullock and two young goats as sin offerings, and a ram as a burnt offering in behalf of his sins and those of the people. The high priest's role was that of a mediator, or one who interceded with the Lord in behalf of the people. His role, of course, was but a type of the great mediating role of the Savior in our behalf. Thus, when Jesus pleaded to the Father for all those who believed on him, he did so as our Intercessor, or Great High Priest.

"The prayer he offered on this occasion had three distinct parts:

"In the first part (see John 17:1–3), Jesus offered himself as the great sacrifice. His hour had come.

"The next part of the prayer (see John 17:4–19) was a reverent report to the Father of his mortal mission.

"In the last part (see John 17:20–26) of his prayer, Jesus interceded not only for the eleven apostles present, but for all who shall believe on Jesus 'through their word,' in order that all would come to a perfect unity, which unity invested Christ in them as Christ is in the Father. Thus all would be perfect in unity, and the world would believe that the Father had sent his Son." (*Life and Teachings of Jesus and His Apostles*, p. 171–172)

JOHN 18

After offering the "Great Intercessory Prayer," recorded in chapter 17, above, the Savior led His weary Apostles to the Garden of Gethsemane. John does not give any

JOHN 18

461

detail here of what transpired in the Garden, rather gives considerable information about the arrest, the trials, and Peter's denial of knowing Jesus. For the details of the Savior's suffering in Gethsemane, you may wish to read Matthew 26:36–46, Mark 14:32–42, and Luke 22:39–46.

The Garden of Gethsemane

1 WHEN Jesus had spoken these words, he went forth with his disciples over the brook Cedron, where was a garden [*the Garden of Gethsemane*], into the which he entered, and his disciples.

"Gethsemane" means "oil press." There is significant symbolism here. The Jews put olives into bags made of mesh fabric and placed them in a press to squeeze olive oil out of them. The first pressings yielded pure olive oil which was prized for many uses, including healing and giving light in lanterns. In fact, we consecrate it and use it to administer to the sick. The last pressing of the olives, under the tremendous pressure of additional weights added to the press, yielded a bitter, red liquid which can remind us of the "bitter cup" which the Savior partook of. Symbolically, the Savior is going into the "oil press" (Gethsemane) to submit to the "pressure" of all our sins which will "squeeze" his blood out in order that we might have the healing "oil" of the Atonement to heal us from our sins.

2 And Judas also, which betrayed

him, knew the place: for Jesus ofttimes resorted thither [*went there*] with his disciples.

The Betrayal by Judas

3 Judas then, having received a band of men [*soldiers*] and officers from the chief priests and Pharisees, cometh thither [*there*] with lanterns and torches and weapons.

4 Jesus therefore, knowing all things that should come upon him, went forth, and said unto them, Whom seek ye?

5 They answered him, Jesus of Nazareth. Jesus saith unto them, I am he. And Judas also, which betrayed him, stood with them [*the soldiers and officers*].

In verse 6, next, it is interesting to see the immediate reaction of the soldiers and those with Judas as the Master announces to them that He is the one they are looking for.

6 As soon then as he [*Christ*] had said unto them, I am he, they went backward, and fell to the ground.

7 Then asked he them again, Whom seek ye? And they said, Jesus of Nazareth.

8 Jesus answered, I have told you that I am he: if therefore ye seek me, let these go their way [*let my Apostles go free*]:

9 That the saying might be fulfilled, which he spake, Of them which thou gavest me have I lost none.

Next, we see Peter's courage and concern for Jesus' safety as he boldly draws his sword and strikes at one of the officers, cutting off his right ear.

10 Then Simon Peter having a sword drew it, and smote [*struck*] the high priest's servant, and cut off his right ear. The servant's name was Malchus. [*Malchus was a relative of the high priest. See John 18:26.*]

11 Then said Jesus unto Peter, Put up thy sword into the sheath: the cup which my Father hath given me, shall I not drink it? [*Should I not go ahead with the Atonement?*]

Luke reports that Jesus healed the servant's ear at that point—see Luke 22:51. One would think that seeing such a miracle would have encouraged the soldiers and officers to leave Him alone and desire to follow Him rather than arresting Him. But verse 12, next, indicates that they went ahead and arrested Him.

12 Then the band and the captain and officers of the Jews took Jesus, and bound him,

Jesus was taken first to Annas, the former Jewish high priest, then across the courtyard to Caiaphas, the current high priest (the chief religious officer among the Jews at the time), then to Pilate (the Roman governor), to Herod (the Roman governor of Galilee who happened to be in Jerusalem), and then back to Pilate, who turned Him over to be scourged and crucified.

These details come from a combination of information taken from Matthew, Mark, Luke, and John.

In the next verses, John tells us about the trials before Annas, Caiaphas, and Pilate. He intermixes this account with the account of Peter and the troubles he faced as he waited elsewhere as Jesus went through the trials before Annas and Caiaphas. Thus, it is a bit difficult to decide which of the next verses deal with the trial before Annas and which relate to the trial before Caiaphas. We will simply note that there was an illegal night trial before Annas and then He was sent to Caiaphas for another illegal trial at night. (It was against the Jew's laws to hold trials at night.) And we will feel sympathy for Peter as he goes through the miserable experiences leading up to the early morning when the cock crows, after he has denied knowing Jesus three times.

Tried before Annas

13 And led him away to Annas first; for he was father in law to Caiaphas, which was the high priest that same year.

Annas had served as high priest, which was the chief religious office among the Jews, for several years, before being taken out of office by the Romans. Even though his son-in-law, Caiaphas, was now the chief officer, Annas still had tremendous influence. (See Bible Dictionary, under "Annas.")

Tried before Caiaphas

14 Now Caiaphas was he, which gave counsel to the Jews, that it was expedient [*necessary*] that one man should die for the people.

Peter Denies Knowing Jesus

15 And Simon Peter followed Jesus, and so did another disciple: that disciple was known unto the high priest, and went in with Jesus into the palace of the high priest.

16 But Peter stood at the door without [*outside*]. Then went out that other disciple, which was known unto the high priest, and spake unto her that kept the door [*guarded the door*], and brought in Peter.

Peter Denies Once

17 Then saith the damsel [*young lady*] that kept the door unto Peter, Art not thou also one of this man's [*Jesus'*] disciples? He saith, I am not.

18 And the servants and officers stood there [*in the courtyard*], who had made a fire of coals; for it was cold: and they warmed themselves: and Peter stood with them, and warmed himself.

19 The high priest then asked Jesus of [*about*] his disciples, and of [*about*] his doctrine. [*The illegal trial by night begins.*]

To read a full account of the illegal aspects of Christ's trial, see *Jesus the Christ*, pp. 644–648.

20 Jesus answered him, I spake [*spoke*] openly to the world; I ever [*constantly*] taught in the synagogue [*in the Jewish churches*], and in the temple, whither [*where*] the Jews always resort [*go*]; and in secret have I said nothing.

21 Why askest thou me [*why ask Me about My doctrine*]? ask them which heard me [*ask the people*], what I have said unto them: behold, they know what I said.

22 And when he had thus spoken, one of the officers which stood by struck Jesus with the palm of his hand, saying, Answerest thou the high priest so [*how dare You talk like that to the high priest!*]?

23 Jesus answered him, If I have spoken evil, bear witness of the evil [*tell Me what I said that was not correct*]: but if well, why smitest thou me [*if what I said was true, why did you slap Me*]?

24 Now Annas had sent him bound [*still tied up to make sure he could not escape*] unto Caiaphas the high priest.

Peter Denies the Second Time

25 And Simon Peter stood and warmed himself. They said therefore unto him, Art not thou also one of his disciples? He denied it, and said, I am not.

26 One of the servants of the high priest, being his kinsman whose ear Peter cut off, saith, Did not I see thee in the garden with him? [*This man had good reason to recognize Peter!*]

Peter Denies the Third Time

27 Peter then denied again: and immediately the cock crew [*the rooster crowed*].

28 Then led they Jesus from Caiaphas unto the hall of judgment [*to the Roman governor's place*]: and it was early [*in the morning; the two previous trials before Annas and Caiaphas had taken place during the night*]; and they themselves went not into the judgment hall, lest they should be defiled [*be made unclean*]; but that they might eat the passover.

It is ironic and sad to think that, even while they were turning the "Lamb of God" over to be executed, they themselves were being very careful not to become unclean in any way that might prevent them from finishing Passover worship, in which they showed gratitude for blessings received by the shedding of the blood of sacrificial lambs, representing Christ.

Tried before Pilate

29 Pilate then went out unto them, and said, What accusation bring ye against this man [*what are you accusing Jesus of*]?

30 They answered and said unto him, If he were not a malefactor [*criminal*], we would not have delivered him up [*turned Him over*] unto thee.

31 Then said Pilate unto them, Take ye him, and judge him according to your law [*you handle it*]. The Jews therefore said unto him, It is not lawful for us to put any man to death [*under Roman law, we Jews cannot execute anyone*]:

32 That the saying of Jesus might be fulfilled, which he spake, signifying what death he should die.

Watch now as Pilate asks Jesus specifically if He is the King of the Jews. Jesus will ask him a question in return.

33 Then Pilate entered into the judgment hall again, and called Jesus, and said unto him, Art thou the King of the Jews?

34 Jesus answered him, Sayest thou this thing of thyself, or did others tell it thee of me [*are you asking because you, yourself, want to know, or because others have told you I am*]?

35 Pilate answered, Am I a Jew [*how should I know what is going on; I am not a Jew*]? Thine own nation and the chief priests have delivered thee unto me: what hast thou done?

36 Jesus answered, My kingdom is not of this world: if my kingdom were of this world [*if this were my time to be king on earth*], then would my servants fight, that I should not be delivered to the Jews: but now is my kingdom not from hence [*here on earth*]. [*The time will come, during the Millennium, when Christ becomes everyone's King here on earth, literally. But that time has not yet come at the time Pilate is questioning the Master.*]

The answer Jesus gives to Pilate, in verse 37, next, is a brief and beautiful summary statement of the Savior's mortal mission.

37 Pilate therefore said unto him, Art thou a king then? Jesus answered, Thou sayest that I am a king. To this end was I born [*for this purpose I was born*], and for this cause came I into the world, that I should bear witness unto the truth. Every one that is of the truth heareth [*hears and obeys*] my voice.

38 Pilate saith unto him, What is truth? And when he had said this, he went out again unto the Jews, and saith unto them, I find in him no fault at all [*I do not find Jesus guilty of anything*].

39 But ye have a custom [*you have a tradition*], that I should release unto you one at the passover [*every year, at Passover time, I release a criminal of your choosing*]: will ye therefore that I [*would you like me to*] release unto you the King of the Jews?

Next, the Jews, who have crowded the courtyard of the Roman governor, and who have been incited by their religious leaders to demand the crucifixion of Jesus, respond loudly to Pilate's question.

40 Then cried they all again, saying, Not this man, but Barabbas. Now Barabbas was a robber.

Ironically, the name "Barabbas" means "son of the father" (see Bible Dictionary, under "Barabbas"). This may be symbolic in that the "imposter," Satan, stirred up the multitude to demand the release of an "imposter," Barabbas, while the true "Son of the Father" is punished for crimes which He did not commit.

JOHN 19

This chapter is John's account of the crucifixion of the Savior. While all four of the Gospels writers (Matthew, Mark, Luke, and John) give an account of the Crucifixion, John adds much that is not mentioned by the other three. The following is a list of verses from this chapter of John which contain unique information or significant additions to what the others recorded:

Unique Contributions of John

Verses in John 19 which contain unique information about the Crucifixion: 1–5, 8–14, 16–17, 20–27, 31–37, 39.

Scourging

1 THEN Pilate therefore took Jesus, and scourged him [*had Him whipped*].

Scourging involved tying the victim to a frame or column, with the arms pulled tightly upward to put tension on the back muscles, and then whipping him with a whip which was made of leather strips with sharp bits of metal and bone fastened to them. Often, a victim of scourging did not survive to continue on to be crucified.

The Crown of Thorns and Mocking

2 And the soldiers platted [*wove*] a crown of thorns, and put it on his head, and they put on him a purple robe [*mockingly symbolic of His being "King of the Jews"*],

3 And said, Hail, King of the Jews! and they smote [*hit*] him with their hands.

4 Pilate therefore went forth again, and saith unto them, Behold, I bring him forth to you, that ye may know that I find no fault in him [*I do not find Him guilty of any crime*].

5 Then came Jesus forth [*where the crowd could see Him*], wearing the crown of thorns, and the purple robe. And Pilate saith unto them, Behold the man [*just look at this pitiful man*]!

"Crucify Him!"

6 When the chief priests therefore and officers saw him, they cried out, saying, Crucify him, crucify him. Pilate saith unto them, Take ye him, and crucify him: for I find no fault in him.

7 The Jews answered him, We have a law [*a law against blasphemy (mocking God) making it punishable by death*], and by our law he ought to die, because he made himself [*claimed to be*] the Son of God.

Pilate Is Afraid

8 When Pilate therefore heard that saying, he was the more afraid;

9 And went again into the judgment hall, and saith [*said*] unto Jesus, Whence art thou [*where do You come from*]? But Jesus gave him no answer.

10 Then saith Pilate unto him, Speakest thou not unto me? knowest thou not that I have power to crucify thee, and have power to release thee? [*Don't You think You ought to answer me. Don't You realize I have power to have You crucified or to set You free?*]

11 Jesus answered, Thou couldest have no power at all against me, except it were given thee from above: therefore he that delivered me unto thee hath the greater sin [*referring to Caiaphas; see McConkie, Doctrinal New Testament Commentary, Vol. 1, p. 809*].

12 And from thenceforth [*from then on*] Pilate sought [*tried*] to release him: but the Jews cried out, saying, If thou let this man go, thou art not Cæsar's friend: whosoever maketh himself a king speaketh against Cæsar. [*If you release Him, you are not loyal to Caesar, because Jesus claims to be the king, instead of Caesar.*]

13 When Pilate therefore heard that saying [*that it could appear that Jesus was undermining the Roman government*], he brought Jesus forth, and sat down in the judgment seat in a place that is called the Pavement, but in the Hebrew, Gabbatha.

14 And it was the preparation of the passover, and about the sixth

JOHN 19

hour: and he saith unto the Jews, Behold [*look*] your King!

15 But they cried out, Away with him, away with him, crucify him. Pilate saith unto them, Shall I crucify your King? The chief priest [*Caiaphas*] answered, We have no king but Cæsar.

The Crucifixion

16 Then delivered he [*Pilate*] him [*Jesus*] therefore unto them to be crucified. And they took Jesus, and led him away.

17 And he bearing his cross went forth into a place called the place of a skull, which is called in the Hebrew Golgotha:

JST John 19:17

17 And he bearing his cross went forth into a place called the place of a **burial**; which is called in the Hebrew Golgotha;

18 Where they crucified him, and two other [*the two thieves*] with him, on either side one, and Jesus in the midst [*middle*].

Next, Pilate frustrates and angers the chief priests by instructing that a sign be placed on the cross. They ask him to rework the wording on the sign, but he refuses.

19 And Pilate wrote a title, and put it on the cross. And the writing was, JESUS OF NAZARETH THE KING OF THE JEWS.

20 This title then read many of the Jews: for the place where Jesus was crucified was nigh [*near*] to the city: and it was written in Hebrew, and Greek, and Latin.

21 Then said the chief priests of the Jews to Pilate, Write not, The King of the Jews; but that he said, I am King of the Jews. [*Don't write "King of the Jews," rather, write "He claimed to be King of the Jews."*]

22 Pilate answered, What I have written I have written [*I will not change it*].

23 Then the soldiers, when they had crucified Jesus, took his garments [*clothes*], and made four parts [*and divided them into four piles*], to every soldier a part; and also his coat: now the coat was without seam, woven from the top throughout [*was woven as one continuous piece of fabric*].

24 They said therefore among themselves, Let us not rend it [*tear the coat into four pieces*], but cast lots [*gamble*] for it, whose it shall be: that the scripture [*Psalm 22:18*] might be fulfilled, which saith, They parted my raiment [*clothing*] among them, and for my vesture [*clothing*] they did cast lots. These things therefore [*to fulfill prophecy*] the soldiers did.

Next, Jesus, despite His extreme pain, focuses on His mother, Mary, and asks John to take care of her after He is gone. This implies that Joseph had already passed away and that Mary was a widow.

25 Now there stood by the cross of Jesus his mother [*Mary*], and his mother's sister, Mary the wife of Cleophas, and Mary Magdalene. [*Mary was a beautiful and common name among the Jews.*]

26 When Jesus therefore saw his mother, and the disciple [*John the Beloved Apostle*] standing by, whom he loved, he saith unto his mother, Woman [*a term of great respect in Jewish culture*], behold thy son!

27 Then saith he to the disciple [*John*], Behold thy mother! And from that hour that disciple took her unto his own home. [*The Savior asked John to take care of His mother from then on, and he did.*]

The Savior's Mortal Mission Is Finished

28 After this, Jesus knowing that all things were now accomplished [*knowing that He had now finished everything which the Atonement required of Him as a mortal*], that the scripture might be fulfilled, saith, I thirst.

29 Now there was a vessel full of vinegar, mingled with gall, and they filled a sponge with it, and put upon hyssop, and put to his mouth.

30 When Jesus therefore had received the vinegar, he said, It is finished: and he bowed his head, and gave up the ghost [*and left his body*].

Elder James E. Talmage points out that Jesus accepted the vin-

egar mixture (verse 30) only after "all things were . . . accomplished" (verse 28). In other words, He refused to accept anything that would provide any relief from His suffering, until all the mortal requirements of the Atonement were satisfied. See *Jesus the Christ*, 1982 edition, p. 661.

Seven Statements from the Cross

Jesus uttered a total of seven recorded statements from the cross. The references for these statements and the statements themselves follow, and are in chronological order:

1. **Luke 23:34**: "Father, forgive them; for they know not what they do."

2. **Luke 23:43**: "Today shalt thou be with me in paradise."

3. **John 19:26-27**: "Woman, behold thy son!"; "Behold thy mother!"

4. **Matthew 27:46**: "My God, my God, why hast thou forsaken me?"

5. **John 19:28**: "I thirst."

6. **John 19:30**: "It is finished."

7. **Luke 23:46**: "Father, into thy hands I commend my spirit."

31 The Jews therefore, because it was the preparation [*time to make preparations for the Sabbath*], that the bodies should not remain upon the cross on the sabbath day, (for that sabbath day was an high day,) besought Pilate that their legs

JOHN 19

might be broken, and that they might be taken away.

Among the Jews at this time in history, the days of the week, Monday, Tuesday, etc., went from about sundown to about sundown of the next day, rather than from midnight to midnight as is the case with our calendar system. Therefore, the Jewish religious leaders were very concerned about violating one of their laws which said people should not be crucified on the Sabbath. Their Sabbath (held on Saturday) would start at about six Friday evening. Jesus and the two thieves had been crucified at about nine that morning (Friday). Persons being crucified often lived two or three days. Therefore, these religious rulers of the Jews asked Pilate to have soldiers break the legs of the three "criminals" who were being crucified to kill them with additional pain and shock, so that their bodies could be taken off their crosses in order to avoid violating the Sabbath. Pilate agreed and sent soldiers to do the deed.

32 Then came the soldiers, and brake [*broke*] the legs of the first [*one of the thieves*], and of the other [*thief*] which was crucified with him.

33 But when they came to Jesus, and saw that he was dead already, they brake not his legs:

34 But one of the soldiers with a spear pierced his side, and forthwith came there out blood and water.

35 And he [*John; see John 19:25, footnote 35a*] that saw it bare record,

and his record [*the Gospel of John*] is true: and he knoweth that he saith true, that ye might believe.

Remember that we mentioned previously that John always refers to himself indirectly in his writing, as is the case in verse 35, above.

Next, John points out two prophecies which were fulfilled by what he just recorded in verses 33–34.

36 For these things were done, that the scripture [*Psalm 34:20, Numbers 9:12*] should be fulfilled [*in order to fulfill the prophecy which says*], A bone of him shall not be broken.

37 And again another scripture [*Zechariah 12:10*] saith, They shall look on him whom they pierced.

Joseph of Arimathaea Requests Permission to Remove the Body of Jesus From the Cross

38 And after this Joseph of Arimathæa [*from Ramah; a member of the Sanhedrin, see Bible Dictionary, under "Joseph"*], being a disciple of Jesus, but secretly for fear of the Jews, besought [*asked*] Pilate that he might take away the body of Jesus: and Pilate gave him leave [*permission*]. He came therefore, and took the body of Jesus.

Nicodemus Helps

39 And there came also Nicodemus [*one of the Jewish religious rulers, see Bible Dictionary, under "Nicodemus"*], which at the first came to Jesus by night [*John 3:2*], and

brought a mixture of myrrh and aloes [*costly spices with which to prepare Christ's body for burial*], about an hundred pound weight.

40 Then took they [*Joseph and Nicodemus*] the body of Jesus, and wound it in linen clothes with the spices, as the manner [*custom*] of the Jews is to bury.

Jesus' Body Is Placed in a New Tomb

41 Now in the place where he was crucified there was a garden; and in the garden a new sepulchre [*tomb*], wherein was never man yet laid [*which had never been used*].

42 There laid they Jesus therefore because of the Jews' preparation day; for the sepulchre was nigh [*near*] at hand. [*There was an urgency to get Jesus' body into a tomb, in order not to violate the approaching Sabbath, and this tomb was close by.*]

Imagine the Savior's feelings, having left His pain-ridden mortal body, as He now enters spirit world paradise where "an innumerable company of the spirits of the just, who had been faithful" (D&C 138:12) await Him. From rejection, mocking, and crucifixion He now enters the realm where faithful Saints welcome Him and anxiously await His message to them. Among other things, He will inform them that their long wait for resurrection is over and that they will be resurrected with Him in a short

three days. He will organize them into a great missionary force through which His gospel will be preached to the spirits in spirit prison (D&C 138:30–34).

JOHN 20

It is early Sunday morning, and the Savior, having come from a joyful reception for Him in spirit world paradise (D&C 138:11-19), has been resurrected and is preparing to appear to His faithful disciples who still don't grasp the fact that He will literally return to them as a resurrected personage (as John explained in John 12:16).

Imagine John's feelings as he records this part of his account. He was one of the first of the brethren to come to the empty tomb after being told by the women (who had already been to the tomb) that the Master had been resurrected. While John only mentions Mary Magdalene here, Luke informs us that other women were with her (Luke 24:10), and Mark tells us that Mary, the mother of James, and Salome accompanied Mary Magdalene (Mark 16:1).

In John's account, he tells us of Mary Magdalene seeing the open tomb first, and then running and telling Peter and John. Then he modestly informs us that he outran Peter to the empty tomb but waited until Peter arrived and then went into the tomb after Peter entered it.

JOHN 20

Next, he shows us that the resurrected Lord appeared to Mary Magdalene and then to the disciples. Thomas is not there for that appearance and declares that he will not believe it unless he sees for himself. Eight days later, he will see, and will believe.

We will now get more details from John's record in this chapter.

Mary Magdalene
Comes to the Tomb

1 THE first day of the week [*Sunday*] cometh Mary Magdalene early, when it was yet dark, unto the sepulchre [*Christ's tomb*], and seeth the stone taken away from the sepulchre.

JST John 20:1

1 The first day of the week cometh Mary Magdalene early, when it was yet dark, unto the sepulcher, and seeth the stone taken away from the sepulcher, **and two angels sitting thereon**.

2 Then she runneth, and cometh to Simon Peter, and to the other disciple [*John*], whom Jesus loved, and saith unto them, They have taken away the Lord out of the sepulchre, and we [*the ladies mentioned above*] know not where they have laid him.

Peter and John Run
to the Tomb

3 Peter therefore went forth, and that other disciple [*John*], and came to the sepulchre.

4 So they ran both together: and the other disciple did outrun Peter [*John outran Peter*], and came first to the sepulchre.

5 And he stooping down, and looking in, saw the linen clothes lying; yet went he not in. [*John waited for Peter to arrive.*]

6 Then cometh Simon Peter following him, and went into the sepulchre [*tomb*], and seeth the linen clothes lie [*saw the strips of linen which Joseph and Nicodemus had used to wrap the Savior's body in*],

7 And the napkin [*burial cloth*], that was about [*was wrapped around*] his head, not lying with the linen clothes, but wrapped together [*folded*] in a place by itself.

8 Then went in also that other disciple [*John*], which came first to the sepulchre, and he saw, and believed.

9 For as yet they knew not [*did not understand*] the scripture, that he must rise again from the dead [*as John explained in John 12:16*].

10 Then the disciples went away again unto their own home.

JST John 20:10

10 Then the disciples went away again unto their own **homes**.

Jesus Appears to
Mary Magdalene

11 But Mary [*Mary Magdalene; see verse 1*] stood without [*outside*] at the sepulchre weeping: and as

she wept, she stooped down, and looked into the sepulchre,

12 And seeth two angels in white sitting, the one at the head, and the other at the feet, where the body of Jesus had lain.

13 And they say [*said*] unto her, Woman, why weepest thou? She saith unto them, Because they have taken away my Lord, and I know not where they have laid him. [*Someone has taken Jesus' body away, and I don't know where they put it.*]

14 And when she had thus said, she turned herself back [*away from the angels*], and saw Jesus standing, and knew not that it was Jesus.

15 Jesus saith unto her, Woman, why weepest thou? whom seekest thou? She, supposing him to be the gardener, saith unto him, Sir, if thou have borne him hence [*if you have taken His body somewhere*], tell me where thou hast laid him, and I will take him away.

16 Jesus saith unto her, Mary. She turned herself, and saith unto him, Rabboni; which is to say, Master.

This is a very tender moment. Mary is very concerned about where the Savior's body has been taken. After turning away from the tomb and the two angels therein, she sees a man whom she assumes is the caretaker. The question comes up as to why she did not immediately recognize Jesus. Several possibilities exist. One is that she had been crying and was so distraught that she didn't even take a good look at Jesus at first. Another possibility is that she hadn't turned all the way around from the tomb. She "turned herself back" from the tomb and the angels in verse 14, yet she "turned herself" in verse 16, implying that she had not turned completely toward where Jesus was standing when she first turned from the tomb. Whatever the explanation, when Jesus said "Mary," she recognized His voice, apparently looked again, and her sorrow was over.

17 Jesus saith unto her, Touch me not; for I am not yet ascended to my Father: but go to my brethren, and say unto them, I ascend unto my Father, and your Father; and to my God, and your God.

JST John 20:17
17 Jesus saith unto her, **Hold** me not; for I am not yet ascended to my Father; but go to my brethren, and say unto them, I ascend unto my Father, and your Father; and to my God, and your God.

The Joseph Smith Translation change in verse 17, above, may solve a bit of a problem otherwise encountered when reading Matthew and then reading John. The common understanding of verse 17 is that the resurrected Lord told Mary not to touch Him. Yet, Matthew 28:8–9 informs us that some women were met by Jesus as they ran from the empty tomb to tell the disciples that the Master's body was gone. They were allowed to hold Him by the feet and worship him. So why was Mary Magdalene not allowed to touch Him (John 20:17)? The answer may be, that she was. The JST changes "touch me not" to "hold me not." The Greek, which was translated as "touch me not" in our New Testament, is often translated as "do not hold me" or "do not hold on to me." The Greek word itself is "harpazo," which is the continuous action of holding. Strong's *Exhaustive Concordance* #0680, defines it as "to fasten one's self to, adhere to, cling to." Thus, it is possible, using the JST as a reference, that Jesus was, in effect, telling Mary "Don't keep holding Me. I must leave." Whatever the case, we will certainly get clarification on it some day.

18 Mary Magdalene came and told the disciples that she had seen the Lord, and that he had spoken these things unto her.

Jesus Appears to the Disciples

19 Then the same day at evening, being the first day of the week [*Sunday*], when the doors were shut where the disciples were assembled for fear of the Jews [*the disciples were afraid that the Jews would arrest them too*], came Jesus and stood in the midst, and saith unto them, Peace be unto you.

20 And when he had so said, he shewed [*showed*] unto them his hands and his side. Then were the disciples glad, when they saw the Lord.

21 Then said Jesus to them again,

Peace be unto you: as my Father hath sent me, even so send I you.

22 And when he had said this, he breathed on them, and saith unto them, Receive ye the Holy Ghost:

In the Jewish culture, "breathed on them" is very significant. The same word is used in Genesis 2:7, where God breathed on Adam and he became a living soul. The symbolism in verse 17, above, seems to be that of "breathing" additional life or "power" into the Apostles. In April Conference, 1955, Apostle Harold B. Lee suggested that it was at this time, after the Savior's death, that He confirmed them and gave them the Gift of the Holy Ghost. This would certainly fit in with Christ's promise to His Apostles that, after He had gone, He would send them "another Comforter" (the Holy Ghost). See John 14:16.

23 Whose soever sins ye remit [*forgive*], they are remitted unto them; and whose soever sins ye retain, they are retained.

Thomas Doubts

24 But Thomas, one of the twelve, called Didymus [*meaning "twin"*], was not with them when Jesus came.

25 The other disciples therefore said unto him, We have seen the Lord. But he said unto them, Except I shall see in his hands the print of the nails, and put my finger into the print of the nails, and thrust my

hand into his side, I will not believe. [*This is how Thomas came to be known as "Doubting Thomas."*]

Thomas Sees the Resurrected Christ

26 And after eight days again his disciples were within [*inside the house*], and Thomas with them: then came Jesus, the doors being shut, and stood in the midst, and said, Peace be unto you.

27 Then saith he to Thomas, Reach hither [*here*] thy finger, and behold [*look at*] my hands; and reach hither thy hand, and thrust it into my side: and be not faithless, but believing.

28 And Thomas answered and said unto him, My Lord and my God.

29 Jesus saith unto him, Thomas, because thou hast seen me, thou hast believed: blessed are they that have not seen, and yet have believed.

30 And many other signs truly did Jesus in the presence of his disciples, which are not written in this book:

John, having born his testimony to us in verse 30, above, now finishes this chapter by explaining why he has selected the things he has written for us.

31 But these are written, that ye might believe that Jesus is the Christ, the Son of God; and that believing ye might have life [*eternal life, exaltation*] through his name.

JOHN 21

In Matthew 26:32, Jesus told His Apostles that He would meet them in Galilee after His resurrection. Matthew 28:9–10 informs us that He told the women to tell the brethren to go to Galilee and there they would see Him. And Matthew 28:16 records that before Jesus' crucifixion, He had "appointed them" to meet Him in Galilee after His death.

In this beautiful chapter, John tells us that they followed those instructions and he gives us details about what took place. There are no JST additions or corrections for this chapter.

1 AFTER these things [*after everything John has told us so far*] Jesus shewed [*showed*] himself again to the disciples at the sea of Tiberias [*the Sea of Galilee*]; and on this wise shewed he himself [*and this is how He showed himself to them*].

As we get to verse 2, next, several of the disciples have already journeyed to Galilee in anticipation of meeting the Savior there. While waiting there, they have decided to go fishing.

2 There were together Simon Peter, and Thomas called Didymus, and Nathanael of Cana in Galilee, and the sons of Zebedee [*James and John*], and two other of his disciples.

3 Simon Peter saith unto them, I go a fishing. They say unto him, We also go with thee. They went forth, and entered into a ship immediately; and that night they caught nothing.

JOHN 21

In the days of Jesus, it was common for fishermen to fish at night on the Sea of Galilee, when the fishing was best. Peter, having been a professional fisherman on that lake before the Savior said "Come follow me," now takes his fellow disciples and they fish all night, with absolutely no success. The "sons of Zebedee," verse 2 above, were James and John, and they, too, had been professional fishermen, before being called by Jesus to follow Him. It must have been extra frustrating for these professionals to have zero success fishing. Watch now as the Savior gets their attention. Perhaps it is appropriate to imagine a bit of a smile on His face and a twinkle in His eye.

4 But when the morning was now come, Jesus stood on the shore: but the disciples knew not that it was Jesus. [*He was apparently far enough away that they didn't recognize Him.*]

Something quite wonderful is now going to happen. The tired disciples have had absolutely no success fishing throughout the night. In the morning, this stranger on the shore asks them if they have had any luck. He then tells them to simply cast their net overboard on the other side of the ship. Perhaps there are few things worse than a stranger telling professionals how to do their work. Nevertheless, they do what He says and suddenly the net fills with so many fish (153 big fish, see verse 11) that they could hardly pull it in.

This rings a bell. An almost identical thing had happened three years ago when He first called Peter, Andrew, James, and John (see Luke 5:1–11). Jesus had come by, and because of the crowd, had requested that Peter take Him a little way out from the shore in his ship. When He was through speaking to the crowd, He told Peter to go out farther into the lake and let down his nets. Peter replied that they had fished all night with no success, but, since Jesus said to do it, he did. Their net filled with so many fish that the net began to break. James and John quickly brought their ship out to help, and the large number of fish almost sank both ships.

Now, the same thing is happening again. Could it be the Master who is on the shore now?

5 Then Jesus saith unto them, Children, have ye any meat [*have you caught any fish*]? They answered him, No.

6 And he said unto them, Cast the net on the right side of the ship, and ye shall find. They cast therefore, and now they were not able to draw it [*bring it in*] for the multitude [*because of the large number*] of fishes.

7 Therefore that disciple whom Jesus loved [*in other words, John, the Beloved Apostle*] saith unto Peter, It is the Lord. Now when Simon Peter heard that it was the Lord, he girt his fisher's coat unto him, (for he was naked [*stripped to the waist*],) and did cast himself into the sea [*Peter jumped in and swam to shore, a distance of about 300 feet—see verse 8*].

8 And the other disciples came in a little ship; (for they were not

far from land, but as it were two hundred cubits [*about a hundred yards*],) dragging the net with fishes.

9 As soon then as they were come to land, they saw a fire of coals there, and fish laid thereon, and bread.

This is a very touching scene. No one in the universe could be busier than the Savior. Yet He had taken the time to cook breakfast for His weary, discouraged disciples who had fished all night with no success.

10 Jesus saith unto them, Bring of the fish which ye have now caught.

11 Simon Peter went up, and drew the net to land full of great [*large*] fishes, an hundred and fifty and three: and for all there were so many, yet was not the net broken.

There is symbolism here. Jesus told the Apostles, when He called them, that He would make them "fishers of men" (Matthew 4:19). The fact that the Savior helped them have such success with actual fish is symbolic of the fact that He will help them have great success in bringing souls into the gospel net and unto the Father.

12 Jesus saith unto them, Come and dine. And none of the disciples durst ask him, Who art thou? knowing that it was the Lord.

13 Jesus then cometh, and taketh bread, and giveth them, and fish likewise.

14 This is now the third time that Jesus shewed himself to his disciples, after that he was risen from the dead.

Next, the Master Teacher creates a teaching moment and uses it to teach Peter, who will become the President of the Church. He repeats the main point of the lesson three times, in verses 15, 16, and 17.

Feed My Sheep

15 So when they had dined, Jesus saith to Simon Peter, Simon, son of Jonas, lovest thou me more than these [*do you love Me more than these fish*]? He saith unto him, Yea, Lord; thou knowest that I love thee. He saith unto him, Feed my lambs.

16 He saith to him again the second time, Simon, son of Jonas, lovest thou me? He saith unto him, Yea, Lord; thou knowest that I love thee. He saith unto him, Feed my sheep.

17 He saith unto him the third time, Simon, son of Jonas, lovest thou me? Peter was grieved because he said unto him the third time, Lovest thou me? And he said unto him, Lord, thou knowest all things; thou knowest that I love thee. Jesus saith unto him, Feed my sheep.

Next, in verses 18–19, Jesus tells Peter that he will be crucified when his mission is over.

Peter Will Be Crucified

18 Verily, verily, I say unto thee, When thou wast young, thou girdedst thyself [*dressed yourself*], and walkedst whither thou wouldest [*and went wherever you wanted to*]: but when thou shalt be old, thou shalt stretch forth thy hands [*you will be crucified*], and another shall gird thee, and carry thee whither thou wouldest not [*where you don't want to go*].

19 This spake he, signifying by what death he should glorify God. [*Jesus thus indicated to Peter how he would die when his mortal mission was over*] And when he had spoken this, he saith unto him, Follow me.

Bruce R. McConkie explained verses 18–19, above. He taught

"'Thou shalt follow me,' our Lord said to Peter on that recent day when the chief apostle pledged, 'I will lay down my life for thy sake' (John 13:36–38). How literally the Master then spoke, and how fully Peter is to do as he offered, he now learns. He is to be crucified, a thing which John in this passage assumes to be known to his readers. Peter's arms are to be stretched forth upon the cross, the executioner shall gird him with the loin-cloth which criminals wear when crucified, and he shall be carried where he would not, that is to his execution (2 Pet. 1:14–15; *Doctrinal New Testament Commentary*, Vol. 1, p. 863).

Jesus Foretells Peter's Martyrdom

20 Then Peter, turning about, seeth the disciple whom Jesus loved [*John*] following; which also leaned on his breast at supper [*at the last supper—see John 13:23*], and said [*asked the question*], Lord, which is he that betrayeth thee?

21 Peter seeing him [*John*] saith to Jesus, Lord, and what shall this man do [*what will happen to John*]?

John Will Be Translated

22 Jesus saith unto him, If I will that he tarry till I come [*if I want him to remain alive until My second coming*], what is that to thee? follow thou me.

23 Then went this saying abroad among the brethren, that that disciple [*John*] should [*would*] not die: yet Jesus said not unto him, He shall not die; but, If I will that he tarry till I come, what is that to thee?

Because of the wording of verses 22 and 23 above, it is not clear from the Bible whether or not John was allowed to remain on earth until the Second Coming. However, through modern revelation, in D&C 7:3, we know that John was allowed to remain. He was translated and will not die until the Lord's coming. Joseph Smith gave us more information about John in *History of the Church*, volume 1, p. 176. He said that at that time, 1831, John was working with the lost ten tribes, preparing them for their return. More information about translated beings can be found in 3 Nephi 28, where details about the Three Nephites are given.

Finally, strong testimony is born to us that the things written by John are true.

24 This is the disciple which testifieth of these things, and wrote these things: and we know that his testimony is true.

25 And there are also many other things which Jesus did, the which, if they should be written every one, I suppose that even the world itself could not contain the books that should be written. Amen.

This concludes Part 1 of *The New Testament Made Easier*. Parts 2 and 3 of this set cover the remainder of the New Testament plus Brother Ridges' book, *The Savior's Life and Mission to Redeem and Give Hope*.

Sources

Doctrine and Covenants Student Manual, Religion 324 and 325. Salt Lake City: The Church of Jesus Christ of Latter-day Saints, 2001.

Ensign. March 1976 and November 1995.

Hymns of The Church of Jesus Christ of Latter-day Saints. Salt Lake City: The Church of Jesus Christ of Latter-day Saints, 1985.

Improvement Era. Vol. 19.

Journal of Discourses. Vol 18. London: Latter-day Saints' Book Depot, 1854–86.

Parry, Jay A. and Donald W. *Understanding the Book of Revelation.* Salt Lake City: Deseret Book, 1998.

Kimball, Spencer W. *The Miracle of Forgiveness.* Salt Lake City: Bookcraft, 1969.

Life and Teachings of Jesus and His Apostles, The. New Testament student manual, Religion 211. Salt Lake City: The Church of Jesus Christ of Latter-day Saints, 1979.

McConkie, Bruce R. *Doctrinal New Testament Commentary.* 3 vols. Salt Lake City: Bookcraft, 1965–73.

McConkie, Bruce R. *Mormon Doctrine.* 2d ed. Salt Lake City: Bookcraft, 1966.

Millet, Robert L. *Alive in Christ: The Miracle of Spiritual Rebirth.* Salt Lake City: Deseret Book, 1997.

Pratt, Orson. *Masterful Discourses and Writings of Orson Pratt.* Compiled by N. B. Lundwall. Salt Lake City: Bookcraft, 1962.

Smith, Joseph. *History of The Church of Jesus Christ of Latter-day Saints.* Edited by B. H. Roberts. 2d ed. rev., 7 vols., Salt Lake City: The Church of Jesus Christ of Latter-day Saints, 1932–51.

Smith, Joseph. *Joseph Smith's "New Translation" of the Bible* (JST). Independence, Missouri: Herald Publishing House, 1970.

Smith, Joseph. *Lectures on Faith.* Salt Lake City: Deseret Book, 1985.

Smith, Joseph. *Teachings of the Prophet Joseph Smith.* Selected by Joseph Fielding Smith. Salt Lake City: Deseret Book, 1976.

480 **SOURCES**

Smith, Joseph F. *Gospel Doctrine: Selections from the Sermons and Writings of Joseph F. Smith.* Salt Lake City: Deseret Book, 1971.

Smith, Joseph Fielding. *Doctrines of Salvation.* Compiled by Bruce R. McConkie. 3 vols. Salt Lake City: Bookcraft, 1954–56.

Strong, James. *The Exhaustive Concordance of the Bible.* Nashville: Abingdon, 1890.

Talmage, James E. *Jesus the Christ.* Salt Lake City: Deseret Book, 1982.

Widtsoe, John A. *Evidences and Reconciliations.* Salt Lake City: Bookcraft, 1943.

Various translations of the Bible, including the Martin Luther edition of the German Bible, which Joseph Smith said was the most correct of any then available.

NOTES

NOTES

NOTES

NOTES

About the Author

David J. Ridges taught for the Church Educational System for thirty-five years and taught for several years at BYU Campus Education Week. He taught adult religion classes, Especially for Youth, and Know Your Religion classes for BYU Continuing Education for many years. He has also served as a curriculum writer for Sunday School, Seminary, and institute of religion manuals.

He has served in many callings in the Church, including Gospel Doctrine teacher, bishop, stake president, and patriarch. He and Sister Ridges have served two full-time eighteen-month CES missions. He has written over 40 books, including study guides for Isaiah, the book of Revelation, the Old Testament, New Testament, Book of Mormon, Doctrine and Covenants and Pearl of Great Price.

Brother Ridges and his wife, Janette, are the parents of six children, have 17 grandchildren, and make their home in Springville, Utah.

Scan to visit

www.davidjridges.com

En busca del río sagrado

Editorial Bambú es un sello
de Editorial Casals, SA

© 2005 Éditions Flammarion para el texto
y las ilustraciones.
© 2008, Editorial Casals, SA
Tel.: 902 107 007
editorialbambu.com
bambulector.com

Título original: *À la recherche du fleuve sacré.*
Les sources du Nil.
Traducción: Manuel Serrat Crespo

Quinta edición: febrero de 2021
ISBN: 978-84-8343-049-1
Depósito legal: M-554-2010
Printed in Spain
Impreso en Anzos, SL –Fuenlabrada (Madrid)

Créditos fotográficos del Cuaderno Documental:
Bettmann/Corbis: 1
Getty Images: 2
Royal Geographical Society/Getty Images: 3
Rue des Archives/Gregoire: 8
Private Collection/The Stapleton Collection/The Bridgeman
Art Library: 9
Rue des Archives/CCI: 10
Bojan Brecelj/Corbis: 11
Rue des Archives: 12
Roger-Viollet: 13
Royal Geographical Society: 14
Bettmann/Corbis: 15
Euan Denholm/Reuters: 16

Mapas:
Marie Pécastaing/Studio jeunesse Flammarion

El papel utilizado para la impresión de este libro procede de
bosques gestionados de manera sostenible.

Cualquier forma de reproducción, distribución, comunicación pú-
blica o transformación de esta obra solo puede ser realizada con
la autorización de sus titulares, salvo excepción prevista por la
ley. Diríjase a CEDRO (Centro Español de Derechos Reprográficos,
www.cedro.org) si necesita fotocopiar o escanear algún fragmento
de esta obra (www.conlicencia.com).

EN BUSCA DEL RÍO SAGRADO

Las fuentes del Nilo

Philippe Nessmann
Traducción de Manuel Serrat Crespo

EDITORIAL

Preámbulo

Donde se descubre que las grandes exploraciones comienzan en los despachos

—*Ni siquiera en tiempos de su esplendor los faraones intentaron saber de dónde procedía...*

Sir Roderick Murchison adoptó un aire solemne. La reunión que presidía a comienzos del año 1856, en un despacho de silenciosa atmósfera en la Sociedad Real de Geografía de Londres, era de la mayor importancia. Para él, para la sociedad que dirigía, para Gran Bretaña y, al menos eso esperaba, para la historia de los grandes descubrimientos.

—*En la Antigüedad, los egipcios consideraban el Nilo como un dios caprichoso y generoso, que cada año les alimentaba con sus crecidas. Sin duda hubiera sido sacrílego querer saber más...*

Embutido en su chaqué, el anciano dejó que se hiciera el silencio, como para dar más peso a lo que iba a decir.

—Más tarde, los griegos y, luego, los romanos quisieron desvelar ese insondable misterio: ¿cómo un río puede atravesar un país tan desértico como Egipto sin nunca secarse? ¿Dónde están, en un continente tan cálido como África, las fuentes de semejante cantidad de agua? ¿En qué lejanas montañas?

Un geógrafo bigotudo susurró, con aire festivo, al oído de su vecino:

—Te apuesto a que nos habla de Nerón...

—El emperador romano Nerón —prosiguió sir Roderick Murchison— envió al lugar una expedición dirigida por dos centuriones. Remontaron el Nilo hasta el actual Sudán. Pero, al sur de Jartum, fueron detenidos por una gigantesca ciénaga, alimentada por mil corrientes de agua. Una de ellas es forzosamente el Nilo, ¿pero cuál? Puesto que no podían recorrerlas todas, renunciaron...

El geógrafo bigotudo se inclinó de nuevo hacia su vecino.

—¿Qué te apuestas a que suelta la palabra gondokoro en la próxima frase...?

—Hace menos de cincuenta años, una expedición consiguió por fin encontrar, en aquella inextricable marisma, la corriente de agua más importante, dicho de otro modo, el Nilo. La remontó hasta que una cadena de montañas, cerca del poblado de Gondokoro, lo hizo impracticable. Los escasos viajeros que se han aventurado más allá, han regresado enseguida. O no han regresado nunca, víctimas de la jungla y de los traficantes.

Sir Roderick Murchison tomó una gran carpeta colocada ante él, en la mesa de su despacho.

–Hoy, las fuentes del Nilo constituyen el mayor enigma de la geografía moderna. Para los hombres y para el país que las descubran serán los honores y la gloria. Y deseo ardientemente que correspondan a Gran Bretaña. Tengo para ello que presentarles un ambicioso proyecto. Su autor no es otro que Richard Burton. Se propone, para resolver el problema, flanquearlo: puesto que no es posible remontar el Nilo a causa de las cascadas y las ciénagas, quiere descender por él. Para ello, piensa dirigirse mucho más al sur, a Zanzíbar, en la costa este de África. La expedición se dirigirá luego hacia el oeste, hacia el corazón del continente, adonde ningún europeo ha ido nunca. Algunos mercaderes árabes afirman haber descubierto allí varios lagos grandes como mares. Si algún río ancho sale de uno de esos lagos y corre hacia el norte, hay muchas posibilidades de que sea el Nilo. Bastará entonces con descenderlo hasta Egipto... Pero «bastar» no es la palabra exacta: la región está atestada de traficantes, fieras, junglas asfixiantes y enfermedades tropicales...

El geógrafo bigotudo se inclinó hacia su vecino.

–No lo he oído: ¿quién quiere aventurarse por ese pequeño paraíso?

–Burton –repuso el otro, molesto.

–¿Richard Burton? Ah, sí, a fin de cuentas...

Sir Roderick Murchison abrió la carpeta y sacó de ella unas hojas y unos mapas.

–Queridos colegas, les he reunido hoy para que discutamos este proyecto. ¿Les parece realizable? ¿Debe financiarlo la Sociedad Real de geografía? Mientras aguardamos recibir a Richard Burton, estudiaremos los documentos que nos ha proporcionado.

El presidente los hizo circular entre sus colegas.

–¿Alguna pregunta?

Acto I

Hacia el lago Tanganika

Capítulo uno

En el palacio del sultán de Zanzíbar
Encuentro con dos blancos
Enrolado a su pesar

Estoy una vez más de guardia en la parte trasera del palacio del sultán, junto a la gran palmera. Puesto que vigilo una puerta por la que nunca pasa nadie, me aburro como el cadáver de un muerto, una vez más.

Para matar el tiempo, intento recordar un viejo proverbio. ¿Acaso: «el que rema a favor de la corriente hace que los cocodrilos se rían», o tal vez: «el que rema contra la corriente hace que los cocodrilos se rían»? Intento meterme en la piel de un cocodrilo e imaginar cuál de ambas cosas es más chusca.

–¡Sidi Mubbarak! ¡Ven!

Es Baraka, mi jefe, el que se dirige a mí.

–¡Ya ves que estoy trabajando! Beberemos más tarde.

–Ven, el sultán quiere verte.

–¡Ah! Si se trata del sultán...

Preguntándome aún qué tontería habré hecho, sigo a Baraka por una serie de corredores muy frescos, hasta la gran estancia del palacio donde el sultán recibe a sus invitados.

—¡Entra aquí, Sidi Mubbarak!

Sayyid Majid ben Said al-Busaid tiene apenas veintidós años. Se convirtió en sultán de Zanzíbar el año pasado, cuando murió su padre, pero se tiene la impresión de que ha dado órdenes toda su vida, tal vez, incluso, ya en el vientre de su madre.

—¡Entra!... Mis invitados quieren conocerte.

Hay allí, sentados en una banqueta, dos hombres blancos vestidos como blancos. Uno de ellos tiene el pelo negro, el otro amarillo.

—Buenos días Sidi Mubbarak —dice el del pelo negro.

Ese hombre me da miedo. Incluso sentado parece alto como un gigante. Sus ojos son tan severos que te empujan hacia atrás. En cada una de sus mejillas tiene una cicatriz larga como un pulgar, como si una lanza le hubiera atravesado de parte a parte la boca.

—¿Al parecer hablas industaní?

Estoy tan impresionado que no lo advierto enseguida: me está hablando en esa lengua.

—Claro —le respondo.

Podría explicarle que soy africano, nacido en la tribu Yao, y que de niño fui capturado por los mercaderes árabes y vendido como esclavo. Mi dueño me llevó entonces a la India. Fue allí donde aprendí el industaní, una lengua de aquel país. Cuando murió mi dueño, me convertí en un hombre libre y regresé a África, donde me alisté en la guardia del sultán de Zanzíbar.

Podría contarle todo eso, pero prefiero callar. Un silencio vale por veinticinco respuestas.

—Al parecer viajaste hasta la India con tu dueño —prosigue el hombre del pelo negro, que lo sabe ya todo de mí—. Vas a acompañarme en un largo viaje por las tierras africanas.

¿Un viaje? ¡Ah no, no quiero! Estoy muy bien custodiando mi puerta, por la que nunca pasa nadie.

Y, además, hay tantas mujeres que me gustan en la isla de Zanzíbar y con las que quiero casarme. ¡No quiero marcharme!

—Sabe usted, sahib, aquí tengo mucho trabajo que hacer para su alteza...

—¡No discutas! —me interrumpe en árabe el sultán— ¡Yo he decidido que vayas!

¿Pero por qué yo? ¿Acaso es un castigo por algo que he hecho mal? ¿Y por qué ese viaje?

—¿Se dedican al comercio de esclavos?

—No, buscamos un río. Se llama Nilo y...

¿Para qué buscar un río? ¡Todos los ríos se parecen! La única pregunta interesante es: ¿qué divierte más a los cocodrilos? ¿Ver a un remero que remonta la corriente o que desciende por ella? Mientras el hombre del pelo negro le habla a las moscas, echo una ojeada a su compadre. Parece algo más joven, veinticinco años tal vez, aunque sea difícil calcular la edad de los blancos. No ha dicho nada desde el comienzo. No hace más que escuchar e inclinar amablemente la cabeza. El jefe no es él.

De pronto, un silencio: la explicación debe de haber terminado.

–¡Nos vemos mañana por la mañana en el puerto!

Con un gesto de su cabeza, el sultán me indica que me marche.

Regreso a mi puesto de guardia, tan contrariado como un borrico entre buitres: ¡no quiero marcharme!

* * *

–¿Cómo se llaman?

–El jefe se llama Richard Burton y el otro John Speke.

Mi amigo Baraka, que es mi superior entre los guardias, es muy curioso: siempre quiere saberlo todo. Esta noche, me ha invitado a su choza para beber vino de coco. Estamos sentados en jergones y me acribilla a preguntas.

–¿Y qué estáis haciendo en el puerto?

–Preparamos el tesoro.

–¿El tesoro?

Me divierte pincharle.

–¡Sí, el tesoro! Los ingleses son muy ricos, llevan rollos de tela, más hermosas que las más hermosas telas del sultán. Y también un montón de joyas y de cuentas. He tenido la suerte de verlas y he quedado tan deslumbrado que los ojos me pican todavía. Metemos esos tesoros en cajas para llevarlos con nosotros. Con eso nos van a pagar los ingleses.

No es del todo cierto: servirán, sobre todo, para comprar comida por el camino. Pero Baraka me cree y abre unos ojos como platos.

–¿Hay muchas cajas?

–Tantas que se necesitarán treinta asnos y treinta y cinco hombres para llevarlas. Y ocho soldados baluchis para defendernos de los ladrones.

–¿Y tú eres porteador?

–Yo, ¡claro que no!

–¿Por qué te han elegido entonces?

Siento la envidia en la boca de mi amigo y eso me gusta. No le he dicho que yo no quería marcharme.

–Porque hablo lenguas. Aquí nadie habla inglés. De modo que los dos blancos no pueden dar sus órdenes. Pero, como han vivido en la India y yo también, me dan sus instrucciones en industaní y yo las traduzco.

–¡Pero también yo he vivido en la India! ¡También yo hablo industaní! ¿Por qué no me han elegido a mí?

–Sin duda porque yo hablo mejor...

–Bah... ¿Y no quieres decirme lo que vais a buscar?

–Si te lo he dicho ya: un río. Pero no puedo decirte nada más...

Apuro mi calabaza de vino de coco y, luego, añado para concluir la cuestión sin mostrar que no sé nada más:

–Es un secreto.

Baraka rumía: le habría gustado tanto participar en el viaje. Él es realmente un aventurero –yo no.

–¿Cuándo os marcháis?

–Hace meses ya que los ingleses preparan la caravana, todo está casi listo. Saldremos cuando acabe la estación de las lluvias.

–¿Y cuánto tiempo durará el viaje?

–No lo sé.

En realidad, lo sé: para mí, sólo durará unos días. Soy un hombre libre y nadie puede obligarme a hacer lo que no quiero. Para no acabar en las mazmorras del sultán, he decidido partir con los ingleses, pero huiré en cuanto nos hayamos adentrado bastante.

Nunca más volveré a ser un esclavo...

Capítulo dos

**En la jungla y la sabana
Mil dificultades para la caravana
¡Valor, quedémonos!**

Se dice que huir forma ya parte del valor.

Sólo me queda aguardar el momento oportuno para ser valeroso.

De momento, es demasiado pronto. El barco prestado por el sultán de Zanzíbar apenas acaba de atracar en el continente. Decenas de hombres, mujeres y niños corren a nuestro encuentro. Algunos se mezclan con los porteadores y se apoderan de algunas cajas. Los dos sahibs están perdidos: parecen gallinas que no reconocen ya a sus polluelos. ¿Eres tú un aldeano o un porteador? ¡Eh, no os marchéis con las cajas!

El sahib Burton, que realmente es muy alto y tiene una mirada realmente muy maligna, se enoja; no obstante, nadie le escucha.

Voy a verle.

–No es bueno enojarse. Hay que dar algunas cuentas a los aldeanos, pues le han ayudado.
–¡Pero si no han hecho nada!
–Déles las cuentas y le dejarán en paz.

El sahib Burton se enoja más aún pero, puesto que es inteligente, acaba comprendiendo que tengo razón y va a ver a los aldeanos con las cuentas. Todo vuelve al orden.

A la mañana siguiente, la caravana se pone en camino. Somos en total casi cien hombres. Said ben Salim el-Lamki, nuestro guía, abre la marcha. En el pasado, acompañó a varios mercaderes árabes que se dirigieron al corazón de África para buscar marfil y esclavos. Conoce bien el camino. Nadie debe sobrepasarlo, so pena de ser multado. Le siguen los porteadores con los fardos de mercancías en la cabeza, van luego los asnos, cargados como mulas y llevados por arrieros. Los sahibs Burton y Speke viajan también montados en asnos. Los ocho soldados armados, distribuidos a lo largo de la caravana, tienen varios esclavos cada uno de ellos para servirles.

Cuando se pone en marcha, la caravana se estira como una lombriz. Rápidamente, los de atrás pierden de vista a los de delante. A veces se alarga tanto que se divide en varios trozos que se siguen en fila, como una lombriz cortada a pedacitos.

Empezamos por tomar un estrecho sendero que se hunde en una densa jungla. Sobre nuestras cabezas, los árboles y las lianas se unen formando un techo verde. Hace fresco y es casi obscuro. De vez en cuando, desembocamos en un calvero con campos de labor y una decena de chozas hechas de barro y ramas, luego nos sumimos de nuevo en la jungla sin fin.

Tras dos horas de marcha, llega por fin el momento de ser valeroso.

–¡Eh, esto pesa demasiado! –grita un porteador dejando su fardo.

Los demás le imitan y todos se sientan en el suelo.

–Sí, es más pesado de lo que nos dijeron.

La caravana se detiene en una confusión general. Lo aprovecho para meterme en la selva.

–¡Bombay!

Bombay es el apodo que me ha dado el sahib Burton: es el nombre de una ciudad de la India. Mis amigos, en cambio, me llaman Mamba, el «cocodrilo», porque tengo los dientes puntiagudos como garfios y me encuentran muy feo. No me molesta ser feo: se acuerdan de mí.

–¿Bombay, adónde vas tan deprisa?

El sahib Burton parece enfadado. Doy marcha atrás.

–Hum... Una urgente necesidad de regar los árboles.

–Dime, ¿qué pasa con los porteadores?

–Oh, nada, las cajas les parecen demasiado pesadas.

–Pero si son de veinticinco kilos, el peso normal. ¡Diles que vuelvan a ponerse en marcha!

–No serviría de nada, sahib.

–¡Hazlo de todos modos!

27

–Pero si no servirá de nada.
–¡Entonces lo haré yo mismo!

Descabalga y, durante unos minutos, grita todas las palabras que ha aprendido en swahili. Naturalmente, los porteadores permanecen sentados.

Yo le contemplo, divertido: un hombre que da órdenes a los guijarros pierde su tiempo.

–No es nada bueno enojarse, sahib. Hay que discutir. ¡Déles un salario mejor!

–Pero acordamos el precio antes de la partida...
–Entonces, si le apetece, siga gritando.

Refunfuña un poco más, luego comprende de nuevo que tengo razón y decide regresar para discutir con los porteadores.

La caravana se pone en marcha de nuevo.

Y yo con ella.

Penetramos lentamente pero con seguridad en territorio de los uamrami, una tribu cuya mayor afición es desvalijar las caravanas de paso. Hace doce años, un hombre blanco llamado Maizan se detuvo en Dege-la-Mhora. En Zanzíbar todos conocen su historia: viajaba solo y era el primer blanco que había llegado tan lejos en África. Mazungera, el jefe de la aldea, lo recibió bien primero. Pero tras algunos días, le reprochó los dones hechos a otros jefes y declaró que iba a morir de inmediato. Ató a Maizan a un baobab y, al son del tambor, le cortó las articulaciones. Comenzaba a cortarle el cuello cuando, puesto que la hoja estaba embotada, se detuvo para afilarla, luego prosiguió su tarea. Luego, Mazungera emprendió la huida y se dice que un dragón animado por el espíritu de un viajero blanco recorre el camino de Dege-la-Mhora, en busca del jefe fugitivo.

Es el camino que estamos siguiendo.

Para apartar a los malos espíritus y a los saqueadores, cantamos, gritamos, golpeamos los tam-tam con todas nuestras fuerzas. Como un gato eriza su pelo para que le crean más grande de lo que es, hacemos ruidos para que los bandidos piensen en una caravana muy bien protegida y muy segura de sus fuerzas.

De momento, funciona.

* * *

Hemos salido del territorio uamrami. Pienso sin cesar en mi proyecto de fuga, pero las lluvias torrenciales me impiden intentar nada de nada. Son tan fuertes que apenas he dicho: «caramba, llueve», cuando estoy ya empapado hasta los huesos. El camino de tierra se transforma entonces en un sendero de lodo. Cruzamos marismas en las que me hundo hasta las rodillas, hasta el vientre a veces. Cuando salimos de ellas, penetramos en una jungla cuyas enormes lianas trepan, se retuercen, se yerguen, se enrollan a los árboles, nos barran el paso. Luego atravesamos una sabana de hierbas cortantes y matorrales espinosos que nos agarran, como para impedirnos llegar más lejos. Porque más lejos hay otras ciénagas.

Cada noche, rígido como un árbol muerto, me digo que lo peor ha pasado. Pero lo peor llega a la mañana siguiente. La humedad lo moja todo, ropas, cajas, asnos y hombres. Un olor a podrido brota de la tierra, como si detrás de los matorrales hubiera cadáveres. Hordas de hormigas con cabeza de búfalo corren por el suelo, de aquéllas cuyas mandíbulas acaban con una rata y no te sueltan ya cuando te han pellizcado. Nubes de mosquitos llenan el aire.

Si huyera ahora, no podría sobrevivir nunca, solo en este infierno.

Me armo, pues, de paciencia.

Por lo demás, llega mi oportunidad: hace ya algunos días que ambos sahibs tiemblan sobre sus asnos, más blancos que el blanco, víctimas de unas feas fiebres. Me siento secretamente satisfecho: cuanto más duro sea, antes renunciarán y antes daremos media vuelta. África no está hecha para los débiles. Sin embargo, cada mañana, ante mi gran sorpresa, los dos ingleses cabalgan de nuevo y nos ponemos en marcha. Me pregunto qué puede ocultar el río Nilo que sea tan valioso, para que les importe tanto...

Y, ¡oh miseria!, África es dura incluso con sus propios hijos. También yo me pongo enfermo. Me duele la cabeza, tengo dolores en los pies, mis ojos arden y siento una gran fatiga en todo el cuerpo. Numerosos asnos, picados por moscas tse-tsé, mueren y nosotros, desgraciados supervivientes, cargamos con sus fardos.

De vez en cuando atravesamos una pequeña aldea. Cuando llegamos, los hombres, las mujeres y los niños huyen a las selvas. Desde hace veinte años, bandidos armados incendian las chozas y capturan a los habitantes. Los venden a las caravanas árabes que, a su vez, los revenden como esclavos en Arabia, en la India o en otra parte. Por ello esa pobre gente tiene miedo de todos los extranjeros, incluso de nosotros que sólo queremos comprar algo para poder comer.

Sé muy bien lo que sienten: cierto día también yo huí, aterrorizado, de la choza de mis padres. Era un niño y no corría mucho: los buitres me alcanzaron, capturaron, arrastraron, vendieron. Nunca he vuelto a ver a mis padres. Ni siquiera sé ya dónde se encuentra la aldea de mi infancia. A veces me pregunto si mi madre se acordará aún de mí... Pero hoy soy adulto y corro mucho.

Huiré y nadie me alcanzará.

* * *

Treinta y cinco días de ruta: saludamos al último cocotero que veremos.

El sendero se eleva hacia las montañas llamadas Usagara y el clima cambia: las lluvias del valle y los hediondos vapores han desaparecido. Cuanto más subimos, más fresco es el aire, más azul el cielo y más agradable el sol. Las ciénagas y los espinosos han dado paso a tamarindos, mimosas y algunos baobabs. Unos pequeños monos se divierten ocultándose detrás de los anchos troncos, mientras las iguanas calientan sus escamas al sol. Unas palomas arrullan entre los matorrales.

Como por arte de magia, nuestras fiebres disminuyen y regresan nuestras fuerzas.

Cada día, tras la dura jornada de marcha, una vez descargados los asnos y montadas las tiendas de los sahibs, pienso en el mejor momento para escapar. ¿Al ir a buscar agua al arroyo? ¿Leña para el fuego? ¿Pero qué voy a hacer luego? ¿Regresaré solo a ese valle hostil?

Cada anochecer, cuando el sol se pone, cuando la ranatoro muge, dejo mis proyectos para el día siguiente, como sorgo y carne hervida para recuperar fuerzas, luego Mabruki saca el tam-tam y me olvido de todo. Palmeamos y cantamos a coro. Danzamos en corro, nos balanceamos hacia delante y hacia atrás, lentamente primero, cada vez más deprisa luego, nuestros brazos se agitan, nuestros cuerpos se agachan, nuestras manos tocan la tierra, el corro se va estrechando, nos aceleramos hasta galopar frenéticamente. Y por fin, en plena excitación, Mabruki hace callar el tamtam y todos nos arrojamos al suelo, con grandes risas.

Sentado en su taburete plegable, el sahib Burton nos observa y, a la luz del fuego de campamento, escribe cosas en un cuaderno. Su negra barba oculta ahora las dos cicatrices de sus mejillas.

A veces, palmea rítmicamente y se ríe de buena gana. Parece menos severo. Enardecido por la danza, voy a verle.

–¿Viene a bailar? ¡Es bueno!

–Me gustaría mucho, pero no tengo tiempo.

–Ustedes, los blancos, tienen relojes pero nunca tiempo... ¿Y qué está escribiendo?

Sonríe y me tiende su cuaderno: nos ha dibujado.

El parecido es tal que nos veo bailar sobre el papel.

–Dibujo, hago mapas de las montañas que atravesamos, escribo palabras en swahili para aprenderlas, anoto lo que ha pasado durante el día. Quiero acordarme de vosotros, de vuestros cantos, de vuestras risas, de vuestro modo de vestir, para contárselo a mis amigos ingleses...

Es casi amable. Sus ojos, tan duros la mayor parte del tiempo, se fruncen maliciosos.

–... y también quiero recordar vuestra pereza y vuestros manejos para que os paguen mejor o para obtener más comida.

¿Habla en serio? En el fondo, creo que nosotros, los negros, le gustamos.

En primer lugar detesta la esclavitud y, además, intenta conocernos. No es como su compañero de pelo amarillo, el joven sahib Speke. Él, tras la jornada de marcha, va de caza; le gusta mucho cazar y trae orgullosamente los cadáveres de los animales. Luego, se encierra en su tienda y nunca se mezcla con nosotros. Los únicos momentos que sale lo hace para discutir con el sahib Burton. No entiendo nada porque hablan en inglés. He visto varias veces al joven enseñando un cuaderno a su jefe. Éste lo lee y tacha algunas palabras, como si corrigiera faltas. El joven Speke agacha la cabeza en silencio, diríase un cachorro ante su dueño.

—¡Dormir, dormir!

Cuando suena ese grito, la música cesa. Todos vamos a acostarnos.

Las noches son siempre demasiado cortas.

* * *

Ya está, se ve ya el final de las montañas y la bajada hacia el valle de Ugogo.

Rebaños de antílopes, cuya cabeza sobrepasa las altas hierbas, nos observan. Los dos sahibs los admiran, tan asombrados como ellos. Luego, de pronto, dan un brinco y huyen ligeros como un sueño.

Cuando llegamos al estanque Diwa, somos recibidos por un concierto de tambores y campanillas. Todos los que necesitan agua se detienen ahí. Al anochecer, miles de pájaros se posan en la ribera. Por la noche, elefantes, jirafas y cebras abrevan ahí. Y de día, lo hacen los hombres.

Una inmensa caravana está acampada ya. Tiene mil porteadores, tal vez más. Sus jefes duermen en grandes tiendas, en verdaderas camas de madera. Viajan con su ganado, cajas llenas de provisiones, medicamentos, tabaco. Llevan también un precioso cargamento de marfil: han terminado pues con el comercio y emprenden regreso hacia Zanzíbar.

¡Zanzíbar!

Mi última oportunidad.

Esa noche no pego ojo; demasiado nervioso. Por fin ha llegado el momento: me uniré a la otra caravana y regresaré a la costa sin temer las ciénagas, ni el hambre, ni a los bandoleros.

De madrugada, seguro de mí mismo y muy excitado, vuelvo a partir con mi caravana, para no despertar sospechas. Sólo debe durar unas horas, pero las horas pasan y me quedo. Luego pasan los días y sigo allí. Todavía podría desandar el camino, pero no lo hago. ¿Por qué? No lo sé. Bueno, sí, lo sé: no soy tan valeroso como quiero creer. Juego a ser un cocodrilo, pero soy sólo un tronco de árbol que flota en la charca. Soy un cobarde.

Y la cobardía acaba pagándose siempre.

Cierta noche, unas hienas atacan a nuestros últimos asnos. Los pobres animales están tan heridos que el sahib Burton ordena rematarlos y vamos a ser también nosotros, los hombres –los negros, no los blancos– quienes nos encarguemos de su carga.

Yo, que no soy porteador, llevo ahora en la cabeza un fardo tan pesado como el suyo. Las jornadas son largas y, al anochecer, el sorgo, la leche agria, la mantequilla rancia, los huevos echados a perder y el agua corrompida, todas esas cosas compradas, sin embargo, muy caras en las aldeas, no apaciguan ya mi hambre.

–¡Sidi Bombay, estás comiendo todo el tiempo! –se burla el sahib Burton.

«Sí, pero yo llevo vuestros fardos y, por la noche, monto vuestras tiendas», le respondo para mí mismo.

Hubiera debido marcharme con la otra caravana...

Cierta noche, me despiertan unos murmullos en el campamento. Es cosa de los porteadores que, aquella noche, se han acostado apartados del guía y de los soldados. A la luz de la luna, les veo moverse, murmurar, reunir sus cosas. De pronto, una quincena de ellos se levantan en silencio y desaparecen en la noche.

Vuelvo a dormirme.

–¿Dónde están los porteadores? ¿Bombay, dónde están los porteadores?

Abro los ojos. Amanece. El sahib Burton está aullando sobre mí.

–Pero... yo no sé nada.

–Ya lo imagino –estalla–. ¡Pero infórmate!

Me levanto, enojado porque me griten cuando no es cosa mía, y hago la pregunta a la veintena de porteadores que se han quedado. Traduzco la respuesta al hombre blanco:

–Han vuelto a su casa.

–¿A su casa?

–Sí, viven en la región y han vuelto a casa.

–Sé muy bien que son de esta región –ladra–, ¡pero el trabajo no ha terminado! Tenían que acompañarnos hasta Kazeh. ¿Volverán?

–¿Les ha pagado ya?

–En parte, sí.

–Entonces no, no volverán.

El terrible Burton se tranquiliza de inmediato: ha comprendido que era el responsable de ese desaguisado. Es extraño cómo la gente que se cree inteligente hace a veces cosas que ni siquiera los más tontos harían. Y, claro está, nosotros, los que nos hemos quedado, tomamos la carga de los desertores. Desde Zanzíbar, parte de los rollos de telas y las cuentas ha sido cambiada por comida, pero queda mucho todavía.

Es realmente muy pesado y cada paso en la tierra seca y ardiente se hace más duro que el anterior.

El sahib Burton lo advierte y se pone a mi altura.

–¿Todo va bien, Bombay?

–Sí, sí, todo va bien.

–Mañana entregarás tu caja a los porteadores. Tú eres mi intérprete, no mi porteador.

–No, no, no sahib, estoy bien.

Por nada del mundo dejaría mi carga: no quiero pasar por una mujer a ojos de mis compañeros.

–Como quieras.

El sahib vacila unos instantes, luego añade, hablando en voz más baja:

—¿Sabes, Bombay?, hay tantos hombres que sólo piensan en llevar la menor carga posible, en robarme cuentas o en desertar que, realmente, tengo suerte de tenerte aquí.

—¿De verdad?

—Lo que estás haciendo es muy duro. Admiro tu fuerza y tu valor.

Creo que está diciendo la verdad.

Y tiene razón: pensándolo bien, ahí, bajo el sol, con mi caja en la cabeza y mis horas de marcha en las piernas, advierto que, si se necesita valor para huir, a veces se necesita más aún para quedarse.

Y yo me he quedado.

Capítulo tres

**Llegada a Kazeh
Un poblado que huele a sangre
Valiosas informaciones**

Hace cuatro meses y medio que seguimos la pista de las caravanas árabes, dirigidos por Said ben Salim.

Esta mañana, el sahib Burton ha ordenado a nuestros ocho soldados baluchis que se pusieran su uniforme, con el sable a la cintura, el mosquete cargado y el escudo decorado. Ha sacado de sus cosas la bandera de su país y la ha puesto a la cabeza de la caravana.

Al son de cuernos y tam-tams, la caravana serpentea por el valle. Cuando por fin nos acercamos, una multitud se apretuja al borde del camino. Nos aclama tanto que no se escuchan ya nuestros propios gritos. Yo no grito, sólo estoy contento de llegar.

Al entrar en Kazeh, varios rostros claros se mezclan con la multitud: comerciantes árabes vestidos con una larga túnica y tocados con el fez rojo.

Uno de ellos se dirige a los sahibs:

—*Salam malecum!*

—*Malecum salam!* —responde Burton.

Los dos hombres discuten en árabe. Desde que oí al sahib hablando con el sultán de Zanzíbar, sé que conoce esta lengua.

—¡Bombay, ven aquí!

Acudo como una gacela llevada hacia el león.

—Vas a traducir —dice en industaní.

—Pero no lo necesita usted, habla perfectamente el árabe.

—No es para mí sino para el capitán Speke.

Snay ben Amir —éste es el nombre del mercader árabe— es alto, flaco y pálido. Por el color gris de su barba, debe de tener unos cincuenta años. Sus gestos son lentos y su mirada penetrante, como los de una serpiente.

Nos lleva a través del poblado. Hay centenares de casas de tierra con techo de paja. Las mayores están rodeadas por un hermoso jardín florido. Los mercaderes árabes, que se han instalado ahí para su comercio, las hicieron construir. Imagino que esos tembes están llenos de tesoros; rollos de tela y cajas de cuentas procedentes de Zanzíbar; montones de marfil y maderas preciosas destinados a la isla.

La casa de Snay ben Amir es una de las más hermosas.

Un pequeño tejado de madera, adosado al muro, alberga una ancha banqueta cubierta de un tapiz rojo. En un taburete de madera esculpida se ha puesto una bandeja de plata. En ella, vasitos para el té.

En una región tan apartada de África, todo eso es un lujo digno de un sultán. Pero a mí me parece que huele a sangre y a muerte.

El mercader árabe nos hace sentar, a los dos sahibs y a mí.

–*Ahlan wa sahlan!*

El joven Speke me mira, algo perdido. Traduzco al oído:

–«Bienvenidos a mi casa, me satisface recibiros».

–¿Que os trae? –prosigue el mercader árabe– ¿Comerciáis con marfil? Puedo ayudaros a encontrarlo. ¡Decidme lo que queréis!

–No –responde Burton–, no estamos aquí por el comercio. Buscamos un río.

–¿Un río? ¡Ah! caramba... Es sorprendente...

Llega un esclavo con una tetera de plata y llena tres vasos. Para mí no hay –soy sólo un servidor. Pero, de todos modos, no habría bebido ese té: desde que he entrado en ese tembe, tengo la impresión de que me cuesta respirar por ese olor a sangre.

–Humm –se maravilla Burton–, ¡té! ¡Es un placer! ¿Lo cultiva usted aquí?

–¡No! Las caravanas nos lo traen de Zanzíbar... ¿Decía usted que buscaban un río?

–Sí, buscamos las fuentes del río llamado Nilo.

El mercader árabe frunce el ceño.

–Espere, deje que recuerde... El Nilo... ¿No corre por Egipto? Sí, eso es, lo recuerdo: cuando vivía en Arabia, leí algunos libros sobre ese país. Es un río muy importante, ¿no es cierto?

Al traducirlo al oído del sahib Speke, dudo en añadir una pregunta que comienza a correr por mi cabeza: «¿Pero qué es eso tan importante que tiene ese río?»

–¿Y creen ustedes que nace por aquí?

–Sí –responde Burton–. Algunos viajeros árabes dicen haber visto varios grandes lagos en la región. El río podría nacer de uno de ellos. ¿Ha oído usted hablar de esos lagos?

–Claro. Al oeste, saliendo de aquí, está el lago Tanganika. Es largo como un mar y ancho como una babosa. Al norte, saliendo de aquí, está el Nyanza. En el pasado, por mi comercio, pude ver esos dos lagos.

El sahib Burton está a punto de atragantarse con su té.

–¿Los... los ha visto? ¿Sabe si algún río sale de uno de esos lagos, un río que corra hacia el norte?

–No, amigo mío, desgraciadamente no lo sé.

El joven Speke intenta decir algo, pero mientras lo susurra a mi oído, es ya tarde, la conversación prosigue su camino.

–¿Tiene usted mapas de la región? –pregunta Burton.

–¿Mapas? ¿Para qué? Las caravanas siguen siempre los mismos senderos.

–Lástima...

–Pero si necesita usted informaciones, no vacile en pedírmelas. ¿Cuánto tiempo se quedarán aquí?

–Unos días, lo que haga falta para comprar víveres.

–¡Sean entonces bienvenidos! Vengan, les ayudaré a instalarse.

El mercader árabe se levanta, seguido por los sahibs Burton y Speke, y también por mí.

Al salir de su casa para reunirnos con el resto de la caravana, tengo la impresión de poder respirar de nuevo: el olor a sangre ha desaparecido.

Sé muy bien que ese olor no existe, que sólo está en mi cabeza.

No conozco al jeque Snay ben Amir, pero no me gusta. No me gusta su casa. No me gustan los demás traficantes árabes y no me gustan sus casas. No puedo evitar pensar que además de marfil venden hombres, mujeres y niños. Algo apartadas de la aldea, he divisado las chozas en las que amontonan a los prisioneros, antes de enviarlos a Zanzíbar.

Sus hermosas casas están construidas con la sangre de los esclavos.

Todos los miedos de mi infancia vuelven a brotar, de pronto, en mí.

* * *

Ayer, día de nuestra llegada a Kazeh, el sahib Burton se instaló en una choza prestada por su amigo Snay ben Amir. Puso allí cajas de cuentas y telas, luego llamó a los porteadores, uno a uno. Tras unos minutos en la choza, cada cual salió con una gran sonrisa en los labios y un pequeño tesoro en los brazos.

Esta mañana, todos los porteadores han tomado sus cosas y, sin decir palabra, han abandonado Kazeh para regresar a su casa.

El sahib Burton está muy enojado. Desde la partida de Zanzíbar, sabía que el trabajo de los porteadores terminaría en Kazeh y que, luego, serían libres de regresar a sus casas. Pero esperaba, secretamente, que se quedaran para continuar el viaje hacia los lagos.

Ahora habrá que contratar a nuevos hombres.

–¡Es perder el tiempo! –grita el inglés en todas las lenguas que conoce, para que todos le entiendan perfectamente.

* * *

«Cuando el gato tiene hambre, no dice que el trasero del ratón hiede.»

Miro al joven Speke, sentado ante mí al pie de un baobab limpiando meticulosamente su fusil, cuando me viene a la mente ese proverbio. Es exactamente eso.

Estamos bloqueados en Kazeh desde hace tres semanas. El sahib Burton pasa parte de sus jornadas y todas sus veladas en casa del jeque Snay ben Amir. El inglés detesta la esclavitud, pero no le molesta, visiblemente, ser amigo de un tratante de esclavos. Hablan de continuar la expedición, de la búsqueda de nuevos porteadores, pero también de Arabia, de las costumbres musulmanas, de libros...

Durante los primeros días, el joven Speke siguió a su patrón. Pero como no comprende sus conversaciones, abandonó.

Y puesto que sólo habla inglés e industaní, la única persona con la que puede conversar soy yo. Y no importa que, desde el comienzo del viaje, casi no me haya dirigido la palabra: ¡ahora le intereso! La otra noche vino a pedirme algo, ni siquiera sé ya qué. En realidad, sólo necesitaba hablar. «Cuando el gato tiene hambre...»

Pero me da igual, también yo le necesito: tiene cosas que enseñarme.

–¿El Nilo? –repite adosado a su baobab– ... Richard te hablaría de él mejor que yo... Pero puesto que me lo preguntas... Es un río sorprendente. Lo vi ya una vez, en Egipto. ¿Sabes? Egipto es un país inmenso, cubierto por completo de arena amarilla. Hace mucho calor y nunca llueve. Ya imaginarás que nadie podría vivir allí si el Nilo no lo cruzara de sur a norte. Gracias a él, nació allí una brillante civilización hace cinco mil años... Construyó pirámides y magníficos templos para sus dioses. Pero nadie ha conseguido nunca saber de dónde procedía esa tan valiosa agua. Y es lo que Richard y yo buscamos... ¿Comprendes lo que te digo?

¿Me toma realmente por idiota o qué? La única cosa que me cuesta un poco imaginar es un país cubierto enteramente de arena. He visto ya grandes playas a orillas del mar, pero una playa del tamaño de un país...

–¿El sahib Burton y usted se conocían ya antes?
–Sí. Los dos somos oficiales del ejército de Gran Bretaña. Estábamos destinados en la India. Allí aprendimos el industaní. Aunque no fue allí donde nos conocimos. Fue después. Hace cuatro años, Richard organizó una expedición a Etiopía. Es un país al este de África. Quería entrar en Harar, una ciudad prohibida a todos los que no son musulmanes. Debía entrar solo, pero necesitaba un equipo de apoyo por si las cosas iban mal. Al principio, yo no debía formar parte de él. Pero otro inglés tuvo que renunciar en el último momento y, entonces, me ofrecí.

Miro, divertido, al joven con su barba amarilla. Le he hecho una mínima pregunta y él me suelta toda su vida.

–Realmente tenía ganas de partir con Richard. ¿Sabes?, en Inglaterra es muy célebre. Cierto día consiguió entrar en La Meca, otra ciudad prohibida a los no musulmanes. Como habla perfectamente árabe y no tiene miedo de nada, se disfrazó de peregrino y a la chita callando, entró en la ciudad santa. Luego escribió un libro sobre el viaje. Escribe muy bien. Adora las palabras. Debe de hablar treinta lenguas distintas. Le basta con oír un idioma para aprenderlo. Estoy seguro de que comprende ya el swahili. A mí las lenguas no me interesan. Pero tengo otras cualidades.

Acaricia su fusil. Sin duda espera una pregunta del tipo: «¿Y cuáles son sus cualidades, sahib?» Pero no quiero darle ese gusto.

–¿Y cómo fue lo de su expedición a Etiopía?

–¿La expedición?... Ah sí... Pues bien, Richard consiguió entrar en Harar. Entretanto, yo debía explorar el río Nogal, donde hay oro. Pero por culpa de mi guía, que era un granuja y no dejó de estafarme, no lo conseguí. Cuando Richard regresó, nos encontramos en la costa etíope, junto al mar Rojo, con dos ingleses más, Herne y Stroyan. Yo compartía mi tienda con Stroyan. Cierta noche, nos despertaron unos gritos. Unos gritos horribles. Saqué la cabeza por la abertura de la tienda. Éramos atacados. Unos indígenas aullaban en la obscuridad y lanzaban jabalinas. Apenas tuve tiempo para correr hacia la otra tienda, la de Richard y Herne. La situación era crítica: nuestros centinelas se habían evaporado. Sólo teníamos nuestros fusiles para defendernos. Disparábamos contra los asaltantes ocultos tras las dunas de arena, y ellos respondían arrojando lanzas. Uno de los atacantes se acercó y cortó las cuerdas de la tienda, que se inclinó hacia un lado. Para no encontrarnos envueltos en la tela, salimos. Los indígenas nos echaban piedras. Aprovechando la obscuridad, uno de ellos se arrojó sobre mí por detrás y me derribó. Cuando desperté, estaba en el suelo, junto a una choza, con las manos atadas. Los salvajes me habían llevado a su poblado. Era de noche aún. Un indígena, viendo que estaba despertando, se divirtió entonces fingiendo que iba a matarme: pinchó mi cuerpo con la punta de su lanza, cada vez más fuerte, hasta hacer brotar sangre. Otros lo imitaron de modo que una lanza me atravesó el muslo de parte a parte. Aullé de dolor y, en un reflejo, me levanté, golpeé a mi agresor y huí cojeando. Los indígenas quedaron tan sorprendidos que no reaccionaron enseguida. Yo corría descalzo hacia la playa cuando empezaron a llover las jabalinas. Pero las evité y despisté en la obscuridad a mis agresores. Luego roí mis ataduras con los dientes y regresé al campamento siguiendo la playa...

Apoyado en su baobab, el joven sahib mira su fusil como si mirara a un amigo.

—No estoy dotado para las lenguas, pero tengo otras cualidades.

El cachorro sabe, en efecto, utilizar sus colmillos...

—¿Y qué les ocurrió a los demás?

—Stroyan, el que compartía mi tienda, había muerto. Los muy sinvergüenzas le habían molido a golpes, habían atravesado su corazón con una jabalina y habían reventado su cabeza contra las rocas. Herne, en cambio, no tenía nada. Por lo que a Burton se refiere, tenía el rostro ensangrentado: una lanza le había atravesado la boca. Había entrado por la mejilla izquierda y había salido por la derecha. Pero estaba vivo. Un milagro.

Un milagro, en efecto.

—De modo que sí —concluyó—, respondiendo a tu pregunta, hace ya bastante tiempo que Richard y yo nos conocemos. Y con todo lo que hemos vivido juntos, se han establecido vínculos...

Capítulo cuatro

Mal presagio
Última parada antes del infierno
En el corazón de África

A veces no es bueno hacer demasiadas preguntas. Tras cinco semanas de obligada inmovilidad, la caravana volvió a ponerse en marcha con nuevos asnos y nuevos porteadores. Kidogo es uno de ellos –un porteador, no un asno. Es alto y fuerte, va vestido con un taparrabos de hojas trenzadas y lleva dos grandes aros dorados en las orejas. Como todos los porteadores, procede de la región de Kazeh, es de la tribu de los uanyamuezi. Entre los uanyamuezi, llevar un fardo es signo de fuerza: desde su más tierna infancia, los muchachos se divierten así.

–¡Soy un asno! ¡Un buey! ¡Un camello! –exclamó aquella mañana, al partir, para mostrarnos su potencia.

De hecho, no es muy listo, justo lo bastante para caminar con un fardo en la cabeza y apartar las moscas con la mano sin dejar caer el paquete.

Hace un rato, me he acercado a él y hemos hablado sin dejar de caminar. Le he hecho entonces la pregunta que no hubiera debido hacerle. Pero, desde hace cinco días, me aguijoneaba como una pulga:

–¿Por qué no han venido algunos de tus hermanos?

Hace cinco días, el sahib Burton anunció que íbamos hacia el lago Tanganika. El joven Speke me explicó que ese lago era mejor que el lago Nyanza para encontrar el río Nilo, pues estaba más hacia el sur y, por lo tanto, más lejos. No comprendí la razón, pero eso carece de importancia. Lo importante es que, cuando el sahib Burton anunció nuestro destino, muchos porteadores prefirieron regresar a casa.

–¿Por qué no han venido?
–Han tenido miedo –me ha respondido Kidogo.
–¿Por qué?
–Porque ya han ido al lago Tanganika y es muy duro.
–¿Por qué es muy duro?
–Porque es realmente muy duro.

Ignoro lo que ha querido decir, pero ha bastado para inquietarme: si es «muy duro» para un uanyamuezi, ¿cómo va a ser para mí?

–De todos modos tú vas al lago Tanganika...
–Sí.
–¿Por qué?
–Porque yo no tengo miedo.

Esto me ha tranquilizado un poco.

—¿Y por qué no tienes miedo?
—Porque es la primera vez que voy.

Hubiera debido callar; ahora, también yo tengo mucho miedo.

* * *

Msene es el último poblado antes de entrar en lo «realmente muy duro».

Las escasas caravanas que se dirigen al lago Tanganika hacen allí una última parada para darse valor.

Las escasas caravanas que regresan del Tanganika se detienen allí para recuperar su gusto por la vida.

¿Qué se hace en Msene?

Varias veces al día, tomo de mis cosas un puñado de cuentas de cristal que el sahib Burton me dio como adelanto por mi trabajo. Voy a la choza de la mujer más vieja de la aldea, la que lleva una pipa en la boca, y cambio las cuentas por algo del palmyra que ella fabrica.

Luego, paso la mayor parte del tiempo con Kidogo y mis amigos porteadores. Tocamos el tambor y bailamos tanto como somos aún capaces, luego hablamos y reímos, tendidos en nuestras esteras, y por fin dormimos.

El sahib Burton viene a vernos a menudo. Quiere que volvamos a ponernos en marcha. Se enoja en todas las lenguas, pero no consigue despertar a los dormidos. Los demás le escuchan en silencio. Yo le respondo que necesitamos recuperar fuerzas, que tenemos mucho tiempo y que aun cuando todos los elefantes de África bebieran el agua del lago, quedaría aún bastante cuando llegáramos. Gracias al palmyra, el sahib no me da miedo.

Cierta mañana, el sahib pierde tanto la esperanza de conseguir que nos pongamos en marcha que se sienta con nosotros, toma una calabaza de palmyra y se la bebe de un trago. El vino de palma le pone alegre por unas horas. Le diviso incluso riéndose con unas mujeres del poblado y haciéndoles cumplidos. Creo que, en Inglaterra, tiene ya una prometida.

El joven Speke, por su parte, suele quedarse en su tienda. Nunca bebe y no mira a las mujeres de la aldea. Sin embargo me ha dicho que no estaba casado. Creo que no le gustan las mujeres. No le gusta nadie.

Salvo eso, nada ocurre en Msene. ¡Ah, sí! El otro día, oí a los dos sahibs peleándose en inglés. No comprendí nada, pero me sorprendió oír al joven Speke hablando tan alto. No sabía que era capaz de hacerlo. Luego me contó lo que había ocurrido. En los bosques de la región de Msene hay muchos leones, leopardos, hienas y gatos salvajes. En las llanuras hay elefantes, rinocerontes, búfalos, jirafas y cebras. Junto a los estanques garzas, grullas y jacanas. El joven Speke adora la caza y pidió autorización para abandonar unos días Msene y buscar rinocerontes. Sueña en matar uno. El jefe se negó, pues la caravana debe poder ponerse en marcha en cualquier momento. Speke piensa que sólo lo hace para molestarle. Por eso gritó una vez, muy fuerte, y desde entonces no le habla ya a Burton.

Estamos en Msene desde hace diez días, pero vamos a marcharnos pronto: a mis amigos y a mí casi no nos quedan ya cuentas para transformarlas en bebida.

* * *

Dos veces al día, el cielo se obscurece.

Grandes gotas cálidas caen sobre nosotros. Tamborilean en mi fardo como en un tam-tam. Por unos instantes me sirve de techo. Pero, rápidamente, el agua chorrea a lo largo del paquete, cae sobre mis hombros, corre hasta mis pies.

Nos encaminamos hacia la estación de las lluvias.

Y, como dice Kidogo, en la estación de las lluvias los caminos mueren. Hierbas verdes y cortantes brotan del suelo y lo invaden todo. Nuestro guía Said ben Salim detiene a menudo la caravana para encontrar el sendero, para descubrir los árboles que las precedentes caravanas han quemado, marcando así el trayecto.

De momento, no resulta aún muy duro. Resiste.

Pero cada día el terreno se degrada un poco más y se hace cenagoso. Un horrible concierto de ranas acompaña nuestra marcha. La tierra viscosa se mete entre los dedos de mis pies desnudos. A cada paso, tengo cuidado de no resbalar, de no dejar caer el fardo. Horribles ciempiés gigantes de patas rojas se cruzan en nuestro camino, con el cuerpo cubierto de parásitos. De vez en cuando, atravesamos ríos de los que salimos cubiertos de sanguijuelas.

Por la noche, tras haber plantado el campamento sobre unas hierbas podridas, encendemos con dificultad hogueras de leña húmeda. Tomo una brasa y la paso por encima de las sanguijuelas, para que se suelten una a una. Como no hay poblados por los alrededores, cada vez tenemos menos comida. No nos quedan ya ganas de bailar.

¡Qué lejos queda Msene! ¡Y Kazeh!... Y Zanzíbar...

Las noches son frescas y húmedas y, por la mañana, despierto con fiebre y con las piernas pesadas. Es preciso recoger el campamento, cargar el fardo y partir, caminar por el barro sin resbalar, avanzar sin pensar en las largas horas de marcha hasta la siguiente parada y, sobre todo, no pensar en la horrible noche que me aguarda sino, muy al contrario, en el pequeño tesoro que recompensará mis esfuerzos, en las cuentas de cristal y la tela que me permitirán, a mi regreso, beber el delicioso palmyra...

—¡Bombay!... ¡Bombay!

Una llamada de socorro. Me aparto del sendero para dejar pasar a los porteadores que me siguen. A cierta distancia, detrás de mí, está el asno del sahib Burton —pero sin nadie encima. Dejo mi fardo y acudo. El inglés está tendido en el suelo.

—¡Bombay, ayúdame!... ¡No puedo levantarme!

Es la primera vez que le oigo, a él, que siempre ha sido severo e inflexible, hablar en un tono suplicante. Debe de ser grave. Me coloco tras él, pongo mis manos bajo sus brazos e intento levantarle. Es pesado y sus piernas están muy flojas.

–¡Llamaré al sahib Speke!

–¡De ningún modo! Pídele ayuda a un porteador.

¿Por qué no a Speke? ¿Aún por esa vieja disputa de Msene? Incluso en dificultades, se niega a reconciliarse: no es bueno eso, el mal orgullo. Y las disputas demasiado largas tampoco, no, eso no es bueno...

Llamo a Kidogo, pero llega Speke montado en su asno. Descubre a su jefe por el suelo y, tras un instante de inmovilidad, se precipita.

Se dicen unas frases en inglés. Yo no comprendo nada, pero vuelven a hablar y eso está bien ya.

–Ven, Bombay –me dice Speke en industaní–, ayúdame a ponerlo sobre el asno.

–¡No! –interrumpe Burton– No lo conseguiréis. Desde hace varios días, cada vez me mantengo menos de pie. Ya no siento las piernas. No es la primera vez que me sucede y no es grave, es la malaria. Sólo hay que aguardar a que la enfermedad pase. Pero ahora, no puedo más...

Yo no lo había advertido. No había demostrado nada. Observo su rostro: se forman arrugas de dolor rodeando sus ojos negros. En sus mejillas, a través de los pelos de la barba, diviso las dos anchas cicatrices. Recuerdo las palabras del joven Speke: el ataque al campamento, la lanza atravesando la boca, el dolor. A pesar de todos estos sufrimientos, el sahib Burton ha vuelto a África. Sea cual sea el dolor, jamás renunciará a su río.

–¡Tengo una idea! –les digo a los dos ingleses.

Voy al bosque con Kidogo y Mabruki y, tras media hora bajo el diluvio, regresamos con mi invento: una rama muy recta, larga como dos hombres, bajo la que hemos colgado una de las hamacas. Tendemos al sahib en la tela y tres portadores, uno delante y dos detrás, levantan la rama y se la ponen al hombro.

–¡Ya podemos seguir! –les anuncio con orgullo.

En el rostro del jefe, como un relámpago de agradecimiento: proseguirá su sueño gracias a mí.

La caravana reanuda su penosa marcha hacia el lago Tanganika. Cuanto más nos acercamos, más duro se hace. La fatiga, los asnos que mueren, la comida que falta, las colinas que deben superarse, los bosques que deben atravesarse, los insectos, la humedad, los fardos que llevamos, el transporte del hombre blanco. Sí, realmente es muy duro. Ahora comprendo perfectamente a los porteadores que no han querido repetir el viaje.

–El bwana blanco se encuentra muy mal –comienza a esperar Kidogo–, tal vez demos media vuelta...

Ya no fanfarronea. Se acabaron, por la mañana, sus: «¡Soy un asno! ¡Un buey! ¡Un camello!»

–No, amigo mío, conozco bien a los dos blancos, y mientras no hayan encontrado el lago, continuarán.

Tras cada colina, interrogo el horizonte en dirección al sol poniente con la esperanza de distinguir el tan esperado lago. Pero nada.

A su vez, el joven Speke se pone enfermo. Entre dos lluvias, cuando el cielo se aclara, la luz se hace muy fuerte, demasiado para los ojos azules del inglés. Ya no ve nada. Dice que no es grave, que ya pasará, pero yo siento muy bien que está inquieto. Se agarra al lomo de nuestro último asno.

Un jefe inválido; el otro ciego. Y nosotros, los porteadores, los guardas y demás, todos afectados por fiebres y dolores, y por el hambre, y por el agotamiento...

Tres meses después de la partida de Kazeh.

Una nueva colina que debe escalarse. La pendiente pedregosa es tan pronunciada que el asno del sahib Speke muere de agotamiento a media altura. Me reúno con el inglés, le tomo de la mano y lo guío hacia la cima. Ignoro cómo va a proseguir. Sin duda tendido en una hamaca, también él. ¿Pero seremos bastante numerosos los porteadores?

—¡Bombay!...

¿Qué pasa ahora? La llamada viene de arriba. Trepamos y, casi sin fuerzas y sin aliento, llegamos a lo alto de la colina.

—Bombay, ¿qué es aquella línea brillante, allí, lejos?

Pongo mi mano sobre mi frente y miro a lo lejos. Una línea gris y horizontal se extiende al pie de las montañas.

A mi espalda, siento al pobre Speke, perdido en su obscuridad, pendiente de mi respuesta.

–Creo que se trata de agua.

Speke lanza un gritito de alegría pero, de inmediato, Burton empieza a gruñir para sí.

–Ese lago es muy pequeño... Los árabes me hablaron de un lago inmenso... Pero ese lago es minúsculo... ¿Cómo puede esa charca ser las fuentes del Nilo?

–¿Algo va mal, Richard? –gime Speke– ¿Qué pasa? Dime, ¿qué estás viendo?

Capítulo cinco

**El lago Tanganika
El ataque de los escarabeos
¿Es el Nilo?**

El sendero desciende serpenteando a lo largo de una salvaje garganta. Siempre que puedo, echo una mirada entre los árboles, hacia el lago. Parece crecer, crecer: sólo a los pies de la jirafa te das cuenta de su verdadera altura.

Tendido en su hamaca, el sahib Burton describe lo que ve a su compañero ciego, sostenido a su vez por dos porteadores. Recuperan el placer de vivir.

Y también yo me siento mejor: mi fardo parece menos pesado ahora que estamos llegando al final.

Después de la selva, la caravana atraviesa campos y poblados. Mi vientre hambriento no cree lo que mis ojos ven. En la plaza del mercado, leche, aves, huevos, tomates, aguaturmas, llantén. Los habitantes nos miran al pasar, sorprendidos al ver dos hombres tan blancos. Tras los campos y los poblados, encontramos por fin una playa de arena sembrada de cañas. Ante nosotros, una inmensa extensión azul en la que el viento forma pequeñas lunas de espuma. En el agua, junto a la ribera, sobresalen ojos, oídos y hocicos: los hipopótamos dormitan. Más allá, en piraguas, unos pescadores echan sus redes.

He aquí, pues, el lago tan esperado. Muellemente tendido al pie de las montañas, se caldea al sol. Es mayor aún de lo que los mercaderes de Kazeh nos habían dicho. De la otra orilla sólo adivino inmensas cumbres grises coronadas de nubes. A izquierda y derecha es tan largo que no veo el final.

El sahib Burton y Speke se asombran en inglés. Tal vez hablen del río Nilo y del país de arena amarilla. Tras unos instantes, dejo mi fardo en la playa y les pregunto en industaní:

—Bueno, ¿y ahora comemos?

* * *

—He aquí lo que vamos a hacer...

El sahib Burton me ha convocado, con el joven Speke, en una choza cerca de Ujiji. Ujiji es el gran burgo de la región. De hecho, es un pequeño poblado ruidoso. En la plaza central, cada día, a últimas horas de la mañana, parece un bazar: decenas de vendedores de la región intercambian alimentos, marfil o telas. A menudo estallan disputas que, a veces, acaban a cuchilladas.

—Bombay, ¿has comprendido bien lo que buscamos? Si el Nilo nace en este lago, como creo, eso significa que un gran río sale por aquí, en alguna parte, y corre hacia el norte, hacia Egipto...

Tendido en su camastro de campaña, tiende el brazo hacia la derecha para indicarme esa dirección. Desde la choza abandonada en la que se ha instalado, se ve un pedacito del Tanganika.

–... Exploraremos esta parte del lago. Para ello, necesitamos un gran barco. Kannena, el jefe de Ujiji, me ha dicho que un mercader árabe tenía un velero amarrado en la otra orilla. Como no puedo caminar, he pedido al capitán Speke que vaya en piragua a buscar este navío.

El joven Speke me dirige una gran sonrisa. Desde hace unos días, sus ojos empiezan a ver de nuevo; se siente muy contento. Parece muy orgulloso de que el sahib le confíe esta misión.

–Bombay, tú acompañarás al capitán Speke y serás su intérprete. Llevaréis con vosotros tres porteadores y cajas de telas y cuentas, para alquilar el navío. Pero a ti, Bombay, te pido además que te informes entre los indígenas para saber si algún río sale del lago, en dirección hacia el norte...

No sé si debo alegrarme de esta misión. Creo que estoy contento: no es arriesgado y tal vez me paguen un poco más.

–¿Cuándo salimos?

–En cuanto el capitán Speke esté listo.

* * *

El agua corre deprisa bajo la piragua. Los remeros bogan desde el alba; nos acercamos a la otra orilla.

El sol ha sido tan fuerte durante el día que, varias veces, he mojado mi mano en el agua para refrescarme. No mucho tiempo: el lago está infestado de cocodrilos.

El joven Speke me explica su plan: el campamento, la búsqueda del barco y de su propietario, la demanda de informaciones sobre el río Nilo. Se toma muy en serio su misión y realmente quiere que sea un éxito. De ese modo, es la quinta vez que me repite lo que debemos hacer.

Ni siquiera le escucho ya. Miro el agua que se desliza bajo la piragua y me pregunto si, en alguna parte, al norte, forma ese río que atraviesa luego el país de arena. Me gustaría mucho saber qué aspecto tiene ese país. Arena por todas partes, mires adonde mires, debe de ser hermoso. Me pregunto si viven allí animales, como los cangrejos en las playas. Cangrejos de arena. Pequeños cangrejos de arena que comerían... ¿Qué podrían comer? Comerían arena y cagarían arena.

Arena por todas partes.

Incluso bajo la piragua.

—Bueno, Bombay, ¿bajas o no?

Hemos llegado: la piragua se ha deslizado hasta la playa.

Primera misión: el campamento. Monto la tienda de Speke. Instalo su camastro de campaña y su mosquitera. Coloco luego la caja con sus cosas: un fusil de caza, una pistola, balas, cuadernos y lápices, material para tomar medidas –no sé cómo funciona–, una escudilla y cubiertos para comer –eso sí sé cómo funciona. El joven sahib está satisfecho.

Segunda misión: el navío. El dhaw está amarrado no muy lejos. Es una gran embarcación muy fina con una vela en forma de triángulo. Supongo que el propietario lo hizo construir directamente en el agua. El propietario, precisamente, es difícil de encontrar: comercia por la región. Finalmente, tras unos largos días, está de regreso. Viendo al joven Speke muy interesado por su velero, lo aprovecha para exigir una increíble suma de dinero. Luego añade que, además, habrá que esperar tres meses pues, de momento, el velero no está disponible. Speke se siente muy decepcionado: lo necesitamos enseguida.

Tercera misión: el río Nilo. Mientras buscábamos al propietario del dhaw, hemos conocido a otros tres mercaderes árabes. Nos han dicho que habían navegado por el Tanganika. Al norte, muy al norte, hay un río, el río Ruzizi. El joven Speke se sentía muy excitado; me dice que tal vez era el nombre que daban por aquí al Nilo. Pero los tres no estaban de acuerdo: para el alto mercader flaco, el río salía del lago. El más pequeño, en cambio, estaba seguro de haberlo visto entrar. El tercero sólo había oído hablar del río, pero no lo había visto y no sabía nada.

De regreso al campamento, tras el fracaso del dhaw, Speke se encerró en su tienda, muy decepcionado al no poder regresar a Ujiji con el velero. Afortunadamente, llevamos al sahib Burton las informaciones sobre el río Ruzizi, aunque ignoremos en qué sentido corre.

En la playa del lago Tanganika, al pie de las montañas grises, la noche ha caído y nuestro fuego se apaga poco a poco. Acunado por el ruido de las olas que mueren en la playa, me duermo imaginando las aventuras de un cangrejo de las arenas y de su cangreja. Parten en busca de su cangrejillo, que se ha perdido. Me pregunto cómo te orientas en un país de arena. No debe de haber carreteras y nada se parece tanto a un montón de arena como otro montón de arena.

De pronto, gritos en la tienda.

–¡Ahhhh!... *Help! Help!*

¿Un ataque? Miro a mi alrededor: nada. Ni lanzas volando ni asaltantes. Nuestros porteadores despiertan también. Corro hacia la tienda. El sahib sale de un brinco a toda velocidad: corre como un loco, aúlla, mueve la cabeza. Se golpea violentamente la oreja con la palma de la mano.

–¿Qué pasa, sahib?

Corre hacia el fuego, busca algo –¿pero qué?–, grita, toma un pedazo de leña, lo suelta, se apodera del cuchillo que ha servido para la cena, se lo hunde en la oreja.

–Aaahhh...

¿Qué le ocurre? Hace girar el cuchillo en su oreja, brota la sangre, lo hunde más aún y aúlla, sus ojos están casi fuera de las órbitas, rasca con la hoja el interior de la oreja, luego se calma por fin, se sienta en el suelo, con la cabeza entre las manos, encogido de dolor.

—¿Está bien, sahib?

Me siento a su lado. No responde, mueve la cabeza de adelante hacia atrás, como un loco.

—Un escarabeo —dice por fin—. Un escarabeo... pequeños escarabeos negros... Los había a montones alrededor de mi camastro cuando me acosté... Me he dormido... Un escarabeo ha entrado en mi oído... Eso me ha despertado... Era demasiado pequeño y se había hundido demasiado en mi oreja, no podía quitármelo... Lo sentía rascar con sus patas... como si quisiera entrar en mi cerebro... ¡He creído que iba a volverme loco! Pero me lo he cargado, ¿no es cierto?

—Voy a mirar.

Aparta la mano. Tomo una llama y la acerco a su oído. Sale sangre, sangre con pequeños pedazos negros, como ramitas: patas.

—Sí, sahib, se lo ha cargado.

—¡Me lo he cargado! —murmura el inglés— Me he cargado al muy sinvergüenza...

Mueve de nuevo la cabeza adelante y atrás.

—Quiero regresar, Bombay... ¡Volvamos a Ujiji!

* * *

La piragua corre sobre las aguas.

Un hombre lleva el compás con su tam-tam y los treinta remeros bogan rítmicamente.

Estoy en la más larga de las dos piraguas. Fabricada con un tronco de árbol vaciado, mide sesenta pies de largo y embarca agua. Tengo las nalgas mojadas.

El sahib Burton está tendido en la proa. Está muy enfermo. Sus piernas siguen sin funcionar y tiene la lengua hinchada, lo que le impide hablar bien. También el joven Speke está mal: un líquido amarillo brota de su oreja con, de vez en cuando, una pata de escarabeo o un pedazo de caparazón. No oye ya nada por este oído y, cuando se suena, silba. Está en la segunda piragua, la de cuarenta pies y veintidós remeros.

El otro día, nuestro regreso a Ujiji fue muy mal. Kannena, el jefe del poblado, había dicho tantas veces a Burton que el propietario del dhaw no pondría objeciones en alquilarlo que se sintió muy decepcionado cuando regresamos sin él.

–Hemos hecho todo lo que hemos podido –se defendió Speke sin mucho convencimiento–, pero el árabe no quería oír nada. No es que no lo intentáramos, ¿no es cierto, Bombay?

Incliné la cabeza. Burton pareció dudarlo.

–Era preciso negociar... –insistió– Los mercaderes árabes dan siempre un precio de salida muy alto, pero hay que discutir... Todo se negocia... Pero sin hablar árabe, claro está, es mucho más duro...

Yo veía por la agitación de sus manos que el sahib estaba muy enojado con su joven compañero: lamentaba haberle confiado una misión. Pero no quería encolerizarse dada su herida en el oído. No se golpea a un perro derribado.

–... En todo caso –prosiguió Speke intentando recuperar su seguridad–, tenemos informaciones sobre el río.

El sahib se incorporó en su camastro.

–Tres mercaderes afirman que hay un río al norte del Tanganika...

Burton me miró; incliné la cabeza para confirmarlo.

–Y ese río –añadió Speke, tras unos instantes de vacilación–, ese río sale del lago.

¡Pero...! ¿Qué estaba diciendo?...

–¡Habérmelo dicho enseguida, Johnny! Eso es formidable. Significa que tal vez lo hayamos encontrado... ¡Hemos encontrado el Nilo!

Speke sonrió. Yo no me moví, temía demasiado que Burton me pidiera que lo confirmase. Afortunadamente, no lo hizo.

–¡Organizaré de inmediato una expedición hacia el norte!

–¿Quieres que alquile piraguas? –propuso tímidamente Speke.

–No, no, Johnny, déjamelo a mí, será mejor...

Heme aquí pues en la mayor de las dos piraguas alquiladas por Burton al jefe Kannena.

Desde hace quince días, subimos hacia el norte. El paisaje desfila, siempre igual, una selva densa con, de vez en cuando, un poblado de pescadores reconocible por las palmeras y los bananos que lo rodean.

Cada noche, acampamos en la ribera.

A medida que avanzamos, los ingleses y los remeros se van poniendo más y más nerviosos. Los remeros a causa de los uabuaris, la tribu que puebla la región. Son, según dicen, caníbales: se alimentan de cadáveres de animales, de mugre y de larvas, pero su plato preferido es el hombre crudo. Los remeros temen verlos aparecer detrás de cada matorral.

Los ingleses, en cambio, están nerviosos porque, diez meses después de haber salido de Zanzíbar, están por fin acercándose a su objetivo. A pesar de su lengua hinchada, el sahib Burton me habla a menudo del Nilo. Le apasiona. En sus ojos enfebrecidos puede leerse el rabioso deseo de descubrir el río sagrado.

–Hace cinco mil años que es un misterio... ¿Te das cuenta? Nadie sabe dónde nace... Y dentro de unos días... vamos a encontrarlo... Tendremos que regresar con otra expedición... dentro de unos meses... descenderemos por el río Ruzizi hasta Egipto... ¿Nos acompañarás, Bombay?

El joven Speke le escucha limpiando su fusil... Está pensativo y silencioso. A veces, tengo la impresión de que se siente inquieto. A veces no. Una oportunidad de dos...

Yo, sólo espero a ver.

Sólo algunos días de navegación.

El lago se hace muy estrecho; estamos llegando al final. Las dos riberas son ahora muy visibles. Puesto que no tenemos ya comida, atracamos en una aldea. Los habitantes gritan y cantan. ¿La alegría de ver que se acerca su cena? No, parecen acogedores.

Nuestros remeros, aliviados, cambian cuentas y telas por plátanos y gallinas. Despliego la cama de campaña del sahib en la playa y le ayudo a instalarse.

–Bombay, ve a buscarme al jefe del poblado, tengo que hacerle algunas preguntas.

Tras unos instantes, regreso con tres jóvenes que visten mantos de corteza imitando la piel del leopardo.

–El jefe no está, son sus hijos.

–Servirán... Pregúntales si conocen el río Ruzizi.

Interrogo a los tres jóvenes. Me cuesta un poco comprender la respuesta pues su lengua no es por completo la mía.

–Dicen que sí.

El sahib Burton se incorpora de pronto en su cama. Los pelos de su barba tiemblan de alegría. Speke se une a nosotros.

–¿Dónde está?

Los tres jóvenes me indican la misma dirección.

–Por allí... a dos días de piragua.

–¡Dos días! –exclama Burton– Dentro de dos días veremos el nacimiento del Nilo... ¿Lo oyes, Johnny? ¡Dos días!... ¿Es un río grande? ¿Mucha agua del lago sale por él?

Hago la pregunta pero, como no estoy seguro de comprender bien la respuesta, vuelvo a hacerla. Idéntica respuesta. Me gustaría hacer la pregunta por tercera vez, pero sé que es inútil. Además, no me quedan ya fuerzas. Busco las palabras para traducirlo.

–¿Bueno, Bombay?

–Dicen... Dicen que el agua del lago no corre por el río. Es a la inversa: es el río el que se vierte en el lago.

–¡No, es imposible! ¡El capitán Speke afirmó que salía del lago! ¿No es cierto, Johnny? ¡Pregúntaselo una vez más!

Hago de nuevo la pregunta, pero conozco ya la respuesta.

–Los tres han visto el río con sus propios ojos. Se vacía en el lago.

Burton suelta espuma de rabia. A él, que por lo general habla tan bien, le faltan de pronto las palabras:

–Pero... ¿qué significa eso? Johnny... Johnny, me dijiste... Afirmaste que el Ruzizi salía del Tanganika...

Speke se aclara la garganta, terriblemente turbado.

–Hum, sí... Bueno... Yo sólo repetí lo que los mercaderes árabes nos habían dicho. Lo que Bombay había traducido...

¡De ningún modo! ¡No es eso lo que traduje!

–Bueno, Bombay, ¿qué puedes tú decir?

Burton me acribilla con la mirada. Siento que todo el asunto se volverá contra mí. Haga lo que haga, me caerá encima. No es el momento de pensar en algo así, pero me viene a la cabeza un proverbio: «Cuando dos elefantes se pelean, siempre es la hierba la que queda aplastada.» Y, ahora, la hierba soy yo. Ni siquiera debo intentar luchar.

–Los mercaderes árabes no estaban de acuerdo. El uno decía que el río salía del lago, el otro que entraba y el tercero que no lo sabía. Creí haber traducido bien, pero sin duda me equivoqué.

El sahib Burton espumea de cólera. Fulmina al joven Speke, luego a mí, luego a Speke, luego a mí. Y de pronto, a pesar de su enfermedad y su debilidad, estalla en todas direcciones con increíble violencia:

–¡Me habéis engañado!... ¡Los dos, me habéis engañado!... ¡Lo único cierto es que este maldito río desemboca en el lago!... ¡Todo este viaje para descubrir algo así! Que no es el Nilo, pues... Todo este maldito viaje para nada...

Luego, como si se hubiera vaciado ya, se tranquiliza, echa la cabeza hacia atrás en su camastro de campaña y repite en un suspiro:

–... todo eso para nada...

Capítulo seis

El regreso tras el fracaso
¡Rumbo al Nyanza!
Speke quiere creerlo aún

Ha aparecido en un recodo del sendero, inmenso.

Speke ha permanecido largo rato inmóvil, sin decir nada, luego ha dicho:

–¡Ése es!

Desde entonces, lo observamos en silencio. Es tan grande que no veo el final: diríase un mar. Su color no es azul ni gris, una mezcla de ambos.

–¡Ése es! –repite Speke–, ¡realmente es ese!

No sé cómo puede saberlo, pero parece creerlo. No puede estarse quieto. Da tres pasos hacia el lago, vuelve hacia mí, se echa la mano a la frente, la quita, vuelve hacia el lago.

–Lo he encontrado... ¡Ése es!... Hay que festejarlo.

Piensa en lo que puede hacer, divisa tres ocas nadando en paz por el lago y arma su carabina.

–¡Bombay, tírales una piedra!

Obedezco. Las aves emprenden el vuelo. El inglés se echa al hombro el fusil, apunta y dispara. Una de las aves deja de aletear y cae como una piedra en la playa de arena marrón.

–¡Blanco!

Los blancos tienen extraños modos de alegrarse.

–Bombay, toma la oca: ¡nos la comeremos esta noche! Entretanto, busquemos un poblado de pescadores.

Tomo el ave, caliente aún, y volvemos a ponernos en marcha.

Hace dieciséis días que caminamos.

He aquí lo que ocurrió después del Tanganika. Tras el encuentro con los tres hijos del jefe, al norte del lago, el sahib Burton quiso ver el río con sus propios ojos. Pero los remeros, aterrorizados por los caníbales, se negaron a seguir adelante. El inglés intentó convencerles con palabras y cuentas, pero de nada sirvió. De ese modo, regresamos a Ujiji y, luego, volvimos a ponernos en marcha hacia Kazeh. El viaje duró tres semanas. Tres semanas terribles para Burton: estuvo enfermo todo el tiempo y, puesto que la expedición es un fracaso, el viaje no le interesaba ya. Prácticamente no dijo nada en todo el trayecto; estoy seguro de que, ahora, detesta a Speke. Conmigo, las cosas van mejor. Llegado a Kazeh, Burton decidió que permaneceríamos allí el tiempo necesario para curarse. Se instaló en casa de su amigo el mercader Snay ben Amir. Speke comenzó entonces a aburrirse, dio vueltas y vueltas y, luego, pidió permiso para ir a ver el otro lago, el Nyanza, al norte de Kazeh. Ante mi gran sorpresa,

Burton aceptó: creo que quiso así librarse por algún tiempo de su compañero. Speke me pidió que le acompañara, con algunos porteadores. Si hubiera tenido elección, me habría negado: desde la jugarreta del Tanganika, creo que Speke no me gusta. De hecho, estoy seguro de ello incluso.

Mientras el sol poniente colorea de naranja las aguas del lago Nyanza, unos niños desnudos, con sus blancos dientes tras una gran sonrisa, corren a nuestro encuentro. Diviso piraguas en la playa y, entre los bananos, el techo de paja de varias chozas.

–¡Acampemos aquí! –anuncia Speke– Bombay, ve a buscarme al hombre del poblado que mejor conozca la región.

Regreso poco más tarde con un anciano de manos arrugadas. Los porteadores han montado la tienda de Speke. El inglés está agachado en la arena, ante un fuego de leña. Tiene en su mano derecha una escudilla llena de agua hirviendo, en la izquierda un termómetro. Todos los niños de la aldea y algunos adultos están de pie rodeándole, observándole.

–Ven a ver –me dice muy excitado–. He medido la altitud del lago y es mucho mayor que la del Tanganika. ¡Es una buena señal!

–¿Cómo lo ha hecho?

–Te lo diré más tarde. No hagamos esperar a nuestro invitado. ¡Dile que se siente!

Speke le tiende unas cuentas de cristal, pero eso no parece interesarle. Mira la escudilla de metal sobre el fuego.

–Pídele hasta dónde ha llegado por el lago.

El hombre me responde que ha seguido la costa en piragua hacia la izquierda y también un poco hacia la derecha.

–¿Ha atravesado el lago? ¿Sabe si hay un río del otro lado? ¿Un río que corra hacia el norte?

El anciano no lo sabe. Dice que nadie ha ido nunca hasta el otro extremo del lago: es demasiado grande para eso.

–¿Cómo de grande?

El hombre se frota el marchito dorso de su mano derecha con el pulgar de la izquierda, reflexiona, luego responde que el lago se extiende hasta el fin del mundo. Sí, hasta el fin del mundo.

Speke hierve.

–Un lago inmenso como un mar y muy elevado... ¡Es éste! En este lago tiene las fuentes el gran Nilo... ¡Lo siento!

Mientras el anciano mira con deseo nuestra escudilla, el inglés examina las aguas obscuras del lago –a cada cual su sueño.

–Regresemos a Kazeh para avisar a Richard. Es absolutamente necesario explorar este lago hasta su extremo norte... Siento que de él sale un río y que es el Nilo.

Imagino ese río corriendo tranquilamente hacia el norte, atravesando primero húmedas selvas, luego sabanas secas, luego una región tan seca que nada crece en ella, ni árboles ni hierba, una región en la que sólo crece arena amarilla, el país de arena –a cada cual su sueño.

–He encontrado las fuentes del Nilo –repite Speke–, ¡yo he encontrado las fuentes del Nilo!

Entreacto

Regreso a Londres

Londres, 9 de mayo de 1859.

Algo había cambiado, pero el capitán John Speke no conseguía saber exactamente qué.

El tiempo era gris y las casas lúgubres, a pesar de una primavera bien entrada ya. Los cascos herrados de los caballos resonaban ruidosamente sobre el adoquinado de la ciudad. Los paseos estaban atestados de calesas, de carrozas, de carros, de carricoches. Unos minutos antes, había estado a punto de ser derribado por un ómnibus de caballos abarrotado, con las damas sentadas en el interior del largo vehículo y los hombres en los bancos de madera instalados en el techo.

El capitán Speke tenía una extraña impresión. Había salido de Londres tres años antes, pero era como si se hubiera marchado la semana anterior. Nada había cambiado realmente: los mismos trajes negros y sombreros de copa para los hombres; los mismos vestidos largos y encorsetados en el talle para las damas; los mismos faroles de gas y los mismos árboles en las calles. Como si el tiempo se hubiera detenido.

Sin embargo, algo era distinto, ¿pero qué? Salió del bulevar por una calleja de tierra batida que llevaba a la Sociedad Real de Geografía. Había polvo por todas partes. Niños harapientos jugaban en el arroyo. Los mismos que hacía tres años.

–*Morning'sir*!

Se volvió y, precisamente cuando respondía al niño, comprendió lo que había cambiado: la mitad de los ruidos de la ciudad había desaparecido. Estaba sordo de un oído. El escarabeo, el dolor, las enfermedades, los lagos, las disputas con Burton, las jornadas de marcha, los animales salvajes, una multitud de recuerdos de África volvieron a su memoria, como un soplo de aire cálido... No era Londres lo que había cambiado en tres años, era él, John Speke.

Cruzó sin dilación la puerta cochera de la Sociedad de Geografía y pidió ver a sir Roderick Murchison.

–¿A quién debo anunciar? ¿Tiene usted cita?

Unos minutos más tarde, John Speke fue invitado a entrar en el despacho del presidente. A sus sesenta y siete años, Murchison había engordado y encanecido. Era difícil imaginarle como explorador. Por lo demás, había sido geólogo más que explorador y había permanecido en Europa.

–¿Ya está usted aquí? –se sorprendió el anciano– Recibí hace tres días un telegrama de Burton procedente de Arabia. No creía verle tan pronto.

Speke vaciló en contárselo todo de entrada. Decidió esperar un poco para ver las reacciones de Murchison.

–Burton estuvo muy enfermo –se limitó a decir–. Se quedó en Aden para recuperar fuerzas. Yo tomé el primer navío a vapor hacia Europa y he llegado esta misma mañana a Londres.

–Bueno, ¿y su viaje hacia los Grandes Lagos? ¿Encontraron ustedes las fuentes del Nilo? ¡Dígamelo todo!

Speke comenzó contando lo del Tanganika y el río Ruzizi; la esperanza y, luego, la decepción.

–De modo que no lo han encontrado...

–Creo que sí –repuso el explorador, como si su vida dependiera de ello.

Contó a Murchison, más atento que nunca, su viaje en solitario hacia el lago Nyanza –al que había rebautizado lago Victoria en homenaje a la reina de Inglaterra, Victoria– y su íntima convicción de haber encontrado las fuentes del Nilo. Luego su regreso hacia Kazeh para anunciar a Burton la buena nueva.

–¿Y qué descubrieron ustedes, cuando ambos regresaron allí?

–¡Nada! Richard se negó a que regresáramos... Ignoro por qué. Me dijo que yo no tenía prueba alguna y que, de todos modos, la expedición había terminado, que regresábamos a Zanzíbar.

–Pero tenía usted pruebas, ¿no es cierto?

–Claro. En primer lugar, el lago se encuentra justamente en la prolongación del Nilo, al sur de éste. Luego, medí su altitud, más de mil metros sobre el mar. Es mucho más que la altitud del Nilo en Gondokoro, que es de cuatrocientos cincuenta metros. Es pues del todo posible que las aguas del lago Victoria corran hasta Gondokoro.

–Son magros indicios...

Speke sintió que vacilaba.

–¡Pero es el lago bueno! No puedo explicarlo, pero estoy seguro...

–No era una crítica, querido amigo. La crítica se la dirigiría yo, más bien, a Burton, que hubiera debido regresar y explorar con usted el lago. Era su deber de jefe.

¿Estaría cambiando el viento?

–Tal vez Richard tuvo miedo de que yo le robara los honores –insistió Speke–. Él era el jefe de la expedición y yo encontré el lago...

Lanzó una ojeada al globo terráqueo que adornaba el despacho de Murchison. En el corazón de África, en una amplia zona marrón, se habían escrito estas palabras: «Tierras desconocidas».

–Si la Sociedad de Geografía lo desea –prosiguió–, si lo desea usted, me gustaría organizar una expedición para explorar el lago Victoria, una expedición a cuya cabeza me pondría... Lo he pensado mucho: podría regresar a Kazeh y, luego, contornear el lago por el oeste para encontrar los ríos que salen de él. Y si, como pienso, el más grande de ellos es el Nilo, me bastará entonces con seguirlo hasta Egipto...

–Interesante... Muy interesante... ¿Podría usted hablarnos de eso, de modo más extenso, uno de estos días?

–Claro.

–¿Sería posible... digamos... mañana? Precisamente presido una reunión de geógrafos.

–¡Mañana! –se atragantó Speke.

Sí, era posible, pero había... antes tenía...

–Debo confesarle... debo decirle que, cuando dejé a Richard en Aden, le prometí aguardar su regreso antes de venir a verle.

Cuando había hecho aquella promesa, realmente pensaba cumplirla. Puesto que Burton era el jefe de la expedición, le parecía normal, aunque ya no se hablaran en absoluto, aguardar su regreso. Sin embargo, en el vapor que le había llevado a Londres, había conocido a un periodista llamado Laurence Oliphan, a quien le había contado la historia. Éste le había explicado que sus méritos nunca serían reconocidos por Burton. Y Speke se había dejado convencer. Debía defender, solo, sus derechos. Por eso, una hora antes, había cruzado sin más espera la puerta cochera de la Sociedad de Geografía.

–¿Está usted seguro de que quiere hacer esta reunión mañana, sin Burton?

Murchison hizo girar maquinalmente el globo terráqueo alrededor de su eje, mientras reflexionaba. Speke contuvo el aliento, como para ayudar al anciano a tomar la decisión adecuada.

–Sí –resolvió Murchison–. Burton tuvo su oportunidad y la echó a perder. Le toca ahora a usted aprovechar la suya.

* * *

Doce días más tarde, Richard Burton llegó a su vez a Londres. Durante el largo viaje en barco, había tenido tiempo de pensar en su próxima expedición. Quería explorar el lago descubierto por Speke, en compañía de éste claro está.

«¡Se han encontrado las fuentes del Nilo!», escuchó en la esquina de una calle.

Se dio la vuelta: era un vendedor de periódicos que pregonaba los titulares para atraer al lector.

Buscó en sus bolsillos, tomó unos peniques, compró el periódico y dio una ojeada al artículo.

El suelo se abrió bajo sus pies.

Speke le había traicionado. Había ido a la Sociedad de Geografía e incluso había convencido a los geógrafos de que le confiaran una expedición. Sin duda había utilizado sus sempiternas sandeces sin fundamento, las que había dicho ya en Kazeh, aquellos vagos «presentimientos», aquellos «lo sé, siento que es el lago bueno».

¡Y los geógrafos le habían creído!

¡Pero qué monstruosa tontería haber permitido que Speke regresara solo a Inglaterra! ¡Qué ingenuidad haber creído que cumpliría su palabra!

Se lo reprochaba a sí mismo. Y lo peor era que la Sociedad de Geografía nunca financiaría dos expediciones semejantes. Puesto que aquel traidor de Speke había logrado la suya, nunca él, Richard Burton, conseguiría otra. Su carrera de explorador acababa de finalizar.

¡Pero aquello no quedaría así! Jamás permitiría que Speke reivindicara tan fácilmente el descubrimiento de las fuentes del Nilo. La batalla sólo había empezado.

Acto II

Hacia el lago Victoria

Capítulo uno

**El regreso de Speke a Zanzíbar
En marcha hacia el lago Victoria
Un ataque de bandidos**

Corro detrás de Baraka por las callejas polvorientas de Zanzíbar.

Y vuelvo a pensar en este proverbio: «Eres dueño de las palabras que no has pronunciado; eres esclavo de las que has dejado escapar.»

A mí el carácter me empuja, más bien, hacia los proverbios con animales: «Un mosquito nunca se aventura por donde aplauden los hombres» o «El mono sabe a qué se expone si utiliza el puerco-espín de taburete» o también «El buey no presume de su fuerza ante el elefante.»

Pero entonces, sin dejar de correr, advierto que, desde hace un año y medio, hubiera debido de mantener en mi cabeza el proverbio sobre las palabras.

Desde mi regreso a Zanzíbar, hace un año y medio, mi amigo Baraka me invita a menudo a beber vino de palma y me hace muchas preguntas sobre mi viaje a los Grandes Lagos. Al principio, le contaba lo que realmente había pasado.

Pero hace algunos meses, puesto que el sahib Speke no regresaba, contrariamente a lo que me había dicho, creyendo que no regresaría nunca, fui un poco más allá de la verdad.

Le conté a Baraka, por ejemplo, que yo era muy amigo de Speke, que me había enseñado a medir la altitud de un lago con una escudilla, o también que quería convertirme en el guía de su próxima expedición.

Le hablé también del país de arena, los pequeños cangrejos que allí viven e, incluso, de una historia de árbol de arena húmeda que crece como un verdadero árbol bebiéndose el rocío, salvo que al morir la arena se seca y se derrumba. Baraka quedó muy sorprendido, pero le aseguré que sí, que era verdad.

De todos modos, no iba a saber nada de la verdad puesto que Speke no regresaría.

Pero Speke ha regresado: hace menos de una hora, Baraka lo ha divisado en el puerto y se ha apresurado a venir a buscarme.

Corro tras él por las callejas de Zanzíbar, y llegamos al puerto chorreando sudor.

Algunos hombres descargan las cajas de un barco a vapor. Un blanco vigila su trabajo, pero no es Speke, ni Burton. El sahib Speke está un poco más allá, a la sombra, sentado sobre un montón de cabos. Me cuesta un poco reconocerle: ha recuperado peso y su pelo amarillo es corto. También su aspecto es distinto; tengo la impresión de que se mantiene un poco más erguido.

–Buenos días sahib –le digo en industaní.

–¡Eh, Bombay! ¡Cómo estás, viejo cocodrilo! ¡Ya ves, he vuelto!

Ya lo veo y sólo me complace a medias. No es que sea bonito, pero a veces soy algo rencoroso: lo que sentí en el lago Tanganika, cuando me echó encima el error del río Ruzizi, todavía me abrasa el pecho.

–¡Pregúntale lo de los árboles de arena! –murmura Baraka en swahili, a mis espaldas.

–¡Sí, sí, está bien!... Pero tú ve a dar una vuelta. No es educado escuchar a la gente. Quiero saludar a mi amigo como es debido.

De hecho, quiero sobre todo librarme de Baraka, que habla también industaní, para que no escuche nuestra conversación. Cuando se aleja arrastrando los pies, me vuelvo hacia el navío y las cajas, y pregunto al inglés:

–¿Es para regresar al segundo lago?

–Sí –responde orgullosamente–, pero esta vez yo seré el jefe de la expedición. No tendremos ya todos los problemas que vivimos con Burton.

–¿Y el otro sahib, allí?

–Es mi ayudante. Se llama James Grant. Es capitán del ejército británico en la India, como yo. Podrás pues hablar con él en industaní... Porque quiero que vengas con nosotros. ¿Querrás ser mi intérprete?

A decir verdad, no lo sé. Justo después de nuestro regreso de los lagos, no habría vuelto con Speke por todo el oro del mundo. Luego, con el tiempo, me dije que, a fin de cuentas, volvería a partir; de hecho, había gastado todo mi dinero. Pero con el paso de los meses ni siquiera me hice ya la pregunta.

—Hum... Ya veremos... ¿Por qué no?... ¡Pero si acepto, me gustaría ser guía!

—No, el guía será Said ben Salim, como la última vez.

—¿Su ayudante, entonces?

—Por qué no, más tarde veremos...

Baraka da vueltas a nuestro alrededor como si fuera una mosca hambrienta. Se acerca por fin y me pregunta en swahili:

—¿Qué te ha dicho? ¡Dime lo que te ha dicho!

Dudo en confesarle que nunca seré guía y que, desde hace unos meses, le he dicho varias mentirijillas.

—Confirma que los árboles de arena existen, ¡tan cierto como existe este barco! Y ha añadido que, en primavera, algunos pájaros hacían incluso en ellos su nido...

* * *

Camino por un estrecho sendero, con un fardo en la cabeza.

Mi cuerpo había olvidado el peso de los fardos y el dolor de los guijarros en mis pies.

A nuestro alrededor, la sabana. Unos antílopes, cuya cabeza sobresale de las altas hierbas, nos observan y luego, de pronto, dan un brinco y huyen como en un sueño.

Desde hace tres meses, hemos atravesado la región de los uamrami, los saqueadores de caravanas. Luego nos hundimos hasta las rodillas en las ciénagas y cruzamos junglas de enmarañadas lianas. Nuestras violentas fiebres desaparecieron en cuanto el sendero ascendió hacia las montañas del Usagara. Luego volvimos a bajar hacia el valle del Ugogo, hacia el estanque Diwa, donde los elefantes beben por la noche y los hombres de día.

Llegaremos pronto a Kazeh.

Comparado con el primer viaje, todo es igual pero todo es distinto.

La caravana es dos veces mayor que la de Burton –casi doscientas personas– y está formada por gente muy distinta. Hay diez soldados hotentotes traídos de África del Sur: puesto que nadie comprende su lengua, siempre están reunidos. Hay también veinticinco soldados baluchis, setenta y cinco antiguos esclavos, cien porteadores más... Por la noche, los que pertenecieron al mismo dueño o son de la misma aldea se agrupan y comen juntos. Speke ha intentado mezclarlos para evitar rebeliones, pero no lo ha conseguido.

Por lo demás, tampoco él se mezcla mucho: pasa todo su tiempo con el capitán Grant. Grant es un hombre muy amable. Todavía no he hablado mucho con él, pero es afable y no se enoja nunca. A veces me recuerda a Speke al comienzo del primer viaje, cuando obedecía a Burton como un niño bueno. Espero el momento en que levante la voz.

Yo, tras la jornada de marcha, me reúno con Mabruki y Baraka. ¡Eso es! Baraka participa en el viaje. Antes de la partida, Speke me preguntó si conocía a alguien que hablara industaní para servir a Grant, y le propuse enseguida a Baraka. Pero, en el mismo momento en que pronuncié su nombre, supe que cometía un grave error. Desde entonces, debo recordar lo que le conté y ver si se corresponde con la realidad.

De momento, salgo bastante bien librado. No soy el guía de la expedición, pero he dicho a mi amigo que muy pronto iba a serlo. Cada noche, ayudo al verdadero guía, Said ben Salim, a distribuir su salario a los porteadores. Tras la partida, aconsejé a Speke que esperara el final del viaje para pagarles, para que no deserten como hicieron con Burton. El inglés me repuso que él no era Burton y se negó. No insistí: un grano de maíz tiene siempre las de perder ante una gallina.

Pero, desde entonces, algunos porteadores huyen casi cada noche. Me pregunto por qué el sahib rechaza mis consejos. Tal vez cree que, si los siguiera, daría la impresión de obedecerme. Y debe demostrar que es el jefe... Me pregunto si es un buen jefe...

Burton, en cambio, sabía escuchar a los granos de maíz.

Con respecto al primer viaje, no son la naturaleza ni los animales los que han cambiado, sino los hombres.

Los de la caravana y los de las aldeas cruzadas: desde hace varios días, los escasos habitantes que divisamos no nos saludan. Nos ven pasar como si tuviéramos una enfermedad grave, como si nos dirigiéramos a nuestra muerte.

* * *

Estoy sentado en el suelo, tras unas cajas amontonadas, con el fusil cargado en las rodillas.

La luna ilumina tan débilmente la sabana que casi no puedo ver nada. El canto de los grillos me acuna y tengo ganas de volver a acostarme, pero mi turno de guardia está sólo empezando. El fuego de campamento me calienta la espalda.

Me aburro.

Hace siete días que estamos detenidos en Jiwa-la-Mkoa, la «Roca-Redonda». Nos faltan porteadores para proseguir: casi todos han desertado. Speke ha enviado dos mensajeros a Kazeh para pedir a los mercaderes árabes sesenta hombres y alimentos. Tardan en regresar.

Anteayer, ordenó que se vigile día y noche el campamento. Hizo poner las cajas en círculo alrededor de las tiendas, para formar un pequeño muro. Ignoro lo que teme.

–Psstt... Ven a ver

El soldado baluchi que vigila el otro lado del campamento, con la bayoneta calada, me hace una señal para que me reúna con él.

–Escucha...

Ruido en las altas hierbas. No veo nada.

–¿Una leona que caza?

–No, tiene miedo del fuego.

–¿Hombres?

–¡Ve a despertar al bwana!

Me levanto, entro en la tienda, levanto la mosquitera, despierto a Speke y le explico lo de los ruidos.

–¡Da la alarma! –susurra– Pero en silencio, conservemos la ventaja de la sorpresa...

En pocos minutos, todos nuestros soldados están al acecho, escondidos detrás de las cajas. Los rumores en las hierbas han cesado. ¿Falsa alarma? Speke ordena permanecer en guardia. Los minutos pasan. Una hiena aúlla a lo lejos. Y, de nuevo, ruidos en las hierbas. A la izquierda, a la derecha y enfrente. Luego, unos gritos. Salen hombres de la maleza, se lanzan corriendo hacia el campamento. Vuelan las lanzas. Una de ellas cae cerca de mí.

–¡Fuego! –aúlla Speke.

Disparos, disparamos contra los asaltantes. Éstos, unos treinta hombres, parecen vacilar de pronto. Algunos se detienen incluso. Creían atacar por sorpresa un campamento dormido y ahora son ellos los sorprendidos. Nuestros disparos aumentan. He aquí a dos que huyen, luego cinco más, luego todos ponen pies en polvorosa como ratas en la espesura.

–¡Alto el fuego! –ordenó Speke– ¿Hay heridos?

No, por fortuna. Todo ha sido tan rápido que me pregunto, incluso, si el ataque se ha producido realmente. La lanza clavada en el suelo, a dos pasos de mí, me demuestra que sí.

El sahib Speke inspecciona el campamento. ¿Cómo ha sabido lo del ataque? A fin de cuentas, tal vez no sea tan mal jefe. Démosle tiempo para probarlo...

Reanudamos nuestra guardia hasta el amanecer.

Por la mañana, mientras desayuno, diez hombres vienen a nuestro encuentro con los brazos levantados en señal de paz. ¿Nuestros asaltantes nocturnos?

–Nuestro jefe quiere hablar con vosotros.

Se lo traduzco a Speke, que acepta.

El jefe en cuestión es un hombre joven de aire altivo. Nos sentamos, Speke, Grant, él y yo, en una tienda.

–Me llamo Manua Sera. La noche pasada os ataqué porque creía que erais árabes... No quería meterme con ustedes.

–¿Qué les reprocha a los árabes? –me hace preguntar Speke.

–Mi padre, Fundi Kira, era el jefe de la región. Yo le sucedí hace dos años, cuando murió. Y como los árabes ganan mucho dinero con las mercancías que hacen pasar por mi territorio, les hago pagar una tasa. Es justo que también yo gane algo de dinero, ¿no?

Speke mueve la cabeza de un modo que no quiere decir sí ni no.

–Los árabes se negaron y amenazaron con destronarme en beneficio de mi hermanastro Mkisiwa. Pero yo no podía tolerar ese comportamiento. No soy una mujer a quien puede tratarse con tanto desprecio. Llegamos pues a las manos: mataron a muchos de los míos y yo maté a muchos de los suyos. Para mi desgracia, me expulsaron de mi palacio. Para su desgracia, ignoraban que yo tenía muchos partidarios fieles. Desde entonces, saqueamos sus caravanas. Han jurado matarme, pero yo quiero la paz. ¿Puede usted ayudarme?

–¿Qué quiere que haga?

–Va usted a Kazeh, ¿no es cierto? Hable con los árabes y dígales que quiero la paz. Para ello, sólo tienen que devolverme mi trono. Y, para demostrarle mi buena fe, le haré un regalo. Hace dos días, capturé un desertor con un fardo de cuentas de cristal. Creo que es de los suyos.

Manua Sera llama a uno de sus lugartenientes:

–¡Trae al desertor!

Speke llama a Baraka y le ordena en industaní:

–Unos hombres traerán un desertor. Le darás cincuenta latigazos.

Tanto al desertor como a Speke, les servirá de lección.

Capítulo dos

Kazeh en la guerra
Un enojoso contratiempo
Baraka, el amigo que ya no lo es

Cuando llegamos a Kazeh, apenas habíamos dejado en el suelo nuestros fardos, recibimos la visita de Snay ben Amir y varios mercaderes. Aunque el anciano árabe guarde altivamente para sí sus sentimientos, los demás han perdido su arrogancia de hace dos años. En algunos siento, incluso, el miedo.

Speke me pide que traduzca.

–Sus dos mensajeros me avisaron de su llegada –explica el jeque Snay–. He retrasado la partida para haceros un buen recibimiento...

–¿Se va?

–Sí, parto a guerrear contra Manua Sera.

–Precisamente me he cruzado con él por el camino, hace unos días y...

–¡Haberle degollado! ¿No degolló usted a ese perro?

–... Y me encargó que le dijera que deseaba la paz.
–¡Demasiado tarde! Desde hace meses, ese bandido provoca nuestra ruina. Se nos acabó la paciencia. Puesto que sólo conoce el lenguaje de la fuerza, le hablaremos en ese lenguaje.
–¿No quiere intentar, más bien, la paz? –insiste Speke, para quien será más fácil encontrar porteadores en tiempos de paz.
–No, estaba a punto de partir al combate con cuatrocientos esclavos cuando supe su llegada. Sólo me he quedado para despedirme de usted.
–Aguarde al menos hasta mañana...
–No, mis hombres me esperan para una gran cena de buey, como exige su tradición antes de una batalla. Esta misma noche nos pondremos en camino. Y si Dios quiere venceremos. *Inch'Allah* !
–*Inch'Allah*! –responde sin vigor Speke, decepcionado al no haber podido evitar esa guerra que retrasará la expedición.

* * *

Kazeh ha cambiado mucho desde hace dos años: el olor del lujo ha desaparecido. En los jardines, los mercaderes no cultivan ya flores sino hortalizas. Algunos tembes han sido transformados en establos. El olor de los purines flota sobre el burgo.

* * *

Musa, uno de los traficantes que se ha quedado aquí, va a contar sus desgracias a Speke: puesto que Manua Sera dejó pasar durante mucho tiempo sus caravanas, los demás mercaderes sospecharon que proporcionaba pólvora a los rebeldes. Por ello desea abandonar Kazeh para ir hacia el norte y propone a Speke hacer una caravana común. Por lo demás, enviará reclutadores por la región para encontrar porteadores.

–¿Cuántos hombres necesitará usted? –pregunta.

–Al menos sesenta –responde el inglés, muy contento ante esa ganga.

* * *

Una semana en Kazeh, ya.

Jafu, otro mercader árabe, ha regresado de una gira de diez días por el distrito para buscar grano. La situación es catastrófica: debido a la guerra, faltan hombres en los campos y las cosechas son escasas. La hambruna mata por todas partes.

–Le aconsejo que aguarde el final de los combates antes de dirigirse al norte –avisa–. Suwarora, el príncipe de Usui, ha dicho que desollaría vivo a quien pasara por su territorio.

El inglés suelta una palabra en su lengua. Debe de ser un taco: diríase que escupe en el suelo.

* * *

Speke se agacha a la sombra de un baobab y traza un círculo en la arena. Dibuja luego un trazo que sale del círculo y sube hacia arriba. Luego, a una mano de distancia por debajo del círculo, un punto.

–Para responder a tu pregunta, he aquí mi plan. El círculo es el lago Victoria.

–¿Nyanza?

–Sí, pero ahora se llama Victoria.

No comprende por qué Speke le ha cambiado el nombre. ¿No estaba bien el que le dieron los africanos? El sahib Burton, en cambio, dejó su verdadero nombre al lago Tanganika.

–El trazo que sube, es el Nilo. Y este punto, debajo, es Kazeh.

Traza una línea que sale del punto y rodea el círculo por la izquierda.

–En cuanto tengamos porteadores, partiremos hacia el norte. Según lo que me han dicho los árabes, atravesaremos Uzinza, Usui, Karagué y Uganda.

–Pero, puesto que el príncipe de Usui no quiere vernos, mejor sería pasar por la derecha del lago, ¿no?

–No, pues es el país de los terribles guerreros massai. Son más peligrosos aún.

–¿Y navegando por el lago?

–Se necesitarían grandes embarcaciones para transportar todas nuestras mercancías, y no las tenemos.

Speke prosigue su curva hasta lo alto del círculo, donde comienza el trazo que sube.

–Si tengo razón, aquí, en Uganda, el Nilo sale del lago. Luego sólo tendremos que seguir su curso hasta Egipto.
–¿El país de arena?
–¿El qué?...
–¿El país donde sólo hay arena amarilla?
–Hum... sí, eso es.
–¿Y luego regresaremos a casa por el mismo camino?
–No, sería demasiado largo. Tú, Baraka, Mabruki y los demás, regresaréis en barco a Zanzíbar. Grant y yo, a Inglaterra.

* * *

Quince días desde nuestra llegada.
Nos llegan noticias de la guerra.
El ejército del jeque Snay rodeó a Manua Sera en una aldea, como se les escapó, los árabes, furiosos, llevaron la devastación a la aldea y el distrito. Matan a las hombres y mandan a las mujeres, los niños y el ganado a Kazeh.
Nunca me han gustado los mercaderes y hoy me gustan menos aún. Sin embargo, guardo para mí mis sentimientos pues, de momento, sólo ellos pueden ayudarnos a encontrar porteadores.
«No insultes al cocodrilo antes de haber cruzado el río.»
Pero de todos modos, no me gustan.

* * *

Puesto que los reclutadores de Musa tardan en regresar, Speke y Grant se fueron durante una semana a cazar el antílope negro. Grant regresó con fuertes fiebres. Nuestro guía Said ben Salim está también enfermo. Y los soldados hotentotes, lo mismo. No soportan el sol de esta región de África. Uno de ellos durmió la siesta sin protegerse la cabeza: al despertar, estaba tan mal que murió por ello.

* * *

Un mes y medio después de nuestra llegada: jornada de llanto en Kazeh. Cuando Snay y sus hombres iban a socorrer una caravana atacada, el ejército rebelde se arrojó sobre ellos. Muchos esclavos murieron bajo una lluvia de lanzas. El jeque, tras haber intentado huir sin éxito, llamó a su servidor:

–Soy demasiado viejo para correr. Toma mi fusil, te lo doy como recuerdo. Yo me acostaré aquí y esperaré lo que Alá haya decidido para mí.

Desde entonces no se le ha vuelto a ver.

Toda la región de Ugogo se ha rebelado ahora. Manua Sera habla de marchar sobre Kazeh.

Nuestra situación se hace cada vez más crítica: no podemos avanzar ni retroceder. Y si nos quedamos, seremos atacados.

* * *

Los reclutadores del mercader Musa han regresado con treinta y nueve porteadores. ¡Sólo treinta y nueve!

–Teníamos ciento veinte pero, al acercarnos a Kazeh, los desastres de la guerra les han asustado. Todos se dispersaron, salvo éstos que hay aquí.

Speke se reúne con Grant, luego me anuncia su decisión:

–Partimos.

–Pero nos faltan hombres...

–De hecho, tú te quedas aquí con el mercader Musa. Guardarás parte del cargamento. Entretanto, yo iré hacia el norte con el capitán Grant, los treinta y nueve porteadores y el resto de la carga. Allí, yo mismo buscaré más hombres. Te los enviaré y tú te reunirás con nosotros llevando el resto del cargamento.

–Pero, sahib, necesita usted un intérprete.

–Baraka será mi intérprete.

–¿Baraka? Pero si no sabe nada... Ni siquiera participó en la primera expedición. ¡Su intérprete soy yo!

–Vigilar el cargamento es una misión de confianza, Bombay, y por eso te la encargo...

Tengo sobre todo la impresión de que Baraka está robándome el puesto.

* * *

Quince días desde la partida de Speke y los demás.

Me pregunto qué están haciendo allí, cómo se las arreglan sin mí. Les imagino marchando hacia el lago. Sin duda cruzan pequeñas aldeas y bosques. ¿Se parecerán las chozas a los tembes de Kazeh? ¿Cómo se deja sentir el hambre? ¿Y qué animales encuentran en la selva y la sabana? ¿Habrá visto Speke un rinoceronte? Hace tanto tiempo que quiere cazar uno...

Me gustaría tanto estar con ellos.

Es curioso: hace cuatro años, cuando el sahib Burton me contrató para el primer viaje, yo tenía sobre todo ganas de dormir a la sombra de un cocotero y de beber vino de palma. Hoy, cuando no sé qué hacer, quisiera caminar, ver de nuevo el gran lago, descubrir Karagué –me han contado cosas muy chuscas sobre las mujeres de ese país. Y me gustaría tanto divisar ese río que los blancos buscan desde hace tanto tiempo, bañarme en sus aguas y seguir su curso hasta el país de arena, que debe de ser maravilloso.

Mis pies son pesados porque permanecen aquí.

* * *

Por fin han llegado algunos porteadores.

Puesto que el mercader Musa está muy enfermo, lo dejo en Kazeh y parto con mi pequeña caravana hacia Mininga, donde me reúno con Speke y los demás. Pero allí, nuestros hombres tienen miedo y se niegan a proseguir: algunos viajeros llegados de Usui han confirmado que el príncipe Suwarora ha construido fortalezas en la frontera y que maltrata a los extranjeros. Speke decide regresar a Kazeh para pedir a Musa cincuenta esclavos, que pagará. Entretanto, Grant se quedará en Mininga con las mercancías.

Mi opinión no tiene importancia alguna, pero no creo que regresando allí tengamos más posibilidades de encontrar porteadores. De hecho, tengo la impresión de que Speke no sabe ya qué intentar para salir bien librado.

* * *

Regreso a Kazeh, pues, tres meses después de nuestra primera llegada. Evidentemente, ninguno de los esclavos de Musa quiere acompañarme.

Nada se arregla; hagamos lo que hagamos, nada se arregla.

–¿Ha regresado usted? ¡Qué alegría! Al parecer necesita porteadores. Podemos procurárselos, pero tendría que ayudarme a hacer la paz con Manua Sera...

Varios mercaderes árabes, temblando de miedo ante el avance del jefe rebelde, han ido al encuentro de Speke. Es divertido verles: en su primer viaje, despreciaban al inglés más que a un perro cojo, porque no hablaba el árabe y sólo le interesaba la caza. Y heles aquí, ahora, implorantes, ¡casi de rodillas!

Para obtener los valiosos porteadores, Speke acepta enviar una delegación de paz a Manua Sera. Se la confía a Baraka. ¿Baraka?...

* * *

Ayer, Baraka regresó triunfalmente con dos ministros del jefe rebelde, uno de ellos tuerto.

Hoy, estamos todos reunidos en un gran tembe, los traficantes árabes, la gente de la expedición y los dos ministros: escuchamos las proposiciones de paz que Baraka hace en nombre de Speke. Yo no escucho, reflexiono, pienso en mi antiguo amigo, en aquél a quien hice entrar en la caravana. Le veo hablar en nombre del inglés, ser su intérprete, al que se envía a las misiones difíciles.

No estoy orgulloso de ello, pero soy muy envidioso.

Tras las proposiciones de paz, los dos ministros se retiran para discutir. Me acerco a Baraka, que habla en industaní con Speke.

–¡Vete a dar una vuelta! –me suelta en swahili– No es muy educado escuchar a la gente. Tengo cosas importantes que decir a mi amigo el sahib.

¡Pero... si es una orden! Eso no es bueno, no es bueno en absoluto. Me alejo un poco, hirviendo de cólera: él, mi viejo amigo, me da órdenes como a un esclavo. Sé que está tramando algo para arrebatarme definitivamente el puesto...

Cuando ha terminado con Speke, le interpelo en swahili:

–Eh, Baraka, ¿no estarás robándome un poco el puesto? ¿Qué le has contado al sahib para convertirte en su intérprete?

–Nada. Nada en absoluto. Él solo vio que soy más inteligente que tú. No tuve que inventar nada para hacerme el interesante.

–¿Inventar?

–Árboles de arena, por ejemplo.

–Ah, ya comprendo... Me estás haciendo pagar mis errores. Gracias, amigo mío, por recordármelo. Pero ten mucho cuidado de no cometerlos tú mismo, ten mucho cuidado...

* * *

Un mensajero del príncipe Suwarora ha llegado a Kazeh. Quiere saber por Musa, al que conoce personalmente, si los árabes albergan contra él sentimientos hostiles. Desea que una delegación vaya a tranquilizarles.

El mercader Musa, cada vez más enfermo, propone a Speke que lleve la respuesta en su lugar. Seremos, así, bien recibidos. Eso nos supone una preocupación menos.

Queda el problema de los porteadores.

* * *

La noche está muy avanzada. Cantos lúgubres se elevan de Kazeh. Los he oído ya en alguna parte, ¿pero cuándo? Speke nos ha reunido con toda urgencia. Por la tarde, todo se ha acelerado: el ministro tuerto ha anunciado de pronto que no había ya tratado de paz y ha huido disparando tras de sí una flecha.

—Partimos mañana al amanecer —explica el inglés.

Baraka traduce y yo rabio —me pregunto qué le habrá contado a Speke para obtener mi puesto. ¿Le habrá hablado de esos estúpidos cangrejos imaginarios y otras animaladas de arena? Espero que no.

—Said ben Salim, eres nuestro guía pero estás demasiado enfermo para proseguir: volverás a Zanzíbar en cuanto las caravanas pasen de nuevo. Llevarás contigo a los soldados hotentotes, demasiado débiles también para proseguir. Los demás salimos hacia Mininga. Encontraremos allí al capitán Grant y el cargamento. Reclutaré porteadores y, luego, proseguiremos hacia Uzinza, Usui, Karagué y Uganda.

De pronto, recuerdo dónde había oído antes esos siniestros cantos: fue aquí mismo, en Kazeh, hace tres meses y medio, la noche de nuestra llegada.

En alguna parte de la ciudad, los mercaderes árabes y sus esclavos están haciendo una cena de buey. Mañana irán a combatir al temible Manua Sera.

Capítulo tres

**En marcha hacia el norte
El kaquenzingiriri contra el hongo
«Encuentro» con el príncipe Suwarora**

P ie derecho, pie izquierdo, pie derecho...
Me satisface reemprender el camino.

El sol es cálido y el sendero pedregoso bajo mis pies desnudos, pero me gusta. El bosque y los campos se suceden. Atravesamos llanuras donde crece una palmera llamada pan de especias. No es el camino de hace tres años, cuando descubrimos el Nyanza: hoy vamos hacia el oeste, para rodear el lago.

Pie izquierdo, pie derecho, pie izquierdo...

En Mininga, encontramos al capitán Grant y el material. Speke consigue contratar porteadores, pero como tienen miedo del príncipe Suwarora, se niegan a marchar más de dos días y exigen, por cada jornada, diez collares de cuentas por hombre –diez veces lo que pagan los árabes. Speke gruñe, pero no tenemos elección: debemos avanzar.

Pie derecho, pie izquierdo, pie derecho...

Parada en la aldea de Nunga. Puesto que los porteadores se niegan a proseguir, Speke sigue como explorador. Toma consigo a Baraka –¡hijo de chacal!– y me deja aquí con Grant y el cargamento. Lo único interesante de la aldea es su jefe, un anciano de pelo blanco respetado por sus súbditos y por sus cuatro esposas. Basta con ver su choza para comprender por qué: en la empalizada, las manos y los cráneos de aquéllos a quienes ha ordenado ejecutar como ejemplo.

Por miedo a cometer una fatal tontería, permanezco muy a menudo con el capitán Grant. Ese hombre me hace pensar en los cortinajes que hay en casa del sultán de Zanzíbar. Son tan finos, tan ligeros y leves que se ve a su través y se olvida incluso su existencia. Grant es igual: es tan amable, obedece siempre sin refunfuñar, no se queja nunca de las fiebres ni la fatiga, se le oye tan poco que olvidas que existe. Espero el momento en que el velo se desgarre y muestre otro rostro, como ocurrió con Speke y con Baraka-la-hiena.

He aquí que, tras quince días de espera, regresan.

–¡Una catástrofe! –se lamenta el inglés– Quedamos bloqueados en la aldea del jefe Makaka. Para dejarnos pasar, exigía un regalo, el hongo como lo llaman. Ninguna de las telas que yo le ofrecía estaba bastante bien. Quería un deolé, uno de esos magníficos echarpes de seda que guardo para los príncipes y los reyes. ¡Pero no para los jefezuelos! Le he dicho que no teníamos, pero Baraka creyó oportuno añadir que, tal vez, buscando bien... Tras semejante confesión, era inútil resistir.

Echo una ojeada a Baraka, bastante contento de su torpeza.

—Y todo para nada: no hemos encontrado porteadores. De modo que cambié mi plan. Quise enviar a Baraka con una misión al príncipe Suwarora, para que nos mandara ochenta porteadores. Pero Baraka tuvo miedo de ir y me vi obligado a enviar, en su lugar, a Makinga, uno de nuestros antiguos porteadores.

Miro a Baraka-el-escarabajo pelotero-torpe-y-cobarde, con tanta fuerza como puedo. Me gustaría tanto que volviera la cabeza hacia mí y, luego, bajara la mirada, pero no lo hace.

—¿Qué hacemos entretanto? —pregunta Grant.

—Usted se queda aquí y yo regreso a Kazeh. Un viajero me ha indicado que el mercader Musa había sucumbido a su enfermedad. Sus esclavos son libres pues. Tal vez nos acompañen al norte...

El inglés se vuelve hacia mí.

—Tú vienes conmigo.

—¿Yo? —digo falsamente extrañado y realmente feliz.

Baraka clava por fin los ojos en el suelo, vencido.

«La mosca puede volar tanto como quiera, nunca se convertirá en un pájaro.»

* * *

Pie derecho, pie izquierdo, pie derecho...

Esta vez, nos dirigimos de veras hacia el norte.

Tras un rápido regreso a Kazeh, por fin tenemos porteadores bastantes para seguir adelante. También encontramos a Nasib, un viejo guía árabe que ha ido varias veces a Uganda. Él nos conduce a través de las campiñas y los bosques de Uzinza. Cada paso nos acerca al misterioso río y al país de arena. Estoy impaciente por verlo.

Tanto más cuanto el cielo se aclara sobre nuestras cabezas: el príncipe Suwarora nos ha enviado cuatro mensajeros para decirnos que, aunque no pudiera proporcionarnos los ochenta hombres pedidos, nos recibiría de muy buena gana. Nos ha hecho llegar también un kaquenzingiriri, una larga varilla de bronce con talismanes colgando alrededor, para que nos ayude a hacernos respetar por el camino.

A pesar de todas esas buenas señales, el sahib está muy inquieto: desde nuestra partida de Zanzíbar, más de la mitad de nuestras mercancías ha sido gastada o robada por los desertores, y otra parte acaba de ser hurtada a Grant mientras regresábamos de Kazeh. ¿Tendremos bastante para llegar hasta el fin? Pues sin cuentas de cristal ni telas, se acabaron los porteadores y la comida, se acabó pues la expedición...

Al acercarnos a cada aldea, la inquietud del sahib aumenta un poco más.

Así es como ocurre: el jefe de la aldea, con una gran sonrisa en los labios, nos desea la bienvenida y nos ofrece una vaca. Una vaca flaca, sólo con la piel y los huesos y unas ubres secas como una calabaza vacía. A cambio, nos pide, si es posible, un regalito, apenas un minúsculo recuerdo de nuestro paso. Speke toma algunas telas en un fardo y se las tiende con ceremonia, como si se tratara de la cosa más hermosa del mundo. El jefe de la aldea echa una ojeada y las rechaza.

–Estoy un poco decepcionado. Le ofrezco la mejor vaca de la región y usted me da ese trapo. ¿Acaso no tiene más valor nuestra amistad? Speke suelta una tosecilla, incómodo, luego añade otros pedazos de tela. El jefe de la aldea los rechaza, con desdén esta vez.

–No solicitaba gran cosa, pero así me siento humillado. Quédese con la vaca, es suya. Volveremos a vernos mañana. Tal vez haya recuperado la generosidad...

Al día siguiente, el jefe de la aldea vuelve a la carga. Speke le recibe con el kaquenzingiriri en la mano -nunca se sabe, eso puede impresionarle, aunque los talismanes no tienen todos sus poderes, pues no estamos todavía en el país de Suwarora. Speke ofrece siempre más tela y, también, collares de cuentas e hilo de latón. El jefe vacila, explica que no es posible comprar una vaca al precio de una cabra; se va, regresa luego. La cosa puede durar horas y horas.

Finalmente, recupera la sonrisa y anuncia:

–A mi esposa sus regalos le parecen muy hermosos y me dice que los acepte.

Speke, aliviado, se dispone a levantarse: es ya hora de ponerse en marcha.

–Y ahora que hemos terminado con los regalos de mi esposa –prosigue el jefe–, hablemos de los míos...

Entonces, loco de rabia, el inglés abandona y me deja proseguir solo las negociaciones –a mí, no a Baraka-el-ñu-destituido. No sé cómo son las cosas en el país de Speke –me ha dicho que los objetos tenían un precio, los comprabas o no, pero que no perdías el tiempo en discusiones–, no sé cómo ocurre allí, pero le cuesta comprender que aquí las negociaciones son un juego. Es un modo de conocerse, de medirse con el otro, de ganar un poco más con ciertos ardides, incomodando, fingiendo que te vas para regresar luego... Por fin, siempre te pones de acuerdo en el precio, te estrechas la palma, bebes vino de palma y los tam-tam anuncian la buena nueva a la aldea.

En la región de Uzinza, jugamos a ese jueguecito con Lumeresi, uno de los principales reyezuelos del lugar, luego con Pongo, un jefe de distrito muy duro de pelar en los negocios, luego con N'yaruwamba, el jefe del siguiente distrito, que rechazaba siempre lo que antes había aceptado –y eso es deshonesto.

A pesar de esas largas paradas, avanzamos y nos acercamos a la frontera con Usui. Allí, todo será más fácil. Los cuatro mensajeros de Suwarora nos dijeron que el príncipe no nos haría pagar nada: sólo quiere vernos.

* * *

—¡Dile a tu bwana que debe pagarme!
—¡Pero si vuestro príncipe dijo que no pediría nada!
—Él no, pero a nosotros tienen que pagarnos por nuestra misión.

Acabamos de entrar en Usui, y los mensajeros intervienen a su vez.

—¡Nunca! —se enoja Speke— Les pagaré cuando nos hayan llevado hasta su Suwarora. ¡No antes!

Los mensajeros amenazan:

—Queremos un brazalete de cuentas por persona, ¡y enseguida! De lo contrario, haremos que les retengan aquí durante un mes...

Ante semejante chantaje, Speke sólo puede pagar.

Reemprendemos la marcha. Atravesamos una gran selva por la que damos largos rodeos, desembocamos luego en unos campos. Sólo las colinas, redondeadas y cubiertas de maleza, no están cultivadas. En plena plantación de bananos se ocultan unos poblados hechos con chozas de hierbas.

—¡Quiero un hongo! —grita el jefe del distrito.

El jefe es también un brujo: lleva en la frente un pedazo de caracola y un pequeño cuerno de oveja en la sien. Ejerce su magia al pie de un árbol del que cuelga una cornamenta de búfalo lleno de polvo sagrado. Una pezuña de cebra, colgada de un cordel, pende sobre un recipiente de agua hundido en la tierra.

—Extraño lugar para la magia —ironiza Speke.

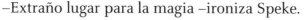

–Muy bien –le responde el jefe brujo–, puesto que es usted capaz de una mayor magia, haga que brote un manantial del suelo.

El sahib reflexiona y me hace responder:

–Lo haré, pero antes, déme usted ejemplo.

El brujo se queda sin palabras y, para no quedar en ridículo, nos deja pasar sin pagar. Escalamos una montaña bastante alta y, en la cumbre, damos con unos oficiales del ejército de Suwarora que –¡qué originalidad!– exigen derechos de paso. Normalmente, el kaquenzingiriri debería permitirnos proseguir sin pagar, pero los oficiales no lo entienden de ese modo. Speke, más irritado que nunca, paga prometiendo quejarse al príncipe.

Descendemos la montaña, atravesamos un valle embarrado, escalamos luego una segunda montaña. Al otro lado, al fondo de un segundo valle, un gran burgo formado por anchas chozas muy separadas. En el centro, rodeado por una triple cerca de matorrales espinosos, una choza tres veces mayor que las demás: el palacio de Suwarora.

Se nos dice que nos instalemos algo apartados, junto a las viviendas de los servidores, a la espera de ser recibidos por el príncipe.

Al anochecer, nos visita un mensajero de Uganda. Ha llegado hasta aquí para pedir, en nombre de su rey, la mano de la hija de Suwarora, conocida por su maravillosa belleza. Pero la infeliz acaba de morir y el príncipe, por temor al rey Mtesa, intenta substituirla por un lote de alambre de cobre.

–Apuesto la cabeza a que Suwarora no cumplirá sus promesas –refunfuña Speke–. Tendremos que pagar nuestra parte del alambre...

Al día siguiente, en efecto, vienen a vernos los negociadores del príncipe. Tras quince días de discusiones, el hongo se eleva a cincuenta rollos de alambre de latón, veinte de buena tela, cien cordones y cuatro mil kutuamnasi, que son cuentas de cristal transparente. Más treinta y cuatro rollos de alambre de latón y seis de tela más, para los hijos del príncipe.

–Pueden proseguir su camino –anuncia uno de los negociadores–. Una escolta les acompañará hasta la frontera de Karagué.

–Pero... no hemos visto al príncipe.

–Tal vez les reciba la próxima vez.

Al día siguiente, levantamos el campo y nos ponemos en marcha hacia el norte, cruzamos la otra montaña que domina el valle y penetramos luego en una hermosa y espesa selva. Graciosas palmeras, huertos de bananos, cardos silvestres la convierten en un lugar maravilloso. Un río de transparentes aguas corre hacia el este, hacia el lago Nyanza.

De pronto, un pájaro khongota atraviesa el sendero. Nasib, nuestro anciano guía, exclama en árabe:

–¡Eso es señal de feliz viaje!

Traduzco al industaní, pero Speke no reacciona.

Perdido en sus preocupaciones, se muerde nerviosamente el labio inferior. Cierto es que nuestra situación no es gloriosa. Yo mismo comienzo a inquietarme mucho: al ritmo en que desaparecen nuestras mercancías, apenas tendremos bastantes para cruzar el país de Karagué y, tal vez, Uganda. ¿Pero que será luego de nosotros?

Capítulo cuatro

**Un recibimiento digno de un rey
Extrañas costumbres
Cacería de rinocerontes
¡Ya le dije que era buena señal!**

Como si le hubiera picado una mosca, el viejo Nasib levanta los brazos al cielo y echa a correr ante sí. Más adelante, en el sendero, otro hombre levanta también los brazos al cielo. Ambos se reúnen, se abrazan, se palmean la espalda, luego regresan lentamente, discutiendo.

–¡Es mi amigo Kachuchu! –exclama Nasib– Le conocí aquí en un anterior viaje.

Traduzco para Speke y Grant.

–Ya les dije ayer que el pájaro khongota era señal de viaje feliz –prosigue–. Rumanika, el rey de Karagué, nos ha enviado a Kachuchu. Por aquí todo se sabe muy pronto. El rey quiere recibir a los dos hombres blancos en su palacio. Kachuchu dice que no tendrán que pagar tasa alguna. En los poblados, los jefes les darán incluso toda la comida que necesiten y el rey la pagará.

Speke esboza una tímida sonrisa: las falsas promesas de Suwarora se agitan sin duda aún en su cabeza. «El que ha sido mordido por una serpiente desconfía de una oruga.»

La caravana se pone en marcha, guiada por Kachuchu. De las ochenta personas que la forman aún no somos ya muchos los que procedemos de Zanzíbar. Están Speke y Grant, unos veinte soldados baluchis, Mabruki y su tamtam, Baraka, yo, y eso es todo, poco más o menos. El viejo Nasib, por su parte, sólo se nos unió en Kazeh. Por lo que a los porteadores se refiere, nos acompañan durante unos días y, luego, regresan a su casa; y nosotros contratamos otros.

Karagué es un hermoso país. A nuestra izquierda se elevan cumbres bastante altas: las montañas de la Luna. Los hierbajos cubren las laderas. Speke observa con ganas los rinocerontes que se refugian en las espesuras de acacias. A la derecha, rebaños de topis ramonean apaciblemente en los valles. Son antílopes grandes y gordos. El lago Nyanza está mucho más lejos, a la derecha, demasiado lejos para que lo veamos.

De pronto, gritos a mi espalda. Hombres y mujeres se nos acercan corriendo y nos sobrepasan; un largo cortejo ruidoso. En cabeza, cuatro hombres llevan en sus hombros un ancho rollo de cuero negro. En el interior adivino, sobresaliendo, la cabeza de una mujer.

–Se ha casado esta mañana –me explica Kachuchu–. Los hombres del poblado la han envuelto en una piel y corren a depositarla en el lecho del novio. Esa es la tradición.

Kachuchu inclina la cabeza para ver mejor a la recién casada.

–¡Es hermosa! Ha debido de costar cara.

–¿Cara?

–Un hombre que quiere casarse debe dar vacas y corderos al padre de su futura mujer.

–¿Y si la mujer no es feliz?

–Puede abandonar a su marido pero debe devolver las vacas y los corderos.

En el siguiente poblado, encontramos de nuevo el cortejo. El jefe, en cuanto conoce nuestra llegada, acude con corderos, aves de corral y batatas. No pide nada a cambio. Speke le ofrece, de todos modos, un poco de tela roja, que el jefe acepta casi excusándose. Es un recibimiento tan relajante como una buena siesta.

Nasib tenía razón: el rey lo paga todo por nosotros. Me pregunto qué oculta tanta amabilidad.

* * *

Rumanika, sentado en el suelo con las piernas cruzadas, se encuentra en una amplia choza. De gran talla y noble aspecto, viste una simple choga negra, que es un amplio manto. Por todo ornamento lleva unos calzones de ceremonia, de cuentas coloreadas, y pulseras de cobre bellamente cinceladas. Su hermano Nnanaji es un gran doctor envuelto en una tela a cuadros, en la que se han cosido algunos talismanes. A su lado, largas pipas de arcilla negra.

–¡Sean bienvenidos!

El rey se esfuerza por hablar en swahili. Le comprendo pues perfectamente y traduzco para Speke y Grant.

–¿Qué impresión han tenido ustedes viendo Karagué y sus montañas? –pregunta orgullosamente Su Majestad– ¿No son las más hermosas del mundo?

Prudentemente sentados detrás del rey, seis chiquillos tienen su mismo rostro oval y sus mismos ojazos inteligentes. Son sus hijos. Vestidos con un taparrabos de cuero, llevan anudado bajo el mentón un pequeño talismán que debe procurarles buenos sueños.

¿Y qué les ha parecido Usui?

El rey sonríe: está claro que sabe ya el detestable recibimiento que nos ha reservado Suwarora. Speke responde que si todas esas tasas no existieran, sería mucho mejor para el comercio.

–Pero ustedes –prosigue el rey–, ¿a qué clase de comercio se dedican?

Speke le habla del Nilo, del lago Nyanza Victoria, de la guerra en Kazeh, de Uganda adonde vamos para ver el nacimiento del río.

Al rey le intriga que se acuda de tan lejos para ver un río.

–¿Pero cómo lo hacen para conocer su camino y saber dónde están?

El inglés le muestra una brújula y el instrumento para medir la altura del sol en el cielo.

—¿Pero el sol —se pregunta el rey—, es el mismo que sale cada mañana o nace a cada aurora un nuevo astro?

Speke le explica que el sol es una bola de fuego y la tierra una bola de roca que gira sobre sí misma, y que por esta razón hay día y noche. El rey se siente realmente muy interesado —y yo también.

—¿Y qué tamaño tiene la Tierra, con respecto a Karagué?

El sahib le habla sobre los continentes y los océanos, el tamaño de cada uno de ellos, los barcos que navegan por los mares, tan grandes que cada uno puede transportar varios elefantes.

Fuera, la noche cae ya, es hora de instalar el campamento.

—Mañana me contará usted el resto —anuncia Su Majestad—. Me han dicho ustedes que iban a Uganda. No se puede entrar allí sin ser anunciado. Enviaré pues un mensajero a mi amigo Mtesa, el rey de Uganda. Para ir y volver necesitará un mes. Podremos seguir hablando de esas cosas tan interesantes.

* * *

Nos aguardan unas canoas a orillas de un pequeño lago. Son tan cortas que sólo dos personas pueden embarcar, además de los dos remeros. Los ingleses van en una canoa, Baraka-el-lagarto-que-se-creía-cocodrilo y yo en otra.

Puesto que me niego a hablar con mi compañero de piragua –mal perdedor, me busca las cosquillas cada vez que puede, como el otro día, cuando quiso hacer creer a los ingleses que yo robaba cuentas de los fardos y tuve que utilizar los puños para defender mi honor–, como me niego a hablar con él, pues, observo el paisaje. Los remeros se abren camino, primero, a través de un bosque de cañas, que nos lleva al agua abierta. La vista es magnífica: un espeso césped cubre las montañas que rodean el pequeño lago. Aquí y allá, bosquecillos de acacias cuya forma recuerda las nubes.

En su canoa, Speke toma notas y hace dibujos. Él ha solicitado visitar las montañas de la Luna y sus ríos. Le servirá para hacer un mapa del país. Para que todo estuviera perfectamente organizado, el rey nos ha precedido por la mañana.

Los remeros remontan la corriente de un pequeño río hasta un segundo lago, al pie de la montaña Moga-Namirinzi. Una última palada y llegamos a una playa. Varias hileras de espectadores nos aclaman con respeto. Speke baja de la canoa, orgulloso como un soberano. A los sones de una música ensordecedora, subimos hacia una gran choza llamada «palacio de las fronteras». Rumanika nos aguarda allí para una comida de plátanos cocidos y cerveza pombe.

A los postres, mientras el rey y los ingleses fuman en pipa, Su Majestad explica los ríos que bajan de las montañas de la Luna, cuenta cómo se reúnen y forman pequeños lagos, de los que sale otro río que fluye hacia el gran lago Nyanza.

–Y más al norte –pregunta Speke–, ¿hay ríos que salgan del lago Victoria... Nyanza?

Rumanika responde que, efectivamente, en Uganda, varios ríos salen del lago.

–¿Está usted seguro de que salen? –insiste febrilmente el inglés– ¿De que abandonan el lago y no que se vierten en él?

El rey confirma la dirección de los ríos. Speke, muy alegre, se vuelve entonces hacia Grant y le dice unas palabras en su lengua. Luego brinca como un mono.

–¡Voy a enseñarle algo!

Corre a tomar de sus cosas un pequeño recipiente y otros objetos. Llena el recipiente de agua y lo pone sobre el fuego que ha servido para cocer los plátanos.

–Mire, Majestad, voy a medir ante usted la altitud del palacio de las fronteras. En primer lugar, meto el termómetro en el agua y espero a que hierva.

Cuando aparecen las primeras burbujas en el fondo del recipiente, toma el termómetro y lee la temperatura.

–A nivel del mar, el agua hierve a cien grados Celsius. Pero cuanto más se sube, más baja la temperatura de ebullición. Aquí, el agua hierve a sólo noventa y seis grados.

El inglés saca su cuaderno y lo hojea hasta encontrar una página cubierta de cifras.

—Según mi cuadro, cuando el agua hierve a noventa y seis grados la altura es de mil doscientos metros sobre el nivel del mar.

Ignoro si Su Majestad habrá comprendido algo; ni se inmuta.

—¿Escribirá usted eso en su cuaderno?

—Claro está.

—Muy bien, eso está muy bien —se felicita el soberano, contento de que le recuerden.

* * *

Hay algo muy curioso en el país de Karagué. En Kazeh, el mercader Musa nos había hablado de ello, pero a Speke le costaba creerlo. Quiere verificarlo con sus propios ojos.

Visitamos pues a una cuñada del rey. Está sentada en el centro de su choza, desnuda por completo, y la cosa supera todo lo que yo pude imaginar.

La muchacha es tan gorda que no puede mantenerse de pie. Ni siquiera consigo reconocer sus formas: sus pliegues se mezclan, los pechos, el vientre, los muslos, los grasientos colgajos bajo sus brazos. A su alrededor han colocado botes de leche.

Para mostrar que forman parte de la familia real, las muchachas de Karagué deben ser enormes. De modo que, desde su más tierna edad, las atiborran de leche: su padre, con la vara en la mano, las castiga cuando no beben bastante.

La cuñada del rey sólo tiene dieciséis años, pero ya tan solo puede moverse a cuatro patas, como un hipopótamo.

Speke le pide autorización para medir el contorno de su brazo, de su vientre, del muslo y la pantorrilla. Orgullosa de sus regias formas, la muchacha acepta complacida. Su muslo es tan grande como mi propio vientre, y tras una buena comida.

Cuando nos separamos de ella, toma un bote de leche y bebe unos tragos para aumentar su belleza.

* * *

También el hombre blanco tiene curiosas y sorprendentes costumbres.

El otro día, puesto que el mensajero no había regresado aún de Uganda, Speke me pidió que le acompañara por la campiña de Karagué, con un guía del rey. Caminamos varias horas y volvimos al pequeño lago. Allí, nuestro guía escrutó largo rato los alrededores, se dirigió hacia un amplio bosquecillo de acacias, luego hacia otro bosquecillo, algo más lejos. Examinó el suelo en busca de huellas, se acercó a una tercera espesura y nos indicó por signos que nos reuniéramos con él.

—¡Por allí! —le dije a Speke.

El inglés se puso el dedo en la boca para hacerme callar. Cargó tres fusiles, me dio uno, otro al guía y se quedó con el último.

La espesura era tan densa que resultaba imposible penetrar en ella, salvo por tres o cuatro estrechos pasos. Speke se agachó y entró en uno de ellos, haciéndonos señales de que le siguiéramos. Fui reculando: sabía lo que nos aguardaba en el interior y no me atraía en absoluto.

Hacía mucho calor y el sudor me caía en los ojos.

A cada lado del paso, había un muro de púas.

De pronto, ante nosotros, se escuchó un ruido sordo, un jadeo.

Speke se detuvo y el tiempo también. Me hubiera gustado estar en otra parte, no importa dónde pero no aquí.

El animal apareció entonces. Ancho como el paso. Una hembra inmensa, más alta que un hombre, con dos largos cuernos en el hocico. Gruñó, pataleó. Estábamos demasiado cerca: iba a cargar. Speke se llevó el fusil al hombro. De pronto, el animal corrió hacia nosotros. Speke disparó. Tocado en la frente, el animal prosiguió su carrera desviándose levemente a la derecha. En un reflejo, el inglés se arrojó hacia la izquierda, en las acacias. Detrás, el guía y yo le imitamos. Las púas me desgarraban el rostro, pero ni siquiera lo advertía. Tenía tanto miedo que sólo pensaba en el animal que me había rozado al pasar. Detrás de él, tan aterrorizado como yo, le seguía una cría.

–¡Venid! –ordenó Speke.

Salimos de la maleza. La hembra herida y su cría huían a campo abierto, en busca de otro bosquecillo donde refugiarse. El inglés corría tras ellos. Me pregunto por qué caza rinocerontes: su carne ni siquiera es buena. Creo que le gusta tener miedo. Reconozco que se necesita valor para enfrentarse con semejantes monstruos, pero, ¿de qué sirve ese valor?

Speke hirió por segunda vez al animal, que trepó con su cría hacia las montañas, hacia un bosquecillo tan denso como el primero y que tapaba la entrada de un estrecho hoyo. Allí había otros tres rinocerontes. En cuanto nos olieron, cargaron de frente.

Speke disparó contra uno de ellos, que se derrumbó tras dar unos pasos. Se apoderó de mi fusil y disparó sobre el segundo rinoceronte, pero falló. Nos arrojamos al suelo para evitarlo. El inglés tomó el fusil del guía y volvió a disparar. Pero las dos bestias estaban ahora demasiado lejos, bajando por la pendiente sin poder detenerse.

La hembra herida y su cría habían desaparecido.

El sahib se acercó al rinoceronte muerto. Muy satisfecho, lo observó y lo midió. Me explicó que, en su país, su casa estaba llena de animales muertos cuya carne había sido substituida por paja. Está muy orgulloso de ello. No comprendo de qué sirve eso.

–Lástima que no pueda llevarme éste a casa –se lamentó–. Le cortaremos la cabeza y se la ofreceremos como regalo a Rumanika.

Los hombres blancos tienen curiosas costumbres.

* * *

A menudo, el rey y el inglés se encuentran y discuten. Hablan de sus dos países, de la historia, de las tradiciones.
Traduzco.
–Pero usted, Majestad, ¿cómo llegó a ser rey?
–Cuando murió mi padre, Dagara, su cadáver fue envuelto en una piel de vaca. Tres días más tarde, tres de los gusanos que había engendrado fueron tomados y colocados en palacio. Allí, uno de ellos se transformó en león, otro en leopardo y el tercero en un palo. Y todo porque él había sido rey. Luego llevaron su cuerpo a la montaña Moga-Namirinzi, y mi pueblo construyó una choza alrededor. Llegó luego el momento de conocer a su sucesor. Mi padre tenía tres hijos legítimos: Nnanaji, Rogero y yo. Un brujo sacó un pequeño tam-tam ligero como una pluma. Pero, una vez cargado de talismanes, el tam-tam se volvió tan pesado que ningún hombre podía levantarlo ya. Ninguno salvo aquél a quien los espíritus reconocerían como heredero del trono. Fui el único que pasé la prueba. Mi hermano Rogero se rebeló entonces y em-

prendió la huida. Mi hermano Nnanaji, en cambio, me aceptó como rey.

Speke escucha con mucha atención. Sé que no cree en los espíritus, en los brujos, en los talismanes, en la magia, en todas esas cosas. Para no lastimar al rey, no lo dice. Pero cuando su mirada se cruza con la mía, siento que me hace en silencio esta pregunta: «¿Cree el rey, realmente, en todo eso?»

Más tarde, los dos hombres hablan de la Luna. Su Majestad quiere saber si cambia cada día de rostro para burlarse de los hombres. El inglés le explica que no, que la Luna es sólo un gran pedrusco que gira alrededor de la Tierra.

–¿Pero cómo nacieron la Tierra, la Luna y el Sol?

–Dios los creó, hace mucho tiempo –responde Speke–. Al principio, no había nada. Dios hizo entonces los cielos y la tierra, luego el Sol y el agua, los árboles y los animales, y por fin al hombre y a la mujer. Lo creó todo en seis días y, al séptimo, descansó. Mucho más tarde, nos envió a su hijo Jesucristo para que quien crea en él tenga vida eterna. Jesucristo es nuestro salvador. Le hablaré más de Él en los próximos días. Cristo hizo grandes cosas y realizó numerosos milagros, como multiplicar los peces, por ejemplo. Después de morir, incluso resucitó de entre los muertos.

El rey escucha cortésmente y, cuando acabo de traducir, me dirige una extraña mirada. Una mirada que significa: «Tú conoces bien al hombre blanco, ¿cree en todo lo que me está contando?»

* * *

Un mes y medio después de nuestra llegada al país de Rumanika, se escuchó el tambor de Uganda. Molá, un mensajero del rey Mtesa, llegó con una gran escolta de hombres, mujeres y niños. De acuerdo con las costumbres de su país, llevaban perros atados con correa y tocaban unas flautas de caña.

–Su Majestad Mtesa –proclamó Molá– ha sido informado de su deseo de conocerle. Y como por su lado el rey está muy deseoso de ofrecer hospitalidad a unos hombres blancos, les pide que vayan a su encuentro sin demora. Mis oficiales les proporcionarán gratuitamente, una vez en Uganda, todo lo que necesiten.

Speke, satisfecho, fue a despedirse de Rumanika. Ambos estaban muy conmovidos. Es sorprendente ver a un blanco, llegado de tan lejos, y a un negro que ha crecido en el corazón de África entendiéndose tan bien, a pesar de sus diferencias.

–Majestad, tengo un último favor que pedirle.
–Claro está, ¿cuál?
–El capitán Grant tiene enferma una pierna. Cojea demasiado para emprender un largo camino. ¿Puede quedarse aquí hasta que cure? Luego se reunirá conmigo.

–Velaré personalmente por él.

Un año y tres meses después de salir de Zanzíbar, nuestro horizonte se aclara finalmente, por las buenas. Al margen de los regalos ofrecidos al buen rey Rumanika, nada hemos tomado de nuestras provisiones. En Uganda, sucederá lo mismo. Y puesto que una buena noticia nunca llega sola, Speke va a librarme de Baraka: decide enviarlo como explorador hacia el norte, al país del rey Kamrasi, por donde pasaremos mucho más tarde, cuando hayamos encontrado el Nilo.

El Nilo, del que jamás hemos estado tan cerca.

Capítulo cinco

Mtesa el sanguinario
Un gatito que se convierte en león
Prisioneros sin prisión

M tesa.

Ese nombre suena en Uganda, más terrible que el rugido de un león. Y cada paso que damos hacia el corazón de su reino nos lo muestra un poco más.

En las aldeas, los habitantes huyen al son de nuestros tambores. Saben que somos huéspedes del rey y que, si levantaran hasta nosotros sus ojos, se arriesgarían a un castigo ejemplar. Los oficiales que nos acompañan lo aprovechan para robar todo lo que encuentran: cabras, pollos, plátanos, grano, cerveza. Puesto que son los «hijos» de Mtesa, no corren peligro alguno.

¡Mtesa!

El nombre acaba llenándome de escalofríos el espinazo.

–Los habitantes de Uganda son un pueblo turbulento al que sólo contiene el temor al verdugo –afirma Molá, el mensajero que ha venido a buscarnos–. En cuanto el rey sepa que han entrado en su territorio, ciertamente hará que corten la cabeza a algunos de sus súbditos para inspirar en los otros un sano terror. Por lo demás, debo avisarle de su llegada. ¡Espérenme aquí!

Speke no se lo cree. Dice que son exageraciones para darnos miedo y quiere proseguir el camino sin Molá. Yo sé que todo es cierto. No conozco a Mtesa, pero siento por instinto que debemos temerle. Desde mi infancia, desde que fui capturado y convertido en esclavo, siempre sé cuándo debo tener miedo. Siento los peligros antes de que lleguen y he aprendido a huir de ellos. Eso me ha evitado muchos problemas en la vida.

Ahora presiento que se levanta ante nosotros un enorme peligro.

Pero Speke no lo cree y, tras varios días de espera, me ordena levantar el campo. ¿Partir sin Molá? ¡Eso es imposible, tenemos que aguardar al mensajero! Mtesa se enfadaría si prosiguiéramos solos.

–Veamos, sahib, tenemos que esperar un poco más. ¿Quién nos mostrará el camino?

–Eso es cosa mía. ¡Limítate a plegar la tienda!

¡Eso no está bien, no está bien en absoluto! Tal vez Speke no vea el peligro, pero yo sé que está ahí. Lo siento con tanta fuerza que los pelos de mis piernas se ponen de punta. No podemos partir. Me niego a arrojarme en las fauces de Mtesa.

Viéndome inmóvil, Speke levanta el tono y, con algunos hombres, comienza a desmontar personalmente la tienda. Se derrumba sobre las mercancías que están en su interior.

Entonces me invade otro miedo, más fuerte todavía que el primero. Grito en swahili a quienes han ayudado a Speke:

−¿Pero estáis locos? ¡Deteneos! ¡Hay un fuego ahí debajo! Y precisamente junto a unas cajas con pólvora... ¿Queréis que todo estalle? ¡Reflexionad antes de obedecer tontamente!

Grito, huyo... Miedo a ver como todo salta:

−¡Cállate! −estalla Speke en industaní− Nada tienes que decirles. Valen más que tú, pues ellos no protestan y me obedecen...

−¡Pero hay pólvora en la tienda y todo puede saltar por los aires!

−Y si me apetece, a mí, hacer saltar lo que me pertenece, es cosa mía. Tú nada tienes que decir... y si sigues desobedeciéndome, te haré saltar también.

Yo sólo quería salvar el material y la expedición. Y he aquí que ahora eso se vuelve contra mí. Me cubren de insultos. ¡Ah!, esa maldita manía de rechazar los consejos. Si no me contuviera... Si no me contuviera... le...

Un puñetazo en el rostro.

Caigo al suelo y me levanto clavando mis ojos en los del hombre blanco.

Un segundo puñetazo.
Me levanto, espumeante de rabia.
Un tercer puñetazo. Con la nariz llena de sangre, me voy, humillado.

–Siendo así, no estoy ya a su servicio.

Camino, loco de cólera, me alejo mucho y Nasib se reúne muy pronto conmigo. Nuestro viejo guía árabe intenta que cambie mi decisión, pero no lo haré. ¡Antes morir! Insiste, me recuerda todo el camino recorrido, el final está tan cerca, el hecho de que si abandono ahora me quedaré solo en el corazón de África. Me explica que lo sucedido no se debe a Speke, ni a mí, sino a la tensión que se ha apoderado de la caravana desde que entramos en Uganda, a esa sombra que planea sobre nosotros.

¡Mtesa!

–¿Quieres darle la razón al rey? –me pregunta Nasib– Intenta dividirnos con el terror. Y, gracias a ti, está consiguiéndolo. Debemos permanecer agrupados. Recuerda que un solo dedo no puede agarrar un dátil.

Nasib es un sabio, me dejo convencer y regreso a la caravana. Al día siguiente, Molá reaparece por fin:

–El rey les aguarda. Ha sentido tanto deseo de ver hombres blancos que, al anunciarle su llegada, ha hecho ejecutar a cincuenta notables y cuatrocientos individuos de baja condición.

A mí, la idea de verle me llena de guijarros el vientre.

* * *

Una caja de hojalata, cuatro hermosos echarpes de seda, un fusil, un cronómetro de oro, una pistola, tres carabinas, tres sables, una caja de pólvora, una caja de balas, una caja de cartuchos, un catalejo, una silla de hierro, diez paquetes de las más hermosas cuentas de vidrio, cuchillos, tenedores y cucharas: cada uno de los regalos, personalmente verificados por Speke, ha sido envuelto en un pedazo de tela.

La bandera inglesa abre la marcha, seguida por el sahib y por doce de nuestros soldados baluchis vestidos con un manto de franela roja, con la bayoneta calada. Sigue el resto de la caravana, de la que formo parte. En nuestros brazos, el hongo real.

Subimos por una gran carretera flanqueada de espectadores que se agarran con las manos la cabeza y gritan: Irungi! Irungi! «¡Bravo! ¡Bravo!» Esto me tranquiliza un poco.

Entramos luego en un patio donde hay grandes chozas. El techo está cubierto de un césped perfectamente cortado. Delante, decenas de mujeres jóvenes, algunas de las trescientas esposas del rey.

En un segundo patio, oficiales con uniforme de gala van a saludar al inglés. Unos jóvenes pajes, con turbante de cuerda en la cabeza, pasan corriendo como si su vida dependiera de la velocidad con la que comunican sus mensajes.

El tercer patio debe de ser el de las recepciones: se oye algunos músicos tocando el arpa. Tras esa empalizada se encuentra el terrible Mtesa. Speke quiere ir, pero el maestro de ceremonias, vestido con finas pieles de antílope cuidadosamente cosidas, se opone. Pide que nos sentemos en el suelo. Algo más allá, unos mercaderes árabes esperan también ser recibidos.

–¡Jamás de los jamases, nunca lo aceptaré! ¡Yo no soy un simple mercader! ¡Bombay, tradúcelo!

¿Pero qué le pasa?

–¡Diles que soy un príncipe y que quiero ser recibido como tal!

¿Qué mosca le ha picado? ¿Ha perdido Speke la cabeza? ¡Se ganará la cólera de Mtesa! ¿Quiere que nos maten a todos? Vacilo unos instantes antes de traducir esas locuras pero, de pronto, mi nariz recuerda la fuerza de su puño y obedezco. Puesto que no hablo la lengua del país, traduzco en árabe a Nasib, y Nasib traduce al ugandés para el maestro de ceremonias. Éste, que nunca ha oído a nadie encolerizándose de ese modo, no reacciona. Speke se enoja más aún.

–¡Bombay, deja en el suelo los regalos! ¡Nos vamos!

Y se va de veras. El maestro de ceremonias, muy inquieto de pronto, llama a unos pajes que salen al galope. ¡Pánico en el patio! Persigo a Speke, perseguido a mi vez por el viejo Nasib y, luego, por el maestro de ceremonias cuyas finas pieles de antílope vuelan en todas direcciones.

–¡Vuelva, vuelva! Pffff... pffff... ¡Todo se arreglará! Pffff... El rey le recibirá primero.

Speke se detiene y, tras unos instantes de reflexión, acepta. Aliviado por el desenlace, acompaño al inglés hacia el segundo patio y, luego, entramos en el tercero.

Allí está el rey, sentado en un estrado rojo. Alto y musculoso, es más joven de lo que yo imaginaba, no más de veinticinco años. Viste una túnica cuidadosamente dispuesta. Su pelo es muy corto, salvo en lo alto de su cráneo donde se yergue una pequeña cresta. Lleva elegantes collares al cuello, en las muñecas y los tobillos, y anillos en cada dedo de las manos y los pies. Tras él, un perro blanco, una lanza, un escudo y una mujer. A la derecha, vacas y cabras que ha recibido, antes, esta mañana.

El maestro de ceremonias invita a Speke a acercarse al rey.

El inglés avanza, erguido como un príncipe.

Silencio.

Ni el uno ni el otro hablan.

Se miran durante un tiempo infinito.

Luego el maestro de ceremonias pregunta a Speke:

—¿Ha visto bien a Su Majestad?

Sólo entonces se comienza a desembalar el hongo. El rey parece satisfecho. Finalmente no tiene un aspecto tan terrible: parece un niño abriendo sus regalos, los hace girar en todas direcciones. Speke tenía razón: los crímenes de Mtesa han sido exagerados para darnos miedo. He sido muy tonto creyendo en ellos. El rey inspecciona minuciosamente la pistola.

–¿Podría usted utilizarla para matar esas cuatro vacas tan rápidamente como sea posible? –pregunta señalando el ganado, a mi derecha.

Speke toma el revólver y mata las cuatro pobres bestias. La multitud aplaude ruidosamente. El rey sonríe, carga una carabina y la tiende a un paje.

–¡Ve a matar a un hombre en el otro patio!

El chiquillo se va.

Suena una detonación.

El chiquillo regresa con una gran sonrisa llena de malicia, como si hubiera encontrado un pajarillo o hecho alguna jugarreta.

–¿Cómo ha ido? –pregunta Mtesa.

–Muy bien –se alegra el niño.

¿Realmente ha matado a un hombre? Ciertamente no mentiría a su rey. Ha debido de hacerlo. Eso me hiela la sangre. Y nadie en la concurrencia reacciona. Nadie intenta saber quién ha pagado con su vida el regio capricho. ¿Un cortesano, un esclavo? Sin duda un esclavo...

Pero todo eso les parece tan normal...

Echo una ojeada a Speke: bajo su aspecto principesco, veo que está apretando los dientes.

Mtesa se toma por un león.

Cuando camina, dirige sus piernas muy a la derecha y a la izquierda y se bambolea, casi como un pato. Sus cortesanos dicen que son los andares majestuosos del león, su primer ancestro.

Esos andares serían divertidos si tuvieran derecho a reírse.

Pero en el reino de Mtesa se tienen pocos derechos. Por ejemplo, sólo el rey puede reposar en una silla. Sus súbditos no tienen derecho a sentarse, ni siquiera en una bala de heno. Sólo pueden acuclillarse en tierra, en el polvo.

Mtesa se toma por un león, pero no lo es: un león mata por necesidad cuando él mata por placer. A veces tengo la impresión de que si nos movemos sin su permiso, si respiramos con demasiada fuerza, no vacilará en suprimirnos.

Por primera vez desde hace mucho tiempo, siento que un viejo miedo se agita en mí, una angustia de antiguo esclavo: soy una presa. Mi vida puede detenerse en cualquier instante.

Estamos muy cerca del río que corre hacia el norte –antes de llegar a palacio, varias personas nos han confirmado que una gran corriente de agua salía del lago, algo más lejos–, pero eso no me interesa ya.

Todo lo que quiero es salir vivo de aquí.

* * *

A petición de Mtesa, Speke, el viejo Nasib y yo visitamos a su madre, que está muy enferma. Su palacio se encuentra al extremo de un largo camino. Cada paso que me aleja del rey es más dulce que el precedente.

Unos guardas provistos de grandes campanas de alarma vigilan las entradas de palacio. Nos hacen esperar en una primera choza, luego nos conducen a otra. La reina madre está en el centro, sentada en el suelo sobre una alfombra, con el codo puesto en un almohadón. Una decena de esclavas se agita a su alrededor, sirviéndole bebida y abanicándola, como hormigas alrededor de su reina. Las despide con un gesto.

Toma una pipa, aspira el humo, toma luego tres bastoncillos de madera.

–Tendrán que curarme de tres enfermedades distintas. Este bastón representa mi estómago, que me hace sufrir mucho. Éste, mi hígado, que me lanza fuertes dolores por todo el cuerpo. Y el tercero es mi corazón, al que debo cada noche pesadillas sobre mi difunto marido.

Speke deja en el suelo su farmacia portátil y también los regalos que le ha llevado: ocho brazaletes de bronce, una bolsa con treinta grandes perlas azules y algunas telas.

–Por lo que se refiere a los sueños, Majestad, es muy frecuente entre las viudas. Se disiparán cuando se resigne usted a tomar un nuevo marido. Por lo que se refiere a los demás dolores, no puedo recetarle nada sin haberla auscultado...

–Traduzco al árabe para Nasib, que traduce al ugandés para la reina.

–¡Imposible! –se inquieta un consejero– Para ello se necesita la autorización del rey.

–¡De ningún modo! –responde la reina madre– No tengo por qué consultar a ese jovencito: a fin de cuentas, al rey lo hice yo...

La miro, pasmado: la madre del león es una leona. Speke la examina y, luego, saca un bote de píldoras de su farmacia. Se las hace probar al consejero, para demostrar que no contienen sortilegio alguno del doctor blanco.

–Tome esto y, hasta mi próxima visita, no beba más cerveza y no coma nada.

La reina madre toma las píldoras y sale penosamente de la choza. Instantes más tarde, regresa muy fresca, vistiendo un magnífico deole que ofrece a nuestra admiración.

–Y ahora, quiero que me muestren los regalos que me han traído.

* * *

Mtesa nos demuestra, cada día un poco más, que está loco. Cada día, o casi, pasa una mujer de su harén con una cuerda anudada en las muñecas, arrastrada por un guardia.

–*Hai, minange! mkama! hai n'yawio!* –grita con los ojos llenos de lágrimas– ¡Oh, mi señor! ¡Mi rey! ¡Oh madre mía!

En la calle, nadie reacciona. Todos saben, sin embargo, que dentro de unos instantes la muchacha será ejecutada. Nadie sabe qué ha hecho para merecerlo.

Nada sin duda.

El otro día, el tirano organizó una excursión por el lago Nyanza. Tras haber cazado hipopótamos, fuimos a una isla para almorzar. El cortejo cruzaba luego una especie de vergel cuando una mujer del rey, muy hermosa por lo demás, tuvo la desgraciada idea de ofrecerle una fruta que acababa de coger. Como presa de la locura, montó en violenta cólera.

–¡Nunca una mujer se ha permitido ofrecerme nada de nada! ¡Agarrad a ésta y matadla!

De inmediato, como una jauría de perros hambrientos, los pajes se precipitaron sobre la pobre mujer que se les ofrecía como pasto. Ésta, indignada, intentó rechazarlos, dirigiendo sus sinceras excusas al rey. Pero los pajes la cogieron y la derribaron.

–¡Por compasión, Mzungu! –le imploró a Speke– ¡Ayúdeme!

Mientras Nasib me lo traducía y yo lo traducía al industaní, Luguba, la sultana preferida, se había arrojado a los pies del rey. Pero éste, excitado por tanta sumisión, se volvía más brutal aún. Tomó una maza para aplastar la cabeza de la infeliz.

–¡No, deténgase!

Speke dio un salto y detuvo el brazo del rey. Nunca antes había intervenido pero, entonces, la crueldad de Mtesa, justo ante nuestros ojos, superaba lo que podía soportar. Contuve largo rato el aliento, temblando en mi interior: el valeroso gesto del inglés podía costarle la vida. Y la mía además.

Los cortesanos y los esclavos presentes se hicieron muy pequeños, por temor a la reacción del tirano.

Pero, tras unos instantes de asombro, al caprichoso monarca, precisamente porque era caprichoso, le divirtió la temeridad del hombre blanco e hizo que soltaran a la infeliz.

Los cortesanos felicitaron al rey por su generosidad.

Yo respiré de nuevo.

* * *

Desde entonces, cada día, Speke es invitado a palacio. Yo le acompaño como intérprete, pero detesto esos encuentros. Los caprichos de Mtesa me aterrorizan. Durante largo rato, juega con nuestras brújulas, nuestros lápices de colores, nuestros cuadernos, nuestros telescopios, como haría un niño... Pero sé que de un momento a otro puede tomar un fusil y pedir a Speke que me mate. ¿Qué haría el inglés si tuviera que elegir entre su vida y la mía? Prefiero no pensar en ello...

–Sería una muestra de gran amistad –dice Mtesa– que me ofreciera usted una de sus brújulas.

Speke, para demostrar que no es su servidor, se niega cortésmente.

—Me complacería, Majestad, pero la necesitaría luego para proseguir la expedición. A este respecto, me gustaría hacer una expedición hacia el este del lago, para ver el gran río que sale de él. Tal vez podría usted prestarme un guía.

Pero el rey, para mostrar que él es quien decide, cambia a su vez de tema.

—¿Podría este fusil matar un cocodrilo?

Me estremezco: el «cocodrilo», Mamba, es mi segundo apodo, porque tengo los dientes puntiagudos y soy muy feo. Pero sin duda el rey lo ignora; es sólo una desagradable casualidad.

* * *

Si me libro, si salimos vivos de aquí, será gracias al sahib Speke.

Lo he criticado mucho desde el comienzo del segundo viaje, lo he comparado con frecuencia a Burton y, a menudo, he dudado de su capacidad, pero debo reconocer que estaba equivocado.

Desde nuestra llegada, hace dos meses, Speke se hace pasar por un príncipe: exige ser alimentado como tal, alojado en una choza confortable junto a palacio. Ha obtenido incluso autorización para sentarse en su silla de hierro.

Al principio, yo pensaba que era un nuevo error, pero el error era mío. Actuando de ese modo, Speke demuestra a Mtesa que también él es un león, no una gacela como los mercaderes árabes o yo mismo: un león que se defenderá si lo atacan. Por ello, el tirano vacila en meterse con nosotros.

El inglés, por lo demás, no tiene que esforzarse para parecer un león: está convirtiéndose en uno de ellos. Hace cinco años, en nuestro primer encuentro, era sólo un gatito inexperto ante el sahib Burton. Daba pequeños zarpazos, pero respetaba a su hermano mayor. Desde entonces, ha crecido y, hoy, también él es un rey a su modo. Cuando uno de nosotros, en la caravana, saca sus garras, él lo pone en su sitio sin miramientos. Mi pobre nariz lo recuerda aún.

* * *

Marcharse. Marcharse de aquí cuanto antes.

Desde hace tres días, no pensamos ya en nada más.

Hace tres días, cuatro meses después de nuestra llegada, resonaron disparos cerca del palacio. Tras un momento de inquietud, vimos llegar una caravana con un hombre blanco a la cabeza. ¡El capitán Grant! Cojeaba un poco, parecía muy fatigado por el viaje, pero estaba ahí, vivo y coleando.

¡Bienvenido al país del rey loco, capitán!

Inmediatamente, el sahib Speke fue a anunciar a Mtesa nuestra próxima partida. Quería obtener su autorización: sin ella, no podríamos dar un paso sin que nos detuvieran. El rey, tras haber hecho varias preguntas mostrando que había comprendido bien lo que esperábamos, respondió así:

–Me gustaría mucho tener el dibujo en color de una gallina de Guinea. ¿Podría usted hacérmelo?

Miró a Speke con una sonrisita aviesa. «Es usted muy fuerte, amigo mío, parecía decir, pero de los dos leones yo soy el más fuerte. Es usted mi prisionero.»

* * *

Huir de aquí.

No sé cómo lo hace el sahib para mantener su calma. Me ha dicho que tenía todavía un as en la manga: la única persona del país que no tiene miedo al tirano.

Sentada en el suelo, acunando en sus brazos una muñeca de fibra de coco, la reina madre nos recibe tras habernos hecho esperar. Sus esclavas depositan ante ella plátanos y calabazas de cerveza.

–Estos presentes son para usted –le suelta al capitán Grant– es un regalo de bienvenida...

Nasib traduce al árabe y yo traduzco al industaní.

–Es muy amable...

–Deja, James –le interrumpe Speke–, yo responderé.

Grant, obediente, calla.

–Es muy amable por su parte, pero no era necesario, el capitán forma parte de mi caravana. No viaja por su propia cuenta. No estaba usted obligada a hacerle un regalo...

La reina madre acusa el golpe: su ardid no ha funcionado. Quería hacer pasar a Grant por un nuevo visitante y obtener, así, que le correspondieran con un nuevo regalo. Pero Speke lo ha comprendido muy bien.

–Sin embargo, si desea usted todas esas hermosas cosas que proceden de mi país –insiste–, puede obtenerlas. ¡Ayúdenos a encontrar el gran río que sale del lago! Luego, haremos que barcos cargados de regalos lo remonten hasta Uganda.

Los ojos de la reina madre se iluminan con un fulgor del que nadie la creía capaz.

–Sí... claro... barcos hasta el lago... Mañana hablaré con mi hijo...

De los dos leones, tal vez sea Mtesa el más fuerte, pero Speke es sin duda el más astuto.

* * *

Ha transcurrido otro mes, durante el que el sahib ha decidido regalar al tirano una carabina, municiones y la brújula tantas veces pedida. Luego, ayer por la mañana, el rey nos convocó.

–Quiere usted abrir una vía comercial por el norte, ¿no es cierto? ¡Es una excelente idea! Le he pedido a Budja, uno de mis oficiales, que les guíe hasta el gran río...

No creíamos lo que estábamos oyendo: ¿éramos libres? ¿Por qué el rey despertaba de pronto, cuando estábamos pidiéndoselo desde hacía cinco meses? Pero no había tiempo que perder con este tipo de preguntas: había que partir enseguida, antes que el caprichoso monarca cambiara de opinión.

Esta mañana, al alba, para dar buena impresión, el sahib Speke se ha puesto al cuello el collar ofrecido por la reina madre y, luego, se ha despedido del tirano. Desde entonces caminamos hacia el este, hacia el gran río que, muy cerca de aquí, sale del lago.

En todos los poblados que cruzamos, los aldeanos huyen al son de nuestros tambores: saben que somos los huéspedes del rey. Los oficiales de Mtesa lo aprovechan para apoderarse de las cosechas, de las vacas, de las cabras, de las pieles, de los tambores, de las lanzas, del tabaco, de la cerveza, de todo lo que cae en sus manos.

Sin quererlo, sembramos a nuestras espaldas la tristeza y la miseria.

¡Mtesa, mal rey, te odio y me siento feliz huyendo de tu país!

Capítulo seis

¿El Nilo por fin?
Un descenso movido
El país de arena

Las cascadas aparecen en un recodo del camino, pero las oíamos desde hacía mucho tiempo ya.

El espectáculo es magnífico.

A la derecha, las apacibles aguas del layo Nyanza parecen dormir. Luego, lenta, muy lentamente, parte de esa agua, ignorando lo que le ocurre, se pone en movimiento, avanza sin agitación alguna. Puesto que las boscosas riberas se estrechan, el agua se acelera, se agita: el lago se convierte en río. Pasa ante nosotros, rodea unas grandes rocas y, luego, se arroja al vacío. Una enorme catarata a cuyos pies el agua ruge, espumea de rabia. Abajo, peces viajeros brincan e intentan remontar hasta el lago. Unos pescadores, en barca, les aguardan con el sedal en la mano. Los hipopótamos pasean su adormecida silueta en las aguas. Más allá, a nuestra izquierda, el agua se apacigua, recupera su curso, se dirige hacia su destino de río.

¡Aquí estás por fin!...

Al sahib Speke le tiembla la voz.

¡Es éste, Bombay, es el Nilo!

Ignoro cómo puede estar tan seguro: no es el nombre que por aquí le dan. Pero el inglés tiene en los ojos las mismas chiribitas que hace cuatro años, cuando descubrimos el otro extremo del lago Nyanza.

–Lástima que el capitán Grant no esté aquí para verlo...

Desde nuestra partida del palacio de Mtesa, hace tres semanas, Grant ha seguido en efecto otro camino. Puesto que cojeaba mucho, Speke le pidió que fuera con el grueso de la caravana, directamente al palacio del rey Kamrasi, donde debe ya de esperarnos Baraka. Cuando Speke le anunció su decisión, Grant puso una extraña cara. Por un instante creyó que el velo iba a desgarrarse y que veríamos otro rostro del capitán. Esperaba yo que se rebelara y declarase: «¡Eso es injusto! Tras todo el camino que he hecho con usted, en el momento de llegar al objetivo, me priva de la victoria final. ¡Quiero acompañarle a las fuentes del Nilo!» Pero no lo hizo: sonrió y obedeció las órdenes.

–Lástima que Grant no lo vea... ¡Mira bien, Bombay, es el río sagrado! Nace aquí ante nosotros... ¡Tenemos ante los ojos la solución al más antiguo enigma geográfico del mundo! Siento que es él...

El inglés tiembla de los pies a la cabeza. Me pregunto si va a festejarlo disparando contra un hipopótamo pero, en vez de hacerlo, bajamos hasta la ribera, se agacha, une sus manos, las hunde en el agua y, muy conmovido, bebe un trago.

Comprendo perfectamente su emoción: hace tanto tiempo que busca este río... Pero debo reconocer que yo no siento nada semejante: sólo veo ahí una cascada saliendo de un lago, un poco de agua. Lo que yo espero realmente es ver el otro extremo de este río. Porque, si el sahib tiene razón, si éste es el río tan esperado, como afirma, si realmente es el Nilo, entonces al otro extremo se encuentra el misterioso país de arena...

* * *

Avanzamos por el agua.

Speke ha alquilado cinco piraguas hechas, cada una de ellas, con cinco largas tablas de madera. Embarcamos en ellas las pocas mercancías que Grant no tomó y descendemos por el río. Las riberas son verdeantes.

Me pregunto adónde nos lleva el río. Supongo que lejos, mucho más lejos, atraviesa arena, arena y más arena aún. A menudo me he divertido imaginando un mundo como el nuestro aunque enteramente de arena, con flores, árboles, lluvia, animales de arena. Sé muy bien que eso no existe. Temo un poco que me decepcione.

Sólo espero que hayamos acertado con el río.

Me gustaría que hubiéramos llegado ya, pero las piraguas son tan lentas. Los remeros no reman: se dejan arrastrar por la corriente y sólo dan una palada cuando la embarcación se acerca demasiado a una orilla. «¿Por qué fatigarse cuando la corriente trabaja para nosotros?», exclama uno de los remeros. «¡El que rema a favor de la corriente da risa a los cocodrilos!»

Caramba, he aquí la respuesta a una vieja pregunta.

Tras dos días de navegación, doce barcas se acercan a nosotros. A bordo, unos hombres armados nos amenazan con sus lanzas. Los recibimos con disparos de fusil. Huyen, pero les alcanzamos y les hacemos hablar: Kamrasi, su rey, se preocupa por nuestra llegada. Según el rumor, los hombres blancos son brujos devoradores de tripas humanas. Además, puesto que Grant entró en el país por la tierra y nosotros por el río, el rey piensa en un ataque coordinado. Para tranquilizarle, abandonamos las piraguas y proseguimos por el camino, donde encontramos a Grant. Tras largas discusiones, Kamrasi acaba por recibirnos en su palacio. Encontramos allí a Baraka, que era mantenido prisionero. Siguen los tradicionales regateos sobre el precio de nuestro paso. Tras dos meses, el rey recibe seis carabinas y municiones, un gran bote de bronce, un cepillo para el pelo, cerillas y un cuchillo. Y nosotros volvemos a ponernos en marcha con una escolta de veinticuatro hombres.

* * *

Puesto que el rey nos ha autorizado a navegar por el río, proseguimos el descenso en una gran piragua.

Cada ribera está flanqueada por un tapiz de cañas. La de la izquierda es baja y pantanosa. La de la derecha, en leve pendiente y cubierta de árboles. Extrañas islas derivan a la velocidad de la corriente: son marañas de cañas, de hierbas y helechos, arrastradas por las aguas en crecida. De vez en cuando, un hipopótamo asoma su cabeza pero se hunde de nuevo, inmediatamente, asustado por los gritos de las gallinas que llevamos a bordo. En la proa de la piragua, el sahib Speke repasa sus cuentas: no nos quedan ya muchas mercancías. Pero afirma que no es muy grave ya: puesto que estamos en el Nilo, pronto llegaremos a un pueblo llamado Gondokoro. Allí, un equipo procedente de Egipto y dirigido por un inglés llamado Petherick nos aguarda con provisiones.

Espero que estemos realmente en el Nilo.

Espero que el equipo esté allí. Salimos de Zanzíbar hace dos años y dos meses: ¿habrá esperado tanto tiempo?

Al décimo día de navegación, los remeros nos dejan en tierra: más lejos, el río se arroja entre dos grandes rocas, luego resbala por una larga pendiente. Y se escucha, más lejos aún, el sordo rugido de una inmensa cascada. Imposible proseguir en barco.

Según el rey Kamrasi, después de estas cascadas, el río forma una curva: se dirige hacia el oeste y se arroja en un lago llamado Luta Nzige, la «Langosta Muerta», pero vuelve a salir de inmediato y asciende hacia el norte. Puesto que toda la región está infestada de tribus hostiles, Speke decide que nos dirigiremos en línea recta hacia el norte. Más tarde regresaremos al río.

Abandonamos pues la orilla y penetramos en el país de Gani. Está cubierto de montañas boscosas y sus habitantes van casi desnudos, al margen de los aros de bronce, las cuentas de cristal y las plumas. Tras siete etapas, regresamos al río y lo seguimos por algún tiempo.

–¡Piraguas! ¡Un campamento!

Ha sido el viejo Nasib, nuestro guía, el que los ha visto primero.

Los dos ingleses se miran, entre alegres e inquietos.

–No estamos en Gondokoro –se sorprende Speke–. Según mis cálculos, no hemos llegado aún...

Sin embargo, el campamento existe en efecto, con sus cabañas y sus piraguas, y sus ocupantes no viven por aquí: van vestidos como soldados de un verdadero ejército.

Disparamos una salva de mosquetes. Responden con otra salva, se agrupan y forman un cortejo militar con banderas y tambores. Tal vez no sea Gondokoro, pero es en efecto el equipo de apoyo. Abandonamos nuestros fardos y corremos a su encuentro.

Un oficial se acerca a los ingleses y, sin saber quién es el jefe, se dirige a ambos.

–*Salam malecum*, me llamo Mohamed.

–¿A las órdenes de quién está usted? –pregunta Speke.

–Petrik.

–¿Y dónde se encuentra, ahora, Petherick?

–Lo verá muy pronto. Tenemos orden de acompañarles hasta Gondokoro.

El sahib Speke le mira y, pasada ya la duda, permite por fin que una gran sonrisa devore su rostro. Se vuelve hacia Grant y le estrecha en sus brazos, le palmea la espalda, muy conmovido. Le dice algo en inglés. Debe ser algo parecido a: «¡Lo hemos conseguido! ¡Lo hemos conseguido!»

Sí, lo hemos conseguido. ¡Estamos salvados! ¡Qué inmensa alegría haber llegado por fin! En adelante, no tendremos ya que preocuparnos por gastar mercancías, por los hongos, los reyes sanguinarios, la búsqueda de porteadores. Hemos llegado y lo hemos conseguido: ¡hemos encontrado el Nilo! Desde el comienzo, la intuición del sahib Speke era acertada: el río nace en efecto en el lago Nyanza.

En brazos del capitán Grant, llora de alegría.

* * *

Pero lo que yo quería ver era el país de arena.

El descenso del Nilo ha sido largo y decepcionante.

Ya no tenía nada que hacer, puesto que el navío llevaba los fardos en mi lugar; me pasaba el tiempo observando las riberas.

Desfilaban lentamente, tan lentamente... Pasamos por regiones verdeantes, por ciénagas. Varios afluentes se unieron al río y aumentaron sus aguas. A medida que avanzábamos, el clima cambió. Se volvió aún más cálido, aún más seco. Durante el día, sudábamos sin cesar, incluso a la sombra, sin hacer nada. Cuando grandes cataratas nos cerraron el paso, desembarcamos, andamos, embarcamos luego en otro navío, algo más lejos. Abandonamos el país llamado Sudán y llegamos a Egipto. Entonces comencé a tener una gran esperanza: tenía tantas ganas de ver en el exterior lo que había imaginado en el interior de mi cabeza. Pero por más que mis ojos se fatigaran, sólo veía ante mí el Nilo y, en sus riberas, cañas, cocoteros, palmeras. Más allá, tan lejos como alcanzaba la vista, había campos de cereales o de cañas. Con, a veces, tristes montañas desérticas y algo de arena amarilla.

–Es normal –me explicó el sahib Speke–, los egipcios cultivan las riberas con el agua del río. La arena está justo después de los campos...

Pero yo no veía nada.

Descendimos casi todo el Nilo, hasta el norte de Egipto, sin que yo viera nada de nada. Y ahora cabalgo en un asno y sigo sin ver nada; pero es normal porque es de noche.

Ante mí, en la obscuridad, los dos sahibs avanzan en sus asnos al igual que el guía egipcio que nos lleva a las pirámides -son, según me han dicho, inmensas construcciones puntiagudas. Los ingleses quieren verlas a toda costa antes de abandonar Egipto. A mí la cosa no me interesa, pero no he tenido más remedio: hace un rato, el sahib Speke me ha despertado y me ha ordenado que le siguiera.

Dejamos atrás las últimas casas de ladrillo de la ciudad, atravesamos campos, seguimos luego por un camino de tierra. La luna apenas nos ilumina. A estas horas, estaría mejor en mi jergón, en el barco, pero al parecer es la mejor hora para ver las pirámides: durante el día, en esta estación, el calor lo aplasta todo.

A nuestro alrededor, siento que el paisaje cambia.

La obscuridad no es ya la misma que hace un rato: era sombría y fría a causa de los campos, es ahora cálida y clara. Me pregunto dónde estamos y por qué son interesantes las pirámides.

Nuestro guía anuncia algo. Habla en inglés. Realmente no sé qué pinto yo aquí –mejor estaría roncando en mi jergón.

Los dos sahibs extienden una gran manta en el suelo y se sientan. Yo me alejo un poco e intento descubrir lo que nos rodea. Hacia el este, al otro lado del Nilo, las estrellas desaparecen una a una y el cielo se aclara. A mi izquierda, adivino sombras gigantescas y puntiagudas; sin duda las pirámides. Algo más allá, una enorme bola redonda parece salir de la tierra. Ignoro qué es.

Poco a poco, el cielo azulea, se enrojece luego. Speke dice algo en inglés y los dos sahibs se vuelven hacia las sombras puntiagudas. En el vértice de la más alta, un pequeño triángulo de piedra es iluminado por los primeros rayos del sol. En verdad es sorprendente. Con el regreso de la luz, las cosas recuperan su forma. Las tres pirámides aparecen por fin, muy impresionantes. Luego, delante, la gran bola resulta ser la cabeza de un gigante tallada en la roca; tiene la nariz rota. A nuestro alrededor no hay nada más. ¡Ah, sí!, en el suelo hay arena, arena fina y tibia que se escurre entre los dedos cuando intento cogerla. Al este, el sol sale de la tierra, crece, rojo y, luego, anaranjado. Los dos ingleses se maravillan ante las pirámides y la cabeza de gigante a la que llaman «esfinge». Todo es en efecto muy hermoso, pero hay algo más hermoso aún, la arena que nos rodea.

Escalo los primeros peldaños de una pirámide y examino el horizonte, del lado del oeste. Tan lejos como alcanza mi vista, sólo hay arena, una arena que pasa del anaranjado al amarillo a medida que el sol se levanta. Detrás de cada duna se dibuja, muy nítida, una sombra negra. Diríase un mar de arena cubierto de pequeñas olas.

–Bueno, Bombay –me interpela Speke–. ¿Te gusta esto?

–¡Oh, sí, sahib, es maravilloso!

–¿De modo que ya no refunfuñas? He hecho bien despertándote esta mañana, ¿no es cierto?

–Sí, sahib, gracias.

Me sonríe.

Antes de bajar de mi pirámide, lanzo una última ojeada al paisaje para que me llene los ojos, la cabeza y el cuerpo.

El país de arena, más hermoso aún que en mis sueños.

* * *

–Todas las cosas tienen un final –suelta el sahib Speke, cuando me dispongo a subir al gran navío de vapor.

–«¡Todas las cosas tienen un final, salvo la banana que tiene dos!»

–¡El maldito Bombay con sus proverbios! Te echaré de menos.

–Yo también, sahib, le echaré de menos.

Ya está, hemos llegado al final del viaje. Hemos descendido el Nilo hasta que se divide en varias corrientes de agua, al norte de Egipto. Hemos navegado por una de esas corrientes de agua y desembocado en el mar, en Alejandría.

Es una hermosa ciudad blanca, con un inmenso puerto. Decenas de grandes barcos atracan allí, cargan o descargan permanentemente mercancías y hombres.

Hasta la vista, capitán Grant; hasta la vista, sahib Speke. ¡Hasta pronto, tal vez!

–No, no lo creo... Ahora que he encontrado las fuentes del Nilo, no tengo ya razones para regresar a Zanzíbar. ¡Adiós, viejo cocodrilo!

Franqueo la pasarela y pongo el pie en el navío que me devuelve a casa. Ahí están mis compañeros de viaje: Baraka, con quien he terminado reconciliándome; Mabruki y su tam-tam mágico; el viejo guía Nasib; los soldados baluchis que nos han seguido hasta aquí...

Abajo, en el muelle, los dos ingleses desaparecen entre la multitud: tomarán otro vapor hacia Inglaterra. Cuando nuestro barco se aleja del muelle y llega a mar abierto, contemplo, acodado en la batayola, las casas que van disminuyendo de tamaño, la ciudad que se encoge.

Me hubiera gustado divisar por última vez el lugar donde el brazo del Nilo desemboca en el mar, pero no lo he visto. ¡No importa! Es pasado ya. Mi porvenir está ahora en mis asuntos: con el dinero que me ha dado el sahib Speke por mis dos años y medio de servicios, compraré una choza y encontraré mujer. Entre mis cosas hay sobre todo lo más hermoso que existe. Una especie de guijarro amarillo que compré en un mercado de El Cairo. Cuando lo vi en aquel puesto, me detuve y lo observé largo rato sin atreverme a tocarlo: era la primera vez que veía uno, pero sabía exactamente de qué se trataba. Con sus pétalos de piedra, no podía equivocarme.

–Se llama rosa de arena –me explicó el anciano que se ocupaba del puesto–. ¿Nunca había visto una? Está hecha de granos de arena y se encuentra en el desierto. Pero no sé cómo aparece.

–Yo lo sé –respondí antes de comprar la rosa.

La guardaré toda mi vida como recuerdo de mis viajes en busca de las fuentes del Nilo.

Siempre supe que en el desierto crecían hermosas flores de arena.

Epílogo

La gloria, el drama y el desenlace

El capitán John Hanning Speke aguardaba en el umbral de la puerta. Lanzó una mirada inquieta hacia la sala que se llenaba cada vez más.

Aquel lunes 22 de junio de 1863, en la Sociedad Real de Geografía había una multitud. En la mayor de las salas se había levantado un estrado con unas mesas alineadas y cubiertas por manteles. Un gran mapa de África se había colgado de la pared, con todas las indicaciones dadas por el capitán Speke referentes a los lagos y al Nilo. Decenas y decenas de sillas se habían colocado ante el estrado. Ya no quedaba casi ninguna libre: los geógrafos, los periodistas, los hombres y las mujeres de la alta sociedad las habían tomado al asalto. Eso era lo que más preocupaba al explorador: toda esa gente. Detestaba hablar en público. Prefería, con mucho, un cara a cara con un rinoceronte colérico.

Pero no tenía elección: desde que había mandado el telegrama desde África anunciando su victoria, todo Londres esperaba verle y escucharle.

Sir Roderick Murchison, de pie detrás del estrado, le indicó por signos que se acercara, y también a Grant.

–Señoras y señores, les presento al capitán Speke, a quien debemos el descubrimiento de las fuentes del Nilo, uno de los más hermosos éxitos de la geografía británica, y a su compañero de expedición, el capitán Grant. ¡Pido que les recibamos triunfalmente!

Aullidos de alegría acogieron la entrada de ambos exploradores. Las mujeres agitaban sus pañuelos de franela y los hombres levantaban sus sombreros de copa.

Reanimado, Speke avanzó hasta la tribuna aclarándose varias veces la garganta. «Señor presidente, señoras y señores», repitió para sí mismo.

En cuanto se acallaron los aplausos, dijo con voz fuerte pero vacilante:

–Señor presidente, señoras y señores, me complace estar hoy aquí entre ustedes para hablarles de...

Y les habló de la expedición, del trayecto, del lago Victoria, de los ríos que se vertían en él, de los que de él salían, de las dificultades debidas a las guerras, de los tiranos sanguinarios y los reyes humanistas, de los extraordinarios animales africanos...

Cuanto más hablaba, mejor se sentía. El público le escuchaba en un silencio de iglesia. Era el héroe del día. Cada una de sus anécdotas daba en el blanco y suscitaba admiración, horror o carcajadas. Todo le salía bien. Se permitió incluso un puyazo para su antiguo compañero, Richard Burton:

–Si, en nuestra primera expedición, yo hubiera ido solo, habría resuelto ya en 1859 el asunto del Nilo, llegando hasta Uganda... pero, puesto que mi proyecto fue desalentado por el jefe de la expedición, que por aquel entonces estaba enfermo y cansado del viaje, tuve que regresar a Inglaterra...

Al finalizar su larga alocución, una tempestad de aplausos le hizo comprender que era mucho más que el héroe del día.

Durante las semanas y los meses siguientes, recibió un telegrama de la reina Victoria, fue entrevistado por numerosos periodistas, fue el invitado de honor de veladas mundanas, obtuvo medallas de varias sociedades de geografía europeas, fue contratado por un editor para escribir su relato en un libro.

Sí, era mucho más que el héroe del día: el héroe del año, tal vez del siglo, incluso.

* * *

Richard Burton no estaba en Inglaterra cuando John Speke regresó de su segundo viaje: cónsul de Gran Bretaña en Fernando Poo, se encontraba en su puesto, en esa isla española ante las costas del África Occidental.

Por aquel entonces, había enterrado ya el hacha de guerra contra su antiguo compañero. Había pasado mucha agua bajo los puentes desde la exploración del lago Tanganika: se había casado con su prometida, Isabel, había viajado mucho y escrito mucho, se había interesado por mil y una cosas. La enloquecida búsqueda de las fuentes del Nilo era ahora una página de su vida vuelta para siempre.

Cuando anunciaron el regreso de Speke, incluso le había enviado una carta para felicitarle por haber llevado a buen puerto tan difícil expedición.

Pero el otro no parecía verlo de ese modo. Apoyándose en su nueva gloria, sintiéndose sin duda invencible, lanzaba a diestro y siniestro flechas llenas de acritud contra su antiguo jefe. Pero, ¿por qué tanto rencor? ¿Por qué quería la guerra? En todo caso, si Speke quería pelea, la tendría: Burton no era de los que rehúyen el combate, muy al contrario. Se lanzó a él, pues, de cabeza.

Primer paso: encontrar los puntos débiles de su adversario. Eran numerosos: así, aunque Speke era indiscutiblemente un excelente andarín y cazador, no brillaba precisamente por su rigor científico. Sus medidas de altitud, por ejemplo, no siempre eran exactas: de creerle, en algunos lugares, el Nilo hubiera debido, incluso, remontar su curso... y además estaba esa «laguna» en el descenso del río, cuando la expedición lo había abandonado para cortar hacia el norte. Según el rey Kamrasi, allí estaba el lago Luta Nzige. ¿Pero quién sabe si no desembocaba en ese lago también otro río? Y si ese segundo río resultaba ser más largo que el procedente del lago Victoria, entonces él sería el verdadero Nilo... Y si ese río más largo procedía del lago Tanganika, a fin de cuentas él, Burton, sería el verdadero descubridor de las fuentes del Nilo.

Segundo paso que Burton debía dar: encontrar aliados. Tampoco aquello le resultó difícil. Desde su regreso, Speke, por su actitud algo altanera, había herido a bastantes geógrafos y periodistas. Se le reprochaba su falta de *fair-play*, especialmente por haber despedido al capitán Grant tan cerca ya de las fuentes del Nilo. ¿No lo había hecho para recoger, solo, los frutos del éxito?

El contraataque de Richard Burton estuvo tan bien llevado que la controversia adquirió rápidamente cierta magnitud. Cada geógrafo, cada periódico, cada inglés tuvo que tomar partido por uno u otro de los protagonistas. Sir Roderick Murchison, que había financiado la expedición de Speke, defendió a su protegido. El muy respetado David Livingstone, que regresaba tras varios años de exploraciones africanas, apoyó a Burton. La duda se infiltró tanto en los espíritus que, al final, nadie supo ya si Speke había o no descubierto realmente las fuentes del Nilo.

Para resolver la cuestión, la Sociedad Real de Geografía decidió organizar un debate contradictorio entre ambos adversarios, con ocasión de su próximo congreso en la ciudad de Bath.

* * *

El 16 de septiembre de 1864, Richard Burton se levantó temprano. Se puso su más hermoso traje y, acompañado por Isabel, acudió a la sala donde iba a celebrarse la reunión de geografía. Se sentía en forma: aguzaba ya su discurso desde hacía varios días. Sabía que sus argumentos, de acero forjado, iban a atravesar al pobre Speke como la hoja de un florete. Y como, además, adoraba hablar en público, no daba ni un céntimo por la piel de su adversario. Al dirigirse a la tribuna desde donde debía hablar, Burton advirtió una pequeña reunión en una sala contigua. Los más eminentes geógrafos estaban allí, con la cara hosca. No se atrevió a entrar y, puesto que nadie le invitó, permaneció largos minutos esperando fuera. En la sala, una hoja de papel circulaba de mano en mano.

¿Qué estaba pasando?

Un amigo geógrafo, al descubrir a Burton, tomó la hoja y se la entregó.

–Lo siento –dijo de entrada.

Sorprendido, Burton tomó el mensaje y leyó:

–«Ayer, a las cuatro de la tarde, el capitán Speke perdió la vida durante una cacería en las tierras de uno de sus primos, algunos parientes lo descubrieron tendido entre los brezos, herido por una descarga que le había atravesado el pecho, junto al corazón. Murió unos minutos más tarde.»

Burton titubeó y se derrumbó en un sillón.

–¿Cómo ocurrió?

–Speke estaba cazando perdices en casa de un primo que vive por allí. En cierto momento, se alejó de los demás.

El primo escuchó un disparo, luego vio al capitán cayendo pesadamente del murete en el que estaba. Mientras buscaban a un cirujano, el pobre entregó su alma... El primo cree que subió al murete, se agachó para tomar su fusil, que se había quedado abajo, cuando se disparó accidentalmente.

¿Un accidente? Richard Burton no podía creerlo. No con un cazador tan bueno como Speke... Cierto día, en África, cuando un hipopótamo iba a volcar su piragua, había visto cómo su compañero procuraba, a pesar del caos, no dirigir el arma hacia sí mismo ni hacia los demás. De modo que un accidente de caza tan tonto, no, no podía creérselo. ¿Y si no había sido un accidente?

–Dios mío... –murmuró.

Cuando Burton fue llamado a la tribuna, no pronunció el discurso previsto sino que, con voz débil y entrecortada por los temblores, improvisó una exposición sobre el reino de Abomey, que había visitado desde la isla de Fernando Poo. Luego, regresó enseguida a su butaca.

* * *

¿Había descubierto John Speke realmente las fuentes del Nilo?

Fueron necesarias varias expediciones aún para llegar a algunas certezas sobre este tema.

En 1864, los esposos Samuel y Florence Baker, después de haberse encontrado con Speke en Gondokoro, exploraron el lago Luta Nzige, al que rebautizaron como lago Alberto.

En 1866, David Livingstone regresó a África, a petición de la Sociedad Real de Geografía, para explorar de nuevo la región de los Grandes Lagos. Pero la parte esencial de los descubrimientos debe cargarse en la cuenta del periodista Henry Morton Stanley. En 1869, puesto que Livingstone no daba ya señales de vida, el director del New York Herald pidió a su reportero que fuera a buscarle. Stanley se dirigió a África, encontró al célebre explorador a orillas del lago Tanganika y se descubrió una verdadera pasión por la exploración de aquel continente. Durante los siguientes veinte años, organizó tres expediciones más, durante las que exploró, especialmente, la cuenca del río Congo, el lago Victoria y el lago Alberto. Gracias a sus pacientes búsquedas, los geógrafos pudieron poner punto final al enigma de las fuentes del Nilo: el río sagrado nace, en efecto, en el lago Victoria.

Desde el principio, el capitán John Speke había estado en lo cierto.

Richard Burton reconoció deportivamente su derrota.

Advirtamos por fin, para cerrar definitivamente esta historia, que en su primera expedición Henry Stanley recurrió a los servicios de uno de los hombres más competentes en materia de exploración africana. Este hombre, cuya existencia suelen olvidar los libros de historia, se llamaba Sidi Mubbarak.

Aunque es más conocido por su apodo: Bombay.

Índice

Preámbulo 7
Donde se descubre que las grandes exploraciones comienzan en los despachos.

Acto I 13
Hacia el lago Tanganika

Capítulo uno 15
En el palacio del sultán de Zanzíbar
Encuentro con dos blancos
Enrolado a su pesar

Capítulo dos 23
En la jungla y la sabana
Mil dificultades para la caravana
¡Valor, quedémonos!

Capítulo tres 39
Llegada a Kazeh
Un poblado que huele a sangre
Valiosas informaciones

Capítulo cuatro 51
Mal presagio
Última parada antes del infierno
En el corazón de África

Capítulo cinco 63
El lago Tanganika
El ataque de los escarabeos
¿Es el Nilo?

Capítulo seis 79
El regreso tras el fracaso
¡Rumbo al Nyanza!...
Speke quiere creerlo aún

Entreacto 85
Regreso a Londres

Acto II 95
Hacia el lago Victoria

Capítulo uno 97
El regreso de Speke a Zanzíbar
En marcha hacia el lago Victoria
Un ataque de bandidos

Capítulo dos 109
Kazeh en la guerra
Un enojoso contratiempo
Baraka, el amigo que ya no lo es

Capítulo tres 123
En marcha hacia el norte
El kaquenzingiriri contra el hongo
«Encuentro» con el príncipe Suwarora

Capítulo cuatro 135
Un recibimiento digno de un rey
Extrañas costumbres
Cacería de rinocerontes
¡Ya le dije que era buena señal!

Capítulo cinco 153
Mtesa el sanguinario
Un gatito que se convierte en león
Prisioneros sin prisión

Capítulo seis 173
¿El Nilo por fin?
Un descenso movido
El país de arena

Epílogo 187
La gloria, el drama y el desenlace

«¿Participó realmente Bombay en los dos viajes de Burton y de Speke como intérprete? ¿Era Mtesa, el rey de Uganda, tan sanguinario? ¿Qué hay de cierto en *En busca del río sagrado. Las fuentes del Nilo?*

Durante sus expediciones por Africa, los exploradores ingleses llevaron algunos diarios que se publicaban a su regreso a Europa. Burton hizo que apareciera *Viaje a los Grandes Lagos del África oriental* en 1860 y Speke *Diario del descubrimiento de las fuentes del Nilo* en 1863. Estos relatos cuentan, casi día a día, los principales acontecimientos de ambas aventuras: la marcha de la caravana, la vida en Kazeh, la decepción del lago Tanganika, el descubrimiento del lago Victoria, el encuentro con el tiránico Mtesa y también el descenso por el Nilo. Más tarde, algunos historiadores se interesaron por estas exploraciones y sus autores. Así, Fawn Brodie publicó, en 1967, una biografía muy completa de Richard Burton (*Diablo de hombre*), que permite captar muy bien su complejo carácter. Todos estos elementos sirvieron para escribir *En busca del río sagrado...*

Pero quedan zonas de sombra. La principal es Bombay. Aunque participó en ambas expediciones, sólo fue en ellas, desde el punto de vista de los europeos, un personaje secundario. En los relatos de Burton y de Speke aparece sólo en pequeñas pinceladas cuando se trata de una misión que se le confía, de sus disputas con Baraka o de una corta descripción de su carácter. Y como el propio Bombay no escribió nada, en definitiva se saben muy pocas cosas de él. El modo como vivió estas dos aventuras sólo puede ser imaginado. Es lo que esta novela intenta hacer.

Philippe Nessmann

Philippe Nessmann

Nació en 1967 y siempre ha tenido tres pasiones: la ciencia, la historia y la escritura. Después de obtener un título de ingeniero y una licenciatura en historia del arte, se dedicó al periodismo. Sus artículos, publicados en *Science et Vie Junior*, cuentan tanto los últimos descubrimientos científicos como las aventuras pasadas de los grandes exploradores. En la actualidad, se dedica exclusivamente a los libros juveniles, aunque siempre tienen de fondo la ciencia y la historia. Para los lectores más pequeños, dirige la colección de experimentos científicos «Kézako» (Editorial Mango). Para los lectores jóvenes, escribe relatos históricos.

François Roca

Nació en Lyon en 1971. Realizados sus estudios artísticos en París y Lyon, su pasión por la pintura le empuja en primer lugar a exponer retratos al óleo. En 1996, comienza a crear ilustraciones para jóvenes. François Roca ha ilustrado más de una veintena de obras y colabora asiduamente con la revista *Télérama*. Vive y trabaja en París.

Descubridores del mundo

Bajo la arena de Egipto
El misterio de Tutankamón
Philippe Nessmann

En la otra punta de la Tierra
La vuelta al mundo de Magallanes
Philippe Nessmann

En busca del río sagrado
Las fuentes del Nilo
Philippe Nessmann

Al límite de nuestras vidas
La conquista del polo
Philippe Nessmann

Al asalto del cielo
La leyenda de la Aeropostal
Philippe Nessmann

Los que soñaban con la Luna
Misión Apolo
Philippe Nessmann

En tierra de indios
El descubrimiento del lejano Oeste
Philippe Nessmann

Las fuentes del Nilo

CUADERNO DOCUMENTAL

Los exploradores

RICHARD BURTON, nacido en 1821, en Inglaterra, pasa su juventud en Francia e Italia. Tal vez de ahí procede su afición a los viajes. Escritor, buscador de oro, aventurero, cónsul, lingüista que hablaba treinta lenguas, viaja por India, Arabia, África, América...
La búsqueda de las fuentes del Nilo sólo es, pues, una de las facetas de su tumultuosa vida. Fascinante, endiablado y autoritario, tiene tantos enemigos como admiradores. Casado a los 39 años, muere a los 69. ¿El libro que le habría gustado escribir? Una biografía de Satán...

BOMBAY, cuyo verdadero nombre era Sidi Mubbarak, pertenecía a la etnia yao. Nacido en los años 1820, es capturado y luego vendido como esclavo. Su dueño lo lleva a la India como criado. Cuando éste muere, Bombay se dirige a Zanzíbar donde entra en la guardia del sultán. Burton le contrata como intérprete para su expedición al Tanganika. Es gruñón y, a veces, pendenciero, pero también taimado y trabajador. De modo que Speke le confía, durante su expedición al lago Victoria, cada vez más responsabilidades.

JOHN SPEKE, seis años menor que Burton, es muy aficionado a la caza: en su casa familiar, reúne una inmensa colección de animales disecados. Capitán del ejército británico en la India, es reclutado por Burton para participar en la búsqueda de las fuentes del Nilo. Solitario e introvertido, es un incansable andarín dotado de un sentido innato de la selva. Verdadero descubridor de las fuentes del Nilo, muere a los 37 años en un extraño accidente de caza, la víspera de un crucial debate sobre su descubrimiento.

El misterio del Nilo

Antes de Burton y Speke, varias expediciones intentaron remontar el «padre de los ríos» hasta sus fuentes, en vano.

① **En tiempo de los faraones,** los egipcios veneran el Nilo, fuente de toda vida, sin intentar encontrar su origen.

② **Hacia 60 d.J.C.,** una expedición romana enviada por Nerón remonta el Nilo hasta las ciénagas de Sudd, donde queda bloqueada.

③ **En el siglo II** el geógrafo Ptolomeo sugiere que el Nilo nace de dos lagos situados cerca de las «montañas de la Luna».

④ **En 1770,** el escocés James Bruce llega a las fuentes del Nilo Azul, el principal afluente del río.

⑤ **En 1840,** bajo los auspicios del virrey de Egipto Mehemet-Alí, una expedición llega a Gondokoro, pero queda bloqueada por la jungla.

¿Qué es un río?

Un río es una corriente de agua que se arroja al mar. Pero cuando se remonta un río y se llega a la confluencia de dos afluentes, ¿cuál de ambos es el río? ¿El más ancho? ¿El más largo?
El problema se planteó con el Nilo Blanco y el Nilo Azul.
Los geógrafos decidieron que el Nilo Blanco fuera el río; el Nilo Azul el afluente.

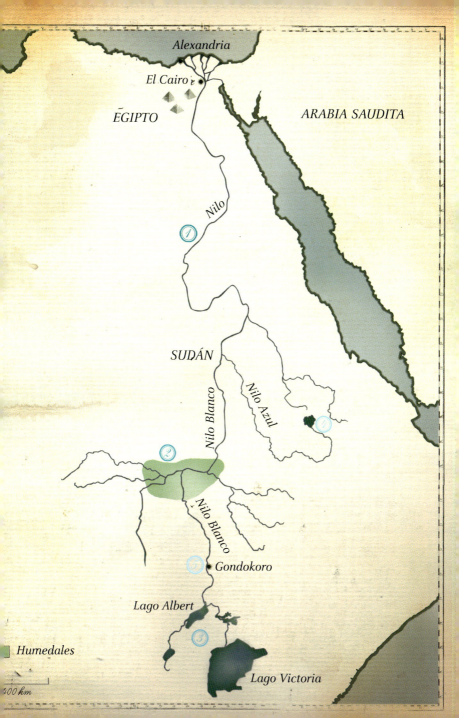

¿Dónde se sitúa la acción?

Puesto que las junglas y marismas impiden remontar el Nilo, Burton y Speke deciden rodear este problema por el sur. Se dirigen a la región de África que hoy es Tanzania. Objetivo: encontrar un gran lago del que brote un río hacia el norte, descenderlo luego y ver si se trata del Nilo.

·········· *Burton y Speke (1857-1859)*

·········· *Speke solo (1858)*

·········· *Speke y Grant (1860-1863)*

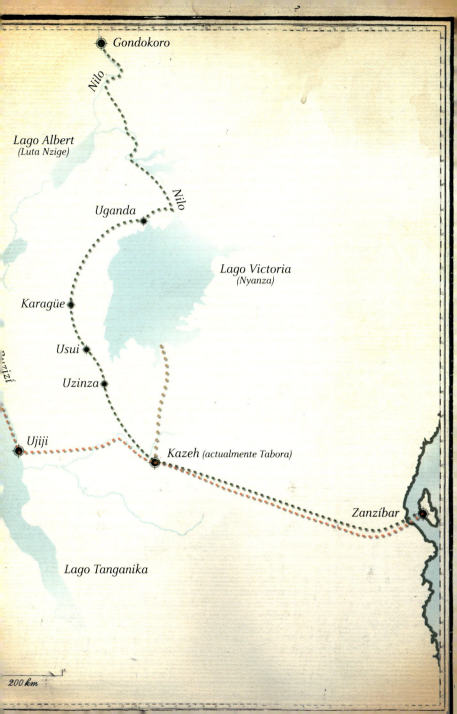

África y los europeos

Hasta el siglo XIX, los europeos no intentan casi explorar el corazón de África. Permanecen en las costas, lo que les basta para llevar a cabo el comercio de esclavos y para avituallar los navíos que se dirigen a la India.

En el siglo XIX, los exploradores europeos –Burton, Speke, Livingstone, Stanley, Brazza...– se aventuran hacia el interior de África descubriendo su geografía, sus habitantes, su fauna... A fines de siglo, se trata cada vez más de tomar posesión del territorio en nombre del propio gobierno: es el comienzo de la colonización.

Con la colonización, los europeos se apoderan de África: franceses al oeste, británicos al este, belgas en el Congo... Objetivo: obtener materias primas (oro, café, caucho...) y revender allí sus propios productos. Pero, para los europeos de la época, se trata también de «civilizar» evangelizando, educando, aportando ciencia y medicina... África, liberada del colonialismo en el siglo XX, sigue aún profundamente marcada por él.

Livingstone leyendo la Biblia

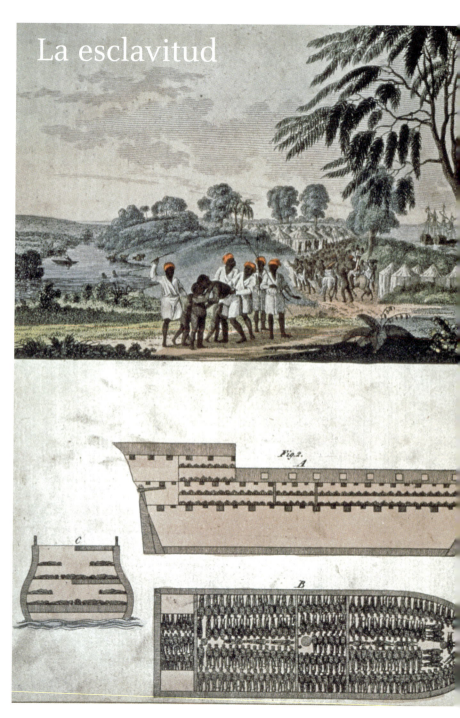

La esclavitud

Los africanos entre sí. En África, la tierra perteneció durante mucho tiempo a todo el mundo. Los hombres y las mujeres eran la única riqueza. Cuantos más esclavos tenía un hombre, más rico era. Éstos eran a menudo prisioneros de guerra. Cuando los árabes y los europeos desarrollaron la trata de negros, los jefes africanos se pusieron a su servicio para proporcionarles hombres.

La trata por los árabes. Desde el inicio del Islam, algunos caravaneros árabes fueron a buscar en África oriental esclavos para venderlos en el Oriente Medio o en África del Norte. En el siglo XIX, la isla de Zanzíbar, donde se instalaron sultanes de Omán, es el centro distribuidor de este tráfico.

La trata por los europeos. Para proporcionar mano de obra a las tierras conquistadas en América, los europeos desarrollaron la trata de esclavos desde la costa oeste de África. Entre los siglos XVI y XIX, más de 12 millones de negros fueron víctimas de este terrible comercio. Gran Bretaña abolió la esclavitud en 1808, Francia en 1848, los Estados Unidos en 1865.

Toda una expedición

Una expedición al corazón de África en el siglo XIX era el equivalente a un viaje espacial de hoy.

Stanley en postura de explorador

El viaje hasta África. Desde Europa, se llega en barco. Para su segunda expedición, Speke tardó más de tres meses en llegar a Zanzíbar, rodeando África por el sur.

El material. Comporta la moneda de cambio para pagar víveres y porteadores (cuentas de cristal, telas, alambre de latón), el material de acampada (tiendas, camastros, camas, sillas, mantas, utensilios de cocina, ropas, herramientas...), el material científico (cronómetros, brújulas, sextantes, barómetros...) y las armas (fusiles, revólveres, espadas, balas, pólvora...).

Las personas. Entre los exploradores, sus servidores, el guía, los intérpretes, los soldados, los esclavos de los soldados, los arrieros y una multitud de porteadores, las caravanas cuentan con varios centenares de personas.

Los desplazamientos. La parte esencial de los desplazamientos se efectúa a pie o a lomos de asnos, a razón de unos veinte kilómetros diarios. La exploración de los lagos y los ríos se hace a bordo de piraguas alquiladas a los autóctonos.

«¡El doctor Livingstone, supongo!»

Una polémica entre Burton y Speke fue origen de un sorprendente encuentro...

El anuncio del descubrimiento por Speke de las fuentes del Nilo (véase página anterior), tras su segundo viaje, hubiera debido poner fin a este enigma. Pero Burton, celoso de su antiguo compañero, siembra tanto la duda que la Sociedad Real de Geografía manda a David Livingstone a África para aclarar el misterio. Médico y misionero, éste está acostumbrado a viajar solo y sin caravana. Deja rápidamente de dar signos de vida. ¿Está vivo aún?...

En Nueva York, el director de un periódico se huele la gran noticia: envía a su reportero Henry Stanley en busca de Livingstone y publicará su relato. Tres años después del misionero, Stanley se dirige a Zanzíbar y sigue sus huellas en el corazón de África. El 10 de noviembre de 1871, el periodista llega a Ujiji, a orillas del lago Tanganika, y descubre a un hombre blanco agotado y enfermo. Stanley se quita el sombrero y suelta: «¡El doctor Livingstone, supongo!» (véase debajo). ¿Quién más podía ser? Por aquel entonces, no había otro hombre blanco en 1 000 kilómetros a la redonda...

Las fuentes del Nilo, hoy

Por lo general se considera que el Nilo nace en el lago Victoria. Pero varios ríos se vierten en ese lago. ¿Las fuentes del más largo de ellos no serán también las más alejadas fuentes del Nilo? En marzo de 2006, tras haber remontado íntegramente el río, el equipo del británico Neil MacGrigor anunció haberlas descubierto. Durante esa expedición, un amigo de los aventureros murió a manos de los rebeldes ugandeses.
A 2 428 metros de altitud, en plena selva ruandesa, un hilillo de agua brota de un agujero lodoso. Son las fuentes del Rukarara, afluente que se vierte en el Kagera que, a su vez, desemboca en el lago Victoria. En total, el Nilo mide 6 718 km. Está en el trío de cabeza de los ríos más largos, con el Amazonas y el Misisipí-Misuri.